# DESERT OF THE SOUL

## Underverse Book 8

By
Jez Cajiao

Jez Cajiao

# CONTENTS

Jez Cajiao

# <u>THANKS, AND AN EXPLANATION</u>

Hi everyone! Okay, so Well, there's a lot to go over here isn't there? First and foremost, I need to apologize for the delay here in returning to the UnderVerse. Essentially there were some issues with a member of the team and I needed to face up to the fact that I was in burnout. *Deep* in burnout.

Now for me, I'd held off the insidious bugger for years, by dancing along the razor's edge, continuing to force myself to higher and higher levels of productivity, and ignoring all those who tried to warn me against it.

My method of choice was to flit from series to series, do two books here, then jump to the next, then two more, which was great because it kept each of the series new for me, enabling me to push harder, but it also meant that there were longer and longer breaks between the stories.

Taking some time out and a good hard look at the situation, as well as some much needed feedback from people, made it clear that it wasn't a viable long term strategy any longer.

Instead I changed my methods, and started closing out the series. As I only needed four books to complete Arise, that was the first to be done.

This meant that as much as I wanted to write the remaining five books of UnderVerse and the remaining five of Rise of Mankind, I had a bit of a quandary.

If I wrote all five of UnderVerse, that's at least a year of solid work, by which time, Rise of Mankind fans have been left waiting two and a half years between releases.

If I instead did all of the Rise of Mankind? Then UnderVerse fans are at three and a half years.

Neither seemed fair, so instead I wrote three of Rise, and then jumped to UnderVerse. Yeah, alright, exactly what I'd decided I wasn't going to do, but it got everyone a story sooner, okay?

Now, fast-forward to today, and here we are;

Arise is complete, Rise of Mankind has two books left in the series, and UnderVerse #8 is done, #9 is in edits, and 10? I'm a third done with writing it!

My plan moving forwards is that I'm going to write the rest of UnderVerse now—there's only two more books after the one I'm working on—and then I'll take a few months off, and then I'll write the remaining two of Rise of Mankind.

After that? Well, I've got a plan, let's just say that.

But for now, I need to thank *you*.

Yeah, that's right. You!

Seriously, thank you for the support, for the friendships and for the love, its been an incredible five years since I released that first draft of Brightblade, beginning the wild ride that is UnderVerse, and while it seems insane that we've come so far, honestly, the best is yet to come.

Thank you, to my beta team, to my editors, to my fellow authors, including that bugger Matt for blazing the trail for us all of late.

Most of all, thank you, you wonderful bugger of a reader or a listener, thank you for giving your time, for choosing to support an indie lunatic, and keeping me listening to crazy music, and hallucinating wildly in my office.
Hopefully I'll see you at a Con soon!

Thanks,

-Jez
26/05/25

# UNDERVERSE BOOKS 1-7 SYNOPSI

# BOOK ONE:

Jax is working a dead end job, in a semi-stable relationship, and searching for his missing brother, while plagued by dreams of the UnderVerse. This terrible alternate reality is where he, and his brother Tommy, are pulled against their will on occasion. When in the dream they inhabit artificial bodies and fight to protect abandoned villages and more, standing between the inhabitants of the Old Empire and the creatures of the night.

They awaken back on earth once the threat has passed, or they've been killed, with their injuries following them. While they heal at a tremendously accelerated rate, it still requires days to recover, and in that time, they hide their injuries, lest they be locked away for self-mutilation.

After one such session, Jax decides to come clean to his GF and explain everything. Badly injured and bleeding heavily, he arrives at her home, only to find her in bed with another man. He loses control, half beating the man to death, and having his skull shattered in turn by her, using the baseball bat he'd bought her for self-defense.

Jax comes to in the hospital, chained to the bed, and is interviewed by the police and warned he faces a significant jail term. While alone and contemplating this, an unknown doctor slips in and assures him it has all been taken care of, before drugging him.

When Jax wakes up this time, it's to find himself restrained, again, but on an airplane heading to meet 'the Baron Sanguis'. A lawyer assures him that should he carry out the reasonable requests of his new employer, then not only will all legal concerns be a thing of the past, but he will find his brother as well. Jax accepts, warned that refusal means death, and meets the Baron, an inhuman monster who admits to being an interplanar traveler, and a member of the original nobility of the UnderVerse, the Realm that Jax and his brother dream of.

To be free and to find his brother Jax must travel to that shattered Realm, and open a stable portal back to this Realm, as the mana here is simply too low in concentration for the portal to be held open for more than bare seconds. Alternatively, a portal from that side, to here, would be secure and enable the nobility to return with servants and forces intact, ready to reconquer their home.

Over the next several months, as Jax is trained for the 'little task', he discovers more about the past of that Realm, including that the voice of madness that occasionally speaks to him, and that he'd written off as himself being mad to some degree, is actually the voice of the Eternal Emperor Amon, a fragment of His soul being all that's left, clinging to the genetic line.

Amon was murdered, by the Baron, His son, and others of the nobility, with the aid of the God of Death, Nimon. In the process, and as his price for this, the followers of the other nine greater gods were purged and their temples cast down. Leaving the God of Death, who dragged one of the moons down to impact the Realm, with a powerful enough surge of His 'aspect' (death) that He managed to banish the other Greater Gods.

Jax grows to hate the Baron, but has nothing left in his life beyond his missing brother, and so takes the opportunity, training heavily, before facing eleven other nobles' choices in the arena to 'earn' the right to go to the UnderVerse. He wins, barely, and trades the remains of his opponents and their personal items to their sponsors, in exchange for several magical artifacts, before passing through the great portal.

Once on the other side, and having made a deal with an opposing noble 'house' for access, he finds himself in a ruined tower. The Great Towers were bastions of the old Empire, powerfully magical, self-sustaining and intended as entire self-contained cities. At half a mile wide at the base, two to three miles high, and sustained by their own mana collectors they acted as garrisons and secure imperial bastions in places of danger.

The Tower that Jax finds himself in, however, was never inhabited fully. It was finished, intended as a research and security station, but had only a skeleton crew when it was assaulted by a SporeMother. The SporeMother, a multi-limbed monstrosity of legend, flooded the defenders with undead and possessed creatures, birthing DarkSpore creatures, parasitical clouds that could puppet flesh, turning the unprepared defenders into attackers, claiming the Tower. The few remaining survivors, beleaguered on all sides, ordered the Tower's controller Wisps to shut the entire structure down, sealing the Wisps themselves away, and preventing the creature from being able to feed on the mana of the Tower to grow stronger, expecting that the Tower would be assaulted and retaken shortly by the Imperial Legion.

Then, before reinforcements could take the Tower back, the Cataclysm came. Seas and mountains rose, islands vanished and the creatures of the deep and of nightmare were set loose to roam. When Jax arrives at the Tower he finds it dark and silent, populated by the ancient dead, with only occasional more recently killed adventurers scattered here and there. He also encounters Sporelings, immature SporeMothers, hidden in the portal chamber, fighting them and locking himself away in a side room.

Jax uses one of the spells he gained, resurrecting one of the Sporelings he killed to form a companion to fight alongside him. Using his new companion, Bob, and his weapon of choice, a bastardized naginata, Jax proceeds to clear the Tower partially, discovering the 'Hall of Memories' and its sleeping Wisp, Oracle. He is gravely injured, and alone, Bob having perished in the fight to enter the room, and when he awakens the Wisp takes the chance it unthinkingly offers, to use some of the stored knowledge of the Hall of Memories, in the form of spellbooks, to enable him to defeat the undead outside the room.

Unfortunately, all magic he has accessed so far has been through books such as this, impressing outside knowledge across his brain and damaging it each time. This final spellbook is one too many, and results in scarring, internal bleeding and more. Jax is dying and Oracle, the newly awakened Wisp, bonds herself to him in an attempt to save him, gaining access to his manapool and enabling herself to cast the needed healing spells to save his life.

Over time Jax recovers, and with Oracle's guidance, reawakens and names Seneschal, the Wisp that controlled the tower, reactivating the mana collectors and beginning the basic repairs the Tower requires, as well as awakening the Goddess of Fire, Jenae. This awakens the SporeMother, now ancient and decrepit, but still powerful. In the fight that follows between Jax, Oracle, the newly reformed Bob and the SporeMother and her minions, the Eternal Emperor Amon makes contact with Jax, guiding him to use an artifact recovered in the Tower earlier. This Silverbright potion (Dragon's blood) transforms his weapon from a standard construction into a basic magical, but evolving, weapon. Jax kills the SporeMother, but is gravely wounded. Over the next day, as he is healed, the companions clear the remaining sections of the Tower, and find the creature's nest underground, along with the remains of the Golem Construction Cradles or Genesis Chambers.

They also find the Wisp responsible for the golems, name him Hephaestus, and take the time to reclaim the single working Genesis Chamber. This begins the construction of the most basic of stone golems to protect and rebuild the Tower. In the process, HeartStones are uncovered, a magical way to send a memory, as a method of communication. Most are long drained of mana, but the fragments that remain make it clear that Barabarattas, lord of one of the two nearby cities, has been trading slaves to the SporeMother in exchange for Sporelings, hoping to raise a captive army of SporeMothers.

The Wisps sense an intrusion higher in the tower and Jax explores, finding a group of slavers, heavily armed, using their slaves to loot an old armory. Jax attacks when seeing a child beaten, killing the slavers, with Oracle's help, and driving off the two airships that had been docked on the balcony. One is damaged and crashes in the courtyard below, while the other escapes to land at a nearby lake to effect repairs.

The freed slaves pledge allegiance to Jax, and while they rest, he takes one of their number, Oren, the captain of the crashed ship, down to the courtyard. He discovers that they were pressed into service, and had no desire to work with the slavers. The remaining surviving crew swear as well, and inform Jax that there is a third ship. This is the warship that was enforcing the City Lord's will, and it was still incoming, having stopped to raid a village along the way. Jax and the slaves use the weapons they have, the remains of the damaged ship and subterfuge to lure the warship in to land, while Oracle disables their engines.

Jax and Bob, aided by some of the former slaves, fight and kill the soldiers aboard the warship, capturing the crew, freeing a group of slaves taken from the villages and locking the crew in those same cages. Jax formally claims the Tower as his, and through the right of blood, having found that he is an illegitimate son of the Baron Sanguis, and therefore noble in his own right, he begins the right of Imperial Succession.Barabarratas, like all nobles remaining in the Empire, with no Imperial House to swear to, had been unable to lay claim formally to the Imperial Throne, but once the succession has begun, sees a way to claim the throne. He threatens war against Jax, unless he surrenders. Jax, being short of patience and self-control, as well as occasionally being an asshole, in turn declares war on Barabarratas and his city of Himnel, taunting him before leading his people in a wake. The end of the book comes to Thomas, Jax's brother, languishing and injured in a jail, before being sold as fodder, the lowest caste of soldier, to the Dark Legion of Nimon.

# BOOK TWO:

Thomas fights his abusive jailor and draws the eye of a Paladin of Nimon, who grants him a chance to prove himself. Thomas is happy to take that chance and prove his worth in battle to escape the rank of fodder.

Jax awakens with a hangover, the wake having gone well, and proceeds to set about trying to repair the Tower. Two of the new recruits, now citizens of the Great Tower, Oren the Dwarf airship captain, and Cai, a Panthera humanoid with a skill for organization, assist him. Teams are formed for hunting and defense, with a personal squad geared around Jax. This is formed from ex slaves who are determined to never be cowed again. Lydia leads them (mace and shield, heavy armor), with Jian (dual wielding swords), Arrin (mage), Cam (Axeman), Miren (archer), Stephanos (archer) and Bob. Jax and his new team go to try and capture or recruit the escaped second airship, but upon arrival at the lake, find the ship deserted.

They are attacked as they search by small four-armed amphibious creatures known as the 'Mer'. In the course of the fight, Jax realizes they are young, ranging from a young adult, to a child, and they were attacked by goblins prior to Jax's arrival, attacking him in pre-emptive self-defense. The young ones are joined by older, more experienced warriors, who agree to a truce at first, and then request help to deal with the nearby goblin horde.

Jax agrees, and three of the Mer join them, assaulting the goblin camp. In the course of the fight, Jax saves the life of one of the Mer, the oldest of the younglings, and upon clearing the ruin, and rescuing the surviving crew of the airship from them, claims the land as part of the Empire. In the process, the goblin cave is revealed as a buried outpost, complete with basic golems, which are claimed and returned to the Tower.

The Mer village remains neutral, but several of their people join Jax, including the youngling, Bane. The leader of the Mer that join the Tower is Flux, an accomplished adventurer, and he supports Bane's desire to be Jax's bodyguard. Several of the older Mer decide to join the Tower, many of whom are skilled, but crippled. Jax heals them, magic being increasingly rare in the UnderVerse since the fall of the Empire, and his abilities and the knowledge stored at the Tower are revealed as being incredibly valuable. The rescued crew join Jax, bringing their ship and joining the resurgent Empire.

The older banished Gods are awakened, and Jax has a disagreement with one, Tamat, the Lady of Assassins. Using a draconic legacy from Amon, Jax manages to beat Her in Her weakened state, before being forced back by Jenae, who begins the process of spreading the worship of the original Gods again. The Gods are weak, but They have abilities They can grant, and information from the past that is relevant. Nimon is unaware They are back.

Jenae, after an earlier disagreement with Jax, helps him to find that his brother was recently in the city of Himnel. Oren and the others implore Jax to free their families, to bring them to the Tower from Himnel. He agrees, pausing only long enough, to have his body inked with tattoos, guided by Jenae, Ame, a Mer runesmith, and a tattooist named Renna.

Jez Cajiao

While attempting to find a hidden entrance to the city, used by smugglers, Oracle, who has fallen in love with Jax, and he with her, is captured and taken deep underground by the Drow, a race of Dark Elves that are scouting the city for an unknown reason. Jax catches some of them, and in a bout of frantic insanity, imbues his body with sufficient mana that he gains a new ability 'Mana-Overdrive' speeding his movements and strength up, but it is short lived, and results in a 'crash' afterward. Jax uses this ability to kill two of the Drow, and then, driven mad by Oracle's capture, pain and fear allows his darker side to come out as he tortures the Drow for information.

Bane calms him down, hides the body from the others, and guides Jax back to himself. Jax's group, now including Barret, a former soldier and a member of Oren's ship's crew, dives underground, hunting the Drow. Over the underground trip, they meet Ashrag, an ancient Cave Spider, who remembers the Empire, and despite her monstrous appearance, was once an Imperial Citizen. Jax resurrects ancient Oaths, claiming them as his own at Amon's direction, and passes out from the mana drain. This convinces Ashrag and, after fighting a group of her brood, she swears allegiance. She agrees, on the condition that Jax free the tunnels of the Drow who view her kind, and their bodies, as a great delicacy.

Jax eventually leads his team through the various dark places, and finds Oracle, captured by the Drow leader, a Drider. The half woman-half spider, has several smugglers held captive and fights the group. Jax is triumphant, but Cam dies at the hands of the Drow. Oracle is freed and the smugglers are mainly compliant, save their leader, who ends up making a comment that Jax disagrees with pointedly, and dies.

The last few Drow fight a retreat, until they are killed by a new threat coming the other way along the tunnel. The three newcomers slaughter the Drow, then, after a tense standoff, are revealed to be Imperial Legionnaires. The Imperial Legion has been dismissed and derided since the Cataclysm, slowly dwindling in numbers and through several bad apples in leadership, have become outsiders in their own homes. They are disliked and disrespected by the locals, even as they march out to fight the creatures that nobody else can.

The Legion is falling apart, its members lost and despairing, until Jax resurrects the Oaths, and finally a chance at a future is given back to them.

The three scouts, Yen, Tang and Amaat swear to Jax, and reveal that they are even now, below the City of Himnel.

# <u>BOOK THREE:</u>

Jax leads the group to the surface, fighting off a group of local thugs who attempt to hunt the Legionnaires, and eventually reach the Arena and Arena Master Mal, one of the local leaders of the Smuggler's Guild. This is the man Oren had recommended as the best choice of an ally in the city. At the same time Jax is in the process of capturing a small group of Djinn, who offer allegiance in exchange for freeing their captured clan mother from the Skyking.

Mal agrees to help, for a fee, and introduces his team; Soween, his right hand, Jay his muscle and Josh his mage and Soween's husband. While Jax is resting, and about to finally get some 'private time' with Oracle, who can assume human form and size at will, Mal receives a message from the local crime lord, the Skyking. He demands Mal turn over the 'Legion' having discovered that it was Legionnaires that killed its people. Mal refuses, and instead, to gain the time they need, arranges a series of arena fights with the 'captured' Legionnaires, including Jax, and betting games.

While Mal makes these arrangements, Jax and his team visit a local healer, intending to get some of the deep seated injuries to his brain that are slowing his ability and level growth addressed. Along the way, Jax is surrounded by the enslaved, seeing the casual cruelty of the people, the way that nobles laugh and stroll, while slaves on the verge of starvation carry their bags. Amon sees this and their twinned rage escapes control, resulting in a temper-tantrum of epic proportions, leveling a section of the city and freeing the slaves, while also releasing Amon to face Jax inside his own mind.

Jax manages to defeat Amon, but in the process, discovers that he's had an unrecognized parasitic inhabitant all this time. He tears it free, gutting himself in the process, and only survives through the intervention of his team getting him to the healer, and the divine help of Jenae.

The Legion, having lost contact with their scouts, and seeing the devastation in the city, send a small, but elite team out to investigate, and with their help, Jax is returned to the Arena. The Legion settles in to protect him.

Jax is drained by the healing, and Centurion Primus Augustus, one of the four Primus of the Legion, fights in his place in the Arena that night, slaughtering all thrown against him.

Jax awakens and meets Mal and the others, works to integrate himself with the Legion and meets the non-human members of the shipyards who've been brushed aside by Barabarattas and his kind as 'sub-human'. They are recruited, and a plan formed. Rather than escaping with everyone through the hidden Smuggler's Path and robbing the city for the Tower's needs, a new more daring plan is concocted.

The airships are built in the shipyards, and Himnel's greatest weapon is under construction, the battleship. Currently it's a bare structure, open to the elements, but under the plan, additional volunteers are brought in, and the battleship is sealed up, and made, minimally, airworthy. The Legion are contacted and given orders, in three days they are to capture the shipyards.

Having little alternative, and no love for the city, as well as a legitimate authority encouraging it, the Legion agree.

Jax fights and recovers that night and trains, dragging Grizz, the Legionnaire into his group, as well as Yen and Tang. The next night, after the fight, he leads his team to raid and rob the Magical Emporium, a golem secured shop. The presence of the golem leads Jax and the others to discover a hidden section below the main shop, unknown by all. They realize that long ago it wasn't a shop, but a golem repair and construction facility. The golems are claimed, the construction facility below ground being ordered to begin repairs and construction, while golems there are used to repair ancient mining golems, which are sent to the Tower, burrowing underground. The rest of the golems are sent to wait in the river for the assault on the shipyards.

The following night the Arena fight is 'fixed', but Jax, with the help of his team, wins, and they launch the assault. Combining the assault on the Skyking with the one on the shipyards, Jax and the small Legion team, along with his own, take the Skyking's tower, killing them all. Halfway through the fight, when confronted with the rarely seen Anubai, a heavily magical species, Jax activates his trump card, his Tattoos. Rather than being decorative, they are in fact magical runes enabling him to channel mana through them, helping him to turn the tables on his foes.

In the fight, they capture the first of the airships circling on 'overwatch' over the city. To capture the others, Jian assumes control of one of the ships and accidentally, being unfamiliar with the controls, fires a giant fireball at the tent city of recruits around the Dark Citadel of Nimon. Jax, as the leader of the group, is blamed and declared Apostate, and a holy war begins.

The ships are brought under Jax's control, and return to the shipyards, to be crewed by his people. In the following confusion, Jax is hit in the head and injured. The ships flee Himnel, having stolen the vast majority of the city's manastone store, which are needed to power the engines of the ships.

Without stones, Barabarattas is unable to give chase, and the ships head out to sea, hoping to leave the impression that they're not from the Tower, and as Jax had ordered. Unfortunately, Nimon is aware of the truth.

The Dark Legion attacks the stragglers leaving the city, and their latest recruit, Thomas assists in killing some of Jax's Legionnaires. Jax awakens when they are far out to sea, close to the Sunken City, a flying city from the old Empire that crashed into a seamount. He confirms the orders to land there, to make the ships secure, and then to make for the Great Tower. He also finally gets some 'private time' with Oracle.

# BOOK FOUR:

Jax meets the Legion leadership, Prefect Romanus, and Alistor, his right hand, as well as the crew of the battleship and many of the refugees. While in transit, Jenae informs Jax that knowledge he needs is lost in the Sunken City, and he vows to find it. Jax is still recovering, but by the time the ship lands, along with its much smaller escorts, at the Sunken City, he attempts to meet the two local parties from both Himnel, and its enemy city Narkolt.

Both are found to be led by 'nobles' but Himnel's is using slave labor, as well as being offensive, and suffers an 'accident' involving a sword. Narkolt's group are slightly more respectful and are given 24hrs to come back and discuss their intentions. The remaining guards from the Himnel group are given the same chance. As part of the discussion Jax uses an Imperial Ability, freeing the city of the souls of the unquiet dead that were condemned to roam it eternally, granting them their peace.

Once this is realized by the nobles, they ignore Jax's warning, and lead their people into the city's depths, searching for loot and artifacts. Jax orders the Legion into it as well, then leads his team in. In searching the depths, they are trapped by a landslide and explosions, set off by one of the nobles from Narkolt, and are forced into the depths.

Jian uses one of two books Jax gives him at this point and summons a demon to assist him, although it becomes clear the demon cares little for anything but gaining its own power. In the search, they are attacked by a group of feral Gnomes, explorers trapped long ago by the undead revenants and worse. These Gnomes were forced into a small pocket that, with typical gnomish ingenuity, they made into a livable space. They were then enslaved by a Skinwalker and its controlled Leviathans, forced to give their water and more to it, leaving them a water source heavily contaminated by metal, to drink and to raise crops from. The result is that the Gnomes essentially are driven feral, regressing and attacking each other. A small group is preserved as best as they can, while the greater population succumbs to madness.

These mad Gnomes attack Jax and, in the process, he and Oracle heal one of them, at least partially restoring his mind. Giint is broken by the things he's seen and done, and joins Jax, not knowing what else to do. The remaining feral Gnomes attack, and are driven back, as Jax and the team attack the Skinwalker and its pets. Jax wins the fight, but the Skinwalker, unbeknownst to them, is inside the creature they just killed, and escapes.

Back with the Dark Legion, Thomas, wounded from long ago injuries, is offered up to the Dark God, allowing His blood to mingle with Thomas' and regaining his magic, as well as sparking to life a dark seed, as he begins to fall in love with Belladonna, his squad leader.

Jax uses an Essence Core and gains the ability of flight and increased mana regeneration through meditation. Jenae reaches out, informing them that a hidden force is incoming, led by the Drow, with captive SporeMothers. Jax orders Oracle to go to the fleet resting overhead. They are to leave immediately and fly at full speed to the Tower to defend it. Jenae makes it clear that the Gnome's original ship, while hidden, is still usable, but the DarkSpore the SporeMothers could release would result in massive casualties if the fleet doesn't leave.

A small number of the Gnomes have been swayed by Giint and wish to join Jax, agreeing to lead him to the hidden ship. He leaves them to prepare, attacking the nearby camp of the undead, led by a necromancer from Earth, a previously sent through 'volunteer'. Bartholomew the Lich, or 'Barry' as Jax refers to him, appears and traps the team, only to have Lydia, in a burst of desperation, seize the hidden power of the Valkyrie, turning the tide of the battle and beginning her own ascension. Barry is killed in the fight, and Jax, when he recovers the rest of the loot from the vault, also awakens a slumbering Wisp. Jax, his team, and the Gnomes race to reach the ship, receiving injuries along the way, but reach it just as the enemy arrives overhead.

The ship is powered up, and the Wisp is permitted to bind itself to the Gnome's ship, gaining control. They use explosives from the Gnomes to free the ship of its hidden location, and then fight their way out of the Sunken City.

One of the enemy ships crashes in the fight, releasing the SporeMother and leaving it behind, while the others follow. In the fights that come, Jax and his team are badly injured, and Stephanos dies, killed by a Drow. Just as all seems lost, Mal appears, flying his own ship and driving the Drow back, having left the fleet to come and help.

Jax and the others start to recover, only to have Jenae reach out, informing them that Nimon has dispatched His Dark Legion, an advanced force, to make a portal close to the Great Tower, and plans to assault it. With that, Jax orders Tenandra, the name the gnomish ship's Wisp has chosen for herself, to get them to the fleet with all haste.

# <u>BOOK FIVE:</u>

Jax transfers ships. Along with his team, and he orders the fleet to land as soon as they are over land again, cross-loading the most skilled Legionnaires and his own team onto a small number of the fastest ships. He leaves the fleet under Romanus' control, and names Augustus as his heir, in case anything happens. Miren, Jian's lover and the surviving archer of the team, quits, unable to keep going.

The faster group flies ahead, securing the Tower and using the majority of the stolen manastones to repair the structure in a massive burst of magic. The next few days are filled with training and meetings as Jax tries to get the Tower's structure, both physical and command, established. Then quests are given by the awakened Gods, and as the Tower is secured. Jax raids the other locations in the path of the oncoming Dark Legion, determined to prevent them from uncovering the golems that could make a massive difference in the upcoming confrontation.

While these are being stripped, Denny, a Legion trap smith, takes an advance force and sets up an ambush for the approaching enemies. Jian's demon rebels and is banished, leaving Jian weaker and furious. He turns to the second book on demon summoning, and heartbroken at the news that Miren has run straight into the bed of a Legionnaire, binds a succubus, Sehran. When Jax finds out, he and Oracle question Sehran, but permit her to stay as a part of the team on a trial basis.

Thomas, unbeknown to Jax, is a member of the closing Dark Legion, and on a side mission, discovers he has a rare gift. As a Dark Berserker, his own nascent power as a berserker is corrupted by the dark gift.

Jax joins Denny and the others, and the trap is sprung, annihilating the majority of the Dark Legion, and Jax, after injuring Belladonna, is beaten back by Thomas. The pair fight each other, unknowing, and Jax escapes, setting off a magical attack that kills several of Thomas' friends in the process. Jax and the Legion take their airship and fall back, while the Dark Legion flee and Jax proceeds to clear local sites of interest.

A hidden interloper, Ronin the Bard, is discovered in the Tower, and joins Jax's team, bringing knowledge, music and a little magic to the team. The Arbuton, a sentient tree, is found living atop one of the old outposts, and deals are struck, with Jax sending a golem to aid the Arbuton, and the Arbuton sending Woodite, a Grove Tender, and its mate, Ha'zel, along with two guardians to assist the Tower.

In the exchange, Jax is separated from the team and dragged underground through a river, only to find a long-buried city filled with kobolds who summon their revenants and attack him. He uses his ability to free the souls of the enslaved within the kobolds' weapons, trapped and ensorcelled revenants, and strips the city of life.

When Jax awakes, having been overpowered by his ability, he finds one of the spirits waiting for him and it offers to guide him out. On the way however, Jax is contacted by Malthus, the 'Administrator of Pelath's View'. The being claims to be bonded to the city, much in the way that Seneschal is bonded to the Tower, and is alone, having been buried for long ages. He offers knowledge and artifacts, as well as a safe fallback position for the Empire should it need it, all in exchange for company. And a song.

Jax agrees, and several hours later, reaches the surface, meeting Oracle and the others, before returning to the Tower, finding that the rest of the fleet has arrived.

Thomas throws caution to the wind, determined to save Belladonna, and has her bound to his back, an IV drip botched together using a vampire's teeth and worse, to share his own blood, and hopefully the healing ability that he shares with Jax, with her. He sets off running to the Dark Citadel, as Jenae informs Jax that She found traces of Thomas… as a Dark Legionnaire.

Jax dispatches Mal and Augustus to Narkolt to try and recruit the Legion garrison there, then returns to clearing the surrounding areas. He and Amon face each other again, this time Amon comes out ascendant, and faces an ancient evil, devastating it, the village, and the land around for miles. Jax has his power torn out of his control, and has a split second to fight Amon, or save Oracle and Bob, who, as bonded companions, need his mana and health pool to live. Jax chooses them, and uses his rising understanding of magic to free them both, forcibly evolving Oracle into a new species.

Lydia faces her past, as well as her father and husband, who sold her into slavery. Jax and the rest of the team watch as she beats them half to death, then the team travels to the slave markets of the Habieen, following the path her mother was taken on to be sold. The resultant fight includes a mana-hurricane, and only the intervention of the Gods keeps Jax alive, but badly broken. Tenandra takes the ship and flies away, attempting to get reinforcements and to draw attention from Jax as he's carried by his people, surrounded by hundreds of freed slaves, into the forests.

The Dark Legion, guided by Nimon, chases Jax, who has recovered consciousness, and his people. Jax sends Lydia and Grizz to free the soul of the last Valkyrie, claiming her armor, rather than letting the following Dark Legion stumble over its resting place. With the rest of the team sent away, Jax is down to Bob, Ronin and Bane, and he sends Bob and Ronin to guide the freed slaves, sending Bane to hunt the Dark Legion's scouts.

The Dark Legion advance teams kill the slowest of the refugees, showing no mercy, and Jax makes a decision, asking for volunteers. They slowed the advance, killing several dozen, but seeing that there's no chance, with the numbers arrayed against them. Jax sends the volunteers on ahead, ordering them to protect the others, as he remains behind to buy them time.

He uses his flight ability, 'Soaring Majesty' to conduct a series of hit and run attacks, drawing the enemy to him, before folding together the most powerful spell he can, literally drawing a firestorm down upon himself, while screaming a challenge to Nimon, the Dark God himself. Then Jax attacks the Dark Legion, determined to sell his life as dearly as possible.

In the course of the fight, the brothers come face to face again, this time Thomas wins, pinning Jax to a tree with a spear, removing his helm to see the light in his enemy's eyes die… only to look into his brother's eyes.

Thomas rebels against Nimon and his weakened blood, drained heavily into Belladonna, allows him to swear to Lagoush, Goddess of Water, and he is accepted as Her champion. The brothers fight the Dark Legion together, but no matter how valiant, skilled, and dangerous, two men cannot defeat hundreds.

At the end, as they both believe it's all over, Augustus steps forward, Mal having gathered all those that he could, and brought them when he realized what was happening at the slave camp. The Imperial Legion faces its antithesis, and wins, driving the Dark Legion back. Jax is collected, and the forces fall back to the Great Tower, the refugees being shepherded by Legionnaires and airships.

Bane, however, is missing…

Jez Cajiao

# <u>**BOOK SIX:**</u>

Jax and Thomas have been reunited, and although the return to the Great Tower was painful, both of them being badly wounded, they have made it back to a secure location and start to rebuild their relationship.

Sint, God of Light and Order, had tasked Jax with recovering His Chosen Champion, and the airship bearing Lucian, Restun's Great-Great uncle arrives. A confrontation between uncle and nephew ensues, as Restun has spent his entire life, battling against the stigma of an uncle that was not only infected with vampiric essence, but that was banished from the Legion.

In the ensuing argument, and with the confirmation of Lord Sint, it is made clear that Lucian was made a scapegoat centuries ago to cover for the then Legion-General's excesses.

The result was an innocent man sent wandering the continent in the aftermath of the Cataclysm, battling evil wherever he found it. Lucian is elevated to Chief Justicar, and set to establish an order of Justicars to enforce the laws.

Jax and Tommy, now going by Thomas, set off and took the fragment of Lagoush, Lady of Water, to the Mer nearby. They continue on to reclaim the tools of Svetu, the God of Gnomes, long lost to the world in an ancient ruin.

The ruin, now populated by insane Goblins and Orcs, is hidden high in the mountains, taking up the front and publicly accessible section of an ancient Imperial production facility.

Jax and his team, assisted by Thomas, loot and recover the site, eliminating most of the inhabitants, and ending up with several Orcs that had been captured and enslaved, as new citizens. The production facility requires several tons of rare ores however, to regain functionality.

These ores were long ago mined by a lost mining golem, and Jax and his team set off to recover the golem, finding, in the process, a clan of Amilith. The mining golem (and the accumulated ore) is recovered, and the Amilith are left in their valley, all save two who are determined to reclaim a member of their tribe back at the Tower.

On the way back to the Great Tower, several fleeing airships are seen, also heading for the Tower, and under attack by demons. Tenandra, in her ship-body, is able to get Jax and his companions close enough to fight the demons and save one of the ships, though the others are lost.

Rewn, City Lord of Narkolt is aboard the lead vessel, having been chased from Narkolt by an assassination attempt by the Drow. Rewn swears to Jax, and agrees to relinquish the city to his control, but in the process of the discussion, is revealed as being a puppet.

Rewn has been 'guided' by his advisors for his entire life, provided a wiling harem, drink and drugs, and told what to say in public. He is utterly unprepared for the realities of life, and breaks down on learning he will actually have to work if he expects to rule in truth in Narkolt.

Bane, missing from Jax and the others since the battle in the forest against the Dark Legion, is found to have been diverted by Tamat, Goddess of Assassins and Dark Deeds, and is currently slaughtering her hated brother Nimon's priests. He rescues a trio of Dwarven women, and they assist him in his slaughtering of the priesthood, as well as their escape, as Bane attempts to return to Jax and his friends.

Rewn attempts to involve himself in the plans for retaking Narkolt, and is handled by one of his concubines, Carmen. He is removed from any kind of leadership position in the short term, while Jax and the Legion assault Narkolt.

Mal is sent ahead, along with a small team of spies, all of whom are captured on arrival, after Mal's lover Alyssa, the owner of the 'Kneeling Lady' whorehouse, mistakenly arranges monitoring of him.

The assault on the city is hard fought, but ultimately successful, and a Drow Drider, a massive half Dark Elf, half spider tears free of the City Keep, revealing the Drow presence for all to see.

In the ensuing fight, a great many good people are lost, but eventually, the city is taken, and Jax turns to mopping up. The Drow, attempting to flee from the city, use a heavily modified transport to try and collect their remaining forces from the 'Kneeling Lady'. They release an immature SporeMother into the city, and Oracle is injured. Jax loses his shit and beats the SporeMother almost to death with his gauntleted fists.

Oracle is exposed as having been changed by the spells and bonding that Jax was forced to bind her with when Amon had torn his connection apart in their last altercation.

Days pass as Jax consolidates his control over the city of Narkolt, and Rewn finally arrives, attempting to declare his ownership, and refusing to learn his place. This results in him being stripped of all rights to the city, and his former lover Carmen, now imprisoned by his hand, being raised up instead to rule the city in Jax's name.

The City interface grants a true Imperial Noble with access rights, a way of monitoring all illegal actions in the city. Jax and his people make use of this to gut the Smuggler's Guild, wiping out the majority of the corruption that has festered in the nobility since time immemorial as well.

Many of the nobles refuse to swear fealty to Jax, and are banished, fleeing with their forces into the surrounding forest. Mal is named a noble, and proceeds to name Alyssa his lady, then brings his father, Hannibal, in to finish gutting the Smuggler's Guild, using the pretense that he was banned from all the 'good bars' by them when he was declared a traitor for helping Jax.

The ancient Imperial Armory under Narkolt is uncovered, and a sleeping Elder God, the original Valspar, is accidentally set free, before being summarily killed in the ensuing chaos when the Gods lend a hand, fearing the result should such a creature regain its strength of old. The Armory contains some working facilities, and they are turned to producing golems and weaponry.

Bane arrives during the fight against the Valspar, and helps to turn the tide, before retaking his position as leader of Jax personal bodyguard.

The city manastone mine is also recovered, an ancient deposit of stones that had been continually converting the city's sewage to manastones since the Cataclysm. This fact had been long lost, and the sewage had been allowed to continue building up, until Jax and his team, literally swimming through the sewage at times, cleared it out and reclaimed it and started repairs.

Barabarratas is inducted into the order of Vampyrs by his assistant Cletus, who in turn is a supporter of Akanji, Lucian's brother. Barabarratas, seeing that his enemy Jax has claimed and secured both the Great Tower, and the city of Narkolt, changing the balance of power on the continent, makes a deal with the Dark Legion and Nimon's priesthood. In exchange for them protecting the city, he cedes some control over it to them.

As Jax and his forces prepare to assault Himnel, a Wisp colony is discovered far to the north, with several of the Wisps being captured by Himnel's forces. One is forcibly bonded to a young girl that is found to have enough of the noble Imperial bloodline. Through Nimon's blessing, she is able to assume control of Himnel, in name only. She is, however, able to command the golems in the city to fight Jax and his forces when the assault begins.

Thomas is sent with Tenandra and a small team to rescue the Wisps, while Jax, with Romanus advising, leads the assault on Himnel. The airship battle is short, the new weapons and methods of manufacturing that Jax has brought to the UnderVerse result in the annihilation of Himnel's forces.

Once the Legion is flown into Himnel's territory, they are deposited and create a beachhead, protecting the area as the Himnel army and elite forces are flown in as well.

Barabarratas orders an assault on their position, one that takes the lives of many Legionnaires, but it ultimately unsuccessful. Romanus is badly injured and Jon takes over as leader of the assault above ground, while Jax and Augustus, along with the remaining Legionnaires and his team, use a mining golem to assault Himnel from below, thinking to avoid the walls, and the deaths of innocents that would come if they were to assault the city directly.

Under Himnel, Jax and his team meet Barabarratas's secret weapon, a captive SporeMother breeding ground, along with hundreds of possessed undead.

Jax fights the SporeMothers, and eventually kills Cletus Thane, Barabarratas's assistant and handler. Several of Thomas's old Dark Legionnaire team are exposed as having been transformed into monsters to track and kill him for abandoning Nimon, and one of them is found and eliminated.

Jax takes control of the SporeMothers, and the hunt for the Vampyrs begins, resulting in several of the coven being killed off, and Alistor, the former Tribune of the Legion of Himnel, being exposed as a traitor and a secret adherent of Nimon.

In the following assault on Himnel's keep, Jax forcibly converts the golems to his side, but only after the deaths of many of the Legion. Jax and the remaining forces assault the remaining enemy forces in Barabarratas's throne room, and in the fight, Jax and Amon bond.

The Eternal Emperor augments Jax's abilities and knowledge, enabling him to easily exert his will over many of those there, and in a pitched battle, Lucian defeats Akanji.

The City of Himnel is taken by Jax and the Dark Legion, along with their surviving priesthood, flee to their citadel.

With the twin cities of Himnel and Narkolt held by Jax, and the airships as well, the Dark Citadel is gradually reduced in power, starving their forces, until after a few days of constant attrition, Nimon takes a direct hand on events.

The Arch Lich Ghastool, empowered by Nimon, leads his forces out of the depths of the ocean and assaults Himnel, Jax and his forces having deployed already before the city in the defensive emplacements they'd been preparing to fight the Dark Legion from.

Grizz is killed in the fighting, and the horror of his failure, the realization that many of his mistakes and the deaths caused by them are down to his own refusal to admit his differences from the others, drives Jax to take a final step, and to accept his power. He bonds himself to Amon.

Jax saves Grizz, returning him to life, and as a newly born Master of Mana. He then lifts into the air, slaughtering the Lich's army and the Arch Lich himself, tearing the mana that was sustaining the ancient undead free in a single act, using that mana to raise his 'Genetic Viability' overall by more than twenty percent though a single spell.

The Heliogifts, magical claymore mines, that had been hidden in the field ahead waiting for the Dark Legion's advance, are set off as the Dark Legion, well, advances…

Many of the Dark Legion elites are slaughtered in the ensuing explosion, and more are killed as Jax unleashes his own war golems, before finally unleashing a spell crafted by one of Amon's highest mages.

The Dark Citadel is destroyed, and Nimon, in a fit of rage, challenges Jax to a battle for his soul. Jax agrees, and the Gods gather round, ensuring a fair fight, reforming his armor and healing him, preparing him for the battle ahead.

Nimon and Jax have equal points agreed, all of Jax's stats are totaled, and Nimon creates a physical avatar with the same points. Unfortunately for Jax, the physical avatar has no need of such things as Intelligence, Charisma or Wisdom, being controlled by Nimon himself.

As such the avatar is physically far superior to Jax, and Jax wins only through a combination of blind luck, and trickery, thanks to his razorwire belt. Jax kills Nimon, cutting His head free, and orders that it be made into a goblet, just because he can.

That night, in the celebrations and festivities, Oracle drops the bombshell to Jax that, regardless of all the perfectly good reasons why it shouldn't have happened, including their being different species, and her having never previously had a body capable of it, she was indeed, pregnant. His life, never simple, got far more complicated.

# BOOK SEVEN:

Jax, having survived to claim the continent of Dravith, was now officially heir primus to the throne of the empire, and had one year in which to hold to his title, before he may climb the crystal steps to the throne of the empire.

Provided, of course, he survived long enough, and could travel to the heart of the empire to do so.

That wasn't the most terrifying change in his life, though. The Prince of the Empire, Imperial Scion and Master of all Dravith, had been struck with an entirely unexpected—albeit not unwelcome—new title as well: father-to-be.

Oracle, his love, his wisp and soul mate, was pregnant, and after sobering up and realizing the implications of this, he turned to the only being he felt he could speak to frankly, and that wouldn't be over-awed by him, or forced to sugarcoat an answer.

The God of Light and Order, Sint.

Unfortunately, due to his divine nature, Sint had never had to deal with such matters, and so gave little advice beyond the immediate to secure the throne and the continent, and to deal with any and all threats as quickly as possible.

He did, however, also give Jax a quest, and a great deal of information, as well as advice, on the next step, regarding the fragment of divinity that Jax recovered from Nimon.

Jax had two choices before him. The first was that he absorb the fragment, and gain a significant boost in power. Although Jax was instantly tempted by that, he was warned that this was, in fact, the lesser of the two paths open to him.

The second was to bind the fragment to his soul, and begin his ascension to godhood.

Ten fragments were required to lift him into the ranks of the lesser gods, on par with Darakin and Issa, Illoth and Asmodeus, among others.

When Jax decided to bind the fragment, and attempted ascension instead of absorbing it, Sint offered him a quest to do so, and then left him to find his path.

Over the ensuing days, Jax battled to bring stability to his fledgling and resurgent empire. He named Thomas as Leader of the Imperial Senate, and others to high offices, before turning control of Himnel over to Duke Augustus and Clan Mother Hellenica.

While trying to bring order to the city, and hand over responsibility for it, an attempted assassination brought to his attention that not all in the city were either devoted, or at least apathetic to his rule.

Instead, in the ancient and forgotten "wizards tower" in the center of the city, a new force had taken up residence…one that had successfully hidden from his forces and his abilities.

In the ensuing fight, he discovered that the notification advising all that he had formally claimed his place in the succession of the empire wasn't limited to only the UnderVerse.

The banished and escaped nobles of his own realm, Earth, had also received such information, and, in a fit of rage, had begun to return, en masse, through forbidden blood magic rituals.

The destructive nature of blood magic meant that the portals used to return them were rendered to scrap afterward, and no control over the location of the far portal was possible.

As such, many of the nobles emerged into long forgotten or ruined locations. There was no way to control or maintain the connection, and many died in transit, but some—including his father—made it through.

Their locations were hidden, but as Jax explored and then destroyed the Himnel tower, he found that it was not the only local emergence point.

Travelling to Narkolt, he led a stealthy search of the area around that city's tower, finding that it, too, had fallen to the enemy.

Although the majority of the legion were training at the Great Tower, and Thomas and his team had been dispatched to secure the imperial production facility—whose portal was also active and under enemy control—Jax was counterattacked by forces of the old nobility.

In the fight that followed, Jax learned more of the secrets behind the fall, and that although Narkolt appeared strong from the outside, even with the infiltrators purged, it stood at the brink of collapse.

Raiders, escaped smugglers, Dark legionnaires, and the local and now displaced nobility who refused to serve the empire had fled into the nearby forests.

There, they raided the villages and caravans that made up the lifeblood of Narkolt, and after the war with Himnel, its own forces were severely depleted.

Jax worried about the team that had been sent to the prax Glorious Retribution—now known as the sunken city—far off the coast, but agreed to hold off on travelling to secure it. Instead, he led his forces to secure the forest, as Restun and Romanus, of the legion, brought in reinforcements to assist.

In the ensuing battle, an ancient harp, the Cursed Harp of Athelas, was discovered. The party nearly succumbed to its lure, abandoning all control, before Ronin, the bard, saved them.

Other camps hidden in the forest were drawn to the sounds of battle. Jax and his party led the rescued and sworn guards saved from the harp's influence to defend the camp, until Tenandra arrived, her ripple fire cannons clearing the field.

Over the next several days, the party recovered, and although emotionally damaged through the influence of the harp's evil magic, they grew closer, as they travelled to the sunken city.

Once there, they found that it, too, had been invaded by the nobles. The party that held the control center had access to a portal, and had captured the group Jax had sent ahead.

In the fight to save them, and to take control of the site, a panicking son of the noble who had laid claim to the structure triggered an artifact, suppressing all use of mana in the area, and trapped Jax in a collapsed section, after they used explosive weaponry from Earth.

Jax, cut off from magic, with his abilities suppressed, spells not available, and significant injuries, was forced to battle his way down to the lowest levels of the prax, to then return upward through a different, and less damaged section.

During the trek, he recovered several large and powerful manastones, giving him limited access to mana but at a horrifically inflated cost, faced foes who had taken over the lower reaches of the city and who had been mutated by the constant exposure to mana, and finally, discovered and rescued a group of semi-feral gnomes.

Using the gnomes, and their knowledge of the prax, Jax recovered some ancient Praetorian armor, and, wearing it, fought his way through the remaining guards of the invaders and to the control room.

Blinded, he attacked, desperate to reach Oracle and his friends, feeling that she and Sehran had somehow been sent far from him. Unable to see, he was forced through a portal to a hidden location, before the portal was again shut.

Trapped on the far side, he discovered Sehran, starving and cut off from her lover, Jian. He bound her to himself, giving her access to his mana and saving her life.

He was, however, surrounded.

Hundreds of both the long dead and the more recently captured attacked him, and he discovered the terrifying reality of the buried city he had been cast into.

It was a long forgotten, and hated, outpost of a creature that was old when the gods first walked the land. For it, mana was inimical to its form: a sentient, distributed liquid intelligence. In forcing its form into these bodies, and the bodies of the soldiers and the other nobility who had been caught exploring its depths, it had learned much about the realm, and now was ready to attempt to lay claim to it once again.

In the deep past, far greater gods than those who currently walked the UnderVerse died in their attempt to cleanse reality of its infection.

Now, with them long gone, the Dark Tide, Xenefier, was returning. In discovering Oracle, a creature both of magic and of flesh in a way it had never encountered, was pregnant, it realized it had found a way to both survive the hated touch of mana and evolve to its highest possible state.

All it had to do was take Jax and Oracle's unborn child and contaminate it with its own form. As that child grew, with its inherited mastery of mana at an instinctual level and access to the imperial throne and all the abilities that inferred, it could finally claim the realm and rule over all.

Jax, Oracle, and Sehran managed to escape, and in doing so destroyed much of the city, fleeing into underground caverns and along long-buried and forgotten passages. But Xenefier survived, wounded, driven back…but not destroyed.

In their escape, Jax and his now much smaller party encountered a second city, though this one was far more recent in creation—a living city, one that was in a constant state of war with Xenefier and its creations, and also with the creatures known as S'barrr, huge reptilian things that hunted the city's inhabitants, the Xon'dike.

The Xon'dike—survivors of a second, much more heavily damaged, crashed prax—had devolved, losing much of their technology and knowledge, reverting into a superstitious and fanatical group, one built around the worship of…the empire.

When Sehran fed on an injured S'barrr and discovered—too late—that its blood was in effect a highly concentrated alcohol, she let slip Jax's identity, and far from falling to their knees and worshipping him, they declared him a blasphemer and heretic.

Jax, Oracle, and a cleansed Sehran were forced to flee, not wanting to kill a bunch of misguided fools who might be recoverable, and after many hours, finally found their way to the surface. Unfortunately, what they found, as Oracle recognized a distant landmark, was that they were even farther from home than they feared.

They were not even on the same continent.

Instead, as they stared out across miles of rolling sand dunes, the heat of the barren desert shimmering, and making the remains of the ancient buried city in the distance seem to hover, they realized that they were alone, far from home.

Jez Cajiao

# **<u>PROLOGUE</u>**

"What the hell do you mean, they're not here?" Thomas growled at Grizz, who stood at attention, facing the brother of his missing prince.

"I mean they're not here, sir!" Grizz replied. The fury that had driven him for the last few days, ever since he'd managed to kill that fucker of a lord and free them all, rose as he met Thomas's eyes.

"Then where the hell is he?"

"We don't know," Lydia said before Grizz could reply, marching tiredly up the slope of the fallen building to reach the others. "He went through a portal, a portal we now can't activate, and he was with Oracle and Sehran. They're all alive, but that's all we know."

"So, what?" Thomas groaned. "He could be anywhere in the fucking realm now? Hell, all the realms?!"

"No, sir," Grizz said. "The portal led to a city, one that was buried underground, apparently, and that they'd been going to and from already. The survivors of the lord's guard on this side told us about it, after a little persuasion."

"And?"

"And they were tricked into going through, then attacked. There's something living on the other side, something that's able to take over the people it catches. No idea how or why, but once it's in them, they can't go back through the portal. They'd come up to the edge, apparently, and try anything to get the guys on this side to go through, but they can't step over to this side themselves."

"Sounds dodgy."

"Very. The son was left in charge of the lord's guard here; he'd been opening it and trying to find his father, or to connect to anywhere else. Apparently, the father went through and took the rest of the keys with him. Something about needing to know where you're going means that, without the right key, you could end up anywhere. Then we attacked, and he panicked, thinking the possessed ones had gotten through somehow. He triggered the mana null field and wiped out all magic on this side. We were hit by some powerful weapons from your home. Jax was lost. He fell down a hole to a lower level," Grizz reported, still standing at attention.

"He's down below? You said…"

"No," Lydia snapped, looking around. "D' ye think we'd be 'ere otherwise? They used some gas on us, and lightning sticks that knocked us out. Then, when we woke up, we were naked, in cages."

"We were trying to get free, then Jax appears, in new full armor and looking seriously pissed. He ran at them, and the dickhead noble triggered the portal, sending him through and closing it after him," Grizz continued.

"So, you let yourselves get fucking captured. Then my brother, who came to rescue you all, *his guards*, ended up being kicked through a portal to some buried shithole?" Thomas snapped. "He could be fucking anywhere and—"

"He's there," Tenandra interrupted, raising a hand and pointing, staring off into the distance over the rolling leaden sea. "I can sense him, although not Oracle or Sehran, not properly. I can feel my bond to him as my master, though, and the Scion…"

"Where?" the others all said at almost the same time, spinning and looking out to sea, ignoring the rain that was being driven in and the heavy storm clouds.

"Far, far away in that direction," she said. "Weeks of travel possibly…maybe months."

"Fuck!" Thomas cursed, turning and walking away, rubbing at his chin as people streamed past, both his squad going to help Jax's, and the crew going to help the crew of the other ship.

"Can you use the portal?" Lydia asked Tenandra. "You were the prax's wisp—could you activate the portal? Get us through to him?"

"Provided you still have the key, it's possible." Tenandra said. "That would be linked to the destination; it should be easy to—"

Lydia shook her head, cutting her off. "We've no got it. The asshole who 'ad it took it with him, but…"

"If the key is gone, then no." Tenandra said, thinking quickly. "Without the key, we would need to repair and activate the command center, and the work needed to repair the pathways and reconnect the portal would be weeks, possibly *months* alone."

"And if we do that, and you can't get the portal working, we've wasted a horrific amount of time," Thomas growled, stepping back in close. "At least weeks we could have been flying to Jax."

"Exactly."

"But we could get halfway, or more, then Jax could use the portal on his end, get himself back through, and the only way we'd know is if you felt it." Lydia looked at Tenandra.

"True." Tenandra turned to Thomas. "I was ordered by Jax that, if I lost contact with him and the others for twenty-four hours, then I was to leave and return with you."

"You left as soon as you were cut off from them," Thomas said. "I already told you that was the right choice."

"It was, but it was also hard, because I didn't want to. I wanted to land and help; I wanted to save the ones I loved and be involved in that, not simply wait while I flew to get help."

"What's your point?"

"You face the same decision now," Tenandra said. "Jax has ordered the empire to remain here, in Dravith. If he is lost, even if only for a short time, then the empire is to pull in and consolidate. The legion are to train the next generation, and we are to go on without him."

"I won't abandon my brother!" Thomas snapped. "He came to this fucking shithole of a realm for me, started a war with that dark dickhead, and you think I should…"

"No," Lydia said, having seen what Tenandra was aiming for. "No, she don't mean yer give up—she means yer need to stay here."

"Here?!?" Thomas looked around at the ruined prax. "Why the hell would I…"

"If *you* stay here, you can recover the golems. You can lead the gnomes and clear out the lower reaches of the prax." Tenandra's gaze grew distant. "As more and more golems are recovered and reactivated, you can repair the most basic functions of the prax, providing power to the systems and beginning recovery. As more sections are repaired, you'll be able to activate the portal, and with the control facilities, you can connect to any portal in its records, rather than using keys."

"No, you could do that better than me." Thomas glanced at Tenandra.

"I'll be with the others, flying straight at Jax. I'm the only one who can both sense and fly an airship to him."

"Then I'll come with you."

"That's a decision you'll have to make, Thomas. If you come with us, then the prax will stay as it is. If, for some reason, like not having the right damn key, Jax can't reopen the portal from his side, then he's trapped there."

"You said the dickhead's son is here and had the key, so he can make another one, right?"

"He did, but as Lydia said, it was snapped in the fight," Grizz said. "We can't get it to connect. The portal powers up, draining us all to do it, but fails at the last point. Arrin and Giint think it's the key not working, but it could be anything, or…"

"Or?"

"Or the portal might be broken."

"Then I'm wasting my fucking time here!" Thomas snapped.

"No, only one with imperial right can command the golems. If, when they're woken up, they go into an attack mode or refuse to listen? Then the only one who can make them obey is you, Thomas. If you come with us, then you make it so that Jax can't come back this way without us finding him by ship."

"Can the golems fix the portal?" Thomas asked after a long few seconds of chewing his knuckle.

"Perhaps," Tenandra hedged. "If the golem is a high enough level crafter, complex at least, then it could fix it…a servitor, maybe. But if they can't?"

"Yeah?"

"There was a second portal in storage."

"Where?"

"In the main hold."

"So maybe at the bottom of the fucking sea?"

"Maybe, but Grizz, you said that Jax turned up in new armor?"

"Yeah, a full set of original Praetorian Guard armor. It was beautiful," he said softly.

"Then the armory is intact, or reachable at least. It was near the storage area. Thomas, you have two choices to make. I *have* to go to him; only I can find him. You can come with me and accept that, if he finds a working portal, then he can make it back on his own to the continent, but not here, or…"

"Or I can repair enough of the prax to power the portal and the control center, then we can go to him," Thomas whispered, closing his eyes. "I stay here and do fucking housekeeping, repair shit, and babysit the goddamn crazy fucking gnomes while we just hope he makes it back to us."

"It be a shitty choice, either way," Lydia admitted. "We can't go an' get more of the legion, so it's just us, flying tae another continent and hopin' we can find him before the locals kill us or our food runs out, or we stay here an' wait for him tae sort it out himself."

"This is the best chance we can give him, Thomas, you know that." Belladonna strode up and laid her hand on his shoulder, her elven ears having let her listen in as she'd approached.

"I know," he said slowly. "I just don't like it."

"You don't have to like it," she said. "You just have to do it. We don't get to choose the way we serve; we're soldiers. You can give him the best chance at surviving by staying here. Tenandra and his squad can go to him. We can cross-load as much food and other supplies as we can to her now, and she can leave immediately. The other ship can return to Himnel and give Duke Augustus a full report. Maybe he'll overrule us, but until then, and until they come back with those orders and more food, you have the responsibility to choose."

"Lydia," Thomas snapped after a few seconds of thought. "Strip anything and everything you need from here; you leave in an hour. Go find my goddamn brother."

"Yes sir!" she barked, fist crashing against her breastplate in salute, before she spun and shouted out orders to the others, sending them running.

"Hold on, bro…they're coming," Thomas whispered, staring out and feeling Bella's hand as it shook his pauldron gently, sharing her presence.

They stood there, watching the seabirds wheel in the rapidly darkening sky, the call of an albatross hanging in the air as it sailed past. Far out to sea, the motion of something under its surface sent a V-shaped wake half a mile long rolling out behind it.

"Maybe that's not all we can do." Thomas watched the wake as it faded, the massive form slipping back into the deep. "Maybe we can send more help his way, after all…"

"What do you—"

"Move it, people!" he shouted, turning on his heel and running for the second ship.

The captain was attempting to restart the engines and scratched his head as mainly feral gnomes clambered over them.

"You!" Thomas snapped, pointing to two of them. "I need you both and that golem."

# CHAPTER ONE

"**W**ell, fuck," I repeated, standing between Oracle and Sehran and staring out across the endless expanse of sand. The remains of the distant city shimmered in the heat haze like a mirage, its destroyed pillars and crumbling dome a testament to just how far the continent had fallen since then, with most of the city entirely buried in sand. "Just how far are we talking here?"

"From here to anywhere actually livable? It could be thousands of miles." Oracle's voice cracked. She wiped tears from her cheeks, the hot wind already drying them.

We stood on the side of a rocky outcropping, several hundred meters up. We stared out at the rolling sand dunes, shimmering in the full heat of the day. In the distance, I could see a handful more of similar small, eroded rocky outcroppings. But beyond that?

It looked the way I imagined the depth of the Sahara did, all rolling sand, baked in the pitiless glare of the sun.

"The Great Altan was always massive, but from what I'm seeing…" She shook her head. "It's spread, consumed what used to be grasslands and forests. That city—I recognize the Dome of Truth!—shouldn't be in a desert at all. Before the fall, this area was known for its fertile fields!"

"Is it all like this?" Sehran shaded her eyes with one hand and squinted out at the rolling sea of dunes. "I mean, the entire continent…could it all be ruined? You said that we're not on Dravith anymore, right?"

"I don't know, but that looks exactly like the dome of truth, and for it to be ruined like this? I just don't know." Oracle admitted, reaching down and rubbing her belly unconsciously in an attempt to soothe our unborn child.

"Wonderful." I shifted uncomfortably in my armor, already feeling like I was being slow-cooked in the rolling heat of the sun. The Praetorian plate had seemed like such a good idea in the cool tunnels below. Now? Not so much. "So what's our play here?"

Sehran peered out from the cave mouth, her wings twitching. "We could fly? I mean, I know your flight costs you health and mana, but Oracle and I could help carry you maybe?"

"No." I shook my head. "You both need my mana to live. I've got maybe enough mana for one short flight, but I can run for a bit as well, and try to regenerate as much as we can before the shit hits the fan next."

I glanced back into the darkness of the tunnel. Distant echoes of pursuit had faded after Sehran's spell brought down the roof, but that wouldn't hold the Xon'dike forever. "We can't stay here either." I sighed.

"We have mana…not much, but we have some," Oracle pointed out.

"Could we make a change to how we're bonded?" Sehran asked diffidently, and we both looked at her curiously.

"Go on," Oracle encouraged.

"Well, I need your mana—or blood—to stay here," Sehran pointed out. "But while I'm trying to limit how much I can take, what if we changed things around?"

"How?" I asked.

"Well, I'm bonded to Oracle at the minute, and I know we talked about changing my bond back to you, Jax, but what if we didn't?"

"You prefer girls now?" Oracle asked archly, trying to interject a little humor.

"Well, you're certainly better-smelling than Jax or Jian…" Sehran smiled. "But seriously, you have your own manapool now, Oracle, and I draw from whoever I'm bonded to, so it's sort of like I'm feeding on you while you're trying to use the pool as well."

"So?" I asked.

"We're not releasing you, Sehran, so don't even think it," Oracle said firmly. "You're family, and I'd rather be without mana and have you anytime."

"And I want to watch you having her," I added unthinkingly, joking obviously, then realizing that to Sehran, that was perfectly acceptable and even much more normal than being with just one person. "Dammit, I meant…"

"You meant what you said." Sehran cut me off with a throaty chuckle. "But I know you were just teasing. It's okay. What I meant was, what if you looked at it as Oracle didn't have her own manapool? That way, if she goes back to using yours as a matter of course, then I can both feed on hers and use it to cast my spells. It means…"

"It means that you're able to add a lot more to the fight." I cut her off. "There's no point in you not being able to fight with everything you have. We need to find you a real weapon again as well."

She tapped a nail on the pair of daggers she'd looted at some point, then shrugged. "They work for now, but yeah, primarily I'd rather use a whip and my spells."

"Let's do it that way." Oracle nodded. "You don't mind sharing with me, my love?" She batted her eyelashes at me, and adjusted her top so that she looked as appealing as possible.

I snorted. "You use my mana all the time anyway, but this way we know which order we're going in. It makes sense. And Oracle? I'm too tired and we're too exposed here. I don't have time for a nap afterward, so you need to behave!"

"Shame." She sighed, then grinned before going on. "Okay, we don't have much time and I doubt a tunnel collapse will hold the Xon'dike for long. So. The Dome of Truth, that bit that we can see from here, was referenced in books as a seat of local government and center of magical research," Oracle offered, her voice steadying as she shifted into sensible mode. "If any of the artifacts survived…"

"They'd have been looted in the centuries since it fell," I finished for her flatly.

"We don't know that, so we have to try." She squared her shoulders determinedly. "There might be a usable portal, manastones, magical items we could use to boost your mana regeneration, or at least a map!"

A faint screech from far out over the desert to our left cut through our discussion, and we all spun. Something large and reptilian dove fast toward a dune in the far distance, furling leathery wings as it screeched.

A small herd of…something burst into view, sprinting up and over the dune. The flying monstrosity twisted in midair and unleashed a second screech that sent a handful of them tumbling from sight, stunned.

The distance made details impossible, but as it vanished between the dunes, the faint death screams carried clearly enough to make it obvious it wasn't a good day for whatever those things had been.

"A wyvern, using some form of sonic attack," Oracle whispered, swallowing hard.

I reached out, putting one hand on her shoulder again, and drew her in close.

Sonic attacks had done tremendous damage to her in the past, and that was when she didn't have to worry about a child in her womb.

"We can do this," Sehran said grimly. "We can!"

"Damn right," I agreed. "Though, I think it's time we moved." I put my helm on the ground, checking straps and quickly working over my armor as Oracle stepped back to give me room. "So, we've got giant flying lizards ahead, religious zealots probably digging their way through the cave-in behind us, and we're thousands of miles from home. Did I miss anything?"

"The heat will kill you in that armor," Sehran pointed out helpfully. "And if you have to constantly use your mana to fight, we'll almost certainly die of thirst before we reach the city."

"Thanks for that." I sighed, before picking my helmet back up and shaking my head in disgust. "I feel thirsty just looking at that mess," I admitted, nodding to the desert before us.

Oracle created a small fountain, letting it splash for a moment as I quickly checked through my bag and pulled out, then filled my canteen and took a drink; then I stepped back, with Sehran leaning in, in my place before Oracle dismissed it. "I can always make water, but it costs mana we can't spare too often," she said. "Not until you've recovered more mana anyway."

"I'm used to less water than you, I think, so I can go without longer," Sehran offered. "One of the joys of coming from a literal hellscape."

"It's not going to make much of a difference," I assured her. "Either I'll recover enough of my mana that we're fine, or we're in so many constant fights that it's used up and we're up shit creek. But thanks for the thought. Besides, it's not like it'll cost us any more to summon the water for us both as it does for me. It's a fountain, remember."

I gestured to where the fountain still bubbled merrily.

"I know, just…" She shrugged and smiled.

"You were just helping, I know." I took one last look at the cave mouth, then out at the city. It had to be at least ten miles away, probably more given how the heat haze distorted distance.

"No, fuck this. We'll wait until sunset, and that'll give me time to fully regenerate my mana," I decided. "Less chance of cooking me alive in this can as well, though we need to be ready to move if the Xon'dike break through. Oracle, could you scout around us? See if there's anything obvious between us and the city we should know about? And watch out for fliers!"

She nodded, lifting into the air. "Be careful," she warned, then streaked skyward.

"Sehran, check out the tunnel, will you? I'm going to try to meditate, see if I can speed up my mana regeneration, and we need to know if they are actually digging at it, or if they've all gone home."

"Of course." She moved to the cave mouth, positioning herself where she could see both in and out. "Though, if you're meditating, you might want to at least take off some of that armor. You're starting to smell like a roast."

I grimaced, because she had a point. But fuck it, it wasn't like we were anywhere safe enough that I wasn't going to need it sooner rather than later. Better to be ready than not, and maybe just relax a few of the cinches. "Wake me if anything moves in either direction, please."

"Even the pretty lizard?" She grinned, showing her dimples…and her fangs.

"Especially the pretty lizard." I settled against the cave wall, closing my eyes. "I've had enough surprises for one day."

The heat pressed in, even in the shade of the cave, but I forced myself to focus. Roughly judging from the sun, we had maybe three hours until sunset. Three hours to rest, recover, and prepare.

My Wisdom was high enough that I recovered fifteen points a minute of mana now; three hours was roughly…two thousand seven hundred mana. My manapool was just over two thousand two hundred. That meant that water and mana for Oracle and by extension Sehran shouldn't be a problem, but fuck it.

I shouldn't be here, not with my damn squad back onboard the prax. I shouldn't be thousands of miles from my supporters. And if I was being entirely honest?

I shouldn't be anywhere but back home in God's country, drinking in a bar in Newcastle.

Should and shouldn't had little to do with my life these days, so screw it. What will be will be.

"They're digging, but it sounds distant. I'll keep an eye on it," Sehran whispered to me at one point, and I nodded, not opening my eyes.

An occasional gust of wind brought a wave of scorching air and stinging sand. I heard Sehran cursing softly, as she scouted nearby, and somewhere in the distance, something roared.

It was going to be a damn long night, so when I started to have issues clearing my mind with everything that had happened, I forced myself to accept that, and rested instead.

Sehran shook me as Oracle returned about two hours later, her wings blurring and vanishing as she landed, moving to sit down close to me and sighing.

I reached for her, taking her in my arms.

Her expression told me everything I needed to know even before she started to speak, and that it wasn't good news.

"There's a watering hole about halfway to the city and maybe three miles to the east," she reported after a long hug, shifting to settle beside me. "But it's…occupied. Some kind of burrowing creatures. They look like a cross between scorpions and crabs, about the size of large dogs. They come up whenever anything approaches the water, so there's a lot of back and forth going on."

"The other creatures in the area need the water to live, so we're gonna be encountering things as we pass it. Wonderful." I groaned, pushing myself to my feet and beginning to buckle my armor back on, glad for even the slight drop in temperature. "Numbers? Could we kill them all and then leave, let the other monsters in the area be drawn to the water and the blood?"

"I counted at least twenty before they burrowed back under the sand. There could be more."

"Of course there could." I finished with the last strap, checking each piece was secure. "Anything else?"

"The city's farther than it looks, closer to fifteen miles. And there are more of those flying lizards. Though I'd guess they'd be the kind to hunt mainly at dawn and dusk." She paused. "And I saw tracks. Huge ones, like something's been dragging itself through the sand."

"Because why not?" I shouldered my bag, checking my naginata was secure. "All right then. My mana is doing a hell of a lot better, even if my meditation was shit. I'm at…" I paused, checking the numbers, and grunted.

"Two thousand and eighty-seven of two thousand two hundred and ten. I was thinking we wait until full darkness, but to hell with it. We stick together, move to the city as quietly as we can, and hope like hell we don't attract attention. As to the water hole…" I paused, looking from one of them to the other. "I don't think we need to go there, do we?"

"Water would usually be a necessity," Oracle admitted, smiling, "But even if we needed to save mana, Sehran could alternate feeding on us and we can keep our mana high enough to easily cover things like that."

"I could not feed…" Sehran suggested, looking ashamed, before Oracle wrapped her arms around the succubus and hugged her tight.

"Don't be ridiculous. It's like asking Jax to just stop eating, or me to quit needing mana. I need it just like you do, and I drained mana, health, and stamina from Jax for a hell of a lot longer than you did Jian."

"Of course that's not all you drain from Jian…" I joined in, winking at her and wrapping my arms around them both. "Seriously, Sehran, it's exactly the same as me needing food or water. You need to eat and drink, and some mana, just like me. No need to be ashamed about it. And we can always share the bond when we need to if mana is getting to be an issue."

"Thank you." The demon smiled at us both, as we stepped back, releasing her.

"So, anything else out there, Oracle?" I asked.

She shook her head. "Not that I could see, but I'd suggest we search the city first. There's signs all around that the area was smashed hard by something, and I'll bet, judging from the Xon'dike we met, it was a prax failing. There's a trail of destruction that leads deeper into the desert, and clearly something massive hit the ground nearby, a long time ago. The Xon'dike said they came from a prax, and if it buried itself, that'd explain a lot of the damage."

"Damn, I don't want to imagine what being aboard one of those would have been like at the end," I muttered.

"It'd have been horrible." Oracle nodded seriously. "I don't know exactly what happened, but when Amon, the Eternal Emperor, was killed and the gods banished, mana across the realm would have gone haywire. Then add in the moon falling and the cataclysm?

"The prax failing and crashing down would have been the last straw. Maybe a handful of the original crew would have survived the crash, but most would have been killed instantly."

"And anyone who was under them as well," Sehran pointed out. "If the prax fell from high enough, could that have caused the desert?"

"Unlikely," I mused, shaking my head. "A desert doesn't just appear. But if it damaged or blocked a river or waterway, that might have led to the desert expanding past its old borders. Have you seen deserts before?"

"Once, though it was only for a single night, and well, we don't tend to get summoned for moonlight walks and exploring." Sehran winked with a throaty chuckle.

"I bet!" Oracle sighed. "You've seen so much more of the realm than me, though, and for forever, it was all I could do to read about it."

"Yeah, a thousand bedchambers' ceilings, and the view…not the best, if I'm honest, though there were also a lot of windowsills I was bent over." She shrugged, and I shook my head at the madness of comparisons.

For me, I'd been a damn barman not that long ago, filling fridges and pouring shitty knockoffs of cocktails in a nightclub that you only attended when you were already so drunk that you could barely walk.

Oracle, in comparison, had been deep in hibernation, an asexual wisp that was forced into servitude to look after the Great Tower of Dravith's magical knowledge. When I'd reawakened her, due to the damage I'd done from using so many spellbooks in a short time, she'd been forced to bond directly to me to keep me alive.

It was only through a very specific set of circumstances that she'd been able to do that, and damn I was fortunate, looking back. Of course, looking forward, I was also the prince of the empire—a fallen and broken empire, but fuck it—and I'd still also somehow managed to get Oracle pregnant. A being that had been entirely magical, until she'd "made" a body to make me happy. Yeah…that seemingly minor decision had opened a whole new can of worms.

I shook the distraction off as I adjusted my armor, shaking my head at the damage I'd managed to do to the ancient Praetorian Guard armor in just a day or two.

It reflected a level of craftsmanship that would make a legion armorer weep for joy, and inside of a day, I'd taken it from gleaming and spotless to battered and scratched. Its red plates that sat over a blackened leather undergarment still admittedly looked impressive and provided incredible defense, but damn. Thorn was going to kill me…and that was only if Restun was too busy having apoplexy to do it himself.

"Ready?" I settled my helmet into place and lifted my naginata, geared up, as I looked over at the other two.

Both women nodded, and we left the cave. The distant sounds of digging had grown noticeably louder even as we spoke.

I strode out into the slowly darkening evening, moving up to the edge of the rocky area the cave jutted out from and idly kicking a shower of small stones and debris over the edge to fall toward the sand far below.

I saw what had presumably once been a cliffside or rocky promontory. The cave we'd been sheltering in was about three-quarters of the way up the side of it, and looking about…

"Damn, it hit *hard*, didn't it?" I asked, unthinking.

"I don't know how they survived," Oracle admitted quietly. "The devastation, coming as it would have right after the bond to the emperor being broken, and the gods going silent? It must have been horrific."

"Well, they had a chance to get that bond back, to make friends and even gain your protection, considering the way they fought those big beasts, but I screwed that up." Sehran said softly, "I'm sorry."

"Don't be daft." I shrugged and settled my armor one last time. "You were off your face on basically a hundred percent proof whisky that ran in the creature's veins, and I told you to feed on it, so if it's anyone's fault, it's mine."

"I still feel—" she started.

"I know." I cut her off. "And I still feel like I should have done more… more in the prax, more in the fight since—hell, I should have figured things out better in the beginning with the damn tower and we could have all been living there with a hell of a lot less stress. Regardless, what we've got is what we've got, so fuck it."

I smiled as a saying that an old friend of mine used to use floated through my mind. "As the saying goes, you can only piss with the knob you've got."

"I don't have—"

"I know!" I snorted. "It means you can only deal with things as they are, not how you might wish them to be. What happened, happened; now we need to deal with it and move on."

Sheran nodded. Then, moving past us and tapping one of my armored pauldrons with a fingernail, she grinned and gestured to the sky ahead of us. "Shall we?" she suggested. "I know it's getting dark, and I know it's dangerous and all, but it feels like a perfect night for flying!"

"We can't fly for long, or at least I can't," I said softly. "As much as I'd rather that, it'll draw attention from the wyverns, as well as using mana we might need. Better that we fly down to the sand, and then jog for a bit, fly for a stretch once my mana's recovered again and then jog…keep doing that until we reach the city."

"You really want to run fifteen miles across sand in all of that?" Sehran blinked.

"No, but I'm going to do whatever I need to, to make sure we get there safe and ready for anything," I said firmly. "And so are you."

"I hate running," she muttered, even as Oracle let loose with a laugh, clearly feeling the same way.

"You two can fly, as long as you stay low to the ground most of the time," I suggested, lifting into the air as I stepped off the edge of the cliff. "I'll run. It'll lessen the mana drain."

"There's no way I was running, I was planning on using the 'but I'm pregnant' excuse if I had to," Oracle added in an unsubtle whisper to Sehran as I soared out ahead, eyes sweeping from side to side, searching for any sign of a threat.

"Thank the gods!" Sehran grinned. Her own leathery wings caught the thermals and sent her soaring, enabling her to glide with little effort. I swooped down, landing a few hundred meters out into the sands and staggering as I caught myself.

The sand shifted underfoot, making each step an effort. Even with the sun setting, the heat was oppressive, like running in a damn oven. For a short while, though, once I adjusted to a better rhythm, I lost myself to the comfort of running, my armor a joy to wear as it flowed with my movements like silk, despite the buildup of goddamn heat.

I was going to be losing a gallon of water a mile at this rate, or so it felt.

We'd made it maybe half a mile when the first tremor ran through the ground. I froze, and Oracle and Sehran took to the air instinctively.

"Movement," Sehran hissed. "About fifty yards back, something big."

"No shit." I watched as a ridge of sand rose up, like something massive was tunneling just beneath the surface. It was headed straight for us. "Ladies? I think it's time for some flight!"

I gathered my mana and prepared to trigger Soaring Majesty. The ridge of sand got closer, picking up speed, and I slowed, curious more than anything else. I was confident in both my ability to escape, or to tear whatever it was a new arsehole.

I planted my feet, almost eager to see what was coming. After the clusterfuck that the Xon'dike had turned into, a straight-up fight would be refreshing. *And let's face it*, I thought to myself. *We really needed to know what the local creatures were like.* After all, those big dinosaur-looking monstrosities I'd fought with the Xon'dike were surprisingly easy.

"Jax!" Oracle called out in warning. "Don't you dare…"

The sand erupted a dozen meters in front of me; a massive, segmented form burst upward. It towered overhead, easily twenty meters long. Its armored carapace glistened with an oily sheen in the fading light. Multiple legs, each ending in wickedly curved claws, spread out from its sides as it twisted in midair. Mandibles the size of my arm clicked together as I stared at something like a centipede with additional leg issues.

They stuck out from all sides: flat paddle-like things—almost bristles, really— that shifted and twisted as it zeroed in on me. Then, like the S'barrr we'd faced oh so recently, additional mandibles slid out, then latched onto the front of the head.

They seemed to lock into place, before dragging back armored chitin, exposing pink flesh and rows upon rows of teeth. And all around the outside, revealed now that the armor was back out of the way?

"Oh, you beautiful bastard," I breathed, hefting my naginata.

The creature's head snapped toward the sound, revealing hundreds of compound eyes that glowed with an eerie purple light.

"It's a sand wurm!" Oracle's voice held equal parts fascination and amazement. "They're not supposed to be this far south!"

"Less biology lesson, more killing it!" Sehran dove from above, her wings carrying her in a tight spiral around the beast's head, drawing its attention as the paddles shifted and flickered. "It's tracking by sound!"

I frowned. "Why have the eyes then? And why the hell do they glow?" I shouted back. "Fuckin' waste of time—what are they gonna see?"

I triggered Mana Overdrive just as the wurm struck, its body coiling like a spring. The rush of power let me dodge the initial strike, rolling to the side as tons of chitin and muscle slammed into the sand where I'd been standing. The teeth burrowed deeper as it dislodged sand, and pebbles fountained from filters on its sides.

My naginata flashed out, connecting with one of the hundreds of legs, and easily severed it; leaving a deep gouge through the flesh behind. The wurm screamed, a sound like metal being torn apart, as I reared back up and it whirled to face me again.

"You know," I called out, dancing back from another strike, "I think I prefer the religious fanatics!"

Oracle's magic lit up the darkening sky; a blast of lightning hammered into the wurm's side. It staggered, giving me the opening I needed. I lunged forward, channeling fire through my weapon as I drove it deep into the creature's side. Then, as it coiled around it, howling fit to burst, I started to move.

I dragged the glowing blade sideways along its length even as it curled up, trying to protect its vulnerable innards.

Instead of attacking, it tried to defend, its chitinous covering closing and locking in tight as it tried to trap my weapon, to lock me in place.

Instead, I channeled a little more mana into the weapon. The bright-blue/white, red, and yellow light of high-temperature flames sent the flesh around it smoking and blackening, and I dug my feet into the sand, pushing and striding onward.

The wurm thrashed, rolling and nearly yanking the naginata from my grip. Its tail whipped around then, catching me in the chest and finally sending me flying. I hit the sand hard, rolling with the impact as best as I could in my armor.

"Jax!" both women called out in unison.

"I'm fine!" I pushed myself up, spitting sand. "Just getting warmed up!"

"Jax, it's using magic…" Oracle called out.

I frowned, looking at the massive wurm.

Small bumps and lumps along its length flared with light, then shifted, changing through the colors all the way to black—that weird UV light stick/purple light that was all the rage in the nineties.

Then the little emitters—because what the hell else could I call them—vanished, and the effect was like looking into a hole in space.

One that was attached to the outer skin and chitinous armor of a segmented wurm.

The effect of holes in space lasted only a split second…before a milky-white substance vomited out, spraying in all directions from each and every one of them.

I'd been knocked far enough back that when I ran to get out of the area of effect, I managed to get clear. But the sand on all sides?

Smoke started to rise, and rise fast. The sand bubbled and roiled as noxious gasses spread, obscuring the wurm, even as it dove, burrowing into the sand.

"Where is it?" I called to the other two, launching myself into the air, hovering higher and higher to get a better view, as they tried to make it out through the smoke.

"It's magical," Oracle suddenly called. "The smoke, it's helping to…oh."

"Oh?" I called when she paused. "What's 'oh'?"

"It's running away." She sounded annoyed. "It's already a few meters down and digging deeper. I don't think it's coming back!"

"Well, that's irritating," I admitted, shifting around and landing lightly on the sand a few dozen meters back from the smoking mess. "So, what? We either have to kill them straightaway, or fucking run?"

"Jax…" Sehran called out sharply, her gaze fixed out on the distant dunes to the east. "I think it rang the dinner bell when it left."

"What?" I looked over. A wyvern launched itself into the air, even as a screech behind me dragged my attention that way a second later.

On all sides, the wyverns were rising, and it wasn't just them, either. Three dunes over, there came a sudden surge in the sand, as what looked like a second wurm began to rise.

"Okay, fuck this, people—head for the city," I ordered.

"Jax, I'm going to use our Chameleon spell," Oracle told me quickly. "It'll help to hide us."

"Don't worry about me," Sehran added, even as Oracle started cast for us both.

I lifted into the air, Soaring Majesty triggering and draining mana, but giving me the boost I needed to fly fast and low across the sands.

As we went, in the distance, I could see that most of the wyverns were staying on course for the smoking sands. But one of them, incoming from just north and west, ahead of us and between us and the city, had clearly spotted us.

"Spread out and take it down," I ordered, my voice grim. "We can't let it alert the others."

I moved into the lead, noting the way that my armored gauntlet and naginata shimmered softly, before blending roughly with the sand all around us.

Glancing over at Oracle, I saw she was the same, the pair of us blending in as best we could, while Sehran…

She'd taken advantage of her species' inbuilt ability to adjust their forms. Normally she was, well, basically a sex kitten on crack. Right now, she was half the size, slimmer, and her skin had adjusted to mimic the sand.

Of course, minor issue—to do that, she'd had to adjust her form enough that her armor no longer fit, and she was busily packing it all away in her bag, while mid-flight, traveling about six inches off the surface of the sand.

"Are you fucking kidding me?" I hissed at her as the ground streaked by. The three of us wove in and out of sand dunes, staying as close to the ground as we could. "Why the hell are you naked!"

"Oracle needs the mana," she hissed. "This cuts the mana needed to hide us by a third!"

"I—" I snarled to myself before agreeing with her.

It literally saved us that mana. It was a sensible choice—it was…it was just fucking weird, that was all! No matter how often she did it, a friend who just kept getting bloody naked and viewed it as common sense freaked me out.

*"Jax, the wyvern!"* Oracle sent to me.

I squinted, searching for it. I'd lost it as we started really weaving in and out of the dunes, but I knew we had to be getting close…

It suddenly screeched, erupting from a nearby ridge, and twisted around, coming from the right and unleashing a barrage of sound. The blast wave sent Oracle cutting to the left, trying to get clear, even as I turned into it.

Sand was blasted up in waves; the very air shook as my skin trembled. My inner ear rolled and flipped, trying to convince me that up was down and left was right.

I pushed through it, squinting, aiming my naginata at the blur ahead of me.

Half a second later, when I braced for the expected impact, my blade extended and reaching, I heard Oracle's shout of anger as a blast of lightning was unleashed. Then I was blinking, bursting out of the sonic wave, and finding I'd completely missed the wyvern's change of direction.

It streaked past me, its wings almost clipping me—a clawed foot missed by a fraction of an inch.

I twisted, slashing up and behind. The blade passed through the air and totally missed, before the second detail I'd overlooked reared its ugly head.

The sand dune I plowed into sent me flipping over and crashing to a halt, even as lightning cracked again and again. *"Oracle?"* I shouted to her through the bond. I pushed myself back out of the sand that half covered me, twisting around, guided by her sensed location, and I saw a second wyvern darting in.

Then I saw that unlike the bug, it wasn't targeting me—it was after her.

"OI, DICKBAG!" I bellowed, triggering my rarely used Taunt ability and diverting its attention for a few seconds.

It shook itself and twisted around, going after her again.

"Jax, it's tracking my mana, I think!" she called, speeding around in a wide arc that brought it closer and closer…until Sehran landed nearby and sang at it.

Now, the wyvern presumably wasn't wired the same way as her usual prey. For a start, I didn't see it getting a beer with others of its kind on the weekend and somehow admiring a female wyvern's tits. But something about her abilities and powers clearly twanged on a nerve still because its head twisted around in mid-flight and its graceful flapping suddenly lost the rhythm.

That was all it took to distract it enough that as it looked back…it did so into our newly upgraded and evolved fireball.

Pyroclastic Blast was the name of the new spell, and it really brought home that although a lightning bolt might have your name on it, fireballs, and all the various evolutions thereof, were destined to forever be addressed as "to whom it may concern."

Oracle clearly wasn't happy about being hunted by the fucker.

As it fell from the sky, its leathery wings and feathered hide ablaze, the first wyvern screamed again, incoming from another dune top.

*"I'm coming to you!"* Oracle sent to me.

I sent her a burst of love and assurance, even as I felt Sehran through the bond as she readied herself for a second attack.

I struggled up the dune, the sand slipping and sliding under my feet, but I didn't dare spend mana to fly the short distance in case it warned the fucker.

I sank to one knee, feeling where Oracle was through the bond, even as Sehran clambered high on a dune to my left, pausing.

"Wait for it…" I whispered, more to myself, as she couldn't hear me from here, but still. "Wait…"

Oracle shot over the dune before me, passing literally close enough I could have reached out and snagged an ankle. Sehran let loose a warbling, magic-enhanced song at practically the same time.

*"Now!"*

I felt and heard Oracle's sending through the bond, and I lunged forward, standing tall and bringing the naginata around with a lick of fire mana to finish the job.

The wyvern had been hot on Oracle's heels, and as it approached the top of the dune, Sehran's cry had distracted it for a crucial second…its head was turned to its right, staring over to my left where Sehran stood.

Then it screeched in pain and horror as my blade passed through first the bones, and then the thin membrane of its left wing, cutting it cleanly off. It flipped over to slam headfirst into the sand on the far side of the dune behind me.

I'd heard the snap as it impacted half a second after my attack. Its speed did enough damage that I knew instinctively it was out of the fight. As I spun, racing down the dune and toward it, I saw Oracle and Sehran hurrying in as well.

"Is it dead?" Sehran called, and I snorted, jumping and skidding down the side of the dune in a cascade of sliding sand.

"Oh, it's dead all right," I called back. With the way the neck was bent in on itself, the creature had died instantly, not so much as a twitch ongoing. I slid to a stop at the bottom, turning to Oracle as she landed nearby. "You okay?" I asked her.

"Yeah, but I think we need to keep magic to a minimum," she said. "It was fixated on me, as was the other one."

"Sehran, are there more incoming?" I called to her.

She changed direction, beating her wings and lifting back toward the top of the dune, turning a full circle as I examined the creature with Oracle.

The wyvern was clearly the survivor of dozens, if not hundreds of fights, and it'd possibly also been used as a "noughts and crosses" board for a lot of years, judging from the oft-repeated and half-healed scars that covered it.

It had stood about four meters in height to the shoulder when alive, with two large back legs that it could clearly walk on, and two arms that also functioned as its wings.

Where dragons were four-legged and then had wings on their backs, wyverns only had the two legs, and were closer to birds in that they were also weirdly covered in small feathers, with a leathery hide underneath, instead of scales.

The tail was shorter and stubbier than I'd expected, and although the neck was long, it was arm length, rather than the great long necks of dragons. Finally, the head was short, with a clearly small brain, but massive eyes and a beak filled with serrated teeth.

All in all, it was a nasty-looking fucker, and I focused on it, checking it over as minor details started to glow, thanks to my Meridian Sight ability.

Important or valuable details became outlined in a subtle blue glow. As I looked it over, I couldn't help but nod. There was a lot of the creature that was valuable, I saw, but as Sehran called out, I cursed and turned from it.

The alchemy reagents would have to be left, as for now, at least, I had no time to fuck around. It was better to leave a body for the others in the area to get distracted by if they started after us, rather than taking the time to gut it, or put it more or less whole into my bag of holding.

"It's clear, if we move now!" Sehran called as she landed nearby. "The other wyverns are fighting one another near that smoke. They're going wild."

"Probably territorial," I guessed, before sighing. "Or fuck it, maybe they're all just pissed it's Tuesday. Who knows."

"So what do we do?" Sehran asked.

"We move," I said. "We head to the city, and we get out of sight. Once there, we can plan the next step."

"What he said," Oracle agreed with a smile, and I gave her a quick one-armed hug, before the three of us set off again.

The flight from here to the city was going to take a while, and despite my mana recovering reasonably fast due to my investments in Wisdom, we didn't dare just push all the way there.

I could have; I knew that. I could have flown all the way, but while the cost in mana and health of using my ability had been reduced, it still wasn't zero; and the last thing I needed was to get there and find it was inhabited by psychotic assholes and that I had low health and mana.

Instead, it meant that the next three hours were stress-filled, alternating between a fast flight for fifteen minutes or so, then an hour of resting, waiting as my mana recovered, and we all had a drink and basically sat around with our thumbs up our asses.

As soon as my mana had fully recovered, we were off again; fifteen minutes later, a break to recover—rinse and repeat.

All in all, it was more than a little frustrating, especially considering that the majority of the creatures we'd faced weren't hugely dangerous to a powerful party like ours.

We just didn't dare go all out when we had no clue whether the next sand dune hid a much bigger and more powerful enemy, and all these were just…well, appetizers.

Finally, the stress that we'd left our friends behind, and not knowing what had happened to them? It all added up to create an uncomfortable mix that left us all worried and on edge.

The first buildings emerged from the deepening twilight like broken teeth jutting from the sand. Centuries of desert winds had scoured their once-pristine surfaces into rough, pitted facades that still bore traces of elaborate, carved patterns.

I slowed our approach, scanning the empty streets ahead as Oracle and Sehran landed atop the final dune beside me.

"Those are imperial markers," Oracle whispered, pointing to a series of half-buried glyphs that glowed faintly blue under my Meridian Sight. "They still have mana, so some part of the collection grid must be active."

"That's a good thing, right?" Sehran asked quietly, and Oracle hesitated before answering.

"It could be," she hedged. "I mean, I can't think how anything could have destroyed all of the grids without literally destroying each and every mana collector in the city, and most major cities had them built into the walls and roads, but…"

I glanced from her to the city in the distance and then back. "Okay, and what aren't you saying?"

"Well, you remember the SporeMother?" she asked. "You remember why it came to the Great Tower, right?"

"For the mana." My stomach dropped. "You're saying that something might have made the city its home to drain the mana."

"I don't see why anything wouldn't," she admitted. "I mean, there's shelter here for anything that can survive in the desert, and if they can access their mana, they might be able to form a siphon."

"The time to tell me that the giant, ruined city looks like a death trap was before we arrived at its wall…you know that, right?" I asked her almost conversationally, and she smiled at me.

"I know, but let's face it—it's the perfect place to find the things we need to survive," she added.

I glared at her, then sighed, returning to examining the city as I refused to dignify that with a response.

I mean, she wasn't wrong.

The central dome we'd spotted from a distance loomed in the center of the city, its cracked surface still bearing the remnants of gold leaf that caught the faint starlight. Around its base, a series of smaller structures created a maze of shadowed passages and partially collapsed archways. Many of the buildings showed signs of violent destruction rather than mere decay: massive gouges in stone walls, impact craters in courtyards, and the occasional glint of melted rock that spoke of magical warfare.

All in all?

It looked like a clusterfuck waiting to happen.

# CHAPTER TWO

We set off "flying," and I used the term loosely.

The truth was, we were basically skimming the sand, hovering an inch or two above the dead ground. High enough not to leave tracks, low enough not to be spotted from a distance, and most importantly, not stirring up enough disturbance to attract another goddamn wurm.

Not ideal considering we were still burning mana, but we were close enough to the city that the trade-off finally felt worth it.

Oracle and I maintained a consistent height without much effort. But Sehran, with her actual wings, had to work a lot harder, the poor bugger, beating them constantly and drifting a bit higher than us.

Still, this approach beat the alternatives. Walking would leave tracks; running, Oracle had said, was what had probably drawn the wurm in the first place; flying high would make us visible for miles. This middle path was the least shitty option, and in my life of late, that was the best I was hoping for.

We slipped into the shadows of the ancient city, ducking under a crumbling archway, only to find barely visible imperial sigils. Their edges, worn smooth by centuries of sand-laden winds, still pulsed with faint blue light here and there. Oracle moved closer, her fingers gently hovering near the markings.

"These are rune markers," she whispered, tracing her fingers across the glyphs. "Protection against predators and…something else." Her brow furrowed. "The inscription's damaged, but it specifically warns against 'those who walk between.'"

"Wonderful," I muttered, adjusting my grip on my naginata. "Because cryptic warnings are exactly what we needed right now."

My mana sat at about three-quarters capacity, a little over sixteen hundred points. Should be plenty for whatever we might face, but thinking like that was what got people killed. Worse, if I just shrugged and marched in…well, that was putting my unborn child at risk, and fuck that noise. We were playing it safe.

Now that we were inside city limits, the risk of wurms bursting from beneath should be a hell of a lot less, considering the whole "sand vs. rock" thing. So we decided it was better to conserve energy and walk, leaving tracks if necessary, than waste mana and leaving a signature everywhere we went. My Praetorian armor felt heavier with each step through the ankle-deep sand that had drifted into the streets. I kept my eyes moving, checking the shadows, searching all directions as we began to explore this gloomy monument to the empire's fall.

Sehran prowled ahead, her altered form blending with the deepening shadows. "There's magic here," she called back softly. "Old magic. But it feels…wrong somehow. It…it smells like it's—" She waved a hand in front of her nose, clearly lost for words at how mana could smell "off."

But even to my mind, it did. Something about the place just felt wrong, and it wasn't just because we were lost, creeping around a silent, deserted city.

Admittedly, it didn't help that I kept imagining all the shit that Hollywood would put in the place to fuck me over either.

Instead, I just nodded, agreeing and trying to ignore how the air grew thicker as we ventured deeper into the ruins. The dome that had guided us here loomed overhead at the far end of the central road that cut through the city, its broken surface catching what little starlight filtered through the dusty air. Around us, abandoned buildings rose like the bones of ancient beasts, their walls scarred by more than just time and weather.

"These marks…" I ran an armored hand across a deep gouge in a wall, noting a dozen more nearby. "Something powerful did this."

Oracle drifted closer, examining the damage. "Yes, and recently, too. See how the edges are still sharp? Sand hasn't had time to wear them down."

"How recently?" Sehran materialized beside us.

"Within the last few months, I'd guess." Oracle's form flickered slightly, a sign of agitation I'd learned to recognize. "And look at the pattern. Whatever did this was strong. It wasn't a repeated blow, instead… I don't know?" she finished on a questioning note, looking over at me.

I nodded, my interest in tracking and limited training coming to my rescue. "Looks like the remains of a fight. Something hit this wall hard enough it left deep gouges in the stone. And considering the building is still standing? Damn strong walls."

Sehran paused and then asked the obvious question, scanning the empty streets around us. "Ability or a monster?"

"Could be either." Oracle moved to examine another set of marks. "Though, if it was an ability, then they were fighting someone who was agile, and it means that the abandoned city isn't as abandoned as we were hoping."

"Yeah, fat chance it would have been," I muttered. "Anyone who sees it would see the same thing we did—a possible source of loot—and they'd either raid it straightaway, or send scout parties to do it. Hell, it makes sense—why wouldn't you raid old imperial sites, looking for artifacts or information you can use."

A distant sound—stone grating against stone—had us all freezing in place. I raised my naginata, channeling a whisper of mana through it, ready to strike. Nothing came out of the shadows, but the feeling of being watched ratcheted up another notch.

"Okay, fuck this. We need shelter," I decided. "Somewhere defensible where we can rest and meditate to recover mana, and we can deal with tomorrow, tomorrow."

Sehran pointed toward a squat building a handful of buildings farther up the street. "That structure still has most of its roof, and the doorway's narrow. Easy to defend."

I studied the building, noting the imperial markings above its entrance. "Oracle? What was it?"

"A guard house maybe? I'm sorry, Jax…I just don't know," she replied after a moment. "Whatever it was, it looks well-made and solid."

"Then it's good enough for us for now." I started toward it, keeping to the shadows where possible.

The short journey to the old building felt much longer than it should have. Every shadow seemed to hold a hidden threat, and the occasional whisper of wind through the ruins sounded far too much like distant voices for comfort. When we finally reached the entrance, I positioned myself to guard while Oracle examined the door's remains.

"There's active magic here," she announced, surprise evident in her voice. "The preservation wards are weak, but they're holding. Whatever's inside might actually be intact."

"Can you get us in without triggering anything nasty?" I asked.

She nodded, moving her hands in complicated patterns as she traced the runes and guttering lights. "Give me a moment… There's a sequence here…ah!"

Her fingers seemed to mist, to lose their solidity, as she dipped them into one of the glyphs that ran up the side of the door. Suddenly, a dozen more flared to life—brilliant blue lines that ran upward along the edge of the door, each symbol different than the one before, and all of them…

"Jax!" she hissed. "I need your essence—put it here!"

"That's what she said!" Sehran said.

I reached over, pressing my fingers to the door, and waited, having to stifle a laugh at Sehran's perfect delivery. Then I cursed, realizing what Oracle was waiting for when she gave me a "really, dude?" look.

I dipped my hand into my bag of holding and pulled out my bloodstone. It was old magic, and it'd been a bitch to make, requiring Oracle and Thomas to literally "bleed" me with a knife over a full day, refining it down and filtering out any contaminants. Making it had granted me access to imperial sites before, though, and as I offered it up, feeding a touch of mana into it to make its signature clear, I was damn glad I'd made it.

The mana signature kicked in, and the door—what was left of it, anyway—swung inward with a grinding protest of ancient hinges. Beyond lay darkness, but it was a different quality of darkness than the desert night outside. This darkness felt…organized somehow. Deliberate.

"Ladies first?" Sehran suggested and moved up, clearly wanting me to step aside and let her enter first.

"Age before beauty," I countered, stepping past her into the gloom. The moment I crossed the threshold, lines of soft blue light began to trace themselves across the walls and ceiling, responding to my presence. Or, more likely, to the presence of the imperial bloodstone.

The interior was a single large room, its walls lined with shelves that still held scrolls and tablets, protected by whatever remained of the preservation magic. Dust lay thick on everything, but it was ordinary dust, not the fine sand that covered everything outside. As we entered, the lights flickered and tried to activate; then a pulse of mana surged and then failed. Crystals set in the wall, magelights, flared and then popped. Some failed entirely; others granted a wan light that actually made more damn shadows.

A second pulse came, strengthening the light slightly, then faded again. I shook my head, looking deeper in. There was nowhere for any hidden monsters to be lurking.

A long desk split the room, clearly designed as a "we sit on the other side and you come to us" kinda power play. But beyond that? The entire room was just bookshelves and ancient scrolls.

"Well," I finally allowed myself to relax slightly, "I guess we found our shelter for the night. Sehran, I don't trust that door, even though it's stone, as well as thick enough it'll be a bitch to kick down. Can you watch the entrance while Oracle and I see what we can learn from all this?"

She nodded, taking up position where she could see both in and out. "Just…try not to wake up any ancient monsters? I could really do with a good night's sleep."

"Yeah, you and me both," I snorted. Looking at the rows of ancient records, each potentially holding who knew what kinds of knowledge or power, I couldn't make any promises, though… It didn't feel like the library I'd found Oracle in.

There, the air literally had been saturated in power, and being around other magical books and scrolls, I realized I'd always felt more or less the same thing.

Here? It felt pretty mundane in comparison…just damn old.

The first scroll I picked up crumbled at my touch, despite the preservation magic.

Oracle made a small sound of distress, quickly moving to stop me from reaching for another. "Jax! No, please…let me," she insisted. Her hands ghosted over the ancient documents. "They need a gentler touch."

I stepped back, feeling a bit crap for destroying the first thing I'd touched, and then decided to take the excuse to remove my gauntlets and start working on the rest of my armor.

The ancient Praetorian armor was incredible, but it was also armor. Although it flowed and fit better than any I'd ever worn, I'd still been wearing it for far too long without a break.

"Anything interesting?" I carefully set each piece of the Praetorian plate aside.

"Lots of requisition orders," Oracle muttered, moving from scroll to scroll. "Complaints about water rationing…oh!" She paused at a particular shelf, her form brightening with excitement. "Here, this is from just before the abandonment."

Sehran glanced over from her position by the door. "What does it say?"

"It's…hold on." Oracle's hands moved in familiar patterns as she drew mana from our shared pool, somehow using it to stabilize the fragile document. "The desert was expanding even then. The noble houses were charging for access to their water mages to help maintain the agricultural districts, but…" She frowned. "The response mentions something called the 'creeping death' advancing faster than expected."

"Sounds cheerful," I commented, finally free of my armor. "Any mention of what that actually was?"

"Not here, but—"

A pulse of mana rippled through the room. The magical lighting flickered, and I felt a sudden pull, a drain on my manapool, much as I had when we first entered.

"That wasn't me," Oracle said quickly, backing away from the shelves.

"No," Sehran agreed, her form shifting as she prepared for trouble. "Is that…is that pull coming from below?"

I grabbed my naginata, cursing the fact that I'd just removed my armor. "Below? This place has a basement?"

"I suppose it makes sense," Oracle confirmed, moving closer to me. "They'd need somewhere secure for the more sensitive documents. I mean, someone could just walk in and do damage. But this feels like…oh!"

Another pulse, stronger this time, and the floor beneath our feet trembled. More of my mana drained away, but this time I felt where it was going.

"Jax… I think there's a wisp down there," Oracle breathed. "I can sense a well! The structure is trying to wake it up!"

I knew that tone. "Oracle, no…"

"We have to help it!" She was already moving toward a section of flooring that started to glow with the same blue light as the walls. "It's been alone down there for centuries!"

"Or it could be trapped down there for a really good reason," I pointed out. But I was already moving to back her up. Some battles you just couldn't win, and trying to stop Oracle from helping another wisp was definitely one of them. "Just be careful, all right? It could be fuckin' mad!" I tried weakly.

In truth, I damn well hoped we'd find another wisp as well—and not for the obvious, "Hey, let's see what form you pick after reading my mind." No, it was because they'd have to have information on the local area. Hell, being trapped in here and linked to a records house or library for the empire, instead of a magical one like Oracle had been?

They'd have had to know a lot about the continent at the very least.

The floor section slid aside with a grinding sound that set my teeth on edge, revealing a narrow stairway descending into darkness. The pulses came faster now, each one draining more mana.

"I need to get closer," Oracle said. "To establish contact."

"Fine." I sighed. "But I'm going first." I turned to Sehran. "Watch our backs?"

She nodded, already moving to a position where she could see both the entrance and the stairs. "Try not to take too long. I don't like the smells I'm getting from outside."

I started down the stairs, Oracle close behind me, her light illuminating worn stone steps that spiraled down into the earth. The air grew cooler with each step, and the mana pulses stronger.

The room below was larger, rows upon rows of old books and scrolls again, but most of them were destroyed. Even the dust in the room looked like it'd been forced back again and again.

In the center of the far wall, I could see a manawell, much as I'd seen before. But here, despite it having access to more mana than Tenandra or Oracle had on first awakening, the pool was empty.

"Something's wrong," Oracle whispered after we'd descended about twenty feet. "These pulses…the wisp isn't responding. It feels…is it gone? Escaped or…oh no."

Before I could respond, a massive surge of power ripped through the stairwell. Oracle cried out as it connected with her, and her form flickered violently. Through our bond, I felt a flood of images and emotions—fire raining from the sky called down by the mages to buy time, the screams of the dying, and a creeping something that consumed everything in its path.

Then Oracle collapsed, and I barely caught her before she could fall down the remaining stairs.

"What the hell was that?" I demanded, cradling her and glaring around, searching for an enemy, a threat.

"Memories," she gasped. "The wisp…it's dead. It has been for centuries. But it left an echo…a warning…" Her eyes met mine, filled with a terror that chilled me to my bone. "We need to get out of here. Now."

"Why? What did you see?"

Before she could answer, Sehran's voice hissed down from above: "We've got company!"

I raced back up the stairs. Oracle floated shakily behind me, and my bare feet slapped against ancient stone. The mana drain had left me feeling light-headed, but there wasn't time to worry about that now.

"What kind of company?" I hissed.

"The kind that we don't need," Sehran replied tersely. She was crouched by the entrance, her form rippling as she adjusted to better blend with the shadows. "And they're hunting."

I hurried to the edge of the door, squinting out into the night and waiting, searching for whatever or whoever was out there. A figure, covered in long, flowing robes and wearing a white, featureless mask, crept out of the shadows on the rooftop some ten houses down and across the street from us.

There was a pause, then three more slowly moved out from the shadows; the center-most of the four held a stone in his hand that he swept from left to right. Flashes of dim light flared from the stone in a pattern, one that apparently meant something as he gestured forward.

The figure to the right of him stopped, head tilted as if listening. Then they raised a crossbow and clearly activated an ability, as energy crackled along its bolt before firing. The shot illuminated the street in a bright flash before striking something farther down the street, a good twenty meters from them—and maybe five meters from us—that had been scuttling across the sand in both of our directions.

The creature—it looked like a scorpion the size of a small horse—was literally blown apart as it crept out of an intersection. Its chitinous shell shattered as the energized bolt detonated inside it.

One of the other assholes burst out laughing.

"Nice shot!" the one on the roof called, their voice drifting down the street toward us. "They're more XP than runners as well!"

"At least they don't cry and beg," his companion agreed with a growl before shouting to the crossbowman. "Though they're worth less coin. Xanna, dammit, how many times can you use that ability before you're dry? Twice? Three times? What if…!"

"Shut it, both of you!" the one with the stone snapped. "Keep your eyes open. Those traces are fresh, and if there are runners hiding in these ruins, thanks to Xanna's stupidity, they now know we're here!"

His order was cut short by a blood-curdling scream from above them and to the left. A fifth member of their group, who had been creeping along a different rooftop that I'd entirely missed until now, had been stabbed through by a massive stinger.

He tried to break free, before being yanked from his feet, then dragged backward. Armor scraped stone as he vanished into the darkness. The screaming cut off abruptly.

Then the ruins came alive.

Scorpions poured from doorways and windows, their armored bodies gleaming in the starlight. Some were smaller, merely the size of large dogs, while others…

"Why the hell did I take my armor off?!" I snarled to myself, quickly gathering as much up as I could and starting to attach it. "Oracle, anything essential here?"

She shook her head, still looking shaken from her experience with the wisp well. "No, whatever happened here, what's left is mostly records, scrolls for administration, or books. I don't sense anything like spellbooks. Nothing worth dying over."

Outside, the night filled with screams and the flash of mana-charged weapons as the trespassers fought for their lives. More scorpions emerged from the surrounding buildings, moving with the coordinated purpose of a colony defending its territory.

I gritted my teeth, frantically pulling my gear on and desperately wondering about the little group of four. Sure, they sounded like dicks, but they were fighting scorpions… Should we help?

"They must have followed someone's trail here," Sehran observed, helping me quickly gather my remaining armor. "Poor bastards probably got taken by the scorpions days ago."

"Fuck it. Their loss, our gain," I decided. The thought of the way that the crossbowman had fired on the first target and had said something about runners and the obvious tracking stone made me decide that they were either hunting criminals, or runaways.

The bolt had been impressive, halfway between a lightning bolt and something explosive. But when I thought about it, it was cool, and I wanted some, but it wasn't anything we couldn't make as well.

Then the cruel laughter and the comments about "paying" secured it in my mind, and the faint guilt dropped away. Mercenaries or slavers. I nodded to myself, securing the last pieces I could manage quickly and dumping the rest into my bag of holding. "That fight will keep both sides busy while we find another way out of this death trap."

Oracle moved closer. "The memories… I have a partial map of the city from them. There're warnings but they're too garbled to make anything out. I think there's an old service passage two streets over, though, and if it's intact, it'll lead us underground. The scorpions are probably too large to use it, and it should lead us toward the dome. If we're careful—"

"Done." I cut her off. "Lead the way."

We slipped out as the battle raged further down the street. The slavers were putting up a fight, but more scorpions kept coming. This wasn't just a small nest, I guessed; the entire ruins had become their colony.

"This place has been stripped bare," Oracle whispered as we moved through the shadows. "Look at the buildings—everything's gone! You were right. It had to have been raided multiple times over the centuries. Anything valuable would have been found long ago."

"Explains why they're hunting runners instead of artifacts," Sehran added. "Nothing left worth taking except people."

I nodded grimly, cursing myself for a fool. If this was back on Earth? Even the cities that Egypt lost to the desert had been looted to fuck over the centuries, and that was when the world had been more or less stable.

Here, when the cataclysm had basically fucked the entire realm, anything useful would have been scavenged at the earliest opportunity. Even the Great Tower had been searched a few times—though the SporeMother had killed the fuckers each time. Expecting that there'd be something here? Fucking stupid of me. The only way that there would be was if there was something powerful enough still guarding it.

I followed Oracle's direction while keeping my naginata ready. The sounds of fighting faded behind us, but in their place came the clicking of chitin on stone, and lots of it.

We needed to find that passage, and fast. The ruins had already claimed enough victims, and we didn't need to add our names to that list.

Oracle led us through a maze of narrow alleys, each turn taking us deeper into the ruined city and farther away from the main thoroughfare we'd walked up originally. Then the growing eerie silence was broken by the whisper of wind through ancient stones and the occasional distant click of chitin on stone.

"Here," Oracle whispered eventually, stopping at what looked like a collapsed wall. "The passage entrance is behind this."

I studied the pile of rubble skeptically. "You're sure?"

"Yes. These weren't random collapses—they were deliberate. The imperial engineers designed them to look like this when triggered." Her barely visible hands traced patterns in the air as she spoke. "There should be a…yes!"

A section of the wall, tight up against the collapse, but just clear of it, right where you'd not be looking—expecting, if there *was* a hidden door, it'd be under the rubble—suddenly shifted slightly.

There was a crunching noise and the runes that had flared to life at her touch guttered and died, making me grit my teeth even as it revealed a narrow gap. Beyond it, stairs led down into darkness.

"Sehran, here." I grunted, passing her my naginata and stepping up close. The doorway had opened by about an inch and a half before jamming on something. I wiggled my fingers into the crack, hoping against hope that there wasn't going to be something on the far side that was feeling peckish, but I couldn't feel anything there.

Instead, I started to heave and strain, trying it without magic at first, then giving in and triggering Mana Overdrive and trying again. This time, with my insanely boosted stats, I managed to move the door a grand total of six more inches before it stopped against something.

"Let me," Oracle whispered, smiling at me, and then slid against the gap, altering her form to allow her to slip through.

I swallowed hard, knowing that she'd not wanted to make physical changes to her body, the larger the child grew, the more space it needed naturally, and while she could still adjust her body to some degree, by the day it grew less and less so. I guessed that there was a lot of her that could be moved and manipulated beyond the womb.

She was quiet for a handful of seconds, then she was back, her face inches from where I leaned against the slab.

"I think I've got all the stone out of the way, but some's jammed in the mechanism. It's not going to move much farther."

"Then we open it as far as we can and I fuckin' lose weight." I grunted, bracing myself. "Ready?"

"Go." She moved back, clearing the doorway.

"They're getting close!" Sehran hissed over her shoulder from the mouth of the alley, backing up slowly. "If you're going to do it, do it now, or we need to run!"

"Fuck it," I snarled, getting as good a grip as I could on the rough stonework and heaving, my Mana Overdrive still active. At first, there was no change; then, slowly I felt it: a tiny shift, then another. Then, all at once, it came loose, sliding back a dozen more inches before it crunched to a very definite halt.

"Come on!" Oracle hissed, moving back out of the way as I straightened and first looked to Sehran, and then back at the gap behind Oracle.

"More stairs going down." I sighed. "Because that worked out so well last time."

"This is different," Oracle insisted. "These passages were meant for evacuations. They're part of the original city design."

A screech from somewhere behind us was followed by the sound of breaking stone. Much closer than I would have liked.

"Talk later," Sehran hissed, her form rippling as she glanced back the way we'd come. "Hide now."

I didn't need to be told twice. We squeezed through the gap one at a time. I triggered Darkvision as soon as I did. I'd been able to see outside more or less normally thanks to my enhanced perception already, but in here I needed more.

Oracle was fine; she was a magical creature first and foremost and had access to all my spells and so on anyway. And as to Sehran? She was a demon. A literal creature of the night. She grinned as soon as we were in a dark, enclosed space, clearly feeling more at home than normal.

As soon as we were all inside, Sehran joined me, putting her shoulder to the rock. The pair of us slid the door back into place with a crunch of grinding rock and the slithering sound of sand cascading from all around. From out in the alley, there came the sounds of chittering just as the wall ground shut behind us with a finality that was less than comforting.

"Well," I muttered, "no going back that way."

And that was true, all of us had to admit, considering there wasn't so much as a goddamn handle on this side.

The passage was narrow—barely wide enough for two people to walk abreast—with a ceiling low enough that I had to duck slightly in my armor. The air was stale but not completely dead, suggesting some kind of ventilation somewhere.

I took advantage of the momentary break to make the others halt, and started to fix my armor. It didn't take long, but damn I felt better once it was all back on.

"These led to safe rooms," Oracle explained as we began our descent. "Every major imperial city had them. Places where citizens could shelter during attacks or natural disasters."

"Like the desert expanding?" Sehran asked.

"Sort of, though that mention of 'creeping death' worries me. From what I saw in the wisp's memories…" Oracle shuddered. "I don't think it was that, or that they managed to save many people in the end."

I was about to ask what exactly she'd seen when a new sound reached us: a soft scraping, coming from somewhere ahead.

We all froze.

"Could the scorpions have found another way in?" I whispered.

Sehran shook her head. "Wrong sound. This is…smaller."

"But yes," Oracle whispered as well. "For all we know, the rest of the building collapsed ages ago and we just snuck in the scorpions' larder."

"That's not helping!" I hissed, torn between a manic desire to fuckin' giggle and an instinct to be very serious, as I knew I should be. Mind you, I wasn't exactly at my best when stressed and I was expected to be serious, as all the examples of me shit talking proved.

There was no light down here beyond that magical lighting, and in the gloom, I could just make out more of those faintly glowing imperial markers along the walls and something else. A shadow moving against shadows.

"There," Sehran breathed, pointing.

I saw it too: a figure, hunched and scurrying, exiting one passage and then disappearing around a bend farther ahead. It looked almost human, but moved wrong somehow, like its joints weren't quite in the right places.

"I'm guessing that's not what you remember the citizens looking like," I said quietly.

"No, and I doubt it'd be them unless they were all elves or dwarves, and then they'd be several hundred years old at least," Oracle agreed. "But it might be what the slavers were tracking."

Another scraping sound, closer this time, followed by what might have been breathing, or might have been the wind in ancient ventilation shafts. Either way, we weren't alone down here.

"Options?" I kept my voice low.

"Forward is the only way," Oracle replied. "These passages all lead to the central dome. But…"

"But?"

"But if that thing came from there, we might be walking into something worse than what we left behind."

I adjusted my grip on my naginata, glad I'd found the time to put my armor back on. "Story of my damn life these days, but fuck it. Let's go see what's waiting for us."

We moved deeper into the passage and the scraping sounds continued, always just around the next corner, just out of sight. Leading us on.

Or leading us into a trap.

The passage began to slope more steeply downward, the ancient stone steps worn smooth by countless feet. The air grew colder, and strange echoes played tricks with our hearing. That scraping sound seemed to come from everywhere and nowhere at once.

"I really don't like this," Sehran muttered, her skin rippling as she tried to adapt to the changing shadows. "Something about this place feels…wrong. And the mana? It makes me feel dirty. And *not* in a good way."

I couldn't help but grin at that. Of all the squad, Sehran and I tended to think the same in a lot of situations. But she was right. The farther we descended, the more the wrongness pressed in around us. It wasn't just the darkness or the cold…there was something else. Something that made the hairs on the back of my neck stand up.

"Oracle," I whispered, "what exactly did you see in those memories?"

She was silent for a long moment, her ethereal form flickering slightly. "Death," she finally replied. "But not just death. Transformation. The wisp…it saw something come out of the desert. Something that forced the locals to look at ways of changing their people."

"Changing them how?"

Before she could answer, the scraping sound came again, much closer this time. A shadow darted across the passage ahead of us, and in the brief glimpse I caught, I saw that it moved on far too many limbs.

"Was that what I think it was?" Sehran asked, voice tight.

"If you think it was someone who's grown extra arms, then yes," I replied grimly. "Oracle?"

"The memories weren't clear," she said quickly. "But there were experiments. Someone or something was trying to find ways to survive as the desert expanded. They…they did things to people. Tried to adapt them."

"And their experiments are still down here," I concluded. "Wonderful."

The passage opened into a larger chamber, its walls lined with more of those glowing imperial markers. Ancient benches and tables lay scattered about, a waiting room of some kind, perhaps. Multiple doorways led off in different directions.

"Which way?" I asked.

Oracle drifted forward, examining the markers. "The dome should be…that way." She pointed to one of the larger passages. "But—"

She was cut off by a sound that made my blood run cold: laughter. Not human laughter, but something that might once have been human, twisted and broken until only the basic pattern remained. It echoed from one of the other passages, followed by more of those scraping sounds.

"They're herding us," Sehran realized. "Like the scorpions with their prey."

"Yes," a voice rasped from the shadows suddenly, as a section of the wall slid aside. "We were."

The figure that stepped into view might once have been human, but that time was long past. Additional arms—crude but functional—sprouted from its torso, and its skin had a chitinous sheen. When it smiled, mandibles clicked at the corners of its mouth.

"Welcome," it said, "to our sanctuary."

More figures emerged from the other passages, all similarly changed, all moving with that same wrong grace. They carried crude weapons, but their extra limbs were weapons in themselves.

"They made you," Oracle breathed. "To survive the desert."

"They made us," the first figure agreed, nodding almost amiably. "Then abandoned us. But we survived. We adapted. And now…" It tilted its head, joints cracking. "Now you will join us, like all the others."

I raised my naginata, channeling mana through it. "I don't think so."

The creature's laugh was like breaking glass. "You don't have a choice. You are here; the desert is here. The slavers, the scorpions…nothing here survives unchanged. No one with a choice comes here, never."

That's when I saw how many of them there were. And thanks to the whole spiderlike limbs, faces, an' shit, I felt my balls trying to climb back up inside my body. Literally dozens climbed down the walls and came out of crevices that, until a few seconds ago? Hadn't existed.

Bane would have probably seen them ages ago. For us? The damn walls were covered in cracks and fracture patterns, or so they'd seemed.

No, I saw them for what they were: nests with sections pulled over to close them off. Now I saw what they held, and who, as they stood facing us with crooked limbs and gleaming eyes.

Worst of all, two had stepped out behind us bearing shields—shields that glowed with runes etched into their surface.

"Join us…" came the call from dozens of throats.

"Ah, hell." I sighed. "Really, dude? Spiders?"

# **<u>THOMAS</u>**

Thomas pressed himself against the wall, lifting a closed fist as the sound of clacking echoed through the corridor ahead. The two squads froze at once, muscle memory from countless drills making their reactions instant and synchronized.

Or…it should have.

They didn't, not all of them, because the damn squads were made up of people from two completely disparate forces that had always hated each other, and a handful of volunteers who were clearly mad already to volunteer for anything of this sort.

Those two sides were now trying their best to forget that the armored figure right by their side—holding a weapon, no less—had probably killed one of their friends only a few weeks back.

Nigret's ears twitched, his feline features tensing as he scented the air. "This one smells death ahead," he whispered. "Death and the salt of the deep ones."

The darkness ahead was absolute, broken only by the steady gleam of magelights that clattered and clinked, attached to their armor as they were.

Considering that only the scouts, Thomas, and Belladonna had their own versions of Darkvision, the lights were both necessary *and* proving to be a nightmare when it came to scouting.

The ancient corridor, even this deep in the prax, showed signs of the original crash. Support beams lay twisted at unnatural angles, and walls bore the scars of impacts that had warped solid metal. And then, if you were to add in the shadowed recesses that were left thanks to piles of debris…then the way that everyone moved, creating rolling patterns of shadows that overlapped constantly?

All in all, it was a nightmare of concealing shadows and confusion.

"Get ready, people," Thomas commanded softly. "Belladonna, take the left. There should be another junction up ahead. If there is, you secure the left passage and center, and we'll do the right and center." He felt rather than saw her nod of acknowledgment, the experience of fighting and fucking together making words almost unnecessary.

The teams separated smoothly. Alistair moved to Thomas's right, shield raised and sword held low.

As he advanced, the weight of Thomas's war axe was a comfort in his hands as Coran fell in behind and to the left of him with practiced ease.

Thomas, as opposed to his mad bastard brother, had always been a man who used whatever was needed to complete the job. Armor. A mace, war hammer or axe, a bow and magic; spears and lances.

Swords were pretty much only for fights against medium and weaker armored opponents, but he'd use them as required. That was where he differed from Jax, who was just too fucking stubborn to change his weapon as needed and insisted on carrying a damn murderstick in busy corridors where he was likely to lop off a friend's arm if they got too close.

That meant that for this excursion, his weapons had been chosen deliberately, with the knowledge of what that mad little bastard Posstoss had warned them was down here. It still wasn't great. The damn creatures had been a pain so far, but

Thomas kept hoping the formerly and still-slightly crazed gnome had been lying about the sheer size of the damn crustaceans that called the wreck "home."

The clacking grew louder, accompanied by the wet sounds of something large dragging itself across metal. Thomas's enhanced vision caught movement, a flash of chitin, the gleam of compound eyes.

"Contact!" Dashiki's voice rang out from Belladonna's position, followed immediately by the distinctive crack of a crossbow firing. As the bolt flashed through the air, so too did a bright light, as one of the mages unleashed their first spell. Ruddy orange and yellow light flared, illuminating the horror that burst from the shadows.

The firebolt—*bolt*, not *ball*, thank fuck—screamed through the air to impact a sodden barnacle-encrusted shoulder, making its wielder screech in fury as it ran at them.

Dozens of smaller ones were in the lead, but the squads only had eyes for the largest, a creature that lumbered along at the rear.

It was massive; easily three meters tall, literally filling the goddamn corridor, with multiple jointed legs and arms ending in serrated claws. Its carapace bore the marks of centuries living in the depths, with coral growths and barnacles creating natural armor atop its badly damaged and malformed shell.

The creatures were obviously bottom dwellers and feeders, heavily armored with claws and mandibles, gleaming and soulless coal-black eyes, and maws that salivated at the sight of so much fresh meat.

They rushed across the ancient metal floors, chitinous legs tap-tap-tapping and tentacles grabbing onto holds to drag them forward faster.

They were a multitude of madness, as almost none of the shapes were identical. Thomas swallowed hard as he realized why.

These were the result of uncontrolled *mutations*.

This was what happened when you spent too much time around a powerful source of mana, and gave multiple generations time to be born and breed.

He'd heard of it before, and he'd seen the abominations that the Dark Legion had nailed to the walls of villages when they were found.

He'd not been "serving" then; he'd been a mercenary, finding the place after a visit and having Dirik, his friend, explain it.

"It's something to do with the magic," he'd said. "Drives your body mad if you're around too much. It's why nobody in their right mind wants to be a mage."

"You like my spells," Thomas had pointed out, and Dirik had laughed.

"A spell now and then? Great for a fight. But spending all your time playing with magic ain't natural, Thomas. These fools? They were trying to ascend, I bet."

"Is it possible?" Thomas had asked, only to receive a shake of the head from Dirik.

"Not from what I heard, and this is only one of the reasons—the Dark Legion don't like others trying to become gods. And if they hear about people trying it? That's the result. You die, and so does everyone you might have influenced."

The entire population of the village had been nailed to the outer wall, left to die slowly. Animals came out of the forest to feed on them, not just the handful of mutated humans who had apparently been spending their time around some source of magic.

What it'd been, Thomas had never found out, as the rest of the village had been looted. At the time, he'd put it down to the madness of the UnderVerse and had moved on, while secretly hoping that his magic didn't one day make his dick drop off.

He'd eventually learned, though, it wasn't the use of magic that caused it: it was being too close to something that generated or focused it for too long.

The Great Tower was fine; it processed and used it, but didn't radiate it. It was controlled, guided, and the ambient mana levels were, if anything, a little lower than normal because the damn place was constantly guzzling it down.

A manastone the size of the thing that Posstoss had described? That was dangerous. Or it was if you tried to spend all your time cuddled up to it, anyway.

Like a nuclear reactor, really, or an x-ray machine. A little exposure was fine. A lot? Well…that led to gingers.

Now, though…now he remembered the signs, and just hoped that none of these fuckers had gained any powers.

"Push forward!" Thomas roared as more shapes emerged behind the first, scuttling out of the cross corridors to stream into the center. "Take and hold the junction! Mages, slow them! Ranged, take down as many as you can!"

The corridor erupted in chaos.

Belladonna and he had agreed to a little "friendly competition" between his squad and hers. The theory was they'd get down to the bottom of the prax, mine the living shit out of a massive manastone that was somewhere down there—according to Posstoss again, but he'd claimed Jax told him and his people in turn—and then they'd separate out and see what they could kill.

Once they were there, both squads would defend the miners, and at the end, there'd be bragging rights on who killed the most.

Not that "bragging rights" was the end of it, of course. For Thomas and Bella, it'd been very quietly agreed-upon sexual favors. For the squads below them, *well…*

There'd been everything from ales and beers to blows, violence to forfeits like a tattoo. Last of all had been the introduction of trading of half a shift of duty.

That wasn't something that was done by the imperial legionnaires, but in the Dark Legion it was common. Trade a shit duty away and do whatever you could to forget who and what you were, while some other poor fool had to cover your shift after their own had ended.

In the long term, with the stated aim of the Imperial Legion to bring peace to the land and to crush all evil, the kind of "fuck it, I don't care" attitude that was shown by trading duties wasn't compatible.

In the depths of a prax, when it was as barren of comfort as it was, and while waiting for reinforcements to arrive, it was the best that they could do.

The Dark legionnaires from both teams sprinted forward, their ingrained response to the threat of the fight to get in there, kill what they could and claim it, while the imperial legionnaires looked on in horror as sight lines were fouled, mages had to jerk spells back under control, and ranged teams nearly shot their companions in the back of their damn fool helmets.

Belladonna started to bark orders, trying to regain some semblance of control as her team—mainly new to the ways of the legion—were the most out of position. While she did that, Thomas backed up the idiots who had charged into the mass of chitinous bodies. His axe, used in dozens of fights and blooded in service to both Dark and now the Light, bit deep into creature after creature as they pushed them back from the end of the corridor, gaining space to deploy the rest of the squads in the narrow passage.

Alistair was a wall of steel beside him, his shield catching blows that would have torn a lesser man in half. Behind and to the left of them, Coran shouldered in as well, his unfamiliar armor just looking wrong to his friend. Coran had refused to ever again wear his Dark Legion gear, even when it'd been recovered, and there wasn't enough of the legion's own to kit everyone out.

As such, he and most of the others who weren't Imperial Legion wore a mismatched and crappy assortment of various grades and styles of armor. He knew his place in the fight, though, and for Thomas, having his friend by his side as they fought against the onrushing tide of carapaces was a comfort.

"Thomas, DOWN!" Nigret's warning came just in time.

Thomas ducked as massive pincers snapped shut where his head had been. The trigara launched himself over Thomas's back, twin swords swinging; the left deflected a second pincer before the right punched forward, sinking through the creature's eyes and into the brain. It reared back, spraying ichor and thrashing wildly. Thomas brought his axe up in a devastating arc that hacked the legs from one side of it, sending the dying creature to the floor, spasming as Nigret kicked it off his blade.

"Form up!" Belladonna's voice cut through the din. "Second row! Get ready to take over when the first line steps back. There's plenty to go around and hours of fighting yet!"

"This means we're close to the manastone?" Sip called to Thomas, who glared at the useless streak of piss as he stepped back, allowing a legionnaire to take his place as he checked the progress of the fight.

"How the hell would I know, Sip, you stupid bastard?" Thomas snapped. "You find a map that you didn't tell us about?"

"Well, no…" the scrawny fighter whined, and Thomas snorted.

"Then shut up and fight," Thomas barked, gesturing toward the battle, before stepping back to stand by Belladonna as she snapped out orders.

She had years more experience than him in a fight, even if most of them had been in the Dark Legion of Nimon, where kills counted for everything from promotion to food. As such, she was much more aggressive than he was in a lot of ways.

He couldn't help but grin as he considered ways that worked out well for him, though. When she caught him staring, she glared at him hard enough to wipe the smile off.

In normal situations, pushing forward to take the middle of the corridor was a damn fool thing to do, instead of defending the front ahead of them and behind. With nice solid walls on either side, you had four directions to defend and fight in.

In normal situations.

Here they were, in the depths of the damn prax, surrounded by walls, floors, and ceilings that felt like they could collapse if you sneezed wrong, and they were narrow enough that, at best, only five or sometimes six could get into the fight.

With the collapses, that was frequently down to two or three, and sometimes the ceiling was three or four meters overhead, and at other times twenty, depending on the room or if the floor above fancied visiting unexpectedly. So, instead of that, wherever possible, they held the crossing and fought what came. It gave more of the legion the chance to fight at a time, gave longer sight lines for the ranged and mages, and best of all, if the shit hit the fan, there was a better chance one of the passages was free and they could all leg it that way.

"We're on the fourth level, right?" he asked her.

She shrugged. "Could be," she admitted. "We've climbed and fallen enough that we could as easily be on the first or the fifteenth."

That was true, he reflected. The prax was a flying city that had been made up of six main floors when it was built, which should make it simple to work out where you were, given that Tenandra, Jax's ship wisp, had been the former wisp of the city, and had given painstaking directions and descriptions as to what should be down here.

Unfortunately, when the city had crashed into the ocean, it'd hit a series of reefs and had taken incredible damage.

As such, in some areas, the floors were virtually intact. But the majority? Some sections had snapped off and had rotated ninety degrees or more, plunging into the depths. Some floors had collapsed into each other and had formed huge caverns. And worst of all, thanks to the city having also been a literal home for thousands, the upper floor had been covered in trees and grass.

Protected by the mana shields, they'd been places for the inhabitants to rest and enjoy. So when the city had crashed, some seven hundred years ago, between the natural growth of the trees, the effect of the crash and the roots, as well as literal centuries of storms and cycles of growth, the city had been written off as an uncharted island when it'd been discovered.

Finally, thanks to the few functioning—more or less—sections of the city being designed for war and possibly horrific damage, meant there were sections that should have flooded centuries ago, and instead had formed underwater grottos and enclosed ecosystems thanks to shields that still tried to maintain their areas.

All in all, it was a madhouse, one of horrific proportions, where turning a corner might bring you face-to-face with a nightmare of the deep, a set of stairs, or a cliff edge, and you damn well never knew what was next.

"I say we hold what we've got, clear the passages, then follow their tracks. Posstoss said that the creatures lived around the manastones, right?" Belladonna asked him.

Thomas nodded grimly. This was what they'd come for. The massive manastone growth that Jax had discovered on his previous visit was exactly what they needed. The stones' power had been steadily growing for centuries, and they needed that power in the first stage of fixing this shit-tip up, reactivating the long-dead golems.

"Sip! Dashiki! Clear those bodies!" Thomas commanded. "Everyone else, push forward! Watch the ceiling—these bastards look like the kind that like to drop down!"

"And if they don't, you know the roof might!" Alistair called out grimly. "Keep your shield up, and your eyes open!"

The fight continued, meter by bloody meter. The crustaceans seemed endless, almost dying away and then a surge of them would appear—smaller ones, large ones, things that squished and rolled along and things that looked like a Salvador Dali painting gone very wrong. All of them were drawn by the vibrations of combat—or, more likely, the smell of fresh blood and meat. Each one they killed only served to attract more as they marched ever onward into the depths.

Thomas called a brief halt after another two hours, letting the squads catch their breath while scouts checked the passage ahead. The floor here was becoming increasingly treacherous, with patches of ancient algae making the metal as slick as ice.

"This whole section's tilted," Alistair commented, running an armored hand along the wall. "Look at the support beams—they're barely holding."

He was right. What had once been vertical supports now crossed the passage at odd angles, creating a maze of twisted metal. Coral growths covered much of it, somehow thriving in the darkness, their surfaces gleaming wetly in the magelights.

"This one has seen that the floor drops away ahead," Nigret reported, returning from his scouting run. His fur was slick with moisture, whiskers twitching. "Ten meters around the next bend, then perhaps forty, fifty meters down. The passage continues, but…" He gestured with one clawed hand, indicating a steep angle.

"Then we'll need ropes," Belladonna finished. She was already pulling lengths of the reinforced cord from her pack. "Those creatures we killed, they were using the walls and ceiling more than the floor. Probably means we're heading the right way."

Thomas nodded, remembering Posstoss's excited babbling about the "big shinies" below. The mad gnome had been clear that the manastones would be where the sea life was thickest, as apparently once Jax had vanished, Grizz and the others had gone to town on the enemy.

While they did that, the mad little bastards had gone deeper again, and had discovered the paths that Jax had used. "How many lines can we secure?"

A quick inventory showed they had enough rope for four separate lines. Thomas split the teams accordingly, making sure each group had a mix of Imperial and Dark Legion members. It wasn't ideal—trust was still an issue—but they needed to learn to work together or die separately.

"Secure them to the strongest support struts," he ordered, testing one of the more solid-looking beams. "Alistair, you and Coran check each anchor point. I don't want anyone falling because we rushed this."

"We'll need to move in relays," Alistair added for the non- imperial's benefit. "As we reach the end of the line, it's resecured and the last man in line moves forward, passing their companions until they're in the lead."

"Then they tie up and the line swings around again." Thomas nodded. "So we need scouts as Ass-End-Charlie at both ends of the rope, people!"

The next attack came as they were setting the last rope. A smaller group this time, but no less dangerous for it. Three of the creatures dropped from above, their leg-claws finding purchase in the coral growths.

"Contact high!" Dashiki shouted, already bringing his crossbow to bear. The bolt took one creature in what passed for its throat, dark ichor spraying as it thrashed, hurled from sight.

The other two landed among the rear guard. One of them—smaller but faster than its brethren—grabbed a legionnaire before anyone could react. Its pincers closed around the man's waist, armor creaking under the pressure.

Thomas was already moving, but Belladonna got there first. Her swordstaff, a great long thing with a wickedly curved blade she'd claimed from a noble's armory, severed the creature's arm at the joint. The legionnaire fell, gasping but alive, as she finished it with a thrust through its central eye cluster.

The third creature proved harder to kill. Its carapace was thick with barnacles, deflecting the first several strikes. It backed away, trying to use its superior reach to keep the fighters at bay while more of its kind skittered and dragged their way up from below.

"Push it back!" Thomas commanded. "Don't let it hold the passage!"

The creature's legs scrabbled for purchase on the slick floor as the combined weight of several fighters forced it toward a hole on one side of the passage. It lashed out desperately, pincers snapping, but Alistair's shield caught the blow.

"Shield-BASH!" he roared, lunging forward with the power of an ability, smashing it back. The creature's momentum carried it over the edge. For a split second, its pincers and legs flailed, trying to grab onto something, anything, before it vanished. Its screech echoed as it fell; a sickening crunch reverberated up and showed that the floor was farther down than they thought.

"Everyone okay?" Thomas helped the injured legionnaire to his feet. The man's armor was crushed but had held. He'd need healing, which most of the legionnaires could do now and clearly some of his armor needed adjusting because he could barely shift his hips, but he swore blind he could still fight.

"We need to move." Belladonna peered down into the darkness. "More coming up the walls. I can hear them."

Thomas gestured to the ropes. "Four groups, staggered descent. Strongest fighters at the second and second last of each line. Mages and ranged in the middle where they can provide coverage." He caught Belladonna's eye. "Your team takes the first and second lines, mine the third and fourth?"

She nodded, already organizing her people. The mixed groups would have to learn to climb, and quickly. The sounds from below were getting louder.

"Remember," Thomas called as they prepared to descend. "Slow and steady. Watch your footing and keep your weapons ready. Whatever's guarding those manastones isn't going to give them up easily."

Looking out over the edge, Thomas swallowed hard. Where the crab thing had just fallen was a literal death drop, one that went straight down to a cavern floor, around a hundred meters below.

There were boulders and metal debris, pools of standing water and what looked like shattered stone. Bodies in their dozens had clearly been left there recently, given the empty carapaces that littered the cavern floor. Even now, the fresh corpse they'd just made was being stripped to the shell by smaller figures.

Weird lights reflected from out of sight, and shadows marched across the walls as something—or some*things*—moved where he couldn't see.

All in all, it wasn't good.

"Couldn't have had a hidden beach down there, could you. Oh fuck no…not an opportunity for a bikini in sight," Thomas muttered. Then he colored as he realized what he'd said, just damn glad that the tiny outfits hadn't yet made it to the UnderVerse. He caught Belladonna frowning in curiosity. "Not important," he whispered, winking at her, knowing damn well if they had been a fixture here, he'd have been paying for that little comment later.

She rolled her eyes and turned back to the teams. "What are you waiting for?" she snapped. "*MOVE!*"

The descent was a nightmare of precarious footing and sudden attacks. The magelights cast dancing shadows across the coral-encrusted walls, creating the illusion of movement everywhere they looked. Worse, the "gentle" slope they'd seen from above had turned out to be deceptive.

"Shit!" Sip's voice echoed as his foot slipped on a patch of algae. He slid several meters before catching himself, the rope burning through his gauntlets. "The whole damn slope's like glass!"

He wasn't wrong. Whatever the original surface of this section had been, it hadn't been steel. Centuries of salt water and organic growth had polished it into a dangerous sheen. The teams were forced to rely almost entirely on the ropes, using them to negotiate past the twisted ruins of what had once been internal walls and support structures as the floor changed from what had probably been a five- to ten-degree cant, to a forty, and then a sixty or seventy.

"Hold!" Alistair's warning came just as a section of flooring gave way beneath him. He swung to the side, shield raised instinctively as chunks of metal and coral crashed into the darkness below. The echoes seemed to go on forever.

"How far down does this go?" one of the legionnaires whispered.

Nobody answered. They all knew that somewhere below them lay the ruins of the lowest levels, and none of them wanted to think about what would happen if their ropes failed.

Thomas caught movement out of the corner of his eye, a flash of chitin in the darkness. "Incoming!" he shouted, just as creatures burst from a hidden recess in the wall. "Protect the ropes!"

The fight that followed was unlike anything they'd trained for. Suspended on their lines, the teams could neither advance nor retreat effectively. The creatures, however, moved across the walls as easily as they did the floor, their claws finding purchase in the rusted metal, the gaps, and occasionally weird fluorescent coral growths.

"Keep them back!" Belladonna commanded, her swordstaff flashing out and punching into restraining limbs, or hacking through carapaces as she fought. "Don't let them get to the anchor points!"

The mages did what they could, but their spells were limited by the need to avoid damaging their own ropes. The cramped space worked against them as well—a fireball here could cook them all.

The majority were small, the size of medium to large dogs, multi-limbed and with distinct "walking" and "fighting" limbs, the pincers separated into a crushing and cutting claw respectively.

Where they had them.

Some were tentacled horrors, the kind that would have had Cthulhu buying drinks and trying to get home for a bit of fun. Others looked like they'd started out as normal crabs…then they'd been put in a washing machine with a handful of large rocks and set to spin.

One thing they definitely were, though, was trouble.

"Use your shields!" Alistair shouted. "Block, then shove!"

That helped to deal with most. A single heavy blow was enough to send them flying—or falling—and the crunches as they impacted far below made it clear that they wouldn't be trying a second attack.

That didn't mean it was all smooth sailing, though.

One of the miners was lost when a large squid-like thing, with dozens of eyes all over its body, launched itself from above, landing on his head with a sickeningly wet *splat*, before the miner's shouts cut off abruptly to the sound of crunching.

The body dropped to dangle on the ropes; blood ran around the mouth of the thing, as it ignored them all and settled into its gory feast.

Another of the Dark Legion, or formerly thereof, was nearly lost as Dashiki totally missed a thrust, slipping and skidding on the slick floor, and the crab batted the blade aside. Its crushing limb ripped the sword free and tossed it aside to vanish into the gloom, before spasming, the hook on the back of Thomas's axe having plunged deep into the back of its carapace as it was distracted.

"Fuck's sake, I liked that sword!" Dashiki raged, stomping over to stare over the side after it, before spitting and swearing, then finally nodding his thanks to Thomas as the larger man broke the spike free with a crunch.

The body flopped and spasmed, sliding from sight to vanish over the near side, and into the darkness after the weapon.

"Thomas!" Nigret called from below as the fight slackened off. "Nigret sees light! *Real* light, not these trinkets we carry!"

He was right. A faint blue-white glow was becoming visible, pulsing slowly like a heartbeat. As they finished off the last of the wave of attackers, they descended farther, moving around a fallen section of flooring. The greater cavern opened up to them, and Thomas could make out more details.

The hundred-meter descent to here, where they'd hoped would be the lowest point, wasn't even close.

Beyond them was a vast chamber. Its walls were covered in limpets; running, mingling streams of saltwater; fresh, red rust streaks; and sheer, gleaming polished metal that refused any damage. There were rocks that had once been below the ocean stabbing up toward the surface overhead that had somehow been caught inside the failing shields that were maintained by these last vestiges of the prax.

Flickering edges of shields allowed the crustaceans to push through, entering and leaving the hidden grotto far below. And in the center? Massive crystalline growths that caught and reflected the light.

"That's it!" Coran shouted. "The manastone formation! Fuckin' hell, that's huge!"

"That's what she said," breathed Thomas unthinkingly, before grinning in embarrassment when Belladonna arced one perfect eyebrow. "Well, you did," he pointed out. The amused look changed to a glare that had him wincing as she apparently noticed others listening in.

"Oh, I'm gonna pay for that…" He sighed to himself as a low round of chuckles were hastily cut off in terror. He started moving along quickly, waving his hands like he was shooing chickens and raising his voice. "Move it along, people! Nothing to see here!"

The crystal cluster dominated the center of the chamber, rising from a pool of standing water like some vast, alien growth. Smaller crystals dotted the walls, and the light they emitted flickered and pulsed constantly, creating a latticework of light that turned the chamber into something from a fever dream.

It also wasn't undefended, of course.

Gathered around the base of the formation were dozens of the creatures, ranging from ones no larger than a dog to massive specimens that dwarfed even the ones they'd fought above. They moved with purpose, seemingly organized in a way the others hadn't been.

"They're protecting it," Belladonna breathed, understanding dawning in her eyes. "They've been living off the mana leakage for centuries. That's why they've changed so much."

Thomas nodded grimly. "And we need to take it from them." He studied the chamber, noting defensive positions and potential choke points. "Think your team's still up for that competition?"

She grinned fiercely. "Winner gets to name their prize, remember?" Her smile faded as she looked back at the crystal formation. "But we do this smart. These things aren't just random monsters anymore. They're acting organized."

"Agreed." Thomas turned to the teams, who were finally reaching a section where it looked like they could spread out and just climb normally. "Rest and regroup. Get ready, people! We're going to need everyone at their best for this."

That done, Thomas turned back to staring out across the chamber, shaking his head at the sheer damn size of it. It wasn't big—the chamber was *vast*, far larger than their magelights could illuminate. Ancient support columns, thick as castle towers, disappeared into darkness overhead, and nearby, what looked to have been a recent collapse had taken out a large section of the flooring for the level above.

The blue-white pulse of the manastones painted everything in ethereal light, reflecting off pools of seawater that dotted the chamber floor.

"Those pools connect to the ocean," Alistair observed, pointing one out with his shield. "Deep enough down here to hide anything waiting on the other side as well. We need to secure the perimeter first and then set up to hold against what could be sent through them."

Thomas nodded. The legionnaire's monster-hunting experience would be crucial here. "We spread out. Belladonna, take your best and secure our left flank. Alistair, you've got the right. I'll hold center with the rest, and the miners stay behind me. Nigret? You're our rear. Pick two others you trust and make sure we're not fucked in it by anything that doesn't buy us a drink first."

Whatever else they might be, the group were all warriors and they all had experience being deep in the shit. They moved with practiced paranoia, shields up as they advanced. The scattered pools forced them to weave between them and the columns, each one potentially hiding death.

The first sign of the new threat came as a wet, slithering sound from their left.

"Movement!" Sip called out, crossbow raised. "I don't—*what the fuck is that?*" he screamed, his voice breaking into a high-pitched whine.

The creature that emerged was nothing like its armored cousins. Where they were all hard angles and sharp edges, this was smooth, almost liquid in its movement. Multiple tentacles, each easily five meters long, propelled it from the pool. Its body was translucent, internal organs visible through gelatinous flesh that pulsed with the same rhythm as the manastones.

"Spread out!" Thomas commanded, eyes widening as he saw a shuddering section near the top expanding. "Don't bunch up—"

The warning came too late. The creature's mantle expanded, and it spat a stream of greenish fluid that splashed across three legionnaires. Their screams were horrible but mercifully brief as the acid ate through armor and flesh alike, until its attack was spent.

"Take it down!" Belladonna roared, already moving to flank the beast. More of them emerged from other pools, their tentacles reaching for prey.

The battle devolved into chaos. Armored crustaceans burst from the water as even more charged from their positions around the manastone formation. As they scuttled forward, their squid-like cousins provided covering fire from the pools. The combination could be lethal. Any fighter who stayed still long enough to engage one threat became vulnerable to the other.

Fire, though…fire was the key.

Those who had it were already launching magic at the squids. As firebolts impacted, the squids burbled and scattered. Whatever else they might be, these deepwater things had little experience with fire. And once they did? They hated it.

Alistair was the first to slam a firebolt into the open siphon of a squid as it was about to unleash its attack, and the result was impressive.

The body detonated a split second later. The acidic compound went up like napalm, and raised the temperature in the cavern all on its own.

The flying chunks of calamari then ignited another that had begun its stream, and almost before anyone could follow the reaction, another went up as well. Suddenly, it was pandemonium.

"Push to the columns!" Thomas roared. "Use them for cover!"

Sip was closest to one of the massive supports. He turned to make a run for it, but as he did, tentacles burst from the depths of a pool he'd overlooked. They wrapped around his legs, armor creaking as they constricted, yanking him from his feet and across the floor.

"Help! Thomas, shit…" he screamed, dropping his crossbow to draw a knife. He managed to sever one tentacle before a blast of acid caught him in the chest. His final scream was lost in the sound of dissolving metal.

"Keep moving!" Belladonna roared over the sounds of battle, hauling a battered and stunned legionnaire to his feet and shoving him in the direction of the fight. "Mourn the dead later!"

The teams rallied, using the columns for cover as they advanced. Legionnaires coordinated their attacks, timing firebolts to detonate the acid-spitters while those that were out of—or low on—mana fought as frontline fighters and engaged the armored ones.

"Something's up," Coran shouted over the din. "Thomas, fuck's sake, you seein' this? Are they herding us away from the crystals?"

Thomas cursed as he saw his friend was right. Every time they tried to approach the manastone formation, the creatures would force them back with coordinated attacks. The largest of the armored ones hadn't even engaged yet, waiting near the crystal base like huge, chitinous generals.

"We need to change tactics," Thomas called to Belladonna. "We're not going to win a war of attrition."

She nodded grimly, dispatching another creature with a brutal thrust. "The tentacle things are the key. They're controlling the battlefield. Take them out, then we can deal with the armored ones."

"Agreed." Thomas turned to his remaining forces. "Mages, focus fire on the pools! Boil those bastards out! Everyone else, form up on me. We're going to give them something to think about!"

The real question was whether they had enough fighters left to see it through. The chamber floor was already littered with bodies—both human and creature—and they hadn't even reached the main crystal formation yet, not to mention having to keep people back to protect the miners.

The battle shifted as Thomas spotted movement near the crystal formation, something different from the mindless aggression of the crustaceans or the tactical retreat of the acid-spitters.

Two dark shapes moved with deadly purpose through the deepest pools, their forms too fast, too coordinated to be just local wildlife.

"Merrow!" Nigret snarled, his enhanced vision picking them out clearly at the same time. "Deep ones, not like surface dwellers. Much nastier, yes?"

Thomas cursed. He'd heard stories of the deep merrow. Unlike their surface or shallow water cousins the naga, who occasionally traded with coastal settlements, these were said to be utter bastards. They occasionally raided shipping, but mainly they existed only in old tales from back when sailors weren't all suicidal. Those who claimed to have seen them in modern times were much rarer, as the fuckers tended not to leave witnesses. Their centuries in the lightless depths had changed them, twisted them into something barely recognizable as sentient.

As if summoned by his thoughts, a third burst from a pool. Its flesh was pale as a corpse, covered in phosphorescent markings that pulsed in time with the manastones. Multiple arms, evolved for the crushing pressures of the deep, wielded coral-encrusted weapons with lethal grace.

It rushed from the pool, shrieking something unintelligible; around it, the bigger, dumber beasts reacted instantly, swarming and protecting it.

"They're controlling the creatures!" Belladonna shouted, noting how the crustaceans moved with suddenly improved coordination. "Some kind of sonic control!"

She was right. The merrow emitted high-pitched whistles and clicks, directing their "troops" with the precision of seasoned commanders. With that pattern seen, what had seemed like mindless attacks became carefully orchestrated movements designed to wear down the invaders.

"New plan!" Thomas roared. "Coran, Alistair, with me. We're taking that formation!"

"How?" Coran shook his head. "Fuck's sake, Thomas, I'll follow you, but I don't see…"

"Explosive Compression! Oracle taught us all, and fuck me if that won't ruin someone's day!" Thomas said to Alistair quickly. "We hit both sides with that, then the three of us charge. We get in close before they can recover and…"

"If they survive; that shit's nasty," Coran pointed out, and Alistair grunted.

"I have enough mana for two spells, and then I'm out with a mana migraine. You sure about this?" he asked.

"We've got a couple of potions—take one." Thomas understood the instinct to horde them until later just in case, but it'd do them no good if they all died before they could use them.

The merrow were clearly intelligent enough to recognize the enemy leadership. One of the creatures started to screech and warble in its own language, before leveling a two-pronged trident—*bi-dent*?—at Thomas.

"If this doesn't work, we've got problems," Alistair muttered, biting the cork in the top of the potion, jerking it out and spitting it aside before chugging the potion.

"We're the legion," Thomas responded, hefting his axe. "And we're taking what we came for."

The pair hurled their spells at the merrow, aiming to land them so that the outer ring of the area of effect was a few meters from the mana crystals. And when they activated?

Whoo-boy.

Thomas shook his head as the first phase started, before taking a deep breath and bellowing out his orders. "Legion… Aaaaad-*vance*!"

The spell was a brutal thing, something only Jax would have come up with. It essentially was a ball of plasma, one that operated right at the edge of stability, and when it was thrown, it broke like an egg.

What came out of the egg, though…that was the kicker. The first phase was a flaming detonation that hammered into anything nearby, knocking them from their feet and giving them nasty burns.

It became interesting, because what came out then was essentially the AOE barrier.

It looped around, creating a destructive dome out from the center, and then it started to drag everything inward.

Anything caught in the field was pulled in toward the center, where they were already burning, and now being crushed as well.

The version Jax had—magic was always a personal thing, and Thomas and the rest of the legionnaires were only able to absorb the most basic version—was capable of gravitational distortions that broke everything inside down to a tiny marble of compressed matter.

The ones they used in comparison were almost laughably underpowered.

*Almost* being the important word here—because when you're dealing with creatures from the bottom of the ocean, and some of them happened to be using a sort of organic acid that they didn't know was at the very edge of being declared a war crime, it burned so well…

*Well.*

Belladonna's squad engaged the crustaceans, keeping them from interfering as Thomas led the assault on the merrow themselves.

The spells yanked all but one out of hiding, as well as two crustaceans and one more of the squids. It crushed, burned, and broke them. The squid burst and its innards ignited in a swirling ball of flame, before releasing them as the pair of spells ran out of mana to roll, screaming, thrashing, and suffering on the floor.

Thomas leapt over a maddened, wildly racing six-legged thing that looked like a coffee table with eyes, and landed with a grunt, swinging his axe around to hack one of the merrow in half.

The creature, now neatly bisected at the waist, continued to shriek and thrash at itself, frantically trying to beat the fire out until it died.

Coran took the other, riding it to the ground as it reared up, covered in flickering flames, to its full three-meter height.

From the waist down, it was a snake, wide-bodied though almost flattened. From the waist up?

They had four arms, spines, and arcing chitinous plates; their faces were fanged monstrosities that opened far wider than anything had any right to.

He slammed into it, and distracted by the fire, the injuries, and the spell that literally just ended, the weight of a fully armored legionnaire was too much for it.

It fell backward, slamming into the cavern floor. As they did, Coran showed the level of brutality that the Dark Legion was famed for. He roared and stabbed, over and over, dragging the blade left and right inside his opponent, using it like a whisk. He rolled his wrist, arcing the blade upward from the belly and coring the creature out as it howled and tried to hit him with three arms—the fourth missing and gouting oily blood already.

Spoiler. It didn't succeed.

The merrow leader was the last; it came straight for Thomas. Its four arms wielded different weapons in a lethal dance as it shrieked and unleashed sonic attacks that sent his insides vibrating and set his ears to bleeding even as he dodged desperately.

"Fuck me, you're *ugly*," Thomas grunted, parrying the two-pronged spear thrust and then dodging a swing from a hooked blade that looked almost organic. "Goddamn squatters!" His axe took one of its arms off at the shoulder, blood spraying, then snap kicked it in the stomach.

The creature's scream was deafening, a psychic blast that stunned everyone nearby.

Thomas staggered, desperately trying to fight through it. He brought his axe around a second too late as the merrow raised its trident again…only to see it stiffen as a swordstaff burst from the center of its chest from behind in a killing blow.

"Mine," Belladonna called to him, before twisting it, then yanking it free and stabbing out at a crab thing that had been running to its master's aid. "Mine as well!"

"Fuck's sake!" Thomas groaned as he blinked and panted, catching his breath and hoping that the sonic attack hadn't just decorated his trousers for him. "She's a goddamn kill-stealer!"

The effect on the battlefield was immediate. Without their controllers, the giant crustaceans reverted to uncoordinated attacks and were quickly dispatched. The acid-spitters were already either dead, burning, or diving for the depths of the nearby pools, considering the floating and still burning mess that covered their surface.

It was like an oil slick had caught fire. The remaining creatures, after a few more seconds of suddenly confused fighting, and having seen their leaders fall, tried to escape but were cut down by coordinated volleys from the ranged fighters.

"Secure the formation!" Thomas ordered, stepping over the merrow's corpse. "Get those miners in and working before anything else shows up!"

"Already on it," Belladonna called back, directing her remaining squad members. She paused, looking at the carnage around them. "Shame about Sip. He had potential…maybe."

Thomas nodded grimly. "He died as a legionnaire, and not stuck with that dick Nimon's fingers on his soul. That's more than he had any right to, but yeah, still wish he'd survived." He turned to survey their prize, the massive manastone formation that had cost them so dearly. "Let's make it worth it."

The aftermath of battle was always the worst part. Thomas supervised the miners while Belladonna organized search teams to check the pools, both for additional threats and for any equipment that could be salvaged from their fallen. The few potions that were recovered would make a hell of a difference, after all.

"How long?" Thomas asked the leader of the miners, a taciturn human who looked too thin and tall to be any good at mining when there were literally dwarves about. But given that they all deferred to him, Thomas was willing to give him the benefit of the doubt.

"Another hour, maybe two," the human replied, chewing his lip in thought. "We can get the first handful free in that time. We have to be precise. Too much force at the wrong point and we'll shatter the whole formation. Too little and we run the risk of spreading cracks throughout it that it can't recover from, and we won't get pieces large enough to be useful."

The massive crystals pulsed with energy, their light seemingly brighter now that the merrow were dead..

"Movement!" Nigret's warning brought everyone to alert, weapons raised, but the trigara held up a hand. "Not hostile. This one sees something…strange."

"Fuck's sake, why the hell couldn't I have died in the arena?" Thomas growled to himself, before pushing to his feet and starting over to the trigara. "*Now* what?" he snarled.

# CHAPTER THREE

I looked at the rune-inscribed shields blocking our retreat and felt Oracle tense through our bond. Wonderful. Somebody had magic shields, and that meant that they probably had access to other things as well.

"You don't want to do this." I let mana flow into my naginata until the blade glowed with a faint crimson light as a warning. "We're just passing through."

"That's what they all say," one of the shield-bearers rasped, squinting into the light. "Before they try to kill us. Before they try to capture us. Before they try to *eat* us." The last word came out as a hiss.

I tried triggering Examine, and got absolutely nothing useful, which kinda wasn't what I was hoping for.

The screen literally fuzzed, expanded, and then failed, popping like a smoke bubble.

I caught Sehran's subtle shift in stance out of the corner of my eye. She was getting ready, her demonic nature bleeding through as she licked her lips and glanced over to me. Oracle drifted closer to me, hands flickering with nervous energy.

*"What the hell just happened?"* I growled through the bond.

*"Anti-scrying spell or artifact, I think,"* Oracle replied tersely. *"Probably to hide them. What do we do?"*

*"Do we fight?"* Sehran asked before I could answer. *"I can probably distract some of them."*

"Look at his armor," another voice called from the shadows. "That's not cheap. That's not a mercenary's gear—he's a hunter! Come to collect specimens!"

"No," I started to say, but the word was drowned out by a chorus of angry hisses and clicks. The crowd of mutated creatures pressed closer, their extra limbs moving in unsettling patterns. Some brandished crude weapons, while others flexed clawed hands.

"The Dark Legion takes our people," the first speaker snarled. "Sells them. Breaks them. Changes them." A bitter laugh. "Your kind never stops!"

Shit. Of all the misunderstandings… "I'm not Dark Legion," I said firmly. "I'm Imperial Legion. The real legion."

That was apparently the wrong thing to say. The entire chamber erupted in screeches of rage and disbelief.

"Lies!"

"Kill him! Take his armor!"

The first wave came at us from three directions at once. I had just enough time to shove Oracle behind me before they crashed into us like a tide of twisted flesh and clicking mandibles.

My naginata's blade left trails of crimson light as I swept it in a wide arc, forcing the closest attackers back, making me seriously reconsider the usefulness of a seven-foot weapon in an underground fucking passage. One tried to duck under the blade, using its extra arms to scramble along the floor like some sort of demented spider. I triggered Lunge and blurred forward, getting some room; I stabbed the figure behind him and simultaneously stomped down hard. Chitin cracked under my boot as I slammed my foot down into the middle of his neck.

He collapsed, squealing. His neck was broken, I guessed by the unnatural stillness. But instead of acting as a warning, it just riled them even more.

Sehran had fully shifted back into her usual form: tall, stunning, clearly fucking sexually active and enticing. She opened her mouth wide, wings spread open in the confined space as she met the attack from our left flank. She let lose a crooning cry, something that staggered the incoming attackers as their attention was derailed, instinctive reactions to what a friend would have described as her "devil whore magic."

Whatever you called it, it broke their furious advance, stunning them and confusing them, until her claws tore through mutated flesh with devastating efficiency. As soon as they started screaming and dying, the spell was broken; for each attacker she put down, two more emerged from the shadows.

"Jax!" Oracle's warning came just in time.

I spun, blade rising to deflect a thrown spear that would have taken me in the throat. The weapon clattered away into the darkness, but I caught the gleam of something else in the thrower's hands. Something that sparkled with familiar energy.

"They've got manastones!" I shouted to Sehran. "Don't let them—"

The chamber lit up with sickly green light as three of our attackers simultaneously triggered their stones. The magic that washed over us wasn't particularly powerful, but it was *wrong*. I felt it trying to seep into my armor, into my skin, seeking to do…something.

They didn't seem to have combat magic, not in the way that we did, but that power? It'd flashed out wildly, surges of something that felt like it could be anything.

A half second later, Oracle's horrified sending reached us both. *"It's something to do with the corruption that changed them! Wild, uncontrolled mana. I'm trying to block it!"*

Oracle's power flared in response. Her form blazed with blue-white light as she threw up a panicked and weak barrier around us. The opposing magics clashed with a sound like shattering glass, sending everyone staggering.

"We need to move!" Sehran called, her voice thick with the effort as she twisted, then fired an Explosive Compression into the passage we'd just come along. The screams made it clear that there was no way we were escaping that way. As I cut and stabbed, she alternated spells, singing that completely distracted and confused them, and then waded into their bodies, claws flashing. "Now!"

I didn't waste breath answering. Instead, I triggered Mana Overdrive. Strength surged through my muscles as time seemed to slow around me. The naginata became a blur of motion as I carved a path toward a passage that Oracle indicated.

The shield-bearers tried to block us, raising their rune-carved barriers. They stood in pairs between us and the passages, clearly placed there just to stop us escaping. As soon as we closed on them, they braced the two shields against each other, edge to edge, then slammed them down against the rocky floor of the tunnel, hard.

There was a flare of red energy, something that surged up and out, extending to the left and right and seeming to anchor itself on the walls.

"Hold them!" I bellowed to Oracle and Sehran, even as those with manastones tried again. The flash of green light that flooded the cavern brought a wave of nausea with it as well.

"Go!" Oracle shouted back, even as she countered, a fresh pulse of healing magic washing out over us all.

I powered mana into my naginata, lunging forward as I damn well hoped that the color meant what I thought it did.

"*Jenae, I could do with some fuckin' help!*" I cast the thought at the goddess, hoping that she could hear me, and really hoping that this was fire mana.

Whatever was going on with the shield, despite my hopes that red basically equaled fire, it—of course—wasn't to be. As the blade slammed into the magical shield, the released energy sent me staggering as my mana and that of the shield fought each other.

Whatever the shields were, they were strong, and seriously so. My naginata had enchantments that made it extra effective against shield spells, and yet still I was thrown back.

Both the figures that wielded them screamed though, growing suddenly gaunt as the shield's light flared again.

Jenae felt… unbelievably distant as she struggled to respond: a sense of concern, of warning, and then a vague squirt of information, a wild hint and she was gone.

I cursed. What she'd sent was a garbled mess, and I had no time to parse it out now. Instead, I triggered Examine, hoping to get some information on the shield or the creature—and I got neither, just a shimmering as a notification failed entirely, making me curse again.

"Jax?!" Oracle called to me. "Anytime!"

"Working on it!" I roared back, falling back on "old faithful."

If the barrier had been fire mana and I'd filled my weapon with that, it'd have slid through the barrier like it wasn't there. That was what I was hoping for. But what I'd seen, first of all, was that the barrier most definitely wasn't fire, or at least not only fire mana, and that the impact of my naginata and the unleashed power that threw me back…had thrown them back as well.

The walls around where they'd been braced looked scoured clean. A meter back from where they currently stood, I saw through the wavering shimmer of the shield. Well, it was far more open than where they stood now.

I took a quick couple of steps back, then ran at them, pulling my Mana Overdrive in and triggering it hard as I impacted, channeling air at the same time into the naginata and making it seemingly weightless. I spun it up, getting as much momentum as I could, and then reversed it, sliding it back to fire just before it hit. The effect was to send them staggering back into the open area. As the shield flickered and surged, reaching out and trying to lock into the surrounding rock, I darted back again.

A fast sprint at them, triggering Soaring Majesty, and then I dropped and slid, taking advantage of the smooth stone floor. My shoulder slammed into one of the shield-bearer's legs, sending them sprawling. Their shields clattered to the ground; runes flared wildly as the bearers lost control and started to scream.

"This way!" I rolled to my feet, gesturing for Oracle and Sehran to follow. Then, on a whim, because they'd already fucked with me once, I stabbed the nearest wielder in the back and snatched his shield up, because why the hell not. More spears were hurled, and I turned, darting after the other two. Some kind of thrown dart, about as long as my arm but without the fletching of an arrow, clattered around us as we ran, the howls of our pursuers echoing off the ancient stones.

We weren't out of this yet, not by a long shot. But at least we were moving. And somewhere up ahead lay our goal: the great dome we'd seen from the desert. Assuming, of course, that we lived long enough to reach it.

I heard the click of chitin on stone behind us, getting closer. These things knew these tunnels far better than we did. This was going to get worse before it got better.

Story of my life, really.

The passage twisted and turned, branching off in multiple directions. Oracle's light pulsed brighter for a moment, illuminating ancient imperial markers at each junction.

"Left!" she called out.

I didn't question it, just pivoted hard and kept running. The sound of our pursuers echoed from every direction now, making it impossible to tell how many were still chasing us or how close they were.

"They're herding us again," Sehran warned, her wings folded tight against her back in the narrow space. "These side passages…"

She was right. Every time we passed a junction, I caught glimpses of movement from the other tunnels. They were paralleling our course, trying to cut us off up ahead.

A figure suddenly burst from a concealed panel, eyes glowing bright, teeth gleaming… Then I was past; my instinctive move to duck my shoulder and plow it into the wall resulted in a series of crunches, a gout of bloody ichor, and a dead bug. I ran on, dismissing it from my mind as an idiot considering I was a heavily armored legionnaire running at full speed.

"Oracle?" I asked between breaths. "Please tell me we're almost there."

"The dome's central chamber should be…" She hesitated as we reached another junction. "This way! Up these stairs!"

The stairway was steeper than the others we'd encountered, rising at a sharp angle. Not the best place for a fight, but we didn't have much choice. I could hear the clicks and scrapes getting closer behind us.

"Go!" I ordered, urging Oracle ahead of me. "Sehran, you next. I'll hold them here for a moment."

"Jax—" Oracle started to protest.

"Move!"

They ascended as I twisted to face back down the passage, fingers working, nearly chewing my own lip off as I cast, then hurled an Explosive Compression spell back into the darkness behind.

As the spell streaked down the middle, the first of our pursuers came into view, scrambling along the walls and ceiling like oversized insects. The sight of their twisted forms moving with that unnatural grace sent a shiver down my spine as literally dozens more of them followed.

The spell impacted maybe the fifth or sixth along in the line: blowing out, smashing them all into the walls, floor, and ceiling, setting fire to them, then yanking them back inward. The sounds of shrieking and burning, cracking bones and creaking metal filled the underground. A handful more burst free of the same passage that the opportunist bug had taken; then, seeing their friends a few meters away being shattered into pieces, clearly decided that a long and rich life had never been what they were looking for anyway and promptly still fucking rushed the magic-wielding warrior in their midst.

I triggered another Mana Overdrive, feeling the familiar rush of power, and met their charge. The naginata's blade traced blurred patterns in the air, as I rolled my shoulders and grinned, moving into a "grass-beater," as my old frenemy West had called it. The blade came up and around, down low to the ground and skimming it and then back up in circular motions, before I swapped my grip and the blade changed from covering the left to the right, keeping them at bay.

I looked cool as hell. But slightly more importantly, the only way to reach me was to literally run into a glittering, spinning wall of sharpened steel. For the two that tried it, it really didn't end well.

One enterprising sod tried to time it to leap past me, waiting until I was engaged in slicing its fellow into kibble, and using its extra limbs to gain purchase on the ceiling. I reversed my grip and drove the blade up and back, catching it mid-jump. The blade pushed through the creature's back, and I whipped it back around, shucking it off the blade and blocking the path of those behind it.

"Jax, hurry!" Sehran's voice echoed down from above. "We've got problems up here too!"

"Of course we do!" I snarled as I started to back up the stairs, keeping my blade moving. The confined space actually worked in my favor here as they could only come at me one or two at a time. Still, there were a lot of them, and that weird magic they'd used earlier…

As if reading my mind, three more manastones flared to life in the crowd below. I turned and sprinted up the stairs as another wave of that corrupting energy filled the passage. Even through my armor, I could feel it trying to work its way in, seeking to trigger changes in my flesh.

I burst out of the stairway into what had to be the base of the dome we'd seen from outside. Pale light filtered down from high above, where sections of the dome's surface had crumbled away. The chamber itself was vast, its floor covered in a maze of fallen stone and ancient machinery.

And we weren't alone.

Sehran and Oracle had taken cover behind a massive piece of toppled masonry. Around them were bodies of some less inhuman, but still clearly spiderlike fuckers they'd just killed. Then, across the chamber, another half a dozen figures crouched in the shadows of the ruined equipment. Unlike our pursuers from below, these were fully human, dressed in loose, battered, damaged desert clothing but armed with proper weapons…weapons that were noticeably pointed at us.

"Slavers?" I panted, joining the others behind their cover.

"Worse," Sehran replied. "I think they're the ones who escaped. The ones those slavers we saw before were hunting."

Before I could respond, one of the figures stood up, leveling a crossbow at our position. "Come out!" a woman's voice called. "Slowly and with your hands where we can see them."

I glanced back at the stairway we'd emerged from. The clicks and scrapes were getting closer. We had maybe seconds before our pursuers caught up.

"We're not with them!" I called back. "We're not looking for a fight—we're just trying to get out of here!"

"You're wearing heavy armor," the woman replied. "And you're running from the Changed Ones. That makes you either slavers or thieves. Either way…you just started a fight that you can't win!"

The first of our pursuers emerged from the stairway, skittering across the ground and skidding to a halt, hissing furiously, even as more burst free behind it. Their twisted forms silhouetted against the darkness.

The woman's crossbow shifted, tracking them, then wavered back to me, then to them, clearly unsure whether the scabrous forms escaping the underground were the lesser threat, and judging from the wide-eyed and horrified look on her face, she wasn't liking the look of them either.

*"Jax, she's afraid of them…"* Oracle sent at the same time as I noticed that.

*"Of course she is!"* I sent back, twisting and checking the walls as the sound of tap-tap-tapping echoed out on all sides.

"Tell them who you are!" Sehran called to me.

I shot her a fast glance, confused, before gritting my teeth. I stepped out from behind cover, keeping my hands visible but not releasing my weapon.

"My name is Jax. This is Oracle and Sehran," I said clearly, inclining my head in their directions as I named them. "I'm wearing this armor because I'm…a member of the *Imperial* Legion. The *real* legion, not the Dark Dicks. But right now, we all have bigger problems than arguing about who we are."

More of the Changed Ones emerged from the stairway, even as more started to appear from shadowy recesses on all sides. The woman's companions had risen as well, weapons ready, forming a loose semicircle. We were caught between them and the monsters, with nowhere left to run.

I tried again, not really expecting it to work, and sighed in relief as this time the Examine worked, then hissed as the information was poured into my brain.

| Changed Ones |
|:---:|
| The Changed Ones, as the name implies, were once very different from their current form. Where the majority were originally imperial citizens, determined people who refused to abandon the land of their fathers, this individual is far from those first volunteers. |
| No longer are the city's inhabitants those brave souls who believed a small alteration would help battle the encroaching wave of death and heat. Instead, the lost and abandoned, desperate souls are seduced into accepting a minor alteration, before being gradually changed beyond all recognition in an experiment that no longer has any meaning. |
| Beware those that once walked between, and beware the corruption they left behind… |

| Weaknesses: Light, Fire, and Water magics | Resistances: 25% resistance to Earth magics & 50% resistance to Death/Darkness spells |
|---|---|
| Health: 182/390 | Mana: 11/40 |
| Level: 17 ||

Sometimes I really hated being right about things getting worse.

A harsh laugh came from one of the woman's companions. "Imperial Legion? Fuck, that's all we need…more of you useless bastards. At least the Dark Legion could be relied on to fight with half a brain!"

"I don't know what you're drinking, but if you think the Imperial Legion can't face monsters better than anyone else, you're crazy!" I snapped back, still absorbing the information I'd gotten. So, the Changed Ones were what? Victims of some scam?

"Damn right, you face them, and then you die like flies!" their leader shouted back. "Oh *shit*—what the *hell* is that?!"

I glanced in the direction she was staring. My little group backed away from the stairwell and the mass of creatures that scuttled free, and I saw it.

One of the Changed Ones, clearly a lot further gone than the rest, had staggered into a patch of moonlight, and I realized what it was. These poor bastards mustn't have Darkvision, or if they did, it was a short-range variant. They'd not see the things in the darkness, beyond blurred movement.

"Well, there's a shitload of these things and it looks like they don't like you either," I replied, keeping my voice steady as more of the Changed Ones filtered into the chamber. "How about we argue over who each other is later when we're not getting surrounded and about to be eaten!"

"Jax," Oracle whispered urgently. "The Changed Ones…they're not just coming from below anymore."

She was right. More twisted forms had already started to emerge from other passages around the chamber's edge. I'd seen that, but now the sound of chittering echoed down from above as well. They moved with insectile ease, heads peering and bodies clambering in through long empty windows, spreading out to cut off any chance of escape.

Whatever else these mutations had done to them, it hadn't damaged their tactical thinking.

"Kaspin!" the woman with the crossbow shouted out into the air in desperation suddenly. "Don't make me do this, Kaspin! We can still be friends!"

Whoever Kaspin was, the Changed Ones chose that moment to attack. They came at us in a wave of clicking limbs and chitinous armor, moving with that same unsettling grace we'd seen below.

The woman cursed and fired her crossbow; the bolt took one of them in what passed for its throat. It fell, twitching, but two more scrambled over its body as they went from moving to surround us to an all-out attack.

"Fuck it," I muttered, then raised my voice. "Oracle, frostfire on the right! Sehran, distract the left flank!"

I didn't wait to see whether the other humans would shoot us in the back. The naginata's blade flared with crimson light as I charged to meet the Changed Ones' attack. Through my bond with Oracle, I felt her power surge as she threw up a barrier between us and the incoming creatures.

"What are you doing?" one of the group of escapees shouted at their seeming leader. "They were offering us sanctuary! We don't know who these three are!"

"They've gone feral!" the woman shouted back, frantically cranking the windlass on her crossbow. "Fucking fight, you idiot! You want to live in the dark with *them?*"

The mass of them were closing on all sides now. Dozens clambered, spiderlike, through broken windows, and pulled themselves through shattered sections of flooring and in doorways.

"Negotiate later, fight now!" I shouted back over my shoulder. My blade removed several of a Changed One's extra arms as it leapt at me; the screaming creature hit the floor and shrieked, before a second slice took the top of its head off.

"They could be slavers!" another of them shouted, presumably talking about us, as I couldn't really see the twisty spider fuckers sitting down to a good deal over dinner with anyone.

"Seriously?" I snapped. "You think I'd be fighting these things just to capture *you?*"

*"Jax, I need your mana!"* Oracle sent me.

I knew what she wanted straightaway. I cut the Mana Overdrive, freeing up as much as I could, and fell back on ingrained and trained skills, as she worked.

The battle devolved into chaos.

Sehran, taking a deep breath, had unleashed a crooning cry that echoed off the walls of the rotunda. A group of easily ten of the incoming figures slowed, drifting as they tried to follow her, mouths falling slack…

Then Oracle slammed down two Frostfire Circles of Cleansing.

That she'd managed two was impressive, and it also took a hell of a chunk out of our mana. But as she slammed the spells down, it changed the field of the fight.

Frostfire Circle of Cleansing was one of the variants that Oracle had worked up based off the original Cleansing Flames spell I'd brought with me to the UnderVerse. Where my flames spell had evolved into Flames of Wrath, dealing far more damage over time, this was a lot closer to the original, and it had quickly become a go-to spell underground while we were escaping.

Like before, it unleashed a ring of flames in a ritual circle, and they both burned my enemies and healed my allies, but these now added a secondary effect that was missing from the original.

As the name implied, "frost" was a great addition, but mainly because it added a debuff to movement. With every second that the enemy was injured and remained in the area of effect, their skin froze harder, their joints stiffened, and they slowed a fraction more.

It wouldn't last forever, and the spell was mana intensive—five hundred mana for sixty seconds, which meant that without a lot of mana potions, I was getting four of them in a fight and that was it. But as it slowed my enemies, as the frost stiffened them, sealing them into place and gave me time to act, the flames also burned them.

There were good, solid reasons; reasons based in physics that meant it shouldn't have worked. Fire and ice should cancel each other out after all, right?

Fortunately, though, magic listened very carefully and patiently as physics explained things like that…then told it to go suck a barrel of dicks.

Both AOEs slammed down ahead of me to my left and right, the narrow field right in front of me left as the only avenue where there was a safe passage for them to attack along…and I stood on the point where the two fields touched.

The healing effect of both fields touching me, the gentle tingle of the flames and the cooling breeze of the frost made me sigh, even as I started to spin my naginata in faster and faster arcs.

"Come on then! Daddy's got something for ya!" I hissed, lunging forward.

The blade sank into the face of one of the monstrosities as it frantically tried to avoid the blue and red flames. Then it slid free with barely a tug as I recovered, bringing the length back and then stabbing forward again.

With both sides now covered by ritual circles, the fight narrowed down considerably, and I went to work, even as the others did.

Sehran's wings spread wide as she launched herself forward, landing then tearing her way through the stunned, and now burning, attackers on my left. Oracle hovered behind me, keeping an eye on everyone, making sure I wasn't about to take a bolt to the back of the head, as the crossbow wielders started to fire as well, taking out those who tried to get around the circle on the right.

More manastones flared among the Changed Ones, sending waves of that corrupting energy through the chamber. It clawed at me, at my skin, digging in; waves of nausea built up. This time, though, I was ready. I channeled mana through the runes tattooed across my skin, using them to absorb instead of fight. Where I'd literally included the runes for "drain" with the intention of ripping the health from my enemies, due to the sheer thickness of the waves of undirected mana washing across us, they triggered and accepted that instead.

I had a split second where I wondered if I'd made a big fuckin' mistake…and then the corruption failed, fizzing out as the mana itself was broken down into a usable form and dragged inward.

"Their magic," Oracle called out, apparently examining the spell on the fly. "It's not just trying to change us. It's trying to *bind* us! They've all been bound!"

That explained the coordination, the way they moved together. Someone or something had done this to them, forced these changes on them, and then bound them into some sort of hive mind as an experiment. The manastones weren't just weapons…they were tools to expand their numbers.

Fortunately for me, as Oracle took the "free" mana I was drinking down and slammed down another circle, they were very poorly managed as well.

A crossbow bolt whizzed past my head, taking down a Changed One that had been trying to flank me. I glanced back to see the woman and her companions had shifted position, taking up firing positions among the ruins.

"Don't think this means we trust you," she called. "But right now, you're the lesser evil!"

"I'll take it!" I spun, blade tracing a perfect arc that separated another attacker's head from its shoulders; the fountain of blood sprayed everywhere as the body fell. "We need to get out of here. Any suggestions?"

"The upper levels," one of her companions shouted. "There's a breach in the dome. If we can reach it—"

He was cut off by a sound that made my blood run cold—a deep, resonant hum that seemed to come from the very stones around us. The Changed Ones fell back. Their movements became even more synchronized as a dozen more moved into sight, all carrying manastones that glowed with a hell of a lot more power.

Even as they did that…sections of rock and pillars that stood beside the exits and doorways on the lower floors all began collapsing in a clearly well-planned demolition.

"No," the woman breathed. "No! It's a trap! We're stuck in here and they're doing it anyway! Kaspin, you promised!" She howled, before turning and screaming at us. "We need to move, *now!*"

"Doing what?" I demanded. But the growing vibration in the floor answered my question. Something was powering up in the depths below us, something I just damn well knew was tied to the same magic that had created and bound these twisted creatures.

Runes flared to life all around us as the chamber's ancient machinery was activated. I'd seen the arms of metal, the great carved symbols that ran along the walls and that described ritual circles on the floor when I'd looked around. But they'd been…well, they'd been just more shadowy crap in a damn place that was full of shadowy crap!

The entire fuckin' UnderVerse sometimes felt like all I had to do was throw a damn rock and I'd hit a buried secret. I'd had enough of this shit!

A Changed One—three arms ending in claws, two normal human ones balled into fists, and practically fuckin' naked—chose that point to leap at me from above, falling with enough speed and force that even if I let the blow land, they'd probably die as well.

I wasn't feeling particularly generous when it came to letting my enemies goddamn touch me right then, so instead, I flipped my naginata around, gripped it by the haft near the base the blade, and swung for the fences.

The far end, that was usually used to brace it against the floor and prevent any damage, was covered in thick metal cladding, and fuck me, the jumper didn't like that.

Or at least I didn't think he did. Neither of the two bits that slid down the far wall and then fell to the ground seemed very happy, at any rate.

I turned, glaring around in a brief second of calm, and saw that yeah, it was all coming to life, panels lighting up with that same sickly green glow we'd seen in the manastones. And in the center of it all, a dozen meters away, a section of the floor began to split open, with more light flaring through the gap.

"It's how they add to their number! They change you into one of them!"

Sometimes I really needed to learn to stop asking questions I didn't want answered, I reflected as I spun, looking for a way out.

The floor split wider; green light poured up from below like some kind of toxic fountain. The Changed Ones had fallen into formation around it, their movements perfectly synchronized now, extra limbs clicking against the stone in a rhythm that matched the humming.

"It's a binding chamber," the woman with the crossbow said, her voice tight with fear and stress. "They're trying to activate the binding chamber!"

"The what?" I kept my naginata ready as I backed toward her position, Sehran and Oracle moving with me. "What the hell did they do to people here?"

"Nothing good." She fired another bolt, taking down a Changed One that strayed too close. "Okay, look. I'm Finna. That's Kered, Bai, and the twins are Jun and Min." She nodded to her companions. "We're from a caravan hit by slavers. We came here looking for shelter; they found us and gave us the choice of joining them and accepting the change, or leaving and going back to the desert to die of thirst and monsters! Considering the slavers are still out there? We were considering it!"

"I'm Jax," I repeated, though she already knew that. "This is Oracle, and that's Sehran. Now, you know how we stop that, or what its range is?"

The humming intensified. Something was rising from the opening in the floor, a column of twisted metal and crystal, crackling with that same sickly energy. The Changed Ones began to chant, their voices a discordant chorus of clicks and hisses.

"The upper levels," Kered gasped, pointing to a partially collapsed stairway that curved up along the dome's inner wall. "If we can reach that breach—"

"They'll never let us get there," Bai cut in. "Not while that thing's powering up. They'll try to drag us back to the chamber, make us like them." Then she seemed to remember my other question. "Kaspin said it couldn't reach past the building, something about a safety for the population, but I don't see us getting out there."

"Yeah, you think that's still working?" Kered, the one who'd been complaining about siding with us, spat. "Nothing here works!"

"Except that," one of the twins shot back. "The one fucking thing we don't want to work still does. Typical—gods pissin' on my luck."

I studied the stairway, then the mass of Changed Ones between us and it. She was right; if we tried to run, they'd just swarm us. And it wasn't like we could keep casting the circles, unless…

"Oracle," I said, an idea forming. "That binding magic they're using, it's like a network, right? All of them connected?"

She nodded her understanding. "Yes, but Jax, if you're thinking what I think you're thinking…"

"Usually am." I grinned, probably a bit manically. "If I can break the machine, you think you can redirect the mana?"

"Not for long, and that's a lot of runes to break," she protested.

"We don't need to break them all, just the heart, then let it go out of control, right?" I asked.

"Oh, well, yeah, if we're just going to smash it…" Her smile brightened. "Yes, okay, if we can block or break the focal point, the mana buildup won't have anywhere to go!"

"The column," Finna interrupted. "That's what they wanted us to be against originally. That's the heart of it, I think."

The chanting reached a fever pitch. More Changed Ones were emerging from the passages, drawn by whatever call was being broadcast through their shared connection. We were running out of time.

"Sehran," I said, "I need you to clear us a path to that column. Finna, can your people provide covering fire?"

"For a chance to destroy that thing?" She smiled grimly. "Just try to stop us."

"Last thing—anyone got any mana potions or stones?" I asked hopefully, getting a snort as my only answer. "Great, always with the negativity," I muttered.

I triggered Mana Overdrive again, feeling the familiar rush of power, loving the fact that these idiots were still pouring out mana in waves. It wasn't much extra, by the time it made it past the cost of the tattoos activating, but it was enough that I was gaining about fifty mana a minute. "Oracle, stay close. When we reach the column, hit it with everything you've got."

"And try not to get us all killed," Sehran added with a devilish grin, her wings spreading wide as she prepared to charge.

"That too."

The Changed Ones saw us coming—it wasn't like there were a lot of options, after all—but their coordination worked against them now. They were so focused on their ritual, on powering up the binding chamber, that they couldn't react fast enough when I hit their lines like a flaming battering ram.

My blade flashed as I carved a path through the chaos, flipping end over end. A touch of mana bled into my naginata and heated the blade to white-hot as it seared its way through their bodies. Crossbow bolts whistled past in a hail of rapid fire, picking off any Changed Ones that tried to flank us. Oracle shared the world around us as we went, allowing me to respond to half-seen attacks, even as she drew in our mana.

We reached the column just as it attained full power; green energy crackled along its length like demented lightning. Up close, I could see there were far more runes etched into its surface than I'd realized, a veritable treasure trove of lost knowledge that Ame would have sold her soul to study.

Well, she was gonna be *soooo* pissed at me over this.

"Now!" I drove my naginata into the column's base, channeling every scrap of mana I could spare into it. Oracle's power joined mine, blue-white light flaring from the blade and then digging into and warring with sickly green.

The tip of the blade punched into the column. Whatever it was originally, it now had the consistence of chalk. A shudder ran through me as I felt the resistance as the blade sank in.

It made a sound like nails on a chalkboard, making me want to vomit, my skin rising in goose bumps like I'd never known…and then the Changed Ones screamed, all of them, as one voice.

They rushed at us from all sides, desperate to stop what we'd started. Sehran met them with voice and blade, fangs and claws, and I released my naginata, spinning to join her, buying Oracle the seconds she needed.

"Jax." Oracle's voice was strained. "It's fighting back!"

I reached up and over my shoulders, dragging both blades free and hacking out with the blades crossing over in an X, as I sliced my enemies apart.

If they were armored beyond their chitin, this would have been a nightmare, but as it was, the vast majority were practically naked. Those that had anything at all on, beyond hairs and strange mottling, wore scraps of clothing. The literal handful that had been wearing armor had been in the lead earlier, I realized as I took another's head from their shoulders. Then Sehran kicked out, folding another around my foot.

I felt it then, the magic surging, the crackling whoosh of mana that rose and fell like a tidal wave.

"JAX, MAKE THEM SWEAR!" Oracle shouted suddenly, struggling with the weaves even as she forced knowledge into my mind, making me stagger.

I saw what she was going to do, if she could get control of the mana. She was going to trigger the frostfire circle, but as we had at the keep in Narkolt. A giant one powered by the mana collectors that we'd used to burn the rats—also known as spies—out of their hidey-holes.

Here, though, it'd kill everything not bonded to us, because she was going to push it out for up to a mile in all directions, that was how much mana there was.

"Shit!" I shouted. "Finna, you need to swear to me, to become part of my party!"

"Fuck you!" she shouted back.

"I'm not trying to—" I retorted.

"We don't have time!" Oracle wailed. "Just do it!"

"I…" I frantically tried to remember how to do this, to push out the offer, because almost every damn time since the first, it'd been her doing it.

Just then, a fresh wave hit, and I was driven back as a larger than average figure literally impaled itself on my blades, clutching my arms and pushing itself up both swords.

It stood nearly two meters tall, with a carapace that suggested it'd been a Xon'dike or similar before the change. But now it had four insectile arms, mandibles that jutted from its mouth, and a dozen gleaming green eyes. Add to that the black hair that grew in tufts everywhere and the patches where sickly diseased skin showed through…

It lunged forward, biting at my helm, and I instinctively jerked back, before pulling back harder and then headbutting it.

Its mandibles cracked. Its mouth had been almost wide enough to fully take my head inside, but it hadn't been aiming to get it in there at that speed.

The jaw broke; teeth, blood, and saliva covered the outside of my helm, and as I shoved it back, freeing my blades again, Oracle screamed.

"Too late!"

The crystal lattice began to crack.

The column shattered with a sound like a thousand breaking mirrors. Green energy exploded outward in a shock wave that sent everyone—us and the Changed Ones alike—sprawling. Oracle had somehow managed to hastily erect a barrier that kept us from being torn apart by the shrapnel and who knew what by the mana, but it did nothing for the sheer force that buckled the floor and sent cracks spreading across the floor and walls.

The Changed Ones' screams cut off abruptly as that same wave of green mana suddenly reversed, flooding back inward toward the column. They collapsed where they stood; their extra limbs twitched as the binding magic that had held them together for so long unraveled. The humming from below turned into a grinding shriek of failing machinery.

"Move!" Finna's voice cut through the chaos. "This whole place is coming down!"

She wasn't wrong. Cracks rocketed through the chamber's floor, racing outward from where the column had stood. The ancient machinery was overloading, decades or centuries of pent-up energy releasing all at once.

"The stairs!" I grabbed Oracle and held her to me with one hand, jamming my weapons into my bag of holding with abandon with the other, before grabbing my naginata and wrenching it free. "Everyone, move!"

We ran for the partially collapsed stairway, Changed Ones lying insensate in our path. Some were still breathing, their mutations apparently permanent even if the binding was broken. Others…others hadn't survived the separation.

"Don't stop!" Kered called from ahead of us. "The whole building's failing. If we're still inside when it goes…"

The stairs weren't in great shape to begin with, and the continuing tremors weren't helping. Pieces crumbled away under our feet as we climbed, forcing us to jump gaps or find alternate routes up the curved wall.

"There!" Bai—I think—pointed to a jagged hole in the dome's surface maybe thirty feet above us. "That's our way out!"

I checked my mana, and cursed.

I had barely enough mana to fly halfway, if I was lucky, or I'd have gotten Oracle clear already.

A larger tremor shook the structure. Part of the stairway ahead of us gave way completely, leaving a fifteen-foot gap between us and the next stable section. Beyond that, the hole in the dome beckoned with the promise of escape.

"Sehran!" I barked, already knowing what had to happen. "Get Oracle out of here!"

"Jax—"

"Do it!"

Sehran grabbed her from me, crouching then beating her wings hard, launching herself into the air and flying straight for the nearest gap. Finna and her people had found another route up, climbing along exposed support beams with the skill of experienced survivors.

The tremors were getting worse. Below, the floor started to cave in, revealing glimpses of the horrors that had been hidden beneath this place. Enclosed chambers, more machinery, literal cells upon cells that showed that they'd either been keeping prisoners, or intending to—all of it was now tearing itself apart.

Oracle glared back at me, despite knowing it was the only way. I raced after her and Sehran, triggering Mana Overdrive in bursts that were a second or less, just enough to get me over a gap, to enable me to kick off a wall, to jump a fraction higher.

It seemed forever, and yet I knew it had only been a brief and terror-filled few seconds before I scrambled up the last several feet to the breach in the dome.

The desert night air had never smelled so sweet as I burst out onto the dome's sloping surface. Its ancient tiles cracked and slid away beneath my feet. The entire structure shuddered now, decades of corrupted magic turning on itself.

"Down there!" Finna pointed to a section of ruins below that looked relatively stable. "Before this whole thing comes down!"

We half-ran, half-slid down the outside of the dome's surface, trying to stay ahead of the spreading destruction. I caught glimpses of other shapes fleeing into the darkness—surviving Changed Ones, now free of the binding but, goddamn, they were still fugly as all hell.

As soon as my boots crashed into the ground—the last three meters were a sheer drop and that wasn't good on the ankles in full armor, but hey, I'd put a lot of points into my Agility and Constitution over the last year—I was off running.

Behind me, I heard the others landing as well. The small group cried out as they impacted…some injured, most fine. But I only had eyes for Sehran and Oracle, who were frantically gesturing to me to go even faster.

Behind us, the dome began to collapse in on itself. Not with the dramatic explosion I'd half-expected, but with a slow, almost graceful implosion as centuries of perverted imperial architecture finally gave up the ghost. Sections of the surrounding walkway, of the road and gardens were next, cracking and sagging, before vanishing in a sound like the end of days.

It took a few minutes to make it to stable ground again. When Sehran guided us to the relative safety of a nearby more or less intact ruin, we turned to watch the destruction. Finna and her people were following still. They also had their weapons trained on us all again, but their hearts didn't seem to be in it anymore.

"So," Finna panted after a moment. "Imperial Legion?"

I nodded, keeping my hands where they could see them. "Yeah, basically. We're trying to rebuild."

"Rebuild…what? The empire's…been dead for…centuries." She panted.

"Not dead," Oracle interjected. "Just sleeping."

"Bullshit." Finna snorted, then studied us for a long moment, before she slowly lowered her crossbow. "You really believe that, don't you?"

"We do," I replied. "Because we've seen it happening. The legion is reforming, reclaiming what was lost. And we could use people like you."

"People like us?" Kered laughed bitterly. "Fuck, you're worse off than I thought if this is the standard you're recruiting. We're caravan guards without a fucking caravan!"

"Just means you're survivors." I grinned. "People who've seen the worst this world has to offer and lived to tell about it are the ones who have a real drive to make it a fuckload better."

Finna shared a look with her companions. Something passed between them, some silent communication born of shared hardship.

"I think you're mad," she said finally. "And we're not joining you, but…there's a camp, a day's travel east of here. People like us, trying to stay free. You can come with us if you want? Rest, resupply. After that…" She shrugged. "We'll see."

"Why were you in there if you knew about this other camp?" Sehran asked, pointing at the collapsed dome.

Finna glared at her, clearly either disliking her because she was hot as hell, or because, well, back there she'd not exactly been subtle about her demonic side.

"Because it's what's left of the caravan we were a part of, and we came here to beg for help. Now we get to go back to them and admit we failed," she admitted sourly.

I nodded, knowing it was the best offer we were likely to get. Besides, we needed information about this part of the realm, and these people clearly had plenty to share.

"Let's find somewhere to rest a little farther back from this shit and then we can see," I hedged. I wanted to meet this group, but also, if I were honest? I was damn well enjoying a little time with only having me and Oracle, and no responsibilities beyond "let's survive." Sure, Sehran was with us as well, but it wasn't like she needed watching over. A caravan of beaten-up refugees?

I just knew that was gonna be a pain in the ass.

As we set off, I glanced back at the ruined dome and scowled. One more piece of the empire's past put to rest, another opportunity to learn, to claim a part of that ancient empire now totally lost. And considering what it looked like they'd been doing?

I couldn't find it in myself to regret that. Sometimes it was wonderful being the Scion of the Empire, knowing that it stood against slavery, that it protected people and it did the right thing. That it hunted down the creatures of the night and fed them their own horns through their buttholes.

Then, on other days, it was like this. I'd be reminded that Amon wasn't a philanthropist. He was a mad dog, one for whom the saying "the ends justify the means" wasn't just a phrase—it was a motto he'd have up in the break room in gold and platinum lettering, possibly on a poster made of human skin.

Fuck it.

Some days it just didn't pay to get outta bed.

# CHAPTER FOUR

"*N*ow what?" I asked Oracle and Sehran through our bond as the others settled down to catch their breath.

"*I think we need to find out who they are, and then maybe we head for the remains of their caravan, see if we can kill whoever stole them,*" Oracle suggested. "*Sehran can distract the guards and draw them off; we take them out and we've got both a thankful group to start off with in the area and some equipment.*"

"*Do we want people?*" Sehran asked carefully, and I looked at her, heartily agreeing. "*Don't get me wrong…I'm not against it. I'm just curious. It ties us to the ground. All three of us can fly, after all, and flying over the desert is going to be a hell of a lot faster than walking. Between being able to summon water and hunting for food from above, do we want to saddle ourselves with freeing prisoners and leading more refugees?*"

"*I…*" I paused, actually forcing myself to think about it, not just go on instinct. There was a part of me that started to say "yes, of course we should; it's the right thing to do," as soon as she said it, even though I'd been thinking exactly the same just moments ago. But the more I thought about it, the more I agreed with her.

"*If we don't, if we stay clear of them all, we could move a lot faster, that's all,*" she went on, and I looked from her to Oracle.

"*Jax, you remember the conversation we had not long after we rescued Decin?*" Oracle asked me instead, and I frowned.

"*We've had a lot,*" I pointed out, already knowing which one she meant.

"*About who we are, and who we want to be,*" she clarified. "*Remember?*"

I paused, then sighed.

Yeah, I knew it. It was when I was starting to get really pissed about the fact that everyone constantly wanted something from me—my time, my gear, just a little more of me and anything I had—*constantly*, when all I wanted was to find my brother and have some actual time off.

I mean, if I'd done things differently, Oracle, Tommy, and I, and possibly Belladonna and a few of the others would all be lounging around in the UnderVerse's equivalent of the Bahamas, right about now.

I could have contacted Barabarattas and told him, "Hey, no worries, all a big mistake…want to buy my tower? Want me as an imperial noble to bless you and fuck off with a load of cash?"

I could have done it, and it would have been a hell of a lot easier than the shit I'd been up to so far.

But…looking from Oracle to Sehran, to the battered and clearly exhausted former caravan guards, I sighed.

"*I remember,*" I admitted. "*We make a choice, Sehran, about who we are, and we stick to it,*" I explained. "*Either we stand against evil all the time, or we open the door to ignoring 'just this' and 'just that' because it's not convenient. None of it's fuckin' convenient, to be clear…I'd rather be on a beach, naked, with rum in my hand and working on lightly toasting my bollocks. So I guess we need to be responsible, no matter where we are.*"

*"I thought I needed to make the option clear, that's all."* Sehran smiled. *"You lead, and I'll follow."*

*"Because you're hungry."* I winked at the joke.

*"I thought Thomas said it was called being 'thirsty'?"* she mused, tapping at a chin, then laughing.

"No offense, but that whole 'talking without talking' is rude," Finna snapped, drawing my attention back to her.

"So was pointing fucking crossbows at us," I retorted. "But fine. Time for some explanations, I think."

"Can we do it while we move out?" she asked. "We need to get out of here before the scorpions start hunting the ruins. This has to have driven them all out of hiding, and I don't want to be here if this turns out to be one of their larders or something." She kicked a section of bone lying on the ground, and I nodded, recognizing what looked to be an old and well-gnawed femur.

"Let's get to the edge of the city and we can talk once we're out of the immediate area," I agreed, looking at it. Yup, a femur.

Or, you know, maybe a giant's finger. Who knew, really.

The night air carried the distant rumble of settling ruins as our small group picked our way through the debris. Every few steps, someone would glance back at the collapsed dome, as if expecting the horrors we'd escaped to come crawling out after us, and the slightest scrape made them all tense up.

The desert wind howled through broken pillars, carrying stinging sand that rattled against my armor, but hidden inside it, I was damn thankful for the protection it offered.

Oracle and Sehran fashioned hoods that they wrapped around their heads as the wind picked up, using some of the clothing I had in my bag. I shifted, pulling out my shield and using it to block as much of the wind as I could from them, even as we hurried along.

"We should put more distance between us and…that," Kered muttered, his crossbow half-raised as I paused, looking around. "No telling what might have survived."

"And no point in marching into a trap," I told him, before turning to Sehran. "Anything?"

"Nothing nearby that's alive beyond us," she said.

I nodded once, starting to move again.

"How'd you know?" one of the twins asked her, and she looked at him with a "really, dude?" expression.

"What am I?" she asked, and the twin shrugged.

"Dunno. You've got horns like the promos, but you're hotter than them. You with him?"

"Promos?" Oracle asked.

"You know, the Prometheans?" Finna asked. "You not seen them before?"

"So you a half-breed?" the twin prodded.

Sehran looked at me, getting a shrug as I made it clear she could tell him whatever she wanted.

"I'm a succubus," she said proudly, standing a little taller.

There was a pause. Then the men all moved a little closer, apparently curious, while the women moved farther away.

"That's new," she admitted, just as confused as I was by the reaction.

"So, uh, you, uhm…" the twin asked slowly, bright red. "Is it true you, uh…"

"She's not available, and she's not a threat," Oracle said firmly, reaching out and taking Sehran's hand in hers.

If anything, the impression given made the men even more excited…until the first twin noticed the way I glowered at him as he stared lustfully from Oracle to Sehran.

"There's a sheltered area ahead," Finna said quickly to break the sudden feeling of imminent violence, pointing to a cluster of partly intact buildings. "We can rest there, get our bearings." She paused, studying me. "And maybe you can explain exactly what the hell the legion is doing out here."

"Fair enough." I rolled my shoulders, feeling the weight of my armor. "But information sharing goes both ways. I'd like to know how you ended up considering joining those…things back there."

Sehran's wings rustled as she folded them against her back, her demonic nature clearly making the others nervous. "And we'd like to know other things as well, like why the area was abandoned and when." She smiled smoothly.

The twins, Jun and Min, exchanged glances. "That's not exactly a simple story," Jun said.

"Nothing out here is," Min finished.

We reached the buildings Finna had indicated, what looked like ancient warehouses, their walls still solid enough to block the worst of the wind, though there was still plenty of it that was getting in as we moved in. Another of their group took up a position near the entrance, keeping watch—Bai, I guessed—while the rest of us settled into a rough circle.

"So," Finna set her crossbow aside but kept it within easy reach, "let's start with the obvious question. You're really claiming to be Imperial Legion? The actual legion, not the dark bastards who hunt people for sport?"

"I am." I kept my hands visible, knowing how twitchy survivors could be. "You clearly know who the legion is, so what the hell's the problem with that?"

"Well, you know." She shrugged.

"No…no, I fucking don't."

"Why you wearing that if you're legion?" One of the twins pointed at my armor. "Thought it was one of your rules that you all look the same."

"Not really." I shook my head. "The legion has different branches, and this is the armor of the Praetorian Guard, that's all."

"Looks weird." The other grunted. "You sure you're legion?"

"You get many people who say they are and aren't?" I countered, and they all seemed amused or disgusted by that.

"Nobody wants to be a legionnaire." Finna sighed. "Okay, look, I'll just come out and say it. Yes, we need help, but you lot? Half the time you can't be trusted not to start a fight, so why the hell should we trust you now?"

"Start a fight?" I asked slowly. "You're talking about the legion, right?"

"Yeah, all that armor, though a bit, well, shittier, and always going on about imperial law and how slavery is illegal?" Finna countered.

"Sounds like them," Oracle admitted. "Jax?"

"It does, but, okay let's roll it back a bit. You said that the legion pick fights all the time, but we're shit fighters? That doesn't make sense."

"Well, they're not," Min admitted, scratching the back of his head, looking a bit embarrassed. "I mean, yeah, they're great fighters—you are, I mean." He glanced at me again, clearly making sure I wasn't taking offense. "But you know."

"No, for fuck's sake, I don't know, so just say it," I snapped.

"All right, I will," Finna said. "We'll take you to the camp, but only because there's fuck all you can do to make the situation worse. We know what you're like, that you always have to charge in and try to save people. But if you're gonna join us, are we gonna have to put a blindfold on you?"

"A blindfold?" I asked, even more confused.

There was a long silence.

"How about this, Finna?" Oracle said slowly. "I'll summon some water, and we all have a drink, then you give us some examples of why you think so poorly of the legion.."

The next half an hour was, well, painful.

It'd have been fucking mortifying if I honestly believed it was all true, but I had to think there was some kind of propaganda at work. Much like the nobles had back in Himnel, smearing the legion as parasites and stupid, here they'd apparently gone all out on the "don't trust the legion" rhetoric.

It wasn't until the end that it suddenly started to make a horrible sort of sense.

"So yeah, four legionnaires, a hundred slavers, all with crossbows, and some of those expansive magical bolts…you know, the ones that explode? The legion told me to go, and it was like they just couldn't help themselves—they just dumped all their stuff, knowing they were gonna die, and ran at them," Bai, who'd swapped over from his place on watch, said.

"They knew they'd die, and they had a chance to hide, to sneak up and use stealth, or any other tactic, even to fucking go and get reinforcements and instead they just ran at them?" I asked slowly.

"That's what they…sorry, *you* do." Finna watched me, confused. "You always do."

"No, we fucking don't," I growled. "Okay, yes, before you ask again, I am…in the legion. Yes, we're rebuilding. Yes, we're reclaiming what was lost. And no, we're not here to conscript anyone, and no, we don't normally come out in teams this small." I gestured to Oracle and Sehran. "We were part of a group exploring a ruined prax, when something…went wrong."

"A portal," Oracle added, her voice carrying as she lied smoothly. "It wasn't supposed to be active, but something triggered it."

Kered barked out a laugh. "A portal? Well, that makes as much sense to be here as anywhere. Welcome to the ass-end of nowhere, where you're so far from anywhere civilized that even the monsters have monsters."

I sensed there was more to that bitter comment. But before I could probe further, Finna leaned forward, her face serious in the dim light.

"So it's just you three?" Finna asked, clearly caught between disappointment that it was, and relief that she wasn't about to find herself in the middle of a legion encampment. "You don't have more with you?"

"Just us." I groaned, taking a drink as Oracle summoned another fountain again, and I smiled at her once I'd finished.

"I understand this will seem strange, but we're from Dravith. It's another continent, far to the west. We could really do with some details on the area, and the current political situation." Oracle smiled as she shook out the sand from her hood. "We'll be finding our way back soon, but it'd save us a lot of time if you could tell us anything you know about the continent, starting with its name."

"Its name?" Finna blinked in confusion. "Carrmor."

"That *was* the Dome of Truth then." Oracle sighed. "I'd hoped I'd misunderstood, because that machine? That wasn't supposed to be in Romesh. Nothing I've seen said they were doing anything like that before the fall."

"The fall?" Min glanced from Oracle to Finna, then his brother. "You mean when the moon fell?"

"That's a myth," Bai said flatly. "Never was no moon fell—can't happen."

"Bullshit!" Min snapped back.

But before they could get to really arguing, Finna held up a hand and they quietened.

"You were honest about who you were, so I'll do the same," she said. "Show you what kind of hell you've landed in." She took a deep breath, hands clenching. "It started with the caravan. We were running a new trading route…nothing illegal, nothing that should have drawn slavers. Just in case, they hired a lot of guards, and we kept the route as quiet as we could."

Finna's voice carried the weight of memories as she told her story, her fingers absently checking her crossbow's mechanism as she spoke, starting to clean it as best she could. "The slavers hit us at dawn. It was a professional job—they'd scouted our route, knew exactly where we'd camp and how many guards we had." A muscle in her jaw twitched. "Lost half our people in the first wave. Didn't help that at least five of the new hires were their people and turned on us from inside the camp."

"We managed to break free," Kered added, pulling out and running a whetstone along his blade with practiced motions.

"We did," Finna agreed. "We ran, gathered up those we could, and we fought a retreat in the only direction they didn't come from—out into the fucking desert, as much good as that did us."

"You're still alive," I pointed out, and she snorted.

"You know how big a caravan needs to be to survive out here?" she asked, swearing as the wind blew another hard blast through one of the missing windows.

"No?" I admitted. "Tell me about the caravan," I suggested as we all got up and moved into the next room, settling in one corner again, trying to get out of the wind that was now growing into a solid storm. I crouched down, then sat with my back against a fallen column. "The real story, not just that it was 'legitimate trade.'"

Finna exchanged glances with her companions before sighing and nodding slowly. "Fuck it, it's not like it could get much worse with you knowing, is it. We were part of the first trek of the Great Northern Circuit, one hundred and fifteen individual caravans joined together. Nearly two thousand people all told." Her voice carried a mixture of pride and bitterness. "Should have been untouchable."

"Biggest new venture in decades," Kered added, his whetstone hesitating, as he spat to the side, clearly bitter. "Merchants, craftsmen—hell, we even let the rabble come, hundreds of people who couldn't even afford a fucking horse, as long as they could keep up and they paid the fee, we'd protect them and guide them along the route. The idea was to challenge the monopoly of the old caravans, you know? To connect some of the more isolated settlements and maybe, just maybe make some coin that we didn't have to give over to them bastards."

"Competing with the established cartels?" I guessed.

Bai snorted from her position by the entrance. "They warned us," she said. "The existing caravan masters. Said we were 'disrupting the natural order.' Offered to buy the bosses out for a fraction of what we'd all invested." Her laugh was hollow. "Jared told 'em to go fuck themselves."

"Should have taken the offer," Kered muttered. "First thing the slavers did when the attack started was gut him."

"Explain that please." I blinked.

"The deal or the attack?" Kered asked.

"Both."

"The caravan routes are part of the guild. You want to use them, you pay the guild fifty percent of everything, and you pay it up front." Finna snorted. "Doesn't matter that you don't know what you'll earn. Doesn't matter that nobody can pay half of what you're going to earn before you earn it. Just matters that the guild gets its beak wet."

"So, you refused," I guessed.

"Jared, the caravan master, he'd run caravans all his life on the guild routes, so he knew all the right people. The last few years, he reached out to us all, each time he'd pass through, those of us who worked with him. He'd talk about the possibilities, about a route that was ours. Not having to pay the guild taxes to use it, but to set one up.

"A caravan is a walking target, constantly drawing bandits and monsters if it's not big enough. And when it is? They just send bigger and bigger bandit groups. Sometimes the slavers try to hit you, but we knew they'd do it. That's why Jared spent years planning this.

"He did deals with us all, hired only those he thought he could trust, made sure that the merchants didn't talk, that the caravans were good, everything.

"He put together a full-on great caravan, two thousand of us, and when the guild sat there fat and happy, expecting to get their cut from us using the guild stations, the roads, and maps?

"That was when he told them where we were going. Not following any of the guild routes, not using their maps, their stations, the backhanders, the dodgy guards and paying their tolls. We were going to tour the whole north, make a route of it, and then finish off at Sonra, before heading back south." She sighed, looking wistful. "It could have worked, too."

"What went wrong?" I asked, not really getting it all, but understanding enough that I was starting to build a picture.

"They told us that if we didn't pay the toll, every market, town, and city would be closed to us. That only the villages would deal with us and they didn't have the copper to make it worth our while. They'd seen the size of the caravan he put together, and they all thought it was going to make them all even richer with their fees. And when they realized that it wasn't? We were told that not a single city would let us camp inside. They'd use their influence to block us from all the stops that we needed." She shook her head, looking sad, and yet proud.

"Jared told them that we'd do it alone, that we didn't need them, and that the places we'd go weren't places covered by the guild charters. That surprised them. But as much as he wasn't an idiot, he thought they'd try sneaky shit, not just go all out. A couple of days before we set off, one of the masters came to Jared, and the next morning we all had a meeting, when they offered us the buyout option. He was honest with us, told us that he'd been offered a Guildmasters Bronze-level badge. If he took it, he'd not be a caravan leader anymore; he'd be a guildmaster, able to run a full guild caravan and take a percentage. It was a nice offer, for him. Rest of those who had invested their gold would have been screwed, though," Finna admitted.

"He asked us all, and when we said no, he refused as well. He was good like that. He hired us guards on a good rate, and most of us had travelled with him before when we hired on as part of the existing caravans, so we knew he knew his shit. Like I said, he'd been planning this for years, and he made deals for the last three years as we travelled as part of the guild.

"Then, when he'd refused, the guild wished us good luck and we set off. Wasn't no surprise when instead of trying to use the guild stops, we hit the villages and found a guild caravan had beat us to it. Routes had been changed deliberately to make sure that the towns and settlements we were going to—places that hadn't seen a caravan in five years—saw two in a month. But we all knew they'd try some shit like that. We took a vote and changed the route. Headed out farther, started winding back and forth across the edge of the desert.

"It was more dangerous, but they couldn't pull that trick then. No sane caravan was gonna do it, not the smaller, fast ones they'd sent out. So we started making good coin. There were more bandit raids out here, though, so when we had the chance, we hired more guards to replace those we lost, and that's when it all went wrong." Finna shook her head as Kered took over.

"The new guards knew the area, and showed us where the watering holes were that were farther from the settlements, and Jared, he trusted them, even when we told him it was too risky."

"The attack was coordinated," Finna continued, drawing lines in the sand with her finger. "Hit our lead wagons first, then the rear guard. Professionals. They knew exactly where to strike." She looked up, eyes hard. "The bastards hadn't just sold us out—the guild had to have paid fucking slavers to hit us. Barely saw them, just heard the screams and saw people being captured. They were as vicious and professional a set of bastards as ever saw a mother's tit. It was a setup."

"You sure it wasn't a coincidence?" I asked.

"Oh yeah." She snorted. "Marlek, one of the new guards, literally shouted that this was what happened when we fucked with the guild, when standing over Jared as he bled out. They *wanted* word to get out. No point in an object lesson if people don't know about it."

"How many got away?" Oracle asked softly.

"Initially? About four hundred." Min's voice was flat. "The desert took more than half of those. Then came monsters, dehydration, exposure." He gestured vaguely eastward. "We're down to maybe sixty now, holed up, waiting for us to bring them the good news."

"And the interesting part," Jun added with a bitter smile, "is what people got to learn about themselves through all of this. They all grabbed what was important or valuable to them and then ran. Some of us had bags of holding. Others just had rucksacks. Some stupid bastards went for gems, posh cloth, and magical items first. Valuable to a merchant, sure, but try eating a fucking ruby or a spell scroll when you're starving."

"While others," Kered gestured to his practical but worn clothing, "spent years on the road. Too poor for our own wagons, carrying everything we owned. We got away with cooking pots, tools…things that actually keep people alive."

"And now the survivors are torn between listening to merchants who own their own estates and have expensive shops, the likes of which would never let us in but have zero fucking real world survival skills. Or the people who couldn't afford so much as a cart and had to carry their gear themselves. Success as a merchant is one thing—surviving, though? Making the decisions that get us through this and keep people alive long enough to get back home and gut those bastards?" He shook his head.

"It's a totally different world." I nodded. "Yeah, we know those lessons."

"That's why we came to check the ruins," Finna explained. "Fifteen of us volunteered. Hoping to find shelter, supplies, anything to help the others survive." Her hands clenched. "Instead, we found…them."

"The Changed Ones," Sehran murmured, her daggers catching the dim light as she checked them over for damage, before smiling hopefully at Kered and borrowing a whetstone when he offered it.

"They saved us, at first," Bai said quietly. "From the scorpions. We thought…" She shook her head.

"Kaspin's offer seemed reasonable." Finna's voice hardened. "Showed us the ones that only had a few minor changes…some darker skin, extra hair, glowing eyes. Just adaptations, he said. Evolution. Like we could become something better, stronger. It was a shitty deal, we knew it, and we didn't want it. But considering the other choice was the desert? We had to think about it, to consider it." She spat in the sand. "Didn't show us what they really were until you came charging through their hive."

The wind outside had picked up, howling, then dropped in one of those weird calm moments, and we all stiffened as the next second, we all heard the distant sounds of combat. I shared a look with Oracle, seeing my own concerns reflected in her eyes.

"Your people," I said carefully. "The ones back in the caves. How long can they hold out?"

Finna's laugh was bitter. "Water for maybe three days. Food…" She shrugged. "Less than that, unless we start eating the leather from our boots."

The sounds of fighting grew louder, and we all tensed. Whatever was happening out there, it was getting closer.

"We need to check that out." I rose smoothly to my feet.

"Could be the slavers getting what they deserve," Kered suggested hopefully.

"Could be," Finna agreed, but her expression said she didn't believe it. "But either way, we need to know."

"Plus, whoever loses might leave gear we need. Let's face it, we need everything," Bai added sourly.

I nodded, checking my weapons. "Then speak up if you see something I miss. Beyond that, fall in and let's go greet our neighbors."

With that, I started forward. Oracle and Sehran moved up to walk with me, even as Sehran tossed the whetstone back to Kered.

Finna's group looked to one another, before she sighed and nodded, climbing to her feet and following, even as she spoke up.

"Don't think this means we're just going to do what you say, Jax," Finna snapped as she hurried forward to catch up to us.

"You been in many fights?" I asked her as I slid my swords out of the bag of holding, putting them back into their sheaths and then getting my naginata out as well. "Sehran, do you want a sword or…?" I offered, and she shook her head.

"I've got more experience with daggers and whips. I don't want to learn a new style of fighting yet, but thank you."

"Whips?" Min perked up.

"Behave, big man." Kered snorted. "She's literally told you she's a succubus, so while it'd be a great way to go, it's not something many men live through."

"He does?" Min pointed out, jerking a thumb in my direction. "I mean, you are all…" He made a gesture that was both crude and poorly made, due to the crossbow he carried, but we all got the meaning.

"It's none of your business, but to be clear, I'm not accepting other work, or donations." Sehran smiled. "I've been tamed, and I'm valued for more than my ability to suck the life—or anything else—out of my targets."

That ended the conversation pretty fast, which I was glad about. But the way that they'd just accepted that she was what she was, I found strange.

Regardless, as soon as I walked out of the smaller room and again out of the building into the street, any other concerns were driven away by the developing storm.

The wind howled through the ruins, driving stinging clouds of sand before it. I kept one hand raised to shield my eyes, though my helmet helped considerably. Oracle and Sehran replaced the makeshift hoods they'd made before, from the cloth I'd provided, but the others struggled against the increasing winds, hefting shields and random junk, then cursing repeatedly under their breath about the sand getting in their eyes.

We turned left and right, trying to get a rough handle on the distance and direction of the fighting, before another bluster of wind sent a swirl of sand past, obscuring everything beyond a few meters away.

It was like a blizzard, but given that it was sand, the effect was a stinging, scratching feeling that clogged mouths, ears, and eyes. We wouldn't last long out here without protection.

"This is going to get worse before it gets better!" Finna shouted over the wind. "These storms can last for days!"

I was about to respond when Sehran suddenly grabbed my arm. "That way!" she hissed. "I can sense life…at least ten."

We'd reached what looked like an ancient marketplace, with the remnants of stone stalls creating a maze of partial walls and shadowed alcoves. Perfect ambush territory. I gestured for everyone to take cover, trying to pierce the swirling sand.

The sounds of combat grew clearer, and with it the distinctive click of chitin on stone, human voices shouting commands, and underneath it all, a deep rhythmic scratching that made the hair on the back of my neck stand up.

"Sehran, check it out," I ordered.

She nodded, launching herself into the air to land on a nearby rooftop, then rocketing upwards thanks to the wind catching her as she vanished from sight.

She was gone less than a minute before she came back, dropping from the same rooftop and attempting to glide to the floor. She was grabbed by a gust of wind and nearly sent headfirst into a wall, kicking off it and furling her wings at the last second with a gasp of pain as something was strained.

"Three groups," Sehran had to almost shout to us all, her voice drowned out by the shriek of the wind. "Slavers…two of the Changed Ones, less mutated than the others…and something else. Big…several of them. I think they're those scorpions we saw before." Then she sighed, shooting Oracle a smile as a healing spell washed over her.

"How big?" Kered asked nervously, bracing one arm and lifting his cloak as a tent to stop the wind as he and Finna leaned in closer.

A distant piercing shriek answered his question. Through the curtain of sand farther down the street, I caught glimpses of massive, segmented legs, easily as thick as tree trunks, moving with terrifying grace despite their size. For a split second, I froze and stared in horror before they continued on, vanishing beyond the cross section and into the storm again.

"The scorpions," Bai breathed. "Gods below, they're hunting."

"The vibrations from the collapse must have drawn them," Min added firmly. "We need to run."

I watched as more details emerged through the storm as the sand dropped again for a brief second. The slavers—five of them that I could see—were making a break for it, and they had two bound figures they were taking with them. Even from here, I could see the subtle mutations: patches of chitin gleaming through torn clothing, additional arms, eyes that reflected what little light penetrated the storm. But they seemed more…human than the ones we'd fought in the dome.

*"The binding,"* Oracle sent through our connection. *"When it broke, we saw some die instantly, and others running away. The slavers caught some."*

"We don't know if they're still our enemies or not," I finished. "But the slavers caught them trying to escape."

The group were trying to flee, that was obvious. The five slavers started to run in our direction. Two of them dragged the freshly caught pair with them as they stabbed and slashed at the smaller scorpions, each "only" the average size of a Doberman.

One of the slaves tried to escape, only to scream as their collar apparently did something to punish them, before being backhanded by one of his captors. Blood sprayed as he fell, stunned to the sand.

"Leave them!" another shouted, running on. "Let the scorpions have them!"

"They're worth good gold!" the one who'd hit his prisoner screamed back. But he only hesitated a second, before cursing and shoving the slave again, starting to run.

"Send them to distract the scorpions!" the lead runner shouted through the storm.

"Varn had the key!" He shouted back, "You distract them!"

The scratching sound nearby grew louder. Through the sand, I saw more massive shapes moving to encircle the group across the nearby buildings, crouching down to remain out of sight to their prey.

"Three greater scorpions, at least twenty smaller," Sehran reported tensely. "They're coordinating."

"Of course they are," Finna muttered. "Because regular giant scorpions weren't bad enough."

I did a quick assessment of our options. We could try to retreat, let the scorpions deal with the slavers. But that would mean leaving those prisoners to die as well. And although they might have been our enemies less than an hour ago, seeing how they were planning to recruit Finna and her people and what the Examine ability had shared, they probably hadn't chosen what was done to them, and we needed information.

Besides that, if we ran now, we might already be too late, considering we were on the edge of the ancient marketplace and the slavers were crossing it, running—Sod's Law—right toward us.

*"Oracle,"* I sent through our bond. *"You think a couple of Frostfire Circles will do it?"*

*"We have enough for two,"* she replied. *"But we're low on mana already, and it'll burn anyone who's not tied to you."*

*"I know."* I drew my naginata. *"Sehran, can you get the prisoners clear when I give the signal?"*

She nodded, wings rustling as she prepared herself. *"Just say when."*

"The rest of you," I addressed Finna's group, "stay back unless you've got a clear shot. And remember, the wind is going to be a bitch here—focus on one target. These aren't normal scorpions…they're smarter, faster, and a lot harder to kill."

"You're really going to help them?" Kered asked incredulously. "After what their kind did?"

"Their 'kind' were victims too," I replied, checking my mana reserves. "And I'm the Imperial Legion. We exist to protect people. Even when they're dicks."

I saw Oracle smile at that, even as she prepared to cast. The slavers still hadn't noticed the danger, too busy threatening their captives. The scorpions had almost completed their circle.

"Besides," I added almost to myself as I stepped out of cover and into the middle of the street, striding forward into the marketplace seemingly alone, "someone needs to remind these slavers that there are laws against their trade. Might as well work some frustration out here and now."

The largest scorpion, its carapace easily fifteen feet long, raised its stinger high. That was all the warning we were going to get.

# CHAPTER FIVE

The largest scorpion struck with stunning speed. Its stinger flashed down through the swirling sand like a bolt of lightning. It punched into the chest of one of the running slavers, impaling him and then yanking him back up into the air. The rest of their group skidded to a halt, staring upward in shock like gormless idiots.

At the same time, I strode out into the middle of the marketplace, relying on the senses that Oracle shared with me as much as my own eyes. The scorpions finally spotted that in addition to their prey, more meat had arrived.

Another scorpion that had been hiding on a nearby roof landed with a crunch as it jumped in, bouncing on all six legs, and then stabbed out with its massive stinger, aiming for me this time.

I twisted aside, letting it slam into the ground where I'd been standing, then brought my naginata around in a sweeping arc that carved a deep gouge in its armored tail.

The beast shrieked, jerking it back, but the wound was superficial. These weren't ordinary scorpions; their chitin seemingly reinforced by age or magic. That apparently translated into making them far harder to kill than their smaller cousins.

That was fine, though, considering I'd not even infused the blade.

"Incoming!" Oracle's warning came just as the last of the massive arachnids emerged from the storm, their smaller offspring swarming around their feet like living waves.

"What the fu—" One of the slavers spotted me, then the other incoming scorpions, his eyes going wide. "Quick! Back to back!"

"Oracle, now!" I triggered Mana Overdrive as she slammed down the first frostfire circle. It was on the left of the marketplace; a second circle flared to life on my right half a second later and caught at least a dozen of the smaller scorpions in its radius. The creatures screamed as ice formed on their shells while flames seared their flesh.

Sehran took advantage of the confusion, diving through the storm to land hard, kicking out and sending one of the slavers flying into a panicking pile of burning scorpions. Then she grabbed one of the bound Changed Ones and launched herself back into the air. The wind caught her outthrust wings and launched her from sight like she'd been fired from a catapult.

The nearest slaver tried to stop her, but before they could do more than shout something, the scorpions were everywhere, leaving no time to use their control devices.

The circles were on either side of the marketplace. I stood in the middle, facing the slavers, with a narrow gap, much as we'd done before, left open as a safety corridor through the fight.

Well, I say "safety," but I was in a bit of a shitty mood, all things considered, and it led directly to me.

I strode forward. Two of the biggest scorpions were running now, having been solidly inside the circles as they activated, and were both burning and freezing. The third faced me, seemingly confused about the fact that I wasn't running and half the world appeared to be on fire. Behind me, I heard Finna and her people opening fire, their crossbow bolts slamming home into chitin armor.

"The collar!" the remaining captive shouted. "They control us through—" A surge of energy from the collar cut him off, dropping him to his knees.

"Shut it!" one of the slavers snarled, before shouting at me. "You want them? Help us, and they're yours!"

I ignored him, focusing on the scorpion to my right. The left, being hit repeatedly with bolts and burning, was distracted enough to leave me be, and the one on the far side had to go through the slavers to get to me.

The stinger lashed out again, stabbing into the sand.

I slid to the left, injecting a touch of mana into the naginata and slicing down as fast as I could. The blade sheared through the tail this time, lopping off the head of the stinger.

It jerked its tail back, shrieking and spraying ichor everywhere.

Instead of giving it time to recover, I darted after it, slashing my blade left to right and leaving a deep wound across its nearest pincer. Then I lunged forward, driving the tip of the blade into its face with a chitinous crunch.

The scorpion spasmed, twitched, then collapsed as I jerked the blade back, its brain pretty much bisected by the blow.

*"Behind you!"* Oracle sent.

I spun, bringing my weapon around. The second scorpion lunged for me, its pincer locking onto the haft and yanking.

As much as I wanted to, physics wasn't something I could entirely ignore. The scorpion was the size of a small house, and as such it had both momentum and size on its side.

That meant I staggered, before I planted my feet, skidded in the sand, then twisted, forcing the pincer aside.

Then I released my weapon, lunged forward, and punched the scorpion with all the power of Mana Overdrive.

It stumbled, then fell as I dragged my fist out of the crater that I'd just driven into the space between its eyes and above its mandibles. Then I grabbed onto one of the mandibles and started to really go to town, punching as hard as I could, literally shattering its face and driving my fist inside its brain with each blow.

That was when I noticed another one had been creeping up on me; Oracle shared the movement, as the stinger speared toward my back.

I stepped to the right, letting the stinger take its friend in the face. I grabbed it, doubling down on Mana Overdrive again, then again, and finally yanking it in—literally reeling it in—as it spun and dug its legs in, trying to run.

Now that I had it from behind, I twisted with the hips, hoicked hard, and swung it around, smashing it into a building, before I dragged it back and swung it overhead into its dying, twitching friend.

It was stunned and its friend was now dead. As a pincer waved too close to me, I grabbed it, twisting and pulling, bracing a foot and breaking the arm off, then tossing it aside, before kicking the scorpion to death.

I didn't realize I'd been screaming in fury until a few seconds later, as, in the middle of a dip in the winds, I heard Oracle speaking calmly to the survivors around me. The rest of the scorpions had apparently either burned to death, or, in the case of the remaining large one, had run as fast as it could.

Apparently they were aware enough to know that anyone who did that, without a weapon, wasn't someone to fuck with.

"When he gets annoyed like this, we find it's best to just let him work it out of his system. There's so many breakable things around, after all," Oracle was saying almost conversationally, as I straightened, my throat raw.

"You know, like cities, mountain ranges, and continents," Sehran added, grinning and striding forward.

I looked from her, with Oracle by her side, the first captured prisoner kneeling behind her and Finna to the others arrayed on either side of the remaining two slavers, one of which was holding a dagger to the last slave's throat.

"Look, you let us go or else..." the other slaver started, pointing a mace at Sehran.

I didn't let him finish. My weapon had been dropped by the scorpion at some point, and I swept it up in a blur. The naginata's blade flashed out, severing his hand at the wrist. He screamed, stumbling back as the mace hit the sand with a spray of arterial blood, followed a second later by his head.

"Wait...you, you don't have to do this!" the remaining slaver cried, frantically shaking his head.

"Slavery is *illegal* in the empire," I growled, even as I forced more of the last drops of mana I had at hand into my Mana Overdrive, moving faster than human eyes could track. "The sentence is death."

"Wait!" The last slaver raised his hands. "We can make a deal! Split the—"

His head left his shoulders before he could finish the offer.

I twisted, seeing movement to the right on the far side of the marketplace. I stepped forward and crouched, ripping a potion bag from the slaver's belt and rifling through it, squinting against the flaring mana migraine.

I didn't spare the time to thank whatever god had seen fit to make sure the slaver had mana potions. But as I downed one after another, my headache vanished. I grinned, resettling my helmet and pointing at the fresh handful of scorpions coming from an adjoining street.

"Your turn," I whispered, before shrugging as Oracle's frostfire circle caught the largest scorpion as it ran between the buildings. Unable to turn in the narrow gap, it was left with no choice but to keep going, even as its smaller brethren screamed their death cries. The creature's movements were already growing sluggish as ice formed across its shell. By the time it broke free, I took advantage of its reduced speed, stabbing forward and driving my blade deep into one of its eyes. It thrashed, then swung at me with one of its claws, as it died.

"They're retreating again!" Kered called out. "But there's more coming!"

He was right. The lull in the storm was ending; the sand whipped around us again. I shook my head. Those who were seeing that they were outmatched were running, but the city had apparently been full of scorpions, and there were still more incoming.

"Jax, we've not got time for you to really let loose, I'm sorry," Oracle called, clearly milking it for our observers.

I grinned in my helm despite myself. "Ah, fuck's sake." I sighed. "I was just getting warmed up! Sehran, can you get to the other slavers' bodies?" I asked. "Recover the key for the collars?"

"Will do!" She nodded, crouching and opening her wings.

"Be careful!" Oracle ordered her quickly. "We have other ways to open them if you can't get them!"

"And potions!" I shouted into the storm as Sehran launched herself.

"We need to move," I said to the stunned group of caravan guards and the slaves, before focusing on them. "Can you both walk?"

They nodded, their mutations more obvious up close: patches of chitin, slightly too large and glowing eyes, but nothing like the monstrosities we'd fought in the dome. They were lucky ones, I guessed. Or unlucky, depending on how you looked at it.

"Then you're coming with us until we figure this shit out. Finna," I called out, turning to her. "Which way to your caves?"

"East," she cried, loosing another bolt into an approaching scorpion. "But in this storm…"

"Is it the rocky outcropping due east?" Oracle asked, and she nodded.

"It is, but we'll never find it in this!"

"Oracle can guide us," I assured her. "Everyone, stay close. Sehran can follow us. Now, move!"

We set off running, or I did anyway. Oracle flew by my side, and the others…well, they sure as shit didn't want to hang around as behind us, the scorpions fought over the slavers' remains. Ahead lay miles of desert, and somewhere beyond that, shelter.

I glanced back at our two newest additions as we ran. "I'm Jax. Imperial Legion. We'll sort out the rest once we're safe," I bellowed to her.

The woman nodded, still looking dazed. "I… I remember who I was now. They took that from us, but it's coming back. I'm Amelia. He's Dex."

"Didn't ask, don't care. Keep up!" I ordered, before turning back to the sandstorm and squinting as the sand was blown with a speed and ferocity that would quickly become lethal.

*"Should we have stayed back there?"* I sent to Oracle.

*"No, for us to be hit by that many scorpions that quickly, and after the survivors ran in all directions, there have to be literally hundreds in the city. Unless you want to start exterminating them, we need to leave."*

*"I could do with the XP,"* I pointed out.

She sent a mental kiss, even as she responded. *"Judging from everything Finna said, I don't think XP is going to be a problem to find."*

*"Point."*

With that, I settled into the run. Oracle adjusted my direction slightly as we went, something about her abilities making it easy to keep a direction. After a few more minutes, when Sehran arrived, we adjusted course again as she'd seen an easier path in another lull in the storm.

It took five hours all told, to make it to the cave, despite them saying it was a damn day away, and that was burdened by the group as we were, but fuck it.

Oracle came up with the plan of using the rope I had in my basic gear in the bag of holding—you can't be an adventurer without rope, after all—to tie us all together.

She also ended up complaining to me along our link that she just needed to make a single flight to get her bearings next time to lead us on the best path.

It wasn't to be, though. Even Sehran had difficulty flying in this, and she was neither as light as Oracle, nor pregnant. She'd not shown many outward signs of the pregnancy, not yet, but at times I felt the exhaustion that ran through her, and being out in the middle of a sandstorm in the desert was definitely one of them.

We shifted to a dogtrot: ten minutes run, five minutes fast walk, ten minutes run, then five minutes fast walk constantly repeating. The group—pulled along by me—managed to keep that up until we made it to our destination.

It shouldn't have taken anywhere near that long—everyone was suffering from the effects of the sandblasting they'd taken when we finally staggered into the caves—but that was just the way it went, especially when people apparently didn't consider physical training important.

I'd been in that boat once, but after the last year and especially the damn daily training with Restun? I was a damn powerhouse now.

I set the pair of Changed Ones down once we were inside, as I'd had to carry them and told Finna to go first. A rough barrier of cloth had been braced over the cave passage farther in to keep as much of the storm out as possible.

Finna broke the cloth loose and called out that it was "Only meeee," getting a few relieved laughs as this was apparently how she often entered a room.

"Well, look who made it back!" a voice called from beyond the cloth barrier. "Tell me you bring good…gods below!"

The shout turned into a warning cry as we entered the makeshift camp. A handful more crossbows were raised, people scrambled for weapons, and children were shoved behind makeshift barriers. All because of Amelia and Dex's visible mutations.

Or at least I guessed so, until I noticed more of the crossbows were pointed at me than anyone else.

"Stand down!" Finna's voice cracked like a whip. "They're with us."

"With you?" A tall man with greying hair and a weathered face stepped forward, one hand on his sword. "Have you lost your mind? Look at them!"

"Yeah, look at them," I growled, stepping between the Changed Ones and the weapons. "Look at the slave collars. Look at their wounds. Then maybe think about what that means."

"We are!" the man snapped, studying first me in my sand-scoured heavy armor, then the others. "You sold us out?" he snapped at Finna, who blanched and shook her head.

"Toren, no! Fuck's sake, how could you…" she said, only to trail off when he waved a hand at her.

His eyes lingered on Oracle, at Sehran's wings and obvious demonic attributes— her body was mostly hidden beneath my spare set of clothing, but still—and then he glared at me and kept his weapon ready. "I'm Toren. These people are my responsibility. Explain yourselves."

"The collars first…I think they think we captured the others," Oracle suggested softly. "Sehran?"

"Shit, we should have done that on the way," I muttered. I should have thought about it, but in truth, with the sandstorm hammering us, I'd just focused on keeping the group going and wondering constantly whether I'd made an incredibly stupid mistake.

Oracle had spent most of the run healing the others, as their skin was literally scoured away by flying particles, but still. I should have thought about it.

On the other side, at one point when I'd been reduced to a beast of burden carrying the exhausted pair, I had used my Examine ability again.

The updated information had shown what we'd hoped it would, that they were no longer part of the hive mind and that they were free at last. But they'd take a long time to recover from what had been done to them.

Sehran produced what she'd taken from the slavers and offered it to me. I took it, turning to our new companions as I hefted the inch-thick, four-inch-long oblong keystone. "Hold still."

The collars clicked open, falling away to reveal freshly burned flesh beneath. Amelia rubbed her throat, tears in her altered eyes. "Twice enslaved," she whispered. "First by Kaspin's machine, then by the slavers when we tried to escape."

"The binding broke when you destroyed the dome," Dex added. "We…we remember who we were now. What we were."

"What we've lost!" Amelia whispered. She closed her eyes and started to weep, turning and pressing her face to Dex's shoulder; he drew her in close, tears running down his own face.

"They were victims too," Oracle explained to the gathered survivors. "The dome contained some ancient magical artifacts, corrupted and twisted. We think it was used to force changes on people, binding them to obey this Kaspin."

"And now?" Toren demanded.

"Now they're free," I said. "And under my protection. I'm Jax. I'm a member of the Imperial Legion. The *real* legion, not the dark bastards. This is Oracle and Sehran." I left out that, well, I was kinda near the top of the Imperial Legion's food chain, figuring if they hadn't seen the notifications, then that wasn't my fault.

For all I knew, they were locked to our continent, or not.

"Are they infectious?" someone called from the back of the room. "I don't want…"

"No," I growled. "They were changed by a fucking artifact, and we broke it when they tried it with us."

"How do we know that?" another called out, and I glared at her.

"I don't know you, and I don't give a damn if you believe me or not. I came to see if you needed help, but clearly if you can be this fucking unwelcoming to us, then you don't need us, right?"

"Wait," Oracle interrupted, gently reaching out and laying a hand on my forearm, seeing I was getting annoyed. She raised her voice and spoke to the room at large. "I can help with most injuries, and I think we can help each other." She gestured, and a fountain of crystalline water appeared, flowing up to bubble and then lift into the air. The stream summoned from the rocky floor drew gasps from the crowd as they desperately surged forward.

It started a scramble, one that it took repeated shouting from Toren and his people to calm down, before people started to move in order of need, the weakest being carried over to drink.

They'd literally been dying of dehydration already.

"But Amelia, Dex…your changes are too deep for regular healing. You'll need a specialist like Nerin to reverse them, if that's even possible." Oracle went on, when things had calmed down enough that she could be heard over the hubbub.

"Nerin?" Dex asked, his voice rough.

"An imperial healer," I said. "She's far from here, though, and I don't know if she could do anything, in truth. I'm sorry…for now, it's best you accept your…condition."

"Yeah." He closed his eyes before clearing his throat roughly and raising his voice. "Does anyone know how long we were in there? How long we were trapped in that city?"

"Our daughter," Amelia added, turning and staring out, her face a tear-streaked mess. "Our daughter was refused. Kaspin said she'd be protected until she was old enough for the change, something about her being too weak. Oh God, he said she was too 'tender'! She vanished—I just know that she vanished, and now I don't remember what happened!" That last was said in a wail, and she broke down as the others started to shake their heads.

"Does anyone know the date?" Dex called out in a hoarse voice, holding Amelia to him as she sobbed.

"It's the fifth of Ides," one of the men called out. "The seven hundredth and forty-eighth year after the breaking?"

"Nine weeks." Amelia whimpered as she worked it out. "Nearly nine weeks we were enthralled there. Please, you have to help us!" That last was directed at me, and I blinked, before cursing.

"Please!" she tried, breaking free of her partner and dropping to her knees. "Please! You're the legion, right? You hunted the monsters? She's eight years old! Eight! She's alone back there, in that, that…"

"That nest." Kered spoke up, roughly clearing his throat as well before going on. "Lass, there's no way anyone could survive nine weeks there, not with the scorpions. I couldn't, and I've lived by my wits and blade for thirty years. A child?" He shook his head as Amelia broke down in sobs.

"Jax," Oracle said slowly, looking to me, even as she rested a hand on her stomach. The thought of a lost child in there made her—and me—think of our own quickly growing addition.

"The chances aren't good," I said softly, looking at her, and she nodded.

"But I can sense life if I can get close enough," Sehran said, and I nodded to her.

"We'd have to go street by street, clearing it out," I pointed out. "And we wouldn't be able to just carpet-bomb it—we might hit her."

"But we could pick a point and draw them to us," Oracle mused. "Maybe have the crossbows set up on the rooftops and…"

"Crossbows?" Toren blinked. "You mean us?"

"You going to leave a child in there?" I frowned.

"You think she's alive?" he countered. "Look, I'm sorry, and believe me, normally I'd hope she got out, but we have to be realistic. If she did? With slavers in the area, the best she can hope is that the scorpions made it quick!"

"You don't know that!" Amelia hissed at him. The sound came out far more monstrous than I'd have thought possible, making a lot of those nearby back up and raise their weapons again.

"No, I don't," Toren admitted. "But I spent ten years as a slave before I was bought and freed by someone with a sense of honor, so I *know* what her life would be." He shook his head. "I'm sorry, truly I am, but if she escaped the scorpions, she'll have died in the desert of hunger and thirst long before she made it to anywhere she could survive. Unless she's a skilled desert walker? A ranger prodigy?"

"No," Dex admitted. Hope died in his eyes with that admission.

"What if I told you I know where there are supplies?" Amelia suddenly said, lifting her head, her eyes shining bright as she dashed aside her tears.

"What supplies?" he asked cautiously.

"Everything looted from the old city, and everything that the people who were changed, like us, brought?" She waved an arm, taking in the whole of the cavern, including the way that the sand was still making it around the edges of the blanket pinned in place over the passage.

"You say she'd need to be a desert walker? What about you! All of you! You've got nothing, less than nothing here!"

"We escaped the slavers with everything we could, but no," Toren admitted. "That was why Finna led her team to search the city, to see what we could recover."

"Well, everything you need, I know where it is!" Amelia hissed. "You want it? I want my daughter!"

*"She's lying,"* Oracle said in my mind. *"Look at Dex."*

I glanced at him, seeing him trying to hide the confusion as he caught us looking.

*"Do we call her out on it?"* I asked, but it was Sehran who replied.

*"Wait, let them come to us."*

*"What?"* I asked.

*"You're the only heavily armored fighter here—real fighter, I mean—and look at the state of the next-closest fully armored fighter."*

I casually looked around the room, picking out the one Sehran indicated, and I barely managed to stifle a snort.

He wore what could charitably be called armor, but as it was clearly looted from a battle and it hadn't been something he'd been wearing before, well…

*"Let them come to their own decision here, and then when they ask us to lead the fight, we make it clear what our terms are. There'll have to be some supplies there—after all, the Changed Ones were surviving on something, so even if she's not telling the whole truth, there's food and some equipment hidden there."*

*"And we can fuckin' cook scorpions if we have to,"* I added with a mental laugh.

*"Go on,"* Oracle prompted, sending me a quick mental kiss as Sehran started to talk again.

*"Thanks to Kered, we know they have valuables, including spells and hard currency. What they don't have is anything to eat. And the way they reacted when Oracle did the water trick? I'm betting they didn't have water for a while, or healers either. We need to leverage that, make it clear that they assist you, and they do as*

*you say. Any loot we find—and there's going to be the slavers' gear if nothing else, though I'm betting the Changed Ones had something at least—all comes to you first."*

"She's right," Oracle said to me quickly, as all three of us watched on passively as Amelia waxed lyrical about the valuable gear they had in the city. *"A minute ago, you spoke about searching the city and the attitude was that we could do it without these people. Toren at least had no intention of helping. That might be because he doesn't think they can do it, or it might be because he thinks that it's not worth it. But either way, you need to take control here."*

"Can you do this?" Toren asked me, and I blinked, glancing from Amelia to Toren and then to Sehran, seeing Sehran's wink.

"Can I do what?" I asked.

"Can you clear the city," he asked, as if it were obvious. "Wait—why the hell am I even asking. If you're legion, you have to, don't you?"

"Me?" I snorted, reaching up and dragging my helm free, then running my hands through my hair. "Clear a city that size, on my own? Kill hundreds, possibly thousands of monsters, then hold off however many of the slavers who raided your entire caravan, driving you all off and capturing the rest, if they decide that the lightshow is an invitation?"

I waited several seconds, looking from one of them to the next, seeing hope dying on Amelia and Dex's faces, as the others joined that group.

I looked at the meager collection of hard tack that seemed to be all the food they had, the way that everyone who could gather anything even vaguely cup-like had frantically filled it with water. And most of all?

I looked at the beaten and broken condition of the group. "I've done more with less."

There was another long silence, before Toren spoke up.

"You mean it? I mean…wait, you think you can *actually* do that? Or is it more of your legion madness?"

"We can." Sehran stepped forward and spoke clearly, probably realizing that I was shit at this side, and certainly remembering that my speech-making skills were somewhere between "that guy we found in the gutter" and "drunk Glaswegian" in both clarity and skill.

"I've seen this man charge armies. On my oath, I've seen him beat a SporeMother to the brink of death with his fists, and then walk away, leaving the experience for others to claim." As she said it, she injected mana into her words; the air vibrated as an oath was made. When the crowd saw that she survived it, they knew that it couldn't have been a lie.

"A SporeMother?" came the stunned whisper, and "They're real?" from another throat.

"He's faced hundreds, *literally* hundreds of Dark legionnaires, he's called their god a dick to his face, and he's still here—they're not. Where we come from, people chant his name when he passes. People worship him. And you're asking if he can do this?" Sehran shook her head, looking amused.

"It's not *if* he can do this…it's if he *chooses* to. He *is* the legion. He leads them in their hundreds, and we're *here*, stranded through an accidental activation of an ancient portal. We're heading home, home to our friends, to those we love, and who need us."

She had moved forward into their midst and turned slowly as she spoke, making eye contact as she did. Her voice shifted slightly as she clearly used some trick of the succubai or of people with an insanely high Charisma score to make her words be better received.

"The question is, why should he risk himself? Why should he delay our return to the people we love, to help you? None of you have offered to help him. He saved you…" She gestured to Finna. "He led us to save all of you, after a running battle through the heart of the Changed Ones' home.

"He saved you too." She gestured to Dex and Amelia. "We heard a fight when we were leaving the city. It wasn't like there was any benefit to us coming to join in the fight, and still we did it. Because he ordered it.

"Then we came here." She turned back to Toren and his party, who looked more uncertain by the second. "We came here, because he told us to, to try to *help* you. We came here to offer you water, to offer healing, before we move on, because as the Imperial Legion, it's our duty."

"Then you should…" Toren quickly tried to interject, only to have Sehran speak over him.

"But there's a prince now, an *imperial prince*, who's claimed Dravith, where we were transported from. As a legionnaire, his first responsibility is to serve the empire. To the orders of that prince. And I can assure you, although the prince would be sympathetic to your situation, he's a realist.

"His advisors would be asking what does the *empire* gain by helping you, by risking one of the premier warriors of his generation…by risking someone on whom the empire depends so heavily, what does the empire stand to gain?

"Not one of you are citizens or have volunteered to swear an oath of allegiance to the empire. What's to stop you from selling the truth of an imperial legionnaire, with information like he possesses, to the Dark Legion? Or to the nobles who'd try to sell him off?"

"You make it sound like he could fight wars on his own," a dwarf to one side said gruffly. "What's a fighter like that got tae fear from the likes o' us?"

"Everyone needs to sleep," Sehran said softly, drawing attention to their own sorry state. "We all need food."

Oracle stepped forward and spoke in a clear voice. "If you want us to help you, then we're not asking for rewards for ourselves. We offer protection and leadership in the fight, but you'll all help, be that by fighting or in other ways. The empire gets first claim on anything that we recover, and we get first call on whatever you have that could help in the fight."

"Hey now!" one of the merchants gasped. "What, you think we escaped the slavers to just give you everything? You're robbing us!"

"No," I said flatly. "This is us asking why we should risk our lives and mission to help you, beyond what we have already. I have no need of gold, or of gems. If you knew what I have already, back home, you'd know how unimportant all of that is to me.

"What we need is information, we need weapons and equipment, and we need fighters. You're in the desert, starving, dying of dehydration, and being picked off by the monsters out here. You were stupid enough to walk into the trap that the Changed Ones offered, and now you want us to sort it all out for you, and for nothing? No." I shook my head.

"If you want my help, it comes at a cost, and it's one you can all easily afford. You all swear to the empire, you swear to the Prince of Dravith, and you swear that on the day that he comes to this continent, you will accept that he is your prince, that the empire is rising again and you will serve it."

"When he comes?" one of the merchants spoke up quickly. "Is he coming now?"

"You swear to serve him *whenever* he comes," I said firmly. "If he's here now, or if he arrives in ten years. As soon as he's here, you serve him."

I felt ridiculous twisting shit around like this, but if I didn't, if they were dodgy enough that they'd swear, thinking they were ripping me off and could then get away with not having to help? They'd deserve it.

And, it wasn't like I could tell them who I was, not without taking some precautions.

On Dravith, I was a nobody long enough that I managed to get support on my own merits, and then survived through sheer bad decisions and good luck.

Here? If word somehow reached the fucking Dark Legion that I was here, and without the Imperial Legion to back me up? They'd dispatch entire armies to come after me.

Nimon wouldn't make the same mistake and agree to face me one-on-one again. No, he'd send his armies after me.

That had come from Jenae. The little burst of warning she'd given me was that I needed to keep my fuckin' head down, and not use any imperial powers, nor summon her and her kin—not until I was somewhere a hell of a lot more secure than in the middle of a damn dead city, anyway.

I had to figure out how to hide the presence of the gods, and that meant doing things *quietly*.

Fortunately, I was a master of subtle.

People regularly talked about how subtle I was.

They pointed at me as I passed, and said things like *'Subtle? That fucker's as subtle as a brick in the face'* and *'He doesn't know the meaning of the word.'*

Damn.

# **CHAPTER SIX**

Finna stepped forward, her voice carrying in the sudden silence. "You want to know if he can do this? I watched him in that city. When those scorpions attacked our people, he didn't just fight them—he dropped his weapon and beat two to death with his bare hands."

She shuddered visibly. "Have you ever heard someone screaming in pure rage while punching through chitin like it was paper? I have. Today. That thing was the size of a house, and I never want to hear it again, but gods below, I'm glad he's offering to be on our side."

"You're exaggerating," one of the merchants scoffed.

"By my blood and breath, I swear I'm not," Finna replied, her voice hard. "Ask any of my people who were there. Ask about the way he moved faster than we could see, about how he kept fighting even when surrounded. The scorpions fled from *him* in the end. Monsters *ran.*"

"If you all swear to this, if you swear that on the day that the imperial prince comes to these lands, you will serve him faithfully for your lifetime, then I'll lead you in this fight and look after you as if you were my own," I said.

"What if we don't know he's come?" one of the merchants asked quickly.

"How about if he stands before us, then we know he's come and we agree. But if we don't see him—we can't be expected to know if there's no way of proving it, after all—then the oath is just to keep secret who you are?" Toren asked.

I looked at him, trying not to giggle at the phrasing. "I could go with that."

A few of the merchants looked relieved.

"What if we're blind when he comes?" one of the more sneaky of the merchants asked, trying to find a loophole. "Or away on business?"

"What if the sky falls?" I countered, my patience wearing thin. "The oath is simple: when the Prince of Dravith stands before you and declares himself, you serve him. No tricks, no games, no attempts to wrangle your way out of the oath."

One of the older merchants, a woman with grey-streaked hair, suddenly laughed. "You know what? This might be the best deal we've had in years. Immediate protection from someone who can clearly fight, healing, water, and all we have to do is promise to serve some prince if we ever meet him? That's practically free."

"Mother!" her son hissed, but she waved him off.

"Look around." She gestured at the cave, where people were still clutching at the water Oracle had created, where children huddled near empty food sacks. "We're dying here. We need help *now*. The future can take care of itself. It doesn't matter what we might lose, when, if we don't, we'll all be dead in two days of hunger and thirst."

Interestingly, most of the rest of the people there showed no issue with swearing to me—well, to the empire—and two of them actually looked excited.

"Do we get armor like that?" Min, one of the excited ones, asked, jabbing a finger at mine.

"If you can pass the tests that Restun, the Praetoria Primus, and the man who decides the members of the empire's most elite forces sets, then yes," I said, unable to stop the smile that came to my face at that thought. "All you have to do is pass his tests."

"So what, you're an 'elite'?" Min asked. "Are there many like you?"

"There's nobody like him," Sehran deadpanned. "Believe me, in the entire legion, when Jax speaks, everyone listens."

"You'll forgive me if we're a little skeptical," Toren said slowly. "This sounds too good to be true, after all."

"And if you think we're saving you without you swearing to follow the empire, then you're going to be very depressed for the rest of your life," I said. "I don't like doing it this way, but you can't be permitted to spread the word of the imperial prince and his retinue when it could spark a war. Oh, and one other thing.

"Children can swear from the age of majority, not as children. So if you've got a child, they don't swear right now. The prince's order is that everyone who swears to him must understand the risks, and must be at the age of majority. What is that here?"

"When you're considered an adult?" Finna asked, and I nodded.
"Depends on the race, really. I mean, elves and dwarves? I think forty is about the average. But for humans, it's what, thirteen?"

"Thirteen." I nodded. "And the dwarves and elves we'll deal with, I guess, considering that I'd not thought about their aging processes before. Dammit."

"Sounds like it's your prince's headache, not yours." Finna grinned.

"Yeah," I agreed flatly. "Who'd want to be that guy, right?" I looked at Oracle and Sehran.

"He has a lot of responsibility, that's for sure." Oracle smiled.

"He fought the God of Death, and won," Sehran pointed out. "One-on-one combat and we were all there. I think we can cut him a little slack now and then."

"Yeah." I smiled. "That was fun."

"Bullshit," Kered said firmly. "Ni—"

"Don't!" I snapped. "Don't name him!"

"We know that naming him can draw his eye. It's not likely, but it can happen." Oracle went on quickly. "You don't need to name him to discuss him, so let's avoid that if possible, okay?"

"Fine, but there's no way this prince could do that." Kered folded his arms and shook his head.

"By my oath, the Imperial Prince of Dravith fought the God of Death one-on-one and banished him from the continent of Dravith when he won," Sehran said formally. The air reverberated with the power of a sworn oath.

"Fuck me," one of the nearby people muttered. "You actually mean that? It's not just some demon trick?"

"What's with that?" I asked suddenly, looking from him to Sehran. "Everywhere else we've been, people are a lot more concerned about Sehran. Here you act like it's normal to have a succubus around."

"Not normal, but yeah, there's a few of them in the Tower of Gaij, so, you know…" another of the refugees admitted.

I looked at him in confusion, then to Sehran as she squealed.

"It's still here?" she asked excitedly. "Wait, they're still there? Seriously?"

"What is it?" I asked.

She shook her head, gesturing for the speaker to go on.

"It's a ruined tower full of succubai. You can go there for…you know…" He shrugged as his face colored. "It's in the center of the city."

"How far?!" Sehran asked quickly.

"Like, three months' travel?" He scratched his spotty beard in thought. "I mean, if you went straight there, it'd only take maybe six or eight weeks. But you'd have to pass through the plains, and that's bandit and slaver territory, so everyone just goes around. It's maybe twelve hundred miles?"

"Sehran?" I asked, again, and she turned to us, slipping into conversing through our bond.

*"It was a place that we could be summoned to, a center of learning for warlocks in the empire, which held a permanently open portal between our realms, where we exchanged knowledge,"* she explained quickly. *"When the fall came here—the cataclysm—the portal shut. Those that were on this side were thought killed, and the tower destroyed. But if they weren't? If they were just somehow trapped here, and they're still there? Jax, this could mean so much to those left behind in the demon realm, and…oh no."*

*"Oh no?"* Oracle prompted.

*"If they stayed here, if they continued to level, to gain classes and specializations, to grow? They'd destroy the fragile order that's maintained back home! There's a reason we're not allowed to grow too strong, Jax. We're demons— even little disagreements tend to be, well…"* She shrugged eloquently.

*"Fucking lethal."* I nodded. *"Okay, so if that's the case, and these demons go back, they'd fuck with the balance of power?"*

*"Jax, I've gained enough strength in the last few months with your party that, as I told you, I'd not be permitted to return. I'd have to be very careful to maintain my expected position back there. If I'd been here for seven hundred years?"* She shook her head. *"Some of the demons on this side should be capable of destroying the realm now, and—"* Then she broke off, as if confused.

*"But if that was the case, why haven't they done something about it, or seized power?"* I asked, thinking the same thing. *"Why don't they rule here?"*

"Excuse me." Oracle smiled winningly at the man who'd admitted to visiting the tower. "Are the demons active in the city?"

"Active?" He frowned.

"Do they do much? Are they commonly seen?" she clarified.

"No…they refuse to leave the tower, I heard," he admitted, though it sounded like he wasn't sure about it.

*"They're feeding off the tower."* Oracle turned back to us. *"I don't know what deal was struck, obviously, but I'm betting that's how the tower still stands…"*

"Is the tower intact?" I asked the man, turning to him, and smiling as I noted the way that everyone waited while we held an obviously private and silent conversation.

"It's a bit fucked. Half of it fell down…though it's weird because what's left looks pretty much perfect, like it's just been finished. The nobles tried to claim it a few times, and the demons have big stone golems that slaughtered them all, and there used to be the legion too."

"Tell me about the legion," I said, my wondering about the tower and its possibilities completely derailed. "Why 'used to be'?"

"They had a base a few miles from the city, on a hill, and the Dark Legion wiped them all out in a big battle, maybe five, six years ago?" He shrugged. "Sorry, uh, legionnaire? I just don't know more than that. It's not really something the likes of us get involved in."

"They all got wiped out?" I asked through gritted teeth.

"Well, most?" He shrugged. "I think there's still some around, but you know."

"No…no, I don't know. Make it very clear," I growled.

"The Dark Legion cut the hands off half of the survivors, and blinded the others, leaving them as beggars," Toren said slowly. "Look, I'm sorry. I know you're all legionnaires, and it's shitty to hear about anyone doing this, but that's what they did. They crippled all the survivors they could catch—blinded half, chopped the hands of the other half—so that everyone knew that if you joined the legion, if you fucked with the Dark Legion, then that's what you got."

"Object lessons," I snarled. "He made them into object lessons."

"Yeah," Toren admitted.

"Right!" I barked, stepping forward. "This is it—make your choice time. Because either I help you now and you agree to serve the empire, or I'm leaving, right fucking now."

The wind chose that moment to howl a little louder, and I ignored the additional sand that managed to get through the covering.

"I can fly, as can Oracle and Sehran here, so if you say no? No issue to me— we'll be leaving. It'll be a struggle to get past the sand and into the air, but once we get above the sandstorm, we can fly just fine.

"I'm going to the Tower of Gaij, after I search the city, and either I'm taking you all, or I'm leaving you here. Pick now, because I'm not wasting any more fucking time while those who *are* loyal to the empire are being maimed!"

There was a long silence, but just as I started to turn from them, Finna stepped forward.

"If we swear to you, will you help us free our friends?"

"Where are they?" I asked roughly. The thought of possibly thousands of good men and women like Grizz being maimed and left to beg on the streets made it come out a lot harsher than it should have.

"The slavers." She gestured vaguely to the south. "They'd not have sent out groups tracking us if they weren't staying to wait for them to return. They'll still be to the south, probably repairing the caravans they stole from us, and getting ready to sell our people off as well. If we swear, will you help them?"

I looked to Oracle and Sehran, both of whom kept silent, but I knew. "If you swear, if all of you swear—not counting those too young to—then yes. We'll start healing you now, we'll begin an inventory of our goods, and we'll come up with a plan."

"And us?" Dex asked before Amelia could. "What about our daughter?"

"I'll sacrifice one day." I held my right hand up, one digit extended. "One day. If I genuinely believed that there was a better chance of her being alive, I'd take the entire city apart to find her, but a lost child nine weeks ago in a city overrun with scorpions and then surrounded by slavers…we will be realistic, and that means we clear out a portion of the city, then Sehran scouts it. She can sense signs of life, so if she lives, she'll find her. That's the best offer I can make."

"There's also the chance that if she did escape then the slavers already took her to the main group," Finna pointed out. "If we don't find her here, we might find her in the city?"

"Either way, you swear now, or we leave." I looked around. "Oracle?" I prompted.

"Can't swear an oath we don't know, boy," the older merchant who had pointed out the advantage earlier snapped, before settling down suddenly.

"I'll handle it," Oracle assured her, before speaking through the bond to the two of us. *"I'll change the oath to reflect what we've agreed. They can get the option to swear the full oath when this is all over. We've got enough potions, maybe, but you'll need to meditate after this."*

The surprised blink from one of the nearby merchants was enough, and I stared at him, noting the way he seemed to stare at something beyond me, before he, and the others, started to speak.

**"I swear that when the Imperial Prince of Dravith stands before me and declares himself, I will serve him faithfully for my lifetime. I will keep his secrets, obey his commands, and work for the good of the Empire. Until then, I swear to obey the one who has offered me this oath—Jax, Legionnaire of the Empire—in place of him. This I swear freely and without reservation. Lastly, I will not be a dick!"**

The addition of the last line made me smile, even as my mana dropped like a stone. I fumbled out potions, chugging three mana as fast as I could, one after the other.

"I, Jax, do swear to protect and lead you, to be the shield that protects you and yours from the darkness, and the sword that avenges that which cannot be saved. As the empire grows in strength, so shall you."

"Jax, several didn't swear, and they're not children," Oracle said clearly. "There at the back."

"Gather your gear and get out," I ordered the trio, who looked suddenly panicked.

"Hey now, I swore!" the apparent leader said quickly, before swallowing hard. "I mean, I was about to… I'm just, you know, I'm just a slow reader, yeah?"

I stared at him, and Oracle pushed the oath out again, our joint mana now absolutely in the dregs *again*. Once again, he hesitated. But seeing the way that the others had moved away from him and the way I stared at him, he forced a smile, sweat beading on his forehead, then started to speak.

He read out the oath, then sat back down, pale-faced as the oath tightened its grip on him.

I took a deep breath and augmented my return oath. "I order you all, by the oath, to step forward and tell me the truth, and to live by the spirit of the oath you have just sworn, not just the letter. Are any of you plotting to harm others in this room, to sell the news of the empire's return, or to harm me and my companions in any way?"

"I…" All three stood suddenly, jerked unnaturally back to their feet.

"I am!"

"I do."

"Me."

"Explain," I ordered coldly.

"We were ordered to follow the group," the leader of the little trio said desperately. "We have a signal stone, for the others to track so that we could capture any survivors!"

"You're one of the slavers?" I asked.

He hesitated, shaking while first one and then both of his companions admitted it.

"Yes!"

"We are!"

"Not…" He struggled, clearly trying to lie, or at least hide something as blood started to stream from his eyes and ears. He sagged to one knee, coughing blood, crying out as he struggled to breathe. "Guard…sent…" he managed.

"You were a guard sent along to watch?" I asked, and he frantically nodded. "A fighter who works for the slavers…you think that's better?" I snorted, shaking my head. "You're wrong."

"Ple…ase…"

"Die quietly," I ordered him, before turning to the other two as he collapsed on the floor, writhing, but utterly silent. "You two, you're slavers and you helped the others to find and capture these people."

"Yes."

"I'm sorry!" the second howled. "I didn't want to…" Then he screamed and fell to the ground, again going silent and writhing at my order.

"You're going to tell me everything I need to know about your masters, the caravans, and their association with the guild," I said to the remaining slaver, as his former leader stilled on the ground by his feet, his other companion starting to scream.

"Anything," he promised, eyes wide and tears streaming down his face.

"You gambled that I'd not think to enforce the oath," I said clearly, looking around the room, as I went on. "Many of you thought that you'd swear anything to get the help now, and then it wouldn't matter because you could wriggle out of the oath moving forward. Well, consider this your proof of what happens when you fuck with the empire."

The grey-haired merchant woman who'd thought she'd gotten such a clever deal earlier had gone pale, her previous confidence replaced by dawning comprehension. Next to her, her son wasn't even trying to hide his panic.

Everyone was silent—including the dying slaver on the floor—as I went on.

"I hate that I need to do this, that I need to magically enforce discipline. It feels too much like slavery to me, but fuck it. You've all seen what was hiding in your midst, so you've got an idea of why it's important, and believe me, I've found hidden vipers in the nest before. Fuck it, let's go all the way."

Toren's eyes widened as realization hit him. He'd been the one to suggest the "when he stands before us" clause, thinking he was being clever. Now he looked as if he'd swallowed something particularly sour as I kept talking.

"I am Jax, also known as Jax Amon, Prince of the Empire, and ruler of the continent of Dravith. I call all of you to serve the empire. Your oath was agreed to, to come into force when the prince was before you, and here I stand."

The silence that followed was absolute. Even the dying slaver had gone quiet. Then the grey-haired merchant started to laugh, a slightly hysterical edge to it.

"'When the prince stands before us and declares himself,'" she quoted her own words back. "Oh, that's…that's just perfect. We thought we were being so clever…"

"Mother," her son groaned, but this time there was a note of anger. "You see what you did?"

"What I did, you young idiot, was agree to a deal that gets us access to an entire new market! A whole territory, a continent no less, where the nobles have no sway!"

"You don't know that!" he hissed.

I watched her, a hint of a smile playing at the edges of my lips.

"Oh, I think I do." She snorted. "Look at him. You think nobles like we've got here are gonna take well to meeting him? You think what, he just marched in and said 'I'm your new prince' and they all said 'Righto then, nice to meet you, boss'? No. He climbed those stairs to the throne on skulls and blades, boy. He's a killer, and a vicious one, unless I miss my bet."

"I am," I admitted. "When you cross me."

"We can all see that." She nodded to the now two dead slavers in their midst, and the last of them, standing silent and trying not to draw attention, as his breeches grew ever more stained with piss.

"So," I said into the silence. "This is Oracle, my right hand and the love of my life, and this is Sehran, my close friend and confidant. I'm going to start meditating, to recover my mana, and you're going to work with them, because as soon as the storm dies down, we're going back to that city."

"To find my daughter?" Amelia asked desperately.

"To pick it up, turn it over and shake the fucker. We're gonna see what falls out, before we go and kill the slavers. Believe me, if we can find her, if she's there to be rescued, I'll do everything in my power to do it."

With that, I moved to the side, settling down with my back against the cave wall in a comfortable position, closing my eyes and focusing on my breathing as Oracle and Sehran began to organize the survivors. Through our bond, I could sense Oracle's methodical approach as she moved through the group, healing the worst injuries first while questioning them about their skills and resources.

I tried my best to block it all out, to focus on the oneness, the silence and create the boxes around my mind. But, as before, I just couldn't; there were so many people I didn't know on all sides. I managed a slight increase in my mana regeneration, and I accepted that as the best I was going to get.

"You were merchants?" Oracle's voice drifted to me, steady and calm. "What kind?"

"Luxury goods, mostly," the voice of the grey-haired woman replied. "Or they *were* luxury goods, before those bastards took everything. I had three wagons of silverspun cloth from the southern kingdoms. Was going to be my big break into the noble market." She laughed bitterly. "Thirty years of careful trading, gone in an afternoon."

"How many others were trading at that level?" Sehran asked, her voice carrying clearly as she helped a wounded former guard over to Oracle to heal his broken arm.

"Five of us," someone else answered. "Most of the rest were smaller operations. Tinkers, general goods, that sort of thing."

The conversation continued as I concentrated on drawing in mana, replacing what we'd spent. Through the bond, Oracle shared what she was learning. There were fifty-nine survivors in total, maybe fifteen of them experienced guards. The rest were a mix: wagon drivers, a couple of carpenters, three tinkers who'd been traveling together, and various family members of those who had been a part of the caravan and camp followers.

"Any healers?" Sehran asked, and I felt her frustration through the bond when the answers came back negative.

"Had two," one of the guards grunted. "Both taken. Slavers always grab healers first."

That tracked with what we knew. Healers were worth their weight in gold no matter where you were.

"We've got some fighters, though," another voice added eagerly. "Some of us were military before taking up caravan work."

"Former military?" Oracle's interest sharpened. "From an army, or…?"

The silence that followed was telling.

"Most were mercenaries. Some were city guards, or adventurers," the grey-haired older merchant supplied finally. "But good ones. They've kept my goods safe for three years now. I brought them with me when we joined the caravan, and they got me and my son out when they saw the fight couldn't be won."

I let the voices wash over me as I continued to meditate, but kept one ear on the inventory Oracle was compiling. Between them, the survivors had managed to save a reasonable amount of coin: fifty-three gold, fourteen hundred and twelve silver, and four thousand-odd copper. Given that they were trading with smaller villages out in the middle of nowhere, the discrepancy to copper and silver from gold made sense as well. They also had some gems, their weapons, and a mass of random-seeming luxury goods. The older merchant, Zyenna, she introduced herself as, was responsible for the cloth that was everywhere in here.

I opened my eyes and glanced at the cloth, having caught it when she named it as silverspun. I noted that it was a little glittery as it moved. Like something that would be worn by a starlet at an awards ceremony, but not, like, the kind of things that the queen would have, if that made sense?

It just looked like thick, expensive cloth that could be made into anything from bedding to clothes.

"You might not think it's much to look at, *my lord*," the old woman called over, having seen me looking. "But it's not finished. The luster of the cloth is much clearer when it has the final treatment, becoming fully waterproof. It has to be dyed first, as once it's treated, it won't accept the dye either."

"So you need to sell it like this to the seamstresses." I nodded my understanding.

"No seamstresses work with the likes of this." She snorted. "Only the weavers can work it, by law."

"Law?"

"Guild law." She nodded when I glanced at her. "A law brought in to maintain a monopoly, so that as only the Caravaneer's Guild can transport it in any real quantity, it keeps the price high. You try buying it and paying an established caravan to carry it? Get ready for a fee that makes buying it look cheap."

"It damn near beggared us to buy so much, and the southern kingdoms thought we were daft when we did it," her son added. "After all, if you can't transport it, it doesn't matter if you buy it cheap, when the main market is so far away."

"So you bought it cheap in the south, then joined the new caravan to get it transported up north to here, thinking to get around the monopoly and make a killing." I nodded. "Smart."

"Most of what we had was in the wagons, but these are the samples, and they've earned their value here keeping people alive." Zyenna sighed. "I'd have loved the profit, but I'd make it with people who actually care. It's been too long I've dealt with snakes in the grass."

"And that was all that you were carrying?" I asked her, before nodding to Oracle as I caught her looking at me, gesturing me back to meditation. "I know, I know," I assured her.

"The rest was smaller—some rubies, some firesticks, a hundred karnaan tails…that kind of thing. That was what we carried in the bags, while the caravans carried the majority of the bigger goods. We emptied all but one of them, grabbing as much cloth as we could, then ran."

"And the others?" I asked.

"Much the same." She shrugged. "A caravan is made up of merchants, and we know what raiders want, so we grab it and run. If we lose only the bulky goods, then we can recover. If we lose everything, we might as well have let them slit our throats."

"Except these weren't raiders, they're slavers, so they'd sell us all as well. Double the profit. Hooray for the Caravaneer's Guild and their wonderful deals," her son added sourly, before spitting on the ground. "So, tell me the truth, are you really a prince?"

"I am." I took a deep breath and called out to everyone. "I release the portion of the oath that enforces the whole truth. You may speak to me normally, and I will do the same."

"A risk, that," Zyenna said softly. "How do you know we won't lie to you?"

"I'd rather you lived when you accidentally tell me a lie and then have the chance to think better of it," I said flatly. "After all, if I think you're lying, I can always order you to tell the truth, and then you know you're fucked, because I'll have learned that you tried to manipulate me and are untrustworthy. You want to run that risk?"

"Not really."

"Then there we go. Look, Zyenna, and, what's your name?" I asked her son.

"Marteen," he said, and I noted others were listening in.

"Right, well, if I'm being honest, I hate that I need to use the oath to compel anyone, but the simple truth is, without it, would any of you have known that those three were your enemies? How do you feel now about those by your side, knowing that they literally cannot harm you, they can't stab you in the back and try to fuck you over, because if they do…?" I gestured toward the mess of blood and the two bodies off to one side.

"I don't like it, but these oaths were common in the old empire, and they ensured that it was a place that you knew you were safe. Is it taking some of your freedoms away? Yeah, it is. But let's be clear: you travelled as a caravan with guards who were spies for the slavers. They literally captured some of your friends. Your family. Some of you have lost sons and daughters to be sold on the slaver's block, because these oaths weren't in place.

"Had you had them? Those hiding in your midst could never have done it. Is it shitty? Yeah, to a degree it is, but considering the alternative? The fucking monsters that you have to deal with otherwise, both literal and figurative—the slavers, the Dark Legion, the vampires, witches, the…" I shook my head. "Hell with it. In exchange for us doing our level best to keep you safe from all of that, I think asking you to agree not to fuck us over, or each other, is a small cost to pay."

"Do you hear anyone complaining?" Zyenna settled back and gestured around. "I don't. They know that they were as good as dead before. We had one last hope, and that was that we could salvage something from a lost city that's been raided before over the centuries. Once that was done, we'd all need to make our own decisions. Some would trek into the desert and try to make new lives, others would try to return home, but we were all doing it with nothing but what we'd brought here.

"Now, instead, we have a chance of recovering it all, and while we might not be free anymore, we're sworn to a noble house, that's all. And believe me, boy, many of the oaths of allegiance that are demanded by nobles are far more restrictive than yours."

"We'll need to discuss that soon," I said. "But for now, basically what you're saying is that beyond some luxuries that are bugger all use here, some nice cloth that's getting trashed being used as bedding in a dirty cave, and a handful of weapons, none of you have anything even remotely close to covering your basic needs?"

"We've got five spell scrolls, none of which are of use here. Seven magical artifacts, four of which are unknown and would only work if taken to whatever device they are attuned to, and three that offer specific, if single-use magics," she said. "Oh, and a handful of gems and enough coin to buy a small village between us."

"What are the artifacts?" I asked, only to have Oracle step in.

"Two are useful in farming, and we have no farmland here, and one is a general attachment for a basic servitor golem to enable it to mine more efficiently. They've been trying to sell it as a mining attachment for a cart."

"So…fuck all of any use?" I asked, and she nodded. "Great."

"You know what would be of use?"

"What?"

"You meditating so I have enough mana to heal everyone and summon water." She fixed me with a glare.

I snorted, then nodded. "All right, I can take a hint." I sighed, leaning back. "Good meeting you both. Sorry it wasn't under better circumstances," I offered to the merchants, before closing my eyes and focusing inward.

Before I buried myself in it, I allowed myself a quick reflection of the situation in the cave.

We had enough. Not enough to thrive, but enough to survive if we were careful, especially if we could find wood to burn so that we could cook the scorpion meat. I had a feeling there was going to be a lot of that, after all.

Then I couldn't help but smile as a thought struck me.

I'd be cooking them already, using my ritual circles, so fuck it. We'd have to check the meat, but I was betting some would be recoverable.

So, we had food; we already had shelter—even if it was a bit shit. More importantly though, they had knowledge. That was what we'd been lowest on. These merchants knew the trade routes, the local powers, which nobles could be trusted and which couldn't. The guards knew the terrain, the threats, the best places to camp and the areas to avoid.

All of it would be useful, especially once we dealt with the immediate threats and could start thinking about expanding the empire's influence here. But first, we had a city to shake down and some slavers to kill.

Through the bond, I felt Oracle's satisfaction as she finished her initial assessment. We had a functional, if ragged, group here. People with skills, with reasons to want revenge, and now with binding oaths to ensure their loyalty.

It wasn't much, but I'd started with less before.

# CHAPTER SEVEN

The plaza stretched before us, a graveyard of broken columns and weathered stone. Centuries of sand had sculpted the ruins into alien shapes, creating shadowed hollows that were filled almost to the brim with wind-blown sand, fucking perfect ambush spots for hiding bugs.

I'd chosen it carefully. Three mostly intact buildings formed a rough triangle around the rear of the open space, their upper floors still solid enough to support those who had crossbows, and yet to reach them, the enemy would have to get past me and the melee fighters.

"Remember," I called out to the gathered survivors, "no heroes today. Work your teams, watch your backs, and if you see something bigger than you can handle, fall back." I caught Zyenna's eye as she finished distributing crossbow bolts to her makeshift squad of archers, and she gave me a grim nod.

Half the people out here were doing it only under very strenuous objection. The rest? They had to be held back.

Markedly, those who were excited were the ones she, or her son Marteen, had under their direction, as they'd both volunteered to lead squads.

The older woman had admitted it to me as we slogged across the sands in the early morning light, watching for any monsters that might be drawn by the group's movement.

We'd had to set off at 'Zero-dark-thirty' to get here and for most they were exhausted before the fight had even begun.

"When you get to my age, you realize that the majority of the levels you've gained, you've wasted," she said. "When I was younger, it was all about the deal— making myself prettier, giving me a better chance of distracting my opponent, tracking the myriad details I needed to build a merchant house. Now? I get up in the morning and the damn thing I need more than anything is Constitution and Agility. Dexterity'd be nice too. But just to not suffer from all the aches and pains of getting old would be wonderful."

Now she was up on the building behind me, leading a squad, determined to earn some levels.

Her son stood by my side, a team of half-terrified, half-excited spearmen and mace wielders with him.

Oracle reached out to me from behind. Her standing on the middle roof with a squad gave them a little confidence that they were important, and it gave her an overview of most of the plaza.

*"Ready?"* I asked both of them through our bond.

*"There's a concentration of Scorpions about two hundred meters east,"* Sehran replied. *"I can sense maybe thirty of the smaller ones scattered across two streets, but there's four of the larger as well, and they're searching for something."*

*"How've they survived this long?"* I asked as the thought occurred to me. *"I mean, they're big bastards. They have to be eating a lot, so what the hell do they eat for there to be this many?"*

*"I'm betting the bigger ones usually hunt the desert,"* Sehran mused. *"It's a natural place for them. And when there are such big monsters out there…"*

*"Makes sense, I suppose,"* I replied with a mental sigh. *"Okay, so, everyone ready?"*

*"Definitely,"* Oracle replied, and in answer, Sehran, who'd been hovering over me, enjoying the warmth of the sun, threw back her head and began to sing.

*"Try not to get yourself killed!"* Oracle sent as the song rose steadily, along with a mental kiss, followed by a very distracting image that made my mind go blank for several seconds. *"It's been a while since we've had any privacy, after all."* She promised, *"Just survive—and win with style, of course—and later we'll sort that out."*

*"Don't mind me,"* shot Sehran. *"I can just watch!"* That was added with a throaty mental laugh, and I shook the thought off.

"I'm happy with one woman, dammit, I don't need two…down, boy!" I muttered, shifting myself as I tried to ignore the thoughts that mental image had sparked.

*"How long until they arrive?"*

*"Less than a minute,"* Oracle replied.

I hesitated, then swore and pulled up my notifications, wanting them out of the way for what was coming.

## *Congratulations!*

**Through hard work and perseverance, you have increased your stats by the following:**

**Agility +1**

**Dexterity +1**

**Endurance +1**

**Luck +2**

**Strength +1**

*Continue to train and learn to increase this further.*

I quickly checked my character sheet, then banished it and took a deep breath. And then, because I couldn't help myself, I flicked through the kill notifications as well.

*

## *Congratulations!*

*You have killed the following:*

- *27x Desert Scorpions of various levels for a total of 31,240xp*
- *5x Giant Desert Scorpions of various levels for a total of 38,290xp*
- *3x S'barrr Beasts of various levels for a total of 17,050xp*
- *35x Changed Ones of various levels for a total of 31,500xp*

- *3x Slavers of various levels for a total of 6,120xp*
- *8x Xon'dike Warriors of various levels for a total of 16,000xp*

*A party under your command killed the following:*

- *14x Desert Scorpions of various levels for a total of 12,880xp*
- *7x Giant Desert Scorpions of various levels for a total of 41,250xp*
- *35x Changed Ones of various levels for a total of 31,500xp*
- *2x Xon'dike Warriors of various levels for a total of 4,000xp*

*Total party experience earned: 89,630xp*

*As party leader, you gain 25% of all experience earned (22,407xp)*

*Total experience gained: 140,200xp + 22,407xp (party leader bonus) = 162,607xp*

*Progress to level 49 stands at 4,638,488/6,455,000*

I nodded to myself, satisfied that it was done, that it was going well, and I fought down the instinctive *"But I want a level, waaaa"* that always came up.

That was probably one of the reasons I left the damn thing so often, I mused, then dismissed it as the first of the scorpions burst into view.

It came from a mainly demolished building on the left of the plaza, its multiple legs carrying it very quickly across the stone and sand. It totally disregarded us all, its focus on the hovering demon that sang a siren song hardwired into all creatures, even these.

The need to mate, to rush toward that beguiling thing in the sky, kept it coming until I stepped forward and stabbed out. The blade of my naginata knifed through its chitinous exoskeleton with a loud crunch.

Its legs spasmed; the stinger lashed forward to slam into the blade hard, bouncing off as instincts drove it, even in death.

Then it was done. I put my boot on the thing's back—it was the size of a small dog, so large enough I couldn't just shuck it off with ease—and I dragged the blade free, before indicating the next in line.

"Spread out, people!" I shouted. "Make the most of the easy experience, and remember, if you're injured, it's fine. If you get envenomed, then call out. We can heal you, but take no unnecessary risks. This is going to be a very long day!"

The first wave came exactly as planned. Sehran swept out over the ruins, her song rolling out in waves and acting like a beacon to draw the predators. I stood in the center of the plaza, weapon ready, as more and more of the gleaming black shadows detached themselves from the surrounding rubble.

They came low and fast, chitin scraping against stone. The next scorpion was barely larger than a horse, its stinger already cocked back to strike as this one apparently noticed me. I sidestepped the initial thrust, bringing my weapon down in a brutal arc that split its carapace. Ichor sprayed across the sand as the creature's legs spasmed.

Two more charged in from different angles. I caught one's claw with my armored forearm, using its momentum to swing it into its companion. Both crashed into a fallen column as crossbow bolts rained down from above, punching through their armor with practiced precision, even as Oracle called out directions and reminders that the bolts were limited.

"Keep them for when we need them. Believe us, there's targets enough for everyone!" she called.

"She's got that right," Finna muttered nearby, and I grinned.

"Left side!" Marteen's voice carried over the sounds of battle. His team of four former caravan guards moved in almost perfect sync, two, like him, with spears as they caught a flanking scorpion in a simple maneuver. The beast thrashed, impaled from multiple angles, before the remaining two of his squad scurried forward, wielding their maces, and started to break legs. The final blow was Marteen's, as his spear bit through the immobilized scorpion's chitin and into its brain.

Those on my right worked in as much sync as they could manage. Toren led them, with Finna and her group of the best of their fighters being kept as backup.

She wasn't happy about that, but as I pointed out, best to have them when we need them, and to get those who didn't know how to fight the scorpions blooded first, before it got nasty, rather than give them a false sense of security.

As the press of the scorpions grew heavier, I called out to Oracle, not bothering to use the bond, instead just shouting, so that our people could hear and feel the relief when I made the decision it was time to narrow the playing field.

Twin Circles of Frostfire flared into existence, spreading across the far end of the plaza, and the mass of racing scorpions began to shriek. Sehran broke off, landing atop the building behind us, next to Oracle, and caught her breath.

There were nearly forty scorpions in sight by my count. All but two were between the size of a Jack Russell dog and a small horse…one of those things that looked like the gods had stuck legs on a barrcl, used up all the hair that was left at the end of the day on the floor at the hairdresser's and then had finished early because it was Friday.

They were almost all killed by the two overlapping circles, flames and frost coating and sealing their fate, with a grand total of four making it out the far side.

Two of those lurched off in the other direction, panicking, and the last two…well, one of them died when it staggered into its smoking and screeching big brother, and the pair attacked each other. And the other succumbed to a terminal case of crossbow-bolt-to-the-face.

"Good shot!" I called out, and snorted when Zyenna shouted out her thanks.

The two bigger ones each had a body that was roughly the size of a medium SUV, with all the weight and insanity that implied.

One was currently shaking its stinger, trying to get the still smoking remains of its sibling off, while the other was running full tilt at me.

I was tempted to fireball it in the face. I mean…multiple legs, fast moving, skittering and insectile—it was close enough to a normal spider to make me uncomfortable, and that was only half the deal. But I also knew that the others needed to see this.

"Here, hold this for me," I said to the man nearest me, passing my naginata over, and strode forward, unarmed.

*"Jaaaax,"* Oracle sent me warningly.

*"Just proving a point, my love,"* I sent back.

She replied with a complicated mélange of emotions—part annoyance, part pleasure at the way I'd thought of her in that way instinctively.

I started to jog, hearing Oracle calling out to the people on the rooftops with her that if they hit me with a crossbow bolt now, I was likely to be very annoyed, so to hold them.

I picked up speed. My boots thundered across the plaza. The high winds of last night and early this morning had left massive drifts of sand in the corners of the plaza, but had uncovered sections of the middle, and the stone under my boots rang out my challenge.

The scorpion took it and responded, raising its pincers and scuttling forward. Its tail bounced menacingly, until we were less than three meters apart.

The stinger flashed out and as I stepped aside, it drove itself into the flagstones, skidding across with a smell of burning, as whatever their venom was set the stone to bubbling.

I'd slid aside, then dove and rolled, easily passing under the scorpion, planting my boot on the far side as it tried to work out where I was. I sprang to my feet, slamming my Mana Overdrive into primacy and punching out, hard.

My gauntleted fist cracked through the chitin underneath. The ventral nerve cord was poorly protected here, and when my fist hit it, it triggered a spasm across the entire creature.

That was nothing compared to what it did when I grabbed on and ripped an entire section of its nervous system out.

I released and rolled, smoothly coming out on the far side as the scorpion's legs and tail gave out. The front half of the creature was still thrashing and trying to figure out why the hell the back half…well, was doing fuck all.

That was when I stood, grabbed onto the end of the tail, and—adding a little more mana so that I could manage such an insane feat—pulled.

The scorpion moved easily, and I grinned inside my helm as I spun it around, building momentum as the next raced forward, only to be met with its sibling being used as a morning star.

The pair of them were almost killed by the impact alone. Certainly, it didn't help when they both started going to town on each other with their pincers. And by the time I strode around the now smoking, frantically battling and immobilized pair, to sprint in and smash the second in a similar way, ripping half its nervous system out and leaving it to collapse to the floor, thrashing, well…

It was all over but the cleaning up.

I turned my back on them and started to walk back toward the stunned citizens who were waiting, whipping the gore off my gauntlets. The pair of massive scorpions, monsters that would have occasioned serious concern and even panic had they turned up at a medium *city*, were now utterly broken and bleeding out.

"Anyone want to finish them off?" I asked conversationally. I paused, dragging a bit of meat out of a joint in my left gauntlet, then took my naginata back from the guy holding it. "Thanks for holding that. Didn't want it getting dirty. Go on, have at it," I encouraged cheerfully.

There were a few hesitant steps as a couple of people started forward, then paused, uncertain whether I was playing some kind of a joke, before I waved them on, and they started to run.

Less than a minute later, they were back, the scorpions were dead, and the general feeling of the battle had changed from "Oh God, oh God, what are we doing…we're all going to die" into "I wonder how much XP I can get from this?!"

As the next two hours passed, the air grew thick with the smell of scorched chitin as Oracle's magic flared. Not only did we use the circles, but occasionally she'd treat herself to a lightning strike that lanced down from above. Each blast of energy illuminated the plaza in stark relief, casting twisted shadows across sand-scoured stone. More scorpions poured in from the surrounding streets, drawn by the sounds of combat and the magical calls of Sehran. But we did our absolute best to maintain control, and only slowly increase their numbers each time.

I lost myself in the rhythm of battle, each movement flowing into the next. Duck under a snapping claw, pivot, bring the weapon up in a devastating arc that split chitin like paper. Roll away from a stinger that punched a crater in the stone where I'd stood. My armor seemed to become more a part of me with each passing minute, as I explored its capabilities, the points where it restricted my movement and where it enhanced it, and I shook my head in amazement.

A particularly large specimen, easily twice the size of its brethren I'd faced to date, charged straight for me. Its claws snapped at empty air as I danced back. The beast was smart, trying to drive me back and break the line, but I'd fought too many of its kind to fall for such basic tactics.

I feinted left, then drove forward as it committed to the attack. My blade found the weak spot where its carapace failed to protect its eyes. With a roar of effort, I drove the weapon all the way up to the haft; three feet of blade was embedded in its body, bisecting its brain. I rolled my wrist, twisting and jerking the weapon side to side, essentially using an egg-scrambler in there. The scorpion's legs collapsed, its massive bulk crashing to the ground as death spasms racked its frame.

When the next wave finally ended, twenty-seven giant scorpion corpses littered the plaza. The sand had turned black with their blood, and the air was thick with the metallic stench of it. I checked my team; a dozen minor casualties had been taken and one major, though Oracle was already moving to heal that, as the cheers started to ring out.

"We're making good progress!" I called out, keeping my voice steady despite the adrenaline still coursing through me. "Get ready, though, because this is very much the 'training wheels' option. From now on, we're gonna start pulling more!"

"More?" one of the men next to me asked, blinking in confusion. "Isn't this, well, all of them?"

"Oh, my sweet summer child," I muttered, shaking my head at his naivety. "Hey Sehran!" I called out loudly.

"Yes, my prince!" She flew over from the rooftop she'd been resting on and hovered overhead as I glared at her.

"How far out have you gone? How much of the city would you say we've covered?"

"Maybe a quarter?" she guessed. "If that?"

"See." I nodded to the talkative guy next to me. "We've got either another, oh, ten hours or so of this, then a mopping up action, or we up the numbers, and get it done sooner."

"I'm exhausted!" he gasped. "Ten hours, like *this*?"

"There's probably a queen somewhere and her hive guards too," I deliberately assured him, clapping him on the shoulder and nearly throwing him to the ground. "Don't worry, it won't get boring!"

"Gods below, we're all gonna die," he whispered, staring out across the field of bodies.

"Nah. Though, I don't know about you, but I am getting hungry." I turned, looking, and found Marteen not far away. "Hey, have we got any chefs?" I asked him.

"Uh, we have a camp cook?" he offered. "No chefs, nothing that fancy, but a cook who usually manages not to poison anyone."

"Excellent. Do they know any recipes for giant scorpion?"

"Oh gods…" The man next to me whimpered.

"It's protein," I pointed out, and he just stared at me in confusion and disgust. "No? Never heard of that? Okay, think of it as meat, that's all!"

"Ah, I don't think so," Marteen said diplomatically when I looked back to him, waiting for an answer.

"You want to ask him?" I suggested. "You never know!"

"Considering he's standing to your left, I don't think it's likely, Lord." He smiled, and I looked at the horrified and no longer talkative man, then sighed.

"Well, look on the bright side," I suggested to my new cook. "You're off the fighting line for a bit, because we all need some food, and that's a hell of a lot of it that's spoiling on all sides right now."

"Want me to start pulling again?" Sehran called down, and I nodded.

"Might as well get to it," I prompted the cook, directing him to a nearby smoking carcass the size of a family car. "We're gonna need a hearty meal, and I don't doubt there's some meat on that thing."

The next few waves were almost routine, if you could call fighting giant scorpions routine.

We'd settled into a rhythm. Sehran would draw them in. Oracle would control the battlefield with her magic, funneling them into set areas where they could be controlled and attacked easier—it helped that because the others were sworn to me, they weren't injured by the flames; instead, they were healed. And I'd lead our forces in cleaning up whatever made it through. The survivors gained confidence with each victory, their movements becoming more coordinated, more assured.

"Another group incoming!" Oracle called out as we started clearing the area around us again; several people had been detailed to just collect and dispose of the bodies. "Smaller this time, maybe fifteen!"

I was about to acknowledge when Sehran suddenly stopped, watching them, then dropped from the sky like a stone. Her wings snapped tight against her back as she landed hard beside me. Her usual grace was gone, replaced by urgent tension.

"Something's happening," she reported quickly. Her eyes scanned the horizon, making sure whatever she'd seen wasn't coming this way. "There's some kind of disturbance in the center of the city, near where the dome was. I can't see what it is exactly—it's underground—but it's big. I can sense a lot of life, like thousands of bodies, and they're swarming." She shook her head. "As many as there are, we can't hold them if they come this way next, not in one wave."

I cursed under my breath. "How many scorpions between us and there?"

"That's just it," she repeated. "They're *swarming*. The group that was incoming just spun around and ran. All of them in sight are doing the same thing. Abandoning everything else and streaming inward in a great wave. I've never seen anything like it. The way they're moving? It's like the things underground, all controlled and moving as one creature. Should I scout for survivors while we have the chance?"

"You think it's them?" I asked, seriously considering falling back if that was the case.

"No, but the way they're moving, I think that if there's a queen in the hive, it's controlling all the other scorpions somehow. Maybe before we weren't worth the bother. Now, though? Whatever's going on is more important than us."

I considered our options quickly. The plaza was secure for now, and we had enough fighters to hold it as long as things didn't get too crazy. "Do it. But be careful. Whatever's spooking the scorpions might be worse."

As soon as she took off, I started to give orders.

"Okay, people!" I shouted. "Looks like there's something going on in the center, so this is going to be your only chance to rest for a while. I want you split into three teams. Those who have been relaxing on the roof are going to form two of those teams. One stays on watch—which group is up to you up on the roof," I clarified, considering that Oracle had made it clear there were several crossbowmen up there with her who were down to their last bolt and were trying to hide that, so that they didn't have to go back down and actually fight.

"The second group gets to recover bolts, and help strip the plaza, get everyone fed and watered, while those who have been fighting down here, in the shit? That group's going to be resting!"

Over the next hour, Sehran made three separate trips, each time returning with small groups of Changed Ones. Unlike the heavily mutated creatures we'd fought in the dome, these were clearly more recent victims. Their transformations were minimal: a few patches of minor chitin here and there, patches that were missing hair, slightly altered eyes, an extra joint or limb struggling to emerge.

"They were taken in the last few weeks," Amelia explained as she came to me after helping one of them, a young woman with faintly glowing eyes, get settled. "The binding was weaker on them. That's why they survived when it broke."

Dex worked alongside her, his own mutations seeming to put the newcomers at ease. They'd found their purpose in this, helping these victims adjust, offering hope that they could still have a future, as well as explaining that there was some hope that a skilled enough healer could help, but that if they wanted more information and to stay with our group, they'd be required to swear an oath.

The last group was just being brought through our defensive line when Sehran came streaking back.

*"Sand wurms!"* she sent to Oracle and me through the bond. *"At least three of them, maybe more. They've breached the foundations under the city center. That's what was causing the disturbance—they're hunting the scorpions!"*

*"The scorpions are their natural prey,"* Oracle realized. *"And yesterday's fighting, all that magical energy we released when we destroyed the binding chamber…"*

*"It drew them straight to us,"* I finished. *"How many scorpions are heading that way?"*

*"All of them,"* Sehran replied. *"It's like watching water drain from a bath. They're all converging on the center, either to fight or flee…I couldn't tell which."*

A plan formed in my mind. *"The wurms will keep them occupied. This might be our best chance to sweep the rest of the city."* I turned to address our gathered forces. "Zyenna, Toren, Marteen, get your people as ready to move as possible, but hold this position. This is now our fallback point if things go wrong."

"And you?" Finna asked, though her tone suggested she already knew the answer.

"I'm going to make sure we have enough firepower to take advantage of this opportunity." I settled into a meditation pose, closing my eyes. "Oracle, keep watch. Sehran, rest and recover. When those wurms are done with the scorpions, they might come looking for dessert."

As I began to gather mana, I couldn't help but smile. Sometimes the gods of chaos threw you a gift—the trick was being ready to catch it when they did.

"Just so we're clear," Marteen's voice drifted over, heavy with disbelief. "We're actually happy that there are giant underground monsters attacking the city?"

"Welcome to the legion," Sehran deadpanned. "Where the worst day of your life is usually just the warm-up act."

# CHARACTER SHEET

| Name: Jax Amon | | | | |
|---|---|---|---|---|
| Title: Godslayer | | | | |
| **Class**: Sorcerer II | | | **Renown**: Imperial Scion, Prince of Dravith, Master of Himnel and Narkolt | |
| **Level**: 48 | | | **Progress**: 4,638,488/6,455,000 | |
| **Patron**: Jenae, Goddess of Fire and Exploration | | | **Points to Distribute**: 0 <br> **Meridian Points to Invest**: 0 | |
| Stat | Current points | Description | Effect | Progress to next level |
| Agility | 82 | Governs dodge and movement | +720% maximum movement speed and reflexes | 1/100 |
| Charisma | 61 (56) | Governs likely success to charm, seduce, or threaten | +51% success chance in interactions with other beings | 21/100 |
| Constitution | 120 (118) | Governs health and health regeneration | 2400 health, regen 160 points per 600 seconds (each point invested now worth 20 health) | N/A |
| Dexterity | 93 | Governs ability with weapons and crafting success | +83% to weapon proficiency, +93% to the chances of crafting success | 7/100 |
| Endurance | 71 (68) | Governs stamina and stamina regeneration | 2130 stamina, regen 52 points per 30 seconds (each point invested now worth 30 stamina) | 9/100 |
| Intelligence | 201 | Governs base mana and number of spells able to be learned | 2210 mana, spell capacity: 102 (100 + 2, +200 mana from items) | N/A |
| Luck | 72 | Governs overall chance of bonuses | +62% chance of a favorable outcome | 1/100 |
| Perception | 70 (60) | Governs ranged damage and chance to spot traps or hidden items | +60% ranged damage, +60% chance to spot traps or hidden items | 87/100 |

| | | | | |
|---|---|---|---|---|
| Strength | 76 (73) | Governs damage with melee weapons and carrying capacity | +76 damage with melee weapons, +76% maximum carrying capacity | 31/100 |
| Wisdom | 100 (90) | Governs mana regeneration and memory | +1350% mana recovery, 15 points per minute | N/A |

# CHAPTER EIGHT

The hour of meditation passed slowly. Despite my recent struggles with sitting still and focusing, the combination of adrenaline and the pressing need for mana should have had little effect. I was used to it, after all—it wasn't like my normal meditation attempts were done in rooms with gongs and whispering fountains.

It was Bane, I realized. Usually the mad bastard was around somewhere, and I could meditate, knowing that no matter what, he was watching over me.

Without him, and with the absolute bowel-numbing terror of Oracle's pregnancy adding to it, I was just so much more unsettled than usual it wasn't funny.

Twice I'd nearly lost her, and twice I'd barely gotten her back, mainly through absolutely excessive violence. And now I wasn't taking any risks.

The distant sounds of combat—muffled roars, the crunch of chitin, and occasional tremors that shook loose sand from the ruins around us—provided a constant reminder of what waited.

When I finally opened my eyes, both Oracle and Sehran were ready. I'd felt them coordinating through our bond during the meditation, planning our approach and—because, oh joy, what we really needed was more enemies—the wyverns had started appearing about twenty minutes ago. First as distant specks against the sky, then growing bolder and in larger numbers as the scent of blood and death drew them closer.

We ended up moving everyone inside the nearest buildings to keep them safe before we set off, and the looks we were getting as we walked toward the exit were telling.

"Ready?" I asked, though I already knew the answer through our bond.

"We're at full mana," Oracle confirmed. "Though I still think this is crazy."

"When isn't it?" I grinned, checking my weapons were secure. "Sehran?"

"Also ready," she replied, her wings twitching with anticipation. "Though I agree with Oracle about the crazy part."

"Want to reconsider the plan?" I asked them both.

"Oh no." Oracle shook her head. "I can't wait. And this is definitely a case of your problems solving each other, if we manage this right."

We carefully moved through the ruins, staying low and using the buildings for cover rather than flying, thanks to the additional observers that now flew overhead.

The sounds of combat grew louder with each block we crossed. The destruction was obvious: entire sections of the city had collapsed inward, creating a warren of broken stone and twisted metal that led down into the shattered under city, with the Dome of Truth as its center.

When we finally reached a position where we could properly see the battle below, I had to force myself not to whistle in appreciation. The carnage was beyond anything I'd expected.

Thousands of scorpion bodies littered the ground, their black blood turning the sand into a toxic soup. The hundreds of smaller ones had been literally crushed or torn apart, while dozens of the larger specimens lay broken and scattered like discarded toys. A sand wurm—easily twice the size of the one we'd fought in the desert—lay dead, its segmented body coiled around the ruins of what had once been a temple or something similar, I was guessing.

"Oracle, Sehran, remember that there," I whispered, pointing to a shattered carving of a deity. "I doubt there's going to be any altars to Jenae or the others here—the dark dick destroyed all he could, after all—but we need to be sure."

The upper floors, well, the usual ground floor of the city, had collapsed inward, revealing hundreds of buried rooms, some as shallow as cellars, but many digging deep into the bedrock underneath.

Here and there, I could see holes that had been bored through, and sections that looked melted and ripped, like the wurms on their way in had been setting up a subway system for the next generation.

In the collapsed sections, the rubble from overhead had filled some of these areas, with the debris creating ramps and caverns, half-buried nooks and wide-open areas that had then been covered in swarming scorpions.

They'd then been reduced to cracked shells and paste by the passage of the massive wurms, each hundreds of meters long, as well as a handful of much, much smaller brethren that had died unnoticed in the battle.

It was a mess of marble, slaughtered scorpions and sandstone, iron and ichor, debris and dust. The fight had been *vicious*.

Regardless, though, it was the ongoing battle that held our attention. Two more wurms, both bearing grievous injuries, were locked in combat with something that had to be the scorpion queen. She was massive, her carapace gleaming with an oily iridescence that put her children's dull black to shame. Where they had single stingers, she had three, each dripping with venom that smoked when it hit the ground.

She was also…wrong.

I guessed it was something to do with the effect of the magical changes that the Changed Ones had been doing over the centuries, but she was covered in additional arms, rippled creases in the chitin, and growths that just looked cancerous.

She was burned and blackened, her injuries clear even from here. Whatever the destruction of the machinery had done to the Changed Ones had clearly affected her as well. Judging from the glowing green eyes, and the whole "three fuckin' tails," I guessed she was more lethal still than her spawn.

Above it all, the wyverns circled. I counted at least eight of them, growing increasingly agitated as they dove and snapped at each other, their territorial instincts warring with their desire to feast on the bounty below.

"The one on the left is dying," Sehran whispered, indicating the more badly injured wurm. "Venom's working through its system, I bet, considering how many stingers are still sticking out of it. The other one, though…" She gestured to where the second wurm had just slammed into a building, using the impact to launch itself at the queen's flank.

"Sehran," I nodded toward the far side where the remains of the Dome of Truth had once stood, "think you can get close enough to spot some weak points?"

She grinned, her form already beginning to blur and shift as she adapted for stealth. "Give me a few minutes."

I nodded and she set off, even as Oracle started to point out the kind of things we'd need, and the most likely spells.

Explosive Compression was going to be doing a lot of the heavy lifting here, considering that although half of the big old capital building had collapsed, there was still around a third of it left.

If we could set off a landslide for that, well, that'd solve a lot of our problems nicely.

The exposed section that the titans were fighting in ran up to the edge of what was left of the building, with the remnants precariously perched there. Half the underneath was gone, and it looked like a few good impacts would be enough to set off another collapse.

If we could angle it this way, though? That'd be a really nasty surprise for the combatants.

The open area we were watching over was roughly a hundred meters at its deepest, and perhaps fifteen at the shallowest point, with several streets and buildings having fallen into massive rents in the earth.

Whatever had been happening down there, the real machinery that did the damage oh so long ago hadn't been constructed originally in the capital building. It'd been spread out over several side buildings and an entire underground complex, with what looked like the main focal point in the Dome of Truth.

That also explained why, when we destroyed it, the collapse of the city had gone on so long, and why the scorpions had fled so wildly.

For a species that saw with a mix of eyes and vibrations—like those bastard spiders as well—it must have seemed like the world was ending.

With them then trying to return and whatever injuries they took in the main event, no wonder the queen had them all riled up.

Last of all, add in that the sand wurms had to be seeing by vibrations as well, and boom. It was like we'd rung the dinner bell.

That raised a bad point, though.

"Oracle, why haven't the wyverns spotted you?" I asked her. "I mean, they did before…they were ignoring me to chase you."

"Meat," she said. "They'll sense my magic, and they'll identify me as meat. I'd imagine that's why they're coming after me—after all, they're not like you, chasing these." She laid a finger on her chest and winked at me. "They're looking for food, and why bother with a tiny snack like me, you, or Sehran, when there is enough meat to keep a hundred of them fed for a week openly on display right there?"

She had a point. The dead sand wurm alone was huge, hundreds of meters long and at least ten thick. And the wyverns? They ranged from my size—plus wings— to about three times that on average, with a single one that was five times my size.

While she scouted, Oracle and I watched the aerial battle intensifying. The wyverns were working themselves into a frenzy, their screeching calls echoing off the ruins as they fought for dominance. That particularly large specimen had already killed two of its rivals, though the victories had cost it part of its tail and it was now dripping blood as it flew.

*"Look at those support columns there,"* Oracle sent through our bond. *"If we time it right…"*

*"We can bring the whole thing down on their heads,"* I finished. *"But we need to be careful. Too much at once and we'll drive them all away. Too little…"*

*"And we waste our advantage,"* she agreed. *"Sehran's found something."*

Our companion's voice whispered through the bond, accompanied by mental images of structural weak points she'd identified. *"There's an entire network of chambers down here. If we collapse the right supports, we can open it all up and turn this whole area into a killing ground."*

*"Maybe we need to drive them toward the dome with a few well-placed circles…just get them closer to that end, and then we take out the supports?"* Sehran suggested. *"Let the whole thing fall?"*

I grinned, already gathering mana for the first Explosive Compression spell. *"Ladies, let's add some chaos to this party."*

Oracle hit her targets first, both closer to our end of the tear in the city, flaring to life and killing or injuring a great swathe of the remaining scorpions, as well as making the less damaged wurm shriek in pain, twisting and heading back away from the frostfire flames.

The result was to drive the wurms back toward the far side, and the scorpion queen backed up as well. Their fight now rolled in that direction, as the last wave of scorpions—that had presumably been farther out in the city—poured inward.

Several wyverns dove, attacking things that were out of sight from where we huddled. But as one started laboriously climbing into the air again, a dead scorpion being carried by the tail, others started to hunt as well.

My first spell hit one of the support columns just as the badly injured wurm made another lunge for the queen. The timing couldn't have been better, from my point of view. The explosion of compressed energy streaked across the intervening distance and passed over the head of the massive creature mid-strike. It cracked into the column on the far side, then detonated, sending chunks of ancient stonework raining down.

More importantly, as it did so, the sections that stood above it shuddered and twisted, aided by Sehran using her own version of the spell. It worked by detonating and shoving outward, pushing everything away from the center of the impact, then pausing and ripping it all back inward.

Oh, and fire—so *much* fire.

My own variant, honed and evolved, could crush bone and meat that would have passed as solid, a meter cubed, into a space the size of an average marble, so when it encountered already weakened, badly overloaded supports…well.

It was effective, put it that way.

Entire sections began to fall, aided along because I wasn't firing one—I fired four, one after the other.

Oracle managed two more, and Sehran managed two. Between them, the first effect was an insane landslide of rock and debris. The second? It opened a section of the upper level, letting shafts of sunlight pierce the gloom.

The buildings overhead fell, and they fell fast. Hundreds of tons of stone and ancient marble tumbled, and one of the onrushing giant scorpions was hit by a statue that had to have been fifty meters tall once, the warrior it depicted achieving one final kill centuries after her immortalization.

The bug practically detonated—blood, chitin, and ichor flying in all directions—and it coated a wurm that had just reared back, about to crush its smaller foe.

The effect on the wyverns was immediate. Three of them dove into the new pit, their territorial screeching rising to a fever pitch as the viscera overrode whatever brains they had.

It was like watching feral seagulls mobbing a beachgoer.

The wurm's momentary distraction cost it dearly, as while it was shaking, trying to make sense of the still ongoing collapse, one of the queen's stingers found its mark, punching through armor-like segments to inject more venom into its already failing system.

Unfortunately, I winced as I spotted what else I'd managed to hit with the falling building.

The temple.

If there was anything in there we could have used, it'd take a team of archaeologists, a jigsaw enthusiast, and a damn Caterpillar construction team to recover it now.

Fuck it—easy come, easy go.

"That's the second wurm nearly done," I muttered, turning back and watching as it thrashed in its death throes. "Think we should help the other one a bit?"

"The wyverns are getting bolder," Oracle observed as another pair dove through our newly created skylight. "But they're still staying high, out of reach of the stingers."

Through our bond, Sehran sent an image of another structural weakness she'd identified. *"That support beam there, it's the only one that's holding on!"*

*"Jax, we're going to need more mana, and soon,"* Oracle added. *"If you can start meditating, I'll hit that."*

I sighed, then nodded. It was instinctive; I wanted to be the one flinging spells, not the glorified battery. But she was right. I settled back deeper into the shadows of the building we were hiding in, as she started to gather mana for another Explosive Compression.

The spell was perfect for this: controlled demolition with just enough boom to make things interesting. If the wurms survived this—or the queen, though—Oracle was right. The wyverns might attack us, keeping out of range of their stingers and jaw to pepper our trio with constant attacks. But we were only in danger of exhaustion at this point.

If we wanted to win this, once the scorpions and wurms were dead, we'd need to focus on them. And for that? We'd need mana.

The next explosion apparently brought down a larger section of the upper structure. More sunlight flooded in, along with a cascade of debris that forced the combatants closer together. The remaining wurm took advantage of the queen's momentary distraction to slam into her side, its segmented body coiling around her in an attempt to constrict.

The wyverns' screeching reached new heights as they dove and wheeled through the expanded opening. Their attacks were still tentative—testing strikes against the wurm's exposed back, quick snaps and lightning bolts unleashed at the queen's waving stingers—but growing bolder with each pass.

*"We should start a betting pool,"* Sehran suggested through our bond. *"Ten gold says the queen takes them all."*

*"Like gold has any meaning for any of us at this point,"* Oracle replied. *"But I'd put twenty on at least half the wyverns killing each other before this is over if we did."*

*"How about a back rub?"* Sehran suggested, and I stifled a groan, forcing the awareness of them aside as I buried myself deeper and deeper in my meditation. *"If you win, I'll give you one. If I win, you give me one. And if Jax wins, we give each other a full-body one, naked?"*

I choked that mental image off with herculean effort.

At least, with the knowledge that the fight was going well enough for them to discuss massages, I managed to block the rest of the world out to a degree that I finally succeeded to activate the first level of compression for my meditations.

The box I imagined consisted of something I thought of as "hard light," though it could be air as much as anything, as it wasn't really either.

I visualized a literal pane of glowing light—or air—that was flat and hovering to the right of me; then I created another, and another. As the seconds passed, I formed all six, then slid them together into what was essentially a solid cube. I placed that around me, leaving me sitting inside the box.

With that done, I visualized the rest of the world—all noises, distractions, sensations and more, discomforts of the body and chaos of the mind—being blocked out on the far side.

Once that was done, then I started the much harder part.

The mana around me was sluggish. It seeped into me, if that was the right word, and into the others around us. It didn't aim to flow in and replace the mana I'd used on doing whatever…it simply *was*.

When there was a vacuum, a space that it hadn't filled…it'd gradually slide into it. And that was the secret—when you increased your Wisdom, you essentially formed some kind of a mental gradient, a slight decline that drew the mana in, ever so slightly quicker.

That wasn't it entirely, as well I knew. There wasn't a natural level that was just filling, any more than mana was a cloud, or a field, or a river or any of the various ways that I'd heard it described.

What mattered was that when there was a gap, it would try to fill it. When I cast a spell, I didn't whisper "Hey mate, you see that big bug over there? Go fuck him up for me, all right?"

Mana didn't whisper back with a Scottish accent that "Aye, nee botha, mate, ah'll go kick 'is fuckin' teeth in!"

It was a force of nature, and now, I knew that it was only part of the equation.

The quest that I'd received that spoke of it being "half" the overall existence made more sense to me when I visualized mana as a floating cloud, a fog that rolled across the ground, then seeped into the depressions that were caused when we used it.

Mainly because visualizing the mana like that—that it flowed along the ground—it also created an impression of a flat surface it floated across the barrier of, one that then had *something* on the other side.

I deliberately didn't focus on that, though, because what I *was* focusing on was the mana and its movement.

The box served to insulate me from all distractions, and when I no longer had them to mess with my mind, I felt the way that the panels of glowing light dragged the mana in that slight bit faster.

Reaching out, I slowly created the panels for the second level, complicated because unlike the first, I couldn't slide a single panel into place and hold it there with glue made up of my mind.

This time, I needed two panels at once. I slid them into place in tandem; the left and right panels glittered as I put them in place on either side of the cube around me.

They were roughly twice the size of the original panels. I held them there, pulling in the second pair, slotting them into place behind and before me.

The square glittered and gleamed, mana increasing in its draw down to me, as I continued to build.

The roof and floor were next. For the first time, as I slid the panel below me into place, I felt…something.

I'd maintained my mental image of the world as I'd visualized it before the plane of the ecliptic forming the floor under me. As I built, I'd created the panels on either side, and for whatever reason, when I'd done that, and I'd created the larger panels of the second layer, I'd set that away on the floor, growing upward as well.

Now, as I tried to slide the next layer into place, the roof had no issue, but the floor?

It felt…sticky?

Like I was rubbing rubber against rubber, the way that you could force it, but it would squeal and rub, doing minor damage to both sections, and…

A sudden cold made me gasp as it struck through into my heart, a cold I recognized—a cold I damn well *feared.*

It was the cold of the grave, the grave where Amon had reached out from long ago to touch me as we were being carried through the streets of Himnel.

It was the cold of the veil between life and death, that second realm where the dead slept, where the souls of those who had gone before awaited now. And as I touched it, as I felt the connection, two things happened.

First, my health dropped. It dropped like a stone as I somehow formed a bridge between the realms, connecting myself literally to the other side of the veil.

Heat, warmth, and sensation flooded free and into that side of the veil. The touch of life in a realm that was entirely its antithesis shifted the walls of reality, and for just a second, I was back there, where I'd once stood with Amon.

A cave, the walls of undressed stone, a ceiling high overhead dotted with stalactites and stalagmites soaring past me, reaching back from the ground upward.

The cavern was small. I could probably reach out with both hands and touch either wall, and yet I also knew that should I try, I'd find that the walls were so far apart, that entire stars could flare and die and never be noticed in its vastness.

The one detail, though, that captured my eye entirely was the veil.

It bisected the cavern, like a pane of water that ran almost crystal smooth from the ceiling to the floor.

The other side, when I'd seen Amon, had been filled by him, and shadowed. Now he was gone, gone to his rest, and instead the "water" beyond looked like I'd thrown a bucket of blood into the sea.

Worse still, as I pushed back instinctively, I sensed the approach of things, creatures that hunted that shadowy realm. Like megalodons cruising in the shallows of Earth's ancient seas, they sensed the nearness of life, and they wanted it.

I pushed back, hard, the place between the realms fading from sight, even as I distantly heard Oracle, her voice hushed, yet panicked and desperate as she shook me.

She called to me to return, to go to her, and I blinked. The last vestiges of the cavern between realms faded, as a new sense bloomed.

I reached my right hand up, and in the air between us, as Oracle was crouched, checking on me, I dragged my right hand downward, focusing on a feeling, on something…

It was another form of magic, something tied to the quest I had. As I slid my hand down—that was all…nothing much more than a gesture—the walls of reality around me seemed to shake like the skin of a beat drum.

A void opened, a void between the realms. For a split second, I saw them; I sensed them on the far side. The Valspar.

They were explorers and wielders of the other form of magic, those that existed on entropy, where time did not touch and all reality was an illusion.

I felt them, and… They. Felt. Me.

The void between us shuddered and fragmented, the air around us being sucked through into the far side, before the edges…*regrew*?

The void didn't seal itself like a door closing. It was more like a wound being stitched together: the reaching, questing filaments of two sides of a cut bonding back together, sealing over and closing as forms of madness and creatures of the depths of time and space—things that should never have existed—reached toward it hungrily.

Again, not knowing what or how I did it, I reached out and smoothed the wound over, smearing the walls of reality back together, as Oracle stared.

The rip faded. Its last segments popped with a faint noise of a soap bubble breaking, and I blinked.

*"What in the Lord of the Depths' left testicle truncator did you just do?!"* Sehran hissed through the bond. *"I felt that! I felt the breaking of the realm, and so…"*

"So did they," Oracle whispered, turning slowly.

I forced myself to my feet, staggering a little, and made it closer to the edge of the building, to where I could see out, to look across the cavern, and the sky, only to find silence.

The monsters below us, wild and terrible things, natural enemies that had for hundreds of years been preying on each other, had stopped their endless battles and instead stared up at us. And the wyverns above stared down.

There was a long moment of perfect silence; then it all shattered as they all screeched in perfect synchronicity. A dozen mouths—of various shapes and sizes— all declared their immediate hatred and need to find me, and fuck me up in *oh so many* fun ways.

# <u>BANE</u>

"**I**'m telling you, Bane, it's goddamn weird, that's all," Grizz grumbled to the multi-limbed assassin as he stretched slowly. "Like Yen *always* knows where I am."

"She's a member of the Speculatores Praetoria, so maybe that's it?" Bane rumbled, his voice as always full of harmonies that the seasoned legionnaire barely understood.

"Dammit, man, that's just it. She's a scout. Sure, they're skilled—they existed to act as the legion's 'diplomatic' sort of Knife in the Dark." He shook his head. "They get called on to do all the crappy jobs, not like the rest of the legion, where we're more there to hunt monsters and fight armies, in the name of the empire. No, she and all her kind were there to make the nobles behave. They were there to sniff out corruption, to have the authority to investigate, and then when they needed to, to literally hang the fuckers with their own ropes."

"Sounds fun," Bane suggested.

"You think?" Grizz snorted, shaking his head as he thought about his new fiancée. "For the last seven hundred years, every time they turned around, they had their responsibilities reduced. They were told, 'We can't do that' or 'Be more diplomatic; make a suggestion, not an example.'"

"Sounds less fun," Bane said. "So, what's the issue?"

"She's back to full authority!" he practically wailed. "I'm a centurion. I lead a hundred of my fellow legionnaires. I'm the last living goddamn knight of the legion. And the worst part of all that? I'm now officially higher in the pecking order than she is, and yet when she gives an order? I jump!"

"Sounds like any mating I've ever heard of." Bane thrummed, his equivalent of a laugh, and Grizz glared at him. "I mean it!" He gestured to Grizz to calm down. "You saw the way that Flux ran for it when Ame was on the warpath yesterday."

"I mean I have to *literally* jump!" Grizz growled. "Literally, I'm compelled by my oath to obey. She's outside of the usual chain of command and now, so am I!"

"You're higher than her?"

"Well, yeah, sort of..." Grizz hedged, now sounding unsure. "I mean, I'm the only legion knight, all right? They came from the speculatores originally, and they're like the, well, the evolution of them. Like the way that the Praetorian Guard came from the legion."

"So, you had a promotion past her?" Bane pushed. "Restun, Romanus, or Jax told you that you were higher now?"

"No," he admitted. "But I mean, that's what they were, right?"

"So you're a higher rank than her, and than, say, Lydia? So you don't have to obey her either?"

"Fuck, no, man—she's the optio!"

"But you're a knight," Bane pointed out reasonably, while knowing exactly what Grizz was struggling with now.

"Fuck, no, man, she's...well, it's different, that's all! I need to, just...because..." He trailed off, and Bane stared at him thoughtfully.

Bane, like Flux and Ame, the other two Tia'Almer-atic—or "mer" as they were colloquially known—had no eyes, seeing instead through a complicated setup that Jax often referred to as a form of "sonar," whatever that was.

It allowed him to pick out the world around him in incredible detail, and as such, it meant that he frequently noticed things that others seemed to miss.

Like the way that the massive legionnaire was doing his best to hide from the woman he professed to love, and he'd sought him out to ask why.

He was also very deliberately not asking questions about the bruising that he could sense below the waist on the pair of them, as judging from the sounds that echoed from their cabin each night, Grizz and Yen certainly weren't having issues with the physical side of their relationship.

All in all, he found the whole situation highly amusing, even more so when Grizz finally admitted why it was a problem.

"Look, I thought—you know, I'm literally the only legion knight around—so I thought that I could get my own back a little. All those push-ups she made me do…I thought, this was my chance to get my own back, so I went for it!"

"And?"

"And yeah, she's *still* outside of the chain of command!" he hissed. "She ordered me to spar with Flux as his training dummy for the rest of the trip, *and* gave him authority over me!"

"He's our trainer and Jax's—he has the authority to order almost anyone, as he's also in charge of Jax's spies," Bane pointed out. "Nothing's changed there."

"It damn well has when my body obeys him instead of me!" Grizz snarled. "The only way it could be worse is if Restun started doing it!"

"Doesn't he…"

"Of course he does!" Grizz half wept, half snarled. "Argh, you don't understand!"

"Not really, no."

"Just because Restun or the primus could order me to do a million push-ups until my arms dropped off doesn't mean they will, okay? The oaths are structured very carefully in the legion. They can't order me to do something against my will that will result in real harm, unless it's for a real reason. Like if I tried to run, instead of standing and fighting?

"They could do it then, though I don't know of any legionnaire who would ever do it. That means that she and Flux are doing this, knowing that it's in my own best interests! They know that I'm learning and improving all the time!"

"And you don't want this?" Bane asked, now thoroughly confused.

"Of course I do, I just… Look, sometimes a guy just needs a little downtime, okay? A chance to kick back, to let the clouds stream past, to watch the sun reflecting off the waves and drink a little ale, and SHE ORDERED ME TO NOT DRINK ALCOHOL AGAIN UNTIL JAX IS SAFE!"

"Ah…"

"AH?" Grizz practically yelled. "Fucking 'ah'? Is that it? What, you think I've got a problem now? I'm a fucking legionnaire, Bane, all right?! I've seen shit you can't imagine, all right? When you were still in the pond, I was being stitched back together after getting gutted by feenals! I…"

He started to rant about how it was ridiculous, that he didn't need any help, and certainly not with his drinking. And that was the crux of it—Bane saw it all clearly. Despite knowing it wasn't the issue, he also understood it. He saw the issue with the chain of command, which was clearly down to Grizz either not believing that he was over her, or that he genuinely wasn't. He knew he'd not had a formal promotion, but had instead been named a knight, but had no background in the Speculatores to draw upon. That put him in a grey area between his old rank and new.

The legion, like many armed forces over the years, had come up with a solution to this, and it was the practice of "claiming" a rank instead.

Much as Lydia had taken the Optio rank, her higher-ups had steered her into a position where she had the chance to step up and claim it, if she was ready, or to stay quiet. Had she stayed silent, a new Optio would have been found and put in command. She hadn't. Just as any soldier would, when the slot was free—if say, the sarge had fallen in battle, and the soldiers around her needed leadership—she'd stepped up, laying claim to the role and rank.

It was formally approved afterward, but in a group as small and close-knit as the legion had become, it was a situation where the right person was steered incredibly carefully.

He'd been put in that position to grow, and when he'd responded to Yen giving him orders, it was because in his heart, he wasn't ready to take that rank yet.

Grizz was many things—and yes, he was an outstanding legionnaire—but in the last fight, it'd been Jax who had rescued them all, and it was Jax, the Prince of the Empire, who had been lost.

He was somewhere thousands of miles to the east now, alone, for all intents and purposes, as he certainly didn't have the legion with him anyway.

He was there, and they were here, and they'd failed the one man who gave them purpose.

Bane got it, and he'd been throwing himself into his training with everything he had, determined to never fail their prince again.

For Grizz—the man who was practically a walking legion recruitment poster—it was worse. As much as the others were all there too, he believed that, right or wrong, the legion would blame him *personally* if anything happened to Jax.

As a member of his protection detail, that was true, but it was made even more so because not only were Jax and Grizz close friends, but Grizz had been publicly ordered by Augustus to literally perform that duty.

He was the designated shield to the prince—a man who was always supposed to take the spell, blade, or whatever that was aimed at the heart of the empire. He'd done it in the past—hell, he'd already died doing just that…twice, for fuck's sake, and Jax had to literally warp reality to bring him back. To make it worse, Thomas certainly had made it clear he did blame him.

Thomas had also been furious at the situation and had been lashing out, but that didn't make it any less valid.

He was a legionnaire with the safety of the prince of the empire personally entrusted to him, and he'd been captured. It'd taken that prince being fired across the damn realm into who knew where to save *them*.

Bane was hurting himself training so hard, but there were healers.

Grizz, on the other hand, had found his solace in a bottle, and when Yen realized it was getting out of hand, she'd been very, very clear that it wasn't going to continue.

As such, until there was a better plan for him, Yen had been ordering him to train, to work out and to improve himself in every possible way she could come up with, in order to keep him from either crawling into a bottle, or doing something even stupider.

Worse still was that none of those aboard ship were any better. Including the gnomes who were constantly rebuilding, tweaking, and "fixing the ship."

That was the reason Bane had been awoken in the early hours as his bedroom wall was sawed through two nights ago. One of the little bastards decided they could shave as much as two hours off the overall transit time if they got rid of "unnecessary weight," and had decided that internal bulkheads qualified as that.

Tenandra had been unimpressed, and the gnome had been given several hours to reconsider making unauthorized demolitions to her ship-body, by being tied to the very top of the central mast and left there.

Now, between the gnomes, Jax's squad, and the ship's highly limited crew, finding a quiet place to consider things was becoming harder and harder.

Add in that Grizz couldn't exactly admit to himself that he'd been on the edge of a breakdown, and the situation only got worse.

"Look, no offense, but if you found me, then she's not far behind, so I'm just gonna…" Grizz started, only to close his eyes and swallow hard as a new voice joined their conversation from behind.

"Morning, Bane, Grizz," Yen said cheerfully as she strode out of the shadows where Grizz had watched her take up station a few seconds ago. "How's training going?"

"Just fine!" Grizz growled. "I'm on my mandated rest period."

"Glad to hear it, Grizz." Yen sighed, as he forced a smile for her, then made an excuse to leave.

"He still loves you, I'm sure," Bane said, after waiting to be sure Grizz had turned the far corner and could no longer hear, seeing her shoulders had slumped. "He knows you're doing it to help him—he admitted that."

"But he's still like this, every chance he gets." Yen sighed again. "What do I do, Bane? How do I break him out of this?"

"Why do you all think I'm good at relationship advice?" Bane asked, his voice full of amusement. "You see my wonderful success there?"

"Point." Yen smiled. "It's more that I'm hoping for a fresh perspective."

"Well, it's certainly not coming from a place of experience," Bane admitted, "but have you tried talking to him?"

"I did. That's when he decided that I was blaming him as well, and he hit the bottle."

"But we were all there."

"Exactly. I think that's what makes it worse," Yen admitted. "That he's feeling it—we all are—and he knows it doesn't make any sense. He's the one Augustus was grooming to replace him, you know that, yeah?"

"As primus of the Third?"

"Yeah." She nodded. "He's never faced anything he couldn't succeed at, but protecting Jax is proving to be exactly that. It makes it even worse that he keeps rescuing members of the squad, and doing things that we know he shouldn't be able to each time. We all train with him, and know where his limits should be. Hell, a year ago, he was basically a tavern wench, to hear him tell it.

"I mean, I know he's the prince, I know he's the chosen of Amon and all that. I know it—but to see that in a year he's gone from slinging beers and talking shit, to, well…"

"Stabbing things and talking shit?" Bane offered, and Yen snorted.

"Yeah, I suppose you've got me there." She sighed. "He does that well, that's for sure. I think it's just that we all train together, and we know he's not that incredible a fighter, you understand? He's a natural, but he's just so…"

"Vicious." Bane shrugged. "If you stabbed him through the heart and loaded him onto a spit, then roasted him for a week, before dropping what was left in a vat of cheelong, then poured out the mess that was left? As soon as you turned your back on it, it'd attack you."

"That's…yeah, actually, that's Jax." She smiled despite herself. "And I think that's part of the problem. We know he's like that, and it's not skill—it's who he is. That we can kick his ass in training, and yet he still does that and ends up rescuing us is a constant annoyance, that's all. Some of us handle that better than others."

"He's not used to failure," Bane guessed.

"Exactly. And he has to work his way through that, before he can grow. Now, I could leave him to find his own way through, but what he doesn't realize, yet, is that when his body is working like this, when he's ordered to give his all in training, he can actually slip his mind into a different place.

"Thomas called it 'running in neutral,' whatever that is, when we spoke about his time in the Dark Legion where they did it as well, but in the Imperial Legion we call it battle meditation." She went on. "When your body is fully running like this, your mind becomes free, free to see everything around you. It's how Augustus can literally stride through entire battles without so much as a scratch, because when you learn to do it consciously, to allow your body to do what it's been fully trained to do, without fear, without delays for assessment because you're that much 'in the zone,' it's terrifying."

"But he's doing it because of his oath of service," Bane pointed out.

"He is currently," she agreed. "But he knows, and all legionnaires do, that you can break that conditioning if you need to. It's deliberately phrased, in our service, that it can only be used to compel in defense of the Imperial Emperor, His direct family, or to compel a legionnaire for their own good. It's phrasing that seems ridiculous, but it means that if the emperor needed to order us into a line to literally soak up dragon fire, he could. And yet our own commanders could never order us to steal, unless we knew it was for a good reason. It maintains the ethics of the legion, not just the laws. If he learns to guide it the way that Augustus did? Grizz will become an unholy terror to anyone who crosses him."

"Why don't all legionnaires do this?" Bane asked.

"Because most people just can't. You need to be able to let go of everything—all ego, all concerns of survival, of consequences—and you need to be dedicated to war at a level that can take centuries to instill. Restun can do it, I'm sure. I think it was Restun who saw the capability in Augustus and taught him. We all try, but nobody but those two have managed it fully, as far as I know."

"And Jax." Bane grunted suddenly. "It's how he does it, isn't it?"

"For Oracle, yeah." She nodded. "I think that he's just that uncaring about anything else, that the entire realm could burn for him as long as he could rescue her, and while that's romantic as hell, it's terrifying as well. Because if he learns to do that fully? I bet he'd be able to gut the dark dick with ease next time they meet."

"You think they'll fight again?" Flux asked.

Bane jerked, then swore, his mentor having snuck up on him *again.*

"You think they won't?" Yen asked curiously. "You think that He'll just accept that Jax cut his head off and ordered it be made into a cup? He'll want revenge, and with the other gods backing him up, there's only one way that He'll get to fight him without a war between the gods starting fully."

"One-on-one." Flux nodded. "In that case, in order to get our prince to the point that he can win that easily, we need to be sure he'll live long enough. With that in mind, his bodyguard needs to be the most elite of us, *not the easiest for me to sneak up on when he's distracted!*"

Bane winced as Flux started to berate him, and Yen beat a hasty retreat.

***

Tenandra made adjustments to their course, the sails, and her engines, watching on in distracted amusement. More than half of her attention was focused on the horizon, on watching the squalls that she could sense in the far distance, and the thickening air.

There were a thousand adjustments required a minute to keep the ship on course and making the best possible time, and she was determined that her passengers—her *family*—would make it to the far side of the ocean in the best possible condition.

It didn't matter that the only contact that Dravith had managed with the continent of Carrmor since the fall had been a single badly damaged and partly sinking ship that was in turn recovered from pirates over two hundred years ago.

They were already approaching the last islands for hundreds of miles between the two continents, and from there? Nothing had made it across the ocean and back since before the cataclysm.

Nothing until *now*, she silently vowed.

147

# CHAPTER NINE

"**J**ax!" Oracle screamed as everything screeched its hatred of me. "What the hell?!"

"Seriously, not my fault!" I yelled in frustration, spinning and gesturing to the passage that led backward from the edge. "Run!"

If I had to guess, the room we'd been in had been part of an old bank; it had the kind of walls that said "Fuck off, you're not on the list…you don't get in" and that'd been great, up until part of the floor fell out and the far wall crumbled.

The other walls were more or less intact, as were the rest of the floor and ceiling. But the farthest wall had partly collapsed, leaving us a hidden—or so I'd thought—place to watch the fight from.

Now, we sprinted back down the passage away from the open end, and headed toward the nearest street entrance.

"What do we do?" Oracle called, flashing along, her feet a few inches above the ground.

"We get up high," I said. "The wurms can tunnel through the ground, the scorpion can chase us and stab us with its fucking 'cat-o-three' tails, and the wyverns can fly and fight us."

"Exactly!" she cried.

"Look, the choice is face the wurms, the scorpion, and the wyverns on the ground, where the fuckers might just tunnel up through the floor at any second, or face just the wyverns in the air!" I snapped.

She snarled something back that I missed, but didn't seem like a viable alternative.

Considering it was something about the "goat-sucking bastard of a dead donkey's dick," I decided not to ask for clarification, despite how proud I was for her rapidly expanding vocabulary.

The passage ahead opened into an old stone entryway. What once must have been a desk had apparently been scavenged for wood and burned, with the brass fittings all melted into slag in the center of the blackened floor.

Sand was—like *everywhere*—blown into all the corners and entirely filling what looked to be a stairwell that led down, meaning we had the choice of climbing out of the window, going up the stairs, or out the front door.

Oracle jerked back from the front door when a scaly form crashed to the ground before us, one leg clearly battered and blood dripping from a dozen wounds, scales rent and its wings badly holed. Even with all of that, still the wyvern had eyes only for us.

Fortunately, Oracle was faster than me, unleashing a lightning bolt on instinct, straight into its open mouth.

The wyvern hurtled backward, tremors and convulsions jerking it from side to side as it thrashed wildly.

Lightning, which was a part of air magic, and apparently something that wyverns had a high resistance to, was still evidently effective. Or at least it was when you rammed ten thousand volts straight down something's throat, it turned out.

What was even more effective, as I sprinted out into the broken street beyond to stab the tip of my naginata into its throat, was cold steel.

"This way!" Oracle shouted, already darting left, and I triggered Soaring Majesty and flew after her.

Screeches and hunting calls rang out from high overhead. The sound of hastily flapping wings accompanied us as I followed Oracle as fast as I could.

She—as a damn creature of magic—was a lot more graceful than I was, considering I essentially had to envisage the winds and air mana under me, pushing "up" to make me fly.

That meant that to change direction, I was less "hummingbird" and more "badly built rocket."

On the upside, though, as I hurtled along, dipping under partly collapsed columns and through gaps in buildings, the wyverns flocking after us were having real issues.

Oracle added to that by triggering a Circle of Frostfire up ahead in the middle of an open area.

It had barely flared to life as I crossed it, but the closest few wyverns that were right behind me literally caught fire and partially froze, distracted by the pain. They then completely missed the juke to the left that was required shortly after to follow the next street, and the wall became their final resting place.

The "slam-splat" of bodies that were several meters long crashing into solid stone walls rang out, along with the sound of breaking bones and the flashing of more notifications, making me smile as I kept going.

*"Isn't this leading us back around toward..."* I sent to Oracle as she took another left; then I whipped my naginata out as another wyvern dropped from the sky, aiming for me.

I carved a shallow divot through its stomach, both of us just moving far enough aside that we couldn't get at each other properly, when we tried to avoid the other's attack.

That was what I'd thought, anyway, until I was hit with a close-range lightning bolt from behind.

My muscles locked up. It was powerful enough it overrode most of my resistances. I dropped like a hurled rock, crashing into the sand and digging a second divot, this one much deeper as it felt like half the desert was trying to become best friends with the back of my throat.

I gasped, shaking myself as I managed to regain muscle control, then threw myself to the right, hitting the sand and rolling at a sending from Oracle, as two lightning bolts slammed into the sand where I'd been kneeling.

A crash of impact rang out as the largest of the wyverns landed then, its truncated tail still leaking blood, as the huge bird-monstrosity screamed and lunged for me.

Its beak snapped shut a few inches from my face; I triggered Mana Overdrive and rolled to the right. It followed, lumbering awkwardly, flapping its great wings for balance, its claws at the end of them reaching.

I came to one knee, slashing up and across, damn glad I'd managed to hold onto the naginata, and carved a leathery flap free. Blood sprayed as I dragged the blade down...then my world was spinning as something hit me hard from the side.

I landed and rolled. Another claw-tipped set of talons crashed down next to my head. I gave up on getting to my feet and shoved with Soaring Majesty, launching myself all of three meters, before a wildly swinging wing caught me and batted me out of the air again.

This time, I crashed into something that was scaly, reeked like an unwashed jockstrap, and promptly snapped at me. A beak latched onto my foot as I crashed down, only to be yanked back into the air and whipped from side to side.

"ORACLE!" I yelled. My inner ear had grown more resilient to this kinda crap, but all I was seeing was leathery wings, beaks, blood, and scales. Every time I thought I could get anywhere, I was being slapped down, hard.

"*JAX!*" she replied, and I felt both her panicked fear and her fury.

A fresh circle flared to life, this time directly under me, and all around me the creatures howled in fury and pain as the flames and ice bore into them.

I was dropped as whatever had been thrashing me about beat its wings and tried to half fly, half hop out of the radius of Oracle's fury.

I landed hard—fortunately on my head, so there was less to damage there—but as I collapsed to the ground, the sound was akin to the collapse of an ironworks. Even as I wearily shoved myself back upright, scrabbling around for my now dropped naginata, I noted the sand that was cascading off the walls nearby, and the way that the wyverns launched themselves into the air.

There was a half second while my banged-up brain connected the dots, and then the wall to my right exploded, as the surviving wurm crashed free.

I launched myself to the right, barely making it to the side as its enormous maw crashed into the sand where I had been. The additional boost of Soaring Majesty was enough that I made it, before I whipped my naginata around and carved a shallow line through its outer skin.

Then the blade was almost ripped from my hands, as more and more of the damn thing kept coming!

I focused, hissing as I fed mana into the weapon. The blade went from the damascene shine to a full-on bright-white light as I dug deeper.

This time, the wurm twisted, trying to drag its flesh free of the searing agony and I snarled, shoving harder.

I managed to cut it for all of a few more seconds, before it broke free; the tail whipped past as it dove into the darkness of its new tunnel. Then Sehran was shouting.

"*Behind you!*" she sent. "*Fly!*"

I launched myself forward and up—the air thankfully almost free of wyverns, considering they'd climbed for altitude—when the scorpion queen rose into view as well.

Unlike its previous combative friend, it hadn't gone through the earth. Instead, it'd climbed the walls of the cavern and then had raced across rooftops.

The fact that it was as goddamn big as most of the largest buildings in the city made it clear that wherever it'd been calling home until now had to have some serious draught issues, because as soon as I lifted into the air, the tails were stabbing out.

I rolled, Oracle and Sehran's vision combining with my own to keep me ducking and diving, even as Oracle started to work on a counter.

It was the "fuck you all" option that she went for in the end, fortunately.

And my God, did she deliver as I twisted in midair and lashed out with my naginata again, carving into the chitin, even as little arms reached out and tried to grab at me.

The Pyroclastic Blast that she unleashed was a recent upgrade to my fireball spell. And as the saying goes, where a bullet might have your name on it, a fireball is addressed "to whom it may concern" because it's that indiscriminately fucky for anyone caught inside its radius.

Well, the upgrade to that spell, the one that every party spent half their lives telling their mage he wasn't allowed to use in virtually every violent, social, or comedic situation, just took it to the next level.

The description made it clear:

**Pyroclastic Blast:**

Pyroclastic Blast is a massively effective weapon, combining all the most fun parts of a volcano's eruption with the ability to reach out and say "You see that guy? Fuck him, and fuck all his friends!"

Concussive effect is tripled within the first five feet of the impact site, dropping by 10% per two feet of distance while radiating outward. Chance to inflict secondary fire damage is increased to 60%. Any pyroclastic flow that impacts anyone will proceed to do massive situational damage until it cools.

Pyroclastic Blast costs 400 mana per casting.

The reality though, was oh so much worse.

It started as a flickering flame, one that roared into existence between Oracle's palms. From there, it grew, spinning faster and faster, as first earth and then water was added; weaves of flaming rock were tangled in with frozen water, which in turn had a core of air that was being compressed down to the point of becoming a liquid in its own right.

By the time she released it, less than seven seconds later, the spell was warping the air around her, dragging in light.

The air around her shrieked with the violation as the spell crossed the space between her and the scorpion in a blur that left a simple afterimage of light behind.

This was the first time I'd seen one of these spells pass me in midair. And considering I was in Mana Overdrive and it still seemed like a bar of solid red and white connecting her fingers to a point behind me, it showed just how fast it was moving.

The crack of displaced air as the leading edge of the spell hit the scorpion queen high on its back rang out, shaking the air. I was picked up and physically hurled through a missing window and into a nearby building by the blast wave.

The effect on the scorpion was something that I put together afterward from Oracle and Sehran's vision as much as my own, as what I'd seen was pretty much my arse and elbows as I was hurled into the sky, trailing smoke and fire.

The spellform had broken on its back, deforming the chitin and flash-searing a few dozen arms into carbon. Then it broke, and the real effect went out of control, like a nuclear accelerator being used as a redneck's still.

The compressed air burst back from its liquid form into its usual volume, and in doing so, rammed the core of ice around it into the swirling magma.

The magma—predictably—wasn't happy about the ice and air in its domain, and it exploded outward in turn.

The effect was like a paint bomb going off and covering everything nearby—except that it added a wave of gravitational force and lastly the paint was replaced with magma.

Magma is not known for its cuddly disposition, as it made known to first the scorpion queen that was now covered in two-thirds of the material, and the swarming wyverns battling to get past her.

Wyverns, it turned out, were highly flammable, or at least they were when they were exposed to the kind of temperatures that turn rock into liquid.

They began falling from the air—screaming, burning—and the scorpion queen just sort of…exploded.

We worked it out later that it was down to the heat. It'd flash-fried the meat and innards of the queen, which then resulted in gasses expanding and they hit the incredibly hot rock…then *boom*.

I staggered to my feet and made my way to the old stone window ledge, bracing myself and staring out at the scene of devastation before us.

Oracle was on the rooftop of a single-story building before the one I was in and one over to the right. Sehran was off to the left, flying toward us from another street along.

The wyverns were, well, either toasty as hell, or they were flying like their arses were on fire, having clearly decided that if discretion was the better part of valor, then moving to the next time zone over was the best way to deal with anything that threw that kind of magic around.

Possibly the next continent, in fact.

The scorpion queen was dead.

*Very dead.*

Its entire upper half had exploded outward and the bottom was in a pile of cooling magma…so yeah, not gonna be looting much of anything from *that*.

The last creature in the area was the sand wurm. And even as I stood there, braced against the windowsill, Sehran sent me a mental image.

The vibrations had fucked it up, I guessed, because there'd certainly been some of those, and it'd turned left when it should have turned right.

The resulting hole, instead of leading it around to dig upward and back toward the fight, let it out in the side of the cavern to fall several dozen meters to the ground face-first.

"Not a terminal injury," you cry, "not for something that big," and you'd be right.

The Explosive Compression spell that Sehran fired at the stunned creature, punching into the wound that ran most of its length before exploding and shredding it, on the other hand, very clearly was.

A few minutes later, Oracle, Sehran, and I sat on the edge of the roof overlooking the battlefield, and watched the smoke rising as we kicked our legs over the side.

"We probably look ridiculous," I admitted after a few seconds, looking from Oracle, who sat to my left, and then Sehran who sat on the far side of her, then down at myself.

"Why?" Oracle asked, confused.

"We're all sitting here, half the city is on fire, there's bits of the giant big-boss scorpion that had to have been landing out in the desert, and as to the wyverns?" I shrugged.

"They did what all animals do when they're scared," Sehran pointed out.

"Yeah, but they're monsters," I replied, cocking an eyebrow, then scratching my sweaty hair. "Damn, I need to get this trimmed again," I muttered.

"Just because they're monsters doesn't mean they're not animals," Sehran said. "Look at me…I'm a demon and a person."

"I'm a wisp and a person," Oracle added.

I nodded. "I mean, yeah, of course. It's just, them literally pissing themselves as they fly away? It was a bit excessive. One minute they're going all in, driven feral by, whatever, and then…"

I paused, then looked at Oracle. "That's a point actually. What the hell happened back there?"

"Which bit?" she asked.

"Uh, the whole everything hates us and wants to kill us, and then the sudden change where everything wants to get the fuck away from here," I said. "Oh, and let's add that spell in as well. I don't remember it being that powerful. Deadly? Sure. Capable of scaring everything around shitless and basically nuking a boss with one hit? Uh-uh."

"Yeah," Sehran admitted. "I was kinda wondering about that, though if you don't mind teaching me the spell, I won't say no!"

"Maybe." Oracle smiled, before bumping the larger demon with her shoulder playfully. "Okay, before we begin, Jax, can you check your notifications please?"

"Okay…" I sighed, pulling them up and going over the "minor" details.

### *Congratulations!*

*You have killed the following:*

- *23x Desert Scorpions of various levels for a total of 28,910xp*
- *3x Giant Desert Scorpions of various levels for a total of 45,000xp*
- *1x Scorpion Queen (level 43) for 65,900xp*
- *4x Wyverns of various levels for a total of 6,140xp*
- *1x Wyvern Elite (level 27) for 9,500xp*
- *1x Sand Wurm Elite for (level 36) for 42,780xp*


*A party under your command killed the following:*

- *217x Desert Scorpions of various levels for a total of 294,755xp*

Jez Cajiao

- ***13x Giant Desert Scorpions of various levels for a total of 205,000xp***
- ***4x Wyverns of various levels for a total of 7,280xp***

***Total party experience earned: 507,035xp***

***As party leader, you gain 25% of all experience earned (126,758xp)***

***Total experience gained: 198,230xp + 126,758xp (party leader bonus) = 324,988xp***

***Progress to level 49 stands at 4,975,139/6,455,000***

"Okay, so I got some XP. But damn, it's annoying. I'm barely moving the dial these days, and these fuckers weren't small targets, despite, you know, the damn size of them," I muttered, reading it all over.

"It becomes more about quests as you get into the higher levels," Oracle agreed absently. "It's why the higher levels tend to be either constantly shut away from the world working on magic, or become wandering monster hunters and so on. Then a single mistake and the latter die off, so the higher levels that people tend to hear about end up as all hermits."

"Ooookay," I murmured, pulling up the next. "I mean, that sort of makes sense and…holy shit."

"Yes?" Oracle almost bounced in her excitement as she accessed my notifications and started to read as well. "Oh yes!"

"What is it?" Sehran asked quickly, the only one who couldn't see the glorious notification that hung before me.

### *Congratulations!*

**You have made progress in your Quest: The Deeper Secret**

In a space between the walls of your reality, you have felt the presence of a new power, and you have seen those who wield it. Although you do not yet have the strength of will to touch it, not to truly understand it, nevertheless, you have made progress in your quest.

Between the stars they exist, those dread wielders who once travelled to your realm, they who were reviled as the antithesis of all life, and yet…you find that they may not be so alien after all.

Whatever they are, though, they have seen you, and they now know you as their path to your realm. The night comes, and when the dawn finally rises, not all that were there before will be alive to see it. Beware, young wielder, for the power that you seek has destroyed realms.

**Forms of Magic Discovered**: 7/10

**Reward:** New forms of magic, 10,000,000xp, Unknown

"Okay, that's creepy as fuck," I muttered. "I discovered a new form of magic, but I've no clue how the hell I wielded it, or…or where it went!"

"That's me, Jax," Oracle interrupted, sensing my frustration. "That's why the spell was so much more powerful than it should have been, I think. I guessed that the problem—the way that they were chasing us and were so fixated on us—was that power, and I could feel it was slowly bleeding away, fading out of our reality, so I just… I shoved it into the spell."

"And it wiped a boss monster out and half the street, as well as scaring the shit out of everything," I murmured, looking down at the still smoking devastation.

"As soon as the power was unleashed, it just…faded?" she said softly. "It was like…"

"Like putting napalm in a firelighter." I snorted. "You overpowered the spell and killed everything."

"And once the power was no longer in you and was expended, the monsters regained their wits and realized that everything was dying," Sehran finished for me, looking over and shaking her head. "I don't know what it was, but I caught a whiff of it and it just smelled…wrong?"

"In what way?" Oracle asked quickly.

"I don't know. I mean…" She paused, and Oracle pressed harder.

"Sehran, this could be incredibly important. Please tell us everything you remember, no matter how small, okay? I'm attached to Jax, so while I felt something of the power, I don't want to contaminate what you felt by saying it. Just explain anything you smelled, you thought…anything at all."

"Okay…" She shifted, frowning as she clearly tried to remember. "It was like a sensation of something being off, like there was…" She chewed on her lower lip, then clearly changed what she was about to say.

"Have you ever had it when you think you're alone, and then there's someone there, and you can feel it?" she asked. "When you sense them, but you can't draw attention to a sound, or a smell or anything that made you aware?"

"Yeah." I nodded.

"Okay, so it's sort of like that, but then take that feeling and make it stronger, like there's someone or something really dangerous there, that feeling that crawls up your spine and makes you all cold, and then…"

She shook her head again, still searching for the words. "You know fresh baked bread?"

"Yeah?" I blinked at the non sequitur.

"Okay, you know how that smell makes you hungry? Even if you've eaten, you just…like it? You want it?"

"And this smell was like that?" Oracle asked.

"No, it was stronger, and more…it was like it was vanishing and I *had* to smell more, like I needed it. That I was hungry and this was all I'd ever wanted, and still, it was fading."

"And the various monsters down there all sensed it at the same time too," Oracle mused. "For me, it was different. I smelled something weird but I couldn't place it. And the sensation of the mana, no…it wasn't mana that was inside you—it was something else. But I could feel it, I could feel it all around, and flowing through you. Even weirder was that it wasn't in me."

"Why?" I asked.

"I don't know, but while I could use it, I could guide it, I knew as soon as I touched it that I couldn't take it. I couldn't use it to keep myself here, to form my body like I used to. I don't know how to explain it. I just know that it wasn't my power."

"It was his?" Sehran asked.

"Yeah. I know that sounds obvious, but, whenever I think of his mana, it's like it's part of me," Oracle said softly. "It responds the same as mine does. It feels warm, comforting, and like it's always been a part of me. Like it always should be. That? It was different—totally separate and it was…"

"Like a pool of water," I said suddenly, remembering the sensation. "If mana is like a stream that we direct, this was like a pool. As soon as I released that other place, I felt the power cut off, and there was a pool of it inside me."

"One that you used up and then it was gone," Sehran finished for me. "Okay, so I get that. I get that it's a limited source of power, that you had it and then you used it, and it massively, incredibly overcharged that spell—but what *was* it?"

"Soul," I said slowly, frowning. "I think it's, well, it's not entirely right but it sort of feels like it could be?"

"Like it's part of the answer but not the whole answer," Oracle agreed.

"Exactly. The power comes from the other side of the veil."

"From death?" Sehran asked.

"No." Both I and Oracle answered at once, then we smiled at each other.

"I can't explain it, not fully," I admitted. "But that power, whatever it is, isn't death. Death is from this side, from the physical realm."

"It's what happens after death. Where what makes us up passes through the veil, and reaches…where we go next, I guess?" Oracle added.

"So, I'm just being clear here, because of the dark dick, as much as anything else, but this isn't His power?" Sehran asked.

"No, definitely not, though I think that gaining that fragment of His divinity might have made it easier for me to reach through the veil."

"It'd make sense, sort of," Sehran murmured after a few seconds of silence.

"What's that?" I glanced over.

"Well, you said that your quest was to find the other side of magic, right?"
I nodded.

"Well, if mana is one side of magic, and it deals with this side of the veil, then what would the other side be?" Sehran suggested. "What are the forms?"

"Uh… Spellforms, potions, incantations, runes, and prayers," I muttered. "That's the first five, or that's what the quest says. No clue why."

"That side is obvious to me at least." Oracle shot me a smile. "Spellforms are a mage using mana through their own controlled focus, and can be used whenever the mage has the power. Potions are mana made physical, ready to be taken and used, but once it's used, it's gone.

"Incantations are similar to spellforms, but they involve another. The focus point isn't the mage's body…it's an external point. Like to summon Sehran originally, the spell is created and cast by a mage, but locked to a summoning point. It needs to use something, like the floor or a wall, to act as an anchor for the passage between the realms."

"You should have seen Jian's face when I came through the portal the first time." Sehran grinned wickedly. "I—"

"Another time." Oracle cut her off. "While I want to hear it—and I do, believe me—this is important."

"Sorry." Sehran nodded, wincing guiltily, and mimed locking her lips and throwing away the key, making me grin at her as I wondered where she'd picked that up.

"So…" Oracle continued. "Then there's runes. Runes and enchantments are similar enough that they're probably classed as the same thing here. They're both a symbol of power that carried the mana, locking it into a solid form, something that can be used over and over again." She paused, furrowing her brow as she thought on it.

"No clue why it's classed the same, while spellforms and incantations are separate, but…" She shrugged. "Maybe that's something we ask Jenae. Regardless, the last form of mana manipulation is prayer. The link between us and the one that we revere as a god, the embodiment of that aspect of creation. It forms a link with a higher—or more powerful—being and they in turn work with us."

"That's a valid point." I nodded. "Mana manipulation. That's probably the most important point there, because that's *not* what I did with Grizz, or what I did when I opened that rift. I just made it real."

"You didn't use mana at all to adjust or influence reality. Instead, you remade reality as you decided it should be," Oracle agreed.

"But *how*?" I asked, infuriated. "I mean, if I can just make things be the way I want, then we'd just step off the edge here and land in the Great Tower." I gestured forward at the dusty, broken stone below us. "It doesn't make sense that all you need is to want it. I mean, that was what I did, right? I just wanted Grizz alive again and he was."

"No, it's not a case of 'want,'" Oracle said firmly. "If it was, then every five-year-old child who wants a pony would ride, and people who are being hurt or killed don't want to be, or at least not usually." She glanced at Sehran, who shrugged.

"What can I say?" She sighed. "It's a living."

"But that's the point." I nodded. "I mean, let's face it. When I'm thinking with the little head, you don't just appear naked and we're teleported away to somewhere private, and believe me, *I want that*. Right now, admittedly I'd rather be back at the prax, to know that the others are okay, but, even that hasn't happened."

"That's because it's not a case of 'want,'" Oracle repeated. "Something about it, about *you*, enables you to manipulate reality. It has to be something to do with the Eternal Emperor. It doesn't make sense for it to be anything else."

"He did do that in the throne room." I remembered when we'd taken Himnel, and Amon and I had fused for a short while. We'd both walked the steps and sat on the throne. A mage had been trying to cast a spell at us, and he'd just clicked his fingers and turned the mage to ash.

There wasn't a spell cast, a flexing of mana…nothing. Amon had simply willed that the mage was dead, and that was it—he'd vanished in a column of flames. A column that was primarily for effect, like the clicking on his fingers.

The goddamn stone under his ashen remains melted, and yet others less than a foot away hadn't even felt warmth.

"The sixth form of magic," I whispered.

"And now this," Oracle agreed.

"But…"

"Yes?"

"What the hell *is* it?" I asked, plaintively.

# CHAPTER TEN

"**I** just don't get it," I growled, some three hours later, shifting around and trying to get comfortable, as I sat on yet another bloody rock, back with the others.

"Jax, if you did, I'd be frankly astonished and terrified," Oracle said as I crossed my arms and glared around. "These are the secrets of reality, something you only have the faintest access to because you have a fragment of divinity, are linked to the Goddess of Hidden Knowledge, and are the direct descendant of, and are blessed by, the Eternal Emperor Amon.

"If you could figure this out in an afternoon, there'd be no point in anyone else ever studying magic, now would there?" she asked, sitting by my side. "I mean, think about it, Jax. I knew arch mages who were in the level seventies, and they did nothing but study. They didn't go out and level by setting fire to continents.

"They did it by discovering the greater secrets of reality…that's what they did, and what you're starting to do now. If you—or I or Sehran—could figure out what that power was and learn to use it in an afternoon, how would it ever have been missed until now?"

She smiled, resting one hand on my arm as she went on.

"What you're discovering is incredible, but to really understand it? I think you're going to need to learn, and learn a lot. Have you thought about asking Jenae?" She cocked one eyebrow at me.

I snorted. "She doesn't want me to call on her unless the shit's hit the fan," I admitted. "She sent me a warning, like a bundle of feelings. I don't really understand it all, but what I did get was that the last thing we want right now is Jenae herself setting foot, even metaphorically, on this continent. Not until we can't help it. Because when the dark dick realizes that She's here, He's going to unleash hell to get Her off it and limit Her power.

"He knows that the only way that He can win against the other gods is to keep them weak. The only way He can do that is to limit their followers. So, when they start showing up over here, He's going to try to kill them all to stop them from spreading.

"Also, and this is kinda important, we're here, and without the legion to back us up. That asshat would drown us in bodies if he could, and sensing her here, considering they're linked to us—sort of—and can only claim territory that we do? The best way for Him to get rid of them, is to kill us. Plus, for some weird reason He just doesn't like me very much." I grumbled.

"Strange that." Oracle smiled.

"Yeah, well, it's basically a case of try and keep our heads down for now and then when He finds out we're here She and the others will come and play, but not before."

"So once word does get around, it's going to be an inquisition?" she asked. "People won't expect that."

"Nobody expects the Spanish Inquisition," I said in ingrained instinct. "Nobody. Our two weapons are…" I saw the look on her face, and I snorted. "Okay, look…ah, fuck it, it's not important."

"Okay, Jax, you're really going to have to explain these jokes at some point, like why you kept denying your arm had been cut off when it had been?"

"Ah, the Black Knight sketch," I reminisced with a wistful smile. "A fuckin' classic."

"You're very strange."

"You sleep with me."

"That's a point. Apparently, I have very strange tastes." She smiled, then nodded, directing my attention over to the left where Toren clambered across the rocks heading toward us.

"Toren." I greeted him. "Everything okay?"

"Well, no, but that's life," he replied flatly, huffing as he arched his back and winced. "Most of the things we need are at the bottom of a very deep pit filled with rubble and dead monsters, and no matter how much you keep telling us that they're not going to come back, we all know that being around corpses is a surefire way to get wyverns."

"Believe me." Oracle smiled. "The last thing the wyverns want is to be anywhere near him now."

"You said that before." Toren squinted at me. "You really did all this?"

"He lost his temper," Sehran called over, as she beat her wings, slowing her descent and landing on a wall nearby. "You remember what I said about breakable things?"

"Like cities and continents." He nodded. "Surely that means that you don't—"

"I do need you." I cut him off. "My magic is powerful, but I'm only one man. I can fight all day and night, but all it takes is a single lucky hit, a slip on blood, or a bad fall and anyone can die."

"Well, that wasn't why I came over," he grumbled after a few seconds of silence. "I wasn't trying to get out of it or nothin', just… ah, forget it." He gave a jerky bow and turned on his heel.

"Was that why you came up here?" I called after him, making him swear under his breath as he turned back.

"Dammit, no, I'm sorry, Lord. Okay, so we've found enough basic supplies that we can probably make it to the edge of the desert from here, but once we make it there, we're going to have nothing left."

"Nothing of value anyway," Marteen added, clambering up the side of the rubble toward us. "Is there a reason you're sitting up here, my lord?"

"Because it's as far away from people as I could get without leaving you all and fucking off," I replied flatly.

"Ah," he replied delicately, pausing and wincing. "I was afraid it might be something like that."

The change in attitude came as a direct result of the fight. The people I'd previously been encouraged by decided that clearly if I could do this—the effect of the rubble-choked streets and devastated bodies had been clear on them—then I obviously should have no need for them at all.

Almost a third of the group had come to me with reasons they couldn't possibly be expected to pick up a weapon against their fellow sentient beings, and why other "butchers like you" should do it, as one idiot had pointed out.

I'd managed to keep from punting him over the far wall of the ruined city, but it'd been a close thing.

There were also—as Oracle had been quick to remind me—others in the groups who were exactly what we needed. Toren was a bit of a grumpy fucker, but he'd been involved in the caravan's management, and the rights of the caravan trail and the overall deals made to date had all come to him with the death of the other more senior partners, making him the new caravan master.

Then there were Zyenna and Marteen.

They were sharks—they really fucking were. I knew that they saw me as a path to power and riches, but the thing was, they were clear and honest about it.

The old biddy kept telling people that I'd managed to convince them it was an easy deal, that they were able to rip me off, and instead I'd ripped them off.

I didn't see it that way. I mean, they were *alive* because of me, and they were leveling like crazy, considering it was in a totally new direction for them.

That had been another little bonus.

One of the reasons I was getting so many experience points for the magic quests was because that wasn't something I did normally. For fighting?

Well, I did that a lot, so I didn't get much XP from it. But figuring out the theoretical secrets of the cosmos? Yeah, not so much.

That was the same for this little group. They were mainly merchants and more, so fighting on a line and battling against giant fuckin' monsters?

Lots of XP was going their way.

There was a lot of XP to go around, to be fair, but still. That was what was annoying me even more—that so many people were willing to risk their lives for the rest of the group and that such a large portion of them just thought "Oh well, why should I risk myself then? Cheerio…let us know when you've sorted it all out."

They'd been quick enough to go when they heard the monsters were dead and the loot was available though, I noted.

Cheeky fuckers.

"Jax…" Oracle whispered, and I glanced at her, then sighed.

I'd been doing it again, glaring around and basically saying nothing, lost in my own thoughts.

"So…my lord?" Marteen asked. "Is there anything I can do to help?"

"No." I sighed again. "Not right now anyway, but thank you," I forced myself to say, grudgingly.

"As I'm sure Master Toren has informed you, we've cleared out and recovered as much as we think is possible to get without additional risk," he told me, before continuing as I gestured to him to do so.

"The buildings' collapse and the subsequent fighting has resulted in a lot of the underground caverns being exposed. The Changed Ones had a substantial amount of equipment put aside, but the reason for it escapes me. Items that were clear trade goods were left to rot in their boxes—not just food.

"Specialist silks, crafting items and collections…there were even what looked to have been memory stones, though the majority were shattered by falling masonry. No; if I was to guess, it's all the possessions of the travelers that they captured and integrated, not so neatly stacked away."

"And how much of it is recoverable?" I asked the question I was dreading.

"Very little," he admitted. "Weapons and armor are reasonably recoverable, and there are some good pieces, if I'm honest, as the kind of people who go wandering in ancient lost ruins generally fall into one of two categories: lunatics with nothing to lose, or professional dungeon divers."

"And?"

"And as such, we find that pretty much the entire group can be outfitted with some form of armor and weapons." He smiled. "Is the armor comfortable? No. Frankly, a lot of it was poorly stored or had been adjusted to fit its former wearer's mutated forms, so there are a lot of places where the armor needs padding, and that's now missing.

"The armor can be worn, though, and better rubbed a little raw, than without it and dying. There's also, as I said, a good collection of weapons, as well as a large number of magical artifacts, though they're generally low level."

"Such as?" I prompted.

"Rings that grant one or two uses per day of healing, a mana boost, six compasses, two magical maps, one small device that has to be gnomish, considering it's a walking stick that on activation deploys a parasol—on a side note, my mother has asked if she can have that. She's not the youngest, and the desert will be hard on her."

"And it's valuable and it'll help her to recover her wealth after all of this when you've got artifacts like that accepted as hers," I added dryly.

"Well, she won't disagree." He smiled, not bothering to deny it. "Anyway, the situation is that inside the hour, we'll have everything that we can realistically salvage from the ruins, and we need to know what you want us to do next."

"I'd ask that we rest for a few hours—a day would be best," Toren said quickly, jumping back into the conversation. "We've got a lot of people who aren't used to hard travel, and who are still recovering. We have copious meat and unlimited water, so a single additional day here…"

"Means that the slavers are going to escape us that bit quicker," Marteen added quickly. "Lord, the slavers will have known as soon as the majority of their spies died. The last one claims that he was just the hired help, I know—and he did say it under oath, so it's most likely true—but the simple fact is that they had a way to let the rest of the group track them. The slavers are either not bothering with us, or, most likely, are going to send out a group to hunt us down and kill us. Either we stay here and wait for them…"

"I'd recommend this," Toren said quickly. "Far better than bumping into them in the open desert."

"Or we make our way back to civilization and try to get them before they can get us." Marteen sighed. "Lord, I agree, if we can, we need to avoid meeting them in the open desert. But they think they have spies in the group, and they know that there's nothing out here. Most likely, they'll split the caravan, send our friends, family, and possessions on to the nearest city with a slave market, and then a smaller hunting team will either follow us into the desert, or more likely, if they can see that we're staying put somewhere, they'll simply wait."

"Wait?" I asked.

"If you have the choice of hunting your prey in the desert, or waiting for it to be driven out of the sands and back toward you by starvation and thirst, what would you choose?" he asked me. "The desert is known to be a monster-filled wilderness, so why risk your own people and punish yourself with the conditions when instead you can sit there and wait?"

"So, you think they'll wait for us to leave the desert, letting us basically weaken here, and then they'll kill us as we escape?" I asked, getting a nod. "Makes sense," I agreed. "If you take into account that they can track us, why would they chase us when they know we're not likely to escape."

"That's just it though, Lord—" Toren started.

I groaned, cutting him off. "For fuck's sake, look. If it's a formal situation, yes, all right, Lord me this and Lord that. Otherwise, just fucking leave it, okay? Call me Jax."

"Okay, *Jax*." Marteen grinned. "The thing you're not taking into account is that any caravan is a massive investment, and if the known goods, as well as the caravans themselves, all turn up as property of the slavers? Well, there's nothing that can be done about that. But if those same caravans all turn up again, as part of the established routes, then word is going to get around, and even the guild can't hide it.

"Some noble will make a point of 'protecting the citizens' and will start lopping off heads, before taking a percentage as payment for him helping maintain the law. It won't be anyone important, but the caravans then would be returned to any families of those who came with us, and to the investors.

"While it sorts out the issues in the short term, what would likely happen is that another caravan would be put together, one with a lot more guards, and they'd be sent out again. Not even the guild can keep doing what they did here, and the uproar against the slavers would result in the Dark Legion being hired to deal with them. At that point, everyone who's involved loses."

"So the alternative is?" I prompted.

"If the slavers have one of the leadership cadre in their possession and they force them to sign the caravan over, then it can be split up. It'd be shown in the guild that the caravan failed and was sold, not destroyed or raided. It's difficult and would mean a lot more work, but then they split the caravans up and use them on the other routes, or take this one over."

"But they can't do that because I was third in command," Toren added firmly. "That's why the slavers were here. If they can take me, or kill me, then the next in line becomes the caravan leader and that happens."

"Why does it matter?" I asked. "Who would know?"

"The guild and anyone who invested," he replied promptly. "And a lot of the nobles took minor shares in it to annoy the guild as much as anything else."

"But…" I trailed off, thinking about how to phrase it.

"How does the guild monitor the caravan?" Oracle asked, and I clicked my fingers.

"Yes! Thank you!" I smiled.

"The caravans are created with a tracking spell woven into their axles." Marteen nodded, finally understanding. "Sorry, it's just common knowledge. Okay." He scratched his scraggly beard and glanced at Toren, who nodded for him to go on. "So the guild, when a caravan route is established, insists on its rates, as we explained before. They don't want more routes, or at least *not ones that they don't control.*

"It's part of the charter, something that was agreed to in order to keep the merchant houses and the nobles from growing too powerful and overtaking one another. With the empire collapsed, and a load of little kingdoms springing up, it was the best way to keep it all nice and stable.

"The nobles have their armies and they run the tax systems and the cities, the merchants create the wealth, and the guilds make sure nobody is taken too much advantage of. They make sure the nobles pay their bills—just because they might have a title doesn't mean they have coin, after all—and if they don't, then that noble can't easily get things anymore."

"No luxuries, no nice prices on their goods, no pretty slaves…all of that." Toren grunted.

"But, to do this, there have to be rules that everyone agrees on, and one of those rules is that the caravan routes, once one is shown to have a minimum profitability and is set, becomes the property of the caravan master. That caravan master then sets the taxes and the guild takes its cut from that, and the various merchants all work to make the route profitable or not," Marteen went on quickly.

"What usually happens in practice, though, is that the caravan master does two or three circuits of the route, adjusts it as necessary, and then sells it to the guild, who increase the costs and pay that caravan master a percentage of the profits until they die.

"Then whoever is marked as the heir to the caravan master takes over, and in a few generations, they're as fat and greedy as all the others," Marteen finished with a shrug. "We invested so that we could get a part of that wealth, and yeah, so did everyone else."

"And if all but a member of the team who the slavers have under their control dies, then they can get them to sell the caravan over, and boom. The guild that set all of this up in the first place owns the route, and they can decide to shut it all down, or run it, and they don't have to share out the profits to the heirs." I nodded, finally getting it all.

"It was the bit about the caravans that was throwing us," Oracle added. "Knowing that they can be magically tracked and identified makes it a lot clearer."

"So, back to the situation with the slavers. You think they're going to get the caravan moving, because they know that as long as they can kill you, then all of this becomes their property, free and easy?" I asked, and Toren nodded. "Okay, and it's how far to the edge of the desert?"

"I don't know, probably a weeks' march," Marteen admitted.

"Across a monster-infested wilderness, with no shelter, no beasts of burden, and little hope," Toren added grimly. "If we stay here, at least there's a little hope that the slavers will have to come after us, and here we can ambush them."

"Because that's the other side of it," Marteen added with grim finality. "If we head out into the desert and meet them coming the other way? Everyone loses. A fight in the desert draws monsters from all directions because it means that there's food."

"Well, fuck." I sighed, rubbing at my face. "Does anyone have any good news?"

"I do." Sehran smiled, raising one hand, and I looked over at her, suddenly noticing the spike of happiness coursing through her.

"Oh?" I asked.

"You remember that little girl?"

"Amelia's daughter?" I straightened. "You found her?"

# CHAPTER ELEVEN

"We found traces of her," Sehran explained, leading me over to where one of the former caravan guards sat, catching his breath, having just jogged into the makeshift camp.

"But she's alive?" I pressed.

"She was," Sehran temporized. "Best if you hear it from him. This is Kalvin, and he's one of the caravan guards, but…"

"But my specialization was as a scout in the army, Lord," he said quickly, sinking to one knee and clapping a fist to his chest. "It's an honor."

"It's good to meet you, my friend." I reached out, taking him by the shoulder. "But my ancestor Amon never required a good man to kneel to him twice, and neither will I. Stand when you talk to me."

"Thank you, Lord." He smiled, then nodded as we both saw Amelia and Dex running up, with a handful of others following.

"You found her?" Amelia cried, and I held a hand up, quickly stopping her before she could ask anything else.

"He's found sign of her, not her directly," I explained. "He's about to tell us what that means, though."

"Yes, Lord." He nodded quickly. "I found signs of her, or at least of three young girls and one boy. Their names weren't clear. They left a carved record in the wall where they'd been staying, but that was partially destroyed. They were taken four days ago—"

"Who took them?" Amelia interrupted in a panic.

"Let him talk," I replied. "Kalvin, go on."

"They were taken by slavers, is my guess, and they're headed south, but it looked like there'd been a fight as well, and at least one of the party was injured by a scorpion. As near as I can tell, there were six slavers. Four of them stayed here in the city, and the other two set off south with the kids."

"That makes no sense…" Toren shook his head as he moved up next to us. "Why split the party?"

"There were empty potion vials around, and the tracks show one of the slavers was injured, badly enough that they were being carried by the children," Kalvin explained. "I'm reading tracks that are four days old and that have been disturbed by the devastation of the city, the sandstorm, and the constant movement of monsters, so it's anything but clear. But that's as near as I can get it."

He looked to me, and I nodded my thanks, before moving to the side, mulling over what he'd said as Amelia and others started peppering the scout with questions, and demanding he take them to the site he'd found.

*"What do you think?"* I asked Oracle and Sehran in the silence of the bond.

*"I think it's the best chance the kids have, and the only reason we had to stay here was that we were worried about bumping into the slavers on the way. As it is, we've got the choice of staying here while those kids have whatever done to them, and they get farther away by the minute, or we go,"* Oracle replied.

*"We're going,"* I replied. *"The choice is, do we take the others, or do we fly straight there ahead of everyone and order them to follow?"*

*"I think we need to stay with the group,"* Sehran said, even as Oracle spoke up in favor of flying ahead.

*"We can fly, and we don't know what those kids are going through now."*

*"True, on both counts,"* I agreed. *"We don't know what they're doing, but I think given the sheer number of monsters out there and the losses this group suffered coming here, we need to move and move fast. Oracle, do you think these people can survive without us?"*

*"No,"* she admitted.

*"Sehran, do you think the kids are safe?"*

*"Not at all."*

*"Fuck."*

*"But..."* Sehran said, then paused, looking to the pair of us. I nodded for her to go on, and she sighed. *"I hate saying this, but I think with the wyverns driven off, the biggest risk is to the group here, rather than the kids and the slavers.*

*"The slavers survived to get to here, so they've got a good idea about desert survival by now, or so I'd think. The kids, if they survived at least nine weeks in the city, surrounded by scorpions? They've probably got more desert survival skills than any of us.*

*"The main group, though? They're going to draw the attention of every sand wurm, wyvern, and who knows what else out there. Just the vibrations alone as the group treks across the sand will be like ringing the dinner bell. Then add in that, as much as we've healed them all, they don't have so much as a change of clothing between them?*

*"They're all covered in both fresh and old blood, sweat, and who knows what else. They're going to need us with them, or they'll be lucky to get out of the desert with ten percent of their current numbers,"* Sehran finished.

Oracle shook her head, speaking up straightaway. *"The group survived to here as well..."*

*"They did it by running like fuck and losing people every so often,"* I agreed, seeing the same realization on her face. *"Not the best survival strategy, that's for sure."*

*"What if you stayed with the main group and I scouted?"* Sehran offered. *"I'm fast enough that I can run from anything I can't handle, and the wyverns usually hunt alone. I can certainly handle even a few of them. And if I spot the kids, I can race back and we make a plan then?"*

*"It keeps us in close enough to the column that we can help them, and if need be, we can run ahead and then back,"* Oracle agreed. *"It's not what I want to do, but it's probably the best option."*

*"So we split our forces,"* I agreed, then turned back to regard the group waiting for us. "Okay, people, listen up!" I shouted, breaking through the arguments that had started already.

"Shut it!" Zyenna barked, whacking one of the louder complainers with her cane. "You want to know what's happening? Shut up long enough to hear it!"

"Thank you." I sighed. I just knew that she and Ame, as well as Nerin, were going to meet up and either become best friends, or each other's most fervent enemies—and I was going to end up paying for it either way.

"So, we have a group of four kids who set off four days ago. They're carrying a wounded slaver, who we can assume was injured by the scorpions and used whatever potions they had to stabilize themselves. If not, we'll find their body quickly enough. Either way, we all need to get to the south anyway, and there's four kids being punished ahead of us.

"I don't know about how it's done here, and certainly not now, but in the empire, and on the continent of Dravith, we kill slavers, we kill monsters, and we damn well protect kids, so this is how it's going to go.

"Toren, gather everyone up. You've got an hour to get people ready to move. Anything that can't be looted and secured in that time gets left." He nodded, and I turned to Marteen.

"Congratulations, Marteen, you just got a promotion. You did damn good work with your fighters. Your position is the most thankless, as you'll be securing the rear. You get half the fighters we have."

"Thank you, Lord." He smiled. "I won't let you down."

"You damn well better not, because if you do, you'll be dead," I replied, leaving it open to interpretation whether it would be me or the monsters taking care of that detail.

"Got it." He nodded, paling slightly.

"Good man." I smiled, then turned to Finna, who I'd noticed on the other side of the group. "Finna!" I barked, making her jump. "Quit skulking around the edges. You're leading the second group, and your role is to cover the middle to the front of the group. We're going to be running in a line, two abreast, across the desert when we leave here, so make sure your people are ready for the shit to hit the fan, because it's not gonna be pretty.

"Where Marteen gets to watch the rear and warn me if anyone's sneaking up on us, you get the sides and to focus on keeping our people safe in the middle!"

"Got it." She nodded.

"Good!" I turned to Zyenna. "And you, you old bugger, you're now in charge of all our gear. From what I've seen of you so far, you probably know the contents of everyone's purses down to the last copper coin, and at least half of what we're carrying was yours to start with. So here's the deal: you maintain it, you make sure that everyone has what they need—be that food, shelter, or whatever—to the best of your ability, and when we're out and all this is sorted? By my word, you'll have made a profit that will make your expected one for the caravan seem laughable."

"And me?" Toren asked, clearly referring to the "profit" bit.

"You all will," I assured them. "Where Zyenna is our quartermaster—or mistress, fuck it—Toren is in charge of the caravan. Between the two of you, you were running things back in the cavern I found you in, so continue that now. Last of all, before anyone asks, yes, I'm aware the sun will be going down soon, and yes, we're still leaving.

"As you all should know by now, the nighttime is the best time to move in the desert. By day, it's too damn hot. And yes, I know you fought a lot today and you're exhausted. But I also know that not one of you is going to suggest we leave four kids in the clutches of slavers any longer than necessary!"

"What will you be doing?" Amelia asked, then blanched. "I didn't mean to imply—" she started, only to be cut off by my upraised hand.

"It's fine," I assured her. "Oracle and I will be with you. I will run at the head of the column, and I'll be hunting any monsters that come close enough. Oracle will be on overwatch, alternating between flying close by me and soaring higher to watch the sands. Sehran, though, is a gifted hunter, and she's going to be scouting for us."

Sehran nodded, knowing what I was going to say.

"She's going to range ahead and back, keeping in touch and watching for the slavers, for the kids, and for anything we need, like a place to camp—which should be, whenever possible, surrounded by rock!

"Once she finds that, she'll return and we'll adjust on the fly. Should we find the kids soon, then we'll rescue them as a priority. If they've already made it to the slavers' camp, then we'll rescue them there. But either way, understand this. My aim is to rescue them all, those kids and your friends, and I'll damn well do it, so get your arses moving!"

"It was a good speech," Oracle assured me as the crowd broke up to run in all directions.

"No, it was terrible." I snorted. "You know it and so do I, but it'll do to let everyone know the next step, so fuck it. Sehran, you ready to scout?" I asked her.

She nodded. "To the south?"

I hesitated, then shook my head. "I know you've done a few passes over the city already, so I'm sorry to ask this, but can you do one more? Anywhere you're not sure about, if there's a chance that there are survivors there, shout out where we are, and then move on. I'd rather not leave anyone here if they're trying to make up their minds on joining us or not."

"Will do," she assured me. "There are a few places that I can sense life, and it's hiding, but honestly? I'm sure it's monsters that are staying clear of us. I'll do one last pass, then I'll follow you all."

"How long will it take?" Oracle asked.

"About an hour to cover the city, if I'm flying fast and just shouting over the possible areas—at least a week if I actually searched properly," she warned us. "It's a city, after all. Even if there hadn't been all the devastation, if the city was pristine, then running from house to house and checking every room could take a week, and they could simply move around to keep hidden. As it is, I'm reduced to flying and using my abilities to sense life, and that's the best I can do."

"That's all we can ask." I nodded. "Catch your breath, then get going."

She smiled, then launched herself into the air without pause, as I turned back to Oracle in the rapidly emptying courtyard. "How you doing?" I took her in my arms and kissed her upturned face.

"I'm good," she assured me.

"Bullshit." I snorted. "We're lost halfway across the realm and you're pregnant."

"I've got you and Sehran, and I've got magic." She shrugged. "Would I feel better if Bane and the others were here? Of course. If I could be back at the tower and everything was back to normal, I'd be a lot happier, but then these people would all be dying, as would their friends. I'd have to be a pretty shitty person to put my comfort over their lives."

"True." I winced.

"Why?"

"I just wish we were there anyway." I shrugged. "Don't get me wrong—I want to save them all and fix things over here, but I want you and our kid safe more."

"Would you abandon them if you could?"

"If I could get you home…" I started.

"No, if I wasn't here, if I was safe at the tower and you had the chance to abandon them and just be back with me, what would you do?"

"I'd… I'd stay," I admitted. "I'm just worried about you, that's all. And everyone else—fuck's sake, I keep pushing that aside but the last time we saw everyone, they were in cages!"

"They'll have gotten free," Oracle assured me. "When you came after us, you gave them a chance at least, and with that lot, that's all they need. We can't affect them from here, so we need to move on as if they're fine, and when we can speak to Jenae and the others, we'll find out the truth."

"We will." I sighed. "Okay, so moving on…" I looked about the courtyard again, noting the way that Zyenna watched us. "Now what?" I asked her, somewhat grumpily.

"Things are moving along nicely," she assured me, stomping over. "One question, though."

"Go on."

"What do we do?" She gestured to herself and a handful of the older members of the group.

"What?" I asked.

"We can't run across the desert for hours after hour," she clarified. "I put all my new points into Agility and Constitution, and now I can move a lot easier than I was, but I'm still not ready for a sustained run."

"Dammit!" I growled.

Zyenna watched me pace for a few seconds, clearly enjoying my frustration, before clearing her throat. "If you're quite finished?"

I turned to glare at her, and she smiled.

"We do have a solution, assuming you're willing to listen, and possibly move the arbitrary hour before we set off back to two?" She gestured, and a thin man with ink-stained fingers stepped forward nervously. He looked barely old enough to grow a beard, though his eyes were older.

"This is Therin," Zyenna introduced him. "He's an enchanter—not a particularly good one, mind you—which is why he was reduced to travelling with us to advance his craft and keep himself fed, but he has an idea."

"My lady does me a disservice," Therin said uncomfortably. "I'm actually quite skilled at enhancement work. It's just that nobody wants the simple enhancements when they could have flashier magic."

Oracle drifted closer, interested. "What kind of enhancements?"

"Mostly load-bearing spells, things to make heavy objects lighter or easier to move. I served my apprenticeship working with the mining guilds before joining the caravan." He gestured to a massive slab of ancient wood that two of the stronger guards were dragging over, clearly at Zyenna's request. "Like this piece we found in the city. With the right enchantments, it could easily carry five people in comfort, or even ten if need be."

I studied the wooden slab. It was easily four meters long by two across, and looked sturdy enough, if absolutely bloody ancient. "And you can enchant it?" I asked. "I mean, to do something useful?"

"I can start the process," Therin hedged. "It won't be perfect, especially not at first, but I can work on it as we travel. The enchantments will grow stronger, more efficient. The problem is power…"

"And that's a problem because?" I squinted.

"Because I only have a small manapool," he admitted. "I need to fill it, to power it and when I do that, I can't be working on improving it. Also, as soon as it runs out of mana, it'll drop."

"We could use the manastones," Oracle mused. "Toren has been recovering them from the Changed Ones' stockpile, and although they're corrupted—whatever they did to them is just a mess—I could probably siphon the mana from them directly into the wood without too much difficulty. We'd need to use those to power it initially, then work with Therin to make the enchantments self-sustaining once we have time to cleanse the stones fully. Then maybe embed one in the…"

"Carrier?" Zyenna suggested, smiling at the sheer madness of the creation.

"It would mean people could rest on it while I worked," Therin added enthusiastically. "Then they could swap with others. We could rotate through the group, keeping everyone fresh enough to maintain pace."

I looked at Zyenna, who was trying not to look too pleased with herself. "And you just happened to have an enchanter with you?"

"Of course," she replied smoothly. "What kind of merchant would I be if I didn't plan for every contingency?"

"Why didn't you mention this sooner?"

"Because watching you panic was entertaining," she admitted. "Besides, he doesn't know anything that's not limited to moving items. He made some small improvements to my wagon, but the prices he was trying to charge meant that nobody else was willing to give him the work."

"And you didn't reduce your prices because…?" I asked, then shook my head. "Let me guess, another guild?"

"The Enchanter's Guild sets the rates, my lord," he apologized. "If I charge less, then I'll be banned and then I'll never advance in my craft."

"Fucking guilds." I shook my head disgustedly. "Okay, how long to get it working?"

Therin studied the slab thoughtfully. "Give me an hour to lay the base enchantments, and maybe another half an hour to test it and power it for the first time. If I rush it, it could explode, so please don't push me to work faster. And it won't be elegant at first, but it will work. I can refine it as we travel."

"Do it," I ordered. "Oracle, help him get started. The rest of you, get ready to move. We've got a lot of ground to cover."

"Ah, one last point." He winced. "It won't move under its own power, it'll just float, so…"

"So, it'll need to be pushed." I sighed. "Is there a limit on speed?"

"No, Lord, just the power needed to maintain it floating. There's enough room on here that I can make it carry more people in more comfort, or I could carry goods."

I looked it over. "You were right with the plan to carry a smaller number of people," I acknowledged. "That way, the gear for the majority can sit on it as well, and people can take turns running and riding."

"Thank you." Zyenna smiled, looking satisfied.

"Next time, don't give me all that shit about watching me panic over a solution. Just tell me," I ordered her, and she inclined her head, before moving off.

The desert crossing would be brutal, but at least now we had a chance of keeping everyone together. I just hoped it would be enough. And seeing the fascinated look on Oracle's face, I damn well knew that I was now going to be flying a lot more than I'd intended, as instead of keeping watch, she was going to have to be working on this.

Joy.

The ancient wood that they'd found was a massive thing, cut from what had to have been a tree once, or maybe…you know what, I didn't know what or where it'd come from, but it was clearly hundreds of years long dead, and desiccated. The grain showed patterns that spoke of centuries of growth, and there were marks where metal brackets had once secured it, to something probably as part of a floor or wall, judging from the shape of it.

It was roughly shaped like a row of seats, but with a dipped section behind the seating that had presumably held something long ago, be that water or…

Fuck it, it held *something* once, and although there were a lot of jagged damage marks and sections where it looked like it'd been hacked at by something, it was large enough and solid enough for our purposes.

As Therin worked—Oracle hovered nearby and occasionally made suggestions that had him alternating between what I guessed was fascination and terror—I examined our makeshift column as everyone got settled back into place.

Marteen had his people spread out in a rough wedge at the rear. He and Finna had split out the most experienced fighters along the column on the outer edges.

They'd stripped what armor they could from the Changed Ones' stores, to augment their own, and although it wasn't pretty, it would stop a claw or pincer.

Finna's group took up positions along the sides of our main body, where the civilians and less combat-capable would march in the middle. I watched as they worked out a rotation, with fresh fighters stepping in every hour to maintain alertness, and those who had been on the outside migrating inward to help the civilians and weaker members of the party.

The floating slab—which Zyenna had already dubbed "the carrier," and the shitty name was catching on, unfortunately—would take up the center of our formation.

Therin knelt beside it now, carefully carving runes into the ancient wood with a silver stylus that reminded me of a soldering iron with the way that smoke floated free of it. Oracle held one of the corrupted manastones, her face screwed up in concentration as she filtered its power into something usable.

"There's a lot of damage," she reported eventually. "I don't know what they did to them, but it's the outside of the stones that's the worst. There's still clean mana at the core. The trick is going to be filtering it out without getting infected by it. And no, don't worry, I'm not willing to take any risks with it. We should be able to power the enchantments for at least eight hours before needing to switch stones, safely, and then I'm going to destroy the stone, and move to the next."

"When you destroy the stones, is that going to be the best choice? And you're sure that this won't explode?" I asked the pair.

"The other option is that we leave the stones lying about. They'll gradually absorb more mana, and then they'll spread their infection to anything they touch." Oracle shook her head. "Destroying them is definitely the best option, though I'll do my best to make it as quiet as possible."

Therin looked up when I repeated my question to him, blinking owlishly before shaking his head, wiping sweat from his brow. "The base matrix is stable. See these containment runes here?" He pointed to a complex pattern that wrapped around the edge of the slab. "They'll safely bleed off any excess energy. Worst case, it just stops floating."

"Which would be bad if we're running from something," I pointed out.

"That's why we're using multiple stones," Oracle explained. "I can swap them quickly if needed, and we should have enough, at my guess, to keep us going for a little over two weeks."

"That's a relief then." I sighed. "Annoying that we're having to waste them on this."

"You wouldn't want to try absorbing their mana into you directly," Oracle assured me, smiling. "That's how the Changed Ones were evolving, and I don't think extra arms and chitin would suit you."

"Definitely not," I agreed.

The sun was touching the horizon by the time we were ready to move some two and a half hours later. Long shadows stretched across the ruined city, and the wind was picking up, carrying the eternal whisper of sand.

Somewhere in the growing darkness, I heard the distant sound of Sehran calling out to anyone who might be hiding that we were heading south and this was their last chance, but nobody had shown up yet.

The carrier…well, it was sort of living up to its name, in that it was covered with a buttload of shit, especially the masses of cloth that Zyenna had been sharing around as bedding. It was also floating, but it was…

Amateurish.

That was the best description, and it wasn't the fun kind, either.

It floated, yeah, but it also drifted constantly; where the ground dipped, it dipped, as the enchantments worked to keep it about four feet from the ground.

That was a good height, sure…a little high for people to get on, but manageable.

The problem was that if the ground was lower on one side? It tilted precariously, bobbed constantly enough that anyone aboard it would have a nasty case of seasickness, and just made me wince as I considered how going across the tops of the dunes was going to work.

It was better than nothing, though, so fuck it.

"Form up!" I called out. "Civilians in the middle—two lines, keep it tight. Anyone who can't maintain the pace stays with the carrier. First rotation of pushers, take your positions."

Four of Marteen's people moved to the corners of the slab. With Therin's enchantments in place, it took only light pressure to keep it moving. The first group of elderly merchants settled onto it uncomfortably, though they relaxed somewhat when nobody accused them of being lazy.

The piled cloth that they'd been using in the caves when we first found them was now layered over and over on the carrier. They rested atop that, making it as comfortable a journey as it could be for them, though some already looked uncomfortably green.

We moved out as the last light faded, passing through streets still littered with scorpion corpses and the occasional pile of smoldering chitin. The destruction we'd wreaked was clear everywhere, adding to the ruined state of the city.

Collapsed buildings, impact craters, and in one place, a section of road that had been partly melted made it clear that, back home? I'd be headed for the Hague for war crimes against history, and I'd probably be lynched by archaeologists.

Of course, as the people who would come here and search for evidence would probably get eaten within a day by the monsters that would return as soon as we left, we were probably safe enough from that.

Sehran soon joined us and started to range ahead, her form briefly visible against the darkening sky before she vanished into the gloom. Through our bond, I could sense her methodically checking each potential ambush point as we approached.

"Seven days," I muttered to myself, as our column snaked through the ruins. "Seven days to cross the desert and find those kids."

*"We'll make it,"* Oracle sent to me from her position floating near the carrier. *"Though I think you're going to have to get used to more flying than you planned."*

I nodded grimly. Between maintaining the carrier's enchantments and keeping watch, she'd have her hands full. Which meant more time in the air for me, something I loved, but I also knew that I needed to be seen slogging along with the people, and I damn well needed the training as well.

That, in turn, meant for the first few days, we'd be keeping Sehran a lot closer to the column than I'd hoped. That was life, though—no plan survived contact with the enemy.

As if to emphasize the point, a distant screech echoed through the ruins, as something big announced its presence, met a second later by another shriek.

"It's gonna be a long fucking week," I growled to myself, then I raised my voice. "All right, people, let's pick up the pace!"

# CHAPTER TWELVE

Sand got *everywhere*. No matter how tightly wrapped your clothing, no matter how well secured your gear, it found a way in. After hours of running, then trudging, then running through the dunes, I was grimly aware of every goddamn grain that had worked its way into my armor's joints.

We moved steadily through the night, our pace dictated by the civilians in the center. It quickly became clear that it wasn't going to be as fast as I wanted it to be.

The carrier proved its worth early, allowing us to rotate the weaker members through without having to stop. Therin hadn't left his position on it, continuously working on his enchantments even as Oracle fed power from the corrupted manastones into his creation.

*"How're you holding up?"* I asked her at one point through our bond as I jogged alongside the column.

*"The corruption is…strange,"* she replied. *"It's like it's alive somehow. But I'm managing to filter it."*

The desert night was surprisingly noisy: the whisper of wind across sand, the crunch of boots, the occasional snarl as someone stumbled and cursed how damn hard it was to run on the sand. Above all, every so often, I'd hear Sehran's wings as she circled overhead, scanning for threats.

Our first warning came just before midnight. A howl echoed across the dunes, quickly answered by others. Through our bond, Sehran sent an image: sleek, predatory forms moving through the darkness, larger than normal jackals and hunting in a coordinated pack.

"Incoming," I called out; my voice carried to the guards as I moved over to that flank. "Desert hunters, some kind of hounds, moving in from the east."

Finna and Marteen's people tightened their formation as the first of the beasts loped into view. They were ugly things, their hides scarred and patchy, with oversized heads and jutting teeth. But it was their eyes that caught my attention. They gleamed in the darkness, making it clear they were nocturnal hunters.

*"How bad?"* I asked Sehran.

"Not bad. Maybe I could take two of the guards, cripple the monsters and let them finish them off?"

"Do it."

That was the way of it. At first, this close to the city, it was small packs or drifting, single monsters. Sehran would stun them, distracting them with her song, then let the guards do the actual work, essentially power-leveling them. Then the small group would gather up what meat they could, and run after us.

The bags of holding were mainly full at this point, but people soon chose to unload things into the carrier for some strange reason, rather than carrying dripping flesh for long.

The first night was the hardest, and with good reason: most of these people had never run a mile in their lives, if you discounted their escape from the slavers in the first place.

That meant that keeping them running required a lot more effort on our part than it should have, and part of that was for Oracle to cast a frostfire circle every so often ahead of the party.

The column would run through; they'd be healed, and then boom. They were still tired, sure, but the actual physical damage that was being done was reversed.

For the first night, I made them keep going for about six hours, before having Sehran find us a rocky outcropping that we set up camp in. Water was summoned—and that caused a few creatures to come looking, sensing that most valuable commodity—and the meat we'd collected so far was roasted.

It was nothing special; literally, there wasn't so much as a vegetable to share around. Instead, it was massive chunks of scorpion and be thankful, or be hungry.

People chose to be thankful, and then slept under the cloth, as instead of lying in it as blankets, we set up a sunshade and maintained a rotating watch.

Most of the little caravan slept the sleep of the exhausted, and when the sun fell, we set off again.

It took a full day before we encountered a pack of the hounds that was large enough and determined enough that we judged it was better off letting them get close.

It also meant that because people hadn't really "seen" the monsters—they'd just heard distant fighting and seen the guards come back each time, unharmed thanks to Sehran healing them as well—they'd been losing their healthy dose of fear.

"A single pack, but they're definitely predators," Oracle called out. "We'll need to kill them. If we drive them off, they'll just follow us."

"Let them come close enough that we can deal with them without leaving the group then." I sighed, already thoroughly sick of the desert.

I didn't like it. I'd rather kill them before they got close to the group, but there were too many for Sehran to take anything less than half the guard to deal with, or our little group. And there were both wyverns following at a distance and other packs of hounds now and then.

I just couldn't take the chance.

The pack split smoothly, trying to flank our column. I counted at least fifteen of them, working with the kind of coordination you'd expect from trained war dogs. Their leader—a massive brute with only one ear and a collection of scars I could have played noughts and crosses on—kept them just outside crossbow range.

"They're herding us," Marteen called from the rear. "Trying to push us west."

"Toward what?" I started to ask, then switched to the bond and reached out. *"Sehran?"*

*"Just found it,"* she replied. *"Something big, buried maybe a hundred meters to our west. The jackals are trying to drive us closer to it, but it's not moving."*

I thought about it for a second, then shook my head. Best not to let them get much closer, after all; an object lesson could come later.

I triggered Mana Overdrive, my movements becoming preternaturally fast as I drew my naginata. "Okay, people, keep the column moving south. Marteen, focus on the rear and don't get driven anywhere. I'll deal with our furry friends."

The pack leader saw me coming and bared its teeth in what looked disturbingly like a grin. Then it threw back its head and howled—not a hunting cry this time, but something that carried power. The sound rippled across the sand, and the sand all around me softened, making it harder to run.

*"Sound-based magic,"* Oracle sent to me. "Be careful!" she added aloud, her voice carrying as I ran, the column streaming past me in the darkness.

I answered with a growl of my own, channeling mana through my blade until it glowed with a crimson light. The pack leader and his friends bounded in, clearly expecting to end this quickly. I lifted slightly out of the sand, my Soaring Majesty freeing me from the softened footing, as I grinned at the incoming pack.

Three of the beasts hit me at once, leading the way. Their coordination was impressive as they bounded in from different angles. My blade carved a crimson arc through the air, catching the first across its left shoulder, then continuing through its face—which was cut in two by the razor-sharp and evolving weapon—and sent it tumbling, thrashing as it died with pained squeals and whimpers.

The second's teeth snapped shut on empty air as I twisted aside, before punting it in the chin and sending it to bark-halla while the third actually managed to get its jaws around my armored forearm.

The creature's eyes widened comically as its teeth failed to penetrate the ancient Praetorian plate. Then I released my naginata with my other hand and brought my fist down hard on its skull, feeling bone crack beneath the blow.

"Bad dog!" I shouted as it let go, collapsing and thrashing in the sand.

*"Watch your left!"* Oracle sent, and I spun to meet the pack leader's charge.

It was fast, faster than something that size had any right to be. Its jaws gaped impossibly wide as it lunged, and I caught a glimpse of something glowing in its throat just before another of those sonic pulses hit me.

This time, I was ready. The sand might be softened, but I wasn't touching it anymore. I met its charge with a thrust that should have taken it in the chest, only to have it twist in midair, somehow finding footing where there shouldn't be any, as it launched itself over my head.

"Clever bastard," I muttered, spinning to track it. Two more of its pack were already moving in, while others had sprinted around me and carried on, now harrying the column's flanks, testing for weakness.

The pack leader howled again. This time, the sound tried to work its way into my mind, suggesting that I should just lie down, just rest for a moment…

*"Jax!"* Oracle's voice cut through the compulsion like a knife. *"It's trying to put you to sleep!"*

I snorted at the simplistic attack, shook off the effect and triggered another burst of Mana Overdrive, snatching back up my naginata.

The world slowed around me as I moved; my blade became a blur of crimson light. Three more of the beasts went down, their bodies literally falling apart as I carved through them, chasing after the damn thing.

The pack leader's next howl was full of frustration. It gathered its remaining followers with a series of sharp barks, clearly preparing for another coordinated assault.

That's when Sehran dropped from the sky like an avenging angel, her claws extended and her wings casting massive shadows in the darkness. She landed atop the pack leader with devastating effect, her natural grace augmented by demonic strength. She literally drove it to the ground, latching onto its throat and biting down hard.

The pack's discipline broke. Most ran, while only a handful stayed, caught between my blade and the guards of the caravan, trying to decide whether running or helping their leader was the best play.

*"The thing in the sand is thrashing around,"* Oracle warned. *"Whatever it is, it's noticed the fighting."*

I nodded grimly. "Time to end this."

I burst forward. The sand under me whipped into contrails that floated away as I hacked left and right, blood spraying as I reduced the first two to kibble. At that point, as their leader gave one final whimper and then lay still, the remaining beasts fled into the darkness, their courage dying with their leader.

Sehran shuddered, lifting herself up and rubbing an arm across scarlet lips, before grinning at me. "Damn, I needed that," she admitted. "There's something so satisfying in feeding on a fresh kill."

"Well, you do you, boo." I snorted, looking to where the column was vanishing in the darkness. *"Oracle, everything okay?"* I sent.

*"Whatever it is in the sand, I don't think it can move—probably an ambush predator, and with the pack...oh, wait!"*

We both got a slightly out-of-focus and dim vision from Oracle of a member of the pack that had strayed too close to the monster in its panic.

It was lashed around by tentacles and dragged, yowling, out of sight and into the shifting sands in seconds. The sound of breaking bones lasted longer than the creature lived.

"Well, on we go." I sighed. "Sehran, you want to catch up?"

"You mind if I take a few minutes?" She clearly wanted to feed some more.

"Nah, I can keep watch," I assured her. "Just catch up soon."

"Will do!" She grinned, her lips and teeth still bloody, and then leaned back down. Her wings closed around, hiding her as she fed on the fresh corpse.

I shook my head as I lifted into the air.

I tended to forget about the more demonic aspects of Sehran until times like this, when I was forcibly reminded that yeah, she was a succubus and lived on both mana and...life-bearing fluids.

It made a lot of sense out of the old tales about them, I supposed. And as long as Jian could walk the next day, I certainly wasn't going to have anything to say about their relationship.

As long as they were both having fun, anyway.

I flew back across the sand, catching up to the column in only a few minutes, then headed higher, checking out the sand all around and the sky.

In the distance, I could see the occasional creature still. Most were smaller, barely appearing before they were gone again. But here and there, larger creatures roamed, including something in the distance that flapped wings that looked to be absolutely huge.

It was illuminated by the distant moon, and whatever it was, I was damn glad it was headed away from us, as it looked to be around half the size of the city we'd just left.

"Any news?" Finna asked as I landed nearby and she dropped back. "Are they still following us?"

"The hounds?" I asked, confused.

"Yeah?"

"No." I shook my head, grinning in the darkness of my helm as I forced myself to remember these people weren't used to dealing with the legion and had little in the way of Darkvision. "They're all either dead or running. The survivors won't be coming after us."

I heard the word being passed back, and the version that Oracle passed back to me had it as there being dozens more than there had been, and the smallest was suddenly the size of a draft horse.

I shook my head and ran on.

We made good time after that. The column settled into a rhythm broken only by the occasional rotation of people to and from the carrier. Therin's enchantments were holding steady, though I caught Oracle wincing occasionally as she filtered mana from the corrupted manastones.

Overall though, the decision was that we were moving a lot faster than we'd expected, and while I couldn't predict how much with any real accurace in the goddamn desert, it looked like we'd beat our estimate out.

The moon was sinking into the horizon when several hours later, Sehran rejoined us, having been scouting ahead again, and now looked refreshed and alert. She drifted in closer, letting our people see her for the morale boost before she vanished again.

*"There's something odd about the desert ahead,"* she warned. *"The sand's...different. Darker in places. And there are these strange formations that look like glass."*

*"Glass?"* I asked, but there wasn't much more she could add, beyond patches of glittery streaks that reflected the distant moonlight.

We found out what she meant an hour later. The dunes gave way to an area where the sand had been fused into twisted shapes, like someone had taken a blowtorch to the desert. The glass formations jutted from the ground like frozen waves, their surfaces reflecting the moonlight.

"This is recent," Oracle observed. "Maybe a few months old at most."

"What could do this?" Marteen examined one of the formations. "Some kind of magic?"

"Dragon, probably," I replied, recognizing the pattern. "Though what one was doing out here..."

"Lord?"

"Hmmm?" I asked, distracted, before Toren spoke again.

"Lord, are we stopping here?" he asked.

Something about his tone made me pay attention, looking away from the streaks of fused glass to the man, and then to the group behind him.

They were all absolutely fucked, covered in dust, sweat stained, and just...wow.

"Yeah," I said softly as I took their condition in. "Let's camp here, I think."

"Oh, thank God..." he whimpered.

I winced, turning to the distant speck that I knew was Sehran, and sent her a call to return, before reaching out to Oracle.

*"We need to—"* I started, only to cut myself off as Zyenna started to speak, directing the people as quickly as she could, while Toren lay down on the sand.

*"She's making a play for his role as well,"* Oracle pointed out to me in the silence of the bond.

I snorted. *"I don't care who does the job. If he does, he can deal with it. All I care about is that the job is done."*

The next ten minutes were filled with groans, declarations of undying pain and the end of the world, and piteous cries to be allowed to rest, even as Oracle and I summoned healing fountains and the camp cook got to work portioning out food again.

He was as fucked as the rest, so I hit him with a healing spell as well, though it made little difference.

The weird glass formations proved useful, once we cleared the area of any obvious threats. They provided anchor points for the cloth, and the carrier itself became a central support, with Therin muttering about resonance patterns even as he drifted off into an exhausted sleep underneath it.

"Two-hour rotations," I told Marteen as he organized the watch. "I'll take first and second. Let everyone else get as much rest as they can."

"You should rest too," Oracle insisted, but I shook my head.

"I've got more Stamina than most of them combined," I reminded her. "Get some sleep. You and Sehran can watch over my stubborn ass later."

The day passed slowly. I spent most of it pacing the perimeter, occasionally catching snippets of conversation from those who couldn't sleep. They spoke in hushed voices about the hound pack, each telling growing more elaborate than the last. By dawn, I'd apparently fought off fifty of the beasts single-handed, each one the size of a small house.

"Your legend grows," Zyenna commented quietly as she joined me for the pre-dawn watch. She looked marginally less exhausted than the others, though that wasn't saying much.

"Let them talk." I shrugged. "If it helps them believe we can make it across this wasteland, I'll fight a hundred ghost hounds."

She studied me thoughtfully. "Tell me about Dravith. What's it like, this empire you're building?"

"Green," I replied without thinking. "Forests and mountains, rivers that actually have water in them. Cities where people can walk the streets without fear of slavers or monsters. A land where the legion is growing, where the gods are back, and they answer prayers and you can get a fair chance."

"Sounds like a fairy tale."

"It was, not long ago. What I'm guessing it's like here…well, it was that way there too. I lost my temper when I was new to one of the cities, when I saw the slavery that was there too, and I kinda destroyed a plaza…or two. It used to be good, though, and it's already a hell of a lot better than it was. Now?" I gestured to our sleeping companions. "Now we're making it real here again as well. One city at a time, one person at a time."

"And what happens to the guilds in this new empire of yours?"

I grinned, though she couldn't see it through my helm. "What do you think?"

"I think I'm going to enjoy watching them trying to bully you," she admitted. "Assuming we survive this little jaunt across the desert."

"Speaking of which…" I nodded toward the eastern horizon, where the sky was beginning to darken. "Time to wake everyone. We need to move while we can."

The next few days fell into a pattern. We'd travel through the night, making what progress we could across the endless dunes. Occasional threats would emerge: more packs of hunting beasts, a few giant scorpions, once even what looked like a snake big enough to swallow the carrier whole. We dealt with them all, though each fight left us a little more tired, a little more drained.

"Gods, I miss beaches," I muttered wistfully to Oracle during one rest period, sitting on the edge of a sand dune and staring out across the endless ridges. "Nice, peaceful beaches with no monsters trying to eat us, the water cool and clear."

"You'd be bored within an hour," she replied fondly.

"True," I admitted. "But damn, I'd enjoy that hour."

Sehran kept us informed of what lay ahead, though the desert seemed to stretch endlessly in every direction. On the fourth day, she reported seeing what might have been structures on the horizon, but they turned out to be more of those glass formations, these ones towering like crystalline mountains.

"The work of dragons, perhaps?" Marteen mused as we made camp in their shadow. "My grandfather used to tell stories about them. Said they'd fight over territory, their battles reshaping the land itself, and that their breath was hot enough to turn sand to glass."

"They did more than that," I replied, remembering what Amon had shown me. "They helped build the empire, once. Before everything fell apart."

"And now they're all dead." Toren sighed.

"Bollocks." I snorted. "Now they *sleep*, mostly. Waiting for something worth waking for." I didn't know much about dragons, but the rare touches I'd had with Tuthic'Amon's mind let me know that the dragons—the greater ones, anyway— were far from extinct; they just didn't give two shits about the rest of the realm anymore.

It was on the fifth day, as we approached what Sehran had identified as a possible resting place—an old caravanserai half-buried in the sand—that everything went wrong.

The first warning was a tremor that ran through the ground, strong enough to drive half the group to their knees.

That tremor was followed by another, and another, forming a rhythm that was definitely not natural. Sand cascaded down the dunes around us as something massive moved beneath the surface.

*"I can feel life,"* Sehran reported, her mental voice tense. *"Three of them, moving in formation, deep down. They're hunting together, and they're…they're bigger than the ones in the city."*

"Of course they are," I muttered. "Oracle, get the carrier to that structure! Marteen, Finna, defensive positions!"

The old caravanserai loomed ahead; its walls half-buried but still solid. If we could reach it, the stone foundation might give the people some protection from whatever was coming. But the distance…

The sand erupted fifty meters to our left as the first wurm breached the surface. Its segmented body just kept coming, rising higher and higher until it towered over us like some ancient monument to hunger.

Its armor gleamed with a weird iridescence in the fading light, and I counted at least six rows of teeth in its constantly moving maw as it twisted around, pointing at us.

The second burst free to our right, while the third…the third was still moving beneath us, its passage marked by the rippling sand.

*"They're coordinating,"* Oracle sent. *"The two we can see are herding us toward the third."*

*"Like the hounds,"* I replied grimly. *"Only bigger. Much bigger."*

The wurm on our left struck first, its massive head plunging down like a hammer. I triggered Mana Overdrive and Soaring Majesty simultaneously, launching myself into the air as its impact sent a shock wave through the sand that knocked half our people off their feet.

"Keep moving!" I shouted, my naginata already beginning to glow as I channeled power through it. "Get to the building! Finna, crossbows on the right one—try to drive it off! Marteen…"

The rest of my orders were lost as the second wurm attacked, its strike clearly aimed not at our people, but at the carrier itself. Oracle's magic flared as she immediately drew power from three manastones, creating a barrier that the massive creature slammed into with bone-jarring force.

Then the third one finally showed itself, and my heart skipped a beat. The beast erupted from the sand directly beneath our column; its armored segments missed our people by inches as it rose like some horrible parody of a snake being charmed from a basket. But where the other two were massive, this one…

"Oh, you have got to be fucking *kidding* me," I snarled.

That fucker was *huge*!

The third wurm kept rising, and rising, and rising. Its armored segments were easily twice the width of the others, and covered in crystalline growths that caught what little light remained. When it finally stopped emerging, its head alone was the size of a small house.

*"They're not after us,"* Oracle sent suddenly as she saw the way they were facing, while people scrambled away in panic. *"They're after the carrier! The manastones we're using to power it…"*

*"The corruption,"* Sehran agreed. *"They can sense it!"*

The massive wurm's head swayed for a moment, then plunged down toward the carrier. Oracle's barrier flared again, but this time I could hear the strain in her mental voice as she fought to maintain it.

"Everyone off!" I roared. "Abandon the carrier! Therin…"

"No, Therin, I need you to…" Oracle snapped, speaking quickly.

I barely caught half of it, as I sprinted toward the nearest, one of the pair of smaller wurms, slashing out with my naginata. The weapon glowed as I fed fire mana into it.

The blade cut deeply, the skin parting like silk. The smell of searing flesh carried free as the wurm I'd targeted roared and twisted around, trying to find me.

Its own segments prevented it getting around at the right angle, and I raced on, slicing it open as quickly as I could.

Sehran fired off an Explosive Compression spell at the largest. The detonation barely fazed it.

*"It's feeding on the mana!"* Oracle sent to us both. *"They want the carrier, so get ready to let them have it!"*

"I'm nearly ready!" the young enchanter yelled. His hands were flying across the runes, carving jagged adjustments into them even as people scrambled clear, crouching down at the edge of the barrier and getting ready to run.

"Run when I say now!" Oracle ordered. "Jax, I need a distraction!"

The nearest of the smaller wurms struck then; its attacks focused entirely on breaking through Oracle's barrier as the one I'd been maiming—or so I thought—clearly gave up on me. The third one reared back, evidently preparing for something bigger.

*"Whatever you're going to do,"* I sent as I crouched and then launched myself into the air, carving a line upward and unleashing a lightning bolt into the parted flesh, *"do it fast!"*

However, the largest had absorbed the mana from the spell that Sehran had cast. They clearly had no such ability to do it when you gutted them and fired a spell inside, as the one I'd been targeting went mental, thrashing and convulsing, crashing to the ground and shuddering as I continued to channel into the wound, smoke starting to rise from it.

"Now!" Therin screamed.

Oracle released her barrier just before the massive wurm struck. Those who had been aboard sprinted in all directions to try to get clear, even as its jaws closed around the carrier. For a moment, I thought I saw Therin grinning manically as his modified runes flared with eye-searing brightness.

Then the wurm dragged our makeshift transport into the sand, and everything went silent.

Silent, that was, apart from the screams of three of the four people who had been aboard it, being sucked down into the sand as the wurm dove deeper.

"Run!" I bellowed to the others, already moving to intercept the second of the smaller wurms. "Get to the—"

The explosion caught us all by surprise. The ground heaved upward as whatever Therin had done to his enchantments detonated, sending shock waves through the sand that I could feel even in the air. The two remaining wurms thrashed wildly, clearly stupefied by the vibrations conducted through their bodies.

*"We need to be quick!"* Sehran reported from above. *"The explosion...the vibrations stunned them!"*

I didn't waste time responding. The second wurm was still reeling, its head weaving drunkenly as it tried to recover. My naginata carved through its hide like it was paper. Black ichor sprayed as I opened its throat from jaw to chest. I did as I had before: firing a blast of lightning into its insides, keeping it up until Sehran's

Explosive Compression flashed past, pushing into the already open wound and detonating.

I flew back—damn fast—to get clear of the radius: the spell exploded, then spread out and yanked inward, basically cutting the wurm in half.

The other one managed to gather enough control of itself to try retreating into the sand, but Oracle was ready. A barrage of lightning bolts hammered into its exposed flesh, cooking the meat and stunning it more and more as I landed next to it. I sent my naginata digging into the flesh again, and this time worked rhythmically to carve my way deep enough that I could sever the head.

It took a long minute, with Oracle shocking it over and over, but as the segments peeled back, I just kept lifting, cutting, and then carving the next bit wider again.

By the time the kill notification floated free, I was covered in guts, the area around us stank of death, and I was down to a third of my mana. But the job was done.

I stepped back, looking around, then sighed and made my way to the caravanserai, seeing the horrified, exhausted faces of those who sat inside, and I nodded.

"That was a bad one," I admitted softly, my words carrying in the silence. "I'm sorry, we did all we could to limit the casualties, but…"

"But a giant fucking wurm just ate my mother," one of the guards interrupted, staring blankly out at the devastation.

"Yeah," I said, unsure of what else to say. "It did."

"I hate the fucking desert," another admitted, and I snorted.

I couldn't help it, and it felt wildly disrespectful to the freshly dead, but a short, bitter laugh tore loose from me. I nodded. "Hell yeah," I agreed. "Fuck the desert."

That started a general low level of agreement, as those who had lost family and friends were comforted by the others. I wandered over to what was left of our transportation, now half-buried in cooling glass where the sand had fused from the heat of the explosion.

"Well," Therin said weakly, tottering over to examine his handiwork a few minutes later, "that could have gone worse."

"Could have gone better too," Zyenna muttered, looking at the place where some of her friends and the last of the cloth had been lost. "Though I suppose being alive counts for something."

"Something," I agreed. "Sehran, can you see anything?"

"I'll go high." She launched herself into the air as I reached out, drawing Oracle to me.

*"We're close now,"* Sehran sent down from above a minute or so later. *"Maybe five more hours to get out of the desert. I can make out trees in the distance and we can—"* She broke off suddenly, her wings beating harder and carrying her higher.

*"Sehran?"* I sent, looking up.

*"Fires,"* she reported grimly. *"A large encampment, maybe two hours ahead of us. And I can see…yes, there's a small group approaching it. Four children and two adults, one being carried."*

"We found them, and we're too late." I cursed.

# CHAPTER THIRTEEN

"We're not too late," Oracle insisted, resting one hand on my arm. "We won't be too late until they're dead, and they're not dead yet."

I nodded grimly, studying the caravanserai's ancient walls. The structure had weathered centuries of desert storms, and although half-buried, its upper levels still provided decent shelter and a commanding view of the surrounding dunes. More importantly, it had a solid foundation, something that would make it harder for more wurms to attack from below.

That being said, I was thinking that three fucking giants of their species being absolutely gutted here would probably send a pretty potent message to any others.

That, in turn, was going to be a problem though, I realized with a groan, as all the free meat was going to draw a fuckload of scavengers.

"Toren." My voice carried in the post-battle silence. "Get everyone inside and start setting up defenses. We're not moving until we have a solid plan."

The former caravan master nodded, already directing people toward the entrance. Most moved sluggishly, exhausted from our desert crossing and the recent fight. The loss of the carrier meant we'd lost most of our supplies as well, though some had managed to grab essential items before Therin's explosive surprise. Most had been taking advantage of the carrier to make their run a little easier.

Well, we were all paying for that now.

*"What are we looking at?"* I asked Sehran through our bond as she circled overhead.

*"I can't see much from here. I'm going to head closer, okay?"*

*"Go for it. Just be careful,"* I agreed, before sighing and looking at the battered and exhausted refugees. All of whom were still trying to recover from the trek, with the absolute shit show at the end just topping it all off.

Half an hour was all it took, but by the time that Sehran returned, and Oracle and I had set up healing fountains for the people, the first of the scavengers had arrived.

"We've got two choices," Zyenna was saying as Sehran landed. "Either we leave and set up somewhere else, or we fortify the entrance and hope that nothing tries to dig its way in."

"Have we got anything we can fortify the entrance with?" I asked.

She hesitated, before gesturing at me. "That fire spell you have…can you use it to melt the sand?"

"I could," I admitted after a look at Oracle. "Though the cost in mana would be high."

"And we'd not be able to get back out," her son pointed out. "Maybe we simply pile the sand up at the entrance? Bury it and mound the sand up, then we stay damn quiet inside?"

"I'd hate to trust to anything not spotting you to keep you safe," I said.

"There's little reason that anything will attack us," Zyenna pointed out. "There's enough meat here to keep a butchery busy for a solid month. And given the choice between a fight or fresh, easily recoverable meat, most monsters and animals will take the easy meat."

"Most but not all," I agreed. "Toren, you're being quiet."

"I think we should move," he said. "Yes, I agree with the 'little reason for them to attack us' argument, but little reason isn't no reason. And frankly, while I like the idea of walls between me and anything that comes looking for all this…meat." He shook his head. "I don't think it's a good idea to be around monsters driven wild by the blood that's been spilled. More and more powerful things will be drawn in, and eventually something will notice us. If the meat's all gone, then it'll eat us next."

"That's a rather grim way to look at it." Zyenna then sighed. "But, you have a point. We wouldn't be able to go far, though. Perhaps a mile, if that."

"A mile would be enough." He shrugged. "If the land here is anything like what we passed on the way out into the desert—and it should be…we could only be a few dozen miles at most from the route we took—then there's going to be places we can camp out of sight."

"Get ready to do that then," I said when they both turned to me, waiting for my decision. "I agree. People aren't going to like it, but that's life. Oh, and get the cook to get some meat—"

"It'll be too acidic." Toren interrupted me. "The wurms produce an acid that their bodies can process. For a normal man trying to eat that, it wouldn't be wise."

"Dammit, and all the food…" I looked at the crater where the carrier had vanished, and along with it most of the scorpion meat we'd taken from the city, and he nodded.

"And most of the waterskins were in there as well," he pointed out.

"Fuck's sake." I groaned. "Fine, give them ten more minutes, then get them ready to move." I turned to Sehran. "Give me good news," I implored.

"The camp is well-organized," she reported. "Multiple rings of guards, not counting the people in the tents or out of sight I counted over six hundred people. I saw at least sixty slaves in the central area, with a hell of a lot of soldiers around the outside of the camp. The children are being brought to what looks like a processing area. They're checking them for injuries before adding them to the main group."

"Any sign they know we're coming?"

"They're alert, but not high alert. The guards are keeping regular patrols. No signs of extra preparations."

"Well, that sucks monkey balls," I whispered, gnawing on a knuckle as I thought. "How many soldiers?"

"Maybe three hundred."

"We can't fight three hundred soldiers." Zyenna came up to us, and I waved a hand at her in agreement.

"I know," I assured her. "Even if I had my normal team here, I'd be wary of attacking three hundred goddamn soldiers. Are they professional warriors, could you tell? Or are they…"

"They're on guard, spread out around the outer edge of the camp, but they're wrong."

"How so?" I asked.

"There's three hundred of them, or close enough, and they're standing at attention, facing out into the night, all of them with weapons and shields at the ready."

"Right." I gestured for her to go on.

"But right behind there, the camp is…well, it's a mess. If they have soldiers who are that disciplined, that alert at all times, then why is their camp a mess?" she asked. "If you take the soldiers away, then it looks like a camp of drink and debauchery. The slave pens are ringed by guards, but while those guards stand ready, watching over their charges, others dressed in silks just swan in and out, claiming slaves or drinking, and…"

"The soldiers, are they wearing a uniform?" Zyenna asked suddenly, and Sehran nodded.

"I think so. Their gear is identical as well. They have a black tabard, or, well, it's dark. It might be dark blue…"

"Could it be green?" Marteen asked sharply.

"A dark green…yeah. I'm looking at a distance in the dark with my Darkvision being flared out by the bonfires," Sehran admitted.

"The Sons of the Deep," Zyenna spat. "Those rat bastards went that far?"

"What?" I asked.

Marteen hesitated, then spoke up as his mother continued to curse. "They're an order of slavers, and a particularly reviled one," he explained. "It's said they sell their slaves twice over—first as they live and then, when they die, they're raised by the caravan's resident necromancer. Where even for most of the slaver bands, that's a step too far, for the Sons of the Deep…they count necromancers as a valued tool, and they force their victims to serve even after death, adding them to their forces.

"The inner grouping of guards will be slaves they've bought from the arenas, skilled warriors who are forced to obey by the use of control collars. Very good fighters and highly dangerous, compelled to obey and protect their masters. Then the ones you'll have seen on the outside of the camp and the guards will be the dead, and that means that we've got a serious problem."

"Oh really, another?" I quipped, and he nodded grimly, not getting the joke.

"It means that we're best off running, because our only chance is to get far enough away that they decide not to come after us. The dead can't be reasoned with, and they're…"

"They're shitty fighters," I said flatly. "Unless they have some kind of special magic way to make them good?"

"Well, no, but they're the dead. They don't get tired, they don't get—"

"They don't level and they can't adjust to changing situations," I pointed out. "And as to their weaknesses, let's be clear—if we can kill the necromancers who raised them, it's all over."

"But we'd need to fight our way through hundreds of them to reach their masters!" Marteen interjected. "Literally hundreds. And when we finally got there, we'd be surrounded and exhausted, and they'd—"

"Die," I said. "They'll die. You said they're enjoying a big party right now, Sehran?" I asked, and she nodded. "Good. Okay, let's move apart from the others. We've got some attention we don't need."

The others were staring at us, several clearly trying to work out what was going on. Right then, the last thing I needed was more questions as I figured out a new plan.

I gathered Oracle, Sehran, Zyenna, Toren, Marteen, and Finna near one of the walls, where we could talk without being overheard. "They still think they can track us," I said quietly. "Which means they'll be watching for movement from the north."

"The tracking stone." Marteen nodded. "The one their spy had. We left it back there, so that should have gained us some space. They probably have others tuned to it."

There was a brief pause, then he let it all out in a rush. "What happened to the spy?"

"What do you mean?" I asked.

"Well, he was inside when we left. You said you were going to question him…" He looked at me, half embarrassed and half nervous.

"Do you want me to answer that?" I asked him after a brief pause. "He had almost no information or I'd not be asking you now, would I?"

"No?"

"No," I agreed. "So, take a second and think about it, Marteen. Do you want me to tell you what happened to him?"

"He's dead," Zyenna said firmly.

"By now? Probably," I agreed.

"Probably?"

"Fine, you want to know, I'll tell you." I shrugged. "We'd killed two of the group, but he had a stone that let the slavers track him. I couldn't risk that the stone might stop working or somehow indicate if its user was dead, so I left him in a situation where he'd not be moving around and he wasn't dead, yet. Now ask yourself…do you want me to explain further?"

"No," Marteen said quickly, even as Zyenna and the others nodded their understanding.

I moved on, amused that although Marteen had led troops in battle, he was still green enough that he was that squeamish. Mind you, I'd been squeamish with some things, but slavers?

I thought back to the state I'd left him in, in the cave, before we'd gone to the city. I'd not enjoyed it, certainly, but he was helping the slavers and he knew exactly what was going to happen to those people when the slavers caught up.

I'd broken his arms and legs, and I'd left him to die of dehydration and hunger. It wasn't nice, but neither was what he'd done. Frankly, my conscience was clear with him.

"So, they're expecting us to either die in the desert or stagger in from this direction, half-dead and desperate." I smiled grimly. "Instead, we're going to hit them from the south. But we need to be smart about this."

"My lord," Finna started, then caught herself. "Jax. These people can barely stand. Even with healing, they're not ready for another fight, and certainly not against overwhelming odds!"

"I know." I glanced at the huddled survivors. "That's why most of them are going to move out and then get some sleep. We'll take a small team, the best fighters, the ones who can still move quietly. And the rest stay to protect the others."

"And what are we going to do? Just run in screaming and die with honor?" Marteen asked skeptically. "Or are you suggesting we leave them here as a distraction and we run away, abandon them?"

Oracle spoke up. "No. They do serve as our distraction, but not in the way that you're thinking. We don't know if the slavers have any other way to detect people, so if they do, they'll be expecting us to approach from the north. If most of our people stay here, that's exactly what they'll see."

"While we circle around and you get ready to hit them from behind," I explained. "While it would have been a lot easier to do this if their sentries were as we thought, this could actually work out better, because they're going to be relying on the slaves and then the undead. If I can take out the necromancers in the first wave, then you'll know when all the dead collapse. At that point, you and your team are going to run in and start freeing the slaves."

"You think that nobody will notice?" he asked in a disbelieving voice. "Or are we the sacrifices so that you can get away? It's been tried before! That's why the slaves in the inner area are all arena trained. They'll just roll over us!"

"Quit that shit," I snapped at him. "I'm not going to abandon any of you!"

"Then how in the seven hells are we going to—"

"While you and your people free the slaves, Oracle, Sehran, and I are going to storm the heart of the camp," I said.

"You're going to what?" Zyenna asked after a few seconds of stunned silence.

"We'll attack the heart of the camp from above," I repeated.

"I don't get it," Finna said. "Look, I'm sorry, but I just don't. If you can storm the heart of the ring, you might win—you *might*. And being able to fly, maybe you can take the leaders hostage and force them to tell their slaves to back down. But if they refuse? I mean, you'd be bluffing hard, but it's still bluffing."

"Who's bluffing?" I smiled grimly.

"You'd have to be," she said slowly. "No, Jax, you don't get it. If you kill their masters, then maybe—and I mean maybe—you could find whatever they use to control the slaves and then order some of them to stop. But you're never going to find them all. They hide things like this. There's a story about one of the leaders of the Sons of the Deep having the controller sewn into himself! It's probably a lie, but if it's not? How are you going to find all the—"

"I'm not going to," I said with a faint smile.

"You're going to use an imperial ability… here?" Oracle shook her head. "Jax, they'll know. Ni— The dark dick will know. Even if you don't claim the territory, the risk that the ability will declare you…it's too high."

"We can try to do it without, but as soon as it gets tight, as soon as the fight starts going badly, I'm doing it, Oracle. Tell me I'm making a mistake."

"You are!" she snapped. "You know you are. Dammit, Jax, we—I…"

"We could lose it all," I agreed. "We could lose it all by activating an imperial ability here, or we could get away with it. Remember, we're not claiming a location—we're freeing the slaves—and the feedback is entirely kept to the artifacts, the items."

"That's not the point," she retorted. "If *He* is watching, if He's paying attention…"

"If that dark dick doesn't know where we are, I'll eat His fuckin' hat." I snorted, gesturing at Marteen and the armored helmet that sort of fit him, more leather than metal and that made it look like he was wearing a pork pie on his head.

"Jax—"

"He's a *god*, Oracle, and I cut His avatar's head off and punted it like a football. I've got a craftsman literally making it into a goblet for me, and I ripped a fragment of His power free and tied it into me. There's no way He's just chalked it all up to experience and turned over a new leaf. If He doesn't already have forces on their way to us, it's because of some random rule that the gods live by. If that's the case, maybe me scratching my arse will invalidate it, and maybe all bets are off when I eat fish on a Friday. My point is that anything that's going to happen will happen regardless, and I'm not abandoning people to torture, slavery, and death because of a maybe!"

As the echo of my voice came back, I dragged down a shuddering breath and tried again for calm. "Oracle, you said it yourself enough times. We can only be who we are. You know who I am, and who I could easily be. If I turn away now, who knows when we'll try to care again.

"We need forces, *real* forces to secure and protect you, and to enable us to survive here. Either we do this right, or we need to accept that we're outmatched and we run. I can sense Tenandra—she's coming this way…they all are. But they're months of travel away, at least. If we abandon everyone, then we can run to her, but then what? Do we just sit on the beach for the next few months and hope nobody bothers us?

"Do we hope that He doesn't know where we are, right up until the Dark Legion marches over the hill and we fight to the death? Without the legion back home, we'd never have stood a chance, and you know it. Oracle, unless we do that again, unless we raise the banner of the empire here, then we're alone. And when you're alone, you've got nobody to help when the monsters come."

There was a long silence then, the others not wanting to interrupt our argument as Oracle and I stared into each other's eyes.

"You're both right." It was Sehran who said it, and I turned to her, one eyebrow raised in question. "You are." She shrugged. "It's a horrific risk, one that you're running for people you don't know, who might just turn around and stab you in the back, at least until you have the oath in place—and Oracle is right about that. The risk is insane, especially for people we don't know." She sighed.

"The thing is, though, there was another risk that you took recently, one that was insane. One that you shouldn't have done. I mean, who in their right mind allows a demon to stay? Grants them powers and their freedom?" she asked quietly. "You set me free, and you let me stay with my Jian. I have a life here, one the likes of which I could never have imagined. And because of that, there's one thing you've forgotten in all of this."

"What?" I asked, my voice rough as I realized the way that Sehran had described herself. Not as a person, not as a friend, but as a random demon.

And she was, back then. It had been mad, but it'd been the right thing to do as well.

"If we can get to the Tower of Gaij, and the succubus are there?" She smiled. "We'll have allies."

"Really?" Oracle asked uncertainly. "I know you want to see them, Sehran. I would too, but…"

"Trust me on this. If my sisters are there, knowing that they could be freed to live like I do? They'll take the oath in a second. I can share my life with them in ways that only another demon can. You think the city would have permitted them to stay free if they had a choice? They'd have been enslaved if they didn't have defenses that could protect them. And I guarantee they'll at least listen to you because of everything you did for me. Trust me on that."

"We love you, Sehran." Oracle pulled her friend in for a hug, before looking at me and sighing. "I don't like it," she warned me.

I snorted. "You think I do?"

"Fine, though if you're going to use the ability, then we do it at the right time." She turned to Marteen. "How many of your people can still fight?"

He considered for a moment. "Eight, maybe ten if we push it. The best are Kalvin, Bai, and the twins."

"And will that leave enough to defend the camp?"

"It will unless it's attacked by something seriously powerful. In which case, none of us would matter," he admitted.

"Good. Get them ready. Armor and weapons only…nothing that will slow them down. I want your best scouts and fighters. We move in two hours. And Finna, you're leading the team here."

"You're taking my son with you?" Zyenna asked, and I nodded. "Then you'll give me your word that you'll do your best by him and not send him into a situation that he can't handle," she insisted.

"No, but I'll do my best by him, that's for sure," I admitted. "We don't get to live without risk here."

"Mother, it's enough," Marteen said. "You know he can't."

"You're my only son!" she snapped.

He reached out, hugging her to him, as she started to argue, and Oracle, Sehran, and I moved off, leaving the pair to their moment.

Oracle drifted closer. "I still don't like it," she said sullenly.

"I know." I wrapped an arm around her waist, drawing her close. "But those kids have been waiting at least ten weeks for someone to save them. I'm not letting them wait any longer."

Through our bond, I felt her approval mixing with concern. "Just…be careful. We're a long way from home."

"Always am," I lied, and she snorted in response.

# CHAPTER FOURTEEN

Needless to say, the plan had changed three times by the time we started off, mainly thanks to about five minutes before we were going to kick everything off, Oracle discovered there was a dome over the camp, one that would be a bitch to break our way through, and that it was probably linked to an artifact.

She suspected she might be able to pass through it with some effort, being a creature of pure magic, but if I or Sehran tried, it would definitely set off some alarms and ruin the whole "surprise" thing.

There was also the issue that it might not just be an alarm; there could be a second layer to the shield that we couldn't currently see, and if that was a solid dome that triggered on the tripping of the alarm…well, that was going to suck.

With the surprise ruined and the dome possibly keeping me outside the camp, we would be fucked.

A little probing later, and yeah, she was sure of two things. So long as the dome was up, we couldn't enter the camp unseen, and if I tried to activate the imperial ability right outside it, there was a good chance it could be blocked.

On the upside, she was also sure that a lot of mana was being drawn, and that nobody was going to donate that kind of mana, literally hour after hour, willingly.

Either they had truly insane numbers of manastones that they were willing to burn through, hour after hour, day after day when there was no apparent risk, or they were powering it from their slaves.

Take out the slaves, and you take out the shield.

That meant I needed to either smash through the barrier—which, when we had no clue how strong it was, would be just plain stupid—or somehow get an invitation into the camp. And considering it was almost guaranteed to go badly, I decided I might as well have some fun and go for it with an open mind.

The eastern approach to the slavers' camp was marked by bonfires that cast wild shadows across the sandy terrain. The scrub grass and hardscrabble dirt that was all that survived this close to the desert meant that sight lines were clear for miles, and I walked openly toward them.

My armor gleamed in the firelight as I approached the outer ring of guards. Their empty eyes reflected the flames as they stood at attention, weapons held ready and utterly motionless.

Up close, I could see the telltale signs of necromancy: the slight stiffness in their movements, the way their chest neither rose nor fell with breath, and almost totally unique for any fighting force in any realm, there were no complaints being muttered or farting competitions in progress.

Plus…there was the goddamn smell of rotting cadavers…you know, subtle things like that.

The Sons of the Deep clearly took pride in maintaining their troops, but there was no hiding what they truly were.

One of the guards raised a hand as I approached, while another struck a massive bronze gong that hung between two posts. The sound echoed across the camp, and I waited patiently as footsteps approached from within.

"Who seeks entry to our humble camp?" a voice called out. Its owner emerged from between the ranks of undead—a well-dressed man with an elaborate walking stick and far too much jewelry—and right on his heels was a small slave boy carrying an incense burner.

"Just a humble pilgrim," I replied cheerfully, "searching for that most holy of relics."

"Oh?" The slaver raised an eyebrow. "And what relic would that be?"

"Why, the Holy Grail, of course!" I sketched out a shape with my arms. "I've searched these lands far and wide. Have you seen it? About this tall, probably glows a bit, grail shaped?"

The slaver blinked in confusion. "I… What?"

"No? Perhaps you've seen a shrubbery then? I was told those are quite important for proper questing."

Through our bond, I felt Oracle's mix of exasperation and amusement. *"Are you quite done?"*

*"Not even close,"* I sent back. *"Keep watching for my signal."*

The slaver had apparently decided to humor the plainly mad warrior before him. "I'm afraid we have neither grails nor shrubbery here. Though perhaps you'd be interested in some of our other wares?"

"Lead on then!" I gestured grandly. "Show me what treasures you've gathered in this delightful establishment."

He paused, clearly wondering at me, then shrugged and gestured. A small stone in his hand glowed blue for a second as I was evidently marked as permitted access, and then the outermost undead stepped aside.

He led me through several ranks of undead, and past the first ring of defenses. I kept my movements deliberately loose, projecting an air of harmless eccentricity even as I counted guards and noted defensive positions. Through our bond, I could sense Sehran and Oracle moving into position high above.

We passed several slave wagons, most filled with huddled figures that shrank back from the light. I was nearly past the main ring of wagons, when I heard a voice cry out in fury: "Fraud! Thief! You, yes, you! The fraud in Praetorian plate! I'll see you dead for this!"

I turned to see a wagon containing about a dozen men and women in chains, their build and general attitude marking them as legionnaires, even without their armor.

One of them, a grizzled veteran missing an eye, was on his feet despite his chains, clutching the bars of the cage with his face contorted in rage, even as others stood behind him, glaring.

"How *dare* you wear that armor! The empire *will* rise again, and when it does—"

"Silence!" the slaver roared and struck the wagon with his cane before turning to me and shaking his head in amused disgust as he started to walk again. "Forgive me. These ones are…difficult. They will be punished for the outburst, never fear. They're former soldiers, you understand. Still clinging to old loyalties. But they can be broken, and for those fitted with control collars, they enforce their good behavior or their death. No risk to you, guaranteed!"

I approached the wagon, studying its occupants with apparent curiosity. "Interesting. Are they for sale? I do love a challenge."

"They belong to the camp lords," the slaver said nervously. "I don't have authority to set a price, not for legionnaires, but they may choose to do so."

I leaned close to the bars, meeting the one-eyed legionnaire's hate-filled glare. "Patience," I hissed quickly. "Listen and be ready, Legionnaire. The empire still stands." Then I turned and spoke to the slaver standing several feet away in a louder voice: "Shame. They seem spirited. Do you at least have the control keys?"

"Only the lords have those. Now, if you'll follow me…"

I allowed myself to be led deeper into the camp, past more wagons and toward the central pavilions, where music and laughter could be heard.

"Perhaps you could tell me of this holy relic you seek?" the slaver suggested.

I nodded, racking my brain, then fell back on the truth. "Brave Sir Robin was one of the searchers, a brave man indeed," I said to get some time.

"I'm sure," he replied.

"He bravely ran away."

"Away?"

"Bravely," I assured him. "He bravely ran away, away."

"From what?"

"Oh, there were terrible beasts." My eyes constantly moved as I tried to pick out weak spots, places where I could expect the keys to be held, weapons stashes… There was a hell of a lot of loot on display, and a huge number of undead, set out in rings around the camp. I went on.

"And the terrible castles as well. One, you'll not believe this, but it was full of women! No men at all. They tried to keep one of my brothers there to help them."

"What with?"

"Oh, I think it was the spanking, and the group sex."

"What?" He frowned, and I kept going, playing to the hilt.

"We're a holy order of knights, sworn to celibacy, and they tried to force him to stay there with hundreds of young women and have sex." I shook my head. "Lancelot saved him, though…stormed right in and rescued him."

"And this castle?" the slaver asked, clearly unsure what was going on, but knowing something was wrong.

"What about it?"

"Why was it important?"

"It had a beacon."

"A beacon?"

"They lit it and it was grail shaped. Drew him straight in."

"So, they knew what it was, this grail?"

He was clearly losing patience and starting to guess something was up when Oracle's cry of rage echoed through our bond.

*"Jax! They're feeding children to the dogs!"*

*"Oracle…wait…!"* I sent, cursing. I was barely halfway to the center of the camp, but it was no use.

I caught a glimpse of her diving from above, magic already gathering around her hands. As she hit the dome, the entire sky flared to brightness as it seemed like morning had come from horizon to horizon in a great wash of golden light.

My guide had frozen, as had most of those around us, all eyes upturned.

I sighed. So much for the subtle approach.

"Well," I said conversationally to my startled guide as I reached into my bag and drew my naginata, "I suppose we're doing this the fun way after all."

The alarm rang out. A clanging of bells and gongs directed everyone to wake, attention drawn upward as Oracle screamed, gathering our mana and punching a hole through the center of the dome.

That made it clear that if the artifact was powering a shield, it hadn't been fully activated—or at least not powered properly—which made a nice change as for the first time in ages, something was going right.

She erupted into clear air, her hands filled with lightning even as the shield over the camp shifted, flaring brighter and obviously being forced to full strength.

Her first spell screamed down like a thunderbolt. The night burst into chaos as she dove, hard; screams erupted from out of my sight, from wherever she was aiming for.

The slaver barely had time to open his mouth before my naginata took his head from his shoulders. As his body crumpled, I was already moving, triggering Mana Overdrive as I sprinted toward the sound of Oracle's fury.

Through our bond, I caught flashes of her perspective: a ring of laughing men, dogs that had been snarling and lunging at a terrified child while bets were placed. Then she came and lightning rained from the sky; the laughter of those men turned to screams.

*"Sehran, now!"* I snapped, and felt her acknowledgment as she dove toward the outer perimeter where Marteen's team waited. The plan might have gone sideways, but we could make this work.

Probably.

I reached within myself, touching that core of power that marked me as Scion of the Empire. The ability I needed was there, waiting, but I held it back for now. Timing would be crucial.

The camp had erupted into chaos. Oracle's attack had drawn every guard in the vicinity, and I could hear shouts of alarm spreading outward as the ranks of undead began to move. Above it all, the slaves—those in cages without the control collars—bellowed in fright and hope, begging to be saved. Others, who had been forced into the control collars and who were new to it, shouted in fear and confusion as their bodies responded to their masters' will, not their own.

"To arms!" a voice bellowed. "Intruders in the camp! Slaves, defend your masters!"

The slave boy who had been carrying the incense burner wailed and threw himself under a nearby wagon, as a pair of undead in heavy armor sprinted toward me.

I'd had a second of thinking that maybe, maybe, I could free the legionnaires and then have them backing me up. But I gave up on that fantasy and instead ran at the undead, naginata raised and grinning tightly inside my helm.

On the other side of them, I saw what looked like two free soldiers—clearly scumbags hired as guards for the slavers to actually have some "normal" warriors—as they watched, unconcerned, as I ran at the undead.

One started to eat an apple, for fuck's sake. That level of disrespect just forced my hand.

I triggered Mana Overdrive and dove forward, hitting the ground and rolling as the first swing of the lead undead's greatsword passed over me.

Then I kicked up, as hard as I could, into the creature's crotch.

Sure, it was dead—yeah, I know that undead are less likely to be affected by a kick in the balls—but the detail that was primary in my mind?

Physics was a bitch, and the undead were lighter than the living.

Even with his armor, he was launched backward into the trailing one. And as they both fell, I flipped myself to my feet, beheaded them both with one elegant slash, and then, for good measure, triggered Lunge and blurred across the short distance to stab the apple-eater through the chest.

His companion panicked, struggling to bring his shield and sword around, only to meet me coming the other way.

I smashed his weapon aside, then kicked him in the crotch. And considering the agonized whimper as he fell, crotch armor was an area he had neglected.

It helped that I was in Mana Overdrive and that I was in full armor. The force I'd put into the blow, with a fast snap kick, was the same as if an American football player, at the height of his game, had a good run up and punted him as hard as he could.

The slaver fell to the floor, the world disregarded as he took up residence in his own personal hell, and I started to move again.

The camp here was busy. Not just with people who ran in all directions—slavers, camp followers, guards, and so on—but also in terms of the layout. There were narrow paths between the wagons that had been drawn up, flaring campfires, stacks of gear and tents, and all of it, when you factored in the running people, just added to the madness.

I almost flew. But knowing that I was going to need both the mana and health—and that should I do that, I was a clear target for anyone with a crossbow or magic—I decided against it. For now.

I burst into the central clearing just as I sensed the first wave of arena-trained slaves charged Oracle's position. She shared the image, and it was all I could do to not change direction and run to her. They moved with deadly grace despite their chains, weapons raised as the collars forced them to attack.

*"Oracle!"* I snarled. *"Fuck's sake!"*

*"Sorry-not-sorry!"* she shouted back over the bond.

Despite myself, I snorted.

"Fuck it. Hopefully this is close enough," I muttered. For the first time, without a speech or being wound up to it by some idiot, I attempted to trigger my imperial ability. Until now I'd been holding back, not wanting to accidentally reveal myself. And when I tried…

Absolutely fuck all happened.

"Shiiiiiiit!" I screamed as I reached for the power and found nothing. *"Oracle!"*

*"It responds to you, to your heart, to who and what you are!"* she sent frantically. *"Reach down, into yourself!"*

"Surrender or die!" came the roar.

As I twisted to see the thing being pointed at me, I frowned.

*That looked like…*

"Get the fuck outta here!" I snarled, lifting my hand and pointing it at the box the idiot was wielding.

He saw that, saw the sparks of magic, and he reacted predictably by pulling the trigger.

The rocket that was fired at me was fired at far too close a range, and without any understanding of what it really was. That should have meant that as the rocket didn't have time to arm its warhead, that the worst it could have done was the impact damage.

The "minor" issue with that was that the impact damage of a rocket-propelled grenade, even at short range, was significant. And then you add in the secondary details that I had magic, that I panicked, and that I lashed out with a spell…

The lightning wasn't the best choice, I later admitted to myself. In fact, it could be argued to be the worst fucking choice as it apparently overrode the arming trigger and detonated the warhead's charge in midair.

Then—because why the hell not add insult to injury—the explosion went off in the middle of the camp between us both, killing half of those who had been running at me, setting fire to the undead who had activated nearby and were rushing me, and finally picked me up and hurled me backward through the air.

I was sent flying, trailing smoke and flames, into the air. I reacted to that on instinct, twisting and activating Soaring Majesty.

It was a catalog of errors, really, that led to me plowing full-force into the wagon that held a handful more of the legionnaires several wagons over from the first I'd seen. But as I forced myself to stay awake and aware, conscious that my naginata was embedded in the frame of the wagon on the far side of the slaves and they looked mightily unhappy to have me sharing their little slice of heaven, I got the last message from Oracle.

It was a scream, one filled with rage, as she saw everything that I'd seen. She felt the pain, the damage that I'd taken—minor, despite everything, but still—and she felt the sudden fear. The knowledge that if these fucks had weapons of that caliber, then we were in serious danger.

She felt it all. And as the world around me swam into focus and the legionnaire next to me in the cage reached out, wrapping his chains around my throat and pulling tight, she gave herself over to it.

The detonation of power that flew out from her was enough to bodily hurl the slaves who were charging her.

Sehran's arrival contributed to the chaos, as she screamed past above the wagon, her voice raised in frantic and unearthly song. And me?

Well, I was being choked out by the people I was most desperate to add to my side.

"You fuck!" the massive man before me snarled, bracing himself against my arms and hauling harder on the chains. "You *dare* wear that armor!"

"Kill him!" roared another legionnaire, chained to the far end of the wagon. "Make him suffer!"

"You're ours!" another voice roared in my ear as a woman grabbed my arms, trying to stop me as I lifted them.

"Stop 'im!" a grim-faced dwarf bellowed, before grabbing a dagger free of my belt and trying to stab me with it.

"STOP!" Oracle thundered in the distance.

"Stop!" Sehran screamed. Her song faltered as she diverted from the plan, arcing around and coming toward me in a panic. "Don't hurt him. He's—"

A second explosion went off nearby, and this time it was clearly magical in nature.

What Sehran was saying was cut off by the explosion, and then by a hail of spells as others—clearly mages and necromancers in the pay of the camp—counter attacked.

The legionnaire who was hauling on me grunted and shifted, trying to get a better grip, the chains literally locked on the bottom of my helm as much as my neck as I struggled to keep them from moving.

They were too large for the gap under my helmet. The helmet had a locking ring that it connected to, but to allow for a full range of movement, that section was by necessity small and a lot weaker than the rest.

It was buckling inward, and if I didn't break free soon, the damn thing was going to pop loose. When it did, the chains would wrap fully around my neck, and I'd have no chance.

I managed to get a hand free, then reached up and grabbed the chain, pulling sideways and twisting my body at the same time, then heaved, breaking my other hand free. And, regretfully, I punched the dwarf in the face.

He jerked back, then drove his dagger at my fucking crotch.

I flinched on instinct, twisting my hips and falling, and being dragged down as the others all pulled on me at just the right time.

"*JAX!*" Oracle screamed over the sound of rapid-fire automatics.

The chains were all I could see. The battered and broken legionnaires who were hauling on them…the hatred in their eyes, the way that they screamed and beat at me…one man had the chains and the others?

They ignored the guards running up outside.

They ignored the blades being shoved in, the glowing steel pokers used to burn flesh and try to drive them back from me.

They were full of furious and righteous rage, at seeing…me in the Praetorian armor.

They'd been captured. I could see burns covering them all. I could see the scarring, the missing eyes, the fingers cut off, the signs of torture…all of it. And yet the reason they were willing to die? To die willingly now, to give their friends a few more seconds of life? It was to kill me. To kill the man they thought had found a set of their greatest armor, the armor that the bodyguards of the emperor wore, and the blasphemy of anyone wearing that was like me pissing on their greatest ideals.

They were going to kill me, because I was pretending to be a guard who was capable of protecting…me.

I saw it all in a second, and I finally managed to get my arms free and into the loop again, grabbing onto the chains. I triggered Mana Overdrive—I had no clue when I'd released it, but I had—and I pulled hard. The legionnaire who had been trying to throttle me was yanked in close and I headbutted him, stunning him long enough to drag him atop me, stopping the others from being able to reach me for a few precious seconds.

"Are you an imperial legionnaire?" I asked him, and he shook himself. "ANSWER!" I roared into his face, my helm pressed against his skin.

"Yes!" he growled.

"Do you serve the empire?!"

"YES!"

"Do you SWEAR it?!"

"I swear on my soul!" he snarled. "I'll be a legionnaire until I die and then I'll curse…"

I spoke quickly as I felt the power of that oath building, before he could make a truly massive fuckup.

"THEN BE FREE!" I roared. This time, the power in me responded. The power rolled through me, filled my words, trembled along my limbs, rose from the heart of all that I was.

Power surged through me as I called out: "In the name of the empire, I break these bonds!"

The wave of power rocked outward like a physical force. Every control collar in its path shattered, their enchantments unraveling as imperial authority reasserted itself over the artifacts of control. The slaves on all sides, scattered throughout the camp, stumbled, suddenly free of compulsion. Deeper in the camp, I heard the screams of the slavers as their control artifacts—the rings, keys, and more—all simultaneously detonated.

The backlash was devastating. Most of the slavers' upper ranks died instantly as their own magic rebounded through them. The ranks of undead tied to the necromancers who were caught in those blasts collapsed like puppets with cut strings. In the sudden silence, I heard Oracle's voice ring out:

"The empire returns! Those who were slaves, take up arms! FIGHT! FIGHT FOR YOUR FREEDOM!"

A roar went up from the freed slaves as they turned on their former captors. The arena fighters were first, their skills now being turned against those who had enslaved them.

More slaves broke free of their wagons, grabbing weapons from fallen guards and turning to free others. Outside the wagon I was in, the world seemed to go mad. On all sides, the slaves started to rebel, and before my eyes, where the legionnaire lay half slumped across me, he raised his hands, totally confused.

The manacles that had restrained him, the chains that had been bolted to the deck and that enabled them to be locked in place without the collars, had shattered too. As he lifted his arms, the remains of the black iron, worn by thousands over the years, crumbled like sun-baked clay.

"What…?" he whispered, totally in shock, until another, the dwarf who had been chained sideways on and had barely been able to reach me at all, dragged his friend back.

"Ah, crap, laddie…" he whispered into a moment of silence. "Ah think ye bin' wailin' on t' next emperor."

"Fuck's sake, he's done a number on my armor," I agreed from my back on the ground, then I reached up. "Anyone gonna help me kill the last of the slavers then?" I asked. "Or do I have to do that myself as well?"

"You're the emperor?" a stunned voice from nearby asked.

I shook my head as someone took my hand and helped me to my feet. "I'm the prince, but I'm working on it," I admitted. "Just gotta conquer a few more continents and slaughter me a few more gods, that's all."

"You killed Nimon," another said. "You killed the fucking God of Death."

"Ah shit," I muttered, as I felt a sudden shift in the realm as calling his name, as naming me as the man who had faced him, drew his eye fully.

The world around us all, across the entire camp, suddenly filled with the presence of Nimon—the cold, the soul-deep chill that came with the God of Death's personal attention. I shoved my way clear of the wagon, dropping to stand on the scrub grass by the side of the wagon. I reached up and unclipped my helmet, holding it out to the side and taking a deep breath as I dropped it.

He knew I was here.

I could feel that gaze, that hatred, and that left me with only one thing to do.

It was unreasonable to expect to beat him a second time.

It was madness to cross him, to upset him anymore.

The last thing I needed was more fuel on the bonfire of his hatred.

So I looked upward, grinned my cockiest grin, and spoke the magic words.

"Found you, fuckface!" I shouted. "You ready for round two?"

The world went black.

On all sides, the light disappeared. A feeling of otherworldly separation surrounded me, and for the first time, as I felt the world vanish, I was alone with Nimon.

I stood in a place between the seconds, facing him, somehow in the realm of the gods, as I knew it. I stood on a cracked and broken stretch of dusty ground—rain had never fallen here—and the breeze that ran constantly flared dust out behind me.

I looked around, seeing nothing for miles—just this dead or dying realm…the cracked, baked dirt, the sky low and foreboding. The wind howled as it began to rise, and I heard as much as felt the distant thunder of an approaching storm.

In the far distance ahead of me, I could make out a mountain range that rose endlessly into the clouds, and on all sides, I felt the attention of others, as things drew closer.

I felt their attention, like the weight of a storm growing before it broke. The change in pressure doubled and redoubled until I wanted to sink to my knees and bow my head. And these weren't even Nimon's "real" allies.

These were the most minor godlings, weak and barely able to claim the title. I felt the presence of their divine nature, and as I did, I felt the presence of their *shards*. Their fragments of divinity were all around me, approaching fast, and I snarled in fury.

Hunger rose in me—hunger to claim their shards, to battle them, to…

That was when the mountain range shifted slightly.

I stared, then stared more as the clouds rolled aside. The mountain range was revealed as only the bottom of the fucking throne that Nimon sat upon.

A huge throne that reared into the sky, that eclipsed the stars, was filled by something that stared at me. A being that was huge enough that entire cities would rest in its eyes glowered at me, in fury over my arrogance, my disrespect, my…

"Nope, fuck this," I said flatly. The one warning that Jenae and the others had given me repeatedly was that the realm of the gods wasn't for the likes of me.

I'd guessed that whatever rules constrained them in my realm weren't likely to hold there as well, and yet there I was, standing at ground zero as Nimon prepared to crush me like a bug.

There was only one thing to do.

# CHAPTER FIFTEEN

An intelligent man would fall to his knees.

A smart man would beg for forgiveness.

Anyone who wasn't a complete fucking idiot would try to just end this little dick-measuring situation with at least an attempt at letting bygones be bygones.

I lifted my right hand, gave him the finger, and activated Aegis.

The world around me vanished as I was suddenly clothed in silver. Scales flowed across my form, adding an additional coating to my battered red armor. And as it closed over my face, I felt the realm of the gods vanish, my feet landed in the scrubland again and the feeling of reality slammed back into me.

"What a rush," I muttered, shaking my head as I came out of it. This time, as I released Aegis and I felt the protection of the elder dragon Tuthic'Amon slip away, I felt the presence of others as well.

Jenae. Sint. Lagoush. All of them were there, suddenly pressing in around me, their divine presence driving others to their knees as I dragged down a deep breath.

*"I see you still act with as much tact and rationality as always, my champion."*

Jenae's voice rolled like thunder around me, and I felt dozens of those on all sides dropping to their knees as the divine presence washed over them.

I tried to subtly lower my hand, folding my finger in and grinning as I saw the looks on the faces of people on all sides, as they saw that clearly, in the time of darkness, where the presence of the one god who was feared beyond all others had arrived, that I'd faced him with a finger raised and I'd been telling him to go fuck himself.

I could feel the sheer disbelief, the terror, and the dancing-along-the-edge-of-the-cliff joy that rose in many of them.

I felt the presence of Nimon, still a black cloud of abject fury that glowered at me and that seemed to fill the world. But with the others here, it was more of a…it was more like that boss you had at work, the one you knew hated you but couldn't get you, not really, because he had no legal recourse.

Like your manager knew about it, and was watching, so you were sort of safe, but not really. You knew he was going to pull some trick out and get you fired still, but it'd have to be when he caught you doing something you shouldn't.

Like shagging in the downstairs glass-walled office in the call center when it was the late shift, as a wild-ass example.

That was one that not even my boss's connections had managed to get sorted for me, though it was hilarious when the security footage was pulled up in the disciplinary.

That wasn't important, though.

What *was* important was that with the other gods watching, with their presence there, he was limited—somehow—and he could only act through his own followers.

Of course, that was scant fucking reward when the notification rolled out.


*Beware!*

**You have been identified as a BLOOD ENEMY of the God of Death, Nimon.**

**He will encourage all those who worship Him to seek your death beyond all others.**

**Beware the Knives in the Dark!**

*

**Nimon has personally intervened to declare any follower of the Pantheon of the Flame, any citizen of the Empire, or any citizen of the continent of Carrmor who does not rise up and seek the death of the Apostate Jax, as an Enemy of the Church of the Dark.**

**All sanctified soldiers of the Church will receive +3 to Strength, Agility, and Endurance when facing the forces of the Apostate and his hated Gods. Killing any member of those forces will make this buff permanent. Furthermore, this buff will increase by +1 for every additional kill those soldiers make.**

*Kill on, Holy Warriors!*


I couldn't help it as I read it over—I snorted, then lifted my face to the sky and shouted back my response.

"You're still a pussy, Nimon! I beat your ass once. Next time, I'm gonna make you braid your hair and add wearing a little dress to the terms!"

*"Jax, as ever, you astound me with your bravery, and your incredible stupidity."* Jenae sighed. *"Perhaps you should secure the camp before picking another fight with a god?"*

"Good point." I grinned. "Great to have you all back, though. I was starting to think you didn't love me anymore!"

*"For the amusement value alone, that is unlikely."* That was Tamat, I knew. The sardonic smile that was sent along with the sense of her wit made me smile.

*"For now, secure your camp, then we shall talk."*

That last one was Sint, the God of Order and Light. Although I'd honestly thought at first that the God of Order and me would never get on well, I genuinely did like him. I nodded, gave the gods a thumbs-up, and turned back to the legionnaires who stared at me in horror.

"Get your arses out of there, get some weapons, and follow me," I ordered them, before turning again and heading deeper into the camp.

I cut through the chaos toward Oracle's position, where she was helping the child she'd saved to safety. Two of the camp lords had rallied their personal guards, trying to restore order, but Sehran and Marteen's team, as well as the freed slaves apparently had them surrounded.

"My lord!" one of the legionnaires I'd seen earlier called out as they rushed to join us. "The necromancer, the master of the dead! He's escaping!"

I turned to see a figure in elaborate robes, surrounded by solidly packed undead, by one of the larger tents, glaring at me. Shadows flowed across him as the remaining undead closed ranks. Unlike his less experienced colleagues, this one had survived the backlash of my ability, though blood ran from his eyes and nose.

"Oracle, Sehran, secure the former slaves!" I ordered, already moving to intercept. "This one's mine!"

The necromancer spun to face me as I approached, lips curled in a snarl. "You dare?" he rasped. "You dare trespass in our lands, interrupt our business, and attack us. You think there won't be consequences?"

"Slavery is illegal in the empire, and these are imperial lands, fucknut," I called back.

"The empire died long ago, whimpering in a control collar, begging for our mercy, and so shall you. I—"

"The empire isn't dead," I replied, bringing my naginata up to guard. "Neither are the true gods. But you, on the other hand…? That I can fix."

He laughed, a wet sound that held no humor. "Did you think we wouldn't be prepared for this? The Sons of the Deep remember the old ways!" His hands moved in complex patterns as he spoke, and the ground began to tremble.

Around us, the bodies of fallen soldiers started to twitch.

"You know," I said conversationally as the first of the corpses began to rise, "this would be a lot more impressive if you weren't bleeding from every orifice."

The necromancer snarled something in a language that made my teeth ache, and the nearest bodies lurched to their feet. But his control was ragged, the movements jerky and uncoordinated. Whatever my ability had done to him, he was running on fumes.

"The empire is dead!" he screamed, spittle and blood flying. The risen undead closed in ever tighter, blocking him almost from view. "The old powers are gone! We built something new from its corpse!"

"Yeah, about that." I triggered Mana Overdrive, my blade becoming a crimson arc as I carved through the first wave of his puppets. "You really shouldn't build on rotten foundations."

Through our bond, I felt Oracle's satisfaction as she and the others secured the camp. The freed slaves were proving enthusiastic allies, particularly the arena fighters. I caught glimpses of Marteen's team leading groups to liberate the remaining wagons while Sehran kept watch from above.

The necromancer's spell oozed out, green smoke that latched onto the bodies on all sides and flowed inside, filling them, forcing them to rise, to stand. And as soon as they tried, I flashed forward, flipping my naginata around, and hacked through a half dozen with a single sweep.

"Fool!" he screeched. "You think you can beat us? We have thousands of warriors! We can drown this land in the dead, and our master remembers the days of the empire. He saw it fall!"

I twisted, unleashing a blast of fire to my left, then sliced my naginata through the last lines before me. I worked, focusing inward, triggering my tattoos, and deliberately taking his next spell head-on.

It slammed into my armor. Sickly yellow lines like crawling fingers of disease washed over it and then fractured, as the spell failed entirely.

My shield flared even stronger; then I punched out, slamming all that naked force into the ground before me with one hand flat against it.

The explosion sent the undead flying, crashing into one another like so many bowling pins, clattering to the ground. I stepped forward and struck again. My naginata took his left hand off at the wrist, then flipped around and lanced forward into his chest. He screamed, clutching the stump as dark energy pulsed around it, trying to hold back death through sheer force of will.

"I am Jax," I said quietly as I straightened, slipping the blade free. "Prince of the Empire, Scion of Amon, and you really should have stuck to honest work."

His remaining hand came up, darkness gathering around it. "Then die like your empire did!"

The spell he was trying to cast was presumably impressive, a churning vortex of necromantic energy that I guessed would have done credit to a master of the art. But he was wounded, drained, and most importantly, he never saw Sehran coming.

Her claws punched through his chest from behind as she landed, lifting him off his feet. "This is for the children you fed to dogs," she hissed in his ear, then ripped his heart back out of his chest, along with half his spine.

The necromancer's body collapsed, his half-formed spell dissipating harmlessly. Around us, the corpses he'd commanded and those he'd been in the process of raising fell still once more.

"Was that really necessary?" I asked mildly.

Sehran wiped her bloody hands on the necromancer's robes. "Yes," she said firmly. "Besides, you were taking too long."

"I was being dramatic!"

"You were showing off," Oracle corrected as she landed nearby. "The camp is secure. Most of the slavers either surrendered or died fighting. The slaves…"

We turned to survey the carnage. The freed slaves had been thorough in their revenge. Very thorough.

"Well," I sighed, "I suppose we should start getting things organized. Oracle, can you—"

A child's scream cut through the night. We all spun toward the sound, only to see a younger necromancer—one we'd thought dead in the initial backlash—stumbling from a tent. He had a knife to a girl's throat, his face a mask of blood and madness.

"Stay back!" he shrieked. "I'll kill her! I'll—"

The bullet took him in the eye, blowing his brains out the back of his head. He toppled backward, the knife falling harmlessly aside as the girl scrambled free.

"That," Sehran said with some surprise but clear satisfaction as she nodded to herself, "was extremely necessary."

I looked around at the remains of the slave camp—at the freed prisoners, the dead slavers, the collapsed undead. We had a few hours to get our shit together, and then we needed to get moving. Because, thanks to Nimon being pulled directly to the fight, I had no doubt he would be sending his forces to stomp us out.

And…in addition to all the rest of the fun that was going on here, I either had an unknown ally, or at least an additional player who hadn't declared their position yet.

"Right!" I called out. "Oi sniper! You know who you are—get your arse in here." I pointed to the largest and most opulent-looking of the tents nearby, which of course chose that moment to make clear that, as a result of the ongoing festivities, was apparently on fire.

As the flames licked up the post and into sight of half the camp, I sighed. "Fuck's sake, Oracle, you and I need to talk, but can you sort that, please?"

"I think we all do," came another voice.

I turned, working on not seeming surprised as I locked eyes on the figure that stood on the far side of the clearing, leaning against an overturned wagon as he regarded me.

"My name is Arlo, and I serve House Granth. The young master ordered me to see to eliminating the scourge of the slavers in the area, and your attack, while not how I'd have done it, certainly provided an opportunity to achieve that."

"House Granth…" I mused. "William's house?"

"Lord Wilhelm," Arlo corrected and straightened from his lounging, apparently surprised that I knew the name, and putting two and two together with lightning speed. "My apologies, my lord. I was unaware this territory had been claimed by another of the great houses."

"Well, it fucking has." I sighed. "Fine, get your arse over here. We can talk, and I need to speak to the leader of the legion here. Anyone survive from the legionnaires?" I raised my voice to carry over the collection of crying, shouts of joy and pain, the begging of the injured and captured guards, and the crackling of flames.

Not to mention the apparently scared animals that were used as pack beasts and to drag the caravans—because the smell of scared animals, a smell best described as "brown," filled the air almost as much as that of the dead did.

All things considered, there was a lot to talk about, and a lot of people who needed in on the conversations. First up, though, before I even started to deal with the bloody gods that I could still sense were hanging around and watching, was Oracle.

She was already headed to my side, having not been far away anyway. When I reached out, she was there, ducking under my arm as I pulled her in tight.

"I know what you're going to say," she said before I could speak. "I shouldn't have started the fight early, I should have waited, and I shouldn't have risked myself. But they were throwing children into a pit to fight with dogs, Jax! I couldn't just let a child be mauled…I couldn't!"

"And you think that I'd expect you to leave a child to be mauled?" I asked her, making her pause, then sigh and shake her head.

"No, you wouldn't," she admitted. "But you are going to tell me it was stupid."

"It was," I agreed. "It was incredibly fucking stupid and could have cost us everything. And you'd do the same thing again if we had to, wouldn't you?"

"I would."

"And so would I." I nodded. "Now, let's go find out what the hell we just got ourselves into, and start dealing with this fucking situation."

"Want me to go get the others?" Sehran stepped up.

I hesitated, not wanting one of the only two people I really trusted here to leave me, then nodded. I'd put my big girl pants on and deal with anything that happened.

"Yes, please, Sehran, and tell them to hurry. We've got a lot of people who are going to need a lot of help over the next few hours. Then we need to get moving, and we still need to try and find Amelia's daughter as well."

"Movin' where, uh, Lord?" a figure asked from beside me.

I glanced over at him. "Legion?" I saw his build, the collection of injuries and the tattoos, and he nodded. "Great. Anyone got any mana potions?" I called out, raising my voice to be heard over the general hubbub. "Strong ones?"

"They'll have some in there." The legionnaire gestured to a tent before ducking his head.

I nodded, moving into the tent he'd indicated. This had been a storehouse of sorts, but as they'd apparently kept some of the control devices in here, and the people in here looked to have been wearing them, there wasn't much in the admittedly lavish tent that wasn't burnt, burning, or covered in blood.

It was literally running down the inner silken walls from the peaked roof. Yeah, it was a bit nasty, but I was actually amazed by how comfortable everything looked.

"First things first," I muttered, starting to search with Oracle's help. It didn't take long, especially as a good dozen people had followed me in, and three of them were legionnaires.

The first bottle that was offered up was barely blue and the effect it had was… Well, I'd not say dirty dishwater did better than it, because it'd depend on the dishes, but either way it wasn't great.

The second one, though, when it was pulled out of a bag of holding from one of the bodies, actually changed the lighting in the room, and I nodded as soon as I saw it.

"Fucking hell yes, gimmie." I held a hand out. The legionnaires who had found it hesitated a second, clearly not sure of me still, then handed it over, watching as I looked to Oracle.

"Better to wait until everyone's here and we'll do it all at once," she suggested, "but I doubt there's more than a dozen who will have sworn the oaths here, are there?"

"What oaths?" the legionnaire asked.

"The oath of allegiance to the empire," I said. "The oath that you take as you join the legion."

"There's a few." He shrugged. "There'll be a few of our trainees an' camp folk here as well, or there were. They might've been separated out already."

"Why?" I asked.

"In the legion, we all be trained tae fight. That means that as that's our profession, we have a solid need fer others in the camp with simpler professions—blacksmiths, fletchers, cooks an' more, ye ken? They do all sign up an' they do all join the legion." He straightened his back and fixed me with a glare. "Now, let me make my position clear, laddie. Ye're an unknown. Ye claim tae be the prince, but we've seen nae evidence, an' ah dinnae know why the prince would be here, thousands o' miles from his lands, pickin' fights with slavers fer shits an' giggles."

"You'll find out," I said. "Look, what's your name?"

"Aellin."

"All right, Aellin, I'm Jax, and yeah, I'm your prince…"

"That remains tae be seen," he said gruffly.

"Fuck me sideways." I sighed, rubbing at my face tiredly. "All right, fuck it. Oracle, you think we've got enough mana for this?"

"We do now." She smiled, pulling a second and third mana potion free of the same bag of holding.

"Excellent. Okay, everyone back outside." I gestured to them as if I were shooing a bunch of particularly large and muscular chickens out of the way. "Come on, daylight's burning."

"It be night," Aellin growled.

"And you're a bit shorter than me, so it'll take longer for the sun to reach you," I snapped back. "So, get your arse out of the way and let's sort this shit out."

"Jax," Oracle said warningly. "No picking fights with people."

"Bugger off." I snorted. "You know it's my second-best skill."

"What's your first?" another of the people, not a member of the legion, asked, and I snorted.

"Well, I could say something filthy, but I think you all felt the dark dick's presence and can feel his annoyance, so pissing off gods is definitely up there. Speaking of which, I need to talk to them, and they're being damn gracious in waiting for me, so here's the rub. I'm gonna down this potion and then I'm going to call on your oaths. You'll all feel and know who I am, and then you get to decide if you're an oath breaker and you can fuck right off, or you can help serve the empire as a thank-you for, *you know*, saving your arses."

I paused, taking a deep breath, and then downed the potion. I wiped my hand across my lips—noting that I really needed to clean the damn gauntlets as my mouth was now dirtier than before—and said the magic words.

"I am Jax Amon, acknowledged Prince of Dravith and the empire," I said, swallowing hard, before going on. "I am Amon's descendant, and I claim his oaths as my own." I wasn't worried about the oath, not this time. I mean, there were what, six or seven hundred people here in the camp after the guards had been slaughtered, and hardly any of them were likely to be legionnaires, so I knew I had to be safe, right?

My mana reserves bottomed out instantly, and the world shook. Light erupted around me as my world vanished. I hissed and sank to one knee as a fresh notification filled my vision:

***You have resurrected the Oath of Imperial Allegiance!***

**Due to lack of mana and territorial control, oath range is limited to a twenty-seven-mile radius. One hundred and eleven Imperial Citizens have been found inside this territory, and their oaths have become active, tied to yourself as Prince of Dravith and Scion of the Empire.**

*"I swear, upon pain of death, to faithfully execute all that the Emperor decrees. I swear upon my soul that I shall stand for the empire when it calls. I shall be strong when the weak need me, generous when the poor are at hand, and merciless when my fellow citizens are threatened. I shall worship the gods of my fathers, respect my elders, and raise up my children to stand tall.*

*"I am an Imperial Citizen. I claim the right to call upon the Legion in my hour of need, to hold those who wrong me to justice, and to be avenged if I cannot be saved."*

**Those who swore the Oath in truth can now sense your location and are pulled to you by its power.**

*

**You have activated the oaths of fifty-three legionnaires and supporters of the Sanketh Legion into the empire.**

"Well, fuck." I groaned, as the word flared around me. Gasps rang out; the legionnaires on all sides—those fully trained, their trainees, and their camp followers—all cried out with one voice.

"All hail Prince Jax! Hail Scion of the Empire!" the ragged voices shouted, and I bit my lip to keep from passing out.

# CHAPTER SIXTEEN

"**D**o I look like I make well-reasoned out choices?" I asked Aellin and the now thankfully much smaller "command team" an hour later, sitting in the far more luxurious quarters of the lead slavers' caravan.

"Well, no, ye don't." He sighed. "But still, maybe it be time tae start?"

"Fuck no. If I started weighing all my options before I did shit, I'd never get anything done." I snorted. "Would a sane man have done what we did?"

"Attack a slavers' caravan of several hundred, with the Sons of the Deep banner flyin' proud?" He shook his head. "Aye, all right, I'll give ye that."

"Well, regardless, we did it and we'll be doing more like it in the future, I've no doubt." I sighed. "Where are we with preparations?"

"We can move in an hour." Toren shifted uncomfortably in his chair. "Most of the caravans have been re-rigged, but the number of dead beasts means we're either going to have to leave five, or move slower as they'll need to be pulled in train."

"Do we have enough space on the wagons for everyone?" I asked. "If we drop those five, I mean?"

"Not even close." He laughed. "We've got a total of six hundred and fourteen people. Half of them are former slaves you've just freed, and the rest were members of our former caravan. The majority of our caravan was already taken, and it's heading to the tent city of Sonra, nearly two weeks from here to the northeast. That is more or less on our path to Gaij, which is the only good news.

"The bad news is that the caravans they took had most of the gear and trade goods. That means at least half of the caravan are going to be walking, which in turn means that we're probably going to be slower than they are."

"Why'd they leave?" I asked.

*"I can answer that, Jax,"* Jenae said softly.

I winced. "I'm sorry, my lady."

I rose to my feet and then dropped to one knee. "Everyone, that presence you feel is the goddess Jenae, Mistress of Hidden Knowledge and Lady of Fire. She leads the Pantheon of the Flame, and is the patron goddess of the empire."

*"Thank you for that introduction, Jax,"* she said, and I could feel the amusement in her voice. *"My siblings and I came when you activated your mantle of right, and we felt Nimon's attention being drawn to you."*

"Thank you," I said. "That was about to get very messy."

*"Your first words to the Dark God of Death were to throw his defeat in his face and ask him for a rematch,"* a new voice rumbled.

I smiled despite myself. "Darakin, Lord of Battles," I called in greeting. "Don't tell me you didn't want to do the same, my lord."

*"And that's why I like you,"* came the amused reply. *"We still need to have that fight."*

"I'll consider it an honor." I lied. Facing the god of literal battles was never going to go my way. The only reason I'd won so far in most of my higher-end battles was through sneaky, underhanded tricks, and I didn't think he'd take kindly to that kind of a trick being played.

*"Regardless, we need to be on with our own responsibilities,"* a new voice grumbled. *"Perhaps we can just give him the advice then move on?"*

"Your advice is always appreciated, Lord Svetu." I lied again, recognizing the voice. The God of Invention was a literal gnome, and I was fairly sure he was responsible for how fucked up that species was. The fact he chose Giint, that mad bastard, as his champion just made me more sure of that.

*"Jax, there are forces arrayed against you here, that's true, but the main foe you face is time. Our gaze is limited on this continent due to our situation, and as such, the advice we can give you is likewise limited."*

Jenae was beating around the bushes as she explained that basically anything she told me needed to be taken with a mountain of salt, and was essentially only advice, because she and the others were so underpowered for this fight it was almost laughable.

*"Grizz and your most loyal team escaped and are travelling to you now aboard the airship* **Lucky Endeavors** *and should reach you, should you continue to head inland, in approximately seven weeks."*

As soon as she said that, I noted the way that Oracle's hand moved to her belly, and I felt a yawning pit open in my stomach at the concern on her face, instead of the relief that our friends were okay.

*"The days grow shorter before your blessing to the realm arrives, however, and due to the nature of it, I recommend you move to a place of power, one that in ancient times was used to protect and nurture your kind, Oracle,"* Jenae went on.

"Where?" I asked.

*"The Cradle of Feshcan'un, an ancient place that was sacred to my supporters, is now beyond my reach,"* the voice of Lagoush, Goddess of Water and Healing, explained. *"Before we were banished, though, many of your kind and others of a magical nature had claimed it as a home and sanctuary. I can feel that it still exists, though not what condition it is in."*

"But you think that's where we need to go?" I asked.

*"To ensure the greatest chance at success and the best start to your child's life, then yes. I cannot guarantee it; I only offer advice. But that was a place of tremendous power for all Life. It was also a place of death for several of those who trod the path you have begun to walk, resulting in a much higher than normal level of mana."*

I worked my way through that, conscious again that she wasn't saying a lot of things. But I remembered Sint explaining that if I had a fragment of divinity or more and I was killed by another who couldn't absorb them, then they'd essentially bleed into the world and create a place of natural power aligned to their fragment.

"Okay, I see what you're saying." I smiled, reaching out and taking Oracle's hand in my own. "And thank you."

*"Jax, the time it will take you, should you travel directly to that site, using these caravans, is eight weeks, meaning that should you decide to wait at a secure location for your companions to arrive, then you will likely cut things very close. That will give you little time to stop along the way. But there are forces between you and this location, forces that are already being made aware of your presence."*

"And if we travel to the city of Gaij on the way?" I asked.

*"You will pass close by it on the trek. A diversion is likely to be less than a day to reach it. But again, although it is close by, time is of the essence when it comes to your forthcoming blessing."*

"Well, fuck."

*"Exactly,"* she said with a trace of amusement. *"However, if you do choose to visit Gaij, I agree, it could be highly profitable for you and your people."*

"Thank you."

*"One more point. The matter you were speaking of…the reason the slavers left?"*

"Crap, yes?" I asked.

*"There is a slavers' market on the Sixth of Rey, fifteen days from now, at the tent city of Sonra. That is where the slavers go, to meet for their annual trade."*

"So, basically we need to get our arses in gear." I nodded. "Either we need to be aiming to get there and free all the slaves, or we need to rescue those we can and run, because I'm betting there's going to be a *lot* of guards there and soldiers."

*"There will be, but as we are no longer hiding our presence on this continent, I believe it is time that I offered a few new quests,"* Jenae said.

I grinned to myself as the first of them popped up.


**Repeatable Quest discovered: Free the Slaves!**

*The Goddess Jenae has always despised slavers, and even more so now, considering the practice has become so commonplace, and the few protections that were once in place have been stripped away.*

*Find the caravan, free the slaves, reunite them, and in the process, learn more of the inner workings of this continent.*

**Reward: ?x followers, 50,000xp, trade goods and wagons**

**Do you accept?**

**Yes/Yes…**


I snorted and took the hint, accepting the quest, which immediately updated. A second one appeared in its place, only to be overridden by the first of a second quest chain.


**Repeatable Quest discovered: Rescue the Legion! (1)**

*The years have not been kind to the Imperial Legion. Where on Dravith they were despised and reviled, on Carrmor they were forced into unwise additions to their oaths, doing tremendous damage to both their reputations and their units.*

*Legionnaires are now openly hunted by slavers, forced to fight to the death in pits and arenas, and at best, are looked upon as dangerous and unstable by the population at large.*

*Rescue members of the Imperial Legion*

- **0/50 Legionnaires freed**

  **Reward: Additional loyal legionnaires, 50,000xp**

**Do you accept?**

**Yes/Yes...**

I kept going, smiling as I accepted and it updated and completed.

**Repeatable Quest discovered: Free the Slaves! (2)**

*Slavers have attacked and despoiled a caravan of hardworking people of many races. Many were killed, and many more were scattered to the winds, but most were enslaved and even now are being driven toward the tent city of Sonra. Catch them en route, or free them at Sonra to gain a blessing from Jenae and her fellow gods.*

*Find the caravan, free the slaves, reunite them, and in the process, learn more of the inner workings of this continent.*

**Reward: ?x followers, 50,000xp, trade goods and wagons**

**Do you accept?**

**Yes/Yes...**

Nice. That meant I'd already gained that reward and it was basically just a bit of free XP.


**Repeatable Quest discovered: Rescue the Legion! (2)**

*The years have not been kind to the Imperial Legion. Where on Dravith they were despised and reviled, on Carrmor they were forced into unwise additions to their oaths, doing tremendous damage to both their reputations and their units.*

*Other legionnaires have been taken, both in towns and cities and the pits and arenas; many of the more dangerous bands of slavers have begun to specifically hunt this most dangerous of game.*

*The reward for a fully trained legionnaire slave, once captured and forced to serve, can be high, more so because although certain restrictions exist—they cannot be made to break their oaths as this results in their deaths—as personal bodyguards or even more so, as guards over treasure vaults and more, they are highly in demand.*

*Rescue members of the Imperial Legion*

- **4/50 Legionnaires freed**

  **Reward: Additional loyal legionnaires, 50,000xp**

**Do you accept?**

**Yes/Yes…**


"Jenae, thank you," I said. "Is there anything I can do to aid you, or your brothers and sisters?"

*"In the city of Gaij, in the Repository of Stone, there are artifacts that hold my power, items I created long ago to help my followers."* Lagoush suddenly spoke up. *"If you can recover them, you will have a choice to make. Carrying them with you will enable you to spread their power, granting health and vibrant life to the area around you, or…"*

"Or?"

*"Or you can break them, and return that power to me,"* she said. *"Should you do that, I will reward you greatly."*

As she spoke, a quest popped up, literally offering those same details, and I accepted it without thought, closing it back down as I sensed her nervousness.


**Repeatable Quest discovered: Recover Lagoush's Artifacts**

**There are a number of artifacts that were gifted by Lagoush to help the city of Gaij and the surrounding territory.**

**The goddess wants them either returned to her, reconsecrated to her worship, or destroyed. Should they be destroyed, the power that has been invested in them will be mostly lost, but that which will reach her will enable a single boon to be granted to the Empire as thanks.**

*Recover, reconsecrate, or destroy the Divine Artifacts of Lagoush*

**Reward: 1x Greater Boon, *or* 3 artifacts, 250,000xp**

**Do you accept?**

**Yes/No…**


*"Should you destroy them, it will be many years before I could replace them. But the bounty that I could unleash in your name sooner would be much greater. And should you desire a boon instead, that too would be possible,"* she promised.

I nodded. "I'll do my best," I assured her, unwilling to commit to either course until I knew more.

*"Then we will distract you no longer, my champion. Please, remember us as you travel, and we shall carry you in our thoughts, lending what small aid we may."* Jenae spoke up, and I smiled.

"Thank you, my lady," I said clearly, "Thank you all, my gods. I will do as you asked, and your advice—as always—is gratefully received."

A few seconds passed as the gods vanished. The palpable sense of relief that flowed over the camp was clearly felt, and I let out a sigh, settling back in the cushioned seat.

"Right then, people, you heard the same thing I did," I said. "It adds some issues, I'll admit. First off, can we realistically catch those caravans?"

"No," Toren said.

"Yes," both Zyenna and Aellin said at the same time.

"Great. You first." I indicated Toren. "Why can't we?"

"The wagons that they took were mainly ours—a full, well-maintained set of specially designed and constructed wagons, built for hard travel and with multiple teams of draft animals. What they left are mainly their own wagons, most of them cheaply made and poorly maintained, with the obvious exceptions of the slavers' residences like this." He knocked on the arm of his chair with a knuckle, and I nodded.

The inside of the caravan that we'd set up in for the conversation was more like a high-end luxury trailer back home, with everything from a large double bed in an enclosed section, to a nice sitting area and a mobile toilet. There wasn't a shower, which I was annoyed at, but there was a bath, and I'd damn well be making the most of that soon.

The sitting area that we were all occupying right now was about three meters by five. Although that wasn't a great amount of space for nine of us, it was enough.

"The soldiers' caravans are the same—well made, but obviously not to this level. They're faster and well maintained, like these are." He went on, and I nodded. "The problems come in when you look at the slave transports.

"To make them as fast as the rest, the slavers usually have their 'stock' push and pull them, hour by hour and day by day, so we're left with the option that either we abandon the slowest and crappiest built ones, and have everyone lend a hand to push and pull still—which I can tell you a lot of the newly freed slaves won't do—or we're stuck at maybe half the speed of our stolen caravan. Oh, and before I forget, we'll need regular rest stops as well. The animals are barely alive as it is—for those wagons, I mean."

"So, they have animals and the slaves to move them?" I scratched at my chin.

"Yes, but again, mainly because neither group is well fed or maintained, and they don't care if a percentage of them drop dead en route." He winced.

"Okay, and why do you think we can make it?" I asked the legionnaire and merchant.

"There are enough of us that we can push, and push hard," a man named Mekkin said. "I'd recommend we give these people the choice—they join the empire, or they don't. Those who don't are set loose here with any equipment and food we can spare, and the rest of us head off after the caravans as quickly as possible."

I nodded, and turned to Zyenna. "And from you?"

"There's a degree of what he said, but mainly we make it clear to the people that they can help rescue their friends and that we won't be stopping. If they want to free them, then they're going to be working damn hard to help and to run alongside."

"That's it?" I blinked and leveled a finger at her. "Don't try to hold it back, you old bugger. You've got more."

"Of course I do." She smiled. "We have an enchanter, after all, and several carpenters. What we do is put them to work. The most damaged wagons are evaluated and we make any repairs we can. Therin rides aboard them and makes fixes as we travel, and he moves from wagon to wagon.

"Then we add in the same thing you did for us when we were running here." She smiled. "That water. If you can give that to the weakest and to the animals, they'll be stronger for it, and they'll be able to pull longer and harder. Then we factor in that the slavers are heading to make a profit, while we're going to rescue friends and family. Tell me, lordling, who do you think will push harder?"

"Point." I smiled. "Okay, anyone have anything else to add?"

"There's also the goods." Another new member of the team spoke up.

"What goods and who are you?" I asked.

"Piotr." He stood and gave a jerky bow. "Sorry, uh, my lord."

"Go on." I nodded.

"I was the headman of a village to the west by three days. It was small, only a dozen of us left after the wells failed, but the slavers came and claimed everything, my people included."

"Go on," I repeated when he paused.

"So, there's a lot of the goods that are part of this caravan that are mine and my peoples'," he finished lamely. "We want to know what's going to happen to them."

"If they're of use to us, then we'll make use of them," I said grimly. "I have sympathy for you, I do, but I also damn well know, and so do you, that three hours ago you were a slave and you're free now because of me and mine. Those goods are spoils of war, and what is needed for the empire belongs to the empire. I don't like it, but I'm being realistic. I don't have time to negotiate with you, so here it is. What we have is mine. If you and your people want to go free, you're welcome to. We'll arrange some supplies—whatever we can afford to share—but that's it."

"But Lord, they stripped my village! I lost everything!" Piotr snapped, gesturing.

"Not yet ye haven't," Aellin said flatly. "What's the lives of yer people worth tae ye, headman? Would ye not have given anythin' three hours ago tae see them freed?"

"Of course, but…"

"Then congratulations, yer prayers were answered," he finished flatly. "As a legionnaire, we tend tae a more pragmatic approach, so ah'll make a suggestion, if ye don't mind, my prince?"

"Yeah?"

"Explain that we're movin' out tae rescue the others, tell the people it'll be a hard slog, an' that ye're only takin' volunteers. Those who don't want tae come with us can loot what we leave behind when we've gone. That way, we get rid of those who don't want tae come with us, an' parasites like these…" He jabbed a callused thumb in the direction of Piotr. "They get tae loot whatever they want."

"I'm not a parasite!" Piotr snapped at the legionnaire, who sneered at him.

"Really? Ye're the only headman in the broken lands that doesnae sell the location of caravans an' peddlers tae the slavers then? Bollocks. Ye couldnae pay yer fees tae the slavers, so they took yer people…don't act like ye're any better."

"The wells failed!" he hissed. "We're freemen, not bound to any lord. You think there's a better option out there?"

"There be yer option, *freeman*," Aellin snapped. "Ye can join t' empire, earn yer place in somethin' greater, or ye can run off an' hide."

"You don't know what we went through out here!" Piotr snapped back.

I held my hand up to stop the building argument. "No, we don't," I agreed. "But I don't care, either. I'm sorry but that's the truth. Aellin, you think many will leave, given the chance?"

"A third to half," he said. "We've tried askin' fer help in situations like this before. When we, as t' legion, arrive t' hunt t' slavers, we get all the sob stories. All do be begging us tae rescue those they've lost, but as soon as we come back wi' 'em, you know what they say tae us?"

"What?"

"'*How soon can we leave*?' They tell us tae go, and they dinnae pay up tha' support tha' they did promise."

"Is that true?" I asked the former headman, who hesitated and then spoke up.

"If we give succor to the legion, then as soon as they leave, the slavers will come and raid us," he admitted. "The longer they're in our lands, the worse it gets, so yes, we ask them to leave."

"An' tae promises o' support?" Aellin spat. "The food tha' ye 'forget' tae send, the young un's to replace those we lose fighting for ye?"

"We're a small village!" he snapped back. "You think we can afford to raise our children then just send them off to die? We need them!"

"*All* t' villages dae," Aellin growled. "They all dae, and then 'cause none of ye support us, ye need us even more the next year, an' t' year after. Where once we could patrol the whole of the empire, now *we're* hunted. The nobles hound us oot o' our bastions, and the fuckin' slavers, t' Dark Legion and t' bandits whittle us doon. You want tae know if we can rescue 'em? Oor people tha' they already left wi' as well as them useless fucks of his?" he asked me.

"I do."

"Aye, we can. We can hit the caravan if we go an' go hard, but I ask ye, ma prince. Why should we?"

"What?" I blinked.

"Why should we waste t' lives of legionnaires tae rescue those who won't care? Who won't help, and who'll stab us in the back as soon as look at us?" He glared around. "That's what life's like as a legionnaire. I say we rescue oor own people, an' fuck 'em all."

"Well, we're going to address that," I said firmly. "Before we go any further, though, I agree on one point—those who don't want to go with us can leave. Toren, Zyenna, I want you both to explain the situation to the people out there. Take the others with you, and make it clear the situation they're in. They can stay or they can leave, and either option is fine. But if they're coming with us, they'll be swearing the oath. What we leave behind they can sort through and take what they want, but we'll be leaving in a few hours. Everything is to be cataloged and evaluated. What we can make use of and that we have space for, we take. If it's expensive and takes up space we need but brings no immediate value, it gets left."

"Who makes that call?" Zyenna asked.

I nodded to her. "You do, because I'm a military man. As far as I'm concerned, I'd take food and drink, weapons and tents, and leave everything else. If anyone interrupts me again to ask stupid questions about what we're taking, that'll be my response on *all* of it, so I suggest, as a merchant looking to make the most of the situation, you make damn sure I'm not interrupted."

"I understand." She smiled. "I'll make sure anything we don't need is left behind."

"Leave some supplies as well, where possible," I said. "Even if these people won't help us, I still don't want them to starve. They're stupid, not evil, I hope."

"Lord," Piotr said slowly, "you don't understand."

"Where I'm from, the legion had been smeared by the nobles of that land as well. They were hunted and abused, abandoned to the night, and I see that's true here to some degree as well," I replied coldly. "They were blamed for the fall of the empire and for the things that went wrong in the cataclysm. It wasn't their fault, but they were a convenient target.

"Here, it's almost worse, because as near as I can tell, you've all been taking advantage of their oaths to protect you. You've been smiling to their faces when you needed them but then you've been going back on your word. At least there they had the excuse of being nobles. Here, you did it yourselves."

"But—" he started.

I held up a finger. "Get. Out."

That was all I said, but it was clear by the cold anger in my voice that now was not the time to test me. He and the others left; Aellin stayed when I gestured for him to do so, joining Sehran and Oracle in the seats as we turned to the last two people in the room.

"Arlo, of House Granth," I greeted him, and he inclined his head, then bowed from a seated position.

"Lord Jax, Prince of the Empire and Scion," he greeted in return. "I presume that given your knowledge and accent, you're the same Jax who went by Jack? Sanguis?"

"I am." I nodded. "I'm a son of that cockwomble Sanguis, though if I have my way, I'd gut him given the smallest chance."

"An emotion that I've heard repeated by others. The lord of your house is not well respected." He nodded with a faint smile.

"He's not the lord of my house," I said coldly. "He was stripped of his position as a Prince of the Empire when he rebelled against Amon. He holds the rank of baron, but I am Jax Amon. I lead my house, and I renounce that fat fuck utterly."

There was a short pause as he clearly worked things out in his mind, before Arlo spoke again.

"In that case, my lord, perhaps I might suggest a meeting between yourself and my house?" he tried. "I'm sure the young master and his family would wish to discuss their options, at the very least."

"Tell Wilhelm I'd welcome a talk with him, and I'm open to a discussion of the possibilities, and our options. But, as you can tell, I have little time and less patience right now. I let you stay in here while we discussed our plans because I damn well know that there are going to be a hundred sly tricks that could be pulled to work this shit out, and this way it saves me fucking around, repeating myself.

"If it was anyone but Wilhelm, then I'd not have given you that chance. But he was someone I thought I could work with, and there were other houses that almost seemed the same. I'm not going to ask about your position and forces, as I know you'll not tell me, so instead I'll ask you this. Do any of the nobles from Earth hold Gaij?"

"Not to my knowledge. Three attempted to claim it. Only one survived and he fled, according to rumor, but I know not whom," he admitted.

"Fine. Well, you know I'm headed there, and if three of the noble dickbags tried to claim it, then I know that you, or they, know what it is. I, however, am the Scion of the Empire. I *will* claim it, so tell Wilhelm this, and invite him to meet me there to discuss our futures. BUT…" I held a hand up, one finger raised. "Tell him that if he breaks his word, he'll regret it."

"His word?"

"He'll know," I said firmly, remembering the oath I'd made him swear to not raise a hand against me, after I'd spared his life in the arena.

"Very well." He stood. "By your leave, Prince Jax, may I depart?"

"One more question." I held a hand up. "When we stormed the camp, one of these idiots aimed a grenade launcher at me. How the hell did he get that?"

"One of our smaller exploratory teams," he said. "They were caught by the undead raiding their camp some three days ago, and it took a few days to track them to here. They didn't understand the 'fire weapons' but had tried to buy some from us. Our house refused and sent the team to shadow them until they were out of our lands. Instead, three days ago, they were killed or captured."

"So you came looking for them." I nodded. "Okay, have you recovered them?"

"Two of the three. One died in the original assault," he said.

"Okay, how'd you get the weapons through the gate without them exploding?"

"Lead-lined, specially designed boxes."

"Yeah, I've seen the same trick pulled elsewhere. One point, and I want to be clear on this—tell your masters that some of the portals lead through to underground cities. If they haven't yet found them, beware. They're inhabited by creatures that will infect your people. Be very careful. The last thing I need is them with fucking Uzis."

"We are aware of the…infection," he said after a brief pause. "Beyond that, any discussion on it is for my betters, not me. May I leave?"

"Go."

He left with his man, the pair quickly getting out of the door, and I sighed, relaxing, before looking over at the legionnaire. "Okay, I need to know who you've got in the camp and what condition they're in," I said. "Names and ranks, specialties and how many. Then explain the setup of the legion here. And lastly, well, tell me your story, I guess, and how you and the rest of your legion ended up as slaves."

"It'll take a while," he grunted, and I shrugged.

"Then give me the overview and you can explain more when we're on the road."

As I said that, Oracle stood next to me and gestured for me to stand.

"What?" I asked.

"You need to get out of that armor," she said. "There has to be clean clothing here, and you can listen while you sort through the armor."

"So I just strip here?" I asked with a snort of laughter.

"He's sworn to you, and a legionnaire," she pointed out. "He was also responsible for some of the damage to your armor and can give advice on repairing it, if there's anyone here who can do it."

"That's a good point." I sighed.

The dwarf legionnaire snorted and shifted around, speaking quickly as he showed me his back. "I be moving tae give yer as much privacy as the room allows, ma prince, all right? Showing yer ma back do no be intended as disrespectful," he clarified.

I gave a short laugh. "Believe me, if you were used to my usual team, you'd know that isn't something that overly concerns me," I admitted. "Fine, tell me what you can then."

"Aye, o' course, ma prince. So, t' legion here do be split between…"

# CHAPTER SEVENTEEN

"So, let me get this straight," I said a few minutes later, as he finished explaining the general structure of the legion, and that all of those with him…weren't the fighters. I got the last of my dented, scuffed, and scratched armor off, and laid out for cleaning and repairs. "You're saying that the majority of your fighting forces were lost?"

"All legionnaires are legionnaires first," Aellin replied distractedly, his eyes already fixed on my armor. His hands clenched and unclenched as he tried to keep himself under control.

"And everyone matters, nobody lies and cheats and steals, and everyone's a good person if you give them the chance. I don't need platitudes, mate, so cut the bullshit. I'm not calling your people out and slagging them off, Aellin. I'm asking a genuine question. And go on, you can look at it if you want."

"Aye," he grunted, moving quickly, dropping to one knee and snatching up one of the gauntlets, peering at it and testing the articulation. "Where'd ye say ye got this?"

"I didn't, but I'll tell you my story when you finish yours. Come on, man, who the hell are you?"

"We're of the Fifth Maniple of the Legion of Sanketh," he replied flatly. "While our maniple was charged with the support of the four active fightin' maniples, that doesnae mean…"

"It means you're the camp followers, the armorers, and the cooks," I whispered, closing my eyes. "Fuck me sideways."

"An' yet we chose tae stand with ye," he whispered, trying to hide his anger.

I snorted. "Actually, you tried to fucking kill me, but let's not even go there." I shifted around and sat back in a comfortable seat, fixing him with a smile. "Aellin, please understand, I'm not upset that you and your people exist—I'm surprised. Back on Dravith, the legion has a small number of support staff. The Fifth Maniple has been folded into the others because there were so few of them, and they are damn well valued for who and what they are.

"My concern here is that I'm going to be leading a charge to rescue a fuckload more people as we set out of here, and instead of an active fighting legion, I have crafters."

"An' we're useless," he finished for me, still looking offended.

"Bollocks," I said flatly. "Are you useless? Are you shit at your job, Aellin?"

"Nae."

"Well then, there we go. I agree you're a legionnaire first and you're trained and experienced as one, despite your specialization being one of crafting rather than battle. What *is* your job, actually?"

"Armor smith," Aellin replied, rubbing at his weathered face. "Though, in truth, ah'm more focused on repairs and maintenance these days. Materials an' skill fer craftin' new pieces are damn near impossible tae come by."

"How'd you end up here?" I asked, genuinely curious. A dwarven armorer for the legion should have been worth his weight in gold, not enslaved in some caravan.

"That's the story of the whole Legion of Sanketh, really." He sighed, gesturing with the gauntlet in disgust. "We were stationed at the fortress of Tor'Sanketh, about three hundred miles northeast of here. Good position, defensible, with access tae the old mines an' trade routes. But the desert…" He trailed off, his expression distant.

"The Great Altan," Oracle supplied. "It's been expanding for centuries."

"Aye. Year by year, mile by mile. The wells started failin' first. Then the crops. We tried everythin'—water mages, irrigation systems, even attempted tae tap intae the ancient imperial waterworks. But nothin' could hold back the sand." Aellin's fists clenched. "The nobles abandoned their estates, an' without the water mages, the people either followed or died. The legion stayed as long as we could, tryin' tae protect those who remained, but…"

"How long ago was this?" I asked.

"Twenty-three years now. We held out longer than most, but eventually we had tae abandon the fortress. Tried tae escort the remainin' civilians tae safety. That's when the slavers hit us." His voice grew hard. "We were exhausted, low on supplies, our numbers already thinned by years of fightin' the desert's monsters. They picked us off, group by group."

I nodded grimly. It fit the pattern: the nobles abandoning their responsibilities, the legion trying to hold things together, and predators moving in to feast on the remains. "How many were you originally?"

"Five understrength maniples, a little under five thousand legionnaires an' support staff total." Aellin's eyes grew distant. "By the time we abandoned Tor'Sanketh, maybe twenty-eight hundred remained. The retreat cost us another two hundred. The slavers…" He shook his head. "At the last rally, there were fifty-three of us left, mostly from the support maniples. The fighters die hardest, but when yer entire existence is one fight after another, we all die sooner or later."

"Why?" I asked desperately. "I mean, you were nearly three thousand legionnaires! Why not set up a new home somewhere?"

"Well, we cannae, can we!" he replied grimly. "We cannae, you know that. An' even iffin we could, where the hell would we go?"

"There's land everywhere!" I gestured vaguely. "For fuck's sake, would none of the other legions take you in?"

"We swore an oath tae protect the people." He snorted. "Ye think that can be put aside?"

"I know but—"

"Nae," he said coldly, shaking his head. "Nae, ye don't. Ye don't understand the effect of the oaths. An' yet we still fuckin' bind new recruits with them. We still ruin their lives an' indoctrinate them, because it's the only way we can survive, an' we have tae. Ye told that arse of a headman tae get out because he wouldnae pay his debt tae the legion, but honestly? As much as ah hate him fer it, ah don't blame him."

"Why?" I asked, wondering.

"Because we're trapped." He sighed. "We cannae move on because our oaths prevent us from leavin' imperial citizens without aid. They claim tae be imperial citizens tae keep us in the area so that we defend them. An' then when we lose people, we come tae them an' we take their people as payment. We replace our losses with volunteers, an' then they get tae see how fucked we all are."

"They protect them?" I asked, confused.

"If they tell us where the slavers are, we're forced by our oaths tae hunt them down an' try an' kill them. Tae be clear, sometimes that's a single fuckin' legionnaire on his own, wounded already an' who'd been headin' back tae try an' heal up and now he's all that's left of his squad, so he has tae try an' hunt down an' kill the slavers—then he'll die.

"When he dies, the slavers go lookin' fer who ratted them out tae the legion, an' they get punished. Then the legion hears about it an' that we've lost more of our own, so we go in—"

He broke off, shaking his head, struggling with his words. "It just gets worse. It never ends. An' the worst part of it all? These villages know they need us at our best strength tae protect them, an' we damn well know that we cannae do it without them, but everyone tries tae hold ontae their own. They don't want tae give their kids up fer the meat grinder. They're barely survivin' as it is, an' fer them then tae hand their sons an' daughters over at fourteen tae join the legion? They cannae do it. They need them, so they lie."

"What do you mean, they lie?" I asked.

"Half the villages send their kids tae the next one along with a new name, where they claim tae be a wanderin' worker lookin' fer a home, an' that village sends their daughter tae live in their place." His voice was bitter now. "They do it tae hide them from us, tae avoid payin' their debt, an' WE KNOW." He swore.

"We damn well know they're doin' it! We don't want tae see their villages fail. We don't want tae go back tae them on our next fuckin' rotation, our never endin' patrol, an' tae tell them that their sons an' daughters died fightin' some slaver, or from an infected wound, or…"

"You're saying there's no way out?" I asked quietly.

"Ye don't know what it's like, prince. We're forced by our oaths tae constantly patrol these lands, tae try an' protect these people, because that was what we were ordered tae do after the fall. We cannae even tell the other legions, because then they'd help!"

"They'd help?" I asked, even more confused.

"They're barely survivin' as it is!" he snarled. "If we told them, they'd be forced tae send help. They'd each lose what they have left, an' fer what? It'd only hasten the end! We cannae win this fight. Every year, fewer an' fewer legionnaires join us. An' those of us are already in? We do our best tae not take others. We take only those who have nae choice!"

His voice dropped lower, almost a whisper now. "We rescue slaves an' we induct them, or orphans starvin' on the streets. But even there, there's a fight fer them! Do ye see that? We have tae fight the gangs tae try an' recruit orphans, that's how shitty it is! That the gangs, the flesh markets an' the goddamn fightin' rings, the arenas an' more are looked upon as bein' a genuine better alternative tae the fuckin' legion!"

He broke off with a shuddering breath, then went on in a quieter tone. "That's where we are, my prince. We're that fucked. Ah can only say this tae ye because ye're legion, but they all know. Everyone knows that the legion is a death sentence."

"So you're saying…" I paused, thinking it through. "You literally can't leave because the villages claim imperial citizenship to keep you here, but they won't actually support you because if they do, their kids end up dead anyway?"

"Aye." Aellin nodded grimly. "An' if we try tae leave, our oaths force us back. If we try tae get help, we doom the other legions tae the same fate. If we try tae save them all, we die faster. If we don't try tae save them, we be forced intae the fight anyway. I wasnae really suggestin' we leave the' others. Ah hell, ah dinna ken how we could rescue just oor people anyway, and it be against t' oath, but damn, you just need tae understand that it's all…"

"It's all fucked. And the slavers know this," I said, understanding finally dawning. "And they know you can't ignore a call for help, so they use it against you."

"More than ye know." He picked up another piece of my armor, examining the damage. "They set traps. Leave a village apparently under attack. Then, when we respond, both side's is them." He shrugged. "Or they actually attack a village, knowin' we'll come. Either way, they whittle us down, bit by bit."

"Until you end up enslaved yourself," I finished.

"Aye. Though that wasnae supposed tae happen." His hands tightened on the armor piece. "We were down tae less than sixty of us. Had a plan tae make one final stand, take out as many of the bastards as we could. But they had a mage with 'em, one wi' spells we'd never seen before. He…" Aellin's voice caught. "He could control the air… When we ran tae fight, an' we be hit by bones, 'undreds o' bones, from all sides. Ye smash 'em, ye break 'em, an' it made no difference. They closed over oor arms an' legs, pinned us. Then, as w' fell, one by one, w' were captured. We be the last. All the rest? They'd bin an' ran outta collars by the time they got tae us. That be why we be left here."

I felt Oracle's horror through our bond, matching my own growing fury. "This mage. He have a name?"

"No one tha' he be tellin' tae the likes o' us." He shrugged. "We just ran tae the fight, an' then boom, it all went shite an' we ended up here."

"Well, that fucking explains a lot," I said after a few seconds of silence, mulling over it all. "Look, I get it, okay? In Dravith, in the cities, the legionnaires didn't get specific orders like it sounds like you did. They were ordered to remain and to protect the people as best they could, but it was a general order by their commanding officer. It wasn't an order someone was forced to follow because of the oath. As such, when the majority of the legion left to return to the heart of the empire, those left behind started to protect their cities," I explained.

"They were undercut and stabbed in the back repeatedly, but it was by the nobles of the cities, and that was to get their hands on the taxes that were supposed to be put aside for the legion."

"Taxes?" He snorted. "There be taxes put aside fer us? Who by?"

"By the nobles of the land as part of their oaths," I said firmly. "If they swore imperial oaths, and they rule by claiming imperial mandate, then there's a percentage of all taxes earned that's supposed to go to you for support. It's only ten percent, but it was enough to clear out the treasuries of the cities when I claimed them, it'd not been paid in so long."

"Damn." He snorted. "Aye, ah dinna think that be the case here."

"Well, we can hope." I said, "Okay, tell me about the local situation—the cities, the continent…tell me everything you know."

He did. For the next hour, he talked, bringing me up to date on history as we worked to get my armor as clean as possible and fix what we could. Most of his gear was gone—taken by the other caravan to sell—but what there was made a hell of a difference. Finally, as I stepped back out into the mid-morning heat that rolled off the desert nearby, I had a plan.

"All right!" I barked, as I walked outside to find the people of the caravan formed up, waiting for me. "Good morning, everyone, and welcome to the first day of the rest of your lives! You have a choice to make, and it's going to be a simple one for many of you, and yet oh so profound!"

I jumped, adding a touch of Soaring Majesty to let me land easily on the roof of what was now "my" wagon. Yes, I knew it was heavy; yes, I knew it was excessive and overly luxurious, but fuck me sideways if I didn't deserve a little of that in my life. It wasn't going to slow us down. It'd been one of the leaders' wagons and was very well made, after all, so it was now my mobile home.

"So, there are a great many of you here, and I know that some of you will want to come with me, and many won't. To make our position clear, I am Prince Jax Amon, and I will be heading from here to hunt down the slavers and rescue those they have taken!"

A cheer rose from the crowd, and I lifted my hands, grinning and damn well knowing that the next bit was going to be the make-or-break one. "You all like that— of course you do. The slavers are going to get punished and I'm going to rescue the caravanners and more of your people. Well, that's great, BUT…"

I paused, looking around at the gathered crowd.

"You all have a decision to make here. I've heard about the way that things work in this land, and how the legion has been 'supported' by you all, and also how they in turn have protected you. It's been a shit show on both sides. The legion were constrained by their oaths to basically constantly hunt the area and try to keep you all safe, and the only way they could do that was to drain you all dry of everything you needed to become successful villages.

"They were a parasite on your lands…" I called out, and I saw the look of horror on the legionnaires' faces and the nods on that of the villagers. "But the reason they did that? The reason they drained you dry?" I asked.

"It wasn't because they were getting fat and happy—it's because none of you fucking *helped*!" That last word was shouted in anger. "None of you took responsibility for your own protection and your own lands. You claimed imperial citizenship, I've been told, as that forced the legion to stay. It literally forced them by magical and soul-bound oaths to fight to their deaths for you. And yet, and this surprised me when I heard about it, it seems you all forgot about the other side of the imperial oaths.

"You apparently sent your children to other villages to keep them safe from the draft, you turned the legion away when they came to you asking for aid and for support, and as for the imperial taxes—the taxes that you swear to pay *as imperial citizens*—the legion has received none."

Silence greeted my words at that.

"Had you fucking paid those taxes, had you supported the legion, they wouldn't have been whittled down to their current size and strength. Had you kept to your oaths, you'd not have ended up where you are. But wait, it gets better!"

I grinned out at the crowd, knowing that I was looking manic now, as I rolled my helmet in my hands. "When I activated the imperial oath, when I reached out with it, I found one hundred and eleven imperial citizens within twenty-seven miles."

Silence.

"That includes the legionnaires, by the way, fifty-three legionnaires, and it includes those who already swore the oath to me, and who came to your aid, here, last night. *Seven* people had actually sworn the oaths, that's all.

"Four were slaves in this camp already, two were taken from the villages, and the last one is some fifteen miles to the east and closing fast upon us."

I looked around.

"That means that you all lied about your oaths. At best, you took advantage of the empire. At worst, you actively conspired to kill my legionnaires."

Now people were getting nervous, and I didn't blame them.

"What's going to happen now is I'm going to lead my people after the slavers. Those who are already imperial citizens will be going with me. Those who were not until now, I choose to believe must have made a mistake, or have misunderstood the situation, and as such, I offer a chance to rectify it.

"You all have the choice to swear to me now and to aid us. You will join the caravan and you will help us to rescue the others. Then you, as imperial citizens, will serve the empire. There are oaths to be sworn, though I assure you they are structured to protect you and the empire, not to enforce suffering or to gain while you do not.

"When the oath is offered to you, I will give you a few minutes to read it over and to make your decision. Those who swear are welcome to come with us, and will enjoy the benefits of full imperial citizenship, which includes me and my people investing in *you*."

I looked around, seeing how many were uncomfortable with what I was saying, and I went on. I needed these people, after all, but I also didn't want people agreeing without understanding, or doing it thinking this was going to be an easy road.

"For those who earn them, there will be spellbooks, skillbooks, and even for those rare few who excel, skill memory crystals. Some will become mages, others bakers. We have airships, literally ships that sail the skies, and that are improved upon daily, sometimes hourly, by gnomish lunatics…I mean, *engineers*." That got some smiles.

"We have full legions that protect our lands, and as you all felt earlier, we have the blessings of the gods. What that means for you is that you have an opportunity to become a priest or priestess of those gods. You could gain power and learn to help people, instead of serving that fucking cockgoblin Nimon."

That sparked a roll of thunder, and I waved him off casually, continuing with my recruitment speech.

"You will get all these chances, and more, but you need to understand that you will become hunted by Him and His kind. You will be joining an empire resurgent, and there are only two sides in this war. You can choose to stand aside and you can remain here. You will go back to your lives—for now—and you can forget about the empire."

Heads nodded, and I nodded back.

"It's a valid choice…for a fool," I clarified. "When I leave, I will not be returning this way again, not like this. The next time you see the empire, it will be as a conquering army and a rising force. You, who have taken advantage of the legion, who have drained my forces, and who I have personally rescued, then denied me, as I ask now for your help, will be left behind.

"Where those who stand by your side rise in my service, where they rescue others and grow strong, you and your villages will continue as you have, wasting away. You can join me, or you can continue to wither.

"What we do now is to protect and recover *your people*. My own are back on Dravith. I *should* be travelling that way even now. I ended up here with my companions thanks to an artifact being triggered, and even now my forces fly toward me, aided by their bond to guide them. Instead, I march away from them. I head from here inland, and to war…and you need to make a decision.

"Those who join me will be running from dawn 'til dusk. We will take the best of the wagons—possibly all of them, depending on how many of you come with us—and we will take that which we need from the supplies. Anything we don't need will be left behind, and those of you who refuse my request and oath can take what you want. I care not."

Some faces perked up at that.

"Those who come with me will learn, they will grow, and that will start in part with physical exercise. Because when I say that we will run, I mean that. We will literally run by the side of the wagons. All of us will run, hour by hour, day by day, to close the gap with the slavers.

"Those who are too weak to do this will be permitted to rest to catch their breath, then they will run again. The wagons will be pulled and pushed by us and the beasts, and we will cover as much ground as we possibly can every day before we rest.

"Magic will be used to heal you all, to grant you the best possible chance in what is to come. And when my forces arrive here, by my goddamn word, they'll find forces waiting to greet them as brothers- and sisters-in-arms.

"For those who join us, I cannot promise victory. I cannot promise that you will win every fight. But I can promise that I would never ask you to do something that I wouldn't do. I can promise that if you stand by my side, I will stand by yours, and that I will help you as best I can.

"I will forge you into the steel that this new age is built upon, and when I'm done, you'll look back and wonder at how weak you were. I ask you all now, to read the oath, to consider your future. And if you want a real chance at becoming all you can be? I ask you to swear it now!"

Sweat ran down my back, and I was mentally cursing myself. My speech was shit. It really was. And yet, as much as I knew that I needed to become better at this, all I could do was speak from the heart. I didn't want to beg. I couldn't make promises that they were going to live in safety and that their kids would grow up to become lords and ladies. All I could do was offer my support, and hope that they'd give me theirs in return.

My mana dropped like a stone as Oracle pushed out the oath to everyone before me. I quickly drank the glowing mana potion, gasping as my mana bar flared to full in under a second and my mana regeneration, per second, was suddenly higher than the fucking maximum I could hold.

I stifled the disappointment that I'd just wasted a potion that was clearly insanely powerful. Instead, I focused as at first one, then a handful, then dozens began to speak the oath.

Dozens became hundreds, and by the time that they had all finished, I was smiling. At least I damn well knew I had a chance, and that was when Oracle spoke loudly.

Four hundred and sixty-six people had sworn by the end, on top of the legion, and damn that felt good.

"Everyone who has sworn the oath, you will now be examined to ensure that the oath was sworn in truth. For anyone who hasn't sworn it, please, back away. This is to remove spies and enemy agents, and will burn any who have not sworn! Please understand, that for those who have sworn, this will actively heal you, not harm."

She started to cast, as people streamed back out of the circles, holding back as long as she dared. But as the Frostfire Circles of Cleansing flared to life—three of them, as I understood what she was doing and cast one as well—a handful of people shouted and screamed, running to get clear. Those who were caught by the spell's active effects and were injured were quickly healed by Sehran. But those who stood inside the circles?

Aside from a few uncomfortable seconds as the flames touched them, they were unharmed.

Then, as the new imperial citizens started to laugh and cry out, the realization spread that we'd told the truth. Not only were they not being injured by the spells, but as they stood there, Oracle had moved quickly onto another spell. Rather than letting the mana go to waste, she was pouring healing into these people.

Injuries that they'd had for their entire lives—bum knees, badly healed breaks, stunted growth through malnourishment—all of it was being reversed. Although she couldn't do everyone, not even with the mana boost we had, she managed to do it for dozens of the worst affected.

By the time the spells ran out and she sagged, exhausted from the strain, more and more of those who had refused the oath saw the bounty they'd missed out on.

"What?" I asked, as I heard the shouted complaints rising and the demands to be offered the chance at the oath again. "Are you fucking kidding me? You think we're going to waste magic like that on people who wouldn't help us?"

I shook my head. "No. Imperial citizens! Legionnaires!" I roared. "Secure the camp. Push those out who refused to aid us and those we go to rescue. They can scavenge what we leave behind *after* we leave. Let's get to work!"

# CHAPTER EIGHTEEN

"What a fucked-up situation," I called out three hours later as we arced around toward the fording point in the river.

Toren guided the lead wagon of the caravan down the long hill toward a clearing by the water's edge. "It is what it is!" he called back philosophically.

I nodded, accepting that, more or less, before launching myself into the air. I flew forward, doing a slow, long pass over the river and searching for anything that might be hiding in its depths.

Toren had added to the information that Finna and the others had given me, and that Aellin had shared as well. I felt that I finally had a good picture of the current state of the continent, and frankly, it was a mess.

I continued to watch over the caravan as it slowed to a stop. The legion and the experienced caravanners took point and split up the jobs, already starting to work well together.

The run so far had been hard, I knew. Hell, I'd felt it, and I was by now at a level of fitness that was frankly herculean.

Most people alternated between running and riding. The wagons were set up and loaded deliberately so that they each carried half their intended load in people, and half in gear.

That meant that the gear was spread out across all forty wagons we'd taken, and at any one time, half of the wagons also held people.

Every half an hour, all the wagons would stop, and the people would jump off and start running.

Then people who had just been running, and who now needed a break, could jump on the alternate wagons, letting the beasts that pulled the wagons enjoy a little respite as they got to pull half-laden ones for the next half an hour.

Then the draft animals would be changed over, a process that got faster each time we did it, and then we'd set off again.

It sounded complicated, but the overall effect was that where the enemy caravans should be able to run for up to ten hours a day at a reasonable speed of four miles an hour, due to the lack of any well-maintained roads, we looked to be able to manage twelve to fourteen hours a day, and five and a half miles an hour.


Every day, we'd close on the slavers at a rate of twenty to twenty-five miles a day—once we took off some breaks—over their speed, because they, unlike us, had no clue they were being chased.

Their average speed was four miles an hour, and they worked for ten hours, giving them a forty-mile range at most a day. We both apparently had the same maps, as they were common to the area, and we'd both be travelling roughly the same route.

We needed to pass through a town that was literally a supporter of the local slave trade, but that just added to the impetus, not detracted for me.

All in all, it meant that they were some hundred to at most a hundred and twenty miles ahead of us, and that if we managed to keep this pace up, including a day to "visit" the slavers' town, we might be able to catch them in about a week, depending on the situation and how hard they were pushing.

I watched from above as the tail end of the caravan wound its way through the dusty terrain. The wagons moved steadily in formation and the people staggered along, exhausted and damn well ready for a break.

The system we'd developed was working well. Alternating runners and riders kept both people and animals from exhaustion. From this height, they looked like a serpentine chain stretching across the landscape, purposeful and determined.

Oracle's voice touched my mind through our bond. *"The next watering point is about two miles ahead. The maps show an old way station, though it's not going to be anything usable or claimable, so don't get your hopes up."*

*"Dammit. Ah, fuck it...everyone could use a break anyway, I guess, and I want to check how the new runners are holding up."*

*"They're doing well,"* she said, and I had to agree.

The ford wasn't a hard one. The river here, for whatever geological reason, was both wide and shallow, with the crystal-clear water running over sandy substrate. Even better, the constant battering across the rocks meant that there was no way that softer-bodied creatures like leeches could survive it.

We were also a large enough party that the few creatures we saw in the distance—which would have normally attacked humans on sight—decided to give us a wide berth.

Lastly, we'd pushed out scouts two hours ahead of us, riding a handful of spare horses. They'd started guiding us, and occasionally sent a member of the group back with things like a freshly killed deer.

That had resulted in a chase when a large bipedal creature called a horak had scented the blood and decided that one rider alone was worth the risk, and that in turn resulted in the reptilian horak being added to our stores a little while later, as the legion scout was in no mood for their shit.

The rest of the horses were integrated into the pool of animals to pull the wagons. There'd been a discussion around whether we should let the weaker and older members of the group ride, rather than run, but in the end, we decided no. Mainly because there weren't enough for everyone, so it wasn't like we could go faster.

And secondly? The only way these people would get stronger was if we made them all run.

If we didn't have healing magic and the ability to let them ride for a bit now and then, it'd be ridiculous and we could have never done it. But as it was? Yeah. It was working well.

The group had wound their way back up out of the little dip around the river and into a series of low hills after the river crossing, and I had to admit, I liked this land.

Unlike Dravith, where everywhere I'd been so far had pretty much been the deep forest, ancient and overgrown, or the cities, which were surrounded by hotly contested farmland, here the land was wide open and empty.

The distant heat of the desert and the general state of the area meant that although there had probably once been huge forests, they were pretty much gone now.

Over the thousands of years of the empire and humanity's history here, the area had been extensively logged, and now?

It was reduced to wide, low scrub grass, massive ranges where in the distance I could make out hundreds, possibly thousands of grazing cattle or similar.

Although it was good for the caravans, it made me damn conscious that for there to be this much land, and almost no people, there had to be something wrong with it.

The earth was shallow and rocky—crap for growing crops—but beyond that, it was fertile enough that it could support vast herds. On Earth, that would have meant that cowboys and more would have followed the herds, creating travelling tent cities. That, I'd been told, was what Sonra, the city that the slavers were headed for, was.

The combination of slavers, a complete lack of any nobles who were willing to invest their armies in pacifying the area, and the apparent love of the wide-open places for certain wildlife, combined to make this a damn dangerous part of the world.

Especially because the wildlife that liked this area went by the name of *dragons.*

Lesser dragons, to be clear—more like flying wurms with little beyond a drive to eat, fuck, and sleep. But I ignored the apparent likeness that Oracle saw between them and me.

The lesser dragons weren't really interested in caravans, but they did like two things beyond their meat on the hoof, the open sky, and getting laid.

They liked precious metals—specifically gold and platinum—and they liked highly magical artifacts.

Trying to cross the territory with too much of either was asking to be hit by a bored—and occasionally horny, which was even more terrifying—lesser dragon. And that didn't end well for anyone, regardless of which you got.

That was the final nail in the coffin, I'd been told by Toren, because if they had earned any great wealth out on this caravan route, they'd have then avoided this particular stretch of land for fear of being raided or visited by a dragon.

Landing near the head of the caravan, I fell into step beside a group of former merchants who were taking their running shift. Their faces showed strain but also determination. The transformation over just these first hours had been remarkable. People who'd likely never run more than a few steps in their lives were pushing themselves beyond what they thought possible.

"How're you holding up?" I asked one particularly red-faced man who Zyenna had named as another former cloth merchant.

"Better…than expected…my prince," he managed between breaths. "The healing…at the last stop…it helped."

I nodded. Oracle and I had established a routine of casting healing spells at each rest point, focusing not just on any injuries that people had gotten on the trek, but on strengthening muscles and easing the strain of unaccustomed exercise. The results made it clear it was worth the effort. People were already running longer and breathing easier.

As another hour passed, I noted that the group was flagging more than ever. I sighed, acknowledging that Toren had known his shit. Although I'd rather have run for another few hours—we were barely four hours out of the camp, after all—he was right that for the first day, we'd need to have a significant rest stop for feed and to recover.

The way station slowly slid into view far ahead, its weathered stone walls still standing after centuries. The sight of the imperial markers, though long vandalized and broken, sent a pang through me. Another reminder of how far this continent had fallen since the cataclysm.

As the caravan finally slogged to a stop, Oracle created her signature healing fountains, the crystal-clear water sparkling with healing magic.

The sight of people drinking deeply, their exhaustion visibly melting away, made me smile despite the grim circumstances that had brought us here.

Toren approached as I moved through the crowds, talking to those who could bring themselves to speak to me, and generally just letting people see me.

"The scouts haven't seen anyone, but they did spot some interesting tracks heading east. Looks like we're not the only ones using these old imperial roads, and it's recent."

"The slavers?" I asked, hope rising.

"Could be, but more likely, it's not just the one caravan." He sighed. "Looking at the tracks, the trail was broken recently, and either the caravan is bigger than we're expecting, or there's been a few using it over a short period of time—a week or two, no more."

I nodded, considering. "Keep the scouts running then, but if they break away from the slavers' trail, we don't investigate. We can't afford delays." I got a nod and a hesitant smile, before he moved off.

The camp cooks had set up their stations with military efficiency; the smell of cooking food drew appreciative looks from the runners. Many of these people had been surviving on bare subsistence for months or years. Watching them eat their fill, the way that they looked at the portions they were given, made me both proud and want to smash someone's face in.

These were trail rations. Literally, the cooks were working hard to prepare food on the wagons while the rest of the people ran, and when we stopped, they'd piled out and had started setting up.

The cauldrons for a very basic stew were going within minutes, and although it was served within the hour, nobody got anything special. We didn't even have time for the meat to cook; it was literally beans and rice, or near enough—some kind of local variants on them—and that was it, and yet…

It was like these people had been transported to heaven.

Just seeing the tears of gratitude flow down one woman's face as a cook asked her whether she wanted more, having spotted her sitting and licking the last bits off her bowl, made me desperately angry, and I did my very best to hide it.

That anyone could reduce people to such a shitty situation boiled my piss, and I resolved to take my fucking time explaining that to someone…very, *very* soon.

The way station was a great place to set up for the night. Large and stone, it had a dozen rooms, and although there were no doors left, nor any comforts, the idea of sleeping in an actual building rather than getting back on the road really would have made them all a lot happier, I knew.

Despite that, I allowed them two hours to rest here—a far longer time than I wanted to, and nowhere near long enough at the same time. Then I forced them all back to their feet, and back onto the road.

The first half hour was a solid walk. Then, when everyone had had enough time to digest their food, I called for the pace to be picked up, and I started to run again with the rest.

This land was beautiful, or it could be, I knew. The things that had happened to it, though? Damn.

Oracle joined me half an hour into the next cycle, as we slowed and got ready to change the animals over, the elderly and weaker among us desperate to take their spaces aboard the wagons for a brief rest.

"You're brooding again," she said softly, landing next to me and taking my hand as we walked.

"I'm just thinking about what Aellin told us. About how the legion here was trapped by their own oaths, forced to watch as everything fell apart around them."

"And wondering if we can change things?" She cocked her head to the side, watching me.

"Something like that." I gestured toward the people stretching and groaning, the legion moving through making sure that people prepared for the next leg of the journey. "These people have courage, determination. But this continent…the damage goes so deep. The cataclysm didn't just break the land; it broke something in the people too."

"Then we'll help them rebuild it," Oracle said. "They're alive, and while there's life, there's hope."

"Yeah, but hearing what was done here? No wonder there's precious little of it," I muttered.

And that was true. The cataclysm had been terrible on Dravith. It'd been an imperial province that was still in need of pacification, and the immediate rise of the monsters, the shitehawks who were always looking for personal advantage, and the lack of any real leadership had caused chaos. But there were also the advantages there.

They were a hardy people, a group who were only a few generations from the original settlers of the land. They had resources and plans to fall back upon. And, as much as I knew I was starting to sound like a broken record, there weren't the dozens of centuries of noble houses sitting around with time on their hands, ready to fuck things up.

Instead, the people had banded together, and although it was hard, they survived. Here?

The moon that Nimon had pulled down had fractured, and a massive segment of it had impacted the land far to the south. On Earth, if the moon fell, the damage would eliminate life. Clouds of smoke and dust would choke out the sun and all plant life would fail, and the carnivores would pass as well.

The seas would boil and the land would break apart; everything would be destroyed, like the end of the world had come for the dinosaurs there. It'd have been worse here, because most of the population lived in houses and weren't hunter-gatherers, used to moving with the food and as needed.

We had neither the hides nor the mentality to survive that kinda shit. And the moon? It was a fucking *moon*.

It was an order of magnitude bigger than the asteroid that had wiped out the dinos, or at least I assumed it was.

The reason that it hadn't ended all life, according to everything people had been told, was because Nimon, who had pulled down the moon in the first place and had admitted to banishing all the other gods, had decided to spare a small percentage of all life, to allow them to follow His ways and worship Him alone.

If that was true or some other bullshit, I didn't know. But what I did know was that part of the moon had crashed far, far to the south.

It was large enough and long enough, that it could have, again, wiped out all life. That it hadn't made no sense to me. But considering I was currently living here, I wasn't going to complain too much in case someone agreed and fixed that.

The upshot of it was that the land that had been there was now basically buried under billions of tons of rubble. Over the centuries since then, it'd settled, thanks to wind and rain, and now there was simply a section of the southern continent that was a lot higher than the lands around it.

Sure, that I got. But what had really fucked shit up was that there were metals from there that you couldn't get anywhere else—or at least that hadn't been found anywhere the people here had access to.

Those metals and minerals really worked well with mana, and had become a primary industry for the southern kingdoms.

They were actually the reason there were southern kingdoms, it turned out, because one "minor" detail was that the land down there?

It was fucked.

Not as in "hey, that looks a bit broken up." Oh, no. Whatever the difference in the land was, it was impossible to grow anything within twenty miles of the moon material. That meant that anything too close to there that survived the touchdown— very little, admittedly—was now dead from contamination.

What had been the midlands was now the southern kingdoms, as the barons and more who had owned that land saw the opportunity, and started to buy up every slave they could. They were sent in teams to go mine the materials out. And considering they were given just enough food to get to the site, mine for two weeks and then return, and anywhere that might be able to grow more food was at least three months' travel away…

Well. They didn't even need to send guards after the slaves.

Just equipped them, sent them off, and kept their borders secure thanks to mages who had staffs made of this magical moon shit.

If it wasn't for the little detail that it was rare as fuck and that making a single ingot was about a month's production, the entire continent would have gained new masters.

Instead, as it was, there were a handful of mages who you did *not* fuck with, and they all came from the south.

Moving on from there, we had a lot to learn about the areas, but little details really stood out. Like the city of Gaij that we were headed for.

It'd once been a great tower, the Tower of Gaij. After this section of the empire had been "pacified," it'd been turned over to research and development, magical learning, and not a huge amount more.

Besides the incredible view up top, the towers were viewed as an anachronism, something that the empire grew out of, and certainly not somewhere that the nobles would want to live.

After all, if they lived there, they had to assist in its upkeep, instead of the empire paying for it, and any building two to three miles high, with tens of thousands of rooms, and hundreds of thousands of fucking windows, required a lot of upkeep.

I mean, the heating bill alone had to be insane in the winter, right?

Anyway, the requirements for serving staff and more were mind-boggling, that was true. And as they came with a legion garrison, any noble who also decided to live there was likely to find themselves under a legion general's eye a lot, which was…not a good thing.

Not when you wanted your life to be based around drink and debauchery anyway.

That meant that when the cataclysm came, there were no "real" nobles near the tower. And those who were around were enjoying a rather nice party in the nearby district mansion, according to the tales I was told.

When the cataclysm hit, well, the great tower wasn't lucky enough to have been reinforced by its entire mana stores the way the Tower of Dravith had been. Instead, it shook through the hellish damage done to the realm, and a building that big can only move so much.

The tower shattered at about a third of the way up. The upper floors fell slowly outward. Doing the one good thing they could still do for the realm, while they carried the leadership of the tower, its resident controller and librarian wisp, and the majority of the research staff and legions to their doom…they also landed atop the nobles' district palace.

Although that did, admittedly, ensure that the entire leadership of the area was wiped out, it also probably made things a lot easier on the local populace once shit was sorted out.

I'd imagine it was a hell of a surprise as well, when these people came to the Great Tower for aid, only to find that the succubai—there as an "exchange program" of sorts with the demon realms—were the only ones left.

They'd claimed as much of the remaining tower as they could, and as they had been granted the identity of "guest" by the now dead leadership of the tower, the golems protected them as they would any other guest.

They categorically refused guest status to anyone else, and although they permitted people to build homes close to the tower, they weren't allowed in unless they paid the fee.

That fee could be paid with trade goods, luxuries, food, or coin, but suddenly "vital fluids" were no longer on the list of accepted trade goods. That was now a freebie that the succubai got when people came to visit.

That visit was a strictly controlled commodity as well, as the succubai had realized the power that they now wielded, though it came at a cost.

They had control of the only safe zone in the area—one that was self-repairing and essentially a paradise in a time when most of the world seemed to be on fire.

A few lucky souls were permitted to visit on a regular basis, getting jobs in the tower serving the succubai—and not in bed— working as farmers and the like on the garden levels.

As time went on, food stopped being as hard to get, and by now there were thousands of refugees around the tower. There'd been a few attempts to claim it, and as nobody left—not the nobles, anyway—had the imperial authority, and those who could have, namely higher legion generals and more, were all dead, things just sort of…continued.

The city of Gaij grew and grew. And by the time the succubai realized that the tower was failing, they were also unable to leave.

The portal home was destroyed, along with the rest of the tower. And if they left? Well, there were a *lot* of people outside who, although they owed their lives to the safety that the tower granted via the golems, were also very aware that they weren't allowed inside where the nice safe places were.

The nobles who had come, all lower ranked and without true imperial authority, wanted to take the tower, be that for themselves or for their people. But either way, they certainly didn't want the succubai having it.

Hundreds of people ringed the tower at all times. Some were the homeless, the destitute, and the desperate. Others were the customers of the tower, and they were well aware that inside, they had to pay. But if their pretties were caught outside?

Well, then all bets were off, as the land descended into barbarism.

The nobles visited the tower and tried everything to get the succubai out; the succubai entertained and enthralled for all they were worth, but they also split their time between "working" the tower, and "working" their guests.

That was what we'd been told anyway, or what had been pieced together by the legion and others. The tower, it seemed, without the upper levels and the controller wisp, couldn't guide itself. It couldn't regulate, and because the mana collectors were based on the crown of the tower there were just no other options that the succubai could see.

The only way that they could survive there was if the golems and the tower were active. The only way to keep the tower active was to donate their own mana, and their lives to it.

The legion knew, and for long centuries they were outwardly seen as "visiting" the succubai just like anyone else, but in truth they'd been working to keep the tower stable.

I had zero doubt that a few horny legionnaires—okay, all the legionnaires—had also been helping with "vital fluid" deliveries…direct ones. But the other thing they were doing was helping the succubai to survive, because the survivors of the Legion of Gaij had been based there. They knew the succubai, and when they'd marched out to go to people's aid, they saw what was really happening.

They had a legion bastion nearby, a training grounds for the legion from ages long past, something that had evolved into basically a small city of its own, but with highly limited capabilities when it came to food and very limited space inside its walls.

That had been most likely the place where the unwise orders that a dying noble had given had forced the legion into a life of travelling and "protecting all imperial citizens, no matter the cost."

Or at least that was, again, the scuttlebutt that I'd been told.

The legion had been forced to start moving, and instead of protecting their bastion and starting to enforce good behavior in the area, they were instead forced out on roving, steadily depleting patrols.

As the land grew more and more lawless, the citizens realized that there was this wonderful supply of good armor and gear, just walking right past. And then, the nobles realized that if instead of the legion, they had control over the bastion and the forges and so on? Well, they could help people too, right?

Yeah.

The legion had eventually been eliminated by its antithesis, the Dark Legion, and instead of as they'd been paid to do, vacating the perfectly good and magical bastion, the nobles all received a complete surprise when the Dark Legion told them to go fuck themselves and started to recruit and equip their people from there instead.

Where the legion had been restrained and had brought order, the Dark Legion brought utter chaos. The strong survived, the weak were bought and sold, and worst of all?

The survivors of the legion, thanks to that fucking stupid oath, were forced out to go and help people again and again, from anywhere they managed to hold up.

That there were any imperial legionnaires left to be recovered was a fucking miracle, all things considered. And one of the things I had planned, and that I was going to do as soon as I had the mana, was rescind that fucking order.

I'd already done it for my small cadre, but I needed a hell of a lot more mana to push it out any further.

Now, as the other nobles from back home were here, there was going to be a hell of a lot of changes coming, because those assholes did have the requisite authority to command the remains of the tower and its golems. And when one of them made it inside, that was going to be the end of the succubai.

Or at least the changing of the guard, and they were going to go from *happy* guests, to "*oh no, it's a fuckin' sex dungeon*" guests.

And that was only two parts of a damn big continent.

The harbor city of Mishrak'Lek, a pearl of the empire that had once been the home of some of the greatest fleets to ever sail the seas, was now, thanks to tectonic shifts, halfway up a mountainside and buried in snow.

Those who had tried in recent years to visit it had never been heard from again.

Then there was a wonderful little detail to consider as well.

The Cradle of Feshcan'un, the very place that Lagoush had recommended to us as a place that would be perfect for Oracle's forthcoming blessing and that we really needed to get her to, was no longer in the lands it had been.

Well, no, that wasn't right. It was where it'd always been—nobody had picked it up and fucked off with it. But where it had been was in the middle of a verdant valley filled with life.

It had been sanctified to Lagoush because it was such a home of overwhelming natural bounties. It had been a cradle of entire species and a holy place because of the incredible gifts it bestowed.

Food grown there had been tightly regulated because an apple from one of their orchards could bestow years of additional life, it was that blessed; and then along had come the cataclysm.

It was now in a desert, supposedly, but it was a desert of life.

Life itself was turned back upon itself there, and simply travelling through the outer edges had killed thousands. There were legends that inside, in the heart, was a blessed land still. But considering it affected even fliers who tried to get across, and the kinds of people who were willing to give everything up to move to such a place were generally not the strongest and healthiest around already…

Well, the place we most desperately needed to fucking get to was in a location called the "desert of life" and surrounded by vast plains, covered in tens of thousands of the dead.

That little detail really sucked balls, but I reminded myself Lagoush wouldn't have told us about it if there was no reason.

There were a thousand other locations. They'd told me about cities where the old ways had been replaced with better: a single location in the far east of the continent, on the coast—and thankfully *still* on the coast—had become a sprawling city of wonders.

They worked night and day and grew food that was used to save people. Anyone who went there was given work, and a home, and supposedly there was a new empire rising there.

If it'd not been spoken of for so long, I'd have written it off as influencer bullshit and have mentally marked it as a territory that one of the nobles from Earth had claimed. But in this situation, it'd been like that for around sixty years, ever since some old noble of the empire had come out of seclusion.

She was an elf, and supposedly had been around before the cataclysm, and had been in a trance for the entire time. When she'd come out of it, she'd been buried and had worked her way out, then had set off to sort this shit out. That was a hundred years ago, and in that time, she'd gone from "long forgotten wanderer" to "ruler of the city," which was nice to hear.

Admittedly, I'd done that in a matter of months, but I was also a man who could do a helicopter and had the nickname of Tripod—and it wasn't because I was just that fucking stable.

All in all, the vast majority of the things I'd been told over the course of the day had washed over me in an endless list of dates and strange names, locations of battles won and lost, and the rise and fall of attempted replacement empires.

Now, as Oracle drew me through the crowds, and up the stairs to our wagon, I sighed in relief. My spinning head of names and details cleared instantly when she led me through to the back, and the bathing area that was filled and ready.

"You've got a choice," she said to me. "There'll be food soon, and you can have a bath with me, or without, and then eat, or…"

"Or?" I looked at the water hungrily.

"Or, Sehran can join us in the bath, and yes, she knows that if you say yes, it's literally a bath only."

I looked at her in question, and she smiled.

"There's not much water," she admitted. "And while yes, I could summon more, the mana to do it could be better spent in summoning that water for these people to drink, rather than us having a fresh bath."

"We could…" I started to say, only for her to talk over me.

"And considering the state of you and her, neither of you are going to enjoy a bath that the other had first," she said firmly. "It comes down to practicalities. She, like everyone else we consider friends, has seen you naked multiple times. You have seen her the same, and we've all bathed together and washed in streams and so on when there's been no privacy. But I understand the concern, and if you—"

"Sehran!" I called, and the succubus stuck her head around the door at the far end of the wagon.

"Yes?" she asked hopefully.

"Get your arse in the bath." I snorted. "We can explain it to Jian if he ever worries about it, but honestly, I don't see it. Just keep your hands to yourself."

"So, no massage?" She hurried along the corridor, her clothes flying off as she came.

"Dammit!" I groaned.

"You said it." Oracle laughed. "However, *I* wouldn't say no to a massage?"

"Dibs!" Sehran laughed, already bumping me with a hip as she moved past me toward the tub, and I started stripping out of my armor.

"This is so unfair," I muttered, unable to keep from watching as Oracle stripped and climbed into the tub as well. "It's gonna take me a few minutes," I pointed out, disconnecting my armor section by section.

"Don't worry, we can reheat it." Oracle purred, as she and Sehran started making the most of the collection of soaps and unguents that sat in a rack by the tub.

"Evil." I groaned and continued to sort through my armor.

In the end, it took me nearly fifteen minutes to disconnect the entire suit of armor, and then, looking at the ladies in the bath, I almost gave in to temptation. But instead, being the dutiful prince of the realm, and more importantly, the legionnaire that I was, I took my armor along the wagon and, stepping outside, gave it to a legionnaire stationed outside. I asked him to summon the armorers and see whether there was anything more they could do with it.

Given how late it was and everything we'd been doing the last few days, I'd not have been surprised if they told me to blow a goat. Instead, the summoned armorers were overjoyed, and I had to order them to do the bare minimum hours working on it, and promised they could play again tomorrow night.

Then I got my ass back into the wagon.

It was…well, the word I had to use was palatial, all things considered.

I mean, I'd never considered that a wagon could have this kind of luxury, and considering the bathroom was yeah, admittedly not huge, but it was also entirely made of fucking marble, it had made me ask a few questions of Toren, who'd confided that the more luxurious wagons were made by specialist enchanters to be both lighter than they should be, and bigger inside than out.

That had explained how there was a tub in the floor that was large enough for three people comfortably, and possibly five if you were very friendly, as well as a ton plus in weight, yet the wagon moved easily.

Now, I moved back inside, peeling the remains of my underclothing off and trying to ignore the flaked, caked blood, sweat, and sand that fell to the floor as I went.

It was probably down to that and the sheer exhaustion that kept my brain on track, as I joined the ladies in the pool, and not the mantra that kept repeating over and over as Sehran rubbed Oracle's shoulders for her.

*"She's your friend, don't look at her... She's your friend, don't look at her... She's your friend, don't... Ah, fuck."*

# **CHAPTER NINETEEN**

The rest of the night—once Oracle and Sehran had finally finished in the bath and I'd then managed to sink to the bottom of the water and scrub every inch clean—was a pleasant one.

First, once I was properly clean, I'd then joined the ladies in the main room, and we'd all eaten. Then, Oracle and Sehran had insisted, and honestly, I really didn't give much of a fight as they both gave me a massage.

It was hard—and it was—but I was good, and thanks to being so tired and her being a friend, I managed to keep from embarrassing myself by imitating a flagpole while Sehran worked on my legs.

It turned out that one of the things demon succubai are damn good at was massages. And, yeah, I supposed it went with the territory, but it was also incredible.

The ladies gave me a massage; Sehran gave Oracle a massage—as apparently I wasn't trusted to behave myself—and when we both offered to massage her, Sehran gave a throaty laugh and refused, saying that we'd both given her enough attention already, and it was time that we had some private time together.

She stayed in the main room, stretched very happily out on a makeshift bed of cushions, while Oracle and I went into the bedroom.

There was a big bed, and a wide collection of what had to be sex toys, as well as chains, manacles, and what was definitely lube. But considering we had no way of knowing whether the previous inhabitants had used things and how, we simply bundled it all up—minus one set of handcuffs, thank you *very* much—and I dumped it all in the main room to dispose of later.

Sehran apparently thought all her Christmases had come at once and happily pointed out that super crabs weren't something that any succubus really had to worry about.

As I left, she was happily tearing through the pile, and I very firmly closed the door between us.

Then, when I returned to the room, and found that not only had Oracle managed to get the clean sheets on the bed, but she was sitting in a very nice little outfit of sheer silk and straps, and closed the handcuffs on her wrists as I walked in the door…well.

When I finally fell asleep, I made a mental note to discuss "if the van's a-rockin', don't come knockin'" rules with the legionnaires.

I slept the sleep of the physically and literally drained. When I awoke the next morning, apparently before the sun had cracked the horizon—thanks to the small, frosted glass window in the ceiling—it was to the wonderful sensation of a hot mouth, working me hard.

I laid there for a few minutes, just enjoying the sensation, loving every second of the love of my life's lips and tongue, thinking to guide a little, when a sudden horrible thought occurred to me, and I jerked the blanket aside.

Sehran stared up at me, her mouth full, then winked.

I fucking *panicked*. My mouth opened in horror, eyes wide, as I tried to sit up, finding that at some point when I was fast asleep I'd been handcuffed to the bed in Oracle's place.

I opened my mouth, babbling, telling her no, that this wasn't right, when she lifted from me, and then…burst out laughing.

She shifted, and once again Oracle was there, half sprawled across my legs, stark naked and grinning at me as my brain struggled to reboot.

"Sorry, I couldn't resist." She chortled, then shifted back.

I stared, horrified, before I noticed the differences and realized what she'd done.

First of all, the form before me right now, although it had *looked* like Sehran at first glance—in the dark and when the little head was in ascendancy—honestly didn't very much when I was looking properly now.

Oracle, sensing what I'd been thinking, quickly assured me that she would never do that, that although she might assume another's form for a joke, to do it for *that* was wrong on all kinds of levels and she'd never consider it.

Then she apologized because although she'd known I would see a succubus at first, and she thought that was going to be hilarious to see my reaction, she also had intended it to be clear to me as well so that even with a split second to look, I'd realize the truth and it'd be okay.

Instead, because I had serious issues around cheating, I'd panicked and I'd totally missed all the differences until she shifted, and now…well, that was kinda the moment ruined.

We talked about it: I explained it, and she apologized. We cuddled, kissed, and she made a point about how she'd literally proved to me that I wasn't that kinda guy once and for all, and then apologized again.

That was it, until she was getting out of bed, about to go and do whatever—get dressed and ready to start the day again, I guessed—and I decided that enough was enough and told her to assume the clearly-a-succubus-but-clearly-*not*-Sehran form. And then I put those horns that curled up from her temples to very good use as handholds.

With hindsight and a very nice sight to consider indeed, I saw that beyond the horns and cloven hoofs, the tail, etc., she actually looked very clearly like Oracle as a succubus, instead of Sehran, and that made everything more or less all right again.

All in all, despite the surprising start to my day, as I walked out into the light of the still rising sun half an hour later, I was a lot more relaxed, and *definitely* lighter on my feet.

The morning went well from there, which, all things considered, was practically fucking unique, in my experience. I found that not only had an armor tree been provided from somewhere for me, but that my armor had been cleaned, assembled on it, and a clean set of under-armor clothing had been found that sort of fit.

I was currently wearing my least funky gear, which was like saying that I was standing naked at the "least" cold part of the North Pole.

It was still funky and I was damn glad to get back inside, peel it back off, and put clean clothing on instead.

Half an hour after that, as the sun finally crested the horizon, the caravan set off. All of us munched on trail rations that had been sorted through for ease of eating, as we spent the first half hour walking to warm our muscles.

By the time we'd all eaten, we stopped for drinks along the stream as we followed it, looking for the next fording point, and then started to run.

That became the pattern of it for the next two days: a slow start, then a hard run, changing over every half an hour, good food, solid effort by everyone, and a hell of a lot of healing for Oracle and me.

We were close to evolving all three of our most commonly used spells, and we knew it'd happen in the next few days for the Circle of Frostfire, our highly used healing spell, and unsurprisingly the healing fountain as well.

Our people healed and grew, and damn, I was getting proud of them.

Although some had been arena slaves for years, and had been kept in tip-top condition, most hadn't and weren't.

We had the elderly, the very young, and the physically weak. Most of the people with us were by no means the kind of people you'd expect to take on a multi-day marathon, and yet, the one thing they had in abundance was cause.

They were coming to help their friends and family, and holy hell that showed through.

Between the good food, the healing, the regular rests, and the well-planned-out stretching, added to the driving force that was making them all push harder than they'd ever pushed for anything in their lives, the pounds were coming off in fat, the pounds of muscle were going on, and damn.

The combination of all those things rolled back the years for the elderly, and as Zyenna ran past me, cackling about how "the young are just lazy these days," I couldn't help but laugh.

I damn well liked these buggers, I had to admit to myself.

Also, the baths, massages, and sexy time each night were definitely working to improve my mood, if I was being honest.

Those two days went damn well. And that was probably why I was so goddamn annoyed, and had such limited patience, when it all started to go wrong.

The first thing that happened was that the lead wagon broke a wheel. Not that surprising in itself, all things considered, until you realized that because these wagons were intended to run in lands without little things like roads, they were designed to not damn well break, or at least not break easily.

Hey-ho though, these things happen, right?

That was when the second wheel broke. And then, as the line of wagons creaked unceremoniously to a staggering, skidding halt, one filled with the lowing of animals, the shouts of people, and the curses of wagon drivers…well, that was when the third wheel broke.

That it was a wagon in the middle of the caravan that went second, and then a wagon at the rear, only made it even more suspicious.

That being said, I think with the gift of hindsight, it was the damn near two hundred motherfuckers in robes who erupted from the scrub on all sides screaming and brandishing weapons that made it clear that this was a fucking ambush.

I spun. I'd been on watch literally until a few minutes ago, and had just landed to go over a few details with Sehran about a particularly suspicious area I'd spotted a mile ahead, when the first arrow slammed into the side of the wagon a few meters from me.

"Incoming!" I roared, sprinting in the direction the arrow had come from, relying on the others to do what they'd been told.

The order of response to something like this was a complicated one. If they were far enough out, then you sheltered in place; you huddled in and protected people, and you tried to counter. If they were close enough, apparently you tried to reach them and fuck shit up.

That was the bare-bones version of the "How to Survive an Ambush" manual by one Jax Amon. Though, in a single concession to the situation, I was carrying a shield this time. Admittedly, I'd been wearing it primarily because the best way to level any skill was repetition, and to provide me with the chance to do just that, Oracle had started to throw stones at me whenever I was near.

It'd become a training game to block and deflect them, and although it wasn't making much of a difference to my skill level with it, it was still a slow increase.

It'd been Aellin's idea, as it was a common tactic in the legion with trainees. I'd adopted it in part because I was trying to lead by example and improve every day in a little way, and partly because it made Oracle happy, throwing pebbles at me, and she kept damn well doing it regardless, whether I had a shield or not.

That meant that when I charged them, following my said manual of tactics guiding principle, I had a shield ready and was fully armed and armored.

The actual truth was a hell of a lot more complicated, as it massively changed depending on who and what the enemy was, what kind of equipment they had, and if they were as these looked to be—lunatics from the edge of the desert—or if they were mages, a fighting force with experience or whatever.

That was why I'd explained to the legion, and to Aellin, that I was better at just going for it, and in this situation, I trusted them to do what they'd practiced doing for hundreds of years.

While they barked orders, the civilians ran inward, toward the wagons; the arena slaves and the legion ran outward. At this point, those groups primarily concentrated on not running into each other, before they could look to start responding to the fight.

While they were doing that, Sehran did what she did best and launched herself into the air, letting loose with an unearthly song of desire and lust, which made very little difference to those who couldn't hear it over the screams and shouts, but certainly confused and distracted the hell out of those attacking from farthest out.

Oracle dove back from the front, despite her usual place being alongside me, helping to bring the pain. When we'd discussed it, she'd agreed that as a healer, and one who had become highly skilled with it, the best place for her in this situation was in the middle of the wagons, healing our new people.

That left me, and three others who had been close by, to rush the screaming, howling line of incoming attackers.

All things considered, it could have been an absolute clusterfuck, had they been intent on killing us all. They could have stood back and filled the air full of arrows—it turned out that the wheels had been broken by specialist shots by their archers—but luckily, we were in slaver territory.

That meant that the dumb fucks were more interested in closing with us and trying to capture us all. And when you brought that mindset to a fight, especially one with freshly freed slaves on the other side?

It wasn't their finest hour.

Two hundred of them attacked. Thirty archers had appeared from hiding and were running up to the top of a nearby raised section of broken rock, and the remaining hundred and seventy or so were racing at me and the other fighters.

The caravan had been winding its way through a natural gully, and it was only because there was such an obvious ambush point about a mile ahead that I'd missed the buggers laid in waiting here—or so I'd console myself later.

As it was, there were cliffs and raised sections of rock on either side of the trail, and where the land had been more or less flat, the group had burst from the ground, shrugging off concealing covers that had been made to look like the ground.

They'd basically dug foxholes and covered them over; then they'd been waiting, presumably well aware of us approaching.

That put me in even more of a foul mood, because had Sehran been the scout for the last little while, she'd have sensed the life concentrated on either side of the trail.

I had no such skill, and as these people raced forward, their robes fluttering in the wind, I roared that fury out.

Two hundred of them, spread across the length of the caravan, laid in wait, armed to the teeth. Their fighters came first, screaming and sprinting in with abandon. Swords were waved frantically, hacking and slashing at the air as they looked to take us down, so that they could capture what were obviously easy targets behind us.

My first spell was a Frostfire Circle of Cleansing, and it did a lot of cleansing—provided I classed that as burning the fuck outta anything in that area that I didn't like.

The initial group of about ten archers who had just sprinted onto the top of the low hill didn't see the spell as it first activated. The lines of the ritual circle spread out in hues of red and yellow, blues and black.

What they did see, a couple of seconds later as the flames rose and ringed them, was that their available space was getting smaller by the second, and that the flames actively changed direction to hunt them.

I was almost to the first of the screaming dervishes when the shrieks began. Although it didn't distract them, it certainly cut down on the incoming arrows causing problems for the civilians.

I locked onto the lead warrior as he ran at me: long, curly black hair bouncing, and a wild, joyous expression that split his face from cheek to cheek. He hacked at the air with a slightly curved blade that reminded me of a tulwar.

He had a smaller, rounded shield, and wore long robes, covered by a tightly bound leather jerkin that covered his chest. The *slap-slap* of his sandals was almost lost in the mad mess of noise.

I grinned in return at him, even though he couldn't see it.

He, like his brothers around him, was a berserker, a lunatic who was wound up and set loose, with the simple aim of killing anything he could, while the slightly smarter in the crowd held back a little and better picked their targets.

That was probably why there was a slight gap between the front line of him and his fellow lunatics, and the next rank of running fighters, and why they were both better equipped, and why they were a mix of races that looked to be experienced fighters.

I could vaguely spot scars and more on the second row, better weapons and armor, as well as what looked like the occasional bag of holding or potion pouch on a hip.

The first guy, though? He was human; he was clearly overjoyed to lead the charge, and he was dead before he knew it.

I didn't bother to use magic—hell, I barely used my *weapon.*

Mana Overdrive was out of bounds for the first couple of seconds until I got an idea how much Oracle was going to need my mana to heal people, so this was all down to muscle memory, training, skill, and an overwhelming need to fucking hurt someone.

I smashed his sword aside with the blade of my naginata, sliced down and through his wrist; the tulwar slammed into the ground, point first—hand still clutching it fiercely. Then I hit him in the center of his shield with my own, and I *really* put my back into it.

His shield was, as stated, a lot smaller than mine, and it was round, with an iron ring that encircled a simple wooden design. It was also a lot lighter, and shittier made, so when it needed to really hold against a pissed-off godling on the field of battle…it just didn't.

The first thing to give was his arm, as it broke behind the shield. The second thing was the pressurized rim of the shield as the wood bent, fractured, and practically disintegrated, and then it burst free.

The ring was apparently hammered together under pressure and locked into place to hold the shield together. It wasn't just hammered and left, oh no.

Someone, at some point in the past, had decided that to give the shield extra strength, it should be locked in and around against pressure…which was a damn fine idea when you're a solid craftsman and know your shit.

When, however, the shield was being made by someone who was at best an apprentice of said craftsman, and probably fired for not knowing that he was shit, it became a very *bad* idea. The bent section of what turned out to be something like spring steel burst free and beheaded its own wielder.

His head vanished upward and backward, and then his chest was hit by the rapidly retreating center of the same shield. He hurtled backward in a spray of blood.

The second row had time to realize that perhaps the enormous man in blood-red and black armor running at them with the great big murder stick and the cool-looking shield was not amused. And then I reached them as well and made my position very clear.

I hacked left and right, carving a rough cross into the barely armored lunatics before me. As my mana dipped slightly, letting me know that Oracle was going for a general healing circle instead of a "oh my fucking God" level of spell, I then treated myself to a little fire mana and set the blade alight.

The magical flames did no damage to me, but they aided in the weapon slicing cleanly through anything in my path. With a roll of my wrist, I flicked the naginata out to a longer handhold, and swung it around again.

This time, instead of "only" killing three people with the swing, I took out five, as their armor—mainly boiled leather—and their weapons—shitty iron and occasionally better that had been stolen and poorly maintained—stopped my attack not at all.

I spun and lunged to the left, then twisted, holding my shield in close against my chest. I again extended my grip on the naginata; I changed to gripping it just before the foot of metal that clad the base, and swung it again, turning in a fast circle.

My weapon was seven feet long, and my grip in the middle of it extended my reach to six feet out, with three feet of that being a blade that cut through iron like a hot knife through butter.

Then add on the length of my arms, and that I didn't stop running, and you got the idea why within thirty seconds the last of those who were only flank had remembered highly important appointments elsewhere.

Admittedly, it helped that my armor was fucking incredible.

I could have worn this and just walked through the middle of them, laughing, as they tried to damage it with their shitty iron weapons. The worst I'd have gotten were some bruises and scratches.

Instead, I spun, launched myself into the air, and spread the love around ten seconds later on the next group in line.

Sehran was still flying, arcing around in ever widening circles and singing, drawing a confused but very ardent second train around behind her, as a bunch of our people lost all control and joined the enemy in chasing her ass.

That was slightly problematic, mainly because our own very limited archers were now having issues picking off the lustful lunatics. I also kinda saw some issues coming from those who already had partners in the caravan who hadn't started chasing Sehran—but hey, that wasn't my problem.

Instead, I landed—and landed *hard*—atop another group, crushing one of them to the ground with an audible shriek and the sound of breaking bones. I slammed my shield into the guy on my left and skewered the guy before me. And considering I'd landed at the rear of a group that had directly charged one of my only groups of legionnaires, the fight was literally over in seconds.

Those who turned to face me offered up their backs to the legion, and no legionnaire lets an ass go unpunished.

Fifteen seconds later, and the legion were running into the flank of another group, and I was having a great time romping through more badly trained enemies who were also badly equipped and poorly led.

My mana dipped drastically; at the same time, a boom of an Explosive Compression spell went off, as Sehran cut her song off and Oracle unleashed fiery death instead.

Thirty seconds after that, with the last of the groups of archers conspicuously not offering cover fire to their forces, the attackers started to realize that their day wasn't going the way they wanted, considering their aim of attacking an easy caravan and looting it, and they promptly tried to run away.

That was when they found that I was chasing them, Oracle was exceedingly pissed about the injuries to some of our newfound friends, and yeah, our ability to not mirror and feed each other's emotions wasn't at its greatest today.

It was when I dragged my fist out of the smashed-in face of a wannabe slaver, after yelling incoherent swearwords, that I realized a new hush had embraced the battlefield.

Turning slowly, and shaking my hand to rid it of some of the bloodier innermost thoughts and feelings of my latest victim, I straightened and looked at the crowd.

"What?" I asked, confused.

"Ah, he was, um…trying to surrender, Prince Jax," one of the legionnaires managed in a cautious voice.

"So?"

"So, we're required to accept the surrender of an unarmed foe," he pointed out, his voice breaking slightly.

I shook my hand again, then looked at the small group I'd managed to drive into a narrow defile in the rocks.

They were pressed as far into the rocks as they could get, with three of them praying, two whimpering, and one who appeared to have pissed himself.

"Were you trying to surrender?" I asked the small group, almost conversationally.

"YES!" one of them shrieked, his head bobbing frantically like a nodding dog and I nodded.

"You're still armed," I pointed out, and cue the sound of many weapons being thrown to the ground as quickly as possible.

"Ah, shall we accept their surrender?" one of the legionnaires asked me hesitantly, his face a strange mixture of pain, anger, and hope.

"Do you want to?" I asked him, still rather confused.

"No."

"That's what I thought. I mean, they're fucking slavers, so why…" I started, then I sighed and shut up, shaking my head disgustedly. "Another fucking oath, right?"

"That's right, my prince."

"Fuck's sake," I whispered. "All right, let's deal with that. And no, you lot don't say anything, and don't do anything," I ordered, pointing one hand at the small group of terrified former attackers.

"Oracle!" I bellowed to the sky.

A handful of seconds later, she landed next to me, the fight pretty much over. She reached out, offering a mana potion to me.

"What's the best way to do this?" I asked her, seeing that once again, she knew me better than I knew myself and was ready.

"Probably to resurrect the original oath only, and then add in that they are to remain loyal to the empire, but that valid orders can only be given by their current direct and sworn leadership and members of the current imperial council. That the laws of Amon are all that they are required to follow and that later amendments enforced by other nobles are null and void. Then, as the Scion of the Empire and its only prince, you can order that they ignore all orders that are given by anyone not in your direct chain of command. That should get us around it." She looked over at the disheveled group of legionnaires for confirmation, and they started to grin like idiots.

"That should do it." I sighed. "Wait, was that noble the only one who gave you these stupid fucking orders?"

"Yes, my lord."

"What was his name?"

"Baren Forthright."

"Then let's do this." I took a deep breath, chugging the mana potion. My mana refilled fast.

"To all legionnaires within the sound of my voice!" I bellowed. "As of now, and until the Eternal Emperor gainsays my word, I, Prince Jax, Scion of the Empire, revoke the orders and changes to your oath made by Baren Forthright, former noble of the realm. You are bound by the oaths that were originally ordered as part of becoming a legionnaire, not the later additions. And furthermore, you are no longer required to obey the orders of any outside of your direct chain of command and my imperial council. As it was of old, so shall it be again!"

That last line that I included was something that the legionnaires back on Dravith had pretty much beaten into them, and I was pleased to see it was the same here. My mana bottomed out. The legionnaires' shouted as their oaths were removed, and then there were the relieved sighs and cheers of them receiving their freedom.

"Lord, do you wish to accept the surrender of the slavers?" one of the legionnaires asked me in a low growl. Not only were these the same kind of slaving fucks who had been torturing, killing, and enslaving his friends for the last seven hundred years, but there was fuck all chance they'd have shown any mercy to them if the tables were reversed.

I turned slowly, looking at the small group of panicking and now disarmed slavers, and I snorted.

"Question one of them. Find out what we need to know about the town that's somewhere ahead, and whoever passed this way before us. Oh, and find out where their stash is, because shitheads like this always have a stash. And beyond that?"

I fixed the legionnaire with a brief smile that he could hear in my voice as I patted him on the shoulder. "You have fun, mate."

# CHAPTER TWENTY

"Should I have accepted their surrender?" I asked Oracle and Sehran a few hours later, as we finally finished the repairs to the wagons.

"Why?" Sehran asked me, confused.

"I just…" I shrugged. "I think it was the right thing to do."

"Why?" she asked again. "Seriously, I'm curious. They're slavers. We know that. The punishment for slavery is death. You've said that before, so at most you'd have accepted their surrender, then had to hang them all or cut their heads off, so what's the problem?"

"I don't know," I admitted.

"I do," Oracle said softly as the three of us watched the caravan starting to pull out of the gorge and climb toward the distant hill. "You don't like the way it made you feel."

"No, I don't," I agreed sadly.

"Jax, you're a product of your experiences, and your genes," she said carefully. "While you have little to do with your father and you hate him, there's always going to be a degree of him in you."

I looked at her in shock.

"You need to hear this so listen, okay?" she said.

I swallowed hard, forcing myself to nod at her to continue.

"You're horrified about the things he did, and more so the things you know you could do. You have ultimate authority over your people and over your lands. And soon, unless we fail, you'll have that authority over tens of millions.

"Cities by their dozens, maybe hundreds will bend the knee to you, and you'll literally be able to order them to stop breathing if you want to. That doesn't even start to cover the divine aspect of your progress, because that power is, frankly, even worse.

"You are approaching the precipice where you have to make the choice. You could be a far worse person than Amon or Sanguis ever dreamed of being, or…"

"Or?" I asked after a few seconds.

"Or you can continue to live by your own code of justice and you can move on," she said. "They were slavers. They murdered, raped, and enslaved people—some of them were no doubt your legionnaires, others were the people who should have been your citizens.

"That means that you were carrying out imperial justice when you ordered what you did. And the fact that you don't like the way it made you feel says a lot more about who you are than anything about any pleasure you got from killing them."

"I know but…" I sighed. "I just worry at times, that's all. Our mum died when we were young…I told you that, right?"

"You did," Oracle admitted. "But Sehran doesn't know."

"Tell me, please," Sheran asked.

I smiled, knowing that she was doing her "succubai aren't just fuck toys" trick, and helping Oracle and me to balance our emotions by the gentle feeling spreading through me.

"Thank you," I whispered. "She died when we were young. And without her to watch over us, to tell us right from wrong, we went off the rails a bit. It wasn't until we bumped into an old friend of hers and had to explain her death—she died of cancer—that we thought too much about it. It'd hurt too much, you see?"

"I know," Oracle whispered.

"Well, when we explained it, and what we were doing—we were 'cleaning up' the area—beating the crap out of the drug dealers and getting the area under our control, at thirteen." I snorted. "Damn, we were vicious little shits back then, but anyway. We were so proud of what we were doing, and Jake, her friend…well, he was ex-army, so we thought he'd be impressed.

"Instead, he just asked us if we thought *she'd* be proud of us or not, and that took the fucking wind right out of our sails," I admitted. "He took us for lunch, a shitty burger in a crappy pub, one that knew we were fucking thirteen, and in my homeland, you had to be eighteen to drink beer. They said nothing and just served us, and he started talking. Told us about a code of honor, and that we could be better men than we knew.

"He told us that we had a choice to make, to be the little shits we were becoming and to become exactly what everyone in the area thought we were, or to become better than that. Gave us some advice, then said he'd be back to check on us in a few months, and then paid the bill and fucked off."

"But you listened," Sehran said.

"Of course we did." I snorted. "He knew our mum, and she liked him. He knew what she'd have wanted, and what we were doing, and we damn well knew it as well. We didn't change, mind you, not really, we just…stopped on the edge. We stood on the lip of going over, and we decided that if he could do it, then we could too, because our mum, she'd liked him. Not sure if they were seeing each other or what at some point, but they were always close.

"So, when he said it was wrong, and we had nobody else we gave two shits about, we listened. Then came a local copper, Johnno—he gave us the benefit of the doubt, mainly because we were doing what he couldn't, and the fancy lawyers stopped happening, and we spread a little justice around.

"So now what?" Oracle prompted, and I sighed.

"Now, nothing changes," I said after a few seconds. "I'm at the precipice looking over and yeah, I get that I could step over it, but it's not what I want to do. I'm going to curb it. I'm going to try not to be a dick, and beyond that, I'm just gonna try, I guess."

"That's all any of us can do," Sehran admitted. "It's one of the things that we learn, or we don't grow up."

"Oh?" I asked.

"In the demon realm…well, it used to be a lot worse than it is now." She smiled. "I told you that we're required to maintain the balance, to not get too strong or else wars start. But what I didn't tell you is that demons, when we're young? We don't tend to listen very well."

"I bet." I snorted.

"So trust me, Jax, when you get worried that you're tiptoeing along the edge of that precipice…believe me that I know. We learn self-control, or we die young. And because I learned that? I get to have my Jian and Tenandra. I get to be with friends, and I get to live an incredible life." She smiled.

"I'm glad." I reached out on instinct and pulled both her and Oracle in for a hug.

"Well, do you feel better?" Oracle asked as we broke the hug and I shrugged.

"More or less," I admitted.

"You know why you really feel wrong?" she asked me, and I shook my head. "When there's something morally grey like this normally, back home on Dravith?" she prompted, and I nodded, getting it straightaway. "What do you do?"

"You're right." I nodded as it all made sense. Back home, *he* was always there…when I'd lost my temper and control when I was dealing with the drow, when I needed someone questioned and it was going to be something that other people were going to get squeamish about.

When it was something that for me was in that morally grey area, where I knew I should have an issue with it, and I really fucking didn't? I had him to step in and deal with things and help me.

"I miss Bane."

# <u>BANE</u>

“**I** hate you,” Bane snarled, forcing himself back to his feet and shaking his head. The world slid in and out of focus as he waited for his head to stop ringing.

“That’s how you know this is doing you good,” Flux replied amiably. “If you weren’t suffering then you’d not be learning.”

“You know that’s one of the stupidest sayings I’ve ever heard, don’t you?” Ame commented from her seat nearby. “Almost makes me think it’s one of the boy’s ones.”

“She’s got you there,” Bane agreed, before leaping forward and striking out with a high kick, followed by three fast jabs and a low spin to sweep Flux’s legs out from under him.

Flux batted the first kick aside, took the three punches and deflected them seemingly effortlessly, then raised the leg that Bane was trying to sweep, before kicking his young protégé in the face.

Bane crashed to the ground on his back, panting, before lifting one hand in a sign of surrender.

Flux straightened, then reached down, expecting to pull him to his feet, and instead had his own feet swept, as Bane rolled onto him, punching.

The next thirty seconds were a frantic blur of attacks, before Ame slapped her hands together and barked, “Enough!” Both mer sagged back, exhausted, before the older woman emptied a pail of warm, fresh water over the pair.

“You got me there,” Flux admitted after a few seconds, as he and Bane recovered, enjoying the lifegiving-touch of the water. “I thought you were too tired to attack again.”

“You got me the same way this morning when I tried that.” Bane shrugged, forcing himself to sit up. “I thought it was worth a try.”

“Never surrender,” Flux quoted.

“Because they’ll only gut you easier,” Bane agreed.

“Are you quite finished?” Ame acidly asked the pair. “Because I have need of some rest, and I’ve no desire to spend the entire night healing you pair of fools.”

“Of course.” Flux nodded. “My apologies, Runecrafter.”

“And mine,” Bane added hurriedly, crossing his arms over his chest and dipping his head in a sign of respect and apology. “Sleep well.”

“I will, once you’re both no longer wasting my time,” she snapped, then stood herself, hitting them one after the other with a healing spell, then grunting as Flux apparently required a second. “You did well there, boy. Cracked his spine in two places.”

“Damn well hurt, that’s for sure,” Flux admitted, before patting Bane on the shoulder. “You might not see it, but I do. You’re improving daily, Bane. I’m proud of you.”

That was all the older mer said, but as Flux and Ame turned, striding off to their quarters and already deep in discussion, Bane couldn’t help but feel elated.

Ten years he’d studied under the older mer, first as a child dreaming of becoming a hunter, then as one of the rare few who were being trained to defend their homes against all aggressors, and then finally, when Jax had come, as bodyguard to the imperial prince.

That the body he was supposed to be guarding was always somewhere else and having just done something incredibly stupid was a source of never-ending annoyance to him.

"He's right, you know," Cheena thrummed softly.

Bane looked over at her and her ever-present shadow, Lio. "I was wondering when you'd show up." Bane sighed. "I swear, you're as bad as Grizz."

"You asked for extra lessons." Cheena shook her head in disbelief. "You know our kind's gifts, you know where and how we strike, and yet still you insist on this."

"You spend your lives in stealth, and still you insist on training to battle like this," Lio agreed.

The shorter human was incredible at stealth and spying tactics; her knowledge of underhanded trickery and rogue skills was a constant reason to be impressed, but Bane needed more. His own failures, both in stealth tactics and outright warfare, had been hard lessons to accept. But when he did, he realized that he had a choice to make.

He could remain as he was, a skilled bodyguard and confidant, or he could push himself to excel.

For the first time in his life, he had access to a group of trainers who were all experts in their fields, and they had little else to do but train, hour after hour, day after day.

Where many of the others—like Grizz—would attempt to find a quiet place and rest for an hour or two, spending several hours a day in training, and then the rest in actually relaxing, Bane had realized that he had an opportunity that was almost criminal to waste.

Now, instead, he practiced with Flux, Lio, and Cheena, and the group had added private sessions at all hours, away from the others' set lessons.

No time was safe. Even in a deep slumber, after an exhaustive day of training, Bane was attacked, driven to sleep with his senses extended. The small group was already finding it harder and harder to surprise him.

Lio spent her time working primarily on the rogue and assassination skills, Cheena worked him relentlessly in stealth, and Flux?

The mer might be the oldest among them, but Bane was closing on him in terms of skill, and already outstripped him in raw speed and strength.

All of these were reasons to be proud, he knew this, but the one reason he could never settle, that he could never just sit back and relax?

Tamat.

Tamat was there every time he did. And as the Dark Goddess of Larceny and Assassination increased in her power, she obsessed more and more over her aspect.

Nimon, God of Death—and as Jax frequently called him "that dark wanker"—had absorbed much of Her aspect into himself after He'd banished the other gods.

Smaller, weaker demi-gods and godlings were permitted to rise in their places. The power that should have fed the greater gods was squandered—aiding and fulfilling the weaker gods. But certain aspects—like darkness—that Nimon himself had always coveted, He kept to himself.

In stealing away that aspect to himself in Her absence, He'd done more than simply banish and weaken Her and the other gods.

He'd stolen a large part of Her power, perhaps the greatest part of it, and still, He held to it.

As the other gods returned, they reached out to grasp their aspects again. Finding them currently being contested by weaker beings, they, in their weakened state, began to fight to claw their powers back.

Inch by precious inch, they grew. Each fragment of power, each prayer they answered or ignored, each interaction of a lesser being and the gods fueled their rebirth.

All but Tamat.

Nimon knew that She'd be wanting to siphon Her power away, knew that She needed to, and that in doing so, instead of weakening His allies, it would weaken Him personally.

He knew it, and He jealously guarded that aspect all to himself.

In doing so, He spent power to prevent Her, in amounts that she simply couldn't match. He burned that power instead to prevent Her rising, and He counted it a win every time.

That left Her two choices: accept that She was lesser and that She'd lost the aspect of darkness, or fight tooth and nail and risk everything She had to claw it back.

The Goddess of Assassins and Theft made an obvious choice, and fought.

To do so, She maintained her pressure on the aspects that She could control, and began to raise new assassins, thieves, and spies, giving each a list of targets that would bring her influxes of power and belief. And all the while, She focused on Nimon and His trespassers in Her domain.

To that end, as soon as She'd seen Bane was headed to the continent of Carrmor, She'd began to work on him, adding more and more targets to his list, pushing and prodding him, demanding more and more.

In some ways, it suited Bane. He'd obeyed her once; when stuck behind enemy lines, he'd gone on a killing spree in one of the centers of Nimon's Dark Legion, slaughtering His priests and generally pleasing Her to no end.

For that, She'd granted him bonuses and She'd reveled in the blood spilled in Her name. But when he'd found out that Jax had need of him, and he'd cut his spree short and had returned to him…

She'd been furious, demanding he kill on, willing to risk the loss of Bane in order to garner higher levels of devotion and fear of Her Knives in the Dark.

Now, although She had more or less accepted his decision—knowing he was bound by his oath to Jax—She was nevertheless adding one more, and just one more, and perhaps another target to his list.

She was determined that her chance to inflict terror and fear would not be restricted to the continent of Dravith any longer, and as such, She teased him mercilessly.

Perhaps teased wasn't really the word, Bane reflected grimly. After all, perhaps "blackmail" and "bribery" were more apt descriptions. But whatever the term he used, She was fixated on forcing him to kill for Her, again and again.

He'd begun to refuse the quests, and when She'd demanded to know why, he'd pointed out—patiently, because unlike Jax he wasn't a damn fool—that he was going to these places to find Jax, and only once he was there could he start to serve Her.

He had no control over where they went and how long they stayed, so he'd insisted that She'd need to offer the quests as appropriate, waiting until he was in an area, as until then, he couldn't accept.

She'd wasted another day pestering him and making demands that he was able to avoid only because of Her place as subservient to Jenae, before She finally fell silent.

That was when he found that as a goddess, She had the power to override little details—like his own settings on his interface—and more so, She had the ability to make small alterations to the quests She'd given him, even those that he'd already accepted.

He'd seen it on a seemingly innocuous one that She'd given him, that he train—and excel—not wasting his time on the crossing between continents.

She'd offered him an additional level in stealth per two stat points earned through training. It was only after he'd accepted it, and checked back after three days to see how it was going, that he'd found the "small additions."

One hundred and fourteen names had been added to the quest, one at a time, for bonus rewards.

For each of them that he killed, he'd gain double, sometimes triple the XP he should have gotten, as well as a slight bonus to a skill—one point to daggers here, one point to stealth there, and a dozen other skills.

He'd thrown all the anger at Her maneuvering him into his training and was seeing results. But still it made him want to scream in fury.

Lydia was pushing as hard as he was, and the support she got from her goddess? Incredible.

She sometimes spoke as they all ate at the end of the day, of the feeling of being watched over by Vanei, of 'knowing She's guidin' me. That She wants me tae be ma best.'

And all the while as she spoke, or the rare times that Giint spoke about the gifts that Svetu gave him, the encouragement of the gods for their champions, Bane quietly seethed inside that his goddess was such a manipulative bitch.

"Bane!" Lio shouted, and he jumped, twisting around to face her, as she shook her head. "What the hell's going on?" she asked more quietly.

"Nothing," he replied shortly.

She shook her head. "Bullshit. Bane, you're getting tighter wound by the day, and you know that doesn't work. You have to let it all go. You have to relax. The more tense you are, the more noise you make; the more noise you make, the harder you have to work to cover it, until eventually you might as well be Jax trying to sneak around for all the chance you've got at succeeding."

"She's right," Cheena said.

Bane shot her an annoyed pulse of Worldsense that carried all his irritation and a clear 'drop it' as well.

Usually, Cheena could be relied upon to know when a subject wasn't to be discussed, but instead, this time she spoke up, and even invoked a right that he'd not expected.

"I'm your trainer in stealth, am I not?" she asked, her voice cold and hard.

"You are," he admitted grudgingly.

"And as such, you agreed to obey?" she pressed. "To do as I order? Even when you cannot see through the depths, you trust me to lead you?"

"I do," he admitted.

"Then tonight we eat together, and we talk," she said. "Or your time as my student is at an end. Because either you trust me, or you don't."

"I'll tell the others you've got things to work out," Lio said casually, before striding off.

Bane spun to fix Cheena with a blast of irritation. "You don't understand—"

"No, I don't," she agreed. "But that's the point. By morning, I will."

"It's not for you to face—it is my problem!" Bane snapped, then he paused as he ran the last words of Lio through his mind again and cursed. "And Lio?" He spun, seeing that she was already gone, before cursing. "She'll be telling them all that we're mating! That the issue we have to work out is that!"

"Is that such a terrible thing?" Cheena asked softly, her voice dropping as she replied. "That they believe this?"

"No!" he snapped. "But they will think—" Her words came to him again, and it finally made it through the layers of frustration and irritation. She wasn't saying 'hell no'; she was asking whether that was a bad thing. That it could happen, not that it was offensive to her.

"Do we care what they think?" She stepped closer. "Flux and Ame have found their way through to calm waters, as have Yen and Grizz, as have Jian and Tenandra. Is the thought so terrible?"

"You know it isn't!" He groaned. "Depths hide and shield me, but no!"

"Then what's the problem?"

"That you don't mean it," he eventually admitted, his tendrils drooping. "That it could be laughed off, and forgotten about as a joke when…"

"When did I ever say that I was against it?" Cheena asked.

Bane hesitated before replying. "You have Fenir…" He named her mate, and Cheena let loose a subsonic thrum of amusement.

"Bane, you're my friend, but you have much to learn of life and the pleasures of mating! I thought you knew that both Fenir and I have others? We always have!"

"But I don't," he said softly.

"No, you *haven't*, until now—not you *don't*. That's the difference. For Fenir and I, we were friends before we were mates, and we will always be both. He has others as do I, and we have no shame in this. Bane, I say this clearly, so that you know where we stand. I do not offer a life mating, nor anything similar. I offer fun, friendship, and nothing more.

"Tonight, you may decide. Come to me. You know where my cabin is, and I will not turn you away. But…this is only when we are away. When I am home, I will be with him. When exploring the depths of another sea, there is no need to be sad and lonely."

There was a long moment of silence before she went on.

"Or, I will find you later, and we will talk of many things. Of life, of our oaths and the things that are causing you issues, but we will not discuss what happens, or could happen, in my cabin. I will not offer again, nor ask. But my door is open."

With that, she turned and marched off, heading to the stairs that led down to her quarters.

Bane, conflicted, stared after her.

He knew that for some that was how it was. He never judged them—it was a choice—and there were many times he wished he was like it, that he could take his pleasure as and where it was offered, but…

He sighed, his mind full of the sights of her, and the desires he'd harbored as a youngling, watching her swim past. He thought of her, thought of the offer and the way that the door to her cabin was *literally* open to him now, and he cursed long and bitterly.

Then he stomped off down the deck toward the entrance to his own cabin. He could fit in another hour's training, before it was time to eat, and to hell with whatever Grizz thought he'd been doing.

# CHAPTER TWENTY-ONE

The clean-up of the wagons should have taken longer than it did, as should have dealing with the injuries, but the answer for both was the same. Magic, baby.

We had three broken wheels, and zero spares, which was a pain in the arse, no matter which way you spun it. So instead, we found the lightest of the wagons, stripped three of its wheels, and put them on the other three.

Then, Therin exclusively focused on the wagon that was down to one wheel for the next hour, while Oracle, Sehran, and I worked to heal those who had been injured.

Five had died; there was no way to prevent that, the attack coming as it did from an ambush. The main mitigating factor was that they'd wanted to capture as many people as slaves as possible. That meant that beyond the original attack to try to spread fear, the rest were deliberately less lethal.

We, on the other hand, weren't trying to capture them at all.

Beyond those five, the majority Oracle had reached straightaway were either able to be healed enough to stabilize, or weren't in immediate danger.

While she and Sehran used their spells, I meditated. By the time the wheels had been changed over and the last wagon was unloaded, it was nearly ready.

Everyone got clear, and Therin, with a wide smile on his face, powered the first enchantments, to demonstrate what he called the future of wagons.

There was a long silence as everyone watched the wagon vanishing into the clouds overhead, before he finally admitted that he'd forgotten the limiting enchantment that would keep it from lifting more than a meter off the ground. And at that point, we started the caravan moving again.

Therin vanished like a fart in the wind, and Oracle went after him to look over the enchantments he'd been doing until now. Mainly to make sure he'd not forgotten anything else.

The decision was made quickly at that point, as she found on examining three different wagons over the course of the next hour, that his project was to be shelved until we had the luxury of a spare wagon to fuck about with, as not one of them was the same as the next.

Standardization was going to rock these people's world, I decided.

Instead, he was to work on a section of spare parchment, and was writing out his plans, while Zyenna essentially performed the role of a rubber duck.

She'd been confused to all hell when I'd suggested the term, and then found she loved it. Although she did actually enjoy learning, this meant that she didn't actually need to understand any of the secrets of the enchanters, or even to respond at all.

Instead, all she needed to do was listen as he talked through his plan, step by tiny step, until he cursed, swore, and cried over the details he realized he was missing.

It was apparently an age-old programming trick, and I only knew of it from an ex who had insisted on me fulfilling that role for her for a few weeks while we dated.

As I'd not really given a shit, and had zero interest in suggesting anything beyond "shall we quit this and have sex," I'd apparently been perfect.

The problem came when a duck tried to offer advice, as that invariably sent the creator off down a new rabbit hole.

In this situation, Zyenna was glaring daggers at him for losing us a wagon and was determined to keep him on track. And it meant that if he was actually to manage what he planned, then we all still won.

For Zyenna, it meant that she no longer had to run, which at first was a relief. But after two hours of his incessant prattling, as I called a halt to rest, she asked whether she could join the front lines and start killing people.

That was how I knew she was perfect for the role.

Regardless, while they did that, and I ran alongside, Oracle started to work. We'd considered the danger side of the fight to come, and we'd decided it was time to start setting up the legion on this side of the ocean for success, much as we had back home. And the first part of that?

Magic training.

I was kicking myself that we'd not started with it already, but starting now was better than in a few days' time, so Oracle had used me for the first three legionnaires. Then, once they were done, she'd started using the spell we'd just taught one of them, to teach more.

I wanted, ideally, to teach them all the usual three spells—Magic Missile, Complex Healing, and of course Explosive Compression—but time being as limited as it was meant that the best bet was to teach them healing only for now.

The other spells were incredible, and I wanted them all to eventually have them. But as it was, we could either spend hours teaching a few of them all three, or less than an hour to teach three of them healing.

That meant that we could get twelve of them taught before we had to stop for the night's entertainment. I'd much rather have twelve extra healers, even if they were shit at it, as that'd mean more of our people seeing the sun rise tomorrow.

As I ran, I found that my brain was comfortably slipping into neutral—or it would have, if not for the flashing of notifications I kept meaning to deal with.

I sighed and pulled them up, discarding them one by one as they meant precisely dick all.

My "running" skill was at level twenty-five—I didn't even remember that one evolving, but I'd clearly accepted it when I had ages ago—my jumping at fourteen; wind-running—which I had no clue about—was at level three. It went on and on, and I dismissed them as quickly as they appeared, until finally, the kill notification finished them off. Or, more accurately, multiple kill notifications, all condensed into one.

*Congratulations!*

*You have killed the following:*

- *10x Desert Jackals of various levels for a total of 3,850xp*
- *3x Sand Wurms of various levels for a total of 31,780xp*
- *6x Slavers of various levels for a total of 1,120xp*
- *2x Undead Warriors of various levels for a total of 400xp*

- *17x Slaver guards of various levels for a total of 3,785xp*
- *2x Necromancers of various levels for a total of 2,140xp*
- *39x unknown desert tribe/slavers/innocents of various levels for a total of 5,680xp*

*A party under your command killed the following:*

- *7x Desert Jackals of various levels for a total of 2,280xp*
- *86x Slavers/guards/undead of various levels for a total of 64,540xp*

*Total party experience earned: 66,820xp*

*As party leader, you gain 25% of all experience earned (16,705xp)*

*Total experience gained: 48,755xp + 16,705xp (party leader bonus) = 65,460xp*

*Progress to level 49 stands at 5,040,599/6,455,000*

I read it, and I hated it.

The improvements to my XP…sure, great—but it was one of the last lines in my section that was why I'd been putting it off: 39x unknown desert tribe/slavers/innocents.

That was down to the indiscriminate nature of the feedback from the slavers' control devices. Innocent people who were just too close when they went off and died. I hated that.

I'd kept meaning to look at it, to read it and get it out of the way, but I'd taken any opportunity to not see it, and this was why.

Mainly because I also knew that there was no way to avoid it. If I didn't use that ability? We'd have to kill the slaves to stop them. We'd cause at least double the deaths that I personally caused through this, and that didn't even include the people on our side.

I couldn't refuse to use my imperial ability, but using it meant that I needed to accept the possible deaths of innocents, which broke my fuckin' heart every time.

It was like shelling an enemy base and knowing that you'd kill some innocent visitors to it, and yet, taking out the base would save thousands of others.

It had to be done—it was the reality of war—but fuck me, it was hard at times.

I banished the notifications and struggled on, slowly doing as I always did, and burying away the pain.

The next few hours until nightfall passed smoothly. As we finally drew to a halt on a hill overlooking the small town we'd been searching for, we were ready.

The dust and broken dirt of the land closer to the desert had gradually shifted over the last few days, moving to less and less arid lands, until as now, the route was more grass on both sides and a beaten dirt road, as opposed to the general dying earth we'd seen before.

Now, as we crested the hill, and I pulled my small team of idiots to the side, I reached down, unclasping my gauntlet, and ran a hand through the stems of green, green grass that shifted in the breeze.

"Damn, I missed this," I muttered.

"Grass?" Aellin frowned.

"Back home, in my…land…I lived in a place that had a lot of rain," I explained as I waited for the others to reach us. The long line of wagons creaked by, deliberately slowly, as the others behind them worked to crest the hill.

"And?" he prompted when I didn't say anything else.

"And in Dravith, there's a fuckload of trees." I locked my gauntlet back into place. "Where I once lived, there weren't many trees. Instead, it rained a fuck of a lot and we had a lot of grass, that's all. It isn't important. I just realized it'd been a while since I'd really felt the grass."

"As yer say." The legionnaire grunted, before gesturing ahead. "So, ha' tha plan changed?"

"Not even slightly," I admitted. "There's no way that a caravan of wagons, on seeing the town in the distance—and that has been seen by the town, because they have to have seen the damn torches at least—wouldn't push on for another hour to reach the 'safety' of the town instead of staying out here."

"That's true." Toren grunted as he came to a halt nearby, puffing slightly from his run. "I'd not have kept going unless there was a damn good reason, and knowing that it's a trade town, there's no reason that any caravan would."

"They might not trust us inside their walls," Marteen pointed out as he and his mother joined us.

"They'd be mad to," she agreed. "But let's face it—they deal in slaves and they're in the middle of the territory, right on the road to Sonra, so they'll be used to caravans of slaves coming through, day after day."

"Anyone who comes this way—any slaver or anyone who's actually able to trade through this way safely, anyway—would have no reason to avoid the town." Toren sighed. "I just don't like the plan, that's all."

"What's wrong with the plan?" I frowned.

"You don't think it's maybe a little too simplistic?" he asked after a brief pause.

"I like simple," Aellin grunted. "Less tae go wrong."

"Well, yes, normally I'd agree. But 'kill them all and move on,' as it goes to cover all the eventualities, I feel it's…somewhat lacking in detail," Toren said diplomatically.

"Of course it is." I shrugged. "Look, Toren, as things stand, we know we've been seen. There was a rider earlier in the day, and they didn't so much as pause when they saw us, just flashed past, right?"

"Yeah."

"So they know that a caravan is coming," I pointed out. "We were damn lucky they saw us when we were eating a meal instead of running. But as it is, they know that we're a large group and we're headed this way. The fucker Aellin questioned earlier said that caravans pass through the town every day. They stop long enough for the caravan guards to visit the whorehouse and to check the local slave market, get goods they need, and then they fuck off."

"And so, they'll be expecting us to stop in the town. But he also said that they close the gates at sundown and that the guards are reasonably strong!" Toren pointed out. "They'd have to be in a shithole like this, or the next slave caravan that comes through would clean them out."

"Exactly." I smiled.

"That doesn't make sense!" Toren virtually pleaded, "This is *not* a good thing. This is why we should be *avoiding* the town, and instead you act like it's the answer to all our problems."

"Aellin, describe the town and everything we know, please," I ordered the dwarf legionnaire, who nodded and stood to attention, as he began to speak.

"The town holds a wee bit under two thousand people, and yet there also be a permanent population, an' no fields under cultivation. All stores do be bought in, or be produced by magic. Visitors tae the town do be issued a pass, an' they must wear at all times. Anyone found within the town limits that doesna display their entry permit do be arrested and sold.

"The slave markets do be the primary source of wealth, though at this time o' the year it's both busier, wit' the caravans passin' through, an' quieter because there do be little 'stock' available, due tae Sonra's great market comin' up.

"Sonra does be primarily a market for livestock, and so has a fuckin' huge amount o' coin tha' changes hands at each market. It takes a lot o' ready coin tae buy a herd, after all. Be that cows, pigs, or whatever…tha' can all be bought there, and that means huge numbers do be needed tae perform the labor.

"Sonra refuses the slave trade, and enforces a strict rule of law that any slave who makes it over tha' border o' their second ring—their city do be divided into three rings—is free. That being said, they dinna give two shits what happens outside their rings, so reet ootside the third ring, does be one o' tha largest annual slave markets in the known realm.

"Because o' the annual market, and the condition o' the local area, anyone with slaves to sell will either try to make a trip to Sonra for the market, or sell here. They'll get a lower price on average if tha sell here, but it also means that those who live local dinna need tae be away from their homestead for long tae sell their slaves.

"If they do be away fer long, they tend tae return tae a homestead that's been pillaged by their neighbors and their families sold, after all, so that's why the market here is still goin' at all. Tha being said, as each caravan passes through, there are less and less, and each caravan has limited space, so there does be a constant trade situation inside the town.

"Then add in alcohol, drugs, an' the whorehouses, as well as tha various less specific criminal enterprises, an' yer see why tha guard here both needs tae be high leveled, an' is kept constantly busy.

"Caravans do be parked outside the city, and only a small number of the caravan's guards do be permitted inside at any time. While they be in tha town enjoying themselves, tha majority do be kept under watch ootside.

"Tha means tha guard needs tae be a substantial size, and well outfitted as well. Usually there be sign o' yer position in the slave market and tha local trade, if ya be invited tae tha 'big house' tae visit tha lord o' Marrow. That be the town's name, iffin ah did ne say before. Marrow. If you're ne important, yer get tae pay a wee tax to pass through, and tha be it. Iffin yer do be important, then yer get an even bigger tax, aye, but yer do be offered yer choice o' slaves from 'is personal stock, who do be all highly valuable an' highly expensive."

As he paused, looking at me, I nodded that he'd said enough, and I took over.

"Admittedly that should sound like a problem," I agreed. "Except that because they close the gates at night and allow only a small number in, this is actually a fucking benefit to us."

I grinned at Toren, who shook his head that he didn't get it.

"Trust me, Toren. Take the caravan up to the right-hand side and get everyone ready. They're to eat, rest, and relax, and I want them doing so, because while half the fucking guard force is watching them, we're going to steal the entire fucking town.

"The guard is used to slavers coming through. They're used to seeing something, and they're going to see it, as long as we don't give them a reason to think we're any different. While you all travel slowly along, me and my little group are going to run ahead, and we're going to get our passes. And while we do so, we're going to bribe our way into the lord's house. We're going to get a meeting with him. We're going to see what slaves he's got, and then we're going to free them.

"We're going to try to do this in a quiet way, and save using the ability for later, instead capturing the leaders and using them to do it for us. But if we can't? I'll use the same ability you all saw me use before."

I left unsaid that the last time I'd triggered it, I'd not noticed it at the time, but now, the more I thought about using it, the…well, more uncomfortable I felt. I didn't know why, just that something felt wrong.

"Once those slaves are free, we're going to take our new friends and our prisoner, and we're going to summon the people in the town who we need. The lord doesn't have to explain himself, after all. So as he pulls in the various assholes, we make them bring their best slaves—and specifically any legionnaires—then we free them, have them swear the oath, and then we bring in the next lot.

"Will we manage to get through the whole town before something goes wrong? No, probably not. And if they use slaves to attack us, and I can't free them any other way, I'm going to have to keep my power as constrained as possible to not free the whole town and kick a fight off that will run house to house. But as it is, it's the best chance we have," I finished.

"That's a wee bit more complicated than 'kill 'em all and move on,'" Toren pointed out.

"It is, but you'll remember that when you asked about it originally, you wanted to know what your part in it was. So for you, it's drive the wagon up to the wall, make camp, and then if things go badly, drive the caravan on, if you can. If you can't, then kill them all and then we move on." I shrugged. "Do you feel better now that you know more of the plan?"

"Not really. We're going to be under the gaze of a lot of guards, guards armed with crossbows and worse, and…" He grimaced, before going on. "We're low on bolts, and arrows as well. Those that we have are mainly the ones that we've recovered from bodies. At best, they're damaged, and at worst, they're probably a danger more to us then the enemy."

"Fuck," I muttered. "Great time to tell me. Have we got any magic ones?"

"Bolts or arrows?"

"Either."

"Na."

"Why the hell did you ask then?" I snapped.

"I wanted tae be sure." He shrugged, looking embarrassed. "But if they attack us from the walls, we won't get many shots off before we're done."

"Great. Would a caravan stop out of bowshot?" I asked him.

"No, we'd want tae be as close to the walls as possible, just in case something happened."

"So if we did that, they'd be suspicious and it'd be more likely that everyone would die in a hail of arrows?" I prompted.

"Aye."

"So there we go." I shrugged. "Look, Toren, this is basically the low-risk plan, because the next stage after this is going to be the slavers' caravan, and then Sonra, all right? We're literally a day or two behind them now, and we might—make sure you understand that—we *might* catch them before they reach Sonra.

"If not, then we're rocking up to a tent city of thousands, in the middle of their largest annual meeting, where slavers from all over the continent are gathering. If we can't take this place, then there's no goddamn chance of us surviving that."

"What do we do if the guards decide to search the wagons?" he asked after a few seconds.

I looked to Marteen, who was ostensibly going to be leading the guards left behind. At least half of which were going to be wearing armor for the first time.

What we'd done was strip as much of the weapons and armor as we could carry—realistically—from the dead we'd left on the field. Then, as we'd approached the town, we'd gotten those people equipped as best we could.

We'd asked for volunteers, and although nobody had been happy to do it, Zyenna had led them, and following her, they'd all felt a little better about it.

They were playing the part of slaves and they were travelling in the wagons, while the other half played the part of guards, marching around in armor, and pretending to be watching the slaves.

I'd wanted us to pretend to be the Sons of the Deep, but as Aellin had pointed out, we didn't know whether they were personally known here, whether there were signs and counter signs, nor whether they were banned, as many settlements refused them due to "fallings-out" in which they stripped the settlements and moved on.

As such, if we turned up claiming to be them, it was likely that we would pay for it, instead of it helping us.

If the shit hit the fan, all the "guards" had to do was use their shields, while the caravans got moving. If anything went wrong in the town, I was betting the guards would have orders to hold the walls, not march out into the field and chase the caravan down.

"I dinna like it," Toren admitted after a brief pause. "Ah'm sorry, my prince, but ah don't. It seems like too much risk fer too little reward. And iffin we do capture the town, what do we do then?"

"We free the slaves, and we move on," I said. "But we do it with everything we can loot from the town, with hopefully more guards, more equipment, and up-to-date intelligence on exactly who passed through this way."

"And what about the townsfolk?" Marteen sounded almost hesitant.

"What do you mean?" I looked at him.

"They're slavers, or at least complicit in permitting slavery," he pointed out. "The entire town is, which means that they all need to be put to death, doesn't it?"

I opened my mouth to say "of course" and then shut it, troubled. I'd been avoiding this as long as I could, but it looked like the bill had just come due. If I said yes, then that meant, by extension, there was an argument for every adult in the town to be executed. I could get away with not blaming the kids, but how did I separate the actual slavers from those who profited by association? And did I want to?

"That's the issue," Zyenna said softly. "And it's going to be a lot more of an issue moving forward. How did you deal with it back on Dravith?"

"Honestly, I declared slavery illegal, and that all slavers were to be rounded up and hung," I admitted. "We had to stop it somewhere, so we left those who weren't outright slavers to go free. And those who had benefitted by slavery, we kinda swept under the carpet, as it meant more than three-quarters of the city. Every business had benefitted from them, from the serving staff in the taverns to the mines to construction, the army to the nobles…everyone had slaves, and we couldn't execute everyone.

"Instead, we freed the slaves, and they were given the chance to remain at their workplace if they wanted—while now being paid a fair wage—and if they didn't want to, then there were suddenly hundreds of businesses that wanted to hire them, having just lost their slaves."

"What did that do to the economy?" Zyenna asked bleakly.

"It crashed it," I admitted. "I created orchards that gave out the fruit free in an attempt to keep everyone fed through the changeover period, as well as employing as many as I could in the army, but yeah. Himnel crashed hard."

"And what will you do here?" she prompted. "If you kill the current leadership and then free the slaves, if you take the guards out of the town—by killing them all, by freeing them if they're slaves, or by making them swear fealty—what happens?"

"The next slaver caravan that passes through enslaves the entire population and sells them," I said slowly. "Everyone becomes a slave."

"Exactly. So what do we do here?" she asked.

We all stared down at the valley ahead of us. The distant town on the hilltop across the valley stood proud, with flickering torches and well-maintained streets, and we all knew how they did it.

They did it through the profits of slavery. And although the people who lived there were about to find their world coming to an end, the hundreds, if not thousands, who passed through or around the town each year would be better off because of it.

"They'll be given the choice," I said after a few seconds. "We cannot be responsible for their actions, only our own. Slavers will be hung. Slaves will be freed to join us or go, stay and live in the town or move on. The people of the town will be given the choice—they can stay, or they can join us. But either way, they'll be swearing an oath. Whether that be that they can't speak of who we were, or the full oath of citizenship, is up to them."

"Then ah don't see wha' we be wasting time fer," Aellin said firmly as the legionnaires gathered round, his hand in that clear. "Any last orders?"

"Just that misplaced words could cause a fuckload of confusion in there, so you're all to refer to me as Jax from now on. I'm never the most formal, and I don't see the point in having people who bleed with me having to stumble over fucking titles. From now on, unless I'm giving an order, or it's a formal setting, I'm Jax. If you have to be formal when there's nobody around, then you can, but understand that I don't need it."

"And when we be around enemies?" Aellin asked.

"Then call me captain." I shrugged. "It's a formal title that most will understand, and it's not as obviously legion as optio or centurion."

"Or primus," Aellin pointed out, and I laughed.

"Are you kidding me?" I shook my head. "My Primus Praetoria Restun would tear my head off and shit down my neck if I tried claiming that title unearned."

I looked around at the shocked looks on the faces of those on all sides. "Seriously. One day, if you're incredibly unlucky, you'll meet Restun, and when you do, you'll understand. He's a force of nature, and I seriously doubt I'll ever surpass him. He scares the hell out of me, as he should."

"When we last had a primus, it do be a long time ago," Aellin admitted, "but ah still remember her, an' she be an unholy terror tae any legionnaire that did'ne live up tae her standards."

"Sounds like she knew her role then." I nodded. "Let's hope you get to meet mine."

"Aye, well, the best chance fer that, is iffin we conquer the whole continent." Aellin sighed, before straightening and looking at me formally. "Do yer wish tae make any changes tae tha' plan, ma prince?"

"No, you have operational authority," I confirmed to him. "You are to lead my guard, and if at any time you judge we need to move from stealth to open warfare, you do it and we'll deal with the fallout later. Everyone else, you know your positions, and I want the legionnaires to gather round now, because it's payday."

"Wha'?" the dwarf asked, clearly confused.

"Payday, the day you get paid on…fuck's sake, man, surely that translates even here?" I frowned.

"Well, aye, but…"

"You're all going drinking and carousing in the town. It's part of your cover…how the fuck will it look if you can't afford a beer?" I asked, grinning around. "Also, obviously I don't need to say this, but the last entire day that Oracle has been teaching you healing spells…well, by an amazing coincidence, alcohol is classed as a poison. As such, a quick healing will get rid of it."

"Don't get so drunk you can't cast the spell, and make sure you keep your eyes open!" Oracle interrupted me.

"Exactly, what she said." I passed out the legionnaires' "wages" for tonight: a gold coin, five silver, and five copper. It was more than most of them had held at any point in literally years, and I saw the shock on their faces.

There was a round of "yes, my prince" and "aye" and "cheers for" and so on. We split up, starting to jog toward the front of the caravan again, with the legion drawn in close around me.

"Have fun, don't get too drunk, and remember, your oaths are solid now. They'll no longer force you into immediate action, but the conditioning of your entire life is going to need to be dealt with. Keep calm, and remember that you're criminal scumbags out for a good time. Sometimes that means drinking, others will visit the whores, and still more will gamble. Hell, maybe there'll be someone who fucks off and they get stabbed in the face…who knows? We're criminals, after all!"

There were a lot of grins and some truly evil suggestions that were being bandied about as I looked at Oracle and winked. But at the lowest level, although the legionnaires' more stupid oaths had been erased, they were still bound to be honorable and to protect the empire and the innocents. As much as I wanted them to have fun, I knew they'd not go too far.

Though, even with oaths in place, if I'd had Giint here, I'd have put a leash on the mad little fucker.

Instead, I just looked around at the drawn-up legionnaires.

There was an argument for leaving them, or at least half of them with the caravan, to make sure our people were as safe as possible. But, in all honesty, this was the best choice, I decided.

They were my guard, and the likelihood of the town guard attacking the caravan was low, beyond a handful of crossbow bolts, arrows, and so on.

Where I was going to be was much more likely to get nasty. As much as I didn't like it, I was the prince, and without me, tens of millions might end up in slavery down the line.

It was time to nut up, or shut up.

The legionnaires fell in around me as I started to run, fifty-three of them, despite me being told that the limit to be allowed into the city was fifty at a time, and with Sehran flying high, and Oracle "running" by my side in legion scout armor.

It wasn't, but as Oracle had always been able to adjust her body however she chose, making it appear she wore armor added to the illusion.

It was about as likely to stop a crossbow as gossamer silk, unfortunately, so as I moved into the lead, she fell back, and only two legionnaires flanked me.

The guard had closed the gate, and as soon as they saw legion plate armor, they went on high alert, as the one really problematic part of the plan made itself clear.

The legion were known for hunting slavers, and this was a slaver outpost.

# CHAPTER TWENTY-TWO

"**S**top or we shoot!" came the hard yell, as we closed to within a hundred meters.

At my gesture, the rest of the legion, that had been jogging fifty meters or so behind me, slowed to a walk.

*"I don't like this,"* Oracle sent me, and I snorted inside my helmet, the sound echoing slightly along with my fast breathing.

*"You think I do?"* I replied, sending her a mental kiss, then lifting my hand in the air and slowing to a walk.

"HALT!" the leader of the guard bellowed.

I pulled my helm off, running my fingers through sweaty hair, and grinned at them. "Ho, lads! Like my new armor?"

There was a brief pause, before the leader yelled out, "You legion?"

"Do you see many legionnaires who paint their fuckin' armor?" I tapped my helmet. "Mind if I come closer? Makes it easier to talk!"

"Just you!"

"No worries!" I called back, before nodding to Aellin as he and the others stopped and made a point of standing around aimlessly, instead of the ordered rows they usually fell into out of habit. We'd expected this.

I strode forward, hands to my sides, my helmet held in the left and my right empty, my naginata in my bag.

"That's close enough," the talkative one, who turned out to be the guard captain, called down.

I came to within a few meters of the base of the wall. The palisade of stone towered over me by five or six meters, and I squinted up to him.

He was clearly short, struggling to peer over the wall at this angle, with greasy black hair peeking out around the edges of his helmet, and a face that made me want to beat him to death with a soap bar on general principles.

His eyes were narrow and so close together, combined with a massive nose, that he looked like one of his ancestors had gotten it on with a rat. Add in the scruffy offense against beards that he was growing to conceal his utter lack of a chin, and he sure as shit wasn't getting laid without paying for it first.

"So, you gonna send someone down to talk to me, or do I throw the fuckin' gold up there?" I called up.

"What gold?"

"The entrance fee!" I barked forcing myself to sound arrogant and confident as I bluffed. "Fuck's sake, I was here nine months ago and you bastards couldn't wait to charge us for coming in. I've been on the road for a month—I need a goddamn drink and a whore!"

"Whose caravan?" he asked.

"Patrin!"

"Patrin's dead," he replied.

"Yeah, he is now." I snorted. "Fuck's sake, it's not exactly a safe trade, is it!"

"How'd he die?" the guard captain asked me flatly.

"No clue. We parted ways eight months ago when he didn't want to pay me what I wanted."

"And now what, you're here?" he asked.

"I hooked up with some boys, we hit an old legion place and stole the fancy gear, then started raiding caravans." I shrugged. "Where else am I gonna go with a caravan full if not Sonra?"

"You got any proof?"

"Like what?" I asked, exasperated. "Fuck's sake, I've got a caravan full of slaves and some coin to spend. You want it or not?"

"How much?"

"How much what?"

"How much you offering?"

"For the gate fee?" I asked. We'd gotten that they paid a fee, but I'd suddenly realized that I'd never actually asked how much that fee was.

"Yeah."

"Get down here and we'll talk about it," I called up after a second, pulling a small ruby out of my bag and making sure he saw it. "I think we need a fuckin' chat, all right?"

"Wait there," he replied after a few seconds of staring.

A minute later, as the sky grew fully dark and the torches popped and crackled, a smaller door in the main gate opened. Two men stepped out, holding crossbows that stayed trained on me. The guard captain moved around them—staying well out of the line of fire—and then looped around, coming to a half a meter from me.

"Keep your hands where I can see them," he snapped as I turned to face him, my hands already clearly in sight.

"No worries." I forced a smile, stifling the urge to ask whether the fucker was blind. "Look, I need a damn drink and a whore, my boys are the same, but I need a favor as well, all right? I know I'm gonna have to pay for it, but you need to be understanding on the cost, because if I'm going to be coming through here regularly, we're gonna need to reach a price that we can both live with."

"To enter the town? Standard fee isn't negotiable. One copper per visitor, three if they're armed." He folded his arms, waiting.

"Fuck's sake, that's gone up!" I snarled, guessing and going for it blind.

"Yeah, well, uncertain times, innit," he sneered.

"Yeah, right, because everything doesn't change every day," I snapped back. "Look, you want a payday beyond this crap, you need me onside, and I need to speak to the boss, you get me? I didn't get an invite to the lord's table when I came through before, I wasn't important enough, but we both know I need one, so what's it gonna cost me?"

"Can't do it," he lied.

"Bullshit. You can, and we both know it."

"Not tonight, it's too late. He's already got guests. Maybe next week, but you know, can't guarantee anything." He shrugged. "Not my problem. I can put in a word, but…"

"We hit a gem merchant," I said flatly. "You want a fucking ruby the size of a hen's egg, you get me that dinner invite, tonight." I showed him a second, much larger ruby, then slipped it back into my bag, before balancing the much smaller one on my thumb, then flicking it across to him.

He caught it, snatching it out of the air, staring at its gentle glimmer before squinting at my bag, speculatively. "What else you got in there?"

"None of your business if you don't get me a dinner invite," I snapped back. "You get me that? Maybe we talk about how I need to meet people, and you'll know just who."

"I want that ruby."

"I want an ale and a blowjob. I ain't getting it standing here though, so no."

"You want me to turn you away?"

"You want to turn down the biggest payday you're gonna see this year?"

"I've got to split it with my boys," he pointed out. "Not much I can do with a ruby, is there? I can't break it down and pass it around until I sell it…might take months."

"That sounds like your problem to me." I shrugged.

"You give me the ruby and five gold," he said after a few seconds of silence where we each stared at the other, waiting for them to break first.

"What?"

"Five gold. You want me to see if I can get you an invite to the lord's table, it's gonna cost you the ruby for me and five gold for my boys. You pay it, *then* we see what we can do."

"How about no?" I snorted. "You get paid *if* we get the meeting. Nothing otherwise."

"I can't leave my post without reason. It'll cost me my job!"

"Does a man with a ruby the size of a hen's egg give a shit about guard duty?" I asked.

"He does if he wants to eat until the ruby's sold," he sneered. "Listen, you want in, you pay the fee. Then, you want to meet the boss? You pay again. I don't promise anything, but…" He paused dramatically, then went on.

"But I want you to come back…I want you to pay to meet the boss again, right? So it's in my interests for you to get that meeting. You pay me, and I'll see what I can do."

"I'll pay for my people to get in," I said after a few seconds. "*All of them*, fifty-four, because four are my guards and are gonna be with me when we go to meet your boss. Fifty get to explore the town, and we pay two copper each. Armed."

"Now hey…" he started.

I held up a gold coin. "This one is for the fee," I said clearly, before taking a second and then a third out as well, holding them all where he could see them. "These two are for you and the lads, for getting your arse in gear and getting up to the boss, see what you can do. If you can't get me in for dinner, that's it, you get nothing else. If you can?" I pulled three more gold out and tapped my pouch suggestively. "You want the ruby and the other coins? You get me that fuckin' invite, *tonight*, because we leave at first light."

There was a long pause, one in which the greasy little shit stared at me, then the coins, then at the little ruby in his hand. He spat on the ground and snatched the coins

I was offering, then jerked his head in the direction of the gate, then hurried back through the open gate.

The two crossbow wielders lowered their weapons, plucking the bolts free and releasing the strain in the arms as they moved through the gate as well. Apparently, the decision had been made that we were anything but legion at the very least.

"Give your names to him," he sneered, indicating a second guard, before hurrying off into the night, giving me my first opportunity to look around and actually see the guards and their shitty little town more clearly.

The guards were universally dressed in what looked like long boiled leather hauberks that had been dyed black, with a reasonable quality, armored chest piece over that, that looked more like a conquistador's than I was used to.

Then add on thick leather pants, a collar that went up the neck and a heavy-looking, wide-brimmed hat, and the look was complete.

They were obviously expected to be out in all weathers, and judging from the thick and high grasses nearby, it was similar weather to England, which meant that it rained here for fun.

I glanced at the clouds coming in and the rapidly darkening skies and snorted, having called it already.

Those who had crossbows were in the minority, I saw now. Most of the guards seemed to have long pikes, or short, nasty-looking cudgels that appeared to have been drop-forged.

I squinted at the nearest, seeing the well-wrapped grip and the star-shaped head, the way that the upper half looked entirely solid without forge marks or the impacts of hammers looking like it'd shaped it. I nodded.

That I did recognize, mainly because I'd been considering it as an option for the tower back home.

I'd watched a load of documentaries over the years, mainly because when you woke up at three in the morning bleeding heavily, having just been killed in a fight in the UnderVerse, you didn't usually want to just roll over and go back to sleep. Instead, we generally watched whatever was on TV, and that was normally documentaries on car plants and so on at that time.

It meant that I had a working, if basic knowledge of standardization and that was going to fucking rock my people's world when it came to the next generation of armor and weapons.

I shook off that thought, and looked from one of the guards to the next as we all filed in, noting that now that we were on this side of the wall, we actually outnumbered the guards. Although I guessed that nearby guardhouse would have more available to come and play if anything kicked off.

"Names," the guard barked, pulling out a large ledger and slamming it down on a lectern under an overhang by the gate.

"Why?" I asked him, and he frowned.

"Whaddya mean 'why'?" he asked after a few seconds, apparently confused.

"I mean fucking why?" I asked. "Half my people have classes that let them change their names; the rest have changed them a dozen times to escape the law since they were kids. Why give you our names? They're not gonna matter." I shrugged, playing the role to the hilt.

"We need names," he growled.

"All right." I grinned, then started to gesture people forward, handing them a handful of silver each as they passed. "This is Bob." I indicated the first in line. "This is his brother, Bob."

The next stepped up, and I named him, then another and another: "Bob, son of Bob; this is Bobbette, daughter of Bob, and this is…"

"Let me guess, 'Bob'?" he sneered, looking up at me.

"Don't be ridiculous." I shook my head, looking disgusted at him for assuming that. "*That's* Bob, for fuck's sake." I indicated the second in the line then pointed at the one he'd asked after, and I named him. "This one's John-Bob."

"We need their names!" the guard snarled.

"I told you. Bob." I shrugged. "Look, you know the name they give isn't going to be real. Shitting hell, you think I know their birth names? I don't!"

"Fuck's sake!" The guard slammed the book shut and stormed off back into the hut, as another guard tried his luck instead.

"You're responsible for them then," he started.

"Nope, your captain took the entrance fee—you're responsible for them until we leave tomorrow. Now, where's that bar?" I asked cheerfully.

"Fuck off and find it yourself," the guard spat, and I laughed.

"Guess you don't want me to be easily found so that you can get the payment then, eh? Your choice, pal." With that, I turned my back on the guards and wandered toward the main street, only to have another guard call out from behind me.

"Might want to take all that legion armor off. They'll not serve you wearing it!"

"They will, or I'll break their bar!" I yelled back over my shoulder, ignoring anything else he said as a handful of the legionnaires closest moved in closer. I started to speak in a low voice.

"We're in a situation behind enemy lines, and we need to make people believe we're bandits and criminals. That means, for each of you, you do what you have to do. Feel free to get into fights, enjoy yourself a little, and if you see something you don't like, do what feels like the most fun."

"Seriously?" one of the legionnaires asked nearby, grinning.

"Listen, for probably the first time in your lives, I'm telling you officially that it's totally fine for you to get into bar fights, meet whores, fuck people up, and lose all your coin gambling. Don't get too drunk, but you can have an ale or two, and stay in small groups. Make sure you all have each other's backs. Go gamble, whore and drink…do whatever you need to. Because until the night's real entertainment kicks off, I need the guard to believe you're all normal criminals. The reason there's so many guards is because they expect fights to break out, so just…have fun."

"What if someone gets hurt?" another legionnaire asked in a hushed, yet hopeful voice.

"Make sure it's them, not you, and that it's not an innocent. You spot a known asshole, someone tries to cheat you at cards, there's a gang that try to threaten you? Remember that in the morning, things are going to be *very* different here, so have some fun. If you lose all your coin, who cares. We'll take it all back tomorrow. This is probably the first time in your lives an officer of the legion can say this to you, but tonight, kick back and relax. However you do that."

"Uh, Jax…" One of the legionnaires struggled just calling me that, and it showed.

"Yeah, Bob?" I grinned.

"Ah…some of the group, it might have been a while, since, uh…"

"Just be careful if you're visiting the whores. I'd imagine they're riddled with diseases here, so make sure you've got a healing potion afterward. And if it doesn't work, Jax and I have some pretty potent healing spells, so don't be too proud to say something," Oracle said.

The legionnaire colored even more, before nodding and moving to the back of the group as low chuckles rang out.

"Hey, he just had the balls to ask what half of you were wondering!" I called out, and that got more laughs.

"There!" one of the legionnaires in the lead called out. "A bar!"

"Go, go, go!" I shouted, grinning as fully half the legionnaires around me started to run.

"That might a bin a wee bit unwise," Aellin said softly. "Ah mean ne offense, but…"

"But they're in need of a drink," I said. "I've been there, mate. I've gotten back from a long deployment and needed to just stop, and I didn't have all the oaths and shit that you did. You've been on deployment your entire lives, not just for a six-month run, and they need this. If they get into fights, it's gonna look like we're more like the usual run-of-the-mill criminals, that's all."

"But if they're taken by the guard…" he started.

"You've forgotten about Sehran already?" I asked, and he hesitated, then visibly forced himself not to look upward. "If they arrest our boys and girls, they'll have a visit paid right before we kick off by a very hungry friend of ours. So believe me, I think we can let our people blow off a little steam."

"I understand yer reasonin', sir. Ah just feel…" He struggled with the words, and I nodded.

"You think it's an unnecessary risk, all things considered," I finished for him, and he nodded. "It is, but either I trust them or I don't. And wearing that armor? If they then act like legionnaires, this is all over. They have to visibly *not* be legion, or we don't have a chance. You know of a better way to do this than have them act like soldiers and have some fun?"

"Ah don't like it, that be all," he muttered after a few seconds as we kept walking.

"Me neither, but it's life." I shrugged. "Let's find another tavern," I suggested. The four guards around Oracle and me, and an additional four who had tagged along beyond that, all continued up the street.

The streets were reasonably wide, clear, and—wonder of wonders—they were more or less paved as well, which was a nice surprise, considering the state of the road that had led up to the town.

The rocks that showed through the muck and horseshit were barely visible, but they were there, and that meant that the streets were practically straight, and the ruts that were left by wagons that passed through weren't deep.

The buildings on either side of the street were clearly open, with torches lit and a handful of animals tied up outside, or closed, with heavy grates over the windows and doors, and in case of a few places, even had a guard under an awning, glaring at anyone who walked past.

"Gem merchant, general store, armory…what's that one?" I asked Aellin as I paused, ticking off our targets for the morning.

"Hmmm?" He glanced over, then shrugged. "Repairs, generally magical artifacts. It'll be a gnome artificer, most likely. Probably enslaved. Poor bastards are always targets."

"Really?" I asked, torn between a growl at the thought of the mad little bastards being enslaved, and hoping that it was as he said, because a gnome on our side was always…an experience.

"Aye, most slaver towns ha' something similar. Basically, they'll make and sell the collars, link up new keys, an' they'll unlock ones that have been damaged. That be why there be a graveyard next door."

"I don't get it?" I admitted.

"Collars can be used again and again and they're no' cheap, while slaves usually are. So, iffin yer got a slave that yer lost or broke the key fer, yer take them tae somewhere like tha', and they can remove tha collar, or…"

"Or?"

"Or yer remove tha slave's head and get rid o' their body in tha graveyard. Then yer get a fresh key all linked up." He spat. "Iffin they want tae make sure the other slaves understan' where tha stand in life now, then they take 'em tae tha graveyard, kill tha one that they need the key fer, and it's all so much more 'convenient.'"

"Why?" I asked. "I mean, I get the rest, but why kill the slave if you need to buy a fresh key to use the collar anyway…"

"A slave costs tae keep, you have tae feed them, and if they're ill, it might no' be worth it. Also, the artificers charge ten times as much tae pair a key if the collar does be active. Somethin' about a magical backlash. So ah've heard o' slavers making their slaves walk up, dig their own graves, then lopping their heads off and retrieving tha collars. That be just another example o' why this town should be burnt tae the ground."

"I'm not disagreeing." I sighed, then gestured to the street ahead, taking a deep breath, and plastered a smile on my face. "But for now, in case we're being watched, we need to play our part. On to the tavern."

It took us all of five more minutes to find a tavern that wasn't already full and that looked like there was at least a chance that the ale wouldn't have dead rats and worse floating in it. And when we did, the sight of ten of us marching into the bar in legion plate drew an instant panicked hush.

I had my helm in my bag by this point, and I forced a grin around the bar, as I spoke.

"And that's why I love wearing my new armor in towns—I get instant fucking respect!"

"You legion?" One of the nearby thugs reached behind him, to where his sword clearly rested against the back of his chair.

"You ever see a legionnaire who painted his armor?" I asked, "Buy me an ale and maybe I'll tell you where I stole it from, though!"

With that, I stomped past him as if I didn't have a care in the world, marching right up to the bar and slamming an armored gauntlet down to brace myself. Then I yanked a stool out from underneath another patron, sending him tumbling to the floor with a yell of surprise.

"Ale for ten!" I bellowed, replacing the stool and sitting down in it myself, while totally ignoring the outraged patron as he climbed to his feet, a dagger in his fist.

"Put the pigsticker away before he makes you eat it," Oracle said in a clear voice as she made her helm apparently vanish into her bag of holding, neither the bag nor the helm really existing.

"Ah would," Aellin grunted, gesturing at the remaining figures rising from their seats on all sides of me. "Believe me, 'e'll clear tha bar iffin yer start a fight."

"I said I wanted a fucking ale," I growled, glaring at the tavern keeper, who spat on the floor behind the bar and gestured to his other patrons to leave it, before speaking to me.

"Three copper a cup."

"I said ale not goddamn whisky. What the fuck kinda ale is three coppers a cup?" I squinted at him.

"The kind that you get served when you wear legion plate and come in here upsetting my people," he grunted. "You want me to call the guard?" He reached out and gripped the rope connected to the bottom of a bell that hung behind the bar, and I snorted.

"You do it, and I'll cut your fucking arm off. One copper."

"Two, or you can fuck off somewhere else."

"I like this tavern." I smiled around warmly, then started to count out coins. When I did that, the tavern keeper let go of the bell and moved closer, only to freeze when I finished counting at fifteen coppers, then lifted my right hand and summoned flames to it. "It'd be a real shame if it caught fire and burned down, wouldn't it?" I said conversationally. "How much was it again, for ten ales?"

"Fifteen copper," the barman grunted after a brief pause.

I cut my hand sideways through the air. The flames vanished, as I sat back.

"You know, I thought that was what you said?" I turned to my companions and the rest of the room, acting surprised at how many were still standing with weapons in hand. "Come on, everyone, we're all friends here. No need for unpleasantness, right?"

"Settle down," the barman added through clenched teeth, "It's not worth it."

"That's more like it. I like a sensible barkeep!" I smiled. "Now then, about that ale?"

"I'll take a wine," Oracle said clearly, drawing every eye, as she smiled widely.

"You heard her!" I gestured to Oracle, before forcing myself not to curse as I found the first fault with drinking in a packed public tavern with legionnaires who didn't really know me.

They were as stiff as boards, and none of them wanted to break the silence.

"Ah, right, so it's like that, is it?" I laughed. "Come on, I promise not to stab anyone who looks at my woman sideways, not again!"

That drew silence through the bar again, until the legionnaires—helped by a swift kick by Aellin—started to loosen up and everyone started talking at once.

Unfortunately, as they were literally with their prince that they didn't know very well, and these were legionnaires, their stories weren't really the kind that fit with the image, so I manfully grasped the bull by its horns and took one for the team.

That had been an education as well, having to start off the conversation with a handful of really bad jokes and stories to break up the uncertain attitude of my companions, and then progressively getting worse and worse until I finally achieved my aim: seeing Aellin snort ale out of his nostrils at the conclusion to an epic tale.

It was an hour, all told, before the guard captain finally found us. And when he did, he looked furious, as well as wet, the heavens having apparently opened recently and drenching anyone unfortunate enough to be out in it. For example, any idiot going from tavern to tavern looking for someone.

"You!" He snarled. "What the hell are you doing here!"

"Drinking an ale," I said conversationally. "You want one?"

"No, I don't want a fucking ale!" he spat. "You're supposed to be having dinner with the lord!"

"Am I?" I blinked. "What an extraordinary thing! And here we were, about to order food as well. Ah, well, another time, my friends!" I called out grandly, before gesturing to the door. "Come on, people. Off to dinner we go."

"It's just you," the captain snapped. "Not your men!"

"It's me and my quartermaster, obviously," I corrected, gesturing to Oracle, who'd been drawing every eye for the last hour as she drank her wine.

"Fine," he snarled. "But…"

"And my guard will be there. But don't worry, they won't cause any issues…probably." I grinned. Then standing and ignoring the guard captain as he snarled and made demands, I downed my ale and turned to the barman.

"I'd like to say it's been a pleasure," I declared with a grandiose wave of my hand, then went quickly on. "But it wasn't, so I won't. That ale tasted like piss, and I think someone drank it before me. Bye!"

With that, I walked toward the door, and the guard captain—who'd apparently lost his hat at some point and was now soaked through—was given the choice of move aside or get walked over. And as he was perhaps half my weight, even wet, he did the sensible thing and got out of the way.

It didn't take long for the furious man to lead us all the way to the "big house." As we trooped up, I felt Oracle spreading a little healing around, making sure that none of us had so much as a trace of alcohol left in our systems.

The streets were deserted by now, as we silently marched through the driving rain. All of us had put our helms back on, and aside from the annoying state of the cleaner, which was now soaked through, I was quite comfortable.

The "cleaner" was the name given to the plume on the top of my helm. It was, I'd been told by the lead legion armorer Thorn some time ago, perfect for "cleaning" the cobwebs away in any low-ceilinged establishment you entered, caves, or as a handhold for "cleaning" your head out of the way to expose your throat, and as such it wasn't well thought of by my legionnaires in general.

That meant that the march for us was a lot more pleasant than it was for the guard, and as we went, I got an opportunity to make a few mental notes.

The town was split into what looked to be three semi-circular districts, I noticed. As you entered, you found the main street that led roughly north to south, and from there, on the left side of the road was the housing area, on the right were shops and storage, and then in the middle, with the other two curving around them, were the homes of the rich and shameless.

The "big house" looked to have been an imperial building at some point in the distant past, considering the high, fluted pillars that bracketed the door—equally massive enough to admit a damn war golem—and the dozen windows that held actual glass, where much of the buildings in the town just had wooden shutters instead.

There was a manicured garden that led up to the door, and a fence that ran around the property, keeping it clearly separated from the houses of those who, I guessed, were the merely rich on all sides.

Add in that they had an actual lawn—well trimmed, I had to admit—and you got the perfect image of a plantation owner's mansion. One that was helped along by the stand that was in place on the far side of the square, and that was surrounded by a dozen large cages.

The cages were open to the sky. Even a quick glance told me that although most weren't occupied, those that were, held slaves that lay uncaring and unable to escape the rain.

"That it for the slaves in the town?" I asked the guard captain, who looked over, raising his head from his sullen silence, then shrugged, only becoming more loquacious as I reached into my pouch and drew forth three gold coins.

"It's what's left." He shrugged again. "Most were sent along to Sonra already. What we had's bin picked over and traded for, so there be some cheap labor and some expensive…nothin' in the middle."

"And they're all there?" I asked again. "In the rain, where they can catch a cold and die?"

"The cheap stuff, aye." He shrugged. "Anythin' else, you'll need to speak to the lord."

"And you can't tell us anything else?" I asked grimly.

"Just gimmie my fuckin' pay," he snapped. "You already fucked my night up enough."

"You'll be surprised," I said softly, handing the coins over, then slipping the ruby out and handing that over as well, knowing damn well that I'd be taking it back from him within a few hours.

He marched us up to the front door, banged a fist on it once, then glared at us all, as a furious-looking chamberlain opened it.

"You're late," he said.

The guard cringed. "They wouldn't come!" He tried to explain, only to be shooed away by the chamberlain, who turned to regard me, clearly picking out the difference in the armor and naming me as the leader.

"The invitation was for one," he said flatly, eyeing my companions.

"Really?" I projected an air of confusion as I turned to look at the guard captain backing away in the downpour. "Strange that your man neglected to mention that. When I asked for an audience, I made it clear that I would have my quartermaster and purser with me."

"And the others?" the chamberlain asked after a brief pause, clearly reassessing me.

Instead of the much more relaxed air I'd shown to the guard, I now forced myself to speak with a clearer voice, much as I did when I was speaking to the nobles in Himnel and Narkolt.

"My guard," I said. "You don't expect me to expose myself to risk, without profit, do you?"

"They'll have to wait outside," he replied after a few seconds.

"They can wait with your guards," I countered. "They're used to eating whatever they're offered, so they won't be a bother, and then I won't have to sit and wait past my welcome while they're rounded up at the end of the meal."

There was a brief pause, then the chamberlain inclined his head and stepped back into the room behind, opening the door wide. He picked a small bell off a table and rang it once, the silvery note hanging in the air.

A young boy hurried from the back of the room, dressed in clean black linens, and he bowed to the chamberlain, the bulk of a slave's collar clear under his shirt as he did so.

"Take these guards to the servants' entrance. Tell Mren that they are to be given space with the lord's guard and fed while their master dines, and pass word to Charla, two additional seats at the master's table."

"Yes, sir," the little lad said rapidly, bowing to me as well, then darting past, speaking quickly to my guards.

"Go with him, and be ready," I said clearly, before turning back to the chamberlain, taking the opportunity to glance around the room as I did so.

It was a tall building, easily twice the height of a normal house, with a grand staircase that led upward ahead of us. Two doors led off from the entryway to the left and right, and then two more ahead led to rooms beyond and on either side of the grand staircase.

The floor was marble, or looked it, and the walls were draped in velvet curtains. The doors themselves were black, the wood clearly lacquered or painted. A massive chandelier hung from the ceiling overhead, shallow bowls of burning oil sending a clear if flickering light out.

The temperature inside was significantly higher than outside, partly due to the fireplaces, which, as the chamberlain led us across the marble floor—our boots filling the air with the ring of metal on stone—we noticed were lit in every room.

"Your name, sir?" the chamberlain asked.

I smiled, taking my helmet off and putting it into my bag of holding. "Jack, and my companions are Oracle, my purser, and Aellin, my quartermaster."

"Very well. The lord is always interested in meeting new bands as they pass through his domain, especially now."

"Now?" I asked, curiously.

"Why, yes," came a cultured voice as we walked into the dining room, and I almost tripped in my surprise. "Now that your masters have returned, everything has changed."

# CHAPTER TWENTY-THREE

The dining room was opulent, with heavy tapestries covering the walls and a massive table that could easily seat twenty, though only seven places were set. Crystal decanters caught the light from dozens of candles, and the air was thick with the scent of roasted meat and spices.

But it was the man at the head of the table who held my attention. He couldn't have been more than thirty, with carefully styled dark hair and wearing what *had* to be a Savile Row suit, if I had to judge. It was impeccably tailored, the shirt almost glowing it was so white, and yet…

It was open at the neck, the wrist, and throat, showing chains that looked to be platinum; he had rings on each of his fingers that, even with the suit, failed to make the man before me look anything but scruffy, especially combined with the spots of dinner that already stained it.

"Come on then, come in, come in," he said impatiently, wiping at his mouth with a thick linen napkin, before tossing it aside and gesturing to seats at the table.

"Earl Sebastian Montero, youngest son of Baron Charlemagne Montero, please allow me to introduce the adventurer Jack and his companions, Oracle the purser, and Aellin the quartermaster of his band."

"Please, join us." Sebastian gestured to the empty chairs. "I so rarely get to meet new…entrepreneurs in our little domain, so it's always a *treat* to see what you bring me."

I forced myself to move naturally as I bowed carefully, then took my seat. Oracle and Aellin did the same, flanking me as my mind raced.

The accent was Nordic, possibly Swedish? Definitely not English, but also clearly from Earth…the suit, the posture, the complete disregard for the world around him and a sneer that said "I've seen it all and you're the idiots I'm playing with."

I glanced at his companions and saw who I guessed to be the former lord of the town—a broken shell of a man with trembling hands and a heavily scarred face, complete with a milky-white blind eye—dressed in finery, and yet clearly petrified and sitting to Sebastian's right.

Two others completed the group: a lean man with a pistol prominently displayed on the table before him, and a younger woman whose fingers kept twitching in half-formed spell gestures and a smile that looked, frankly, fuckin' deranged.

"I must admit," Sebastian continued as servants began to lay out some food for us, and the noble started to eat again, "I find it fascinating how readily the locals adapted to my presence. A few demonstrations were all that I needed to make, and suddenly they're falling over themselves to accommodate us."

"The locals can be quite accommodating," I agreed carefully, after swallowing, then picking up my glass and smelling it, studying the wine as I thought quickly. "I confess, though, you have an advantage. I wasn't aware any noble houses had decided to seize power here. I'm used to dealing with the likes of him, but you seem different." I gestured at the trembling former lord as I spoke.

Sebastian's laugh was sharp as he looked from me to the old lord by his side. "Oh, we're quite new to the area. But my family has extensive experience in…establishing order in primitive territories." He gestured to the broken man beside him. "Isn't that right, former Lord Marrow?"

Marrow flinched, mumbling something inaudible.

"Impressive." I took a careful sip of wine. "And you found taking control easy? I've found that you need to be brutal, and strike fast to take control. But when my partners and I have done it, there's usually more signs left behind. I was expecting someone like him. I had no clue another had taken control."

"That's because you're all primitives," Sebastian scoffed. "You locals still think science is magic, and where I come from, we have a lot of experience in dealing with those of lesser status. No offense intended," he added with a smirk that made it clear he meant every bit of offense.

The assassin—because that's clearly what he was—reached out and adjusted his pistol slightly, lining it up unerringly with my chest, before smiling at me hungrily. The mage's fingers twitched again and she let loose a slight giggle before covering her lips and shushing herself.

"None taken," I replied, spreading my hands. "Though I'd be curious to hear more about your experiences. The road to Sonra can be treacherous, I'm told."

"For the locals, perhaps." Sebastian waved dismissively. "But we've found that proper organization and superior weaponry make most problems…manageable. Though I'm always interested in expanding our operations. I understand you have quite the collection of merchandise with you—forty wagons and more? Anything that's worth my time?"

"That would depend on what you're looking for," I hedged. "I have over two hundred ready for sale, though some are more valuable than others."

"Such as?" he asked casually, staring at me fixedly.

"Judging from your clothing, perhaps the pair of tailors I have would be of interest? A journeyman and an expert—though the expert has a wasting disease, and I need to find a healer for her. Do you have healers?" I bullshitted, trying to get some time.

"Use a potion." He shrugged.

"We've tried. It's resistant."

"Resistant," he mused, watching me before taking a drink of his wine and then pointing at me with the hand that held his wine. "That's an unusual word for one of your kind. Where'd you say you were from?"

Oracle tensed beside me, though she maintained her neutral expression. Through our bond, I could sense her readiness at Sebastian's obvious suspicion.

"The north. My father was…" I snorted, then shrugged. "He was mad," I said.

"In what way?"

"Said that he was from another world. Taught me things and words, but he still died the same as anyone else when the legion hung him."

"And yet now you wear their armor?"

"He found a place with some relics, and I've plundered it over the years as needed. The armor was one of the bonuses, though for some reason none but him or I could retrieve it. So, if you're wanting to buy some, you'll need to make me an offer that's attractive."

"Why?" He sat up straighter. "And who was your father?"

"My father?" I blinked. "No clue. He simply called himself Boromir when people asked. Why? Did you know him?"

"Boromir? Huh. Strange name to choose, but it means he was probably…" He glanced at the mage. "You. Examine him."

"I don't have much mana left, Lord. You said that I had to—"

"Then get a potion!" Sebastian snapped, before drawing in a deep breath, then looking back to me as she got to her feet and hurried from the room. "You said that you found the armor in a site with relics. Describe it. What kind of relics?"

"Valuable ones." I smiled. "I sold them over the years and…"

"You stole relics and sold them?" he hissed.

"Hey, they were from the old empire, all right?" I shrugged as if I were unconcerned. "It's not like anyone from the empire is going to come looking for them, is it?"

"You'd be surprised," he said coldly. "Where was it?"

"That's information you'll have to buy." I smiled. "And I have five hundred trained killers to make that point for me if you want to try to argue it, instead of make a deal."

"You have less than a hundred, and I think most of them are in my town, currently drunk as skunks, so you'll watch your mouth, or I'll nail it shut."

"How do you know that?" I pretended to be worried as I sat up straighter.

"We have our ways." He smiled. "Now, your slaves…how many do you have and what do you need?"

"You want to make a bargain?" I asked.

He shrugged, clearly playing for time as his mage got the mana potion. "Indeed." Sebastian leaned forward. "Tell me, have you encountered any of the old Imperial Legion in your travels? We've found them particularly…valuable when properly motivated."

"That's a relief. I was getting ready to fight my way out." I grinned. "So—"

I was cut off as a distant and sudden scream rang out, followed by an explosion that shook the building. Sebastian's head snapped toward the window as shouts and screams began to fill the night air.

I smiled, all pretense dropping away. "Funny you should mention the legion."

The mage burst back into the room just as another explosion rocked the building. Sebastian's eyes narrowed as he looked from me to the chaos outside, then back.

"What have you done?" he demanded, his carefully cultivated accent slipping.

"Me?" I spread my hands innocently. "I'm just sitting here having dinner. Though, I have to admit, your reaction to mentions of artifacts and relics is…interesting. Almost like you're looking for something specific."

"My lord!" A guard burst through the door, armor singed and smoking. "The legion! They're—"

The assassin's pistol cracked; the guard's head snapped back as the bullet took him in the throat, clearly having been mistaken for an attacker.

Before the assassin could spin on me again, I was already moving. My hand snapped out to grab the decanter of wine and hurl it at the assassin's face, even as Oracle unleashed a bolt of lightning at the returning mage.

The mage shrieked, blasted backward, caught off guard while carrying a potion pouch and looking inside. The assassin reeled drunkenly, one hand rising to his face, blood and wine and broken glass all painting the area.

"You know what really pisses me off?" I asked conversationally as I stood, my chair crashing backward. I dipped my hand inside my bag and yanked my shield free, settling it on my arm, just in time to deflect a pair of bullets, before Oracle's own shield snapped into place over us.

"It's not the slavery—although, believe me, we're gonna address that. It's not even your contempt for the 'primitives.' It's that you noble pricks came back through to my fuckin' realm thinking you could just take whatever you wanted."

Sebastian's face had gone blotchy with fury and fear. "*Your* realm?"

"Yeah, about that whole 'mad father' story…" I grinned as Aellin deflected a fast shot from the assassin, then stormed around the table toward him. The handgun unloaded into the dwarven legionnaire's shield as they discovered the difference between legion plate and regular cheaper armor they might have faced before. "I might have exaggerated slightly."

The mage was screaming, Oracle's lightning having blown her halfway across the room. The assassin was scrambling to eject and replace his magazine; his nose streamed blood from where the decanter had landed. And Sebastian…

Sebastian was pulling something from his jacket, something that glittered. "You have no idea what you're dealing with," he snarled. "We didn't come here unprepared!"

"Actually," I cheerfully corrected him as I channeled mana into my tattoos and sprinted forward, "I think it's you who's in for a surprise, my old fuckeroo!"

The artifact in Sebastian's hand flared with a bright-white burst of energy. Tendrils of power writhed outward as he held it up triumphantly. "You think you're the only one who can find relics? Unlike you, we can use them!"

"Oh, for fuck's sake," I sneered, recognizing the rank insignia in his hands. "Please tell me you activated the control chair first? You didn't just flood the fucking insignia with mana and wake them up?"

His triumphant expression faltered slightly. "What?"

"*Jax!*" Oracle snapped to me through the bond. "*He's activated some kind of emergency spell. It's not golems—it feels more like a defensive net, but I don't know what's live and what's…*"

"*Can you claim the control room?*" I asked her, our minds meshing at a thousand miles an hour.

"*Maybe?*" she sent back. "*It might accept me, considering the…genetic material.*" She meant our child, the fact that she was pregnant with the child who would be the next prince or princess of the empire, provided we damn well managed to sort this shit out.

"*Go!*" I barked at her.

She flashed back out of the room through the nearby open doors, clearly searching with her magical senses in ways my own mundane ones weren't capable of.

The tendrils of energy suddenly snapped taut, stretching between Sebastian and the walls, floor, and ceiling. The room itself seemed to pulse as ancient mechanisms ground to life.

A handful of guards burst through a concealed entrance at the back of the room, on the other side of the table and closer to Aellin, who spun to face them, dropping his shoulder behind his shield and bellowing "shield bash" and slamming into them like so many bowling pins.

"You absolute cockwomble." I sighed, triggering Mana Overdrive as Oracle released the shield. "So, for your fucking information, if you're so dumb you don't know, you just activated an imperial site. What it does, no clue, but I'm willing to bet my authority is higher than yours, fuckface!"

The assassin reloaded, his hands steady despite the blood streaming down his face. The mage tried to crawl toward the potion bag she'd dropped, still smoking from Oracle's lightning. And Sebastian… Sebastian's eyes had gone wide as the energy began to wrap around him instead of reaching for us.

The assassin slammed the replacement magazine home and darted forward, grabbing onto Sebastian's shoulder and trying to drag him clear, even as he unloaded the entire mag at me.

With Mana Overdrive in place, I jerked the shield into position and held it as the bullets slammed home. The shield rang with the impacts, until the assassin shouted something.

"What's happening?" Sebastian demanded, trying to drop the trigger, finding that instead of going, it remained fixed to his palm, pulsing faster as he screeched at whatever it was doing. "Make it stop!" he yelled at the mage and assassin both.

"Sorry, mate," I shrugged, "but that's what happens when you play with toys you don't understand. Time to learn just how fucking unstable magic can be!"

The walls groaned as more mechanisms activated. Sebastian's face had gone from red to white as the energy began to crawl up his arm. "You…you're not just some primitive!"

"Nope," I agreed cheerfully, stepping forward as Aellin moved to cut off the assassin's retreat. "Prince Jax Amon, at your service. Scion of the Imperial Throne, and yeah, your fuckin' master. Though I think I've seen you once before, back when you sat in a fucking arena, watching as your betters fought on the sands below."

The look of horrified recognition on Sebastian's face was almost worth all the pretense. Almost.

The assassin chose that moment to make his move. I saw it out of the corner of my eye as he yanked the pin from a grenade and threw it at Aellin, who'd just finished with the last of the guards. He jerked his shield around, clearly recognizing an attack, even if not the method. The clang as it locked into place against his shield rang out and I cursed, guessing it was magnetic.

"Fuck!" I yelled, bracing behind mine again as another staccato pattern of gunfire slammed into my shield and then my legs, hunting for weaknesses. "Aellin, throw your shield!"

"What?" the legionnaire asked, totally confused.

"Throw your shield away, Legionnaire!" I roared, and as he hesitated again, I bellowed again, "That's an order!"

He shucked it off then, fast and clean, and hurled it aside. The tip clanged off the wall before it bounced back toward the ground…then exploded.

He crashed to the ground even as a pair of freshly arrived guards were evicted from the room via the window, on fire.

I cast Lightning Bolt, wanting to take the fucker—or at least his gear—intact or alive, and hurled it at the retreating assassin as he paused, ejecting his mag and slotting a fresh one in its place.

He was picked up and punched into the wall. His pistol went off wildly; the bullet ricocheted around the room before embedding itself in the ceiling, and at the same time, he fell. The snapping of bones and the way he crashed to the floor, limp and unresponsive, made it clear that I'd put a bit too much mana into the spell, considering he was now smoking.

Sebastian clearly saw an opportunity, and gave less than two fucks about his people, because he suddenly rose, looking haggard but no longer with the insignia attached. I glanced down and grunted as the mage started to convulse. The artifact was no longer attached to Sebastian and now glowed brighter and brighter on her back as it drained her of mana and life to reactivate the ancient structure.

"My father will…" Sebastian started, then screamed as a bolt of crackling power slammed free of the wall nearby, punching into the floor and cracking a section of marble free. It revealed a disc of gold that glowed with power, making him sprint back toward the nearest wall to get clear of it. Lightning burst free again, carving blackened lines across the walls. The mechanisms within groaned louder.

"Your father will what?" I yelled after him, genuinely curious. "Because last I checked, he was still stuck back there. And even if he made it here… *I'm the prince, bitch*! How'd that go down with him when he found out?"

"You dare! *You* are the interloper, the fool here. I shall—"

Whatever he was about to say was cut off as a massive explosion rocked the building. Either the prick apparently had one last trick up their sleeve, or it was the imperial structure giving up the ghost. The blast caught me in the back, sending me staggering forward as chunks of the ceiling rained down.

Through the smoke and chaos, I caught a glimpse of Sebastian being dragged through a suddenly open section of wall. The assassin, somehow back on his feet along with a pair of freshly appeared guards, helped him escape despite his injuries. Then the ceiling really started to come down.

"Time to go!" Oracle shouted, as she burst into the room again. Another shield sprang up to protect us from the worst of the debris.

"But—" I started to protest, gesturing wildly at both the fleeing prick and the artifact that was clearly channeling a fuckload of mana into itself.

"We need you alive more than you need to chase him!" she cut me off. "The control center is destroyed, and now the building is going to blow!"

She was right, damn it. The whole building shook worse and worse by the second. I snarled in anger, spinning to see that the old lord, the fucking idiot still sat in place at the table, and the damn chamberlain and the kid were both standing in the doorway still, not a one of them running.

"What the hell are you doing!" I barked at them. "Get out!"

"We can't!" the old lord wailed. "We're slaves!"

"So?" I shouted as a section of the ceiling crashed down in the next room.

"We were ordered to stay!" the chamberlain called out desperately. "We were ordered to return to the master to await orders…"

"Get out!" I bellowed, and none of them moved. For a second, I almost grabbed them and carried them out physically. Then I remembered that there could be dozens, or hundreds in the building standing exactly the same, and I roared in impotent fury.

"Goddamn you idiots!" I took a deep breath.

I gathered it all—the anger, the frustration at such stupidity and the outrage that anyone would be so, so, fucking arrogant and idiotic. Then I yanked it back up. The room suddenly blazed with a bright, white light. I lifted a few feet into the air; the power surrounded me, filling me and crackling out to lick at the walls and floor on all sides. I took the chance, reaching out and grabbing onto the mana that was running out of control in the building.

I triggered my Mana Manipulation ability. I desperately needed to get more practice with it, and like so many of my abilities, I swore that I'd take the damn time to learn to use it properly soon. But for now, as manic as my life had been of late, I was stuck at the most basic levels with it.

It was the entry level version of the skill Amon had, Master of Mana. I'd gained access to his skill—with his help—when the shit had hit the fan in Himnel.

I'd used it before, and yet when I'd lost Amon, when he went to his final rest, I'd been left with a half-formed skill that sort of worked and sort of didn't, meaning I could do more with my spells than I should be able to, and yet oh so much less than I could only a few weeks ago.

Then I'd hit my first double century in points invested in my Intelligence stat, and I'd regained access to the baseline version.

I could manipulate the mana of the realm around me so much easier with it than I could before—and a brief flare of remembrance made me guess I needed to adjust my meditation techniques because of this—but the important detail?

I'd gained the ability to again reach out and not just cast with the mana inside me. I could now, with difficulty and a lot of effort, but I could affect mana that wasn't my own.

In the case of a wrist-thick bar of destructively unleashing mana that was carving holes in the walls and floors, I made the most of it, dragging it into me and feeding my ability with it. I yelled out the words, frantic to get as many people freed as possible with this free boost.

"By my imperial right as Jax Amon, Prince of the Realm, Scion of the Empire, and master of this land, I declare all bonds to be broken! Those who have been enslaved, YOU ARE FREE!"

The power left me in a rush, blasting outward and up, tearing free the roof of the building and hurling rock and debris out and away to uncover the night sky.

It tore through walls and floors, a great circle of power that picked the slaves up around me and hurled them clear of the building.

It was also like a hammer to the back of the head—the power left me stunned. A feeling like I'd plugged myself into a power outlet ran through me, even as I pushed it through and out.

Like so long ago in Himnel, the walls and floors rippled with power, flowing as if a sleeping giant beneath them shifted, like a dolphin swam just beneath the surface.

And they moved...the slaves all around me—dozens in the manor, and hundreds more outside in the town—were found and touched, enveloped in a bright light and held safe, invulnerable, as all around them buildings collapsed.

Control collars that had rubbed skin raw for decades were suddenly shattered like clay, their parts cascading to the ground as the injuries of the slaves were healed.

That wasn't all, though: where the control collars were destroyed, the power that maintained them was redirected.

The matrices of the rings, keys, bracelets, and more that granted control of their bonded partners suddenly found themselves being filled, then overfilled with energy.

Such artifacts—often on the sharp edge of overload already, barely understood, and frequently poorly maintained—detonated under the onslaught.

The pressure wave of my power rang out across the town, fueled by both my ability and the freely triggered and unleashing mana. And as the slaves were freed, healed, and protected, their masters were anything but.

Rings exploded, maiming their wearers; keys superheated and melted to slag, or again, exploded. Nightstands where the control devices were set vanished in pillars of flames. And in tavern after tavern, the richest of the town, those who could afford to enslave their fellows and had then grown ever richer on their labor, screamed and died.

I saw it all, my consciousness carried by the expanding wave until it petered out. Then I crashed to the floor, the entire town mapped to within an inch of its life in my mind, even as my knees buckled, and I barely managed to stay upright.

My mana was gone, like literally gone, and my health had taken a hell of a hit as well. But Oracle, at least, no longer required my mana to survive, even though she drew on it to use our spells, so although it was a kick in the tits, it wasn't dangerous.

Something hit me from the side, and I grunted. The effort required to lift my head felt like I was trying to lift a semi-truck with my neck muscles alone. But as I struggled, I heard his voice.

"Ah've got yer, ma prince!" Aellin rasped.

With a herculean effort, I managed to look at him. Another pair of legionnaires burst into the room, sprinting to my side and helping to take my weight.

Where the solid dwarf had seemed uncomfortable before, almost uncertain, listening and knowing intellectually that I was the prince but never quite a hundred percent mine...now?

Now his eyes shone with fervor.

He saw the legion, he saw the empire, as it again could be, and he *believed*.

They set me down outside, the grass lit by the flickering of the dozens, possibly hundreds of fires that were steadily consuming the town on all sides. I felt her presence as Oracle pressed a mana potion to my lips, her own mana almost fully depleted, with Sehran using as little as possible in turn, lightening the load for us all.

"What happened?" I mumbled. I fought to clear my head; a wave of confusion and grogginess poured through me, as I could hear fighting distantly on all sides.

"You don't know?" Aellin laughed. "My prince, you freed them—*all* of them, again, just like at the caravan!"

"Prince?" the chamberlain asked, confused.

I forced myself to look up, having to close one eye to better focus, and grinned at him, having felt the connection to him as his collar—a much more streamlined, but still a fucking device of enslavement—had been destroyed.

"Yeah, sorry, I'm a little…" I waved a hand in vague explanation as Oracle took up the story.

"His name is Jax Amon, Scion of the Imperial Empire and Prince of the Realm, ultimate commander of the Imperial Legion, and yes, freer of slaves. Most of those titles pale into insignificance when you consider his last one, though."

"What?" The boy was the one to ask, his piccolo flute of a voice rising higher as he warbled on the brink of puberty.

*"Godslayer."*

# CHAPTER TWENTY-FOUR

I accepted more potions, and around me, I heard Oracle and Aellin barking orders, and distant crashes and the crackle of spells. A few times, I heard the dull thump and then the powerful crack of explosive spells. But most of all, I sat there, the backlash of freeing and healing so many, and most definitely of tapping the discharging power of the structure, leaving me feeling like I'd been cored like an apple when the power had run out and I'd fed it from both my own mana and health pools.

Now I was left feeling unbalanced, exhausted, and with a mana migraine that was flaring and dying as I teetered on the edge. My mana slowly started to refill, then vanished as Oracle needed to use it.

"Jax?" Oracle asked me gently, and I forced my head up to squint at her. "It's okay. It's all under control, and your people are safe. You can rest."

I let out a sigh of relief, having been battling to keep myself upright.

"Your mana…" she started to say, hesitating, and I waved a hand at her.

"Our mana," I corrected. "You do what you need to do, and I'll rest and meditate."

I lay back on the grass and took a deep breath, reaching up to run my fingers through my hair—at some point, someone had removed my helm and gauntlets. I watched the flaring cinders of fires float upward.

My mind was too beaten to meditate properly—I was too distracted, too exhausted—but I managed to relax. Instead of forming the boxes, which I knew was quicker but also beyond me at this point, I simply relaxed, opening myself to the realm and drinking its glorious skies in, as my mana increased slightly faster.

I watched the gentle wheeling of stars, and I slowly felt the world settling again. The blue-green of an aurora faded from view, and at last, with the sky showing the first crack of dawn, I managed to sit upright, finding a dozen legionnaires standing around me in a protective ring.

They were in full armor, their shields on one arm and spears held at the ready, their butts grounded and set. There was a faint breeze, and it carried…it carried a song?

I blinked, confused, as I struggled to my feet, only to find Sehran there, and then my Oracle.

"What happened?" I asked again, and this time, I was conscious enough to hear the answer.

"The town do be pacified, ma prince," Aellin declared, moving through a gap the legionnaires opened for him, and then dropping to one knee. "They stand ready to swear."

"Swear?" I looked at Oracle.

"We sorted through the town," she said quickly. "It wasn't hard. Most of those who we were warned to look for were already dead or dying. The backlash killed at least half, and the freed slaves killed most of the rest. Then there were plenty in the town who knew…what's that saying?"

She paused, then nodded to herself. "They knew 'where the bodies were buried,' and they weren't shy in showing us. Sometimes literally."

"And?"

"And we took care of things," Oracle said. "There were more than a dozen legionnaires of various ages and conditions within the town, most having been bought over the years from passing slave traders and then used as guards on the locals' strongrooms. Their oaths prevented them being used for things like blood sports against innocents, but there was a small arena that had a handful, and the rest were held ready in case their masters got robbed."

"Another eighty-seven of my brothers and sisters are free now because of my prince, and they stand ready. Whatever orders you have, no matter the cost, we're yours. We're still searching, so there may be even more still locked away here, but that many?" He shook his head in amazement and was unable to keep the disbelieving grin from his face.

"Thank you," I whispered, only to feel Oracle as she reached out to me, speaking in the silence of our bond.

*"He means what he says, my love. If you thought the Dravith Legion was fanatically loyal, you've seen nothing yet. These men and women would charge hell if you asked it of them."*

"Thank you, all of you!" I said again, raising my voice and projecting as loud as I could. "I came here to free as many of you as I could. I'm only sorry I couldn't make it sooner."

"Command us, ma prince," Aellin begged, lowering his head. "Let us prove ourselves."

"Aellin, what gives?" I asked in a softer voice. "Fuck's sake, man, you ran by my side for the last what, four days?"

"Ah did, and ah will never discharge tha' shame of ma actions there," he replied grimly.

"What?"

"Ah thought yer another noble, one perhaps more interested in what we stood fer, but either way just another noble, an' ah thought tae use yer tae try an' save th' empire."

"And now?"

"Now ah see ma prince!" He looked at me, his eyes afire with fanatic light. "I cannae use ye tae save tha empire—'cos ye ARE the empire! Every man, woman, and child tha' lives now, is because of yer mercy. We owe oor lives tae ye, oor souls, and by tha' soul, we will NO fail ye again!"

*"Shitfuck,"* I grunted internally to Sehran and Oracle. *"What the hell happened to him?"*

*"I don't know, but we need to keep an eye on him,"* Oracle agreed. *"I don't think he's dangerous, I really don't, but I think that he didn't really get to see it properly when you freed them all back at the caravan. Here, already freed himself, he saw it all, and he's seen who you are over the last few days. I think, well, he's just a fan, though a very intense one."*

"Aellin, you've been fighting to survive for so long, that you've forgotten much of what the empire was," I said slowly. "The empire existed to protect its people.

Where you offer your life for mine, you offer to serve and protect me, you have to understand, that in turn, I will give my life, if needed, for you. For *all* of you."

"No, ma pr—"

"Don't you fucking do it, Aellin," I growled. "I've got a name and you know it."

"Prince Jax…" He shook his head. "It's no' appropriate fer me te—"

"I'm a goddamn man like any other, Aellin!" I barked. "I damn well put my pants on one leg at a time and I fall over when I trip. Don't make me into something I'm not or I fucking swear I'll order you to braid daisies into your beard and fuckin' dye it pink!"

"If…if ma prince wishes…" he replied, swallowing hard.

"Don't. Don't you dare." I leveled a finger at him. "Fucking help me, yes. Serve me, Aellin—I'll accept that, and I need it. But worship? Amon didn't want it or need it, and neither do I!"

"But—"

"I'm just a man!" I snapped. "A man like any other!"

"A Godslayer," someone whispered.

I hesitated, then cursed. "All right, yes, okay? I fought the dark dickhead and I have his skull being made into a goblet, but that's not… I mean, who the hell wouldn't!"

"Fight a god?" someone asked, and I snorted.

"All right, yeah, okay, I get that might be a slightly lower pool of people who go for that one, but the goblet is reasonable! Who the hell wouldn't want one!"

"His actual skull?" the child who had helped in the manor house asked, eyes wide and round.

"Well, it was just his avatar." I shrugged.

"What's…" the boy started to ask.

"It's a body made entirely from scratch for one purpose—for a fight to the death," Sehran replied for me. "It was the perfect body that the god of death deliberately created for the single purpose of fighting Prince Jax, and Jax still killed him in single combat."

"He was limited!" I snapped. "Limited to the same number of points I had."

"He was, and he also didn't have to waste any of them in things like Intelligence, or Wisdom. Tell me, Jax, of, oh say, your top three stats, how many of them are mental stats that he got to assign to physical traits instead?"

"Don't make me into something I'm not, Sehran," I growled.

"How many?" she repeated.

"Two of his top three are mental stats. Intelligence over two hundred and Wisdom is a hundred," Oracle said proudly.

"I don't know what it was then…that was weeks ago." I tried to wave it off.

"Weeks." Sehran nodded, before raising her voice. "You hear that, Legionnaires? It doesn't count, because he fights so frequently, he's leveled since then. You know, since cutting the God of Death's head off and having it made into a goblet!"

There was a sudden rumble of thunder and a feeling of oppressive pressure filling the air as a divine presence made itself felt, and not a friendly one.

Sehran fell silent, as did the others as the thunder rolled again.

"Oh, fuck off!" I shouted into the air, all my pent-up annoyance breaking free as I lunged to my feet. "You heard me, Nimon, you cock! Unless you want a second go, right here, right now and I'll fight you for this continent like I did Dravith? Well?"

*"You go too far!"* The voice was like the dropping of leaden weights, and I snorted.

"Fuck off, do I! Which of us pulled down a moon, eh? Who slaughtered billions just because he could and killed Amon! It was you who started this shit, and I'll finish it with my boot up your arse! Now fuck off, or get down here and fight me again!"

*"Jax…"* The new voice was firm, but clear, and I paused, listening.

"Sint?"

*"I recommend you do not push further, Champion of my Sister. Nimon is a god, remember."*

"Exactly. You'd think he'd be too busy to come running and whining every time someone says something he doesn't like, or at least have some self-respect. Look at Tamat!"

*"Jax!"* Sint snapped. *"Beware…"*

*"What about me?"* Tamat sounded dangerously interested, her presence suddenly shouldering into the group.

"Lady Tamat, Goddess of the Assassins and Dark Deeds!" I called out. "Mistress of the Knives in the Dark. A goddess with all the fucking reason in the world to be the one running around and listening to anyone who names her, and yet she's not the one who comes running and likes throwing thunder and lightning around, is she?

"You claimed her fucking aspect, Nimon! You pretended it was always part of you and that you should have control over it, but you're nothing more than a coward and a thief! You tried to take it all, and yet even as pissed as she is, she has better control and self-respect.

"Then there's you, ya fucking cock! Hiding from me and hiding from judgment! Well, I remember! I remember you, and I remember that fucking lightning bolt in the forest!"

I could hear the hisses of anger from Tamat and the sudden presence of other gods, gods on both sides as the ruined town was rapidly becoming ground zero for the next war of the gods.

"I remember when you were supposed to be constrained against acting against me directly, and yet YOU STILL DID IT! You hit me with a fucking lightning bolt in the middle of that forest, all because I was kicking the shit out of what…a hundred, *two* hundred of your Dark legionnaire fucknuts all on my lonesome!"

The silence was thick enough I could have used the fucker for a blanket. All around me, I saw those who weren't legion, Oracle, or Sehran backing the hell away, both from my incandescent rage and the clear epicenter of the next divine smite that was going to arrive.

"Well, I'm sick of it!" I yelled, waving one hand in a dismissive gesture that then morphed into me flicking my middle finger at the sky. "So, either get your arse down here and face me, give me one of your fucking followers to gut, or fuck right off. I don't care which, but the next time you come sniffing like a desperate puppy just because someone mentions your name, I'll rip you a new arsehole!"

*"Very well!"* came the response.

For a brief heartbeat, elation and absolute terror surged in me at the same time. *Was he going to do it?*

"You'll fight me for the continent?" I asked, desperately hoping, even as I damn well knew I'd really not picked a good time for this, considering how exhausted I was.

*"No, but I'll name a champion to face you again for your impertinence, one that will remove the stain of your existence from the face of the realm!"*

I opened my mouth to speak, then shut it with a clop as he went on.

*"Illoth, you wished to punish this whelp? I give you leave! March from your depths and make his suffering something to speak of for the next thousand years anytime a single human thinks of leaving their caves!"*

"Oh, it's fucking on!" I grinned. "Come on then, you bitch, get your spidery arse down here!"

*"You think to face me, child?"* came the hissing, furious voice. *"You wish to face me in truth, to die by my hand? Very well! Even though you have no chance, I will still lower myself to face you in the flesh!"*

"No chance?" I called back. "I fucked up your boy Nimon, bitch! You think you're harder than him? Why're you his follower then? You literally just called him weak, if I've no chance against you and I kicked his ass, so come on, let's do this!" I gestured people back, though in truth the ring of people on the outside of the gardens was getting a lot bigger as everyone except the legion had run for it when the gods started throwing threats around.

"Move back, guys—I'm gonna need some room for this!" I called to the legion. "Come on, Lolly! That's your name, right? Lolly the Turd Spider? Sorry, but you've not ranked high enough in my enemies for me to *remember your fucking name!*"

There was a screech of absolute fury, and the earth shook all around me. I grinned, not believing this was actually working. It hadn't started out intentional, not really, but if I could goad the stupid fucker into actually facing me as limited as Nimon had made himself last time?

I had a chance.

If I was realistic, facing the fucking God of Death was insane.

His throne was the size of mountains; he could drop his goddamn dinner plate and shatter a continent. And there was no way that a flea—which I was to him in size in that realm—was going to take him out.

It just couldn't happen…there was no way. *But…*if I could goad him into a fight, into putting himself or one of the other gods within reach of my divine fragment's ability? I could actually fight them and have a chance!

The more divine fragments I could get, the more power I'd gain. And then, with that power, the safer I could make my people.

As much as I didn't want it, the thought of having a living god sitting on the throne of the empire should be enough to make anyone else who might want to fuck with me back the hell up and rethink their lives.

All I had to do was force the gods to face me in fucking combat, which should be easy, right?

***"You think to taunt me? You think to insult me, and that I am a fool?"*** Illoth hissed.

"What, you think that just because I tore Nimon a new arsehole I can't do it to you? Might want to be careful there, Lolly. You just called your boss weak and now a fool for facing me in honorable combat! All you need to do now is call him a fucking coward and I bet he squashes you like the bug you are!"

Silence.

Things went dangerously quiet as she apparently replayed the things she'd said, and then realized what she'd implied.

"Come on, Lolly. I'm waaaaaiting! You remember what I did with your altars? Where I had the pieces put? They're in the *latrines*, Lolly. Every time my people go for a shit, they do it on you and your memory!" I called.

"What, you want to scuttle out of the light, go fuck off and hide under your blankets like the cowardly bug you are? Hell, I bet you were planning on sending a spider to do your work for you, weren't you?

"You don't even have the guts to face me—it was going to be a disposable bug! That way, if you somehow managed it, you could claim the kill, and when you failed miserably, you could hide it! How many of your pets have I squashed now? How many of your followers have told me how powerful you are, how incredibly dangerous, and despite all that? HERE I AM."

I snorted, then spat on the ground.

"You've not got the balls," I said derisively, trying to do anything I could to infuriate her and push her into a fight instead of sending a legion of spiders after me at night. "Tell you what, I'll give you an out, seeing as you're too much of a coward to face me, one-on-one right here and now!"

I turned and pointed at Aellin, speaking quickly.

"How long until we get to Sonra?" I demanded.

"Six days?" He swallowed hard, feeling the eyes of the gods on him.

"A week from now, I'll be at the tent city of Sonra," I yelled up toward the sky, turning slowly, my arms out to the sides as I threw the challenge far and wide. "It's a massive place where tens of thousands will gather. Now, I know you're too dumb to find it without help, and you're too much of a coward to face me here and now, so how about this? A week from now, at the tent city of Sonra, I'll call you out and you face me? You say that only a fool would face me—well, I think you're right on that at least.

"I think Nimon *is* a fucking fool. He thinks he's not and that facing me in single combat was worth the risk. As much as I hate the shitfuck, I've gotta give him respect for that. You, though? Not you…we all know you don't have it in you. So, let's go, bitch. Either you're a fucking coward and you don't dare face me, which you'll prove then and there before the eyes of the gods and men. OR…" I grinned, letting it hang in the air.

***"Or you prove that you believe your master to be an idiot, and that you believe you know better,"*** Jenae said, the feeling of her divine presence rolling out to join the others. ***"What will it be, little spider? Will you scuttle off and hide? Proving to your master that you think he's a fool, knowing what will come of that? Or will you face my champion and be banished from this continent and Dravith both when he kills you?"***

*"I accept!"* came the hiss. *"Seven days from now, we will meet, and I'll eat your heart!"*

"Good luck, bitch. You're gonna need it!" I called out. For a long few seconds, I waited, hoping, until finally, the sense of the enemy gods' presence faded, and I let out a long breath of relief.

"Jaaaaax!" Oracle snarled, and I winced, knowing that now I was in real trouble.

*"You are, as always, braver than a pride of lions, and more foolhardy than a child prodding that lead lion's testicles."* Jenae sighed.

I smiled at the mental image.

"I like that description," Oracle agreed.

*"Jax, this was foolish…"*

*"I think you mean impressive,"* Tamat purred. *"It was impressive the way that you manipulated them so easily, forcing them into a situation where she must insult her master—who would have punished her—or face you directly."*

*"Tamat, he barely survived the fight against Nimon,"* Jenae snapped.

*"True, and yet if he wishes to grow, to gather more divine fragments, his only chance is to face those who wield them. Although taunting Illoth to her face was foolish, as a gamble it was more sensible than leaving himself open to her pets. A moment of distraction was all they would need, and only his unpredictable nature has kept him safe from them so far."*

*"Yet offering to fight Nimon?"* Jenae asked.

I shrugged. "I didn't think he'd go for it, but let's face it, if he had? If I won, then we gained a hell of a breathing space. And if I lost…well, Augustus and Tommy are there to pick up the pieces."

"And you'd be dead!" Oracle snarled.

"I would, but the only way we're gonna win here is by taking risks, and frankly that was a good one to run."

*"Against Illoth it is, as if you win, you will not only further reduce her power, but you will gain much strength. Against Nimon, I doubt you would survive a second meeting. But against his pets? Perhaps."*

"Thank you for your confidence, Lady Tamat." I beamed.

*"Oh, don't thank me yet, boy. I think you're going to die—I just expect the show to be worthwhile! On a side note, should you fail, I wish you to agree that Bane would be released from all imperial oaths at the point of your death."*

"Why?" I frowned.

*"He insists that he is bound to serve you first, and if that bond transfers to another, he will again attempt to follow that instead of doing as he should as my champion! He and his companions draw closer by the hour, and I have targets he can begin punishing, rather than being wasted by your empire."*

"Go to hell," I snarled. "You accepted he was mine first when you chose him—you don't get to steal him away because you want shit done!"

*"You're looking very vulnerable when you sleep, Jax…remember that,"* Tamat hissed.

"And I can find you just as easily," I snapped back.

*"Jax, Tamat!"* Jenae barked. *"You are allies, and on all sides are potential followers—remember that!"*

That brought a few seconds of silence, before I sighed, then nodded and sank to one knee.

"Lady Jenae, my goddess, I apologize. Lady Tamat, I can't release Bane. I need him. But I shouldn't take out my irritation on you, and…" I forced myself to say, knowing that as always, my mouth had been writing checks my ass couldn't cash. "When I cut Illoth's head off, I'll let you pick the latrine it ends up in as an apology."

*"Tamat…"* Jenae drew out her sister's name in encouragement, making me feel like we were two kids being forced into making up after a playground fight.

*"I want a goblet,"* Tamat replied after a brief pause. *"Make me a goblet to match your own, Prince Jax of the Empire, and I'll come down and drink with you to all disagreements being long forgotten!"*

"Deal." I grinned. "Though you'll need to wait for me to get back to Dravith to get mine."

*"For this, I'll personally recover yours from your home and bring it!"* she promised, making me laugh.

*"Very well. Now that you've managed to ensure the entire realm knows where and when you'll be available as a target, I suggest you consider a range of disguises, my champion, because I believe, as we have discussed before, there are some on this continent who would be pleased to claim your head."*

"Wait, what?" I blinked, and that was when Jenae apparently removed the block that she'd somehow put on my notifications, and they all crashed in.

# CHAPTER TWENTY-FIVE

"Ah, fuck," I muttered, wincing as I read, accepted, and dismissed notification after notification.

The first few weren't important at all: kills and skill upgrades; I'd not made it to another level, and the skill increases were all piddly little ones, not worth the time. With the goddamn big flashing ones that took pride of place, I barely bothered to note them.

**You have made progress in your quest: "Divine Is As Divine Does."**

*The God of Light, Sint, advises you DO NOT attempt this quest before a minimum of level 50, and yet you have chosen to disregard this, and begin early. He is unamused, and yet unsurprised at the same time.*

**The Goddess Illoth of the Drow—also known as "Lolly the Turd Spider"—has agreed to face you in single, open combat at the tent city of Sonra, seven days from now.**

**The winner of the fight shall claim a fragment of divinity from the loser, as well as their enemy's corpse.**

**Seek out and acquire fragments of divinity, aiding you in both your ascension of the Crystal Steps to the Imperial Throne and to Godhood.**

**Seek out and harvest fragments of divinity from those who hold them: 1/10**

**Reward: True immortality, Ascension to Godhood, 5,000,000xp per fragment**

Obviously I'd accepted that already, so that reminder was good but it changed very little. What did change things, though, was the next one.

*Let all be aware!*

**Jax Amon, former son of the disgraced House of Sanguis, and Godslayer, has formally challenged Illoth, Goddess of the Drow, named by the Empire as "Lolly the Turd Spider" to formal combat.**

**A fragment of the divine shall be claimed by the winner of the fight, as well as dominion over the local area—100 square miles—and all who dwell within those bounds.**

**As this is also a time of war in the Imperial Succession, Prince Jax of the Empire's title and position will be deemed secure for this period, and will transfer to his heir, Duke Augustus of Himnel, should he perish.**

**The Imperial claim shall be judged continuous, unless his successor declares his claim null and void.**

**Should the Goddess Illoth win, then she shall claim a fragment of divinity and the life of Jax of Dravith.**

**Should Prince Jax of Dravith win, then he lays claim to one tenth of her power, condensed into a fragment of her divinity, and, as per the previous challenge, claims the Continent and strips his opponent of any access, but not others of the Pantheon of the Dark.**

**HOWEVER: The continent of Carrmor is currently classed as contested, and not currently under his direct control. As such, each territory that is claimed by the Imperial Throne and Prince Jax shall be cleansed of Illoth's hand only once it declares for him. Should Prince Jax succeed in claiming all the continent, then she—and by right of connection, any others who bear her mark—shall also be removed.**

***The Imperial Succession continues!***

**All those who wish to contest the rise of Jax now have less than one year to state their grievance and face him.**

**If he still stands in control of a Greater Territory and as a Prince of the Empire, then and only then may he ascend the Crystal Steps and be proclaimed Emperor!**

**All Hail Jax Amon! All Hail the Prince of the Empire!**

As I finished reading it, I started to swear, before a thought came to me, and I started to laugh instead.

"Ma prince?" Aellin asked, confused, as Oracle started to snigger as well.

"She's a fucking idiot," I crowed. "Who added that bit?"

*"I did,"* Sint rumbled, and I couldn't help but laugh aloud.

"She thinks she's getting off lighter because she doesn't get booted off the entire continent if I win, doesn't she?"

*"I assume so. She will perhaps regret that,"* Sint said. *"In the future, Jax, I suggest a little more caution when you summon the gods. But either way, I must admit, your empire looks to be a place of constant surprises."*

"Love you too, mate." I grinned as once again his presence and that of the other gods vanished.

"Ah don't understand," Aellin admitted. He and the others around me visibly relaxed now that the sense of divine presences had ended.

"Any city that has an issue with the drow has just gained a way to remove them all from their bounds in a single fell swoop, should you win," the chamberlain said clearly, before bowing to me, deeply. "I am Othair, my lord, and I'd like to offer myself and my team to take care of any needs you have."

"Thank you." I nodded. "I'm sure we can find a use for you somewhere."

"Wait, any city?" Aellin suddenly grunted. Then he started to laugh, clearly rereading the notification. "Shit, all they have tae de is declare fer Prince Jax, don't they! Iffin the leaders o' the city swear tae accept him as their prince, they get all the drow booted out, *instantly*. It be a divine-level house clearing that'll remove every damn sneaky spider fucking bastard one o' them, an' at the same time, it gets yer sections of the continent that yer've never even heard o' declaring tae follow yer!"

"Exactly." I grinned. "What Sint did just gave us a chance to gain entire territories without me ever even having to set foot in them. Sure, there'll be issues with governance and dealing with shit, but once they swear, I can activate their oaths, and then they're imperial citizens. I can free the slaves, the legions, everyone, and bind them to me!"

"And even more so, given the situation with the lost cities," Othair added, smiling.

"Lost cities?" I turned to look at him in question.

"The cities that failed, like Romesh, an ancient city of the empire now long lost to the desert, my prince. I was a scholar once, and the empire was something of a passion. The original cities were set up in places of power as well as natural resources. If they were claimed, and a minimum operating population installed, I believe they would requalify as the capital of the region. In fact…it probably should easily, as the current nobility have no imperial ratification for their titles. Should you name that as a capital of the territory, declare a member of the caretaking team as its lord, then anything within that territory would also become part of your holdings."

"It'd be a way to quickly expand across the continent, and to kick the drow out of it as we go," Oracle added. "I like it. Othair, you and I are going to have a lot of conversations moving forward, I just know it."

"It would be my honor, uh, lady purser?" he tried.

"Shit, let's sort that out." I sighed. "Ah, can we get everyone in and listening? As many of the local population as possible, our people, and we're gonna need a shitload of mana potions or stones." I smiled. "Let's…"

**Attention, Imperial Citizens!**

**To "Prince Jax Amon," House Sanguis formally refutes your claim to the throne and demands you step down, naming Baron Sanguis, head of that line, in your stead.**

**Should you do this, you will be permitted to retain the continent of Dravith as your personal holdings, until such time as the Imperial Succession is over, at which point you shall be formally acknowledged as High Lord of Dravith.**

**Do you accept: Yes/No**

Obviously, I snorted in disgust and refused it. But as soon as I did, a second took its place—word for word almost identical, simply changing the name of the house for another that demanded my surrender, then another.

As I refused them, more notifications appeared, until finally there were no more and in their place:

**Attention, Imperial Citizens!**

**A war of succession has been declared, a civil war for the heart and soul of the Empire. As of this time, you are offered two choices: declare for your rightful**

**master, Baron Sanguis, or the impostor and warlord "Prince" Jax of Dravith. Be warned, however: taking a side in this most grave of situations will mark you eternally, and neither side is likely to forgive nor forget...**

"Jax, don't accept or decline anything else!" Oracle quickly spoke up, and I glanced at her as the same declaration, minus a few minor rewordings, popped up again and again. "The next...yes, there it is!"

**Attention, Imperial Citizens!**

**Baron Sanguis Declares WAR!**

**To the pretender, Prince Jax of Dravith, you have been given a chance to step aside for your betters with your honor intact. Instead, now shall you face wrack and ruin, your lands shall be salted, and your people bled to the ninth generation for your temerity!**

**Baron Sanguis Declares WAR!**

**Do you accept:**

**Yes/No...**

"Don't!" Oracle snapped.

I frowned, looking at her. "What's the problem?" I asked.

She shook her head, making sure I wasn't about to go for it anyway, and then when I didn't, she let out a low breath before going on.

"If you accept that, you'll be able to see where he is. Where they *all* are," she said. "It didn't matter with Barabarattas, because he wasn't an imperial noble, he was just a pretender, basically. But for an imperial noble, you'd get access to their location, one that's kept up to date through the imperial throne's power."

"Why?" I asked, confused, before a pulse of memory flared, and I cursed. "Fucking hell, Amon!" I snarled.

"Exactly," she agreed. "He claimed it was to make sure that anyone who declared war knew the consequences, the real ones, as nobles would usually try to bargain for their lives and avoid them. If the war went poorly, they could run and hide, while their forces would die.

"For the nobility, the consequences could be a loss of coin and other resources, but it wasn't likely to be more than that, until he put this system in place. When the nobles realized that a war between them would open them up to real-time tracking that could be shared with assassins? It cut down on the wars very, very quickly."

"So that worked great for then, but for us, not so much." I grunted. "Every single one of these idiots would have gotten my location, and there'd be all their forces on the road in minutes—snipers, assassins...the works."

"Exactly." She nodded. "As it is, there's no way we can hide that we'll be at Sonra, but until them? We need to keep a low profile."

"Shit."

"Yeah." Oracle rubbed at her face. "We were already skirting the edge of the risk. You sent word to Wilhelm, after all, and that asshat Sebastian will be spreading the word as well, if he survived. But at least they're likely to only tell their own families, and they'll be limited by range."

"No satellites to enable cell phones." I nodded. "And although some will have keys for the towers and portals, we know most are locked, so they're gonna have to conquer the territory on foot. Hell, no maps—most of them will have no clue where Sonra is. And even if they do know, they're unlikely to be able to reach it in seven days, considering we know where it is, and it'll take us six. No vehicles and the weapons they did bring are limited."

I scratched at my chin, then nodded as all the issues with carrying tech through the portals, starting with the likelihood of detonation, ran through my mind.

Every single gram of matter that passed through the portal was massively expensive in terms of mana needed, mana that just didn't exist on the far side in any great quantities.

That meant that as the magic of the portals tended to set explosives off, the only way to carry any kind of modern weapon through—and batteries as well—was in heavily lead-shielded boxes.

That in turn massively limited the number of bullets and the number of people who could make it through. There were likely to be less than a hundred of each lord's retinue. And due to the damage done to and the range of the portals across the realms, I was betting that they couldn't just be opened from this side again, not ever.

We'd gotten some information from the dickhead nobles we'd already faced and questioned, and that their use of blood magic had basically precluded those portals ever being any use again. I knew there were other reasons, such as the stability of "minor" portals and their likelihood of collapse while they were being used.

That was why the baron hadn't just ordered me to get through and open the portal wherever, so that he could march through with an army.

He'd been *very* insistent that I get here, then go straight to the capital and open *that* portal to him.

It'd not been said directly, as near as I could remember, but Falco's daughter Sintara had made it clear that each connection, and the longer the connection was made, damaged the portals.

Now, thinking about that, if there wasn't a reason that any portal on this side could be connected to the portals back there, then the baron would have simply had whoever got through use that key in the portal if they survived and boom.

He'd be home.

Instead, he'd demanded that only that portal was acceptable.

That meant, I was betting, that he'd only be able to get through once, and once it was done, the portal—again, as Sintara had mentioned regarding the ongoing damage to the great portal—would be destroyed.

Working through it logically like that, now that I knew more of the pieces of the puzzle, I could make a few educated guesses.

I'd been told that a portal could only be opened to a place that a portal had been opened in the past, as the area of space and time was weakened and folded to permit it. That was why he couldn't just jump through, then set a new portal up and designate the coordinates as the imperial throne room.

It had to be a site that had previously held a portal, and that still had a working portal. Those were rare as hell, because although there had been hundreds, perhaps thousands back before the cataclysm, that had all changed on that fateful day.

Some would now be at the bottom of oceans, or buried underground. Still more would be in positions that, although they could accept the connection, wouldn't end well. If it was up against a wall for example, or buried in a landslide, then the simple action of stepping through would kill you.

I'd go from being my size, to a quarter of an inch thick and the consistency of jelly with interesting bits, or worse, if something was in the way. I'd be pinned until the portal ran out of mana, and then whatever hadn't made it out the far side would be destroyed as the link closed.

That didn't even include those that were broken, and then there came the majority: locked portals.

Any portal that was locked could only be opened by someone with a relevant key, or the appropriate authority. If Sanguis, even still marked as a baron, decided to portal across to my great tower, he'd be in for a world of pain, because as my authority was higher and I'd locked it, he'd slam into a barrier and be rejected.

Even if his authority was high enough, like mine—none now had a higher level of authority over imperial devices—but it was set to a full lock, then he couldn't access it. Then came the personal issues.

If the portal wasn't a general imperial portal, if instead it was locked to a particular house as a personal portal, then only those with a key could open it.

That was why Sintara Falco had given me a key specifically for this tower. Admittedly, she'd not fucking warned me it was a SporeMother nest, and she'd not helped me at all there, but that was life. She might not have been aware of the true situation.

What all of this meant, though, was that there was a good chance that the nobles who had come here were scattered far and wide. And as such, although Sanguis might be mouthing off, he also might be ten million miles away and trapped, unable to do anything at all.

I wanted to see where he was, I really did—having his head mounted on my wall was a genuinely heartfelt desire, after all, but… I couldn't run the risk that he was half a mile away, with a hundred troops with sniper rifles.

If I opened the door to this shit, then I'd be reduced to permanently hiding, to using body doubles and worse.

No, for now, I couldn't accept the declarations, as it was the only way I could protect Oracle and Sehran, as well as my new people.

"My prince?"

I blinked, turning and looking at Othair the chamberlain, as he waited, clearly trying to get my attention.

"What?" I snapped, then sighed. "Sorry, let's try that again. What is it, Othair?"

"The majority of the people are heading here now. Many had already gathered, and those who were concerned about the presence of the gods…" He paused, searching for the words.

"They already fucked off?" I suggested, and he nodded. "Fair enough. I don't blame them." I sighed. "Okay, first things first. Legionnaires, let the man through, and we need to start the ball rolling with getting to know each other."

At some point while I'd been lost in thought, he'd clearly gone off and the legionnaires weren't sure whether he should be allowed too close to the imperial person. I'd need to address that and... I looked around and spotted Aellin heading over with a tall woman by his side. Her grey skin and underbite, not to mention her tusks, made it clear she was of mixed race.

"Prince Jax." He clapped a hand to his chest in formal greeting for some reason. "This do be Daralen the Red, Primus o' the Third Maniple o' the Legion o' the Tower o' Gaij."

"My prince," Daralen said respectfully, bowing as she clapped a fist to her chest in salute as well.

"Primus!" I nodded my greeting to her, unable to keep the grin from my face. "Goddamn, it's good to meet you!"

"My prince, I will serve, if you will have me?" she asked carefully.

I frowned.

"Ah can confirm both her rank an' suitability." Aeillin spoke up quickly. "Please, ma prince, Primus Daralen do be an excellent officer. Ah highly recommend that yer permit her tae retain her rank an' assist yer."

"Why the hell wouldn't I?" I asked her. "Are you kidding me?"

"I am, as you can see, of mixed blood," Daralen said carefully, before struggling on. "Many of the nobility I have dealt with have had…issues…with my presence," she admitted.

"Oh, for fuck's sake." I shook my head. "Daralen, we're gonna have a good chat after this, and I'm going to need an explanation of a lot of things, as well as confirmation of your rank once you've sworn, but I sure as shit don't care what anyone says about your suitability based on your blood."

"Thank you, my prince," she whispered, a hint of relief in her eyes.

"He means it, Daralen." Oracle stepped forward. "I don't know how common people with your background are here, but in Dravith they're rare. That being said, Thornapple, another of your kind, is the second-in-command of the legion's armorers there, and that's because she stepped down when a smith with more experience came. Jax fought to convince her not to, not the other way around."

"Her armor kept me alive on multiple occasions," I agreed.

"She crafted this?" Daralen asked, eyes stunned.

"Ah, crap, no." I shook my head. "Sorry, no, her armor was what I was wearing until I recovered this. This armor dates back to the cataclysm, and it's an original."

That apparently wasn't the thing to say to set her at ease at all, as she now stared at my armor with a kind of hunger that I rarely saw on anyone's face.

Except Oracle's, now and then.

"Okay!" I said suddenly, realizing that we'd all fallen into a brief moment of silence. Even the legionnaires on guard started to stare at my armor, and me at Oracle, thinking of…well.

Oracle gave me a wink and a shake of her head, mouthing "naughty" at me, and I grinned. It looked like she was at least forgiving me a little for the whole "picking fights with the gods" thing again.

We set off—Othair guiding us—to a raised section of the main square, one that as soon as I climbed the stairs to it, I recognized the uses it'd been put to.

There was a nice section that was clearly supposed to have the "real" people standing to discuss their wares and the value thereof, and a lower section that was rounded and stood before it, with steps leading up and then down the far side.

From above, it looked like a smaller circle that I could stand on, with a sort of half-moon of raised ground directly before it, and then the space arrayed all around it was open for those who were in the market for a new slave, to stand and watch.

The slave could be brought up and paraded before them—no doubt sans clothing—and then the offers would be made and the bidding started.

I stood there and looked out over the people gathered. Likely, a significant percentage of those who stood there, watching me, had walked it and been sold. I swore.

"Fuck's sake," I muttered, marching forward and looking out over the crowd. "Morning, all!" I called.

"First things first, this isn't going to work for any of us. I'm not talking to you all from the front of a fucking slaver's bidding post, and you're all half terrified, so let's change this right up."

I looked around, then pointed back at the grassy lawns across the plaza. "There, those big gardens! I want you all to march over there and sit on the grass. I know, I know…there's going to be complaints about you getting grass stains on your high-quality clothes, but fuck it, I'm willing to risk that, rather than have our relationship start out from a slaver's pulpit."

Considering most of the people there were wearing at best, filthy clothing, and in the case of a literal handful of the whores who had been freed from the brothels, blankets, that got a few hopeful smiles and titters.

"Okay, everyone, if you can make your way over there, please, except for you." I pointed at the former lord of Marrow, who'd been standing very quiet in a wide-open space all his own. "You can get your arse up here," I growled.

He swallowed hard then nodded and started moving as the people around him parted to let him through.

"First off, let's do this nice and quick so that we know where we each stand. Legionnaires!" I called out, and Oracle pushed the oath out to them as I pulled the top from the mana potion and held it ready.

**_You have resurrected the Oath of Imperial Allegiance!_**

**Due to lack of mana and territorial control, oath range is limited to a twenty-seven-mile radius. One hundred and ninety-six Imperial Citizens have been found inside this territory, and their oaths have become active, tied to yourself as Prince of Dravith and Scion of the Empire.**

*"I swear, upon pain of death, to faithfully execute all that the Emperor decrees. I swear upon my soul that I shall stand for the Empire when it calls. I shall be strong when the weak need me, generous when the poor are at hand, and merciless*

*when my fellow citizens are threatened. I shall worship the Gods of my fathers, respect my elders, and raise up my children to stand tall.*

*"I am an Imperial Citizen. I claim the right to call upon the Legion in my hour of need, to hold those who wrong me to justice, and to be avenged if I cannot be saved."*

**Those who swore the Oath in truth can now sense your location and are pulled to you by its power.**

"Fuck me sideways, that many?" I gasped, then downed the potion, followed by two more in swift succession, grunting as a fresh mana migraine flared and threatened to fuck my day up.

"I didn't have time to adjust for the new legionnaires only," Oracle explained.

I downed another potion, letting out a sigh as my mana bounced like a hooker's arse for a few seconds, and then started to refill.

"Still, we have damn near two hundred of the legion found and brought home." I sighed. "Well done!"

"It's true," Daralen whispered, looking at me as I grinned at her.

"Damn right it is, sister," I said. "You're legion, and you're family. We might be a fucking dysfunctional one, but we're all family, and that's how this works moving forward."

Then I paused, eyeing her and the other legionnaires on all sides. "I mean, that is if you want to remain legionnaires?" I asked, as a sudden fear rose. "I mean, if you want out…"

"No!" she barked, then repeated in a lower voice as she sank to one knee before me. "All hail Jax! Hail Scion and Prince of the Empire!"

A hundred and ninety-five throats roared the same at me a heartbeat later.

I let loose a sigh, before nodding and hauling her to her feet.

"Thank you!" I called out to them all. "I'll be administering oaths to the populations that we recover as we move forward, but for now, know this. There is no more 'just' the legion. You are never 'just' a legionnaire, and I am incredibly proud to stand by each and every goddamn one of you! Also…"

I paused, remembering the phrasing I'd used and pushed more mana into it as Oracle, reading my mind, reached out, guiding me to touch each of them, so that I wasn't wasting mana.

"As of now, and until the Eternal Emperor gainsays my word, I, Prince Jax, Scion of the Empire, revoke the orders and changes to your oath made by Baren Forthright, former noble of the realm. You are bound by the oaths that were originally ordered as part of becoming a legionnaire, not the later additions. And furthermore, you are no longer required to obey the orders of any outside of your direct chain of command and my council. As it was of old, so shall it be again!"

"SO SHALL IT BE AGAIN!" The roar came back as they all felt their conflicted, crappy additional oath-bound orders falling away.

I grinned and turned back to the Primus, noting that Aellin had dropped well back and stood with a bunch of the others.

I almost pulled him forward again, until I saw the way he swallowed and broke eye contact, making me realize what was going on.

He'd deliberately gone looking for a higher member of the legion, and when he had? Instead of standing by my side as someone who wanted to rise up the ranks would have, he'd quietly stepped back. He was a member of the support legion, and even now, when I looked at him, I could see the relief that there were once again legionnaires for him to support.

"Primus," I said firmly, after nodding to Aellin that I understood it. "Was the lord of Marrow someone who gained from the slave trade, and a willing slaver, or someone who fought to make the lives of slaves better in some way, fighting against the degradation and pain?"

I already knew, but fuck it, there were a lot of people hanging back, wanting to see what was about to happen, so I might as well make it clear.

"He was a willing participant and frequently availed himself of his female slaves, until they fell pregnant, often selling them at that point or their children," she said clearly.

I turned to the lord as my anger rose. "He regularly raped his slaves and then sold his own bastard children if they fell pregnant," I translated coldly.

"That is correct, my prince," she said.

I nodded once as the former lord of Marrow started to sob.

"If this piece of shit town was worth claiming as an imperial location, I'd order you to hand it over, but it's just not," I declared before turning to my new Primus. "I want you to make sure he tells us of anything of value he's concealed."

"And then?" she asked as he collapsed to his knees, blubbering out his thanks, attempts at explanations, offers of bribes and more, clearly thinking he was being forgiven and given another chance.

"Hang this scum."

"Yes, my prince!" Daralen declared joyfully.

"Gather up everything he owns and add it to the imperial treasury," I ordered as I lifted into the air, my Soaring Majesty ability drawing gasps from those who saw it. "And Daralen? Feel free to make his passing painful."

With that, I flew across the plaza. People moved as the legion smoothly decamped from the plaza and ran over; only a handful of legionnaires stayed to "discuss" matters with the former lord.

I noted that as much as Daralen clearly wanted to, she wasn't one of them, and my opinion of her grew.

Landing on the far side, now back in the grassy garden and feeling a bit stupid—I was fairly sure I was less than five meters from where I'd been napping earlier—I gestured for people to sit.

It only took a minute or so, though I had to admit the occasional meaty smack or pained wail that drifted over the crowd from the former lord and his new friends definitely helped to keep them all quiet.

"Listen up!" I called out, looking across the sea of faces before me. "I'm not gonna lie to you—the empire I'm rebuilding isn't going to be easy. But it's going to be worth it."

I stood tall, letting my voice carry. "Right now, you're all asking yourselves if you can trust me. If this is real. Well, look around and look at the notifications that you received since I arrived here. Look at the legion who stands with me. Look at those sitting next to you who were slaves an hour ago, now free. That's what the empire means.

"I've got legionnaires who were slaves. I've got members of the Imperial Senate who were slaves and everyone including the bloody bakers who were slaves. I've got people who thought they'd never amount to anything, who are now masters of crafts thought lost for centuries. Why? Because they chose to stand up. They chose to fight back.

"You want proof? I'd love to tell you to ask any of my people about the skills they've gained. The memories they've recovered. The ancient knowledge that we're bringing back. But they're not here. Why aren't they? Because they're back in my home!

"I was fighting to save a team of legionnaires when I was trapped, thrown across the realm by a portal, and I ended up here." I paused, making eye contact with several in the crowd. "I could have turned around. I could have headed for the coast. Hell, I *could* be sitting in a tavern with the woman I love and our friend right now under an assumed name. It'd be a lot easier and frankly, I could sure do with an ale.

"I'm not, though, because I met some people when I first arrived here, people who were escaped slaves. They told me about their lives, and they asked for my help. They're at the back there now. Feel free to ask them about what it means to be free. Really free."

I gestured to where Zyenna and others stood by the wagons, grinning manically and clearly enjoying being the 'old hands' now.

"Now, I'm not gonna pretend this'll be easy. We're going to Sonra next, and yeah, we're going to do our best to free every damn slave in that tent city. Then we're marching on Gaij. There will be blood. There will be pain. And some of us won't make it.

"But I swear this to you: I will never ask you to fight a battle I won't fight myself. I will never abandon you to face the darkness alone. The legion stands with you. The gods—the real gods, not that dark cockwomble's puppets—stand with you." I paused, taking a deep breath and then going on.

"Those who've profited from slavery? You've got a choice to start making it right, and right now. I know that many of you have—there's no way around that in a town that was full of slaves—and while I really hate this, I need to be realistic. From now on, slavery is banned, in every form. If you're alive now, and not horrifically injured, it means that you didn't have a slave control device on you at the time of my freeing those people. That means that, for most of you, you didn't have them. For those who did and you were just goddamn lucky, that it was out of reach, or whatever…

"If that's you, I suggest you either approach a legionnaire and explain your situation, or you run. If you explain it, there's a chance you'll be made to make things right, but you get to live and do better in the future. Alternatively, as I said, you can run. And believe me, I'll remember who runs. Or you can stand with us. Help us free others. Help us rebuild something greater than any of us.

"The empire isn't just about power. It's about standing together. It's about looking at the person next to you and knowing they've got your back. It's about building something that will last long after we're gone.

"So, make your choice. Stay or go. But know this. If you join us, whatever comes next, whatever armies march against us, whatever gods think they can break us, we face it together. As citizens of the empire. As free people."

I stopped there, wanting to say more, feeling like there was so much that still needed to be said and explained. And instead, I forced out a breath, then smiled, before turning to Oracle.

"You ready?" I asked her, and she nodded.

"Better to sit down for this one," she said firmly.

I nodded, turning back to the crowds. "My partner Oracle is going to share the oath with you now. You who don't wish to take it? That's your choice, and I wish you good luck. As such, you can leave. Those who do wish to become citizens of the empire, who want to gain more than they lose, speak the oath, and be welcome!"

I sat, popping the mana potions, and laid four around me, ready. Each was a greater mana potion that Daralen had handed over and could replace four thousand mana at a time. Even with that, and my own manapool as it was, I just hoped that I'd not need them all.

The first voices started to rise a bare heartbeat after I felt my mana drop like a stone.

Oracle had pushed it out, and already people were speaking the oath, not even waiting to read it, which I suppose was a sign in itself.

*"I swear upon pain of death, to faithfully execute all that the Emperor decrees. I swear upon my soul that I shall stand for the Empire when it calls. I shall be strong when the weak need me, generous when the poor are at hand, and merciless when my fellow citizens are threatened. I shall worship the Gods of my fathers, respect my elders, and raise up my children to stand tall.*

*"I am an Imperial Citizen. I claim the right to call upon the Legion in my hour of need, to hold those who wrong me to justice, and to be avenged if I cannot be saved.*

*"I swear to obey Prince Jax and those he places over me; I will serve to the best of my ability, speak no lie to him when commanded otherwise, and treat all other citizens as family.*

*"I will work for the greater good, being a shield to those who need it, a sword to those who deserve it, and a warden to the night."*

*"I will stand with my family, helping one another to reach the light, until the hour of my death or my lord releases me from my Oath.*

*"Lastly, I will not be a dick!"*

The new oath that Oracle had shared was plain and simply a mixture of the other two: the original oath of imperial citizenship, and now the second oath that named me directly, binding these people to me, as there was no emperor.

I spoke up, as the voices trailed off, the taste of the third mana potion minty on my lips as I did.

"I, Lord Jax, do swear to protect and lead you, to be the shield that protects you and yours from the darkness, and the sword that avenges that which cannot be saved. As the Empire grows in strength, so shall you."

That was it, I reflected as hundreds of new threads, each connecting me to a brand-new citizen of the empire, settled into place inside my soul.

"You'll note that important last line there in the oath, that you won't be a dick. For those who aren't sure what that means, it's simple. Look at the things you do and the way you live your life. If you flip it around, and you were on the receiving end of that, how would you feel? If you ask yourself 'am I a dick?' and you don't understand the question, chances are, you're a dick. As such, let's try to help each other a little moving forward, and remember that we're all one family.

"The simplest way to think of it, and I mean this, is that you need to think of everyone around you as family. And yeah, for those who just sniggered and drew a link in your mind between your sexual partners and your family, congratulations— you're a dick.

"For the rest of you, though, think of the people around you as those brothers and sisters. You might not like your brother very much, and hell, the gods know there's days I don't like mine. That's fine. Anyone who wants to hurt him, though? They come through me first. *That's* family. That's us and the rest of the world defined right there. We look after our own, always."

I felt them all—the light of their belief and trust, their love—as the last sections solidified into place, and I drew in a deep breath. From the connection, I could feel the threads that bound us. As opposed to when I did it in Narkolt and most of those who had sworn to me in the throne room were the blues and greens of honor, here, I had the silvers of dedication, shading toward the gold of love. I could literally feel their devotion feeding back to me…their desire to help, to serve, to prove themselves as worthy of being freed.

I didn't have the mana to burn to make the threads visible to all, and thanks to the way that many of the threads passed through others to lead from the originator to me and back, it was difficult to make out who had and who hadn't sworn, but here and there it was obvious.

I felt patches in the tapestry of light that stretched out from me into the hundreds of people on all sides, as those who'd not sworn remained silent, or mumbled along, thinking that it'd be enough.

"Thank you all!" I called out. Then, grinning as I remembered the effect on the gnomes in the depths of the prax, I spoke again. "Now, those who are injured still, please come forward, and I ask everyone else to step back." I pulled three more of the greater potions out and got them ready.

"If you chose to not swear, that is your right, and I respect it. As such, I ask that you leave now, both because things that I share with my people are not for your ears, but also because in order to heal these people, I will draw upon the mana of the area. That is safe to do, for me and my citizens, but it will rip the mana from those who are found to not be aligned, and I have enough deaths on my conscience as it is.

"If anyone thinks that they may have made a mistake in the oath and perhaps it didn't activate fully, then I invite you to go to the wagons there, and speak to Toren or Zyenna. They will protect you and stand ready to bring you to me to take the oath when I'm done."

There was a sudden nervous silence that was then broken as here and there people started to shift.

"Again, if you haven't taken the oath, you have five minutes to leave the town. Please, I don't want you getting hurt, so I suggest you start to run, and right now!"

*"You're evil,"* Oracle whispered to me, and I snorted.

*"You love it."*

*"Oh, I do,"* she agreed. *"I'm going to start building a spell. It won't do anything, but it'll look impressive, and I think I can spare the mana considering it's literally going to do nothing. Warn them that the first phase is starting."*

"We're beginning now. Any citizen who needs healing, please step forward!" I called, feeling the spell as Oracle began to build it. At the same time, I cast Frostfire Circles of Cleansing around me, causing a sudden series of screams as those who were caught in its radius felt and saw the flames.

"Don't panic!" I roared. "They're safe to any citizen!"

There was a brief uproar, but it fell away as people who had moved forward were suddenly lifting injured hands, stripping away bandages, wiping bloody injuries and revealing healed skin beneath.

As the disturbance faded away, Oracle let loose a suppressed giggle and unleashed her spell, a take on the ritual circle that we used for several spells. But in this case, literally all it did was mimic the glow and form a perimeter, one that was much, much larger, covering well out to the wagons and all around us.

Those inside it when it went active, having seen the flames that were climbing over people, suddenly realizing that "maybe" they'd not actually taken the oath and were about to be burned, stampeded out and ran for it.

There were perhaps two dozen across the entire group who hadn't sworn the oaths and who hadn't already left. But as soon as they went, Oracle confirmed to me in the silence of our bond that she could feel no others, and that it was now just our people.

"Okay, everyone. If you've been healed, please move back and I'll recast the first spell here again. It's going to heal anyone who steps into the circle, so if you need it, please step forward!" I called out. Some people had nervous looks on their faces, but the kids were excited to see 'real magic' as a few dozen more moved in and out of the target area. "Don't be afraid. Those who have left hadn't sworn the oaths and were just hanging around for some strange reason…" I let that hang dryly in the air for a minute.

"Now that they're gone, though, let's get a move on! We have wagons here, but not many, and I'm sure that there's more stashed around. The other thing you'll have is supplies, goods, and more that are valuable to us as a group. If you're a merchant, and you owned those goods until now, please go to Zyenna. She's the older woman over there who looks a little too predatory for her own good. She'll make a note of what you're handing over, and I'll make sure you receive fair compensation for it later.

"Make no mistake, though: in three hours, we leave this town. And once we leave, I intend to see it *burn*. There won't be a town here to profit from the slave trade for the next caravan that comes along. I know that means that for many of you, you'll be seeing homes go up in smoke. That's going to be hard on you and I understand it, but frankly this town's a shithole and it deserves it. If you want to live out here, in the middle of a slaver alleyway, then you can rebuild and I hope you learn from the experience."

I paused, then clapped my hands together.

"Legionnaire Primus Daralen, Legionnaire Aellin, Othair, and Toren, I want a word with you now. Everyone else: I suggest you get to work!"

# CHAPTER TWENTY-SIX

"**R**ight, then." I looked at the small group gathered before me as the sounds of organized chaos erupted all around us. The legion again folded around us, forming a little bubble of privacy that also included both Oracle and Sehran. "Primus Daralen, first things first. Please confirm that was your rank and that it was obtained genuinely."

"I was named Legion Primus of the Third Maniple by our legion general after working my way up the ranks, my prince," she replied stiffly.

"I thought that was going to be the case, but considering that you're about to become the de facto legion commander for me for this continent, until you die or I find someone better, I needed to be very sure. I'm sorry, and I hope you understand that. Now, I need a quick assessment of our combat capabilities. How many of your legionnaires are genuinely combat ready? And please don't spin me some bullshit about a legionnaire always being ready. We have nigh on two hundred who have been enslaved until this morning. I don't believe they're all going to snap out of that overnight."

The half-orc straightened, her bearing purely professional despite the earlier emotional moments. "One hundred and twelve are combat effective, my prince. The rest…" She grimaced. "The rest need time to recover, both physically and mentally. Many were used as arena fighters or guards, but weren't permitted proper training or equipment maintenance. And many are also missing limbs, or are otherwise unable to serve as they once did."

"Oracle?" I glanced at her.

"Depending on the severity of the injury, we can probably heal anywhere from five to thirty a day," she said. "Fingers, for example, won't be too bad; entire legs will take a lot longer and more mana."

"That'll be the first step, though I'm sorry to say, Daralen, that means we need to focus on those who are most likely to be able to assist us first. Those who are physically broken but mentally fine will be the priority, as shitty as I feel saying that. Those who are incapacitated will be cared for. We'll do everything we can for them, but to keep them safe and make sure they get that chance, the combat-capable must be brought up to peak condition first. Of those combat effective, how many can march at legion pace?" I asked, already doing calculations in my head.

"Perhaps seventy, though that number will improve rapidly once proper equipment is distributed." She glanced at my armor, then quickly looked away.

"I don't have more armor with me," I said. "And most of the legion's equipment that we do have was literally the armor that those legionnaires had. I don't suppose there are any supply caches in the area you know of?"

"If there were, we'd have raided them long before now," Daralen admitted. "Though some of us were permitted to retain our armor, most had it sold out from under them. Some of the shops in the town have it, though, or other, lower quality equipment."

"Send people to recover it, and anything you feel we need," I said. "Those who refused to swear to the empire are not to be attacked unless they attack you, but this town is now under the control of the empire. We will honor a debt to those merchants who joined us for the equipment claimed, but that's going to be paid further down the line. And frankly, it'll be on a case-by-case basis.

"If they were abusing slaves to make their fortune but simply were lucky enough to not be caught, then they're not going to like how they're 'repaid.' If they weren't absolute shits, then when we get some space and can work things out, they're going to do well out of it. All of life is a risk, though." I shrugged.

"If those who haven't sworn attempt to lay claim to items that belong to the legion and the empire?" Daralen asked formally.

"Then they're thieves," I said. "Make them aware of the distinction, and give them a chance to change their position. If not, then remove the items with as much force as is necessary. I don't like it, but frankly, this was a town full of slavers. They ought to be damn thankful any of them besides the freed slaves are being given the freedom to breathe my air.

"I also want you to check on the guard, as I know you'll have had the chance to meet them by now, and I'd imagine you probably have your own experiences with them. See how many swore to the empire and how many are actually trustworthy. Question them. If you believe they can be rehabilitated, then they join the caravan as guards. If not, then let me know. I seriously doubt many would have joined us when they could have run instead, knowing how the legion and the empire views slavery, but there's always one idiot somewhere. If you need me, come see me and I'll release them from their oaths and send them running. Or we can look at a form of service to make up for their past crimes."

Daralen nodded, a quirk of the lips letting me know how ready she was to deal with the guard.

"To be clear, my intention, here as it is back on Dravith, is that *all* forces we take are to serve as part of the legion. That may be as auxiliaries or to join the legion proper. Regardless, the legion command structure will be one they obey, so they might as well get fuckin' used to it now.

"Othair." I turned to the chamberlain. "You know this region. There was a caravan that passed this way most recently, a day, two at most ago. What's the fastest route to catch up to them, then on to Sonra that can support our numbers?"

The chamberlain didn't hesitate. "The main road would be quickest, my prince, but it's also the most watched. Local bandits will have informants watching along the trails. There is another route, through the eastern grasslands, but it adds perhaps half a day's travel."

"And requires us to feed and water several hundred people while crossing open country," Oracle added, her practical nature coming to the fore. "Though I can help with the water, the slavers we're chasing would draw ahead again."

I nodded, considering our options. "Aellin, Toren. What's your assessment of the wagons and supplies we've gathered?"

The dwarf legionnaire stepped forward, his earlier uncertainty forgotten as he focused on logistics. "We've fifty-three wagons now, my prince, including those we brought. Good solid construction mostly, though some will need work. The issue isn't transport capacity, it's speed. A wagon train that size will move slowly, especially across open ground."

"What if we split our forces?" Sehran suggested, causing everyone to look at her. "A fast-moving advance force to catch the slavers, while the main group follows at a safer pace, with scouts to hunt down any spies on the road."

I saw Daralen nod approvingly at the tactical suggestion, but Othair shook his head. "The slavers who left yesterday morning had at least two hundred fighters with them, and, forgive me if you're unaware, but they met the…gentleman you fought earlier and the former lord of Marrow. They are led by a member of the Sons of the Deep—one of their founding fathers, to hear him tell it—and a small force would be at severe disadvantage."

"Unless," I smiled, "that small force happens to include a group of legionnaires who are rescuing some of their own."

"Jax…" Oracle's warning tone was clear.

"We stormed this town and took it with fifty-four legionnaires. I'm willing to go on faith that a group of fifty legionnaires can take out two hundred slavers."

"They'll be supplemented by at least another several hundred of the undead. This is a Sons of the Deep caravan, after all," Aellin pointed out.

I snorted. "Fucking please." I shook my head. "We were chasing them with our group until we hit the city. If you thought we were going to have issues taking them down with just fifty-four legionnaires from the support maniple, what's the problem with fifty legionnaires from the Third?"

"Well, you see, my prince…" Aellin said slowly, as if trying to share a sensitive secret. "We might be the Fifth Maniple, I admit, but we were the Legion of Sanketh. The Legion of Gaij, although they're very good people, they tend to do a lot less real work, and spend a lot more time in the tower…entertaining."

There was a long, drawn-out moment of silence, as I looked from the smile that threatened to break out on his face to the slowly spreading look of outrage on Daralen's. Then I burst out laughing.

"Aellin, I love it." I grinned. "Daralen, I should point out to you that I'm an ex-enlisted myself, what you'd count as a legionnaire, and I tend to run my empire with a rule of formality only when required.

"Aellin just landed that one perfectly, and I can't wait to see how you get him back. Seriously, though, can you do it, and can you give me fifty legionnaires?" I finished, looking at her.

"I can," she said grimly. "Though I believe the first rule I will be reinstating for all legionnaires will be mandatory fitness assessments as soon as we've finished this meeting."

Aellin winced at that, though I also noticed that the horror and look of stunned betrayal on her face had vanished, replaced by a slight smile that tugged at the corner of her lips.

"They can be from whatever legion you decide, any mixture of skills, as long as they can damn well fight," I clarified for her. "And as long as those left behind can guarantee the caravan's safety."

"There are no guarantees in this life, my prince," she replied calmly. "Though I will do the most that is possible with what I have."

"That's all anyone can expect or ask." I nodded. "Okay, for the avoidance of doubt, let me make myself very clear on this, and the chain of command. I am the Prince of the Empire, yes, but back on Dravith, I have a named heir, should anything happen to me. He is Duke Augustus of Himnel, a primus of the Legion of Himnel, and frankly a far better man than I'll ever be. He spent his life in the legion, and is an absolute unholy terror with any and all weapons."

I saw the look of interest and approval on the faces of both Aellin and Daralen at that.

"There is, however, soon to be another heir." I smiled, reaching out and taking Oracle's hand in my own. "This is Oracle. She is the love of my life, my partner, and one day when we sort all this shit out, she'll be my empress. She is also pregnant with our child."

I saw the way that the legionnaires on all sides shifted slightly at that declaration, and the way that their interest and focus changed.

"I am not human, not entirely," Oracle declared. "I was a wisp, originally bound to my Jax through magical means to save his life. As our bond strengthened, in a fight with a creature known as the Valspar, one of the ancient enemies of life, and thanks to the intervention of the Eternal Emperor Amon himself, I was changed."

She left out that it was because he almost killed her, being a fixated dick on a rampage.

"Jax and I now share a soul, meaning that as well as my form being changed to one that is unique in the realms to the best of my knowledge, my life is now bound ever more deeply to his own. Should he perish, so shall I, and so will our child."

"So," I said very clearly, "if Oracle gives an order, I want it understood that she's giving that order as if it was my word. We share a soul, a link that enables us to speak privately across great distances, and will soon share a throne. As such, you will protect her. Do I make myself clear?

"The unborn child she carries will most likely take my place on any throne we claim, and where I and Augustus can and will rip anyone a new arsehole who tries to attack us, that child is currently unable to defend itself. Their future, the *literal* future of the empire, is in your hands."

"We will NOT fail you, my prince!" she swore, her eyes bright, and I nodded.

"I didn't expect you to, or I'd not be having you lead the legion here," I said bluntly. "Oracle will be close to me most of the time, but no matter the situation, I need her safety to be an absolute priority for your people. Back in Dravith, I have a small team of stealth experts who act as bodyguards, and although it annoys me frequently, I also know that they're absolutely needed and we will be looking to add to their number."

"I…" She paused then hung her head, almost ashamed. "I regret to admit that we have no stealth specialists." She sighed. "Those who were skilled in those areas were generally ordered to escape when the rest of us were captured. And should there be many legions out there operating still, they will be making extensive use of such members."

"Then we'll recruit and train," I said. "I'm not precious about them being from the legion only. Hell, only a handful of my closest, literally my personal unit, are legion, or were at the beginning.

"Now they're led by an Optio, and she's…well." I couldn't help but smile proudly at the thought of Lydia. "She's a Valkyrie and an absolute legend in her own way. The first of a new class, and she's both their leader and, knowing her, their big sister—not to mention being utterly furious at me for getting so far out of her sight. When she arrives, you'll see her temper firsthand."

"That sounds like a treat to behold," she said.

I sighed. "It is what it is. You'll all no doubt have questions about Sehran as well…" I indicated the gorgeous succubus who stood close by, watching over us all. "She's a member of my team, and for the avoidance of any doubt, we're not fucking, and she's not, to the best of my knowledge, looking for 'friends with benefits.'" I made air quotes, before growling to myself as I remembered that nobody here had a clue what they were.

"I'm not," Sehran clarified. "I have two lovers, and they are approaching now, but they're still many weeks out. We aren't looking to expand our group, though I thank you for the interest, if that was in your mind."

"Regardless, she's, as I say, a member of my team, and not because of any sexual antics. She earned it on her own, and her loyalty to me is in no doubt. She has all the abilities of the succubai, but as you'll understand, if you think about it, those being used against your enemies make a hell of a difference. Especially when they're not expecting them."

"I'm reasonable at stealth, but better at distraction." She smiled.

"I'm sure." Daralen seemed to have relaxed a little, and I was willing to bet that a lot of her racial concerns had been put aside when she realized that the new prince was to marry—one day—a creature of mixed races.

That had to give her some hope that in the future, she'd not be quite as looked down upon by the new nobility for her own mixed parentage.

The legion had clearly accepted her for all she was, as evidenced by her making it to primus, but the nobility?

"Now that you know who these two reprobates are, returning to our tactical situation." I looked around at them all. "We need to catch those slavers before they reach Sonra, and I'd personally love to do it before they link up with any other caravans. We also need to get there in time for my little appointment with a goddess."

"Seven days," Oracle reminded me. "Less now."

"Six and a half." I nodded. "Othair, tell me about the route options again, but this time include any potential dangers or advantages we should know about."

The chamberlain straightened, inclining his head, before spreading out a map on the ground, showing the local area. Although it wasn't magical, it was impressive with how detailed it was.

The town of Marrow was a speck on the map by the bottom right, and looking over it, I realized that it didn't actually show much of the continent at all, just fading out the farther it went.

Instead, the map showed the entirety of the "great plains" and showed Sonra as a series of marks. A trail of imperfectly rubbed out prior marks made it clear that it was updated on a regular basis.

Sonra was moving through an area of the plains that appeared to be higher than the land we were on, and I grunted, having noticed the hills far in the distance.

They were apparently reached through a series of either sharp or rolling inclines, or through specific passes that were marked as well-worn roads.

I guessed that made it a lot more convenient for raiders, but as the caravans passing through here mainly dealt in human misery, I didn't really give two shits.

"The main road, here, as I mentioned, is the fastest but most watched. It runs through three small settlements before reaching Sonra, each with defenses. The eastern grassland route is less traveled, but crosses through territory claimed by the horse clans."

"Horse clans?" I glanced at Daralen, who nodded grimly.

"Nomadic raiders. They breed and train warhorses, and they're not fond of outsiders crossing their lands. They also have…arrangements with the slavers. Information for coin, mostly."

"And the western route?" Sehran asked.

"Marshlands." Othair shook his head. "Impassable for wagons, and home to things far worse than raiders."

I considered our options. "The slavers took the main road?"

"They always do," Daralen confirmed. "The roads themselves are primarily made by the slavers. As much as Sonra claims to hate slavery, they never try to stop the market. And when it coincides with their annual gathering of the clans like this? It's huge. Tens of thousands attend.

"That's why the slavers are gathering, caravans passing through daily. They're all heading to Sonra to buy and sell with the expectation of becoming very, very rich."

"Tell me about Sonra," I asked, and it was Othair who started it off.

"The tent city of Sonra is a nomadic one, wagons and tents that follow the great herds—bison, mammoth, varm, and horses mainly—and it's run by three clans.

"The inner ring is clan territory only. If you're not a full member of the clan— and that means by birth *and* standing, not one or the other—you don't get into there.

"The second ring of the city is for their relatives; no guests or merchants are allowed deeper than the first few rows of tents. They also make it very clear that it's a territory that is free. No slave is a slave once they set foot inside the ring, and anyone who uses a control device to drag a slave out—or injure them in any way— is stealing from the clans.

"They're executed and their group banned from Sonra. And by group? That can mean their friends and family. Or, if they're wearing colors, like they're guards from a nearby city, then any member of that city is banned until 'the way has been cleared' between Sonra and them.

"I have no way of knowing the details of such negotiations, but generally from the rumors I've heard, they include ten times the value of the incident being paid to Sonra. That might be a gold coin, or a wagon full. They assign 'value' in ways that aren't always clear.

"The clans of Sonra run everything. They're nomadic, as I said, and are split into a dozen smaller and three larger clans, with a council-based system of governance. Sonra is split up into twelve camps, each based in the first two rings."

"Do we know the names of the three greater clans?" Oracle asked, and Othair nodded.

"The Vhyrakai, led by Matriarch Ilena Vhyrakai; the Kreonar, led by the brothers Daven and Malik Kreonar; and finally, the Suntari. The Suntari are led by Lord Commander Reth Suntari, or they were as of the last information we have.

"The Vhyrakai breed the horses, and have both great horse herds, and a smaller varm population…"

"Varm?" I held up a hand to stop him.

"Ah…similar to deer?" he suggested. "Fast moving, light on their feet, but primarily meat eaters. Hence the small herd. They're both valued for food and for scout mounts, as they can survive on pretty much anything that breathes."

"Got it. Sorry, carry on."

"Yes, my prince, ah…okay, the Kreonar are primarily responsible for the bison, mammoths, and other larger beasts, as well as overall the health of the town. Where the Vhyrakai guide the largest of the herds, the Kreonar look after the people and are the primary negotiators. Many of the nobles across the great grasslands wish Sonra to pass through their lands due to the increased fertility—a year or more down the line—such a movement causes."

"But it fucks the little people in the short term." I nodded. "Got that."

"Very much so," Othair agreed. "The final group is the Suntari. They are the warriors of Sonra, both a police force—with very few laws—and a defensive group. They claim to never start a fight, but will always finish it."

"Considering their elite ride mammoths into battle, they don't tend to leave many around after to make complaints." Daralen scowled. "The legion and Sonra should be natural allies, due to our stance on things like slavery, but we're not."

"Why not?"

"Because if they decide the legion breaks their laws—like fighting to free slaves in the third ring—then we're banned from Sonra and hunted down."

"They hunt the legion?" I growled.

"Yes, but also…" She hesitated, clearly wanting me on her side with this, but needing to be truthful. "They have a point, and they make it clear whenever we enter the city. They also don't hold us all responsible for the actions of a group, which is in itself unique. They punish that group—they do. I've lost friends and legionnaires to Sonra killing them for fighting in the ring, but they also accept a token payment, when others are punished a lot harsher."

"Okay, sounds like there's something there." I nodded.

**Quest discovered: What Secrets Does Sonra Hold?**

*Your Goddess Jenae is curious: why do the guardians of Sonra grant special privileges to the legion, and yet execute them unwaveringly for their transgressions?*

*Discover the truth and you shall be rewarded…*

**Reward: ?/? followers, 50,000xp**

**Do you accept?**

**Yes/No…**

I read it as it popped up and snorted, then accepted it. Clearly Jenae had given up on the whole 'staying at arms' reach' and was now watching over me again. I focused and grinned as the others blinked, apparently receiving the quest that I shared as well.

"Thank you, my prince…" Othair smiled, and I nodded.

"No worries, but in the future, when it's like this…please, for the love of the gods, quit with the formality?" I asked. "Call me Jax if you want, all of you. When we're in public and there's a need for formality, fine. But when we're in conversations like this, it just grates on me and wastes everyone's time. Now, go on."

"Thank you…Jax." He nodded. "Where was I? Ah! So, the inner two rings are made up of the twelve clans, while the third ring is primarily merchants and support groups, or those who follow the city and have no fixed place in it—wagons of minor clans and mobile smithies, tinkerers, etc.—there are strict rules in there.

"One of the main rules is 'no fighting' but that comes with very unusual workarounds, as things like challenges for honor are commonplace. There're three arenas that are generally spaced out across the third ring and the 'outside,' and they have set spaces in them for honor battles as well as regular fights.

"There are also less honorable things done there, gambling on things such as animal fights, and fighting between the weak, destitute, and children against monsters."

"So why the hell are the legion getting killed for fighting, if you can fight for honor there?" I asked.

"Because when a legionnaire sees a slave, we have to intervene by the oaths," Daralen said. "If a slave is being beaten, forced, or injured in some way, we are compelled to intervene, and when that happens…"

"Got it. That's why I removed those fucking stupid additions," I growled. "So, to be clear, it's more a case of the legion not doing it by their laws, than a case of they don't like the legion. Okay. Also, there are slaves in the third ring?"

"Occasionally," Othair said. For the first time, there was an edge of anger in his voice. "Most slavers don't want the risk, and they know that Sonra and her people disagree with slavery, so they don't want to annoy them. But others, like the former lord of Marrow, like to take their slaves up to the line of the second ring and order us not to cross, then place bets on whether we can survive disobeying them."

"And you die if you disobey." I nodded. "Got it. Basically, it's a torture game, and one they make money on. The Sonra don't stop it?"

"Some will; some guards of Sonra join in the bets. There are twelve clans spread out across the second ring. Many of them don't agree with the no slavery rule."

"Great. Okay, third ring is all merchants, shitehawks, and camp followers. What else is there?" I asked.

"The third ring is much, much larger than the first two. It is also separated from the inner two by the herds, tens of thousands of animals. So, the third ring isn't like the first two in that it's a heavily populated area; instead, it's more lots of camps that are set up around the others, with the herds filling the gaps.

"The 'outside,' which basically covers everything that Sonra doesn't care about, or at least professes not to, includes the slavers and camps that are set up to provide things they won't permit inside. Like the death pits, places where those with the coin to pay for it can buy slaves and literally murder them for whatever reason. Some of those are smaller arenas, generally dirt ones with spectators, and others are specially designed tents or wagons to shield the noise. They're also set up a minimum distance of a mile back from the third ring, meaning that on arrival to Sonra, you're likely to see other smaller, spaced-out camps first. These are those who aren't permitted closer, and are invariably the kind who are most likely to be hostile to your rise, my prince.

"As a final explanation of those places, they tend to have whorehouses attached, so that if the visitor wishes for a different kind of entertainment, or if they decide they're willing to pay the fine, they can enjoy themselves both ways."

"Fuck me sideways," I growled. "And Sonra permits that?"

"It's outside," he pointed out. "They don't claim to police the world, just inside their rings."

"Okay, so first off, they hate slavery?" I asked for clarification.

"They do. Although they won't involve themselves in it outside their rings, if a slave makes it inside the second ring, they're free, and they also buy slaves, and free them."

"Go over that." I nodded, interested.

"They buy specialist slaves, and they're brought inside the rings and are given their freedom. They get to live in the second ring, but they're warned that they owe their cost to Sonra, so for however long, they earn that back. I will say, though, Sonra provides basic sustenance, shelter, protection, and all to their workers, and they don't charge them for it. The average slave is paid off and free in three to five years, according to rumor."

"And more expensive slaves?" I asked.

"It depends. They're all paid a flat wage against their debt as they work, so a higher skilled slave will take longer. But given the choice, I guarantee those slaves are happy they've got the chance."

"But add in that there's a lot of slavers who surround Sonra all the time and the general scum that a nomadic city with lax laws and set boundaries brings, not to mention massive wealth, and you can imagine how many of those former slaves ever leave Sonra again," Aellin pointed out.

"So, still a borderline 'are they bastards or not' situation." I nodded. "Okay, so as we get closer to Sonra, there's going to be a lot of people, but there's roads here, and you said that the city is nomadic. Why aren't there rambling roads going in all directions if people all want to get there?"

"Sonra tours the Great Plains, and despite their size, the herds move slowly. The city is generally set up in a single location for about two days, then it's broken down and moved again. With the herds always on the move, the city simply sets up at the head of the herd, then it's at the middle, then the back, and moves again." Othair gestured clearly to make sure we understood the way that it moved constantly.

"To tour the entire Great Plains takes an average of thirty years for such vast herds, and they limit their 'visits' to places that pay them enough and that can sustain the herds. As such, there are limited passes and locations to access the plains, moving from the area around us. It's simply logical to include certain stops along the route. Then the caravans reach the plains and trek along, following the route until they reach it."

"Fair enough." I grunted, having not been that interested anyway. "The slavers ahead of us…if we take fifty of the legion and we leave everyone else to protect the caravan, which takes the longer, safer route, we can catch them?" I asked.

"Depending on the route they've taken and how fast they're going, I'd estimate that you could catch them within perhaps two days. They made it clear that although they were travelling to Sonra, they intended to make several other stops along the way to trade as they went," Othair said. "Though that is based on little more than conjecture. I am unsure how quickly the legion could move, unburdened."

"Daralen?" I asked.

Daralen's expression turned predatory as she did the calculations. "Unencumbered by wagons, and with only legionnaires? We can maintain roughly forty miles per day, more if we push it. At that pace, we'll catch them at this pass within two days at most. Depending on how hard they're pushing, perhaps as little as a day."

She pulled the map around and tapped one of the stopping-off points that had been marked up.

"That fast?" Othair looked startled. "Even the fastest messengers only manage thirty…"

"The fastest messengers aren't legionnaires," Daralen replied with quiet pride. "And they're not trying to rescue their own."

"Or chasing slavers," I added with a grim smile. "All right, let's talk specifics about this pass. What are we looking at?"

Daralen gestured, sketching a rough map in the dirt with a knife. "The cliffs rise about two hundred feet on either side. The road narrows to maybe twenty feet at its tightest point. Caravans have to go single file through there."

"Perfect killing ground," Sehran observed.

"For either side," Oracle cautioned. "We need to control those cliff tops."

I nodded, amused by the tactician side to my love. "Agreed. Daralen, I want your best climbers. We'll take the high ground first, then hit them from both sides when they're in the narrows."

"They'll have sentries," Othair pointed out.

"They will," I agreed. "But they'll be watching for bandits or maybe cavalry raiders. They won't be expecting legionnaires scaling cliff faces in the dark to get into position."

"And they certainly won't be expecting me," Sehran added with a predatory smile.

"Or a pissed-off prince." Oracle sighed, but I could see the hint of a smile. "Just…try not to bring the entire pass down on our heads?"

"Hey, that was *one* time…" I protested, playing along, then turned back to Daralen. "How soon can you have your fifty ready?"

"Give me thirty minutes to select them and gather equipment. We'll need climbing gear, light rations, water…"

"Take what you need, but remember, speed is our priority. The lighter we travel, the faster we move. And we can provide water, through spells, that will also heal injuries."

She nodded sharply. "Understood. Permission to begin selection?"

"Granted. And Daralen?" I caught her eye. "Pick the ones who most want those slavers dead. We're not taking prisoners this time."

Her answering smile was fierce. "That won't be a problem, Jax."

As she strode away to begin her selections, I turned to the others. "Aellin, the main caravan is yours to protect. Keep them moving but don't take risks. Better to arrive late than not at all."

"We'll get them there," he promised. "Though, honestly, I'm not that high a rank. I was hoping…"

"You *weren't* that high a rank," I agreed. "That'll be changing, though. You did well, my friend, and if you don't want more responsibility…well, that's tough. Where I come from, it's called the 'curse of competence' and you're infected with it. Besides, I trust you." I cut him off as he tried to say something. "These people trust you as well. Besides," I grinned, "someone needs to keep Zyenna from taking over the whole operation."

That got a reluctant chuckle from him. "Fair point. Gods help us all if she decides she's in charge…"

"You think it's bad—she's a damn merchant, not a caravan master, and she's still telling me how to run the caravan," Toren muttered to the legionnaire.

"Start standing up to her then!" I laughed. "If I wanted her running it all, I'd have named her to it. Toren, you want to run the caravan, it's time you started acting like it."

"I wish I'd stayed home," he muttered, to a general chorus of laughter.

# CHAPTER TWENTY-SEVEN

My fingers found another crack in the rock face as I hauled myself higher, the stone cold and rough against my armored gauntlets. The moon was a bare sliver above, providing just enough light to make out the larger handholds, but leaving the finer details to touch and instinct for those without Darkvision or other such ability.

Two hundred feet below, the narrow pass wound like a black ribbon through the cliffs.

We'd pushed hard to reach this point, running for nearly twenty-eight hours straight. Even with Oracle's healing spells at our brief rest stops, I could feel the bone-deep weariness in every legionnaire around me. But not one had complained; not one had slowed.

The thought of their enslaved brothers and sisters so close to hand had driven them on.

*"Ten more feet,"* Oracle sent through our bond. She floated nearby, keeping watch while we climbed. Through her eyes, I could see the scattered positions of our people along the cliff face, fifty dark shapes moving with careful precision upward.

A loose stone clattered down somewhere to my left, followed by a muffled curse. I froze, every muscle tensed as I listened for any reaction from below. The slavers' caravan was still a mile back down the pass, their torches visible as dim points of light in the darkness, but sound carried strangely in these narrow walls.

"Clear." Sehran's voice drifted down from above. She'd taken point, her flight and ability to sense life making her perfect for scouting the route. "But there's a handful of figures on the opposite ridge. Looks like they've posted sentries after all."

I eased myself up another few feet, finding a narrow ledge that let me brace and take some weight off my arms. The rock was treacherous here. Centuries of wind and rain had worn away any sharp edges, leaving deceptively smooth surfaces that could crumble without warning.

*"How many?"* I asked through the bond.

*"Three that I can see,"* Sehran replied after a moment. *"Two with crossbows, one with what looks like a signal horn. They're not paying much attention, though...more focused on staying warm than watching."*

I nodded grimly. Overconfidence would work in our favor. The Sons of the Deep were used to being the predators, not the prey. They wouldn't be expecting an attack from above, especially not one led by a pissed-off lunatic and fifty equally angry legionnaires.

*"Keep an eye on them. Let me know if they see us,"* I ordered her, and I felt her agreement.

The climb had taken longer than I'd like, but we needed everyone in position before the caravan entered the narrowest part of the pass. From what we'd seen of their pace, we had maybe an hour before their lead elements reached that point. Enough time to get set up, but not much margin for error. And that the bastards were determined to camp at the top of the pass, instead of the bottom, had made things so much worse.

We'd expected them to stop for the night—they *should* have stopped for the night—but clearly, they were pushing on. I didn't like what that implied.

*"Another handhold just above your right shoulder,"* Oracle guided me. *"But be careful, the rock's not as stable as it looks."*

I tested it carefully before trusting my weight to it. Even through my gauntlet, I could feel the way the stone shifted slightly. Getting up this cliff was one thing; getting back down might be a lot quicker, though, if I allowed myself to keep getting distracted.

It was also a hell of a lot harder, because I'd expected that there'd be a general stripping off of armor to do it. No such luck. The legion were used to doing this kinda shit in full armor, because all too often when they reached the top, there were monsters, maniacs, or worse waiting for them.

When it took even an experienced legionnaire at least a few minutes to clamber into their armor again, it was just a better idea to train them to live in it.

I, because of course I had, had decided that if they could do it, so could I. I enjoyed climbing years ago, though doing it in full plate armor was a different and much more humbling experience. It also meant that I was close enough that if someone fell, I could fly and catch them.

That was my excuse, anyway, and I was damn well sticking to it. It wasn't because I felt like if I flew up and sat waiting it'd be a shitty thing to do.

A sudden gust of wind sent loose pebbles rattling down the cliff face. I pressed myself closer to the rock, feeling the bite of cold through my armor. The night air carried the scent of rain. A storm was coming, which could either help or hurt us, depending on timing.

*"My love."* Oracle's mental voice held a note of concern. *"The undead in their group...they're being unloaded. Something's making the slavers more cautious."*

*"Have they spotted us?"*

*"I don't think so. Not at this range. It might just be what we thought, that this is the perfect place for an ambush, so they're getting ready for one."*

*"Well, that's not happy making."* I sighed. *"How long until they reach us?"*

*"Hard to tell in this light,"* Oracle replied. *"But based on their current speed and the terrain...maybe forty minutes? They're carefully moving their wagons, especially with the undead on foot now."*

I finally reached the top, hauling myself over the edge and rolling to take cover behind an outcropping of rock. My armor scraped against stone despite my best efforts at silence. Around me, other legionnaires found their own positions, spreading out along the cliff edge in prearranged groups.

Daralen appeared beside me like a ghost, her mixed heritage giving her excellent night vision. "All teams are nearly in position," she whispered. "But we have a problem."

"Besides the undead being deployed?" I asked dryly.

"Look at their formation." She gestured down at the approaching caravan. "They're not moving like they're worried about bandits. Those undead are being staggered in rows, but I didn't understand the pattern. It might be something I'm just unfamiliar with, but we need to be cautious."

I studied the scene below, letting my Darkvision adjust.

There were seventy wagons in all, I guessed. Forty or so were filled to the absolute brim with trade goods, presumably the remainder of the wagons that had made up the caravan. Then came the wagons that I guessed that the Sons of the Deep had brought, as they were little more than mobile cages. There were six wheels on them, a massive, iron-barred monstrosity of a cage complete with manacles that hung from the roof, and a gate at one end, to load and unload the "stock" from.

The roof was made of bars as well, presumably because as they apparently didn't bother to stop for things like bathroom breaks, the wagons would stink to high heaven in short order. Instead, the rain washed them clear. Looking them over, it was obvious that either they reserved the collars for certain slaves, or they simply only carried a certain amount, magical as they were, as dozens wearing them marched alongside each wagon, or as now, were standing listless and hopeless, awaiting their next orders.

The wagons with the manacles presumably were to hold the majority in as efficient a manner as possible.

I saw that, and then I saw the wagons on either side of the slaves.

They held row upon row of silent undead, standing in what were apparently boxes to prevent degradation and damage from the elements, because they, unlike the slaves, were valued.

Ahead of the slaves and their keepers were the masters. And they, in comparison, travelled in the lap of goddamn luxury.

Three articulated wagons like the one that Oracle, Sehran, and I had been using were next, clearly keeping ahead of the slaves and what I presumed was a general smell, no matter what you did and the rain that fell.

These wagons were lit by the flickering light of candles or fires, glowing manastones and torches depending on their inhabitants' taste, and had warriors who stood atop them, who rode by the sides, or who sat next to drivers.

Small sections of each had, again like my own, a covered portico where the masters could stand out of the rain and give orders, and for two of them, that was what was happening.

One appeared to have nobody currently in it, but it was the unique wagon at the back that drew my eyes the most. It, like the others, had a few smaller boxlike wagons ahead and behind it for the undead to be transported in their containers.

It, however, was clearly the home of the caravan's primary necromancer, and it was a hive of activity.

The entire wagon at this distance seemed to be made of bones and leather, with ten undead riding it, spaced a few meters apart, standing tall on the roof. They were armed and waiting, with a single unimpressive figure waving his arms wildly in their midst.

Daralen was right. The shambling corpses that were still unloading from the transports weren't just wandering alongside the wagons; they were moving in disciplined ranks, with what looked like more aware undead directing them.

"Fuck me sideways," I muttered. "They've got at least a few with actual military experience, and the undead look a lot more prepared than the usual."

"More than that," Sehran whispered. "They're setting up defensive positions at regular intervals. Someone down there knows what they're doing."

"Makes sense," Oracle added. "The Sons of the Deep have been doing this for years, maybe centuries. They'd have picked up tactical knowledge along the way. And if they have a skilled enough necromancer, he could harvest the knowledge of others to create a leader."

I watched as more undead were deployed, their movements eerily precise in the darkness. What I'd hoped would be a straightforward ambush was rapidly becoming more complicated.

"Options?" I asked quietly.

"We still have surprise," Daralen pointed out. "And the high ground. But we lose a lot of that advantage if we don't strike before they're fully deployed…"

"And they're forty minutes away, so no chance of us beating that. And I'm guessing that they know someone's here, so there goes the surprise as well," I finished. "How many of your people are in position?"

She did a quick hand signal check with her subordinates. "Forty-three up, seven still climbing. Five minutes at most."

I nodded, mind racing through scenarios. The undead complicated things. They didn't feel fear, didn't break ranks, and had to be completely destroyed to stop them. But they also had weaknesses…

"Oracle, what's the maximum range we can cast the frostfire circle?"

"I think we can manage about fifty meters, but that's going to be the maximum range," she admitted. "And it's going to cost double."

"Okay, so let's look at the ground with the plan changing to a magical attack." I shrugged. "We can't attack the wagons with it, but we could…"

"Hsst!" Another legionnaire waved to get our attention.

I looked over, seeing Daralen scowl at the increased likelihood of us being spotted due to the movement.

It was worth it, though, as he pointed at the far ridge, and the trio of watchers fighting another group of figures.

"Okay…what's going on here?" I asked, even as Sehran grabbed my arm, gesturing into the distance.

"There!" she whispered.

I nodded, seeing, at the very limit of my vision, figures hurrying from rock to rock, forming up in small groups and clearly ready to hit the slavers.

"Shit, now we know why they're forming up," I growled. "There's an attack coming. Raiders maybe?"

"No, we're not raiders," called a new voice.

I spun, hands coming up and ready for a fight, fists balled. Three more figures stepped out of stealth only a handful of meters away from our outermost pickets.

I checked left and right, feeling Sehran stiffen; her grip on my armor made it creak as she hissed.

*"There's at least two dozen of them stealthed still! I'm sorry!"*

*"Just be ready,"* I replied, knowing that if the front line were good enough to hide from her in stealth, then there was no way that the legionnaires—after Daralen had pointed out that they had literally nobody who was any good at stealth left—could be expected to have seen them.

That meant this was on me, because I was so used to Tang, Bane, and Yen clearing the way for us. When Sehran had spotted the figures on the far side, I'd just assumed that meant there was nobody else around, and I'd damn well ordered her to focus on them.

Now, even as I glanced back, I saw that those on overwatch for the enemy had been eliminated, and we were surrounded.

"Ah, ah, ah!" came another voice.

I looked over to my right, seeing a figure holding a crossbow that was just this side of being rated as a siege weapon.

"The first hint of magic from any of you, or a song, and I fire."

It was also aimed squarely at Sehran.

She was many things but what she wasn't, was faster than a crossbow, and certainly not when the bolt wouldn't look out of place hanging under a F16's wing.

"I fucking hate stabby-stabby bastard rogues!" I snarled.

"Well, we hate you too," the first speaker said coldly. "Right now, the only reason you're alive is that we're curious, so don't do anything to piss us off, or you'll regret it."

"Save your breath," the crossbowman said quietly. "You know what they are."

"That's yet to be seen," the first figure said. "If you want to live, you stay silent, and still. We've got a hundred of us up here, and we've been watching you climb for the last hour. These crossbows will punch through your armor easily at this range."

*"I think I can pick out, maybe forty?"* Oracle sent through our bond.

*"I've got five,"* I sent back. *"They're probably bluffing about their numbers, but they've still got us at a disadvantage."*

The speaker moved forward slightly. In the dim light, I could make out scarring around his neck. The kind left by a slave collar worn too long. His eyes held the hard look of someone who'd seen too much and survived anyway.

"You're wearing legion armor," he stated flatly. "But they don't paint their gear. So what's your game?"

"We're Imperial Legion," Daralen replied before I could, her voice carrying pride despite our predicament. "We're here to free—"

"The Imperial Legion?" another voice cut in with bitter laughter. "Where was the Imperial Legion when we were being sold? When our children were being taken?"

"Not you incompetents!" another hissed. "By the burned one's left tit, I was hoping they were bandits wearing stolen gear."

"Incompetents?!" a legionnaire growled, and I frantically waved at him and Daralen to settle down.

"Fuck's sake, calm down, all of you," I snapped before I raised my hands slowly, keeping them visible. "We're here now. And we're after the same thing you are—to stop those slavers and free their captives."

"Fuck off."

"That's why you're here, right?" I pressed. "To save them?"

"Yeah, and that's why we want *you* out of the way. Just remember, we could have killed you, so maybe you just sod off and keep your heads down. Don't screw this up for everyone, all right?"

"Pretty words," Crossbow-man sneered. "But we've heard them before. The legion makes lots of promises. Then they get themselves killed or captured, and we're the ones who suffer for it."

That explained some of the hostility. Failed rescue attempts would have brought harsh reprisals against any slaves left behind. No wonder they viewed us with suspicion.

"We're gonna free our brothers and sisters, and then we're gone, all right?" the first speaker said flatly. "You all stay the hell out of the way, keep your mouths shut and your weapons in their sheaths, and maybe you get to walk away after you learn something."

"Look," I said carefully. "I understand your distrust. But right now, we've got maybe thirty minutes before those slavers are in position. You want to stop them? So do we. We can either work together, or we can fight each other and let them get away."

"Or we could just kill you now," one of the figures suggested. "Save ourselves the trouble later."

"You could try." I kept my voice level. "But I'm guessing you've been watching long enough to see we climbed the cliff in full armor to get here. You're not even curious about why?"

"Nope," he replied. "We don't care, and yeah, we've been watching you for the last *three* hours. We even killed two of the slavers scouts who saw you, which is why they're spooked now. So, here's the deal. Sit down, shut up, and stay out of the way. Any legionnaires in there?"

"We think so," I admitted.

"Great, fine, whatever. If there's legionnaires, you can take them with you an' fuck off."

"We can work together to do…" I started and got a low round of chuckles in response.

"You're all the same. You promise and you fuck it up. So Sanna here's gonna lead you back out of the way, and you get to wait there, like good little boys and girls, sitting on your hands while we do what you can't. Remember, we've got people watching you. Any talking, any attempt to interfere, and we shoot. You want your people free? Fine. Stay here and don't fuck this up and you can have them."

"You're making a mistake," Daralen ground out.

"No, the mistake would be taking any of your idiots with us." He snorted. "What, you think we'd trust some of you lot in our base? Fuck off."

"What the hell's with the aggression?" I glared at him. "We're here to rescue the slaves. You should be—"

"The only way this works is if we pull it off. *Go*," he snapped. A dozen more of their people dropped their stealth, showing that we were practically surrounded: the cliff at our back and these nice people with crossbows aimed at our faces.

"Jax?" Daralen asked, and I hesitated, then shrugged.

"Should we just let them lose their people?" I asked her. "When they fail, we'll have lost the element of surprise, but they'll have hopefully learned a valuable lesson and they'll have whittled their numbers down for us."

"This is a mistake," Daralen growled at a crossbowman who was aiming solidly at her. She and the others started to stand, moving casually but quickly between the crossbows and Oracle, Sehran, and me.

"Go on, get out of the way and let real heroes do what you can't," another of their number sneered. "Get out of the way, all of you."

"You got a fucking problem with me?" I growled, noting just how many of them were seriously pissed at the legion. "Fuck's sake, we don't have to be enemies here, all right? See, I respect what you're trying to do here. I really do. But I don't think you understand—"

"We understand plenty," the leader cut in. "We understand that every time the legion tries to help, it's the slaves who pay for it. It's us who die. So, *move*."

A gust of wind rattled loose stones, and at that moment of distraction, I caught Oracle's eye. Through our bond, I could feel her tension, her readiness.

"Look, one last try, all right? Look at them. Those undead down there? They're in military formation. Those aren't mindless shamblers. They're being controlled by someone who knows what they're doing. And you're about to walk right into their trap! Those are your people down there, aren't they? They can't see what we can from up here!"

"We know what we're doing," another of their group snarled. "We've freed more slaves in the last year than your legion has in ten."

"And how many survived?" Daralen asked quietly. The bitter silence that followed was answer enough. "How many did you lose when the slavers chased you down?"

"Look at their deployment," I hissed, moving and gesturing to the group below winding their way into the pass. "Those aren't random patrols. They're setting up kill zones. Someone down there is expecting an attack, and they're ready for it."

The leader hesitated for just a fraction of a second. "You trying to tell me how to do my job?"

"No, you moron. I'm trying to stop you from getting your people killed. Because right now? You're doing *exactly* what they want you to do."

A commotion from below drew everyone's attention. More undead were being deployed, but now I could clearly see the pattern. They were deliberately leaving gaps in their lines, creating what looked like weak points in their defense.

Worst of all, from here I could see that the group getting ready to attack them, hiding amongst the rocks and bushes, had no clue they were about to march into the meat grinder.

"See those openings?" I asked. "They're not mistakes—they're *funnels*. Hit them from any direction, and you'll be channeled right where they want you. Then those units on the flanks will close in and—"

"Shut up!" The crossbowman shifted his aim slightly. "This is our fight, not yours."

"It's everyone's fight." Oracle spoke up, her voice carrying quietly across the ridge. "And right now, you're about to throw away any chance we have of winning it!"

The leader studied us for a long moment. Below, the caravan continued its careful advance, unaware of the drama playing out above them.

I thought I had him; I thought, for a long second, he was about to break, to listen. And then he spoke.

"Fuck it. Move or we shoot. Not another word out of you. Back. Now." The leader jabbed a finger toward a section of rock twenty meters from the cliff edge. "And stay there."

I briefly met Oracle's eyes, seeing that our choice was either start a fight here, early, or get out of the way and clean it up when it all went up shit creek. After a brief pause, I gestured to Daralen. No point getting our people killed before the real fight even started. We retreated to the indicated position, keeping our movements deliberate and non-threatening.

Four of their number kept watch over us as we went, with one incompetent actually trying to order me to hand over my weapons. I snorted and ignored him, as did the rest of the legion.

The group of would-be rescuers took our places along the cliff edge, setting up hurriedly. Their crossbows were impressive, especially the couple of big ones that were clearly designed for particular species to carry, judging from the way the wielders were struggling with them. Unfortunately, they moved with the coordination of people who'd done a lot of sneaking around, and very little actual fighting.

"Just watch," one of them sneered at us. "This is how real heroes handle slavers."

I glanced at Daralen, who looked horrified by what was clearly about to happen, and I shook my head. "Either we let them do this and hope there's more to the plan than we can see, or we fight them. We risk our own losses but either way, the element of surprise is fucked in the ass."

"I don't like it," she said.

I nodded, opening my mouth to respond.

"Quiet!" snapped one of the crossbowmen, a boy of perhaps fourteen who was having problems keeping the crossbow steady, and was spending more time staring longingly over at the others crawling up to the edge or at Sehran's tits than he was watching us.

Fifteen minutes later, in what had to be shitty positioning for the trap to be sprung, all hell broke loose.

The attack started well enough: a coordinated volley of crossbow bolts raining down on the caravan below. But the slavers weren't unprepared. Shields had to have been in place, and the groans from the group as well as the reflected flare of light from the shield—that even we could see back here—made it clear that they'd failed to break through.

"Second volley!" someone shouted. But before they could fire again, a second shout rang out, warning that there were undead archers.

"Get down!" I shouted, almost making the kid watching us shoot me in his surprise, but it was too late. Arrows flashed past in a wave, filling the air, forcing the idiots back from the edge. Two went down screaming. Then the arrows came again, and this time I saw a tactic I recognized from back home.

The first volley had been to break them up and drive them back from the edge of the cliff, but this—this was the *real* counterattack.

Volley-fired arrows flashed up in response, soaring high overhead, then a second volley, then a third. Arrow after arrow filled the sky, with only a slight change being made to the angle.

This was an old tactic, and worse, it was one that would clear the field.

"Legion!" I barked. "Shields!"

The legionnaires all around me ripped their shields free of bags and raised them, moving fast to lock them together—forming a turtle, I thought it was called—even as I shouted to the idiots who had fucked this all up to get over here.

A handful obeyed; most didn't. I cursed again, seeing panicked fools trying to outrun arrows by the hundreds, even as the first ones came thundering down.

It was a tactic that on Earth had been the decisive one for the English longbowmen: filling the air with hundreds, sometimes thousands of arrows, and literally destroying opposing armies wholesale.

We moved quickly, covering the ground to those we could reach who stood a chance of survival with our shields locked into place. The front row faced theirs out at ninety degrees; the others held theirs overhead, flat.

The arrows slammed home. Even where we were, off to the side, we took a good dozen impacts. Long arrows made of some kind of metal crashed down hard.

Most did little more than scratch the legions' shields. But for those without such protection, the effect was terrible.

Dozens of crossbowmen appeared from stealth, pierced through and pinned to the ground, screaming in agony…for those who lived long enough to do even that.

The boiled leather armor they wore did precisely dick against the well-made and clearly heavy arrows.

I snarled as I barked another order. "Legion, advance!"

We marched across to the edge and around. The whole point of us being up here, and specifically us climbing the cliff where we had, was because the pass that led up to here was in clear sight from below.

Cliffs rose on either side, the passage narrowing until it was barely wide enough for a wagon to pass through to our left. We'd been forced to climb where we had to make sure we were out of sight, to maintain the advantage of surprise. But now that was gone?

It was time for the main event.

We quick-marched into the middle of the ravine entrance. The front row dropped to one knee and held their shields across their fronts; the row behind—which I was a part of—slotted our shields against theirs, and angled left to right as well.

When the rank behind me held theirs overhead, it created a shield wall that let us see out, and yet offered practically no chance of an archer getting an arrow through the gaps.

Now that we could see the fight, though, it was clear that it wasn't going well. The "rescue" group's melee fighters had apparently burst from hiding, charging the caravan's flanks. For a moment, it looked like it might work, until the slaves in control collars were forced forward, brandishing weapons.

"No…" I heard one of the crossbowmen—apparently, they'd stayed, terrified, in the middle of the formation with us—and he whispered curses as the slaughter began.

The undead moved with terrifying coordination, cutting through the attackers like scythes through wheat. Controlled slaves, their collars glowing with cruel light, were forced to fight their would-be rescuers. And everywhere, screams carried clearly in the night air.

Arrows clattered against our shields again and again as those left out on the ground around us died, but none got through to us.

"Look!" I grabbed the idiots' leader's arm, forcing him to watch the carnage below. "Look what your pride has cost!"

He tried to pull away but I held him firm. His people were being butchered, cut down by the very slaves they'd come to save. The undead archers kept up their relentless fire, forcing anyone still alive to stay pinned down.

"Now," I snapped grimly, as someone apparently saw us and the first of the undead started to charge us, the melee fighters who had raced at the caravan already either dead, captured, or running for their lives. "Your fucking pride caused this, now watch! Shut your fucking mouth, and see how professionals do it."

He stared at the slaughter below, his face ashen. "I…we…"

"Oracle!" I called out. "Light them up!"

The first circle was exactly where I'd have put it. The undead raced silently up the ravine, weapons raised, shields held at the ready, and as soon as they stepped into it, they were lit up by flames.

Where the flames healed those who served me and burned those who didn't, for the undead, they were an even worse—or better—option.

Healing, we'd found ages ago, did indeed damage the undead instead of 'fixing' them. And when they were semi-sentient flames that burrowed deep and ate through them?

Yeah.

The lead undead didn't even make it halfway through the circle. The second and third ranks did little better, and as Oracle refreshed the mana to the circle, they fell as well.

Dozens collapsed in smoking, rolling bits. Then more ran in behind them, until the necromancer realized his mistake and ordered them back.

That was when they hit her second circle. The outer edge literally unfurled as they bunched up, and they raced forward, nearly thirty undead compressed into a small space between the two glowing circles.

Then Sehran opened fire.

She'd grown to love the Explosive Compression spell, and she couldn't help but grin as she demonstrated her new evolution for it.

The first stage was the same, an explosion that flung everyone near the point of impact outward, followed by the second, which pulled them all inward, crushing them as gravity was warped.

Bones broke, metal bent, and life, even unlife, was extinguished.

Then the third phase, the new addition, went active: the entire cycle began again, as what had been compressed inward was fired out again, violently.

The few undead that had escaped until now were smashed bodily from their feet and into the guttering circles, thrashing and stumbling as they died.

"Not bad!" I shouted, making sure everyone heard. "I think that's seventy undead for three spells. And now that the goddamn first rank of pests are cleared, the real fight can begin! Oracle, Sehran—I want those archers dead!"

"Again?" Sehran asked gaily, and I snorted.

"Behave or you're going over my knee!"

"Promises, promises!" She laughed, and I shook my head.

"Legion, at the ready!" I turned, looking at Daralen. "Primus, this is your legion. Would you like to do the honors?"

"With pleasure, my prince!" She grinned, the whites of her eyes gleaming through the slit in her helm. "Legion…*aaaadvance!*"

# CHAPTER TWENTY-EIGHT

The pass echoed with the sound of armored boots striking stone as we advanced in formation. The burning circles cast flickering shadows across the cliffs, making the ravine feel like the entrance to some hellish domain. Which, considering the smoking remains of undead scattered across our path, wasn't far wrong.

"Legion, at the ready!" Daralen's voice carried clearly as the first line of legionnaires reached the edge of Oracle's spell. "First rank, maintain shield wall. Second rank, prepare to attack!"

I stared through the flickering flames as they died, and nodded to myself as the forces on the far side formed up again, this time in ranks with the undead at the back, and a fuckload of slaves wearing control collars in front of them.

Beyond that, the slavers were regrouping. Their undead archers had fallen back behind the wagons. Clearly seeing that they weren't doing anything to us, the necromancer had shifted their aim, and they were now making damn sure the running "rescuers" were dying in droves.

I nodded to myself again, then looked over at Daralen as the enslaved warriors were being forced forward. Their control collars pulsed and made them scream out when they tried to rebel.

Behind them all, I caught glimpses of robed figures underneath magical shields, the necromancers and slavers responsible for such a disciplined undead force.

"We're going to have to kill our way through the very people we came to save, to get to the slavers and necros," Daralen pointed out. "Unless you feel up to a demonstration?"

"I'm thinking what we really need are those slavers and the necromancers in as close together as possible," I purred. "Oracle, Sehran, you think you can land some spells around and get them to bunch up more?"

"Easily." Oracle nodded. "I'm going to switch to Flames of Wrath. It'll do more damage in the shorter period, and there's nobody down there sworn to us yet, so the healing aspect would be wasted anyway."

"I've got enough for four Explosive Compressions," Sehran said quickly, pulling out a mana potion as she gestured to the walls of the ravine. "If I hit one on either side, and then…actually, can we hold for…thirty seconds?" she asked in a rush.

"Hold here!" I barked.

"I'll get out and fly high, fast as I can. Start your trick when I start firing, okay?" She grinned in the dimness under the shields that still protected us all, before spinning and pushing her way back, slipping through the gaps the legionnaires made for her in their lines. "Sorry…pardon me…oops, sorry about your foot!"

That last made me smile because I knew it'd been both deliberate and on one of the crossbow wielders. Because any legionnaire who cared about a woman, even a succubus, stepping on his foot when he was wearing armored sabatons had issues.

"Jax?" Daralen asked.

I nodded to the forces forming up and waiting for the spell to fail, even as Oracle slid it a bit more mana to keep it going a little longer.

"If we can get the necromancers in close to the slavers and then I can create a feedback loop, that should be enough to detonate the control devices. Chances are at least one of the necromancers will have devices on them that will kill them. But ideally, if they're in close, then the others' devices will finish off the job if they don't."

"Like in Marrow?"

"Exactly, only this time, if we can get them all in close and behind their pretty little shield, it'll serve to pin them with the blasts as well."

"So, we need to hold until they're close and you've done your thing?" she asked me.

"Yeah. Then we need to be ready to pass through the freed slaves. I don't think they're going to want to fight us at that point."

"Maybe not, but that's not something we can rely on," she disagreed. "Most of them are likely to be slaves, being forced to this life, but others will be assholes who were hired. And some of the slaves are likely to be so indoctrinated, they just continue."

"We don't want to kill them, though…our people, I mean," I said.

She lifted her voice instead of responding to me directly. "Okay, listen up!" she barked, everyone going still and silent as their primus gave out her orders.

"Magic is going to pin their leaders in place. Then the prince is going to use his powers! Be ready! When he frees the slaves, the line is to split on the right. Position one and two, you're to break free and fall back; take up position to the rear, facing out.

"Position three, turn and lock. I want a free path running down the side of the ravine up and out, but there's to be not a single inch that some asshat can get at you, understand? If you fuck up and dare die, you're gonna embarrass me, and anyone who embarrasses me better pray that the gods protect you because I'll rip your soul free of the veil and beat it!"

"Damn," I muttered, impressed by the speed and clarity of her orders compared to mine.

"Now, as last time, this is likely to draw the eye, and the slaves are going to be confused to all hell. So, when they're free, and that passage is clear, we get ready! Any who are left are likely to be killed, recaptured, or used as shields, so I want everyone ready to run!

"At my order of 'break,' the legion is to break into pairs. You know your battle-buddies by now, and if you don't, goddamn find one! Get out there and take down anyone with a weapon who threatens the empire! I'd rather we saved everyone, but if they attack us, they go down, *hard*. Do. You. Get. Me?"

"WE GET YOU, PRIMUS!" the legionnaires bellowed back.

I couldn't help but grin.

Daralen turned to me, waiting expectantly.

I paused for a second; then, mentally cursing, I closed my eyes and focused. Searching.

The ability wasn't easy to use. It was linked to the imperial throne, and every time I'd used it successfully, I was either in a fugue state, my conscious mind pretty much stuck in neutral, or I'd been filled with righteous rage.

The one thing that I did really understand about it, though, was that for it to work, it wasn't so much about mana—though I needed a shitload of that as well.

No, it was about me. It was about them. And it was somehow tied to the other forms of magic that were out there.

I needed mana to do this, as with part of it, I healed them—these people, these slaves—of all their injuries, where I could. That took an incredible amount of mana, considering at times I could bottom my pool out over and over healing a single person if their injuries were bad enough.

Also, establishing the feedback loop in the control devices, blocking and protecting the slaves' end of it, and forcing the controller end to detonate? That took a fuckload of mana as well.

Finally, creating the little bubbles of protected space around each slave, when I genuinely had no clue who, where, or how many of them there were, should have taken an amount of mana that I could have never held.

I'd managed it with a fraction of what it should have taken, which—I'd realized more than once, while lying awake on many a cold floor or deck—had to mean that I was using more than just mana.

If I could use mana, then it seemed to respond better. Things like the incident before I found Tommy, where I'd started a flare of light that had been seen for hundreds of miles, was not the way to go about it, given the choice, but that was just it.

I was fumbling in the dark, and doing it all on instinct.

Here, I decided to try it with a little of both sides. The knowledge that Amon had shared with me as a master of mana, joining with my half-formed ideas and suspicions of the other sides of magic, and specifically the imperial abilities meant that I now understood more than I ever had, and yet…

Understanding was going to be a hindrance, I was sure.

I'd done this the first couple of times without a single goddamn clue how I was doing it, just relying on rage and…and love.

Love for these people. Hope, and…and belief.

I wasn't some tree-hugger hippie-dippy dickhead, so I didn't believe that love could make anything work. If that was the case, no kid would ever be ill and only dickheads would die.

That meant that it wasn't some mystical power of "love"; it was something that it was linked to, that the force of love was touching, that…

Belief. Belief and a rock-solid need.

It wasn't just the belief that you could do something. It was belief that it was right. That it *should* be done, that all of reality should give way and that this was how it was.

That was what I'd done.

What I'd done when Grizz had been dying. What I'd done when I pressed my soul into Oracle and remade her as part of me and her own magical new form.

What I'd done when I'd freed the revenants, the fighters of the empire that had bound themselves to the prax Glorious Retribution, in shame at their having failed the empire. And yet only with a few words, they'd moved on.

They hadn't *heard* me, not all of them, and even if they had, there was no way that hearing some random guy speaking about how all was forgiven would have changed anything for them.

They'd killed thousands, possibly millions of creatures over the years that they'd protected and patrolled the prax, both those who came from above and those who trespassed from below.

I had no fucking doubt at least a few of their victims had to have tried begging for their lives and at the point of death, I had to think their words would have been more impassioned than my angry ones had been.

No, what I'd done was warp fucking reality with the power of my belief, the power of me, and who was I?

"I'm Prince Jax Amon," I whispered, feeling my way along the ability in my mind, feeling surges of power, of 'almost' as I fumbled to a realization.

A fresh flight of arrows struck the shield wall, the undead trying again, even as the crack and boom of Sehran's spells slammed down in fast succession.

The ravine funneled the explosions, channeling them, hurling bodies about, shattering and destroying undead, tracing lines of fracture patterns in the sides of the cliffs. I felt Oracle pushing out the ritual circles. The Flames of Wrath surged, destroying the undead that stepped into them and forced them to back up, the slaves to retreat, and the small bubble of the shields that protected their masters to flare as debris, bodies, and undead brushed against them.

"I am Jax," I whispered, seeing more than I ever had as I mentally traced the power that I had used, feeling it fading again. I shifted to follow it, focusing on what I had grasped so far.

Power didn't just "exist." It couldn't.

That power that I'd been tapping into couldn't just exist in a vacuum, having always been there and never touched. It had to come from somewhere. And I was betting it went somewhere as well. It went…it went…

It was an *imperial* ability. It was tied to the empire. It was tied to Amon. And that meant that the only way I could use it, the only way that I could have ever used it, was through him.

I'd been accessing it since he went to his grave, but it'd been far more mana-based. I'd drained the area; I'd pulled in huge quantities of mana when I'd tried to do it without understanding what I was doing.

I'd drained the valley when I fought the slavers at that fair. I'd dragged in all the mana for miles and I'd used it up, badly fucking myself up in the process because my body couldn't handle such a transfer of mana.

I'd been barely able to hold myself together, and yet I'd felt that power racing through me to save those people and I'd done it.

I'd lost fifty stat points. It hadn't been a punishment by "the system" or whatever; it'd not been a consequence of my actions because I'd been naughty.

It was damage because I'd overreached and I'd fucked up. I'd accepted that. I'd bound a fucking fragment of the divine and still I knew I was barely struggling at the edge of comprehension, because the power I used wasn't something that should be wielded through me.

No, that was wrong—it *should*. In fact, it *had* to be wielded through me. For me to be freeing people and altering reality like this, it wasn't something the system was letting me do because I'd gotten a marker that said "imperial prince" and I'd had some kind of access provisions permitted.

I'd not been granted a 'staff of immense power,' no 'boots of unbelievable funkiness.' No, I was reaching out blindly and forcing reality to bend to my will.

The power required to do that was incredible, and yet it was only *one* of the imperial abilities.

I searched my memories, trying to ignore the shouts around me and the clash of weapons and armor as I struggled to make sense of this, stuffing down and aside the knowledge that people were dying because I wasn't ready yet.

I'd sensed Amon's memories as he used the abilities, but it was rare, and it was only ever for the greatest of needs. I used them every few fuckin' weeks, but the power levels…

I was basically shifting a tiny aspect of reality; in comparison, I was affecting a few dozen meters, if that, when I usually freed the slaves, up to a few miles at most.

Him? I remembered him sinking *island chains*.

He'd faced dragons, ancient ones…ones that should have destroyed him, that even Shustic had been wary of, and she was the greatest dragon to have ever lived, according to him.

Amon had folded his arms and watched as one of those dragons had put everything it had into a blast of dragon fire that turned obsidian to gas. And at the end, as the dragon paused, expecting to see a hole in the ground and some sooty strands, it'd seen Amon, standing there, looking *pissed*.

He'd killed it, and it wasn't with so much as a punch. He'd simply willed that the space between its ears and that all the way to its eyes, the literal interior of its brain, was cold, hard rock, and it had been.

I saw it all, as that massive dragon collapsed, dead as fuck—and not just the dragons, but the fucking gods had. They'd watched Amon in sheer stunned amazement, because he'd wielded the powers of a god, because he'd used an imperial ability, one that was like theirs!

HE was a step below the gods, and a fucking small one at that. Nimon had banished them; he'd killed Amon. Why?

Why did he do it?

I was fumbling along the edge of something, and I knew it…a greater secret, something that explained it all, but beyond me right now. Meters ahead, people were dying. Right now, they fought and bled, and they didn't have to.

There was no point to this, because at last I understood how that power worked now.

"I am the Imperial Prince, Jax Amon," I whispered, opening my eyes, and feeling the way the legionnaires around me shied back, looking away as a sudden light blazed from me.

I felt the shields on either side of me being pushed back inexorably as I lifted upward. Oracle called out in joy as the power that rolled off me reached out to her too, accepting her, forming a conduit that flooded her body with power.

She was strengthened by that power, and it touched, caressed, and protected our unborn child as we lifted higher.

I stared out, seeing the lines of power, the oaths and obligations, the gossamer threads that ran from each and every one of the powers I could see, out across the curvature of the realm.

I could see a billion lines, from the black of fear to the red of pain to the gold of love. I saw imperial obligations, I saw oaths of fealty, and demands that had twisted love to enforce obedience.

There were lines of lust, of shame, of regret and hope, and they joined the billions of others, weaving a tapestry across the realm.

I saw the lines that led from me out, soaring across miles in their thousands to reach those I'd left behind.

I saw golden glows that burned the eyes they were so bright, and I saw the silver of hope, changing to belief, love, and awe, as those around me watched as I lifted higher.

"I AM JAX AMON!" My voice shook dust free of the walls, causing rocks to tumble off the cliffs and cascade down, as the fighting stopped.

"I SEE YOU ALL. I SEE THOSE OF YOU WHO HAVE BEEN TAKEN, THOSE WHO WERE HURT, AND THOSE WHO WERE BROKEN. I SEE OATHS ABANDONED, AND LIES THAT FESTER. I SEE HOPE FLICKERING AND I SEE PAIN.

"I SEE ALL THAT HAS BEEN DONE TO YOU. I SEE THE FAILURE OF THE EMPIRE, AND I SEE THE HARM THAT WAS DONE TO YOU ALL."

I paused, seeing it in truth. For a fraction of a second, I saw these people below me—not just the slaves, but the slavers. I saw the warriors and mercenaries. And I saw the dead—the bodies that were puppeted around, that had been forced to pretend to live again, that still carried trace fragments of the souls that had driven them.

I felt it all: the rising tide of terror and pain and hopelessness, and finally the tiny fragments of light.

I saw the slave who hid their child to give them a chance. I saw the warrior who never returned home, because he knew, knew in his heart, that those he loved were better off without him. I saw the mother who cradled, then pushed away her child as she was captured in their place.

I saw the joy of those who found love, those rare moments where the world all seemed to just work, and I understood. Even the slavers loved; they left partners and children behind as they worked. They dealt in human misery, but they still loved their kids and fought to help their friends...most of them, anyway.

All of them had been failed by the fall of the empire, the descent into lawlessness that had come about and the centuries of barbarism.

They and their ancestors had been failed by the promise of the empire, because they'd been reduced to squatting in the corpse that survived, instead of building something new.

That was the truth, and all of it had been because Nimon had been...afraid.

He was afraid of what we—what Amon and now I—was becoming, and I saw *that* as clear as day.

I reached out, walling off the collars. I closed the matrices that funneled the mana of the realm into maintaining the devices of slavery, and I compressed them. Then I looped a single strand around each and every slave I could feel. I reached out to those who had been trying to rescue them; those who still lived, pinned to the ground in some cases by dozens of arrows, bleeding out, I touched as well.

I felt their form, their existence, and I felt the gaps in it, the faults, where their injuries had broken their ideal.

I found them all, and I removed them. I decided they were intact. And they damn well were.

"I AM the empire, and I declare you to be *free*," I whispered. The world around me shook as reality warped, and then settled.

The slavers' devices exploded as one. Their shields held long enough to constrain the detonation, to trap it inside as the shields were painted red from the inside, blood and fire making the walls of the shield clear.

Then they failed. All that was left inside were broken bodies, and blood that fell to the ground as the form it had coated now vanished, leaving only the dying.

The vast majority of the undead just outright buckled, their strings cut. But those that remained upright, the elites atop the last wagon, moved with terrifying speed as the rest simply collapsed, bones rolling free and armor clattering.

Slaves who had been forced to march forward, weapons at the ready and those who had been in battle, forced to fight the legion, who were desperately trying to block and not injure those poor fools in turn, collapsed as well.

They fell, gasping as their collars shattered, as control over their limbs returned, and along with it, stunned hope.

Hundreds of slaves who had been transported in the wagons or been made to march alongside them, their collars enforcing their behavior, had been used as shields.

They'd taken arrows and ricochets; burns and breaks were commonplace. More than half had some kind of long-term injury that had healed imperfectly. And as they lay in piles, gasping and shaking, they did so with bodies that no longer shrieked in agony, that bled, or were restrained.

The other undead, though, had moved with stunning speed, and they stood at the ready. No longer interested in attacking us, they stood with weapons bared and pressed to the terrified former slaves, waiting for an order.

The slaves who were free of the undead scrambled and crawled, ran or hid as soon as they saw me, drawing back as I flew forward. The legion moved quickly, marching to keep as close to me as possible. Oracle slid around to hover behind me, and Sehran swooped down to beat her wings, taking up station behind me and to the left, opposite Oracle.

There was one of the enemy left alive—or at least one, anyway. Because although most of the undead had collapsed, those that had been standing atop the bone wagon still stood. Eight of them now stood over fallen slaves, with two atop the wagon still.

They'd stopped again, and now fully half of them stood stock-still in what I recognized as legion plate.

It was old, and yet clearly still imperial, with the rank insignia of four optios, and a single primus. They had been atop the wagon, along with their companions, though these wore the armor of the Dark Legion, the followers of Nimon instead.

As I flew forward, the last two of them suddenly moved. Instead of the attack I expected, they stepped inward smoothly, reaching down and grasping handles set into the roof, then pulling.

A hole appeared, offering entrance to the wagon and shining with welcoming candlelight. From my angle, I could just make out a stairwell that led inside, formed out of long bones.

"Stay with the legion," I ordered Sehran. "Be ready to pass orders along."

She nodded, flaring her wings, then arcing around to drop to the ground before the legion as they ran in. I heard Daralen barking orders, and the line opened for her, letting her in without compromising the overlapping shields.

*"Jax, I don't like this,"* Oracle sent to me.

*"I know. Neither do I,"* I admitted. *"But if we don't accept the invitation, I'm betting we lose half the slaves."*

*"Can you..."* She started.

I shook my head, feeling the strain. Somehow—though I didn't know how or why—I knew, without knowing how, that using imperial abilities wasn't something that could be done over and over in short succession. Not without serious consequences. And if I forced through and did it anyway, next time I needed it, I might not be able to do it.

I couldn't risk arriving at Sonra and finding that all the slaves we needed to free couldn't be helped because I'd chosen the easy path here. So, instead, I risked it.

I felt her understanding as I began to descend, as well as her hating the separation, but knowing that it would be insane for both of us to go inside. She instead climbed higher and higher, weaving magic quickly to hide herself, even as she slipped to the right and swung wide, keeping watch over me.

I landed at the top of the stairs. My mana rose inside me as I prepared to lash out with a handful of spells at the first sign of trouble. Instead, I found…

A single figure waiting, who gestured me to come down and join him, before turning and hobbling out of sight.

I strode down the stairs, noting the way they folded back as I lifted my foot from each, locking back into place on the walls, and looked around the interior of the necromancer's wagon.

Everywhere, there were bones: arms and hands made up tables, legs and rib cages formed chairs, and long, thick rugs were clutched by skeletal fingers.

Weapons were in evidence here and there, but they were notably magical, held in place as more of a collector's piece than a ready threat. As I glanced from a lance that ran along one side of the long wagon, I noted that the sword next to it had a splayed hand in the wall directly behind the hilt.

"Will you sit?" He gestured to a seat that unfolded from the wall; leather and rugs flowed along from a storage device to drape over it, waiting.

"Will you attack me?" I asked.

"Not unless there is a reason to do so," he said clearly. "Will you swear to do the same?"

"No."

"Then why should I bind myself?" he asked, before sighing and sinking into his own chair with visible relief. "Old bones." He forced a smile.

I snorted, striding forward and coming to a halt halfway across the wagon from him.

"Old" was an understatement, I reflected, examining him first with my eyes, wary of casting magic at him until he made a move.

His skin was draped over bones that seemed too small, the color of it making clear it rarely, if ever, saw daylight. It had the fragile quality of the very old, and his wispy white hair added to the impression of an ancient man.

His ears marked him clearly as elven, as did the slightly tilted eyes and the otherworldly hints of what had presumably been good looks.

Once.

Now he sat back in his chair, an arm extending out from it to hold a staff at the ready, even as he reached down, accepting a potion that was lifted up for him.

"What's that?" I asked gruffly.

"Healing potion," he said. "I find they help to stave off the pains of old age nicely."

He took it and drank it, sighing in contentment before dropping the empty flask to the side unconcernedly. Another hand shot out from the side of the chair, grabbing it and dragging it back out of sight, behind the old man.

"Now, what to do about you?" He sighed again, before shaking his head. "You've cost me a considerable investment in time and effort, boy."

"And you've cost me the lives of my citizens," I said coldly.

"Until they swear to you, they're not yours," he pointed out. "Or else I could argue that you've stolen them from me, and demand imperial redress."

"I am…"

"Jax Amon, Prince of the Empire…yes, I'm well aware." He sat back and watched me, folding his hands comfortably over his stomach. "Tell me, boy, how old do you think I am?"

"Old. Beyond that, I don't care much."

"Well, let's see what you can tell without magic, shall we? I'd ask that you don't use a spell. Instead, use your brain, if you have one."

"That's rude," I said softly, flexing my fingers in my gauntlets and hearing the creak of leather and plate.

"As I say, you've damaged an operation I've invested much time and effort in. I'm feeling considerable annoyance right now, and I'm trying to maintain my equilibrium. I suggest you don't fuel it."

I watched him for a few seconds, well aware that outside there were possibly hundreds of lives in the balance. As much as I wanted to smash this old fucker's face in and finish the job of the undead off, I needed to try to protect those people.

"Okay, you're elven, and you're the oldest of that race I've seen."

"True." He smiled and shook his head. "If you've seen older, I'll be surprised."

"Considering that I've been told your kind live long enough, it might as well be forever, and yet you look like a stiff breeze might finish you off. I'm guessing that you're very old. Pre or post cataclysm?"

"Pre," he said with a faint smile. "And yes, that means that I recognize that armor, and the desire not to see it damaged is in part why we're having this conversation."

"Oh?" I lifted a gauntlet, looking at the deep scratches in the lacquer.

"Further damaged," he amended. "I see from the enchantments that it's an original set. Probably the work of Grenelda and her team, judging from the flow of mana."

"Grenelda?" I asked.

"Imperial armor smith, an imperator in fact." He nodded. "Quite the wonderous creator. I searched for her for many years, but alas, long lost now."

"She survived?" I asked.

"You show your ignorance, boy." He sighed. "No. The Imperial Reserve was destroyed outright. The mana forge that powered it and kept it afloat for so long detonated, and those aboard all perished instantly. Even if they hadn't, the *Reserve* was two miles up. Nothing without wings could survive the drop. So, unlike her limited contingent of Valkyries, the imperial servants aboard her had little chance to escape."

"So, you were searching for her body," I said grimly. "Let me guess…you could strip that knowledge from her."

"I could, even then." He nodded. "Though I'd have given her a choice, as I do all who I awaken from those times: serve me, or slumber on. Their bodies hold much of the secrets that their souls once did, and when you're as old as I am, you learn many tricks. No, as it was, none of the bodies I could find were more than servants or lower-level artisans.

"The legionnaires I raised were driven mad with grief, limiting their use, and in time, even their empty corpses failed. It was five generations before the bite of their failures faded enough for them to be useful after death again."

"So you stole the bodies of my people, and now you're complaining that their dedication to the empire was an inconvenience?" I asked.

"Fwah!" he spat. "Boy, you've clearly been raised to take your place as Amon's heir. I bear you no ill will for that, but you're a product of these times. I bet you think the empire was some monolithic edifice of good! A bastion that held the line while outside her borders, it was all barbarism and the sacrifice of innocents! I tell you, it wasn't!"

"No, it wasn't," I agreed, and he paused, fixing me with a gimlet glare. "The empire was a fucking mess, telling people to do this and not do that, while it did the opposite whenever it needed to."

"It did, and it's a surprise to hear one such as yourself admit that. A pleasant one, though it changes little."

"It did good, though," I added, sitting down in the offered seat and watching him, waiting for the inevitable attack. "For every innocent who was injured, a hundred or more had the chance to live good, safe lives."

"Did they?" He smiled. "That's interesting. Tell me, boy, how did you escape entropy? Because of the two of us, the only one who walked the streets of the old empire is me, unless you're a more interesting tale than I'm expecting."

"Perhaps," I said. "What's your game here?"

"No game," he said softly. "Just curiosity."

"Then have your undead step back and let the slaves go free and we can talk," I said.

"Why?"

"What?"

"Why would I do that?" He gestured with one hand as if brushing something aside. "By the rules of the empire, they belong to me. We are no longer within the limits of her boundaries; this land is unclaimed by any successive noble of the empire, and as such has reverted to its original ownership."

"This is imperial territory," I said firmly. "Slavery is—"

"Legal." He cut me off, smiling sharply. "You show your ignorance again. *'No land that is unclaimed by the empire is bound to its laws. Slaves purchased or acquired outside of imperial lands are of no concern to the empire unless they are her acknowledged and sworn citizenry',*" he quoted.

"This, like many other lands that were annexed in the days of expansion, were brought into the empire under specific treaties of conquest. The one that applies here was *'Imperial lands, undeeded, that are unclaimed for a period of five hundred years, consequently shall be released to their regional inhabitants.'*"

"Bullshit," I snapped.

"This land is imperial no longer, boy. She is free, and as such, your vaunted freeing of slaves under imperial law won't work." He smiled at me coldly. "I saw what happened out there, and I felt the effects. You'll be feeling backlash, I'd imagine."

I stared at him for a few seconds.

"Do you understand what it is?" He reached out to the staff and gently ran a hand down it. "The source of those powers, I mean? And how incredibly limited they are?"

"I do." I lied. I had a suspicion, but I needed time to think.

"Lies." He snorted. "I appreciate the sentiment, boy, but if you understood it, you'd neither waste it like this, nor would you use it outside of the bounds of claimed territory."

"What do you know?" I asked.

"Things that you cannot imagine." He sighed. "I was a power in those days, boy, and I've spent long ages learning. The things I've learned are beyond possibly all others. Spells? I rival the emperor at his height in knowledge. Wealth? I have the wealth of nations hidden away, ready for the day that I need it—not only gold and platinum, but artifacts of the past. Things that would make that wisp of yours beg to serve me."

He smiled knowingly. "She's old, boy, though her kind mainly age from experience, not time. And unlike you, I could grant her freedom, true freedom. She'd not have to bind herself to me like she has you, no. She'd be free after a time, ten years perhaps. I feel her watching me out of your eyes, and she's considering it, isn't she?"

*"Not even slightly,"* Oracle breathed in my ear along our bond. *"He's old and he knows some tricks, but all he's doing is trying to distract you, to weaken you."*

*"My imperial abilities require absolute certainty,"* I sent to her. *"He knows that, somehow, and he's trying to put a kernel of doubt in, hoping it'll stop me."*

"It's rude to whisper." He glared at me. "Summon her in. She may sit too."

"No," I replied.

"I didn't ask you, boy."

"No, you're right…you demanded. I'm sorry. My response should have been clearer—go suck a bucket of dicks." I smiled at him.

# **CHAPTER TWENTY-NINE**

There was a long moment of silence as we stared at each other. I waited, unsure whether this was going to be the moment that kicked it all off.

He threw back his head and laughed. "You misunderstand my purpose, young prince," the necromancer said, his voice calm and even bloody amused. "The Sons of the Deep have watched and waited for centuries. We've preserved knowledge that would otherwise be lost, maintained order in our own way."

"Through slavery and death," I spat. "You're nothing but carrion feeders."

He smiled, showing teeth that seemed too sharp. "We are the future. The empire you dream of rebuilding is dust. Join us instead. Your power, combined with our knowledge…" He shrugged and let the offer hang in the air.

Through our bond, I felt Oracle's warning: *"He's stalling, Jax. I don't know what he's planning but I can feel mana in all the bones around you. Something's building, subtle, but it's there."*

I watched him for a long few seconds, then sighed. "Give me a minute." I reached into the bag of holding and popped free a medium-grade healing potion—a hundred health it'd heal, no more, but that wasn't the point. What I needed wasn't a lot of healing, and I damn well knew this was going to suck.

I took a deep breath and snorted as he stiffened. Then, rather than saying anything else, I triggered my bonus ability from my Reanimator spell.

Technically it was a skeletal reanimator, but fuck it, because the important detail here was the bonus ability it had gained when I hit the last evolution.

> **Magically Active:** Bones that have long been infused with magics will reveal themselves to you now, and you will sense ways to tease the power from them, granting your creation unique Abilities and Bonuses dependent on the materials used to upgrade it.

Basically, it granted the ability to learn more about the bones I saw and the magic in them, by simply looking at them.

That was great and all, but the side effect the first time I'd used this ability was to literally burn my fuckin' eyes out.

They let me see the magic of bones, and what they were infused with, in theory to aid me in making more impressive minions. Such as giving Bob—and damn I missed the big, bony bastard right now—the ability to cast spells, to resist certain kinds of magic, and more.

That was all great and its main use, but it also enabled me to see or sense bones that were hidden, as well as what particular magics they held.

Triggering that ability on an airship over the remains of a five-hundred-year-old magical battlefield had resulted in a horrific pain and my losing my eyes.

Here and now, in a fuckin' wagon that was literally made from magical bones? I knew ahead of time it was going to suck balls.

That being said, as I closed my eyes, mentally prepared myself and then slowly opened them again, it was…less horrific than I expected.

At first, yeah, sure, it was like staring into the midday sun, except that every damn bone on all sides glowed with it all. I hissed in pain. But right before I was about to cut it off and start healing myself, I noticed something.

It was like when people wore those transition sunglasses, where they were almost clear one minute, and then pure black glass the next.

The world slowly tinted back to almost normality, with each and every bone on all sides standing out with shimmering power woven through them.

I squinted as my eyes slowly adjusted. The difference made up by my already insane accelerated healing meant that after ten seconds or so, I sighed and was finally able to look around.

"What's going on?" the old bugger asked curiously.

"I have a sight ability that lets me see magic," I admitted. "It's more than that, but obviously considering the magic in here, I decided it was worth having a closer look around."

"Oh? You could have asked," he pointed out.

"And you could have not invited me down into your lair of fucking dark decrepit weirdness, but that's life," I replied. "It's impressive how many bones you've got here, and how many of them are from different consecrated gods."

"You can tell that? An unusual ability indeed, young one. Tell me, what else can you see and why would I do this?" He settled back, releasing his staff and watching me across steepled fingers as he waited.

"So that you've got weapons that do additional damage against particular foes, as well as defend better against them."

"And just like that, you betray how ignorant you truly are." He sighed. "I had such hopes when you saw such details, and yet, as usual, the current generations disappoint."

"Okay, why would you then?" I asked him.

"Why should I share secrets long earned with you?" he countered.

"Because you're complaining that this generation doesn't know shit without being willing to teach means that you're a hypocrite otherwise?"

"You seek to offend me, is that it? I'm nearly four thousand years old, boy. You'll need to do better than that to entice me to share my secrets."

In truth, although I was curious, I also wasn't going to believe anything he said. I was more interested in getting as much of a warning as possible before he launched an attack. The mass of bones was impressive, and yeah, I wanted a lot of them for Bob regardless. Beyond that there were different ones…there wasn't much to learn here, I decided.

"Okay, then tell me about the Sons," I said, buying time while scanning for weaknesses. "How many of you survived the cataclysm? How many of you are there?"

"There are enough," he replied. "Enough to maintain our traditions, no matter the damage you should think to do. And yes, I see the way you're fishing for information. The Sons as a group aren't that old, perhaps two centuries if that. I started them, along with a few others with similar backgrounds, when we found one another."

"You're all necromancers?"

"Yes, though it's less that we're evil because we raise the dead, and more that we have little regard for the common view of our kind. Many necromancers are shunned by society, do you know that? Where once we were accepted as a part of the pattern, respected for the gifts that we possessed…those days are no more."

"Gee, I wonder why?" I drawled. "Maybe because you're murdering, slaving scumbags who use the dead to capture the living and sell them to other assholes? I mean, what an example you're setting!"

"When I was young, boy, I was renowned for my ability to speak with the dead. I served the empire as a necromancer, and I made it possible for the living and the dead to speak. For the living to say their last goodbyes, for the dead to pass on their secrets, and for those who perverted the natural order to be punished!" he snapped, glaring at me.

"And now you enslave the innocent?"

"I was the *victim*, boy. I was the one punished for those who couldn't bear the truth! When a justicar didn't like the answers I gave, they did their best to shut me up! They told lies that meant I was banished from my village, and all for 'the greater good'!"

"What?" I frowned. "They can't do that, can they? I thought their oath meant—"

"Their oaths are meaningless!" he spat. "Like all the rest of the empire, they could be set aside if they decided that the greater good required it!"

"Explain that," I demanded.

"One last secret for you, boy, one last hint for free—then comes the time of bargaining. Just this to show you that I do know all." He forced a sour smile, then went on.

"When the empire fell, the cities and towns began rebelling, and as part of that, many lives were lost. Sometimes it was necessary—of course it was. But other times? A case of mistaken identity meant that an innocent woman was hanged. When her husband petitioned the justicars, they brought me in. When I agreed, communed with her and shared the truths of her soul?" He shook his head. "They turned on me."

"What was the truth?" I asked. "Why'd they…"

"She was innocent. She couldn't have broken the law, because when she was supposed to be smuggling, according to the case, she was actually riding the captain of the guard! I showed them. I proved it to them. And when the husband refused to accept it, the captain of the guard was called in. The justicar sent the husband out, and questioned the guard, who admitted it!"

"And they covered it up?" I asked, stunned.

"The justicar said that they couldn't afford to have the guard captain removed and the proof spread that the guards themselves were no longer bound by their oaths!"

"Wait…"

"Their oaths, boy! When the emperor died, the nobility lost their right to the land. With their rights diminished, the oaths that were sworn to them were weakened as well. Those who believed, truly believed that what they were doing was right found they could do anything! That was the secret—those put in place as justicars could set aside their oaths, in service of the greater good for the empire! Nobody else could,

could they? Oh no. Your precious legion? They died in their tens of thousands for stupidity!

"But those personally entrusted with carrying out the imperial will? Why, boy, they could have smiled to your face, and eaten babies! They could commit any crime, slaughter entire cities to keep their secrets, and the rest of us were forced to accept it!"

I stared at him for long seconds as I thought about it, wondering whether that was the case. Then he started to speak again.

"That's why I started as I did, boy, why I started to look to my own protection. The guard captain knew that I was the only one who could prove that they'd gotten it wrong, so he set about discrediting me! It came down to either they were right and that meant I was wrong, or they'd hung an innocent woman, a woman who the guard captain had been engaging in adultery with!

"They couldn't have that. So, instead they spread around that my gift, like that of the priests, was failing! That the souls of the dead that I summoned? They were illusions! I was hounded out of my job in the town. And then, when I returned to my village, they followed me there! Accusations, vile stories, and then the attacks came. It was all I could bear, and then…then they destroyed my servants!"

"Servants?"

"The dead I'd raised!" he snapped. "I'd spent years working to recover their secrets, teasing this or that memory loose, and then I instilled them all in a small handful of the dead. I raised them. I gave them meaning, and memories, and then I started to use them, having my smith create armor that was as good, if not better than that of any smith in the villages!"

"And?"

"And they burned them!" he snarled, spittle flying. "Ten years of work, lost in an instant just because I refused to sell to them at a discount!"

"A discount?" I felt ridiculous now, constantly repeating the fucker, but this was going around in circles.

"They expected me to sell my armor at the same price as those who made lesser work! They expected me to only supply them? After all they'd done? No! I told them, either they pay, or the raiders would! I'd take my creations and the raiders would buy them, then I'd have my revenge!"

"Why?"

"All because I'd stripped the bones of the smith's ancestors to build my own! They were long dead—it's not like *they* cared! I gave them a chance. I told them, with my powers, we would raise the long dead of the village, harvest them for their secrets and then I'd force out the corrupt in the city. I'd lead the dead back to retake it and from there? We'd have all the corpses I needed to create incredible creations! The old empire was crumbling, and it was time for the necromancers to rise again!"

"And then they refused, and burned you out, destroying your creations?" I asked, finally seeing it.

"Exactly!"

"Okay, so what I'm getting from this long-winded load of bullshit is that there was a fuckup and they tried to cover it up, the justicar doing it in fear that there was already a rebellion in the offing and seeing that as the only way to head it off. They hounded you out, which yeah, I agree, pretty shitty even if they believed it was the right thing to do for the empire.

"Then you set up in a village and tried to make your fortune by robbing the graves of the villagers' loved ones, and then harvesting them of their secrets; you set up your own forge in direct competition with the village forge, that about right?"

"They weren't using the dead, and I spent long years honing my craft!" He nodded as if I were agreeing with him.

"Oh, and wait, I forgot a detail. Using the memories of the smith's ancestors, you made armor and weapons that were better than they could, demanded a premium for those weapons, and said that if people didn't pay it, you'd sell them to the raiders. I'm assuming they were slavers and fucksticks like you?"

"You know nothing and still you judge." He sighed, shaking his head. "You understand so little, and yet you think you have the right to judge me. So like the empire, so like Amon."

The mention of my predecessor's name sent a surge of anger through me, but I forced it down. "And you think that I should just toss aside the old empire and its values, stab the legion in the back, and what do I get in exchange?"

"Reasonable guidance of your reign. The empire reborn, but *wiser*. No more foolish restrictions on necessary practices." His eyes gleamed. "The strong should rule the weak, after all."

"The empire *exists* to protect the weak, not to rule them," I countered. "To bring order and justice."

He laughed, a dry sound like rustling autumn leaves. "Justice? Order? Pretty words that mean nothing. Power is all that matters, but clearly you don't understand that. I offer you a chance, boy. Listen…*learn*. Don't be blinded by the lies of the empire, nor the ridiculous fantasy that so many spread. Lies that 'all are equal' and such rot. The only time that all are equal is when they lie in the house of the dead!

"When they pass through the veil, then truly all are equal, because they *all* exist to serve my kind! You have Bonesight, and some variation on it? Fine, you can learn. You have clearly touched on the secrets of the grave, so…" He reached forward, resting one hand on his staff again. It began to glow. It was old, gnarled wood that looked to be as ancient as him, and yet the crystal that was gripped in a tangle of roots at the tip glowed a sheer, malevolent yellow.

"Apprentice yourself to me, boy. Serve and learn, and I will guide your feet along the path to glory," he whispered. "Your mistake was in coming within reach of me at all, so let me make it clear. You will serve me. You will bend the knee, or you will die. And when you lie, broken in death, I shall raise you up again, and use you to lay claim to the rotting corpse of the empire.

"Serve me and rule, or die and serve me for all of time!" he hissed, spittle covering his chin as he grinned, nodding to himself. "Now, let me show you *true* power."

The wagon's structure came alive with sickly green energy. Bones began to shift and flow like water, walls becoming fluid as an army of skeletal hands reached for me. I triggered Mana Overdrive and launched myself backward, smashing through the bone ceiling as Oracle's warning scream echoed in my mind.

I erupted into the afternoon light just as the wagon exploded outward, bones splitting, half into a mass that spread across the ground, latching onto the bodies of the dead. They pulled more and more bones free, adding them to the morass as the rest of the wagon collapsed to the ground.

A handful of chests and blankets were picked up and carried by piles of bones across the ground, clearly being moved aside so that they didn't get dirty.

Beyond that, the entire wagon and each and every bone that was within reach was already being rebuilt, locking against the cliff sides. They spread out, forming a literal floor of bones, one that had hundreds, if not thousands of hands, all reaching for the bodies of the living and the dead beyond it.

The undead legionnaires and the Dark legionnaires hacked downward, killing the slaves they stood atop of, and then spun, sprinting full bore at the living legionnaires who outnumbered them so much.

The other half of the bones, though, were moving as well, assembling themselves into a massive construct. The necromancer rose at its center, his frail form now crackling with emerald lightning as he directed his creation. Shields popped into place as he laughed maniacally.

"Legion, form up!" I roared, landing among my soldiers as they raised their shields. "Oracle, Sehran, get high and get ready!"

The bone monstrosity towered three stories high, a writhing mass of skeletal arms and legs forming and reforming into weapons. Skull-faced warriors emerged from their flanks, charging our lines as the necromancer began to weave a spell that made the air itself feel dead and heavy.

"You could have been so much more," he called down, his voice booming with unnatural resonance. "Now you'll join my collection, young prince. Your bones will serve a greater purpose than you know, and unlike with the living, bones never disappoint me!"

"Your bone disappointed the living?" I shouted back at him, before grinning at the look of confusion on his face. "Well, there it is, ladies and gents…the real reason the necromancer fuckstick is evil. His whisky dick disappointed the living."

I raised my naginata as Oracle and Sehran took flanking positions. Around us, the legion locked shields as the first wave of undead crashed against their line, and I still grinned down at him, watching as he restructured his creation.

The bone construct shifted and flowed like liquid mercury, its form constantly changing. I flew around it, burning mana to keep aloft as I tried to work out what the hell I was going to do with this.

Massive arms of fused femurs and spines lashed out, trying to sweep our lines apart while skull-faced warriors charged. Beyond that, and on all sides, tremors started in the ground as more and more undead appeared, dragging themselves out of shallow graves.

"You think this is the first time we've been ambushed here?" he sneered, the contempt clear in his voice as it rang out even over the clatter of bones. "Two hundred years I've rolled around this route, boy! Two hundred years I've spent making preparations. Entire *legions* have fallen to my creations!"

*"Jax, on the cliff tops!"* Sehran sent, and I got a sudden picture of dozens, perhaps hundreds of undead digging themselves out of the ground, already armed and armored.

"First rank, hold!" Daralen's voice cut through the chaos as the massive arms crashed down again. The legion braced, spreading the impact across them all by the use of the same legion ability I'd seen demonstrated back in Himnel.

The magic of the shields was basic, incredibly so in comparison to the armor that had been in play back when the empire was strong and young. But for something like this, it didn't need to be fancy. All it did was spread the impact out, the force disseminating over a surface that was made up of the entire legion turtle, drawing grunts from the men and women, but little else.

"Second rank, spears ready!" she bellowed.

The legion moved with practiced precision. Shields were already locked together and now spears thrust through small gaps, skewering the first wave of undead.

The first rank were easily dispatched, but the next group that hit the line did so with the force of a bone-pile driver. These weren't mindless zombies; they were the ten resurrected dead that were his elite guard. They fought with the skill of veteran legionnaires, the fearlessness of the undead, and an absolute lack of any restrictions on their stamina.

Oracle's lightning crackled overhead, blasting apart clusters of bones before they could fully form. Sehran dove through the air, her Explosive Compression spell hammering into the bones and detonating, even as her claws raked through skeletal warriors. But for every one she destroyed, two more rose from the expanding bone field.

She started to grab skulls, launching herself up and away from the fight, hurling the skull at the rocks and shattering it. But unlike fighting the more regular undead, that did nothing. These weren't controlled by a single spell that bound them together from the heart or head.

They were bones. Bones that were fully imbued and ready for anything.

I darted forward, lashing out with my naginata and smashing a dozen bones that were thrown up around me, then falling back as more and more came.

Each time I tried to get in close, bones would spray from the ground, striking out, desperate to wrap around and crush me.

When I flew higher, he'd switch from me and attack the legion. If I came within reach, I was hammered over and over with the bones. And as much as I normally liked a target-rich environment, when they were like this? Not so much.

The undead that were throwing themselves into the fight were mindless, beyond the ten elites, but fuck me they were coming in literal waves.

"Your mockery shows your ignorance, boy!" the necromancer's voice boomed as his construct reshaped itself. Ribs and vertebrae wove together into massive tentacles that whipped toward our flanks. "Let me educate you!"

I triggered Mana Overdrive again, leaping to intercept the bone tentacles before they could wrap around our formation. My naginata blazed with fire as I carved through the writhing mass. But even as the severed pieces crashed to the ground, losing cohesion…a minute later, it simply flowed back together.

"*Jax!*" Oracle's warning came just as a wall of jagged bone spikes erupted from the ground beneath my feet.

I twisted in midair, barely avoiding impalement. A second attack caught me across the shoulder, scraping against my armor and making me hiss in pain as it went numb, the joint almost dislocating with the force.

"The Praetorian plate," the necromancer called out. "Such a waste on one who doesn't understand its true purpose. Perhaps I'll preserve it, after I've added your bones to my collection!"

I fired off a fireball. Well, no, that's not right—a *Pyroclastic Blast* that fuckin' slammed into the old bastard's shield...and then sank into it. The broken and breaking bones that had been starting to fall free were suddenly torn back into the mass as it roared in triumph, and he bellowed in laughter.

*"Great, his shield can absorb and redirect mana,"* I snarled to Oracle and Sehran.

*"We need to hit it with physical attacks, break it with that or all we're doing is helping him to keep his undead active."*

*"Or, we break all the undead and make him run out of mana,"* Sehran suggested, before cursing. *"If he's this prepared, he's probably got a load of manastones and a massive manapool."*

*"Physical it is,"* I agreed, looking over the rest of the fight for a second to get my bearings.

The bone field spread rapidly now, creeping across the ground like a living thing. Everywhere it touched, more warriors rose. Our lines were holding, but I could see the strain on the legionnaires' faces as they fought opponents who never tired, never hesitated.

The ten they were facing were...well, they were impressive, no matter what I thought of them. Combined with the weight of the armor and their weapons, when the first ones had bounced off the still powered shield that the legionnaires kept up, the others split their attacks.

Half went high, forcing the legion to block there, while the rest went low, stabbing out into the ankles, sabatons, and cuisse of the legionnaires.

They wore heavy armor—the majority, at least—and "minor" things like a spear hitting that, when there was so little of the legionnaire available to be hit, to get a good strike going, should have been something that could be shrugged off.

Against the more regular undead, that was certainly true.

Against these?

They fought in disciplined pairs, where one broke the line with a spear punching through, then wrenched it sideways. The second kicked out, breaking the lock and separating the shields.

As that was done, the next two darted in. For the living, that would have been it: they'd have been taken down hard...these were legionnaires they faced, after all. But as undead, little things like a stab to the gut or losing an arm didn't faze them.

As the first of the undead legionnaire collapsed, its head finally removed, the others streamed inward.

The turtle that had shielded the legion ironically proved to be its undoing, as the close quarters meant that none of the legion could get enough room to hit with any real force.

That, in turn, meant that as the first undead fell, two more legionnaires fell in short order.

Then the true horror of the necromancer was shown as the seemingly injured legionnaire who had fallen rose again. Their friends to either side gave them room and tried to let them through to tend to their wounds…only to be stabbed in the back, as they were revealed to have died and been reanimated, the freshly arisen undead taking their former companions down.

This wasn't a battle we could win through attrition. We needed to reach the necromancer himself, but his bone construct kept shifting and changing, making it impossible to get close. And with every passing second, his power over the battlefield grew stronger.

The battle was rapidly turning against us. Through our bond, I felt Oracle's rising concern as more legionnaires fell, only to rise again as puppets of the necromancer. The tightly packed formation that had been our strength was becoming a death trap.

*"Jax, we need to break the pattern,"* Oracle sent through our bond. *"He's fighting a battle he's won hundreds of times before."*

She was right. This ancient bastard had perfected this ambush over centuries. The ravine, the slavers, the bone field—all designed to funnel enemies into this killing ground.

Shit, it was perfect, I realized; the location was absolutely *perfect* for an attack, for an ambush. Except that anyone who attacked this wagon in these perfectly positioned choke points wasn't the ambusher—they were the ambushed.

"Daralen!" I shouted. "Break formation! Scatter to the high ground!"

The primus immediately understood, bellowing orders that sent the legion moving in practiced groups of three, abandoning the traditional shield wall. Their discipline showed as they executed the unexpected maneuver, preventing the undead from exploiting the gaps.

"Oracle, Sehran, keep up high and give me a fucking magical solution to this! Use the ultimate spell!" I yelled, launching myself higher into the air to draw the necromancer's attention. I dove down and rolled around, flashing past him as I let off an almost pathetic barrage of Magic Missiles—not one of which managed to do more than shift his shield from clear to, literally, slightly darker.

*"What?"* Sehran asked. *"What do I do?"*

*"A distraction. Get ready to distract him, that's all,"* Oracle assured her. *"Jax is going to use his naginata. It has a shield breaker enchantment, but he needs to actually reach him to make it work."*

*"I bet I can distract him!"* Sehran sent a mental giggle, one that was half evil and half excited.

"Ultimate spell? Show me! Show me the pathetic magic that you're so proud of!"

The ancient elf's face contorted with glee as he directed his construct to lash out at me; bone tentacles stretched impossibly to try to snare me, whiplike. But that's exactly what I wanted. His focus on me, not on the two women who were now positioning themselves on either side of the battlefield.

*"Ready?"* Oracle asked through our bond.

*"You're the distraction this time,"* I sent back, grinning despite the pain in my shoulder as it reknit. *"Make it count."*

I dove straight at the necromancer, naginata blazing with fire. The bone construct surged to meet me, shields forming and reforming to block my approach. I poured mana into my weapon, the blade glowing white-hot. I hacked through the defenses, making it look like I was pouring my all into this.

"You think you're the first to try a direct assault?" the necromancer cackled. His withered hands directed more bones to reinforce his position. "I've faced *dragons*, boy!"

"Yeah, but they didn't have them," I yelled, pointing behind him. "Go, go, GO!"

Oracle's ritual circle flared to life beneath the construct. Flames of Wrath spiraled upward through the mass of bones, doing bugger all, but making him look for something else.

At the same time, Sehran launched her attack, flashing forward toward him and bypassing Oracle. She didn't attack with claws or explosive magic, but with something far more fundamental to her nature.

The succubus hovered directly in the necromancer's line of sight. Her form shifted, radiating waves of pure desire as she let loose with the most powerful song of lust and need that she could manage, targeting the ancient elf's most primal instincts.

For all his power and age, he was still bound to his original form, with all its weaknesses. His concentration faltered for just a second as Sehran's magic took hold. His eyes widened, fingers loosening on his staff.

That was all I needed. I released the second Pyroclastic Blast spell, the one that I'd been holding ready, but this time I didn't aim for the necromancer.

Instead, I aimed for the golem, a headless, formless trunk that served simply as a focal point for the mass of bones to erupt from. It was like a cup, risen from the earth, with the necromancer floating atop it like a bubble cresting waves.

The spell impacted, and instead of hitting the shield, it detonated in the midst of the bones, sending razor-sharp bone shards in all directions.

They hit the underside of the shield. The non-magical nature of the impact meant that instead of feeding it, it drained it—not fully, but enough that the shield went entirely black in response, cutting the old bastard off from the rest of the world.

That was when I slammed into the shield. My naginata drove straight through what had been layers upon layers of bones that were there to keep me back, and what was now an unprotected section. The blade punched through layer after layer of magical defenses before being deflected by a final shield of bone over the necromancer's chest.

He shrieked, shoving forward; bones slid from a ring on his finger, deflecting a second blow and a third, as he tried to reform the shield.

His shield flickered and failed to form even as we both fell, battling as Oracle's flames consumed the bones supporting him.

"Fool!" he snarled. "You cannot win! I am eternal. I am—"

He made a weird noise, half a whimper and half a squeal like a stuck pig, and lost concentration for a split second. The bones all around him suddenly splayed in a dozen directions as I struck, ramming my blade into his chest.

"You're just another dead asshole," I finished for him, twisting the blade.

The construct began to collapse around us as the necromancer's control slipped away. I grabbed his staff as he desperately tried to pull it in close and instead ripped it from his grasp. He tumbled free, no longer able to keep himself afloat, feeling the ancient power thrumming within it.

He slammed into the pile of bones, sending them flying and rolling as he slid down them, staring up at me in shock and horror…and what looked like a little surprise as well?

Guess he didn't expect to be fucking defeated then.

All across the battlefield, the undead legionnaires stumbled, then fell in a great clatter of bone and metal. I dropped from the sky, landing atop the pile and standing over the necromancer, watching as his body began to crumble, the centuries finally catching up to him. But his eyes still burned with hatred as his lips formed final words.

"The Sons…will never…let the empire rise again," he forced out in a pained, fury-filled, and still confused voice.

With his death, the massive bone construct collapsed completely, sending shock waves across the battlefield as thousands of bones clattered to the ground.

Oracle and Sehran converged on my position. The three of us watched as a handful of undead that had somehow survived were dispatched by the legion.

"That was too close," Oracle whispered, reaching out to me as I pulled her in close, the three of us staring at the evil, ancient old bastard's corpse.

"And too easy," Sehran added, her eyes scanning the battlefield. "A necromancer that powerful wouldn't just…die."

"I think he did," I countered. "I think he's dead. I think he was close to becoming a lich, but just hadn't made the final transition yet, that's all. Mind you, there's definitely something about him, about that fight that just rang weird to me."

"Oh?" Sehran asked, with a twinkle in her eye.

"Yeah, I mean, that fight was close. He was good and then suddenly he just…" I shrugged. "Like he lost control of his power for a second."

"Like he lost all control?" she asked mischievously.

"No, but he was close." I frowned, looking at her, and seeing the grin tugging at her lips. "Okay, you minx, what did you do?"

"Well…" She bounced suggestively. "You know that for me to do…what I do, I need to understand what my master, my mistress, or my target wants, right?"

"I get that, and please stop bouncing." I sighed, closing my eyes.

"Nope, because we both know you like it."

I opened my eyes, glaring at her as Oracle laughed and Sehran grinned totally unrepentantly.

"What's important, though, is that for me to do that, I get into your head. Now, for most people that's hard, but if I can get there, I've got a lot of control. Don't worry…I couldn't make you do things, not really. It's more a suggestion. And once you're aware it's there, you can block it easily.

"It's something I can only really do once, and it's tied to the centers of your mind and body that I…well, that I get to play with. I couldn't make someone walk around and do things because I'd have no clue how to do it, how to control all the muscles and so on. But I can, and I've learned how, through a *lot* of practice, to grip a certain muscle."

"A muscle…" I muttered. "Wait, you can mentally grip that and—"

"I gripped it and pumped it a bit, that's all. Along with a feeling like a finger rammed where he wasn't expecting it." She smiled sunnily.

I burst out laughing, not sure whether I should be horrified or impressed, or even disgusted considering he'd been in mid-fight with me at that point and she'd…

"Well, I guess the fight didn't have the happy ending he was hoping for." I sighed, then grinned as both Oracle and Sehran groaned. "Oh, come on, you know it's true!" I laughed, deciding it was funny.

"Okay, we need to see to the legion and any slaves who were injured again," Oracle said. "You need to do the whole 'lord and master' bit." She indicated me. "And you and I need a talk about appropriate behavior in a fight." She indicated Sehran.

"You want me to teach you to do it, don't you," she deadpanned.

"Obviously!" Oracle crowed. "Do you know how much fun I could have distracting Jax in meetings with that! Not to mention during his speeches, or over dinner—all of it!"

"Fuck my life." I groaned. "Right, back to work!" I ordered, shaking my head in mixed horror and hope for the future.

# CHAPTER THIRTY

The aftermath of battle was a mess of broken bones, both literally and figuratively. As the legionnaires began the tedious work of clearing the battlefield, I sat on a chunk of what had once been the necromancer's fancy-ass bone wagon, watching the organized chaos unfold, and trying to get into meditation mode.

Daralen was in her element, barking orders and organizing recovery teams with crisp efficiency. Eleven legionnaires had been killed outright in the fighting, with another dozen sporting injuries ranging from "walk it off" to "how the fuck are you still breathing?" Oracle moved among them, her healing magic mending flesh and bone with practiced ease.

I'd been reduced to a walking mana battery—or, more accurately, a *sitting* mana battery—and for now, I agreed that was for the best. It also gave me a few minutes of peace and quiet to sort through the emotional roller coaster of the last few hours as well.

Despite everything, there were some niggling little concerns that the bony bastard had been right about things with the empire.

Worse still, I knew he had a point. The justicars would have tried to hide something like that in those days because a rebellion, when it was all going tits up, helped nobody, and hiding it, yeah, it wasn't going to bring back the woman who'd died.

All it'd do would get a load more people killed, and frankly, there was no point. Especially not when people were barely surviving back then.

It was still wrong, and a part of me wanted the city guard captain nailed to the gate by his balls, as an example. But then, considering all the other shit that was happening back then?

Fuck it. It wasn't like it was anything that we could really do anything about at this point.

The surviving members of the would-be rescue party were a sorry sight. Of the hundred or so who had started the attack, maybe thirty remained. Most were wounded; all were shell-shocked. They huddled together, eyeing us with a mix of suspicion, gratitude, and lingering resentment.

Their leader—the same asshole who'd been so certain we'd fuck things up—sat on a rock with his head in his hands, blood seeping from a wound across his scalp.

*"You should talk to them,"* Oracle sent through our bond as she finished healing a legionnaire with a nasty gut wound. *"They've lost everything, and they need to understand what just happened."*

*"I think you mean that their brilliant plan got most of their people killed and nearly fucked us all?"* I shot back, then immediately felt like an ass when I caught her reproachful glance.

*"They were trying to save people,"* she reminded me gently. *"So were we."*

She was right, as usual. I sighed, pushing myself to my feet and wincing as my shoulder twinged. The bone spike that had caught me had done more damage than I'd initially thought, and I made a mental note to have Oracle look at it once she'd finished with the serious cases. Until then, our mana was better spent on them, and there was no point in wasting a potion when all I needed was a little time to replenish that.

Oracle was down to the last half dozen or so injured, and I looked from her to the idiot, and then popped a low-grade mana potion to replace the meditation I was losing out on, and examined the five artifacts that had been brought to me.

The freed slaves—nearly three hundred of them—were being looked after already, and I wasn't needed there. Most were still where they'd fallen when their collars had shattered, too stunned by their sudden freedom to move. Others had begun helping the wounded or searching for friends and family among the survivors. A few had simply wandered off in shock, only to be gently herded back by patient legionnaires.

There were also, although not as many as we'd hoped, more legionnaires in the mix. The seventeen we'd rescued had all taken their places alongside their brothers and sisters with profuse thanks and determination.

Six of the legion were currently engaged in "battlefield recovery," which was a euphemism for "looting everything not nailed down, and if it's nailed, we'll have the nails too."

That had turned up a small supply of usable items like potions, and an insane supply of various consumer goods, more of that cloth that Zyenna had brought at such cost, and a million and one other items.

It also resulted in five magical artifacts, and whoo-boy were they good!

| The Dusk Warden | Further Description *Yes*/*No* |
|---|---|
| **Details:** | This lance was forged during the last days of the Empire from the bones of a dying black dragon. Its shaft is midnight-black adamantine wrapped in leather made from the hide of the same dragon, with runes of binding and death etched in silver along its length.<br>Wielded by Commander Vexius of the Legion of Arentine during the Twilight Campaign, it was lost when his entire legion was swallowed by the sands during a magical storm. The lance absorbs life essence with each strike, storing it within the crystallized dragon heart at its core. The wielder can release this essence to create a field of necrotic energy that slows enemies and gradually drains their vitality while bolstering allies with temporary vigor. |

| **Rarity:** | **Magical:** | **Durability:** | **Charge:** |
|---|---|---|---|
| Legendary | Yes | 68/100 | 0/100 |

That was impressive—hell, it looked cool as fuck. But damn, knowing that it had lost its charge meant that at some point, the fucker had to have used them up. The only way to make it useful for me was to kill people with it, and a lance? I'd need a mount.

Bob, on the other hand, though…that I could see working.

I grinned evilly, intending to give it to him, along with a makeover.

The next one was cool as well.

| Soulrend | | Further Description *Yes/No* | |
|---|---|---|---|
| **Details:** | | This greatsword has changed the fate of kingdoms on three separate occasions.<br>Its blade is forged from enchanted ice that never melts, bound to a hilt of ancient ironwood wrapped in the preserved skin of a frost wyrm. The guard is crafted from platinum inlaid with sapphires, and the pommel holds an orb of condensed ice mana. The sword emits a constant chill that forms frost on nearby surfaces and can unleash waves of freezing energy that slow and gradually petrify enemies.<br>Those slain by the blade rise temporarily as frost wraiths that serve the wielder for a short time before dissipating.<br>The sword's most terrifying ability is to trap the souls of particularly powerful enemies within the sapphires, allowing the wielder to consult them for knowledge or torment them for eternity. | |
| **Rarity:** | **Magical:** | **Durability:** | **Charge:** |
| Legendary | Yes | 47/100 | 3/5 |

The description was a little freaky, sure, but that it held souls already? That said to me that they were powerful. And, knowing the dickhead who had held this beforehand, I was willing to bet they knew a lot as well.

I mentally chalked this one up to personally check it out later on.

| Worldcleaver | Further Description *Yes/No* |
|---|---|
| **Details:** | This massive great axe was supposedly forged from a fragment of the moon Ishtic that fell during the Cataclysm.<br>Its blade is a crescent of midnight-black metal that seems to drink in light, with |

| | a haft made from the heartwood of a grove guardian. Worldcleaver is infamous for its ability to cut through almost any material, even those warded against conventional damage.<br>When swung with sufficient force, it can create rifts in space that linger briefly, allowing the wielder to step through them to appear elsewhere within sight. Extended use is known to weaken the boundaries between realms, sometimes allowing glimpses of other planes and occasionally attracting the attention of entities best left undisturbed. BE WARNED! |
|---|---|

| **Rarity:** | **Magical:** | **Durability:** | **Charge:** |
|---|---|---|---|
| Legendary | Yes | 16/100 | 23/50 |

That one…considering I'd seen the shit that lived on the other side when I'd faced the Valspar…yeah, that was a hard pass. I mentally marked that up as something to be investigated, and then possibly melted down.

The last thing I needed was Grizz chopping a hole in reality and ending the world.

| **Crown of Whispers** | **Further Description** *Yes/No* |
|---|---|
| **Details:** | This seemingly simple circlet of tarnished silver set with a single opal appears unremarkable, but conceals terrible power.<br>Created by the mad sorcerer Valthis during the necromancer wars, it allows the wearer to hear the thoughts of the dead and communicate with spirits, *continually.*<br>The crown enhances necromantic magic significantly, reducing the mana cost and increasing the power of such spells. Its most dangerous ability is soul tethering—the wearer can bind spirits to themselves, drawing on their knowledge and power.<br>However, each tethered soul exerts its own influence on the wearer, gradually changing their personality and desires. The crown is rumored to contain the bound souls of seven ancient |

|  |  | necromancers, including Valthis himself, who offer their knowledge to the wearer but constantly vie for control.<br>After prolonged use, wearers report dreams of a vast underground chamber filled with countless whispering souls, and a growing sense that the crown is not merely a tool, but a gateway to something far more sinister. |
| --- | --- | --- |
| **Rarity:** | **Magical:** | **Durability:** | **Charge:** |
| Legendary | Yes | 4/100 | 6/7 |

That was a hard pass. Just fuck to the no. I put it straight into my bag of holding and just noped the hell out. I'd deal with it later.

| **The Faithful Centurion's Cuirass** | **Further Description** *Yes*/*No* |
| --- | --- |
| **Details:** | This magnificent breastplate bears the insignia of the Imperial Legion's elite Praetorian Guard, those sworn to protect the Eternal Emperor himself. Forged from an alloy of adamantine and mithril, it is inlaid with gold runes that pulse with magic, and set with five blood-red rubies representing the five pillars of Imperial power. The armor absorbs a portion of any damage dealt to the wearer, converting it to mana that can be used to power a temporary shield of force, enhance the wearer's physical abilities for short bursts, or heal wounds by accelerating the wearer's natural recovery. Most impressively, once per day, it can make the wearer completely invulnerable for a few seconds— enough time to survive what would otherwise be a fatal blow. Legends claim the armor will gradually mold itself to better fit a worthy wearer and may grant additional abilities to those of imperial blood. |
| **Rarity:** | **Magical:** | **Durability:** | **Charge:** |
| Legendary | Yes | 4/100 | 4/100 |

The last one? That was cool as fuck, and had it more than four points of durability left, I'd have been swapping my own out for it right goddamn now.

There were also a handful of "minor" trinkets, though clearly all were necromancer or lunatic focused. I checked the first few, then put the others aside to go over later, seeing that they really weren't anything that was going to make much of a difference at this point.

| Bone Dice of Fate | | Further Description *Yes*/No | |
|---|---|---|---|
| Details: | | A pair of six-sided dice carved from the knucklebones of a prophet. When rolled and imbued with the user's mana, they momentarily reveal glimpses of various possible futures before settling on a result. The visions are brief and often cryptic, but always tied to events that might soon affect the roller. | |
| Rarity: | Magical: | Durability: | Charge: |
| Rare | Yes | 66/100 | N/A |

That one freaked me out while also making me think about how cool it was. First of all, I didn't believe in fate; secondly, how many fucking prophets were there going around that their knucklebones could be recovered and made into goddamn dice for this set to "only" be rare rather than legendary or unique?

| Shroud of Passing | | Further Description *Yes*/No | |
|---|---|---|---|
| Details: | | A tattered black cloth that, when wrapped around a corpse, preserves it perfectly for transportation or ritual purposes. It also masks the presence of the dead body from both mundane and magical detection. | |
| Rarity: | Magical: | Durability: | Charge: |
| Uncommon | Yes | 71/100 | 74/100 |

That was kinda cool, even if it was a bit macabre.

| Shadow Lantern | | Further Description *Yes*/No | |
|---|---|---|---|
| Details: | | A small brass lantern that, when lit, casts shadows that move independently of their sources. These shadows can be mentally directed to gather information, scout areas, or deliver simple messages, though they cannot interact physically with the world. | |

| Rarity: | Magical: | Durability: | Charge: |
|---|---|---|---|
| Uncommon | Yes | 27/100 | 33/100 |

The remainder of the artifacts were things like rings of healing, personal shields that had been drained until they were broken, several rings of plus one or two to health. A ring called the Serpent's Chance that could produce poison when channeled into, though what grade and strength wasn't stated, and a handful of other trinkets, making it clear that although there were a lot of magical artifacts here, the "good stuff," beyond the old prick's staff, was hidden elsewhere.

There were also fifteen bags of holding, that went all the way from two more bags of spatial folding—one to Oracle and one to Sehran, thank you *very* much—down to barely worthy of the title. But the sheer amount of random knickknacks, what had to be drugs, and sheer fuckin' weirdness I found?

We could have made the tower into a wonderful home for people with some of this shit and yet, as it was? I was seriously considering leaving most of it here, feeling dirty by association just by touching it.

"Jax?" Sehran landed beside me, her wings folding neatly against her back. Despite the battle, she looked remarkably composed. A trait I envied. "Those idiots from the cliffs want to talk to you. Well, not 'want,' exactly. More like 'need to before they do something else stupid.'"

"Yeah, I'm going." I rolled my shoulders, settling my armor more comfortably. "How's the leader doing?"

"Still breathing, which is more than he deserves." She snorted. "I hit him with a heal before coming to get you, but he's feeling sorry for himself. Survivor's guilt is hitting him hard."

I nodded, understanding all too well. "Keep an eye on our people. I want an inventory of anything salvageable from the wagons. Especially manastones. We're going to need a lot of shit just to get these folks to Sonra, and I don't doubt that if these dicks have seen the opportunity to be gained by raiding, others will have as well."

Sehran gave a mock salute that made me roll my eyes, then took flight again, heading toward the far end of the wagons.

As I approached the survivor group, I could feel the tension rise. Several of them reached for weapons before thinking better of it as the nearby legionnaires growled and grabbed their own. That gave me a little hope. At least they weren't completely stupid.

"Your plan was shit," I said without preamble, stopping a few paces away from their leader. "You got most of your people killed, and you nearly fucked the rest of us in the process."

The man looked up, his eyes red-rimmed and hollow. "We've been fighting these bastards for years. Saving who we could, when we could. And you…" He gestured weakly at me. "You just waltz in and what? You expect us to be grateful?" He shook his head.

"What?" I asked.

"Why?"

"Why what?"

"Why did you let them die? My friends, my family, and you just let them fucking die, you asshole!" He was on his feet, stalking forward, tears in his eyes as he started screaming. "You fucking dick! You did this!"

"We saved you, motherfucker," I growled.

"You could have stopped us—you *should* have stopped us!" he screamed, shoving at me, and bouncing off when I didn't move.

"We tried talking you out of it!" I slapped his hands aside, then held out a hand and called out as every legionnaire in sight went on point like a hound after a rabbit, weapons being fully drawn now. "It's all right! Settle down!"

"This is your fault!" he spat. "You might as well have killed us yourself!"

"Berin…" one of the others spoke up, and he waved them off, continuing his rant at me.

"You say you're the legion? Bullshit! We *know* the legion! They fucking run in and pick fights with entire armies and they die! All of them, every time!"

"The legion, as you knew it, was being forced to obey stupid goddamn oaths from seven hundred years ago!" I snapped back. "You see them now? You see how they did this? They're professionals, the best fighters in the world, and you told them to fuck off. You had crossbows on us and threatened to fire unless we let you attack. What did you expect us to do? Ruin the piss-poor element of surprise that you had left by fighting you? We all lost people today."

"We had no chance!" he yelled. "Don't give me that! They killed almost all of us and then you lost what? One? Two?"

"We lost eleven, and that was because we had training, resources, and a plan," I replied, softening my tone slightly. "And we've got more than that. With every step, we gather more of the empire behind me."

A harsh laugh escaped him. "The empire? The fucking empire's been dead for centuries, and good riddance!"

"Not anymore." I held his gaze, letting him see the certainty there. "I'm rebuilding it. One free person at a time, if that's what it takes."

A murmur ran through the group, and I realized I had an audience. Not just the survivors, but many of the freed slaves as well, drawn by the conversation. I stood straighter, raising my voice to address them all.

"My name is Jax Amon, Prince of the Empire and ruler of Dravith." The words carried across the clearing, silencing the murmurs. "What you saw today wasn't just magic—it was an imperial ability. The same powers that built and preserved the empire in the first place, and the power that will rebuild it now."

I looked around, meeting as many eyes as I could. Some wary, some hopeful, all attentive.

"The old empire wasn't perfect. It made mistakes—serious ones. It let power corrupt it, let scumbag nobles twist things until they could bring about the fall. And in the end, it too fell." I paused, letting that sink in. "But at its core, the empire stood for something real. Protection. Order. Justice. The idea that the strong protect the weak, not prey on them."

One of the older slaves stepped forward, the signs of manacles around his wrists and ankles still visible. "I done heard stories of the empire since I were a bairn. Tales ma grandmother told, passed down from her grandmother. But they just be stories."

"No. They're not just stories anymore," I replied. "But I'll need help to make it real again. I'll need people willing to fight for something bigger than themselves."

The leader of the rescue group—Berin, apparently—spat on the ground, swaying slightly. "Pretty words. But we've heard pretty words before."

"Then judge me by my actions." I spread my arms. "You're free. All of you. Not just from the collars, but from what comes next too. Anyone who wants to go their own way can do so, and we'll give you supplies and weapons from the captured wagons. I won't force anyone to follow me."

That caused a stir. Even among the legionnaires, I caught a few surprised glances.

"But," I continued, "for those who want to be part of something greater—for those who want to ensure no one else suffers what you've suffered—I offer a place. Swear to the empire, and you'll never stand alone again."

The silence that followed was heavy with potential. Then the old slave stepped forward again.

"What about the drow, my lord?" His voice carried clearly. "The messages appeared to those of us not in the collars, even in the pens. You've challenged Illoth herself."

That revelation sent a fresh wave of murmurs through the crowd, and I grinned despite myself. Clearly, an imperial prince challenging a goddess was newsworthy enough that people had remembered it.

"Yeah," I acknowledged, feeling Oracle's concern through our bond. "I've challenged the Goddess of the Drow to combat at Sonra in less than a week's time."

"You mean to fight a goddess?" the rescue leader asked incredulously. "Are you insane?"

"Probably," I admitted with a grin that made several people step back. "But I've already faced Nimon. Illoth's just next on my shit list."

That did it. The mention of killing the God of Death—a feat they *had* to have seen the notifications for—even if more than a few disbelieved—sent a shock through the gathering. Many stepped back farther, making what I guessed were religious or warding signs. But others moved closer, expressions shifting from wariness to awe.

"In less than a week, I will face Illoth at the tent city of Sonra," I continued. "And after I defeat her, I will free every slave in that city and beyond. That's my promise to you all."

The old slave looked at me for a long moment, then slowly sank to one knee. "Then I will follow you, my lord. If only to see such a thing with my own eyes before I die."

One by one, others followed suit—first a trickle, then a flood. Not all, certainly. Some held back, watching with skepticism, outright fear, or even anger. But enough. More than enough.

Berin stared at me still; his face expressed his internal struggle with his pride, as a small number started to leave.

"Stand," I said after a moment. "All of you. The empire doesn't need subjects on their knees. It needs citizens on their feet."

As they rose, I caught Daralen's faint smile, and she nodded to me, standing surrounded by filthy, exhausted-looking men and women who were out of armor.

I guessed that they were the rescued legionnaires, and I smiled as I looked at them. "Legion, I am Jax Amon, Prince of the Empire, and I say we're gonna fuck some slavers up and kill anyone who gets in our way. Are you with me?"

The roar in response was enough to make a few of the hesitating figures join those who were clearly joining us, and I nodded my thanks.

"Okay, people, those who wish to come with us will be swearing an oath as a citizen and to follow me. Don't worry, it's just to make sure you're safe from each other, and I can rely on you. If once you see the oath, you decide not to come with us or swear? I understand, and I will, as I said, ensure you get some supplies and a weapon.

"However, you won't be travelling with us if you're not sworn, so you can go in any direction you like, *except* toward Sonra. That's because the last thing I need is someone selling the details of our route and who we are to the scumbags who will no doubt be waiting for us there.

"You've got a few minutes while I drink these potions, and then the oath will be coming out to you all. One last point, and please take this seriously—we will be offering regular healing to our citizens, as well as skill and spellbooks, and when I have them again, skill memories. I've done this already for literally hundreds back on Dravith, the continent I've come from.

"The spell uses flames to burn out any kind of infection and heal you. Oracle, could you please?" I asked, and she nodded, casting the Frostfire Circle of Healing off to one side. Before I could ask, Daralen marched forward, having to order the other legionnaires with her to wait until they'd sworn before they entered the flames.

When she was fine, people settled down again, and I went on.

"If you were thinking of not swearing and instead pretending and then following along for the free food, weapons, armor, training, and homes, then please don't. If you are not sworn to me and you set foot in the circle, you will be identified as an enemy. Please don't risk that, as unless we're very fast…." I shrugged, seeing the rising uncertainty in the faces of many.

"It sounds bad," Daralen barked. "I know it does, but it's literally free healing. You're standing there now, free, because he decided to free you. You're going to have full bellies and clothes, freedom to live your life however you choose, as long as you help your fellow citizens and the empire, and what has all this cost you?"

There was silence, until Berin, the prick, started to open his mouth, looking angry. One of his friends grabbed him.

"It's cost you nothing. Three hours ago, the best you could hope for was that you might find a kindly master who wouldn't abuse and beat you too much. For the legionnaires? We were most likely destined for the fighting pits. Being made to fight to the death against monster after monster until we fell.

"Two days ago, I was a slave. Today, I'm a legionnaire in service to the empire again. And tomorrow?" She shrugged. "Who knows? I don't, but I guarantee it'll be better than being a damn slave."

Oracle had finished with the last of the wounded and now stood at my side, her presence a comfort. Sehran stood farther back, clearly trying not to be a distraction, her expression unusually serious.

"We've got three days of hard travel between now and when we meet up with the rest of the caravan, though," I said. "Because for those of you who were in the caravan that was raided originally?" I looked around, seeing faces filling with hope. "There were other survivors and people we freed from that camp as well. Toren leads that caravan now, along with Zyenna, which for anyone who knows who they are, means that you know they're constantly arguing and they both want to be in charge," I finished dryly. "That means that we really need to get back to them before one kills the other, and there's a lot of work to do before then. Let's get started."

"Okay, everyone, I'm Oracle, and I'll be pushing the oath out to you in a minute. If you don't want to take the oath, we understand, but please move off to the other end of the ravine. We don't want you getting hurt while we heal everyone else. We'll sort some food for you when we can."

She smiled and acted sweet and innocent, and damn me, in that tiny speech, she'd made it clear that they got fuck all healing and they were an afterthought if they didn't swear.

I couldn't help but smile, and she winked at me, feeling my love.

The oaths were a clear success. Twenty-seven people refused, and of the people who refused, nineteen were members of the "rescuers" who had started the fight off so badly. A total of three hundred and eight additional people joined us. Between the original fifty legionnaires I'd brought, the eleven who were lost and the seventeen who were rescued, we were up to fifty-six legionnaires again as well.

The organization took hours. Wagons had to be repaired, supplies inventoried, routes planned. The dead—both our own and the enemy's—had to be properly tended to. Through it all, the strange mix of legion, former slaves, and rescue survivors worked with increasing coordination. Though, if I were honest, I didn't know what the hell I was expecting, considering how far out we were from anywhere.

By nightfall, campfires dotted the ravine, and the mood had shifted from shock to something approaching determination. As I moved among the fires, checking on preparations and speaking with small groups, I was struck by how quickly common purpose united even the most reluctant allies.

"You did well today," Oracle said as we finally retreated to our own small fire at the edge of the camp. "They believe in you now."

"Let's hope I can live up to it," I muttered, finally allowing myself to feel the bone-deep weariness the day had brought. "Fighting a goddess in front of a crowd isn't exactly how I planned to spend my week."

Sehran snorted, sprawling gracefully by the fire. "Since when has anything gone according to plan since you got here?"

"Fair point."

We sat in companionable silence for a while, watching the stars appear overhead. Tomorrow would bring its own challenges: the long trek to Sonra, the preparations for battle, the inevitable complications that always seemed to find us.

We chose not to sleep in the luxury wagons that we'd gained, instead enjoying the little camping session, and that even as the stars wheeled overhead, legionnaires came and went.

I'd done their oath as well, and claimed Amon's oaths as my own; Oracle ensured that the "footprint" of the spell was limited to a mile in radius.

Everything was moving nicely into place, which was why it was such a fucking predictable surprise when the former "rescuers" left the camp in the dead of night.

Twenty of them left without a word, only one making the trek through to my campfire. And when he did, I recognized the man who had gagged their leader when I was speaking to the crowd.

As soon as he approached, not being legion, he was stopped. A ring of steel had "mysteriously" appeared around my little campfire as legionnaires took turns guarding me.

At my call, they let him through, and when he reached me, he went to one knee.

"What's going on?" I asked him curiously as he stayed silent.

"I... I..."

I didn't want to assume, as it'd be pretty fucking embarrassing if I had Oracle push the oath out and then he told me to fuck off and he just had a stone in his shoe or something. But after a few seconds, he started to speak.

"I'm Kajha, and you, um, today you saved my life," he said. "I'd have been dead, or a slave now if you'd not done what yer did, so…ah, crappit." He shook his head. "Look, Lord, I'm sorry, all right? I'm sorry Berin's a dick. He doesn't mean to be, but his girl, she were out there with the fighters an' she died. He planned this—he talked us all into it. Iffin it's not your fault, then it has to be his. That means…"

"It means it's his fault that the woman he loves is dead." I nodded. "I get it."

"Look, he wants us to all go back to the others, an' I will, but, can we come back?"

"Come back?" I asked.

"Yeah, I mean if we go, if we go to get the others, if we talk to them, and they want to join you, can we?" Then, before I could answer, he pushed on. "And if I do, if *we* do, I mean, can we keep hunting slavers?"

"No," I said. "Fuck no, man."

"Uh…" His face fell.

"There's no goddamn way I'm sending you back out after slavers until you can at least hold your own in a fight. If you want to join us and you want to do that? Hell yes, I'll take you. But you'll do it with real weapons, real training, and some fucking tactics! Not to mention spells. I mean, fuck's sake, have any of you got even a basic healing spell? A firebolt? Anything?"

He shook his head, and I sighed. "Look, Kajha, you want to join us? I'll take you, so long as you swear the oath. I'll even take Berin. I think we both know he's a bit of an idiot, but the way you did this today? You're lucky to be alive. You need training, experience, and damn, you need a plan."

"Thank you!" he said quickly. "Look, I can't tell you where we're going, or how many of us there are, but we're going to talk to the others when we get back. Berin says it's all your fault, but he knows it isn't, so we should be able to meet you at Sonra, maybe in a week?"

"A week?"

"It's four days from here," he said.

I nodded, deliberately not saying that it meant that it was at most a day from here to their camp, if he was going to get some time to talk to people there. The look on his face showed he at least knew he'd said too much, and I smiled.

"Go on, man, go meet your friends. And yeah, in a week, we should be at Sonra. If we've moved on from there, there'll be people who know where we went, I'm sure."

"Thank you." He then bowed his head again jerkily, clapped his fist hard enough to his chest that it had to have damn well hurt, then bounded to his feet and ran out of the firelight, nearly getting stabbed by the legionnaires for moving too fast.

Then, that was it. As I lay there, listening to the celebration of the members of the camp on all sides, I couldn't help but smile in the darkness, before sighing and pulling up the goddamn notifications.

### *Congratulations!*

*You have killed the following:*

- *79x Undead of various levels for a total of 9,660xp*
- *1x Ancient Necromancer (Level 59) for 38,000xp*
- *86x Slavers/guards/innocents of various levels for a total of 14,221xp*

*A party under your command killed the following:*

- *214x Undead of various levels for a total of 61,910xp*
- *86x Slavers/guards of various levels for a total of 59,330xp*

*Total party experience earned: 121,240xp*

*As party leader, you gain 25% of all experience earned (30,310xp)*
*Total experience gained: 61,881xp + 30,310xp (party leader bonus) = 95,770xp*

*Progress to level 49 stands at 5,236,369/6,455,000*

It broke my damn heart again that I'd killed more innocents, but the reality was that as much as I hated it, I would do it again tomorrow as the only viable method of saving so many.

Jenae's words about assaulting a city to end a war came back to me…that a rock from a ballistae could crush an orphanage and that was just bad luck, basically. I was paraphrasing as I couldn't remember the exact words, but basically, tough fuckin' titty was the message.

I *hated* it, but knowing that to save a million people I might have to allow the deaths of a thousand or more? A few short months ago, I'd have refused that, and if it was in front of me, I probably still couldn't do that math, I knew. But as it was?

If I didn't, then the slaves that the enemy had would be forced to fight us. We'd have to kill at least half to stop them, and in the fighting, my own people would die as well.

If we did that, at least ten times as many would die who didn't deserve it. I had the option: choose that, or the overload method, and accept that those people were dying.

Amon had said it once ages ago, and that single, short conversation that had been one of the most coherent we'd had—outside of battle—had stuck with me:

*"We do what we must; we blacken our soul 'til naphtha seems like sunshine, and in return, the little child can see that light. They can condemn us, curse us, and revile us, but because of the things we do, they live to do these things.*

*"Welcome, my heir, to adulthood."*

I forced myself to keep going, seeing finally a nice notification pop up, and smiling despite everything. It was *always* good to see that I'd gained points through goddamn hard work, and basically running my ass off for days at a time in full legion plate. Then, climbing cliffs? Yeah, if that hadn't done it, I'd have been pissed!

**Congratulations!**

**Through hard work and perseverance,
 you have increased your stats by the following:**

**Agility +1**

**Endurance +2**

**Perception +1**

**Strength +1**

**Continue to train and learn to increase this further.**

**You have made progress in a Quest: Rescue the Legion! (2)**

*You have freed more of the legion, hunting down and rescuing them from a life of captivity that they would never have imagined when they first signed up to protect the empire. Go forth, Prince of the Empire, and earn your legion's devoted worship.*

*Rescue members of the Imperial Legion!*

**Reward: 17/50 Legionnaires, 50,000xp**

Lastly, to the sound of snores, farting, and the occasional disbelieving laugh, sob, or the scattered sounds of conversation, I pulled up my stat sheet, read over the last details, and then closed my eyes.

Tomorrow would come soon enough, and frankly, it was going to be a pain in the ass.

Jez Cajiao

# CHARACTER SHEET

| Name: Jax Amon | |
|---|---|
| Title: Godslayer | |
| Class: Sorcerer II | Renown: Imperial Scion, Prince of Dravith, Master of Himnel and Narkolt |
| Level: 48 | Progress: 5,236,369/6,455,000 |
| Patron: Jenae, Goddess of Fire and Exploration | Points to Distribute: 0<br>Meridian Points to Invest: 0 |

| Stat | Current points | Description | Effect | Progress to next level |
|---|---|---|---|---|
| Agility | 83 | Governs dodge and movement | +730% maximum movement speed and reflexes | 4/100 |
| Charisma | 61 (56) | Governs likely success to charm, seduce, or threaten | +51% success chance in interactions with other beings | 29/100 |
| Constitution | 120 (118) | Governs health and health regeneration | 2400 health, regen 160 points per 600 seconds (each point invested now worth 20 health) | N/A |
| Dexterity | 93 | Governs ability with weapons and crafting success | +83% to weapon proficiency, +93% to the chances of crafting success | 21/100 |
| Endurance | 73 (670) | Governs stamina and stamina regeneration | 2190 stamina, regen 53 points per 30 seconds (each point invested now worth 30 stamina) | 4/100 |
| Intelligence | 201 | Governs base mana and number of spells able to be learned | 2210 mana, spell capacity: 102 (100 + 2, +200 mana from items) | N/A |
| Luck | 72 | Governs overall chance of bonuses | +62% chance of a favorable outcome | 41/100 |
| Perception | 71 (61) | Governs ranged damage and chance to spot traps or hidden items | +61% ranged damage, +61% chance to spot traps or hidden items | 11/100 |

| | | | | |
|---|---|---|---|---|
| Strength | 77 (74) | Governs damage with melee weapons and carrying capacity | +77 damage with melee weapons, +77% maximum carrying capacity | 3/100 |
| Wisdom | 100 (90) | Governs mana regeneration and memory | +1350% mana recovery, 15 points per minute | N/A |

# <u>THOMAS</u>

Y ou've got to be fucking kidding me, right?" Thomas whispered, staring up at the deck overhead. It was canted to the right, dropping away and downward at a forty-five-degree decline before shearing off and plunging hundreds of meters straight down.

Even better, across the far side, and slightly lower then where they stood, right where they had worked out they needed to get to, a dozen creatures stood stock-still, staring.

"Nope, they're DarkSpore, all right." Alistair sighed. "That means we've got at least one more SporeMother aboard the damn place, and considering the state of it? Yeah, that's not gonna be fun."

"What's the problem?" Bella leaned on her swordstaff and looked over the significant gap.

"Well, besides that they're there, where we need to go, and we're here you mean?" Thomas asked sarcastically, and she glared at him.

"Exactly," she snapped. "A legionnaire I *thought* I knew would have been overjoyed at the discovery of a SporeMother in the basement."

"Why?" Alistair asked, sounding genuinely curious.

"Because it's an opportunity to kill, to grow and to level, not to mention the loot that there must be over there just waiting to be recovered!" She shook her head disgustedly. "Honestly, boys, if this is too much for you, then you go back. Me and mine will take care of it."

"It's a SporeMother," Alistair ground out. "It's not your average monster. And even if it was, it's over there, and we just spent the last day climbing to get to this point. Now there's a hundred meters of empty space from this side to the next section.

"We're going to have to climb all the way back down there, then up the other wall and try to climb across the gantry, then rig ropes to get up to there, and the entire time, they're going to be attacking us."

"Don't forget that the gantry and those supports look like they'll collapse if you sneeze wrong." Thomas gestured at the mess. "I mean, look at it. There're dozens that have fallen already, the entire 'easy' route up is gone, and recently…"

"Recently?" Alistair repeated, looking at the long gouges in the wall, the collection of debris at the bottom of the gap, and the fresh scratches on the metal. "Damn, yeah, you're right. This isn't that old. What, a few weeks?"

Thomas nodded grimly, running a hand through his sweat-matted hair. "And looking at that side, there's even more. Whatever brought that section down did it within the last few hours. Which means…"

"The DarkSpore have been trying to cross in their puppets," Belladonna finished, her voice dropping to a mocking whisper. "They're scouts. Meaning that the SporeMother is active and hunting."

The DarkSpore-infested undead across the gap remained motionless, their dead eyes reflecting the squad's magelights in eerie pinpricks. Most were clearly former explorers and scavengers, their bodies twisted by the parasitic spores, weapons still clutched in bloated hands. Two larger shapes hulked at the back of the group, the misshapen forms of dead crustaceans, their shells cracked open by something that now allowed the dark tendrils of the spores to weave through.

Nigret slipped forward silently, his feline features tense as he scented the air. "This one smells rot and brine, but also something else. Acrid. Like burned metal." He pointed to a section of the floor near the edge. "There. That is different."

Thomas cautiously approached, crouching to examine the deck plating. A section roughly a meter wide was discolored, the ancient metal bubbling as if exposed to extreme heat. He reached out, then thought better of it and pulled back.

"Some kind of acid," he muttered. "Strong enough to eat through whatever alloy they used to make this place. The question is why?"

"To stop us getting over there, obviously." Bella snorted. "Come on, Thomas, I know you tend to think with your staff, but it's not that small."

"I don't know if I should high-five you for that or put you over my knee," Thomas muttered, before sighing. "All right, though, seriously, let's think this through, not just charge in."

"Boring," Bella whispered, before winking at him.

"The crustaceans maybe," Alistair guessed. "Either deliberately to bring down whatever was left of the passage across, or when they tried to climb over?"

Coran drifted up beside Thomas, his mismatched armor creaking. "So, what's the play? We can't go back empty-handed after all this. Four days we've been down this time, man. I'm telling you, the miners are getting pissed."

"We're not," Thomas replied, straightening up. He scanned the vast chamber, taking in the twisted metal, the various levels of collapsed flooring, and the gap between them and their destination. "Dash, what's your range with that crossbow?"

Dashiki—a former Dark legionnaire with skin the color of midnight and a perpetual scowl—stepped forward, hefting his crossbow and grunting as he started to wind the windlass. "Hundred meters accurate. One-twenty if I don't need to hit anything vital."

"Good enough," Thomas said. "Those creatures haven't moved since we spotted them. They might be in standby mode, waiting for movement or sound before they attack."

"Or they're bait," Belladonna offered. "Drawing us across the gap into an ambush."

"Either way, we need to get over there, and we need to know," Thomas said. "Dashiki, put a bolt into the floor about five meters in front of them. Let's see how they react."

Dashiki nodded, raising the crossbow and sighting down the length of the bolt. It shot across the gap, hitting the metal flooring at an angle and ricocheting with a dull *thunk* that echoed in the cavernous space.

The bolt slammed into the crotch of one of the standing adventurers—who had to be thankful he was already dead at that point—and the reaction was immediate.

The DarkSpore puppets jerked into motion like marionettes with their strings suddenly pulled taut. Their heads swiveled in unison, focusing on the bolt, then swept across to track back to Thomas's group.

The largest of the crustacean puppets shuddered, then opened its maw. Instead of revealing the expected mandibles, it extruded a writhing mass of black tendrils that flowed outward, forming a grotesque proboscis.

"Down!" Alistair shouted, already backing away.

Thomas followed suit, dragging Coran with him behind a chunk of fallen bulkhead as a stream of viscous black fluid arced across the gap. It splashed against the wall behind where they'd been standing, hissing and bubbling as it ate into the metal.

"Well, that answers that question," Thomas muttered. "They're definitely not in standby, and it's them that did the acid attack."

"They're defending something," Belladonna observed from her position behind a support column. "They have to be. Why else leave them there?"

"Guarding something," Alistair agreed. "Something the SporeMother doesn't want us to reach."

Thomas's mind raced through the possibilities. The SporeMothers were intelligent, in their own alien way. If one had established itself down here, it would naturally be drawn to sources of power, the manastones they'd already harvested being the obvious target.

If it'd been here, though, why the hell hadn't it found a way down? Why stay there, watching the stones, instead of going down and claiming them? More to the point, the damn DarkSpore didn't need air, so why the hell not march them down and out into the sea? Sure, the SporeMother couldn't survive—he thought—at the bottom of the ocean, but its creations could, couldn't they?

It wasn't like they'd end up *more* dead, right?

And even if it'd found the location too late, and the bulk of the crystal formation was already harvested by them between this and their previous trips, why then wait and watch? If Thomas and the others had found a way down, surely they could too?

"The map," he said suddenly. "Bella, remember the lower storage areas? The emergency power sections—could they be above that?"

Her eyes widened in understanding. "The golem storage? The one Tenandra said we needed to reactivate?"

"Exactly. If the SporeMother found a way in there…"

"Why the hell would she be there, though? The manastones are below her and…" Alistair groaned, then went on. "Fuck me, that's all we need. I bet she's been listening to us! She knows where we're going, and that we need to take the fucking manastones there, so why go to all the trouble of climbing down, when all she has to do is sit and wait for us to reach her?"

"Why have a dog and bark yourself," Thomas muttered, before waving off the confusion on the faces of the others. "All right, so she's listening to us?"

"Probably."

"Burn her out," he ordered, lifting his hand and starting to cast. A flame appeared as the few others capable of magic started to do the same, searching.

His plan had been more to get her to pull the DarkSpore back to protect it, rather than seriously managing to kill it, considering all the hiding places nearby, until Bella pointed out the most likely location for it.

"If it's not hiding under us, I'll eat your cooking for a week," she said laconically.

They all looked at the pitted, rusted, and broken flooring.

That sparked a round of groans and swearing, because although the DarkSpore was a semi-sentient cloud of darkness and would have no issue sliding through the shattered underside of the floor, the heavily armored, armed, and muscled legion squads had no chance of squeezing into those gaps.

"Fuck, whispers from now on!" Thomas snarled, before hurling his fireball across the intervening gap to take a hulking figure in the face.

The splash damage set fire to three more, and he sighed and nodded when Alistair asked him whether he felt better now.

"A little, but fuck me. I'm sick of this place," he admitted.

One of the miners, a stocky woman named Petra who'd remained silent until now, cleared her throat and leaned in, whispering. "There's another problem, sir. Those supports we came up through? They're weak as all hell. I'm not sure we can get back down the way we came, not safely."

Thomas cursed under his breath, moving back to where he could look down. She was right; the weight of the group slogging up to this point had done more damage to the ancient structure, and the condition it was in meant that it was only a matter of time until it collapsed.

"Forward is the only way," he said finally, gathering his small team together and speaking as quietly as he could. "But we need a plan that doesn't involve us getting melted or infected by DarkSpore before we reach the other side."

"I have an idea," Coran said, a familiar reckless grin spreading across his face. "But you're not gonna like it."

Thomas sighed, already knowing that whatever his friend was thinking would be most likely stupid and suicidal. "Hit me."

"We make them waste their acid. Those big ones can only produce so much before they need to regenerate, right? And with the whole 'being dead' thing, I don't think they're gonna be able to make more, so once they've fired it all at us, that's it gone, right?"

"Then what?" Alistair asked gruffly. "Fuck's sake, Coran, what do we do while the acid eats through the already weak floor?"

"Then we use fireballs and magic to pick them off, and we hope that gives us enough cover to get a rope line across."

"And how exactly do we make them waste their acid without, you know, bringing down the entire floor?" Belladonna arched an eyebrow.

Coran's grin widened as he pointed upward at the network of pipes running across the ceiling. "We don't cross where they're expecting. We go over their heads."

There was a long silence as Thomas and the others stared at the darkness above: the hidden shadows where a thousand DarkSpore could easily hide, and the sheer number of damaged pipes that looked like they had already fallen free.

"I say we volunteer Sip," Dashiki suggested brightly, before his face fell. "Damn."

"Yeah," Thomas agreed with a growl. "He's dead, but you spoke up, so congratulations."

"I didn't volunteer," Dash tried to say, before dropping silent at the looks the others were giving him. "I hate my life," he muttered.

"Don't worry, mate." Thomas grinned.

"I don't have to do it?" Dash perked up.

"No, you do, but it's okay, because we hate your life as well." He snorted.

"You'll have to do it without armor," Alistair added thoughtfully, the glare Dash gave him washing off the older legionnaire. "After all, the added weight will mean you almost certainly fall. And if you do?"

The group looked over the side at the almost three hundred meters straight down at this point, and Dash started to swear.

"Good point. You'd only waste the armor." Bella nodded. "Strip down to your underwear and leave anything you have that's valuable."

"You robbing me as well, Sarge?" Dash asked grimly.

"Not at all, Legionnaire!" She grinned mirthlessly. "The empire appreciates your donation. Now move!"

"Fucking bastards," Dash whispered, before starting to strip.

"You were happy to send Sip to do it," Thomas pointed out.

"Yeah, but I didn't like Sip!" Dash snapped back. "He was fuckin' useless!"

"And now he's dead." Bella nodded. "And I don't like you, so shit rolls downhill, doesn't it?"

That kinda finished the conversation.

Thomas winced, watching as the others gathered up, drawn by his whistle, and Alistair started to explain the plan in a low whisper from group to group.

"You got a rope?" Thomas asked, getting a glare as the only response. "Dashiki, someone needs to get over there. It can't be someone with spells as we're needed on this side to pick off the DarkSpore before they can attack you. It can't be a regular imperial legionnaire…"

"Because they're important and you like them, and you hate me." Dash interrupted him.

"Actually, I don't, but the imperial legionnaires are twice the size of you, and they're a lot better fighters. I need them when we get to the other side, and they're certainly too fucking heavy. Name one person in the group who has the strength to do this, and a low enough weight that they won't break the pipes, besides you?"

"Sergeant Belladonna," he snapped back hatefully. "But you're not gonna risk her, are you, not when she's sucking your—"

The hand that clapped over Dash's mouth shut him off before Thomas could, but it wasn't his. Instead, it was Alistair's, the big legionnaire moving before anyone else.

"I'm going to explain the realities of life to this legion aspirant, sir, if you don't mind," he said cheerfully.

Thomas, glaring at the idiot, nodded once, before moving off.

"There a problem?" Bella asked laconically, and Thomas grunted. "That's the difference between the Dark Legion and the Imperial," she pointed out. "In the Dark, we'd not have thought twice about sending the little shit out there."

"I know," Thomas growled.

"But now you feel like you shouldn't, even though he was happy to send a battle brother to face that risk, and even though he's the one with the best chance of success?" she asked.

He nodded.

"Fuck it." She shrugged. "When you've got a few more years in the rank, you'll understand, Thomas, but sometimes, no matter the situation, you just have to hope for the best and deal with it. Nobody lives forever, and in what world, in what army, do you send a sergeant to do a job that an aspirant is the best choice for?"

"I know. I just don't like it," he admitted. "All right, people, get ready. On the count of ten…"

Dashiki, stripped down to a tight-fitting undershirt and shorts, gave Thomas one last venomous glare before turning his attention to the network of pipes that crossed the ceiling. Alistair had finished his "explanation," which had apparently involved gripping the smaller man's shoulder hard enough to leave finger-shaped bruises.

"If it helps," Thomas said quietly, "I wouldn't ask you to do this if I didn't think you could make it."

"Go fuck yourself," Dash muttered, but there was less heat in it now. He tested the coil of rope slung across his chest, then flexed his fingers. "Just don't miss when those things start spitting."

Thomas nodded grimly. "I'll see what I can do."

The plan was simple but dangerous. Dashiki would climb up to the pipes, using a nearby section of broken wall as support. Then he'd cross the ceiling using the network of old pipes and conduits, doing his best to make the most of the fact that until he reached the far side, he should—in theory—be out of sight of the enemy due to the angle of the damaged roof. While he did that, the team's mages would create distractions, drawing fire from the DarkSpore puppets. Once Dashiki reached the other side, he'd secure the magically reinforced legion rope, allowing the rest to cross on a makeshift zip line.

"Mages ready!" Thomas called quietly, looking to the small group of legionnaires and mages who had access to magic.

"Start counting," Dash said, taking a deep breath as he braced himself against the wall.

Thomas raised his hand, fingers spreading one by one. "Ten…nine…eight…"

Dashiki began his climb, finding handholds in the damaged wall with surprising ease. For all his complaints, the man moved like a spider, his lean muscles working efficiently as he scaled the pitted and broken vertical surface.

"Seven…six…five…"

Across the gap, the DarkSpore puppets remained motionless, their dead eyes fixed on the main group. The crustacean monstrosities stood like sentinels, claws or damaged chitin clacking occasionally.

"Four…three…"

Dash reached the first pipe, testing it with a gentle tug before committing his weight. It creaked but held.

"Two…one… NOW!"

Thomas thrust his hand forward, unleashing a ball of flame that screamed across the gap. The other mages followed suit, filling the air with elemental fury. Fire, lightning, and concussive force slammed into the gathered DarkSpore, scattering or destroying dozens of them. The larger crustaceans reacted exactly as hoped, spewing streams of caustic acid that hissed through the air toward the group, who scattered.

Above the chaos, Dashiki moved with focus, swearing for every inch he crossed, and occasionally whimpering as a bug or rat shifted, scampering away.

The pipes climbed high to the left and then along the junction point where the wall met the roof, leading to a section of the floor on the far side that was empty of the majority of the enemy. Presumably that was because it was farther away than where they'd gathered to glare at Thomas and the others. But when they understood what he was going for, that'd soon change.

Until then, they had a chance to hammer the enemy back and create a beachhead, one that Dashiki was going to have to hold when he made it over, alone, until more of the squads could follow.

Hand over hand, he inched along the pipes, his body a dark silhouette against the distant magelights. Every few meters, a pipe would groan under his weight, forcing him to scramble to the next support as he frantically moved, his grip getting weaker by the second.

"Keep them occupied!" Belladonna shouted, launching a throwing knife that embedded itself in a puppet's eye socket. The creature staggered but didn't fall.

Thomas alternated between watching Dash's progress and directing the assault. "Alistair, left flank! They're regrouping!"

Another volley of spells crashed into the DarkSpore, sending chunks of rotten flesh flying. The crustaceans continued their assault, but Thomas noticed with satisfaction that their acid sprays were becoming thinner, less pressurized.

"It's working," Alistair muttered beside him. "They're running dry."

Halfway across, disaster struck. A pipe that had seemed sturdy gave way beneath Dashiki's weight with a screech of tearing metal, swinging out until a section of bracing slowed it. He dropped several meters before catching himself. The rope around his chest nearly slipped free as he swung and shrieked, legs kicking and fingers barely holding on.

"Fuck you, Thomas!" The cry echoed across the chamber as Dash hung suspended, legs still kicking in empty air.

The movement drew the attention of the crustaceans. One turned, its distended maw tilting upward as it tracked the motion overhead. The proboscis extended, preparing to spray.

"Dash, move!" Thomas bellowed, launching a fireball directly into the creature's face. The spell hit with a wet *thump*, setting the exposed tendrils ablaze. The beast thrashed wildly, its acid spray going wide and splattering against the ceiling.

Dashiki didn't need to be told twice. He swung his body, using the momentum to propel himself forward, grabbing the next pipe in a desperate lunge. His palms were slick with sweat, but he held on, continuing his precarious journey.

Thomas turned to Bella. "We need to cross as soon as he's secure. Who goes first?"

"Your squad, then the miners," she replied without hesitation. "They've got the manastones. Then my squad."

"And you?"

She flashed him a predatory smile. "Last. Someone needs to bully them across."

Thomas wanted to argue but knew she was right. As a sergeant in the Dark Legion, she'd been trained to do what was necessary no matter the cost. The longer they waited, the more likely that the rope, the floor, or the pipes would snap, stranding one or more of them on this side to try to fight their way through somehow. "Fine, but I'm staying with you. We need magic to keep them under control and hammered back."

"Wouldn't have it any other way," she replied, her eyes locked on the battle.

Across the gap, Dashiki had finally reached the opposite wall. He clung to a section of pipes that merged into the bulkhead, fishing out a piton from the small bag of holding at his waist. With practiced movements, he hammered it into a joint, then secured the rope, staying as high in the shadows as possible while the DarkSpore infected creatures burned.

He waved quickly and nodded frantically that it was ready.

Thomas had a momentary horrible suspicion that this was where Dashiki betrayed him and lied about the line…before he dismissed it. They were the Imperial Legion now, or they would be when they all passed the tests.

The past was the past; they were sworn to Jax, and to each other, and as much as that was weird in itself, they were damn well living it, so to hell with it.

"Alistair, get the zip line ready," Thomas ordered. The big legionnaire nodded, immediately setting to work with the pulley system Thomas had salvaged from an old mechanical elevator mechanism two days earlier.

It wasn't complex, it certainly wasn't pretty, but a pulley with a pair of handholds and a second rope attached made a hell of a difference in this situation, and he'd come up with it after only a few days of climbing up one side and down the other of the entire bloody city.

Now it was a lot easier, and certainly much more fun.

You attached the pulley to the zip line, made sure the second rope was attached to that, then you gripped the hand holds and clung on for dear life.

It'd not have worked as well in a world without magic, but here, where the ropes were reinforced to take a fully armored legionnaire without issue? Even a squad when they all had to climb at the same time?

Yeah.

Alistair was the first, as always, grabbing onto the pulley, lifting his legs and streaking across the slight decline with the aid of an enthusiastic push by Nigret.

He reached the far side in seconds, dropping from the rope and hitting the ground hard. He rolled then popped to his feet, before firing off a barrage of Magic Missiles. He drew a dagger with his shield and set himself, ready to fight the magical little bastards with the armory's equivalent of a butter knife.

It was tiny, but Thomas had seen Alistair put it to good use too many times this trip already.

The DarkSpore, finally realizing that their prey was on the side they were as well, launched a final, frenzied assault. The remaining crustacean puppet spewed the last of its acid in a wild spray, most of it splashing harmlessly against the floor. The humanoid puppets surged forward, shambling toward the big legionnaire, even as Dash stayed partly hidden in the ceiling.

"Time to go!" Thomas shouted as Nigret finished yanking the pulley back up the line. "My squad, go!"

Thirty seconds later, Nigret was on the far side. Thomas unleashed barrage after barrage of Magic Missiles as more and more of the legion flashed across the gap.

Less than a minute later, with the DarkSpore-infested undead staggering back in disarray, his squad was over and he bellowed again.

"Miners, go, go, go!"

Petra and the other miners hooked themselves to the line one by one, carrying their precious cargo. They zipped across the gap, and the pulley was yanked back. The system groaned under their weight but held. Finally, they were followed by Bella's team.

As the last of their forces made the crossing, Thomas turned to Belladonna. "Your turn."

She shook her head. "You first. I want to watch that ass and hear your screams." She grinned. "They're so pretty!"

"Fuck's sake!" He half laughed, half groaned. Then he was moving, knowing of the two, a rock would give in before Bella did.

He landed on the far side with a grunt, quickly checking himself; then Bella slid in moments later. Her boots skidded on the metal floor as she dismounted, coming to rest against his chest.

"Told you I'd be right behind you," she said with a smirk, before kissing him, and then shoving him hard to get him moving.

Thomas allowed himself a brief moment of relief before refocusing on their mission, staggering and looking around. "Everyone accounted for?"

Alistair nodded. "All present and temporarily whole, sir."

"Good." Thomas turned to Dashiki, who was pulling his armor back on with shaking hands. "Nice work."

Dashiki paused, clearly surprised by the acknowledgment. "Thanks," he muttered after a moment. The word sounded as if it had been physically wrenched from him.

"Anyone think we should send Dashiki back to untie the rope?" Thomas asked loudly, getting a choked groan from the smaller man. "Ah, fine. Good thing I've got a spare then!" He laughed.

"Bastard." Dashiki muttered glaring at him.

"No time to rest, people!" Thomas ordered, going on. "Whatever the SporeMother is guarding, we need to find it before she realizes we've broken through her defensive line."

"And if she's waiting for us?" Coran checked his weapon.

Thomas's expression hardened. "Then we finish the job."

"Thomas?" Alistair winced.

"Yeah, mate?"

"What one of the DarkSpore see, the SporeMother sees. She knows we're here."

"Ah, fuck!" Thomas groaned, as the sound of frantically rushing feet echoed down from a nearby stairwell. "You couldn't tell me that before we trapped ourselves on this side of the gap?"

"Thought you knew, sir, sorry," Alistair apologized, the honorific showing he was actually embarrassed. "You know, considering the monster is what it is, and that your brother's killed so many now."

"Yeah, well, I didn't, and he's a dick." Thomas sighed. "All right, people! Form up and get ready. Today just keeps getting better!"

# CHAPTER THIRTY-ONE

When I finally cracked my eyes, I was met by a vision of absolute loveliness… Unfortunately, it was Sehran, who was apparently in a playful mood.

"Fuck's sake!" I gasped, jerking back from her. The evil bugger had apparently felt that I was stirring and had positioned herself a quarter inch from my face, staring into my eyes as I first blinked the sleep from them.

Now, as the sun climbed above the horizon and painted the sky in flames of orange and red, I collapsed onto my back and tried to calm my thundering heart. Oracle let loose with peals of silvery laughter through our bond, letting me know the whole thing had clearly been her idea.

*"I hate you,"* I told her, stretched out on my bedroll, feeling the usual litany of aches and pains that came with sleeping on rocky ground in the aftermath of a major battle. I again reconsidered, as I had several times during the night, the sheer stupidity of lying there in the open, where everyone could see me and see that I wasn't too good to sleep like they did.

Oh no, I wasn't too good for it at all. The problem was that had any of them been offered the master's wagons and the fluffy pillows, the deep mattresses, and yeah, a bit of privacy for some sexy time, I now had to admit they'd have taken that chance like a rocket.

Only *I* was so stupid as not to.

I sighed and sat up, deciding that tonight we were getting a room, and I was going to pay Oracle back for that trick. I sent her a mental image and grinned to myself as she sent me a message back through the bond that was basically "yes please."

Now fully awake, I stood, pulling my gauntlets and helm out, having slept fully armored beyond that, as we were in hostile territory.

"Look alive, your beauty sleep isn't making enough of a difference to keep going," Sehran's voice called from where she'd retreated to somewhere above me. "The wagons are almost ready to move."

I squinted up to see her hovering a few meters above the ground, wings beating lazily as she grinned down at me. She looked far too cheerful for this ungodly hour.

"What time is it?" I called to her.

"Twenty minutes to sunrise!" she called back. "It's early enough that we can make up some of Toren's lead. Oracle's been up for hours, organizing the wagons and sorting supplies."

That got me moving. I couldn't have my pregnant partner outworking me, even if she did have the advantage of not needing sleep as much as I did.

I growled to myself as I worked, latching the last sections of my armor and tightening where I'd let the tension off here and there for comfort through the night.

Around the camp, legionnaires moved with practiced efficiency, breaking down tents and loading supplies. The former slaves worked alongside them, some still wearing the remnants of their previous position like unwanted reminders. I made a mental note to make sure that everyone at least got some proper clothing once we had time. The constant reminder couldn't be good for anyone's mental health.

Especially not when I saw that some of the former slaves were in little more than rags, and others… Well, clearly certain outfits had a bedroom connotation, let's just say that.

One guy bounced past with a massive smile on his face, and little else besides tiny red leather straps across his body and for me, that sealed it.

I was a proud man—I didn't need a depressing sight like that before my goddamn breakfast.

"Morning!" I greeted Daralen as she approached. "How's it going?"

She moved with the confidence of a career soldier, her armor gleaming in the morning sun.

"Fifty-eight wagons are operational, my prince," she reported, coming to attention. "Six more needing repairs beyond what we can manage on the road, and the last few are basically scrap wood after last night. We've salvaged what we could and left anything that's neither valuable, nor supplies. Food and shelter are…adequate. Water will be our biggest concern."

"Oracle and I can help with that," I replied, gesturing toward where my partner flew past the head of the column.

"Thankfully." Daralen nodded. "I've taken that into account, but didn't want to press for it. If you are both willing to summon water as needed, then things go from uncomfortable to, well, as comfortable as life ever gets, really. As for our people, morale is improving, though many are still…processing yesterday's events. The healing done means that most will be able to run alongside the wagons, with only the youngest children, several expecting mothers, and the eldest needing to ride."

I nodded, taking in the information. "And defenses?"

"Thin," she admitted with a grimace. "We have fifty-six combat-capable legionnaires, perhaps another forty from the freed slaves with actual fighting experience, and the rest…" She shrugged. "They're willing, but untrained."

"We'll work on that as we go," I decided. "Training exercises during rest breaks. Basic drills. Even an untrained fighter who knows how to form a defensive line is better than a panicked civilian."

"And our route?" Daralen asked. "We're still to meet up with the others?"

I jerked a thumb westward, away from the pathetic excuse for a road. "Yeah. Definitely time to cut across the plains. We'll meet up with Toren and the others, then continue to Sonra together. We're avoiding the main routes—too many chances for an ambush."

"Off-road will be harder on the wagons," she cautioned.

"Better broken wheels than broken necks," I countered. "We're a few days to reach the rendezvous point. Then it's a couple of days to Sonra and we get some rest, fun, and I get to kill a goddess."

She nodded sharply. "I love the way that you say that like it's nothing, Jax. Okay, I'll organize scouts. Two-mile perimeter, rotating shifts. Twenty legionnaires in close, ten on you. The remaining twenty-four will be scouting."

"Good." I clasped her shoulder briefly. "Let's get moving."

She hesitated, then spoke quickly, as if not liking it, but needing to say it. "Jax, there's something I need to warn you about. There was a lot of legion equipment mixed in with the lot that we took."

"Okay." I nodded. "Good that we recovered it then."

"It is, but most of it is old. What I mean is…"

"They've been raiding legion burial sites," I finished for her, and she nodded. "That old necromancer basically admitted it."

"That means that the others were probably doing the same, you know that, right?"

"The other Sons of the Deep? Yeah, I guessed."

"That means that we've got a chance to recover a lot of the older armor that was buried with the legionnaire it was made for," she said carefully.

"Okay?" I agreed slowly.

She watched me for a second, then sighed and went on. "Jax, we've got bugger all spares. We've got a handful of legionnaires who are classed as armorers, but because of the way that we live and the constant travelling, they spend all their time fixing broken gear, not making new."

"And the legion who are with us now?" I asked, looking out and seeing that they were all wearing their armor.

"They're wearing most of what we have," she finished.

"I'm missing something, aren't I?" I asked.

"I mean that the others back with the other caravan gave their armor up to provide a fully armored unit for you, and this armor that we've recovered means that some of them can have their armor back, if you'll allow it?"

"Of course I will. Why wouldn't I?" I asked, confused.

"Because there are legion rules and customs about a legionnaire being buried in their armor for their final duty," she said. "This flies in the face of custom, but…"

"The dead don't need their armor," I finished for her. "Fuck's sake, Daralen. Yes, please, as we go, if you get the chance to recover any armor, take it. I have, and I will. The first time I met members of the legion, I was in armor that some adventurer had died in. Pants too, which believe me, made my skin crawl."

"Thank you, sir." She sighed. "It'd been a concern among the boys and girls, especially because some of that armor, the stuff that the elites wore, is old, and damn well maintained. It's rune enhanced, and to a level we've not had in a long, long time."

"Then share it out to the most deserving and in need and do what's right, Daralen. You should have told me last night," I ordered her.

As Daralen strode off to relay orders, wearing a relieved expression, I finished strapping on my armor and made my way toward the front of the column. The camp was almost completely packed now, the last few cauldrons and the rare couple of tents coming down as I passed. People nodded or saluted as I walked by, some with respect, others with naked awe that made me uncomfortable.

Word of yesterday's confrontation with the necromancer had spread overnight, many of the slaves having been stunned or flat out passed out while it was happening. And apparently some of the legion had spread the word about Marrow as well. The tales were growing with each retelling until I'd apparently single-handedly saved them all, rather than being part of a team and just stabbing a really old elf with questionable fashion sense.

I found Oracle at the head of the column, consulting with a group of former slaves who seemed to know the terrain.

"Morning." I came up beside her and nodded to the others. "Heard you've been busy while I was lazing around."

She smiled, the expression lighting her beautiful face. "Well, I know you…someone had to make sure we didn't leave half our supplies behind," she joked.

Through our bond, I felt her warmth, her love, and beneath it, a current of tension. *"We need to talk,"* she sent privately. *"About Sonra. About the fight to come."*

*"Later,"* I promised. *"When we're on the move."*

She nodded slightly, then turned back to the group. "Jax, these men were guards before they were captured. They think they know the best routes across the grasslands." She left unsaid that to have been working in these areas, they might have been protecting the slavers or worse.

A fresh start, I reminded myself. Some of these people were born here and had to do whatever they did to survive. They'd been slaves when we met them, and now they had a chance to make things right.

An older man with a weathered face stepped forward, bowing deep enough he almost fell over. "Name's Horace, m'lord. Been crossing these plains for nigh on thirty years."

"And where would you recommend we go?" I asked grimly.

*"It's not what you think. I asked around after you went to sleep. Even though there weren't official caravan routes passing through here, there were small private merchant groups that passed through without the guild's knowledge. They were part of one of those before they were raided,"* Oracle sent to me.

I straightened, suddenly feeling a whole lot better about listening to the fucker.

He scratched his grizzled beard. "Depends on what you're avoiding, m'lord. Main roads are patrolled by the slaver and raider groups. Normally we'd be in a smaller caravan, faster moving and have at least this many guards, but…they'd not be legionnaires."

"That's a good thing and a bad." Another of the group spoke up. "Legionnaires are targets, while us? Normal guards wouldn't be, but this many legionnaires could easily take out most raider groups we're likely to meet."

"The northern route has more water, but bandits know it and they'll be camped at the watering holes. Means we'll need to fight over and over, I think. Southern route is drier, but less traveled, so more monsters and we might cross paths with the Watchers or some raiders, as they'll be out looking for free stock for Sonra," Horace added.

"Watchers?" I asked.

"Ah, I don't really know, just rumors that if you see them, they're a bit…weird, and not to mess with them. If they tell you to move on, or that a tree is sacred, you need to honor it or they'll attack. But they're generally not interested in the affairs of others."

"Okay, interesting. Well, we need to head west, then southwest, depending on the speed we can manage," I said. "We're meeting up with the rest of our people, then on to Sonra."

Horace exchanged glances with his companions. "West takes us through the tall grass country. Good cover, but easy to get lost without markers. And the grass hides things…things that hunt."

"What kind of things?" I asked.

"Plains cats, mostly," another man offered. "Big as horses, some of 'em. Smart, too. Hunt in packs. This many people might scare 'em off, but it might just draw more as well."

"Sounds delightful," I muttered. "Anything else I should know about?"

"Not much else out that way," Horace said. "Few settlements, mostly just grass for days. But if we're heading for Sonra after, we'll want to avoid the direct migration path. Herds make the ground treacherous, and where there are herds…"

"There are predators," I finished for him. "Great."

"We can handle predators," Oracle reminded me. "And the tall grass will provide cover for us as well as them."

"There's also the little detail…" Horace added nervously, "of, uh…ex… escrimin… excrim…I mean, poo."

"The shit that the herds leave behind?" I asked, guessing at what he was trying to pronounce.

He sighed, nodding, clearly thinking I'd have been traumatized by the mention of shit for some reason. Nobles, I mentally berated myself. Of course, he was used to thinking of the local nobles standards.

"Yessir." He nodded.

"Well, we can try to avoid as much as we can." I shrugged. "It's not like it's going to hurt us."

"It can," Oracle corrected. "Disease spreads in its path, so for a few weeks after the herds pass, the ground is going to be horrible. Then it'll dry out and the first shoots will start growing through it, and it'll get better."

"And the people, Lord. Most haven't got so much as a shoe between them. They march through that, they'll get rot in their feet. You see if they don't." Horace nodded to himself.

"Great, so we need to skirt the edge. Will that do?" I asked, and he nodded. "And that's where the predators will be." I sighed.

"Again, we can handle them." Oracle smiled. "Or the legion can, anyway."

She was right, of course. Between the legionnaires, our magic, and my own abilities, natural predators weren't a major concern. Most monsters would have been culled by the group as they passed in the first place.

No, the real threats would come from two-legged hunters, and at least in the long grass we would be less likely to draw their attention. No more likely than anyone else, anyway.

"Tall grass route it is," I decided. "Horace, you and your people will guide us. Oracle will work with you on the specifics, but speak to Daralen for security."

The old guard nodded, clearly pleased to have a purpose again.

With our route settled, I gave the order to move out.

The wagons lurched into motion, massive wheels grinding against stone before finding purchase. The column stretched out behind us, as I flew upward with Oracle and Sehran, staring out at the mass migration.

It was a motley assemblage of legionnaires, freed slaves, and captured wagons that most of the drivers had no clue how to guide. So they kept stopping and starting, pulling in different directions and shouting at each other.

Not exactly the triumphant march I'd imagined leading the second half of the caravan back to the first, but it was a start.

"Daralen," I said as we took our positions at the head of the column, "have you been to Sonra before?"

"No, but I know the city itself is enormous—tens of thousands of people, with the herds numbering in the hundreds of thousands," she said. "Due to the oaths, it's one of the places that legionnaires can't go—not in recent times. In the past, we could. When we had large enough numbers that we could smash the slavers and so on, but now?" She shrugged. "The oaths would force us into action even against overwhelming odds, and then we'd either die, or be taken."

"So you avoided the place," I growled.

"Not by choice," she hastened to add. "You've no idea how much we've wanted to clear it out. And in the past, we were always welcomed by the families. They hate the nobles, and view the majority of the city dwellers with a lot of suspicion. Given that we were made to be pretty nomadic as well by our oaths, they seemed to respect that about us."

"That's a point," Oracle said suddenly. "When you were forced into moving, how did you do it?"

"What do you mean?" Daralen asked curiously.

"The actual moving…I mean, did you march or…"

"Ah!" She smiled. "No, while we could, the majority of us—when travelling the grasslands especially—would go by horse. We used to have tremendous horses." She sighed regretfully.

"Ah shit, and now I'm making everyone run everywhere." I winced.

"What happened to the horses?" Oracle asked.

"We gradually sold them off or lost them to ambushes, monsters, and battle," Daralen admitted. "That's the reality of life—when you have a horse, it's another mouth to feed. When the legions were supported, that was fine; it enabled us to make fast strikes and to scout or pass word quickly.

"Since then, though, with the losses we've incurred and the loss of support, they were just additional costs that we couldn't maintain." She shook her head. "Eventually the herds were sold to Sonra, and then from then on, they were dispersed. What happened to them after that, who knows. But I remember when we had some smaller stables still."

"Okay, so that sucks, but it's still a bit better than Dravith for that. They never had horses, not in any great quantities—it was all on foot," I admitted. "Mind you, just wait until you see airships."

"Airships?" she prompted, curious.

"Literally what it sounds like." I smiled. "A ship with mana engines on the sides, great sails, and then beyond that, well, they're ships. They have flattened bottoms, and legs that can be folded down to brace the ship, or lifted away when in flight, but they fly in the clouds, and believe me, it's incredible."

"I bet." She sighed. "Now *that* would be an upgrade."

"You have no idea." I grinned. "It's like sailing, in that you're aboard ship, but they're faster. There's, well, not *no* monsters, but less, and my people generally split their time between training and relaxing as they travel."

"Jax, on the other hand, spends the entire day working on alchemy or training." Sehran shook her head. "Honestly, it's terrible. It also drives Lydia, the optio of his personal squad, to push the squad harder than she needs to."

"You've never told me that." I frowned. "Lydia isn't that bad, is she?"

"Well, no, but that's because the entire rest of the squad is as insane. You put a relatively normal person into those situations and they'd give up in a few days."

"They're normal people!" I disagreed.

"Really? Name one."

"Well, Lydia…"

"Is a Valkyrie, ex-slave who even the Legion Primus Praetoria points to as addicted to self-improvement."

"Okay, well…uh…"

"Bane is an insane, mass-murdering mer who's also the champion of Tamat, Goddess of Assassins. Grizz is the first knight of the legion in seven hundred years and has died, what? Three times? He's insane by anyone's standards and pointed to as a perfect legionnaire, formerly being groomed to become a primus. Then there's Arrin, a thrill-seeking mage ex-slave who had to be stopped from putting his head inside the maw of a giant cave spider soldier as a party trick because it was traumatizing the poor thing…" As she spoke, she counted off names on her fingers.

"All right, well, yeah, they're exceptions…" I tried.

"We've got Ronin, a 'bard' who's actually an imperial truth seeker and well, he's a sex pest—and I'm a succubus saying that. Then there's me—there's my Jian…"

"Yes! Jian's a normal guy…" I pointed out.

"Who is both an airship captain, started a war between the empire and Nimon by accidentally firing an airship cannon at their encampment…"

"It was like a fireball but ten times the size," Oracle pointed out in an aside to Daralen. "He did it when we were plundering a city."

"And he's not just my lover, but he's also sleeping with the ship's wisp, Tenandra. He's amazing, and not just for those reasons. Dual wields swords like he was born to it…and dual wields Tenandra and me too," Sehran went on proudly. "Oh, and he's a warlock. Obviously."

"Then we've got Bob. He's a giant undead who's fully sentient and gets rebuilt practically every week. And that doesn't even touch on Giint."

"Yeah, let's leave him out of this," I said. "Ain't nobody wants to touch Giint."

"He's a gnome artificer and badunka rider," Oracle pointed out to Daralen. "But when we met him, he was both a cannibal and completely mad, as well as feral, having been drinking contaminated water and eating, well, you can guess, for most of his life. Even now he's borderline feral."

"And the personal champion of Svetu," I added helpfully.

"And I see why you say that there are so many unusual people in the squad." Daralen smiled.

"What about Yen?" I suddenly crowed. "Yen's normal!"

"She's a member of the Speculatores Cohortes Praetoria, and she's sleeping with Grizz. That's two things that mean she's either mad or very, very good."

"But she's not mad," I clarified. "Sure, she's a special case in terms of her being really efficient and a sort of scout who moonlights as a justicar, but she's not insane."

"And she's the most 'normal' of your group?" Daralen asked, smiling as we picked up the pace, moving from a walk to a jog as the wagons cleared the ravine and turned, heading out across the open grasslands.

"Exactly!" I assured her. "Perfectly normal!"

"They're also on an airship now—Tenandra, I'd bet—and are headed to us," Oracle pointed out. "They're closing the distance, and considering I can't feel the connections to any others getting noticeably shorter, so there's at most twenty or thirty others with them. Most likely the ship's crew and at most a small contingent of legionnaires as support."

"Exactly."

"On their own, having been dispatched to cross the oceans on the first airship that will have been seen here as far as we know." She went on. "Alone to try to rescue the prince of the empire."

"Don't make this worse." I sighed. "Look, yes, they're a good bunch. Yes, they're friends and my squad, but they're normal, ish."

"Shall we talk about Thomas then?" Sehran suggested. "The former Dark legionnaire who nailed you to a tree with a spear, and is both your brother and the leader of the Imperial Senate? The dark berserker who betrayed Nimon for you, then got named as the Champion of Lagoush and is screwing a Dark Hunter?"

"You deliberately made that sound worse than it is!" I snapped, to much laughter. "Look, let's change the subject, all right? What can we expect at Sonra?" I asked both Daralen and Horace, who sat on the wagon bed next to the lead wagon's driver, listening in as we jogged.

There was a long few seconds of silence as knowing grins were exchanged, before they apparently decided to move on and stop teasing me.

"The inner ring will be closed to you. The second will be willing to deal with you if you bring enough gold or platinum, the trade goods in the wagons and so on, but they'll not accept your authority, Prince," Horace admitted carefully as I looked at him first.

I gestured for him to continue and he did.

"The outer ring will be a mix of merchants and slavers. Both groups will welcome you as someone to fleece given any chance, and then it's all down to the outriders and herds."

"What are outriders?" I asked.

"Literally what they sound like." Daralen spoke up. "The outriders are always in motion, a mixture of warriors and herdsmen who keep the herds safe from poachers, both monsters and people, and who keep the peace of the camp. They look out for troublemakers and essentially refuse you entry if they think you'll be an issue. They're small groups, but they keep in sight of each other, and as there's massive herds, there's a lot of them. If you try to force your way past them, they'll attack, and you don't want that."

"Better to be friendly and just pretend to be another caravan," I agreed. "We should be able to slide in. There must be a lot of caravans every day that join them, right? We'll just be one more."

"We could be, if they didn't know that there was a prince of the empire travelling to Sonra, one who had already announced he was going there to face Illoth," she corrected. "Which, by the way, is still one of your more insane ideas."

I grinned at her. "Just one of many."

Oracle didn't smile back. *"Jax, this isn't a joke. Illoth is a goddess—diminished, perhaps, compared to the height of her power, but still, it's a hell of a risk,"* she sent me through the bond.

*"I've faced Nimon,"* I reminded her.

*"And nearly died,"* she countered. *"And that was with Amon."*

The mention of my predecessor sent a familiar chill down my spine. The Eternal Emperor's presence in my mind had been both a blessing and curse—his knowledge invaluable but his methods, and hell, his mind? Broken and often brutal. Since the fight with Nimon and my claiming of the divine fragment, I'd felt him slipping away. Almost as if he knew that I didn't need him, or that it was time for me to tread my path without him.

Or, he was being a twat still and had decided that this was the most inopportune time for him to fuck off. There was a part of me that was gloomily convinced that was true as well.

*"I'll be ready,"* I promised, more confidently than I felt. *"But first, we need to reunite the caravan and get to Sonra. There's a lot of shit that can go wrong between here and there."*

The plains stretched before us, an ocean of grass shimmering in the morning light. In the distance, I could make out the hazy outline of low hills. Apparently, they were our first landmark to watch for. Behind us, the ravine where we'd battled the necromancer was already vanishing into the distance.

I took a deep breath of the clean morning air, feeling the weight of responsibility settle on my shoulders once more. Three hundred plus lives depended on me getting this right. More than three hundred new citizens of an empire that was seven hundred years dead, and looked to have been almost entirely killed here.

"One step at a time," I murmured to myself.

"What was that?" Oracle asked.

I shook my head. "Nothing. Just talking to myself."

"Careful," she teased with a smile. "People might think you're mad!"

"If they think that just because I'm muttering, then they don't know me yet." I smiled. "Are you happy to start magical training again for the legion?" I asked her, knowing she was.

Daralen almost fell, with the way her head had whipped around to stare at me, a mixture of hope, fear, and surprise painted across it.

"Definitely!" Oracle declared. "Sehran can sit with me for the first group, as that way I know I'm safe from you when I'm distracted!"

"When the succubus is a better choice, you know you're getting a bad reputation," Sehran pointed out to me, giving me a bawdy wink as a few scattered chuckles rose.

As the sun climbed higher, we rolled down a long, gentle decline with the grass rising from ankle to knee, and then higher over the next few hours, leaving the rocky terrain behind.

With a sea of grass ahead of us, slowly swaying in the constant breezes, I couldn't help but smile. This was right. This was a sea of green, and damn, the grass was a lot shorter back home, but it looked healthy and open.

I had the illusion of open vistas and being able to see for miles without a single threat, for all of thirty seconds more.

Then a small rodent-like thing sprinted past my feet, making me stagger and swear, as a second, larger catlike thing flashed after it, the yowl and shriek of their passage hanging in the air.

# CHAPTER THIRTY-TWO

By midday, the tall grass surrounded us completely, rising well above the height of the wagons in some places as we dipped and rose, following the curve of the ground.

Horace had proved invaluable already, sending ahead a small party on some of the captured horses to break a trail. Twice they'd led us around collections of rocks that would have caused issues, and by the time the rest of us ran through—we'd formed up a trail-breaking group into a column that was ten across and five deep, jogging twenty meters ahead of the wagons—we left a nice, clear path for them to follow.

The landscape had changed dramatically—from rocky ravines to an endless ocean of green grass that whispered secrets with every breeze. The sky above was a glorious blue, the sun a hammer beating down upon us. Occasionally, a brief rain shower would sweep across, coming and going in literal minutes, before the sky returned to baking.

That was weird as well. Back home, we were entering into winter. Here? It was summer, if I was any judge, at least as hot as any I'd dealt with back home on Earth. According to Daralen and Horace, this was late spring, if that.

That meant two things. First, if there was such a thing, then we were below the equator, and second, if not, I had no clue how the geography of this fucking realm operated.

Given the size of the realm pre-fall, the very least I could work out was that if it was a round world like Earth—and I couldn't imagine a way it wasn't—then it was the size of fucking *Jupiter*.

Even the gods didn't know how big the realm was, just that it was seemingly infinite, and that if you explored long enough in one direction, you just never came back.

That said to me that there were forces out there making sure you didn't return. But for a civilization that had giant war cities like the prax, and that created magical golems and shit, and had done for literally hundreds of years?

That gave me the willies, frankly.

As it was, I was sweating my tits off, and that was while jogging. The "lowlands" that we'd come through had been markedly cooler, even closer to the desert. Again, that made little sense to me, but to hell with it. Even so, sweat plastered my under-armor gear to me and my hair to my forehead. Most of the legionnaires were doing okay, their training enabling them to run for hours in far worse conditions. But more and more of the former slaves struggled, unused to exertion in the open air after years of confinement.

The last caravan had it easier with the lack of grass to have to trample over, but beyond that, we were doing well, I decided, considering it felt like we were running in a furnace.

"We need to call a rest break," Oracle said, floating beside me. Unlike the rest of us, she showed no signs of discomfort from the heat. "Some of them won't make it much farther without water and shade."

I nodded, scanning the terrain ahead. "Horace," I called to our guide. "Any good spots ahead for a midday rest?"

The old guard squinted into the distance. "There's a stand of trees 'bout half a mile on, m'lord. Would give some shade, at least."

"Trees in the middle of these plains?" I asked skeptically.

"Ancient ones, m'lord. Grow near the underground springs. Water's brackish, but drinkable in a pinch."

That decided it. "Spread the word. Rest break at the trees ahead. One hour, no more."

As the message rippled back through the column, I caught sight of Sehran circling overhead. Her wings gleamed in the sunlight as she executed a graceful dive, landing beside me with barely a sound.

"Trouble?" I asked, noting her expression.

"Not yet," she replied, folding her wings. "But we're leaving a trail a blind man could follow. And I've spotted movement to the northwest—could be natural, could be something else. It's at the limit I can see."

"How far?"

"Ten miles, maybe more. Honestly, it's really hard to judge in this terrain…it's about as far from my normal habitat as it's possible to get." She winced. "It could be more, or less…"

I considered our options. If they were hostile, ten miles gave us some time, but not much. The wagons couldn't move any faster than they already were in this terrain, and fighting in the tall grass would be chaotic at best.

"Let's push some scouts out to keep an eye on it," I decided. "But we keep moving toward those trees for now. These people need shade, we need water—though it'll be what we can summon—and as you said, we're leaving a trail a blind man could follow. Not that there's any other option."

I damn well knew my eyesight wasn't going to be much better in this—the grass was already making things far away seem a lot closer—but I'd still have a look myself and soon.

Sehran nodded, then launched herself into the air again, wings propelling her aloft with an ease a lot of the people around me seemed to envy.

Mind you, she'd found an outfit that more or less fit her, and although it was leather armor, it'd been clearly intended for someone with less…her.

She was bursting out, and being Sehran, she was happy as a pig in shit about the looks she was getting.

Some of the older men looked like, between the exercise and the sight of her, there were going to be heart attacks soon.

I passed the word to Daralen, and then Oracle and I took off, flying up high and having Sehran point them out.

From here, it was clear that *something* was moving through the grass. But with the blazing sun, the distortion with the waving grass, and the low angle of them to the grass there, it could just as easily be a small group of riders, a wagon, or even a small group of monsters.

Oracle moved closer, her concern evident both in her expression and through our bond. *"If those are riders, they could be slavers—or worse, Dark Legion."*

*"Or they could be nomads, or other merchants, or any number of other things,"* I pointed out. *"Let's not borrow trouble."*

*"Says the man who calls the God of Death 'that cockwomble,'"* she replied dryly. *"And you know that's not how our lives work out."*

I couldn't help but laugh. *"Fair point. Okay, let's keep an eye on them. They're cutting our trail, so either they're heading in the same general direction and it's a coincidence..."*

*"Which is unlikely considering why we're going this way is to deliberately avoid others,"* Oracle pointed out.

I sighed. *"Yeah, all right. We keep an eye on them and see what Daralen's people bring back."*

The trees, when we reached them, were a welcome sight. A small cluster of massive, gnarled trunks rose like islands from the sea of grass. Their bark was pale, almost silvery, and their branches spread wide to create pools of blessed shade beneath.

On the approach, we'd had to climb some small hills that were dotted around the area. When we crested the ridge, well, the little bowl-shaped depression looked heavenly. The ground around them was relatively clear, the grass giving way to a mix of low scrub and bare earth, with a small pool at the center.

Daralen had already organized the legionnaires to secure the perimeter as the wagons circled the largest trees. The former slaves gratefully staggered in, then collapsed into the shade, many dropping immediately into an exhausted sleep.

We chivvied a bunch of them back on their feet, lining them up, and then summoned fountains. The healing magic made several cry in abject gratitude as broken skin and blisters were soothed away.

That was when I found the first of the issues that I'd not truly considered about running through the grass like this.

The stalks were long, strong, and fucking sharp, meaning that people in their dozens were leaving bloody footprints behind them as they walked.

I was horrified—and then it was made even worse by how accepting these people were.

The vast majority had been slaves for years, and little things like that? Totally unworthy of comment in the grand scheme of things. But a healing? That meant a lot to them. Rations were passed out and we spent the next twenty minutes moving along the line, summoning more and more fountains, checking on people and generally doing some hearts and minds work.

Eventually, I found a spot under one of the larger trees and sank down, my back against the rough bark, grinning as the legionnaires who were by now a constant guard moved up and spread out their things all around me by an amazing coincidence. Oracle settled beside me, summoning another fountain for everyone, and this time taking the time to drink a little of the healing waters herself.

"How are you feeling?" I asked quietly.

She knew what I meant. "The baby is fine, Jax. It seems to be thriving, if anything. My energies have been...fluctuating, but it's manageable."

"And you?" I pressed. "Not just the baby. You."

A faint smile touched her lips. "I'm still adjusting to having a physical form that can carry life. It's…strange. Beautiful, *wonderful* but strange." Then she laughed. "I'm going to be a hell of a surprise to them if we *do* find some other wisps."

"I bet." I smiled as I reached for her hand. "We're going to figure this out. All of it."

"I know." Her confidence warmed me through our bond.

We took a few minutes, that was all, to sit and just relax, before finally she sighed.

"You ready to start again?" I asked her.

"Yes, but right now, I think we have a fresh problem." She drew my attention to Daralen, who was approaching with a small group. One was Horace, and beyond a few who I recognized as scouts, the other was a younger woman, one who really didn't seem to want to be brought over.

I pushed myself back to my feet, reluctantly leaving the cool shade to check on our people.

"Daralen," I greeted the legion primus. "Horace. Okay, what's up?" I looked around the small group, listening intently as he pointed toward the horizon.

"All is well, my prince. Just telling these lot to avoid the Sinking Fields," he said. "Lost a whole wagon there three seasons back. Ground looks solid, but it's not. We've got a choice to make after these trees."

"Explain." I peered down as he started to sketch a rough map in the dirt.

"We're here." He pointed to a mark representing the trees. "Need to head southwest to reach your rendezvous point. Two ways to go." His finger traced the first route. "Follow the higher ground. Slower, more exposed, but safer. Or…" He traced the second route. "Cut through the lowlands. Faster, better cover, but that takes us near the Sinking Fields."

"And these fields are…?"

"Quicksand, bogs, and worse, I think," one of the scouts explained. "Near impossible to spot until you're already sinking. I heard say it's old magic from the cataclysm, but who knows? Never seen anything magical about it, an' I've travelled that route plenty before. All I know is the ground swallows men and beasts alike. If you don't watch for it."

I studied the crude map, weighing our options. Speed versus safety, the eternal dilemma of any journey.

"And what about those trails behind us?" I asked as I thought.

Horace frowned. "Could be anything, m'lord. Nomad riders, hunting parties, slavers. Or just wild herds roaming."

"Daralen?" I asked.

She shook her head. "Scouts I sent haven't returned, but I'd not expect them to yet. They're more following along as a rearguard than outright backtracking. I could send them direct and order them to check, but if they get attacked, they'd be alone, and if they're travelling out here in a small group…" She lifted a hand, waggling it from side to side uncertainly. "They're either dangerous as hell, or know that land if they're riders."

"Dangerous as hell and we want more people to go check them out, and if they know that land well, our scouts aren't going to catch them," I said. "How fast could they reach us?"

"If they're riders and they spotted us?" Horace scratched his chin. "Before nightfall, easily."

That settled it. "We'll take the lowland route," I decided. "The cover is worth the risk, and we need to make up time. But we'll send scouts ahead to mark safe passages."

"The wagons will slow in the lower ground," Daralen pointed out. "Mud, if there's been any rain."

"Better mud than arrows," I replied. "Oracle and I might be able to help with magic, maybe dry the ground out a bit?" I looked at her, and she sighed and nodded that she'd think on it, before indicating the last little member of the group who'd still not said anything.

"This is Annabeth." Daralen introduced her. "She's the former caravan leader Jared's daughter. I was made aware of her identity by another of the freed slaves, and thought you might wish to meet her."

"Certainly." I smiled at the young girl, who looked, frankly, terrified. "Are you okay?"

"I'm fine, m'lord," she said quickly. "All good."

"I'm sorry for your loss," I said, and she looked at me, terrified.

"I won't take it," she blurted. "I won't try an' sell it, I promise!"

"What?" I asked, taken aback.

"The control of the caravan," she babbled. "You don't have to do anything to me, I promise!"

"Ah, you…" I trailed off, thinking, and then nodded. "You're worried I'm going to do something to force you to hand over the rights to the caravan?"

She stared at me like a rabbit in the headlights.

I sighed. "You were right to bring her over, Daralen, thank you." I waved the others off as Oracle reached out and gently took the girl's hand.

"Annabeth, I'm Oracle. You're in no danger from us, I swear."

"No?" she asked, still clearly terrified. "I mean, no, of course I'm not."

She was agreeing to anything, I saw, and I forced a smile.

"Annabeth, do you know Toren?" I asked, and she nodded, a sharp, jerky motion. "Okay, he already surrendered the caravan to me, and even if he hadn't, we captured it after it'd been taken by slavers. Please don't take this the wrong way, but those facts mean that I'd have a right to the caravan anyway. Add in that I'm the prince and I freed you all, and I think it's pretty straightforward, so what's the issue here?"

"N…nothing."

"Annabeth, please, we're not a danger to you. Just tell us what you know," Oracle said. Then, when she still stared at us, terrified, she sighed and called Sehran in.

Sehran landed less than a minute later, smiling widely as she was introduced to an even more terrified girl now, before nodding as Oracle explained the situation through the bond.

The succubus sat, drawing the girl down to sit with her, and Oracle started to speak, talking of general things as Sehran started singing.

I looked from one to the other, then took the hint when Oracle jerked her head aside. I buggered off, leaving the ladies to their work.

Instead, I decided to check on the rest of our makeshift camp. Food was being distributed—more simple rations of dried meat and hard bread, salvaged from the slavers' wagons—not exactly a feast, but more than enough to keep everyone moving, and for most of the party, far more than they'd had in months.

As I accepted a portion from one of the legionnaires, I caught sight of an older woman sitting apart from the others. Her hands worked methodically as she stripped fibers from a handful of the tall grass stalks, her meal done.

Curious, I wandered over.

"What are you making?" I crouched beside her.

She looked up, startled, then quickly lowered her eyes. "Just twine, m'lord. I'm sorry, I didn't mean to disturb. It's just an old habit."

"May I?" I gestured to the neatly twisted fibers in her lap.

She hesitantly held out a length of the twisted grass, and I took it. It was surprisingly strong, a testament to her skill, and I bent it, surprised at how solid it was for a bundle of bloody grass.

"Where did you learn this?" I asked, genuinely impressed.

"Was a weaver, before," she said simply. Meaning before slavery, though she didn't say it aloud. "Plains grass makes good rope…baskets, too. Waterproof, if you treat it right."

An idea struck me. "Could you make sandals? Teach others?"

She blinked, confused. "I…suppose, m'lord. Not much to teach, though. Sandals…well, it'd just be either a fast loop of twine like this through a piece of wood, or I could make shoes, but they wouldn't last more than a few days."

"A few days of these would mean that people would have shoes," I said. "If you teach them, then when we slow, they could be weaving. Hundreds of people all doing it will give us usable materials quickly, and each time people make their own pair, they'll get better. They'll earn a little experience, and more than that, they're doing something for themselves. It's more important than you know," I explained. "Rope, baskets for carrying water, even simple mats for sleeping. Things like that, that belong to the person making them? That's valuable."

For the first time, she met my eyes directly, a spark of pride kindling there. "I could teach, yes. Would need more hands, though. I can only teach a handful at a time, after all."

"You'll have them," I promised. "I'll speak with Oracle—she's organizing our resources. For now, have a think on organizing that, and we'll talk soon."

As I walked away, I couldn't help but smile. One small interaction, one tiny step toward building something lasting. It wasn't just about fighting and freeing; it was about creating a future where people could make things for themselves again, own something, and I bet that would make a hell of a difference.

Besides, what did it cost us?

We were literally running through the grass. It would make little difference to the trail we left, and if by the time we reached the path to Sonra these people had even a rudimentary goddamn set of shoes, it'd be worth it.

I looked around, noting that the legion guard had split, most staying with Oracle and two staying with me. "Give me a minute." I waved them back, then took a deep breath and sank to one knee, assembling the weaves and plucking free a filament of fire, building the spell with that in primacy, and reaching out to the goddess Jenae.

*"Jax,"* she greeted. ***"What can I help you with?"***

*"Hey, my goddess, I'm going to be speaking to the caravan soon about you all, and then we'll set off running again. When we stop for the night, I was thinking to try to lead them in a little prayer or two, get them in the right mindset, but will that do anything?"*

***"Without a temple, an altar, or a focal point, not appreciably,"*** she admitted. ***"You are, however, not far from an old temple of Lagoush's. She was debating asking you to visit it, but didn't want to cause further issues, given the situation."***

*"How far out of the way is it?"* I asked.

***"About four hours' run to the north—hard running, to be clear."***

*"That's a long way."* I winced.

***"It is, but it would enable you to reach a place of worship specifically to her. It has long been abandoned, and the altar was destroyed, long lost now. But the ground still holds traces of her presence, and a prayer there would reach hungry ears."***

*"Okay, what if I send a scouting party and had them recover some of the building?"* I mused. *"Just a few dozen rocks?"*

***"They were part of a consecrated building,"*** she agreed. ***"Any prayer made holding such an item would reach Lagoush."***

*"And can she share that mana?"*

***"If she chose to,"*** Jenae confirmed.

*"So just as a wild thought here—if we got everyone here to start praying to Lagoush with those sections of the temple nearby, then she might get that mana and then share it out among you all, right?"*

***"I believe so."***

*"Okay, so what if, just as a thought here, but what if we needed a little inventing help, a little quest maybe from Svetu to help these people, specifically to help them in learning how to make shoes out of grass?"*

***"That…is a strange and particularly mundane request,"*** Jenae admitted, leaving me unsure whether it was offensive or just weird.

*"I know. What I'm thinking is that he was the God of Crafters and Invention, so if they were to be praying to him as they work, would that not help him?"*

***"Perhaps…"*** she hedged.

*"Because it would help them as well,"* I said quickly. *"It'd be an opportunity for them to get something of their own again—not something we give them…something that they make. It'd mean something to them, and more than that, it'd be a chance to get some XP. Also, they damn well need shoes, Jenae. We're going to be running across literally miles of shit soon, and as it is? They're already getting their feet shredded by the grass.*

*"If they can do this, and he can give them a quest to do it, it gets them some shoes and XP, it gets Him some worship, and it keeps their minds occupied. Sooner or later, one of them is going to think about the place we're heading to and all the slavers there, and they're going to start getting damn scared. They need this, and so do I."*

Jez Cajiao

*"Leave it with me, Jax, as issuing the quests to these people, especially a repeatable one, would cost us much. But I admit, the idea has merit. If we do it, it would cost all the mana that Lagoush receives and more, though."*

*"But it'll also show these people that you're there, and that you're watching over them. And, if they start praying every night..."* I left it unsaid, and Jenae sighed.

*"A valid point. An investment, if you will. Very well, Jax. I'll speak with Lagoush and Svetu."*

The sense of her presence faded, and I stood, blowing out a long breath, hoping it'd work.

The remainder of the hour passed quickly, and soon the call to move out rippled through the camp. People rose reluctantly from the shade, gathering their meager belongings and returning to the wagons. I watched from a small rise, assessing our formation with a critical eye.

"They're moving better," Oracle observed, appearing beside me. "The rest helped."

"It's not enough," I muttered. "We're too slow, too obvious."

"We're doing what we can with what we have," she reminded me gently. "Even the empire wasn't built in a day, Jax."

I smiled despite myself. "Neither was Rome. Ha, you sound like Tommy."

"Gods forbid," she replied, but there was humor in her voice.

As the column began to move again, we took our places at the front. Horace led the way, and we took up station alongside his wagon, with the trail-breaking teams ahead.

The lowland route took us into even taller grass. The slowly shifting and now golden stalks towered a good three feet above the tallest wagons. It created an eerie tunnel effect. Our world narrowed to the trampled path before us and the strip of blue sky overhead. Sounds were muffled by the surrounding vegetation, giving an illusion of isolation despite the hundreds of people behind us.

"I don't like this," Daralen murmured, joining us at the front of the column. "Too easy for an ambush."

"That works both ways," I pointed out. "They can't see us any better than we can see them."

"Still prefer open ground for fighting," she grumbled.

I couldn't disagree with that. Fighting in this grass would be a nightmare of confusion and friendly fire—literally with fireballs—but the cover it provided was worth the trade-off, at least until we knew more about whoever was trailing us.

As if summoned by my thoughts, Sehran dropped from the sky, landing in a crouch beside us. "Riders," she reported tersely. "Definitely not natural dust. They're moving in formation, about eight miles away now and definitely following us."

"Or heading to the same destination," Oracle suggested.

I considered the possibilities. "How many?"

"Hard to count from this distance," Sehran admitted. "At least thirty, maybe more. They're riding in single file, which made it a lot harder to be sure."

Thirty riders were too many for a simple hunting party, but not enough for a slaver force. Raiders, perhaps, or scouts for a larger group, but for thirty of them, they were no threat to a group this large.

"Keep watching them," I instructed. "If they pick up the pace, we'll need to know immediately."

Sehran nodded and took to the air again, her wings carrying her swiftly above the grass canopy.

"Should we prepare for an engagement?" Daralen asked.

"Not yet," I decided. "We'll continue on this route, but pass the word to be ready. Thirty of them following us makes no sense, unless they're trailing us and others are setting up an ambush ahead."

She nodded sharply and moved back through the column to relay the orders.

*"You're worried,"* Oracle observed through our bond.

*"Cautious,"* I corrected. *"Thirty riders could be anything. No point in panicking everyone until we know more."*

*"And if they are hostile?"*

I flexed a gauntleted fist and grinned. *"Then we deal with them. I could do with letting off some steam."*

Oracle sighed, kissed my cheek, and then returned to the wagon, working to teach the three spells to more legionnaires. I couldn't help but grin when I heard quiet questions and muttering, wondering whether others could learn too, and just how long a legion term of service was.

The rest of the afternoon passed in tense anticipation, but the riders neither approached nor disappeared, continuing to follow at a range of about seven miles. It was almost worse than an outright attack—the constant uncertainty, the feeling of being watched.

As the sun began to sink toward the horizon, bathing the grasslands in golden light, Horace called the column to a halt.

"Need to make camp soon, Prince," he explained. "Not safe to travel these lowlands after dark. Too many sinkholes, too much wildlife hunting."

I nodded reluctantly. "Recommendations for a defensible position?"

He pointed ahead. "There's a rise about half a mile on. Old burial mound, if the stories are right. Ground's solid, gives a good view of the surrounding area."

"Burial mound?" I raised an eyebrow. "You sure that's a good idea?"

Horace shrugged. "Been used as a camping spot for generations, m'lord. Whatever spirits might have been there are long gone or used to the company."

That was less reassuring than he probably intended, but we had limited options. "The mound it is. Get us there before sunset."

"Yessir." He smiled and started to pick up the pace.

I turned to Oracle as she joined me, clearly wanting a break from the magic lessons.

"Hey you. You okay?" I asked her, getting a smile and a kiss. "So, what did you find with Annabeth? Is she okay?" I asked, remembering, and she smiled.

"She is. I was wondering if you were going to ask."

"I figured if you needed to tell me, you would. And honestly? I forgot." I grinned at her, before explaining what I'd asked Jenae for, and Sehran, who'd landed and was running alongside at this point, immediately offered to go and scout it out.

"If we could find it, it'd be worth the visit for the stones alone," she suggested. "Wouldn't it?"

"It would, but at the end of the day, although I owe Lagoush a favor, I want her to be clear on this one—if she wants us to do it, there's a hell of a risk sending you or a scouting party off to check it out," I said. *"I owe her for saving Tommy, but I don't want the favor hanging over my head forever. If she asks us to do this, it's a down payment against that debt,"* I said through the bond.

*"Good point,"* Oracle replied, before speaking aloud. "For Annabeth, it turns out that if you remove the various leaders of the caravan, the ownership reverts to the family of the caravan master. They had no formal claim, as Annabeth had no formal position in the caravan. She was along to help her father out, and to learn.

"That muddied the waters a little, in terms of who was in charge when the slavers took over, as they'd expected to have killed the last few leaders and having her in their grasp…"

"And that's why they split the caravan." I grunted. "If they could kill or capture Toren, then control reverted to her; she signs it over, then boom. The guild gets control and the slavers sell her off."

"Exactly. She was hiding as she didn't want to be more of a target, and frankly, she'd just seen her father slaughtered. And the methods of persuasion they were using on her…well, if she could have signed it over, she would have."

"And now?" I asked.

"Now she's just a scared young girl and she's desperate to find her way in the world. She doesn't really have any hope of returning to her home. And even if she did, there were precious few friends and only distant family there. Her life was travelling with the caravan. She didn't grow up in it—her mother loved the city life and kept her close. But when Jared returned from his last expedition, it was to a wife who had been carried off by a sickness, and a daughter who was terrified, being pursued by suitors who wanted access to the caravans and never her."

"Poor kid." I sighed. "All right, well, I guess we look after her then, just like all the rest. Is she happier now she knows we don't need to pressure her for anything?"

"Yes and no." Oracle winced. "As it was, she was the heir to the caravan, provided she could survive to take control or sell it. Now she's a pauper, just like everyone else."

"And we're sitting pretty with her caravan, just like we are with all the merchants' goods and so on." I grunted. "I know we need to, but damn. Still feels a little shitty."

"Yeah," she admitted.

And with that, the conversation broke up, moving to occasional little details, as we ran on.

# CHAPTER THIRTY-THREE

The alleged burial mound, when we reached it, turned out to be a big earthwork. One that climbed maybe twenty meters above the surrounding plains. Its top was weirdly flat, and there was enough space for our wagons to circle the entire mound in a defensive formation, which made Daralen happy at least. The grass was shorter here, barely knee-high, giving us better sight lines in all directions as well.

As the sun dipped below the horizon, long shadows stretching across the plains, our first proper makeshift camp took shape. Fires were lit in pockets around the base, the smallest that would do the job, so as to limit the range anyone could see us from. Around the edge of the camp, the legionnaires established a watch rotation, their armor gleaming dully in the fading light, and between every legionnaire was at least one volunteer.

The slaves had, after all, learned in the worst possible way the value of keeping an eye open when there were potential slavers about. Now they were determined not to run that risk again.

I stood at the highest point of the mound, watching as stars began to appear overhead. In the distance, pinpricks of light marked our mysterious observers' camp—they had stopped as well, which was starting to piss me off.

I was in the middle of complaining to Oracle about it, toying with the idea of flying over and introducing myself, when Sehran joined us. I stopped her reporting—seeing that she wasn't concerned—and waved Daralen, who was jogging up the side of the mound, to join us.

The rustle of grass in the evening breeze seemed louder than it should have been in the unnatural quiet, like the whispering of ghosts. After such a long day of running, I could see the exhaustion etched into every face. But at least we had a defensible position for the night, and although the vast majority were practically asleep on their feet, or collapsed already, I saw shelters being erected, campfires lit, and more.

"The perimeter is secure, my prince," Daralen reported, coming to a halt.

"Good." I nodded, still scanning the darkened plains. "Any movement from our friends out there?"

"They've sent a pair of scouts—one leading, the other twenty meters behind, probably in case they're ambushed—and they're headed straight for us. The rest have set up a camp about seven miles out, keeping their distance the same as much as possible," Sehran said. "It doesn't look like an attack. Why send just two, after all, but still…"

"Probably want to make contact in the dark," Daralen suggested. "If they're locals and are used to the area, they'll be able to get away a hell of a lot easier than we can pursue."

"Keeping their options open," I agreed. "They're either curious or cautious. Either way, it's looking like a peaceful attempt at contact, so fuck it, let's play nice. For now."

The night air carried a chill that hadn't been present during the day's heat, and I was suddenly grateful for my layers. Even now, I could feel the layers of armor and the under armor helping to keep me warm. The freed slaves huddled closer to the fires below, wrapped in whatever scraps of cloth they'd managed to salvage, or using the trade goods that we'd doled out to everyone.

"Everyone's settled for now. We've already done the healing fountains and that seems to have made a hell of a difference to them all," Oracle added next. "I spread the word, as did Daralen, about that weaver. She's giving some basic classes, but the wounds…" She shook her head.

"How bad?" I asked. I'd moved up the mound when we first arrived to check the local area out; then I'd stayed there when I'd seen that Daralen and Oracle had things well enough in hand without me adding more to it.

"Bad enough. The grass cuts like razors in places. Some of the children have feet that were basically ribbons of flesh. Older people generally have harder skin and it's getting damaged but less than the kids. We're healing them, but they need proper footwear before we set out again tomorrow—or they need to be riding. Their parents and those who were more unlucky than the rest didn't want to be a bother, as they've still got it in their heads that they might be discarded or killed if they draw attention in the wrong way or at the wrong time."

"Fuck's sake. That's madness. We can't have kids running about, crippled for—" I shook my head. "Even if we truly didn't care, we're leaving blood trails that are going to draw monsters, surely? Fine, okay, I'm working on that next," I replied, reiterating my conversation with the old weaver and my request to Jenae. "If the gods agree, we might have a solution, and I know they won't want to waste much time as we'll miss the chance at the temple."

"It would certainly help," Oracle agreed, then turned as Sehran smiled and started to speak.

"One other thing. Our incoming guests were swinging around to make sure they approached from downwind."

"Smart," Daralen observed. "They're experienced, whoever they are. And, no offense, Lord, but probably not human then. If they use smell as a tracking guide, they'll be able to tell a lot from that and we'd not smell them in return, but…" She looked out over the camp. "Honestly, we probably don't smell much better than a slave camp. We'll smell of fresh and old blood, stale sweat and filth. It's not like we've managed to stop anywhere that people could wash and get fresh clothing."

"Want me to intercept, check on their races?" Sehran asked, a predatory gleam in her eyes.

I considered it briefly, then shook my head. "No. Let them approach. I want to see what they do when they reach our perimeter. If they're hostile, they'll try to strike quickly. If they're just gathering information…"

"Then we might learn something about who they are," Oracle finished.

"Exactly."

We fell silent, each lost in our own thoughts as we watched the darkened plains. Eventually, Daralen excused herself to check on the legionnaires, and Sehran took to the air again for another reconnaissance circuit, apparently loving flying again, especially here.

I also had a suspicion that certain nighttime predators were getting a final, demon-shaped surprise as she went, knowing her.

Oracle remained beside me, her presence a comfort in the stillness.

"You're worried about Illoth," she said suddenly, and it wasn't a question.

I let out a long breath. "I'd be an idiot not to be," I admitted quietly. "But I'm doing my best not to show it and act all 'Billy Big Balls' for those watching."

"You've faced a god before."

"And nearly died," I reminded her. "Plus, I had Amon with me then."

Oracle reached out, her fingers brushing my gauntleted hand. "You're stronger now than you were then I know we've talked about this before, but I can feel the stress in you."

"Maybe." I wasn't convinced. Amon's presence had completely faded. "Also, Illoth's got an advantage that she can prepare, and when we get there, I get the feeling that she's not gonna show up with an open field and lots of clear sightlines. She's a spider goddess, so the whole thing is gonna be freaky."

"We need to consider our approach as well," Oracle said. "Thinking about it, if she could kill you off by a knife in the back before the fight, I bet she'd be a lot happier."

I grunted, and she went on. "I mean it, Jax. As much as you're worrying? I bet she is more. She's a weaker goddess than…*him*…and you killed him, then stole a fragment of his power. She's weaker—she can't afford to lose that power to you. He couldn't as well I'm sure, but that's not the point. If she wins the fight, her master is going to be pissed, and she'll pay for showing him up. If she loses? She loses face, control, and a massive part of her power. The only way she can win here is by not facing you at all."

"So, assassins." I groaned. "Stabby-stabby bastards."

"Exactly."

"I'm going to need to ask Daralen to beef up my security, aren't I?" I asked sadly. "I'm sorry."

"Why?" She frowned.

"I just hate having too many strange people around us. I like a little privacy with you," I admitted.

"They're our people now," Oracle corrected gently. "Each one swore the oath."

I smiled despite myself. "Our people. You're right."

We stood in companionable silence until a soft alarm sounded from the darkness overhead—three short whistles, Daralen's prearranged signal for approaching strangers.

I straightened, hand moving automatically to my weapon, even as I sent my thanks through the bond to Sehran.

"Showtime."

The scouts had shifted around to approach from the east, keeping low in the grass. They'd made it within two hundred yards of our perimeter before they realized they'd been spotted. And then, rather than retreating when discovered, they'd frozen in place, waiting.

"Smart," I observed again as I took up position in the shadow of a wagon. "They want to see how we react."

"Nervous, too," Oracle added, from beside me. "They've been still for nearly ten minutes now."

I nodded to Daralen, who we'd joined, and she gave the order to move out. Four legionnaires headed out into the grass, spreading wide to flank the position where the scouts had been spotted. I watched their disciplined movement with approval—even exhausted after a day of running, they moved like the professionals they were.

Several tense minutes passed before one of the legionnaires returned, approaching and greeting us with a crisp salute.

"They're coming in, my prince, Primus Daralen," he reported. "Two riders, hands visible. They've agreed to leave their weapons with their mounts. One wanted to hang back, but we stopped that just in case they're planning something."

"Good work," Daralen replied, then turned to me. "Jax?"

"Sounds good. Well done," I said, not sure what she was looking for from me, but getting a nod.

We moved to the eastern edge of the camp, positioning ourselves where the firelight would illuminate us clearly while the legionnaires formed a loose semicircle around us. A show of force, but not too aggressive a one.

The scouts emerged from the grass like ghosts, both figures wrapped in dust-colored cloaks that made them nearly invisible in the darkness. They approached slowly, hands held out empty and visible at their sides. As they entered the circle of firelight, I got my first good look at them.

The first was a tall, lean man with skin weathered to leather by a life outdoors in the wind. His face was crisscrossed with thin scars—ritual markings, I guessed, not battle wounds. The second was a woman, shorter but no less imposing, and with the same scars. She had close-cropped grey hair and eyes that missed nothing as they scanned our camp—both clearly, as Daralen had said, not human.

They were trigara, the same race as Nigret, if I had to guess, seeing the thicker cheeks, the feline features and the patterning. I instantly wondered how that mad bastard was getting on now.

Both wore simple, practical clothing beneath their cloaks, reinforced leather in places that suggested armor without the bulk or weight of metal. No visible weapons, as promised, but I'd have bet my last copper piece that they had knives hidden somewhere.

The man spoke first, his voice low and raspy. "You're a long way from the trade roads."

"As are you," I replied evenly.

A slight smile touched his lips. "We live here. These plains are our home."

"Must be a drafty house," I commented, earning a small chuckle from the woman.

The tension eased fractionally. The man studied me for a long moment, taking in my armor, my stance, and the obvious deference of those around me.

"I am Called," he said finally. "This is Whisper. We speak for the Watchers."

"Interesting names," I observed.

"Earned ones," the woman—Whisper—replied, her voice surprisingly melodic. "As all true names should be."

I nodded in acknowledgment. "I'm Jax. Prince of the Empire and ruler of Dravith. This is Oracle, my partner, and these are my people."

Called's eyes widened fractionally at my title, though he recovered quickly. "The empire fell long years in the past. The Watchers remember this."

"I'm bringing it back," I replied simply.

The scouts exchanged glances, having a silent conversation in the way that only longtime partners can.

"The Watchers have been watching your group since you entered the plains," Called admitted. "You are many, and passing our lands, such a large column…"

"You thought we were slavers," I guessed, wondering at the slightly weird way they spoke.

"Or worse," Whisper agreed. "The Watchers know this route isn't used by the honest. Too dangerous, too many ways to disappear."

"We're not slavers," Oracle said firmly. "In fact, most of those with us were slaves until recently."

Called nodded slowly. "So we have heard. The voices tell us that you are different. Your people are distinctive. Our ancestors didn't expect to find any left alive in these parts, not after the Dark Legion's purges."

A cold anger settled in my gut at the reminder. "The Imperial Legion endures."

"It must, or it breaks," Called agreed, then hesitated. "We came to see for ourselves you weren't raiders looking for stock. Now we know."

I studied them carefully. "And what will you tell your people when you return?"

"That a caravan of freed slaves passes through, led by the ancient honor bound, and claiming to serve a reborn empire." Whisper's tone was neutral, revealing nothing of what she thought of this assessment.

"Will that cause us problems?" I asked bluntly.

Called shrugged. "Not from us. The Watchers mind our own." His gaze swept over our camp, taking in the wagons, the people huddled around fires. "You're heading to the uplands?"

"That's right."

"Toward Sonra."

It wasn't a question, but I nodded anyway. "We have people to meet along the way."

"The rest of your caravan," Whisper said. At my surprised look, she smiled thinly. "We've been watching them too. They're camped about a day and a half's journey from here, travelling this way. You should catch them tomorrow, if luck and the wind serve you."

That was useful information, though I wasn't sure why they were sharing it, or how they knew, considering the distances involved. "And what should we expect between here and there?"

"Bog lands for half a day," Called replied. "Then rising ground toward the foothills. Game is plentiful there, if you know how to hunt it. And predators, if you don't."

"And the herd migrations?"

"Already passed and upland. Scouts pass still, but no more."

I nodded my thanks for the information. "And your people? Will we encounter more of the Watchers?"

Called's expression closed off. "Perhaps. Perhaps not."

"You won't tell us where your settlement is," Oracle observed.

"Would you, in our position?" Whisper countered.

"Fair enough."

A brief silence fell, interrupted only by the crackling of the campfires and the whisper of grass in the night breeze.

"We leave you now," Called said finally. "Our people will be waiting for our words."

I nodded. "Safe travels."

"May the wind speed your travels and carry the scents of summer." Called hesitated, then added, almost sounding less mad for a minute, "Watch the northern edges of the bog. The ground looks solid but isn't. Many caravans have lost people there."

"Thank you for the warning," I replied sincerely.

The scouts nodded once in acknowledgment, then turned and melted back into the darkness as silently as they'd appeared.

"Well," I said once they were gone, "that was less than informative."

"And somewhat reassuring," Oracle added. "At least they're not immediately hostile."

"Not immediately," I agreed. "But they're clearly fucking mad as well. You catch that bit at the end? He almost sounded like someone else."

"They're sharing their bodies," Sehran said softly.

"What?"

"They're sharing their bodies with another. It's rare. I've only heard of it. But if you raise a spirit, it can be done…to invite them in, and let them live in your flesh with you."

"That sounds all sorts of fucked up," I said firmly. "How do you know and why would they do that?"

"I don't, but the changing speech patterns, the way that everything is 'we' and 'the Watchers,' it matches. Though why? No clue."

"Should we follow them?" Daralen asked.

"Maintain the watch," I confirmed. "They seemed honest enough, but I'd rather be cautious. Double the guard until midnight, then normal rotations after that."

She nodded and moved off to relay the orders.

"What do you think?" I asked Oracle once we were alone.

"I think they're survivors," she replied thoughtfully. "People who've found a way to live out here, away from the cities and the slavers. They're cautious but not aggressive."

"Agreed." I gazed out at the darkened plains. "And they're watching both halves of our caravan, which means they know these plains well, and they can somehow pass information faster than a horse can ride."

"Do you trust what they told us?"

I considered it. "About the terrain? Yes. I don't see what they'd gain by lying about that. About their own people and intentions?" I shook my head. "Out here, who fuckin' knows, if I'm being honest."

With that, we returned to the center of camp, where the freed slaves were settling in for the night. I noticed with approval that several small groups had formed around the older weaver, watching as she demonstrated how to strip and twist the grass fibers. Good. They were already starting to work on the problem without waiting for divine intervention.

Speaking of which…

I found a quiet spot away from the main fires and knelt, focusing my mind and gathering the strands of mana and then building the spell, reaching out to Jenae. The familiar warmth of her presence washed over me almost immediately.

*"Well met, Jax."* Her voice was warm in my mind. *"Your timing is perfect. I've spoken with the others about your request."*

*"And?"* I prompted when she paused.

*"We are in agreement,"* she replied. *"Lagoush is particularly pleased with the idea. That temple had been long abandoned, and the recovery of even a small portion would be meaningful."*

Relief washed through me. *"Thank you, my goddess."*

*"There are conditions,"* she cautioned. *"The party sent to recover the artifacts must be small—and they must do no more damage than necessary. It was a site of worship for her, after all, and the final resting place of many of her followers. I ask that you show respect when you go there."*

*"Of course. What else?"*

*"Each evening, as you suggested, your people will pray to Lagoush, who will share that power among us until proper altars can be established. In return, we will each offer a boon."*

*"What kind of boons?"* I asked, cautiously.

*"Svetu offers a repeatable quest to create grass sandals and other basic necessities, as well as more advanced crafting for those with the capacity. Those who complete his quests will gain experience and his blessing, which will slightly enhance their crafting abilities.*

*"I will enhance your campfires each night, granting those who rest nearby a small bonus to health regeneration. Tyosh offers aid in meditation, allowing those who seek his guidance to recover mental energy more efficiently, and to process the things that they have experienced. This may help many in ways that your own healing and that of your companions can't.*

*"Ashante will ensure that game is plentiful along your route, allowing your hunters to more easily find food. Sint will grant a blessing of endurance to your scouts, making them run faster and for longer.*

*"Tamat…"* Jenae hesitated. *"Tamat offers to guide the hand of any who seek vengeance against those who enslaved them, though I caution you to be careful with her gifts. They often come with…complications."*

I nodded, understanding all too well. *"And the others?"*

*"Vanei will send favorable winds to speed your journey when possible. Cruit will strengthen the earth beneath your wagons, reducing the chance of becoming mired in the bog lands. Darakin offers to enhance the combat abilities of five warriors of your choosing during one battle of your choice…or…"*

*"Or?"* I prompted.

*"Or he offers to spar with you. Directly. As a god in an avatar's form. One that he will create especially and that, as such, you will not need to fear injuring. There are additional conditions on that, and both Sint and I have agreed upon them."*

*"What conditions?"*

**"That neither side may claim anything beyond the lessons of the fight, that you may not kill each other, and that the fight ends at the end of the bout, with no repercussions for anyone."**

*"Sounds good. Did he agree to it? Were you worried he was going to try to…"*

**"Jax, these conditions are primarily aimed at YOU,"** she said. **"We need Darakin, and we need you, but of the two of you, at this point, we need you more. And frankly, you're also the one most likely to lose control and cross a line. That's also why we insisted on him creating an avatar instead of using his humanoid form."**

*"Oh… I mean, seriously? You really think I'm that bad?"* There was a long silence, and I snorted, then moved on. *"And Lagoush herself?"*

**"She will ensure that any water summoned by you or Oracle carries additional healing properties for the next seven days, will guide your people safely through the bog lands, and because we both know that you're going to take Darakin up on his offer, she will boost the healing that you'll need afterward, as well as step in should she judge you to be injured too highly."**

I considered the offers, impressed by their generosity. *"And in return?"*

**"As agreed, prayers each evening, and the recovery of artifacts from her temple. There is one more thing,"** Jenae added. **"Issa."**

*"The God of Light in Dark Places,"* I remembered. *"What does he offer?"*

**"He asks that when your people pray, they remember those still enslaved in Sonra and beyond. That you, and they, agree to try to free them. In return, he will grant a small boon to any who attempt to free slaves in the coming days—a moment of clarity in confusion, a shadow where one is needed, a distraction at a crucial moment."**

*"That seems more than fair,"* I agreed, thinking of the probable thousands still enslaved in Sonra. *"Please convey my thanks to all the Pantheon. We'll dispatch a team to Lagoush's temple at first light. They need to rest at least a little first."*

**"Be careful, Jax,"** Jenae warned. **"The temple ruins have long been abandoned for good reason. When such tragedy has struck, it leaves marks in the soul of the realm. There are many who will avoid such places, but others…they may be drawn to them. We cannot see whether the temple is inhabited or not, so be ready…"**

With that cryptic warning, her presence faded, leaving me alone with my thoughts as I rose and rejoined the camp.

Oracle approached, having sensed the conclusion of my communion with Jenae. "Well?"

"They've agreed," I told her, outlining the conditions and the promised boons. "We'll need to select a team to retrieve the artifacts from Lagoush's temple."

"I could go," Oracle said immediately.

I shook my head firmly. "Absolutely not. You're too important, and with the baby…we can't risk it."

She frowned but didn't argue the point further. "Sehran, then. She can fly, which gives her an advantage if there's trouble."

"Agreed. And a couple of legionnaires for muscle, plus maybe one of the former slaves who knows the area."

"Horace?" Oracle suggested.

I considered it. "He's proved reliable so far. He's done a great job leading the wagon, but fuck it, he can recommend someone else, I imagine, so yeah, that works. We can give them horses as well."

We spent the next hour moving through the camp, checking on our people and sharing the news of the gods' blessings. The response was a mixture of awe, skepticism, and cautious hope. After so long without any kind of divine protection, with knowing that beyond the Dark Pantheon, no god cared about the realm, the idea of gods taking an interest in their welfare seemed almost insane.

I found the old weaver, now surrounded by a dozen eager students as she demonstrated how to twist grass fibers into usable cordage.

Considering the state of people's feet, even now after the healing, I instantly knew why. The group who sat around her included a hell of a lot of kids as well, and I guessed that if these people surrounding them weren't their original parents, they were as close as we were going to find now.

"Looks like you've got a following," I observed, crouching beside her.

She glanced up, her weathered face creasing in a smile. "People want to learn, m'lord. Especially when it means not having their feet cut to ribbons tomorrow."

"I've got good news on that front," I told her, explaining about Svetu's quest. "Those who learn to make sandals will gain his blessing, making the work easier and the results stronger."

Her eyes widened. "The old God of Inventors himself? Taking an interest in our humble work?"

"That's right. Every pair of sandals made, every length of rope twisted—it all honors him. And he'll reward those efforts."

She bowed her head, momentarily overcome. "Never thought I'd live to see such a day."

"Spread the word," I told her. "We'll have a proper prayer service before we sleep, but anyone who wants to start working on sandals now can begin earning his favor."

She nodded eagerly, and I left her organizing her impromptu crafting circle with renewed vigor.

Oracle joined me as I made my way back toward the center of camp. "The legionnaires are setting up a simple altar using stones from the mound," she reported. "It won't be much, and it won't serve to channel the mana either, but it will serve for tonight's prayers to help people understand."

"Good." I looked around at the camp. "I should have thought of this before." I sighed.

"You're learning," Oracle teased gently. "Sometimes leadership isn't just about charging into battle. And Jax? Nobody else thought of it *at all*. You did, so accept the win, okay?"

"Meh, and I do enjoy the battle part," I admitted with a grin.

"I've noticed."

As the night deepened, our makeshift altar was completed, a simple arrangement of stones with a small fire burning before it. Around it, freed slaves and legionnaires alike gathered to offer their first prayers to the gods of their ancestors.

I led the service, feeling ridiculous as my voice carried clearly through the night. I called on each of the gods in turn, explaining their domains and the blessings they offered. The legionnaires joined in confidently, while the former slaves followed hesitantly at first, then with growing conviction.

When it came to Lagoush, Goddess of Water and Healing and the last of those to be named tonight, Oracle spoke up. "To Lagoush, Lady of Peaceful Passages, we give special thanks tonight. For her promise to guide us through the waters that lie ahead, for healing our wounds, and for sharing our prayers with all the Pantheon until proper altars can be built for each. We vow to recover what was lost from your temple, to honor your name and your gifts."

A murmur of agreement rippled through the gathering as the people repeated the prayer. I felt something shift in the air—a tension, a building of power that raised the hair on my arms despite my armor.

Then, as we finished, a ripple of red and yellow light passed through the campfires, transforming ordinary flames into something more. The fires burned higher, brighter, their light carrying a sense of warmth and healing that was more than physical.

"Jenae's blessing," Oracle whispered to me, and I nodded, recognizing my goddess's touch.

As the ceremony concluded, people drifted back to their sleeping spots, many lingering near the enhanced fires, drawn to their healing warmth. I noticed that several groups continued to work on their grass weaving by firelight, inspired by the promise of Svetu's blessing.

"I can't believe it worked," I said to Oracle as we made our way to one of the luxurious master's caravans near the edge of the mound. There were already legionnaires surrounding it, and I smiled as Oracle put down a Circle of Frostfire as soon as we reached it. "They needed this."

"They did," she agreed. "And so do we. And yes, I know you, so you're thinking that we just cast that to make sure Illoth can't sneak any spiders in to get us, and that's right. No, we can't do it for the entire camp. Yes, you need a proper night's sleep in a real bed. No, you can't sleep on the ground again. Just because there aren't enough beds for everyone doesn't mean that the prince of the empire should go without."

I grinned at her, then nodded. "We're gonna need to change the sheets," I pointed out. "No telling what was done in them before now."

"Already done. No, we don't know, and yes, when we can replace them with completely new ones, we're burning the old ones. Lastly, no, you need to actually sleep and rest, so it's sleepy time, not sexy time," she finished, smiling.

"You know me so well." I laughed.

We settled down for the night. Daralen had pointedly refused my offer of standing a turn at watch, and the camp quieted around us.

I lay there for a while, drifting off to sleep. Oracle was cradled in my arms, me naked—her pointedly wearing a nightdress that literally covered her completely and having put a pillow between us down there for added safety.

It really didn't help overly as she actually slept, and I considered poking her with it anyway to try to wake her up. Eventually, I sighed and drifted off to sleep, knowing I needed to be good, and already plotting when I could fight Darakin, considering that a training session with the God of Battle was definitely the best preparation I could manage for facing Illoth.

Sometime in the deepest part of the night, I woke suddenly.

Oracle stiffened, sensing it too—a subtle change in the air. A stillness that went past the normal quiet of a sleeping camp. The few nightbirds that had been calling fell silent. Even the grass seemed to stop its endless whispering.

I rose to my feet, looking at her as she changed into her 'fighting outfit' and I started to swear, dressing hurriedly.

As soon as I was minimally dressed, I left the wagon, standing bare-chested with Oracle by my side as we scanned the darkness. Even Sehran was asleep now, and lay undisturbed by the fire nearby. The few legionnaires who had the watch over us glanced from us to the night.

Nothing moved on the plains surrounding us. The perimeter guards maintained their vigilance, unaware of the change I sensed.

For long seconds, I thought I must have imagined it—a bad dream forgotten or a cramp that never quite started—until Oracle spoke up.

"Something's coming," she whispered.

Before I could respond, a faint glow appeared at the edge of my vision. I turned, squinting into the darkness, and saw them—pale, translucent figures rising from the earth of the burial mound itself. They emerged slowly, without sound, their forms indistinct yet somehow clearly human.

"They're spirits," Oracle breathed, moving to stand beside me. "The mound's inhabitants."

I counted at least a dozen of them now, their ghostly forms drifting upward from the earth, gathering in a loose semicircle before us. They made no threatening moves, simply watched us with eyes that held centuries of patient waiting.

"Can you communicate with them?" I asked Oracle quietly.

She frowned in concentration. "Not directly, but I can sense…impressions. They're curious. We've disturbed their rest, but not in a way that angers them."

"Maybe I should…" I started, thinking of my clairvoyance spell.

"It won't work here," Oracle said definitively. "Just wait."

One of the spirits, taller than the rest, drifted forward. Its form was that of a warrior, ancient armor hanging from its spectral frame. It raised a hand in what might have been greeting.

"They've been here a long time," Oracle murmured. "Centuries, waiting."

"For what?" I asked.

"I'm not sure. For someone to remember them, perhaps. For something, though."

An impulse struck me. "Should we release them? Send them on to whatever waits beyond?"

Oracle caught my arm as I began to gather mana. "No. That's not what they want."

"What then?"

"They want…" Her brow furrowed in concentration. "They want to be remembered. To be known. They were guardians once, defenders of these lands. Now they're forgotten, their names lost to time."

The lead spirit drifted closer. Its featureless face turned toward me expectantly, as people on all sides stirred, many shocked, but none shouting or crying out. Whatever this was, the feeling wasn't one of a threat. Instead, it was somber, but hopeful.

"What do I do?" I asked quietly.

"Acknowledge them," Oracle suggested. "Honor their watch."

I straightened, facing the spirit directly. "I am Jax, Prince of the Empire. We recognize your vigil here, guardians of the mound. Your service is not forgotten."

The spirit inclined its head slowly, and a ripple of movement passed through the gathered ghosts. They seemed to stand taller, their forms becoming momentarily more distinct.

"Tell them," Oracle prompted, "that the empire remembers its defenders."

"The empire remembers," I repeated, looking from one to another of them. "And honors your watch. When we have rebuilt what was lost, you will be recorded again, your service acknowledged."

A sigh seemed to pass through the assembled spirits—not of release, but of satisfaction. The lead ghost raised its hand to its chest once more, this time in what was unmistakably a legionnaire's salute. Then, one by one, they began to sink back into the earth, returning to their long vigil.

The tall warrior was the last to go, its form lingering for a moment as it gazed at us. Then it too faded, and the normal sounds of the night returned—the rustle of grass, the soft call of nightbirds, the crackle of campfires.

"What was that about?" I asked, still staring at the spot where the spirits had disappeared.

"They needed to know they weren't forgotten," Oracle replied softly. "That the oath they swore still matters. They'll rest easier now."

"They're not moving on?"

She shook her head. "Not yet. Their watch isn't over. But now they know it has purpose again."

"They weren't legion," I whispered as some extra details struck suddenly. "They were from a long, *long* time ago, weren't they?"

"I think so," she whispered. "I think they sensed us, sensed you and the attention of the gods, and they just…wanted to be seen, maybe?"

I nodded slowly, understanding. The ghosts of the burial mound were like the legionnaires from the prax themselves—holding to oaths made centuries ago, waiting for something. Now their vigil continued, but hopefully with a little meaning, maybe? That made me wonder just how many places like this existed out there. Places where the long dead refused their rest. Where secrets lay forgotten, while the realm had just…moved on.

Wide awake now, we returned to the wagon, though this time we sat on the roof. The last hour or so of the night passed uneventfully from that point. As the sky began to lighten with the first hint of dawn, Oracle suddenly stiffened beside me, her gaze fixed on the edge of the mound.

"Jax," she whispered, pointing.

I followed her gesture and saw them—the spirits, returned with the fading darkness. They stood in a silent line along the eastern edge of the mound, facing the lightening horizon. As the first rays of the sun crept over the plains, they raised their arms in unison, a silent salute to the dawn.

Then, as the light touched them, they faded from view, returning to their eternal watch below the earth.

"Whoever they were, they worshipped the sun," Oracle guessed. "They must come here on occasion, showing the realm that they remember."

I nodded, unexpectedly moved by the gesture. "And so will we."

# CHAPTER THIRTY-FOUR

We broke camp with the rising sun. The burial mound fell away behind us as we set our path out toward the bogs and the rest of the caravan again.

The small team destined for Lagoush's temple—Sehran, two legionnaires named Vislen and Tarra, and Horace to guide them—split off to the north with a promise to rejoin us hopefully before nightfall if they pushed as hard as they could, and as well as the three horses, they took three spares. I watched them go with serious misgivings, but Sehran's confident wave reassured me somewhat.

It was weird not having her in the bond anymore. For a start, I was used to the constant bag of emotions, feral madness, and barely suppressed sexual tension she radiated continually, and not having that, it made our bond feel almost quiet.

Vislen had a good manapool, though, and when we'd explained Sehran's needs, he'd happily volunteered.

The way his eyes had bugged out and he'd had to nip off to deal with something suggested that having a horny succubus in your brain, one who wasn't making any offers and yet was also not shielding her own desires, wasn't just a problem for me.

The rest of us continued, the column spreading out across the plains. Already I could see the difference in our people—sandals made of woven grass adorned a handful of feet, but many more were being crafted as we traveled. Spirits were higher, conversations more animated, and there was a new sense of purpose in the way they carried themselves.

By mid-morning, we reached the edge of the bog lands Called had warned us about. It was a vast stretch of deceptively placid pools and seemingly solid ground that could swallow a man whole if he stepped wrong. Oracle flew ahead, guiding our path with Lagoush's blessing, identifying the safest routes for the wagons.

The going was slow, the wagons frequently bogging down even with Cruit's blessing strengthening the earth beneath them. More than once, we had to halt the entire column to drag a wagon free from sucking mud, everyone straining together under the watchful eyes of Daralen's legionnaires.

It made me seriously damn thankful for Cruit's help, because judging from how hard this was, we'd have lost at least half the caravan if we'd tried to bull our way through any other way.

"This is taking too long," I muttered to Oracle during one such delay.

"It takes as long as it takes, Jax," she replied, smiling gently. "Lagoush guides us. Without her blessing and Cruit's, you're right that we'd have lost wagons by now, not just time."

She was right, of course. By midday, we'd navigated more than half the bog lands without major incident—a minor miracle given the treacherous nature of the terrain. I flew up occasionally to scout our path, noting with relief that the ground rose steadily beyond, promising firmer footing ahead.

The sun was beginning its descent, the wagons finally climbing free of the last stretches of bog, when Sehran's familiar form appeared in the distance, winging her way toward us at top speed.

"Trouble?" Oracle wondered, as her figure grew larger.

"Possibly," I replied, watching her approach, and waving to Daralen, who hurried over to join us as well. "Or good news."

Sehran landed before us in a flurry of wings, her expression both excited and tense. "We've got company," she announced without preamble. "But not the kind we expected."

"Explain," I prompted.

She gestured southwest. "Scouts from the other half of the caravan. They've been riding hard and spotted me flying and approached Vislen and Tarra. They're making their way toward us now—should reach us in a little over an hour."

I felt a surge of relief and worry. "That means we're on track, but that our other scouts missed the incoming group if we're that close without a warning!" I groaned.

"After the time in the bogs, we're lucky to be still moving," Oracle pointed out. "A little mistake is understandable…"

"Tell it to Daralen." I winced, knowing that was going to go down like a lead balloon. The legion primus had flared nostrils and her 'it's fine' smile had a lot of teeth. It reminded me of the *Jaws* movies—and not in a good way.

That damn movie had put me off the sea for fuckin' life.

"There's more," Sehran added. "They say Toren's group was attacked yesterday—raiders or possibly amateur slavers testing their defenses. They drove them off, but they're expecting another attempt."

"Then we need to hurry," I decided, already calculating distances and travel times. "If we push, we can reach them by tomorrow evening."

"The people are tired," Oracle cautioned. "They've been slogging through mud all day."

"We'll rest tonight," I conceded. "But first thing tomorrow, we make all speed toward the rendezvous. I'm not losing any more of our people to raiders."

Sehran nodded in agreement. "About the temple mission—we found it. The ruins are impressive, even after centuries of abandonment. We took what was left of the old altar and a handful of other things that seemed, I don't know, that seemed personal to the goddess? I have them here." She pulled out an example, a wooden carved votive offering bowl, long since cracked, but that even I could feel was, well, connected to a goddess.

"Any trouble?" I asked her, channeling a brief burst of two hundred mana into the bowl as a general 'thank you' to Lagoush, and feeling a shiver run through it in return.

"Nothing we couldn't handle." Her casual shrug told me there was more to that story, but now wasn't the time to press for details.

"Good. Daralen, keep an eye out for those scouts, please. I want to know the moment they arrive."

With renewed purpose, we urged the column forward, seeking higher ground for the night's camp. The last of the bog lands fell away behind us, as we returned to rolling plains and distant foothills. Somewhere beyond them waited the rest of our people—and after that, the city of Sonra with all its dangers and challenges.

One step at a time, I reminded myself as I scanned the horizon. First, we reunite the caravan. Then we prepare for what awaited us in Sonra. And somewhere in all of that, I needed to figure out exactly how I was going to kill a goddess.

The scouts, when they arrived, were both riders I recognized from swearing the oath, but they were also more faces in a damn sea of faces of late. I ended up hitting them with an Examine before they got too close, then greeted them as if I'd known their names all along.

It felt like a bit of a shitty trick, but honestly, I was just so fucking relieved when they told me about the caravan being okay, and that the group who had raided had been weirdly incompetent, that I just smiled.

They were fed, given messages and general support as well as two fresh horses, and sent back to the others. Then, as we were utterly exhausted, Oracle, Sehran, and I all went to bed.

The night was shorter than I'd like, both in terms of 'oh my fuckin' God, I want more sleep' and the state of the people all around me, but having Sehran back was a relief.

Admittedly, Vislen had been almost reluctant to hand her bond back, and kept shooting gazes her way, making me think I might have another budding warlock on my hands, but that was life.

The next morning was a hell of a surprise for me and again, one of those situations where, as a man, you're left with the whole "I shouldn't look…but what the absolute fuck."

This wagon wasn't as fancy as the other one with Toren. Instead of a bath, it simply had a sort of tub, one that was wide and shallow, but was clearly meant for observation, because it was right in the middle of the main bedroom.

You know, where I'd been sleeping.

I was woken up to the squeals of laughter and complaints of cold, as Oracle summoned a healing fountain and Sehran gave herself a good scrubbing.

It was apparently *very* cold water, and I quickly covered my face, trying to stop certain anatomical reactions as I both genuinely tried to banish the view from my mind and hoped that I would fail.

Then they both made it worse.

"Jax, could you summon some fire?" Oracle asked, and I pulled the pillow aside, squinting at her as she "innocently" smiled at me, standing—completely naked—by the same tub. "I think we'd both like some hot water instead and…"

"I hate you both," I growled.

"No, you don't!" Sehran laughed.

"You're doing this deliberately to see if you can get a rise out of me." I tossed the pillow aside, sitting up. "And Oracle can discard the dirt at any damn time she wants!"

"So, you don't want to watch us in the tub then?" Oracle asked coyly, stepping into the water and giving Sehran a cuddle.

"YES!" I snapped, standing up and making it very obvious how much I wanted to. "Fine, yes, all right, you win, Sehran!"

"Oh goodie!" She laughed, seeing that the thought—and the view—was definitely having an effect on me.

"Seriously, you're my friend—you don't have to tease me like this," I growled. "And as for you!" I jabbed a finger in Oracle's direction. "Either behave or bend over because I'm not going through the entire day with a hard-on I could beat someone to death with!"

"Sehran…" Oracle smiled. "I think this means you've won, so…?" she prompted, and the succubus sighed.

"You're right. Thanks for the help, Oracle." She grinned at me, before looking me up and down as she settled back in the tub and started to scrub. "Either you can wait until I'm out of the room—I'll not be long—or you can start now and I'll just watch. I know which I'd prefer, but you've never let me before, and—"

"Wash, dry, and get dressed," I ordered flatly. "Because I'm pretty sure Jian wouldn't want you getting yourself off watching me screwing Oracle's brains out."

"He doesn't mind." She smiled and shrugged. "He knows I like to watch him and Tenandra almost as much as joining in."

"Yeah, but that's…" I damn well knew that she knew what I meant, and that she genuinely didn't see the issue.

The worst part was that neither did Oracle, and I knew that Jian would probably shrug the whole thing off as well. That meant there was a great chance that I could have some fun right now, and get a fantastic view as well and maybe…

I choked that traitorous thought off, opened my mouth to order Sehran out, and again, choked off what I was about to do, when Oracle reached down for Sehran.

My brain totally derailed for a second, and then…

"Lord Jax, the scouts are returning. We request a moment of your time!" came the cry from outside.

And I, Prince of the Realm, Scion of the Empire, High Lord of Dravith and the Godslayer, let out a whimper that would have startled anyone who heard it.

"Ah, too slow." Oracle sighed, straightening up and stepping out of the tub. Clothing appeared over her as she blew me a kiss and set off for the door.

"Dammit. I'm horny!" Sehran snarled. "All I wanted was half an hour and to watch—is that too much to ask?!"

She stood, water streaming down, and I whimpered again, before turning around and rubbing at my face and head.

"Out, out!" I cried. "Images out!"

"I can stay for a bit if you want to make sure you can remember all the details?" Sehran offered. "Oracle said she doesn't mind me watching, as well, you know…"

"I'm a married spud, I'm a married spud," I muttered to myself over and over, refusing to explain or elaborate as I got dressed.

Ten minutes later, I was marching along with Daralen and Oracle, while the caravan started off and Sehran flew overhead, reveling in the bright, warm sunshine.

"What's the situation?" I asked, accepting a piece of flatbread and some random unidentified meat and vegetables. Apparently, the entire damn camp had been ready before me, and while I'd been getting totally distracted by other things, the legion had been trying all the traditional methods to make me aware I was running late.

Banging the side of the nearby cauldron and ordering—loudly—that it all needs clearing away so that the march can begin…that kinda thing.

With Sehran and Oracle naked, it'd all been reduced to meaningless babble.

"The scouts have returned and they warn that the raiders number at least a two hundred. Though, again, as per the report last night, they seem a little sloppier than I'd expect and stupider, even for raiders," Daralen said, clearly annoyed by that.

"Explain that, please."

"There's fifty of them, roughly, following Toren and the others. They've been harrying them along, but refusing to actually engage. According to the scouts, Aellin asked to run them down and kill them all, but Toren and Zyenna refused, on the grounds that there could be more out waiting for such an opportunity."

"And you think that was the wrong choice?" Oracle asked.

"Yes and no. If they didn't have the scouts to maintain the perimeter or other forces, I'd say no. But in all honesty, Aellin could have taken them and reduced the risk to the caravan with only a small force. Instead, they're being driven along, and our own scouts have found the anvil that they're being driven to."

"An ambush?" I asked.

"Not entirely." She snorted. "Unless there's a much more subtle plan in place, then what they appear to be doing is driving the caravan to exactly where we're due to rendezvous."

"Right?" I blinked.

"It's a watering hole that was marked on the map, one that fell out of use due to the limited settlements in the area, which is why we chose it. But it seems this group have set up in it. The confusing part is that there appears to be less than two hundred all told. A lot less, possibly. There are at least a hundred fighters we've identified, and they're split up into two groups. Our scouts provided the top estimate in case there are more forces hidden and waiting, relying on the maximum number the limited tents and hovels at the watering hole could hold."

"So we've got two small groups who are trying to take down the caravan?" Oracle asked.

"Exactly. And although I believe that Aellin could defeat both groups individually or together with considerable ease, it gets more ridiculous, because they don't appear to have spotted us yet either."

"Wait, so the group that's driving them toward their camp—" I broke off.

"They're expecting reinforcements to help them attack a larger caravan. Why they believe they'll succeed, I'd imagine, is because the majority of the legionnaires with the caravan gave us their armor to enable us to better protect you, and free our brothers and sisters."

"And we lost nearly as many of you as we freed." I sighed.

"We did, but those who fell died free, protecting the literal heir to the empire and freeing their fellows. There could be no greater honor," she finished sharply, before clearing her throat and going on.

"Regardless, Jax, should we instead change our direction slightly and pick up the pace, we could attack their base, clear it out and be waiting when the caravan arrives. We could even send a small force to help the caravan if needed. But I think if we were to get into place and set our own ambush, it would be far more effective, as well as a very important learning situation."

"And the lesson is?" I prompted.

"Never fuck with the legion." She smiled, and it was a cold, predatory one at that.

# CHAPTER THIRTY-FIVE

"**I** fuckin' love a good ambush," I muttered later that day, grinning as I lay belly-down in the tall grass overlooking the watering hole.

The enemy camp sprawled below us, a collection of mismatched tents and ramshackle shelters clustered around a small pool of dirty water.

I counted roughly eighty fighters and camp followers milling about, cleaning weapons, eating, or just lounging in the shade—the very picture of overconfident raiders who hadn't yet learned that the universe had a way of balancing its books.

The minor fact that we'd estimated fifty and arrived to find another group of at least that many again had ridden in would normally have been concerning. But honestly? At this point, having had the time to look them over, I'd have bet on Giint attacking the camp alone.

Mind you, he was fucking mental and would probably win even against triple that number, not to mention leaving any survivors with therapy needs that would give a generation of psychiatrists orgasms.

"They have no perimeter scouts," Daralen whispered beside me. Her tone made it clear she found this level of incompetence personally offensive. "No defensive formations, no watch rotations. It's like they've never faced real opposition."

"Or they're bait," I countered, almost hopefully, scanning the surrounding terrain again. "Though I'm not seeing any evidence of a larger force."

Oracle lay next to me. Through our bond, I felt her annoyed assessment of the situation. *"I've checked the area twice. There's no magical concealment, no hidden forces. These are exactly what they appear to be: poorly organized and apparently idiotic raiders."*

I nodded, still not entirely convinced. Things rarely went this smoothly for us. "And the other group? The ones herding our caravan this way?"

"About five miles out and closing," Sehran reported, from beside us. She'd flown a wide sweep around the camp before joining us at our observation point. "Our scout reached them, and they know the plan. Aellin's running interference with a small squad, keeping them at bay, but they're pushing the wagons hard and doing their best to make it look authentic."

Daralen traced a rough map in the dirt before us. "If we hit the camp now, we can secure the watering hole before the second group arrives. With the terrain, they won't know anything's wrong until they're within bowshot."

I studied the crude map, then the camp again. "Oracle, what do you think?"

"It's almost suspiciously convenient," she replied, echoing my earlier thoughts. "But I think Daralen's right. We take the camp, set up our own ambush, then let the caravan pass through us and catch the second group between us and Aellin's forces."

Decision made, I turned to Daralen. "You sure about the plan? I mean, you're the primus, I'm only the prince." I grinned at the half-orc who looked just pleased as fuckin' punch with the opportunity to lay down the hurt.

Her smile was cold and predatory. "It is simple, surgical, and overwhelming. Based on everything we've seen so far, I see no reason to change. Three teams. One comes in over the laughable back wall, the second comes up that stream from the far side, and the third…" She sighed. "We're all above them here already. I think we just stroll down and kill them all."

"Works for me." I rolled onto my back, staring up at the clear blue sky, before an evil thought occurred to me. "You know what, though…how about we go all out? Invite a special guest to the party."

Oracle gave me a questioning look. "Jax?"

"He did offer." I grinned, gathering mana and focusing on a combination of different weaves, and then, reached out and just hoped he was listening really, considering it wasn't like he was tied to fire, like Jenae. The divine connection formed almost instantly with Darakin, the God of Battle. Either he'd been expecting my call or he was particularly attuned to the prospect of combat.

Or more likely, he was bored and watching with the divine equivalent of popcorn and a beer.

*"Prince Jax,"* his voice rumbled through my mind hungrily. *"I sense you stand on the precipice of battle."*

*"That I do, Lord Darakin,"* I replied silently. *"A small engagement, nothing worthy of note, but I didn't know if you were busy, and I wondered, if you'd already created an avatar to spar to face me, if you might like to join us for a little fun? Then afterward, we can have that sparring match we discussed?"*

A sound like distant laughter rolled through our connection. *"You invite me to bloodshed as one might invite a friend to dinner. I knew you were a worthy foe!"*

*"Is that a yes?"*

*"It is. A thousand times over yes. Long have I grown bored, sitting, watching! I shall manifest when the battle begins. And afterward, yes—we shall test your mettle properly, Prince of the Empire."*

The connection faded, and I opened my eyes to find Oracle studying me intently. "He's coming," I told her, pushing myself back into a crouch. "Says he'll manifest when the fighting starts."

"The God of Battle joining us against these amateurs?" Daralen shook her head. "I almost feel sorry for them."

"Don't," I replied, my voice hardening. "These are murderous scumbag raiders. They've killed, enslaved, and terrorized people across these plains. Today, they learn there's a price for that."

Daralen nodded sharply, accepting the rebuke. "Teams are ready on your mark, my prince."

I hesitated, then let it go. As much as I wanted to tell her that it was all right, that I didn't mean it like that, it was best that she got to know me as her ultimate boss as much as someone she could talk to normally.

It sucked monkey balls, but more and more, I found myself thinking of Romanus's early comments of late, and accepting that yeah, he had a point. I did have to be 'prince of the realm' with a lot of people, and only occasionally show 'me.'

I drew my naginata, feeling its familiar weight settle in my hands. "Oracle, give the signal for our legionnaires to move into position, please. Everyone else stays back with the wagons until we've secured the area." I hesitated. "They really haven't spotted the fucking entire caravan? I mean, I can hear them from here!"

"To be fair to them, they're in a depression in the land and they did have scouts out." Daralen sighed. "They were pathetic. Two of the three were asleep, but they *did* have them."

I snorted, and I felt Oracle and Sehran both slipping away to join the other two groups, ready to pass along the signal. Through our bond, I felt her determination, and frank annoyance at these raiders being so amateurish.

If they were going to cause issues and interrupt our day, they could at least be worth the effort, after all. And they just didn't look like they were even worth drawing a blade for at this point.

*"How long until the other group arrives?"* I asked Sehran through the bond.

*"At their current pace, just under an hour."*

*"Perfect."* I settled back to observe the final preparations. The legionnaires moved with silent efficiency, spreading out to encircle the camp. From here, they really were a fearsome sight—disciplined, focused, and utterly lethal.

"They've missed this," Daralen observed quietly, watching her people deploy. "Fighting with purpose again."

"I hope they remember how to show mercy," I replied. "I probably should have said this before, but we need prisoners for information."

Her expression grew guarded. "Of course, my prince."

I snorted, considered passing it to Oracle and Sehran, then sighed and decided I really couldn't be bothered. There'd probably be someone left over at the end of the fight to question—wounded, most likely. And if there wasn't…well.

These things happened.

"Daralen," I said quietly, "as soon as we've cleared these up, you sure we can set up the ambush in time? It's going to be tight."

"It would be if we were building real traps and dealing with a larger, more professional force," she agreed. "As it is, though, I think simple works best. I'll stagger two groups of fifteen on either side of the incoming path, and let them get some practice in with their new spells. Once our people are past, we'll wait until the enemy are close, then simply kill half of them outright with the first volley."

"And the other half?" I asked.

"Well, the second volley of course." She smiled.

"Ah, all good then." I grinned, seeing that in all honesty there genuinely wasn't any more to it than that for them.

"We have spears and shields, and all our shields are legion, so they can not only be locked together, but they can be powered to form the legion shield wall," she reassured me. "If they charge us, we simply form the wall and let them break themselves against it. It'll be a shame for any horses that they force onto the spears, but my boys and girls will be fine. If they run, we pick them off with our new spells. And if they escape, we track them down. After all, we have scouts, supplies, and a succubus." She smiled and nodded. "And you, my prince? Will you be joining the second stage?"

"Possibly not," I admitted. "I'm keeping a sparring appointment with a god, so it depends if he enjoys himself or not. If not, we'll face each other. If he does, maybe he'll take half and I'll take the other half."

Her eyebrows rose fractionally, but she simply nodded again. "Then perhaps 'good luck' is in order?"

I took a final sweep of the camp below, seeing all the benchmarks of amateur raiders—poor guard rotation, weapons left carelessly about, no proper fortifications. It was almost insulting how easily they'd fallen into our path.

"Ready?" I looked from Daralen to Sehran.

Both nodded.

"Then let's teach these fuckers why you don't mess with the empire. Go." As I gave the order, I reached out and shared it with Sehran and Oracle as well, and they passed it on.

Every legionnaire moved in almost perfect unison, rising from the grass and charging the camp from all sides. The element of surprise was total. Half the raiders didn't even manage to grab their weapons before the first wave hit them.

I triggered Mana Overdrive and launched myself from the hill with Soaring Majesty. Daralen and her legionnaires raced after me as we cut a path straight toward the center of the camp. My naginata flashed in the sunlight as I landed, rolled, and then came to one knee. A sweeping, wide arc took down three raiders with a single strike. They weren't even wearing decent armor—just leather scraps and mismatched pieces.

I'd cheated slightly, in that I added a lick of fire mana to my naginata. Sure, it did carve its way through them like a hot knife through butter, but that wasn't the point.

The confusion in the camp quickly turned to panic as legionnaires breached the perimeter from every direction. Unlike the random violence the raiders were used to, the legion struck with clinical precision, running forward and barely slowing to knock weapons aside before limbs, heads, and entire torsos were hacked in two.

I carved through the chaos, moving with Daralen toward what looked like the command tent at the center of the camp. A group of better-equipped raiders had formed a hasty defensive perimeter around it, their weapons raised as we approached.

"Take the leader alive if possible," I called to Daralen, who nodded grimly.

The raiders, seeing they were about to be overrun, made the utterly wonderful and completely suicidal choice to charge us. I blocked the first man's clumsy sword thrust, hooked his blade with my naginata, and sent it spinning away before slamming the butt of my weapon into his crotch and lifting him at least two meters into the air with the sound of breaking bones. He dropped like a stone and presumably died fairly quickly, because there was no way a human should make a noise like that twice.

Daralen was pure efficiency. Her blade flashed in the sunlight as she systematically disarmed and disabled three raiders in rapid succession. Each of her strikes were lethal, and if I was honest, after seeing these raiders, knowing what their kind did in these lawless lands, I genuinely didn't think it was worth reminding her to offer the chance for surrenders.

My people had been shit on from a great height for many years, and a bunch of slavers and raiders appearing like this? Well, either I could be annoyed about it, or I could view it as I was: an opportunity for everyone to let off a little steam.

I reached the central tent first, slicing through the entrance flap and diving inside. A startled man in slightly better gear than the rest lunged at me with a short sword. I parried the blade aside, spun, and brought the flat of my naginata across the back of his knees. He collapsed with a howl of pain, and the sword clattered away.

"You must be the brains of this operation." I placed the tip of my blade against his throat. "Though that's not saying much."

"Who the fuck are you?" he spat, eyes wide with fear despite his defiance.

"The wrong person to piss off," I replied. "Order your men to surrender."

"Fuck you."

I sighed, pressing the blade just enough to draw a thin line of blood. "Let me be clearer. You have exactly five seconds to order your men to stand down, or I'll—"

The air around us suddenly thickened, a pressure building like the moment before a thunderclap. The raider's eyes widened further, true terror washing over his face as he stared at something behind me.

***"Or he'll let me decide what happens to you,"*** a deep voice finished.

I glanced over my shoulder to see a towering figure materialize in the tent's entrance. Darakin, God of Battle, had chosen to manifest as a warrior in his prime— seven feet of corded muscle clad in simple, perfectly crafted armor that seemed to shift between various historical styles with each subtle movement. His face was neither young nor old, bearing the weathered look of a lifetime campaigner, with eyes that burned like banked coals.

"Lord Darakin," I acknowledged with a nod of my head and a tap of my fist to my chest in respect. "Your timing is impeccable."

***"Prince Jax."*** He inclined his head slightly, then turned his burning gaze to the raider cowering on the ground. ***"Your opponent appears somewhat…underwhelming."***

The raider made a strangled sound somewhere between a whimper and a moan.

"He was just about to order his men to surrender." I raised an eyebrow at the man. "Weren't you?"

"S-s-surrender," he stammered. "Everyone…surrender. Now."

Darakin's laughter was like distant thunder. ***"Wise, if belated."*** He stepped aside as Daralen entered the tent.

"My prince, the camp is secured," she reported. Her eyes widened fractionally at the sight of Darakin before she mastered her expression. "Zero casualties on our side. The enemy is dead."

"Excellent. No prisoners then? Ah well, shame. Guess he should have made that decision sooner then." I smiled down at the now terrified man on the floor. "The second group will be here soon, so let's start the party, shall we?"

"Already done," she replied. "Oracle has set up observation points and our archers are moving to position."

I nodded, impressed as always by the legion's efficiency. "And our guest?" I inclined my head toward Darakin.

Daralen bowed deeply to the god. "Lord Darakin. We are honored by your presence. If you wish to observe the coming engagement, we've established a command position with clear sight lines."

Darakin's smile was all teeth. ***"I prefer a more…direct approach to battle."***

"As you wish," she replied, completely unruffled. "The enemy approaches from the north. They appear to be driving our caravan before them."

"Then let's prepare a proper welcome." I grinned as Oracle stepped into the tent. "My love, do you think you can get some details from him?"

"Easily." She smiled at me, curtseyed to Darakin, and then thanked Daralen when she ordered two legionnaires to stand on either side of the prisoner, making it very clear that his options were cooperate, or be gutted like a fish.

*"Sehran, I think it's time to move on with the plan. Can you go to Aellin and get ready to relay orders, please?"* I asked her, and got an evil laugh in return, as well as the sensation of her discarding a dried husk of a body.

Her snack had been enough to make sure she was feeling fully ready for a short flight and some more violence.

What was left of the hour passed in a blur of activity as we fortified our position, and prepared for the arrival of the second raider group just in case we were missing something. The path leading up to the watering hole now bristled with hidden legionnaires; those with spells were positioned on every vantage point, and Sehran had flown ahead, staying low to the ground, to join the incoming caravan in preparation.

The one change to the plan, though, was that I'd asked that the legion only get involved if they judged it was needed now.

Darakin observed it all with an amused expression, occasionally offering a suggestion that invariably proved tactically sound. The legionnaires, after their initial shock at having a literal god wandering through their midst, adapted with professional calm—though I noticed they worked with even greater care under his watchful eye.

Oracle joined me atop a small rise overlooking the northern approach. "The caravan is two miles out," she reported. "Aellin sent a scout ahead. The raiders are still pursuing, but holding back just enough to avoid a direct confrontation."

"Driving them right into our arms." I nodded. "Any sense of who's leading them?"

"From what I've gathered from the prisoner, they called themselves the Bloodmoon Company," she replied. "Recent arrivals to the plains, they're a mixture of bully boys driven out of the towns to the west and an escaped group of highwaymen who had the rest of the gang eliminated by some nobles and the Dark Legion. They've been preying on isolated settlements and caravans for about three weeks."

***"Amateurs playing at being warlords,"*** Darakin rumbled, appearing suddenly beside us. ***"A shameful example of combat."***

"Perhaps," I agreed, "but they've killed and enslaved, so they earned what's coming to them."

The god's eyes gleamed with approval. ***"Indeed. The measure of a warrior isn't only found in glorious battle against mighty foes, but in the protection of those who cannot protect themselves."*** He gestured toward the horizon. ***"Your caravan approaches."***

I squinted, making out the distant dust cloud that marked their passage. "Time to finish this." I drew my naginata. "Oracle, keep in touch with Sehran and Aellin. Tell him to keep on, and be ready to pass through our lines, please."

She nodded and closed her eyes, sending the message through the bond to Sehran, who would relay it to our forces with the caravan.

"Stay with the command post, please, my love," I told Oracle. "Coordinate our forces."

"And you?" she asked, though she already knew the answer.

I grinned, glancing at Darakin. "I think it's time the God of Battle and I introduced ourselves."

Darakin's answering smile was savage. *"Let us hunt."*

We moved swiftly down the hill and through the hidden legionnaires, many of whom touched fists to hearts in salute as we passed. At the edge of the camp, we paused in the tall grass, watching as the first wagons of the caravan crested the final rise before the watering hole.

The pursuing raiders didn't take long to come into view as well. A ragged line of horsemen almost overtook the rear wagons, whooping and yelling, shouting muffled and unclear things that floated on the breeze. They maintained distance, clearly intending to drive the caravan into their allies' waiting arms before closing in for the kill.

*"Sloppy,"* Darakin observed sadly. *"No scouts, no flanking maneuvers. They rely solely on limited numbers and intimidation."*

"Their mistake," I replied, watching as the lead wagons began their descent toward us. "Shall we?"

The god's only response was to materialize a weapon in his hand—a beautifully crafted swordstaff, its blade gleaming with an inner light that seemed to shift between colors with each subtle movement.

We moved through the grass like shadows, splitting to either side and waiting, the path between us clear for the caravan's approach. The raiders, focused entirely on their prey, never even noticed us standing there until it was far too late.

I watched the relieved grins on the faces of the caravanners and the refugees as they streamed past, the joy at seeing me and knowing that if I stood there so calmly, waiting, then it was payback time.

Then I noted the way that more and more sensed Darakin's presence, despite him dampening it down as much as he could.

The passage down into the camp was narrow, with scrub brushes and short, twisted, and stumpy trees that stood on either side. The caravan was reduced to two at a time, and the refugees were running alongside in a panic that was only partly feigned.

That meant that for the raiders who now decided to bully their way past, there was only a very small gap on either side of the trail they could fit through. And that, in turn, meant that only the lead horseman on either side of the last wagon saw us before it was too late.

The first rider to us died without ever understanding what a truly monumental fuckup he'd made.

He'd been riding at full tilt, yelling and whooping, clearly having simply the fuckin' best time, and then he saw Darakin, standing there, in his archaic armor, a swordstaff in hand and smiling widely.

Someone with even the slightest something about them would have wondered at that. But he didn't.

Instead, he adjusted his course, hunched down over the horse's neck, and tried to ride the literal God of Battle down.

Darakin stepped to the right in a movement that was so smooth it made me feel clunky and graceless, and whipped his blade up and forward.

Darakin's blade passed through his target's throat with almost surgical precision: in under the right-hand side of the rider's chin, then up and back, across to the left, then ending with a little flick that popped the head free.

It sailed over and over, with the body still clinging to the horse; the horse ran on, utterly delighted at the change in its rider's condition.

I claimed the second kill. My naginata swept the legs out from under his horse before a reverse stroke separated his head from shoulders as he started to fall.

A horse isn't a light creature, and especially not when they're running at full tilt with a rider on its back and all the usual riding gear included—saddles, packs, bedrolls, and weapons…never mind armor.

That was why I'd taken the legs.

I didn't like it; I wasn't really a horse lover—my memories of a riding lesson to help seduce an ex that hadn't ended well…far too many bruises—but I liked animals generally.

I didn't like many people, but that was a different story.

No, the reason I'd deliberately killed the horse was because I was nowhere near as graceful as Darakin. And had the horse run into me full speed, it'd have ruined the whole competition.

Not to mention it'd have damn well hurt.

There was also the advantage that a load of spraying blood and a big body that partly blocked the path behind me, narrowed the space even further as the last caravan rumbled past.

The third raider noticed something was wrong and opened his mouth to shout a warning as we both stepped out into the path, clear and ready. Darakin's thrown dagger took him in the throat before sound could escape.

Then the real fight began.

Four more horsemen came at us in the next wave, two in the lead, side by side, whipping their horses and yelling encouragement, then two more directly behind them.

The third rider's horse, on seeing the pile of steaming horsemeat behind me, smelling the blood, and seeing the other now riderless horse crashing through the bushes and off in a random direction, decided that it would really like to explore the area on its own for a change, and took a sharp left.

The next horse in line, its rider armed with a stupidly long spear that was only a hair off being a damn lance, was staring ahead, open-mouthed in confusion as he finally realized something was wrong, tried to jink right, and then caught a full-on glimpse of Darakin.

He was currently making himself less of an overtly divine level of threat so that he could have some fun. But horses were stupid creatures and it apparently didn't get the memo about being subtle.

That meant that when it suddenly reared back, stiffening its legs and basically yelling 'fuck to the no' in horse-ish, it found it had an additional few unexpected problems.

First, it'd just smacked its rider with the back of its head, and he was tumbling free. Secondly, inertia is a bitch. And thirdly, the big shiny thing the rider had been carrying on the end of the long stick had introduced itself to the ground.

The rider was catapulted out of the saddle and over our heads, his nose broken, streaming blood and yelling in terrified confusion.

Then the horse tried to jink to the side out of the way, and Darakin graciously let him.

The horses behind, however, were now all trying to adjust their headlong run, and there was very little space.

I stepped to the left, leaned against the nearest tree, and stuck my naginata out, adding a little fire to it again, and then started casting Magic Missile, even as Darakin started to weave from left to right, side-stepping horses like it was great fun and skewering their riders.

Inside of thirty seconds, the riders who had been hard-pressed together in close pursuit now crashed into one another, tumbling and screaming, and generally caused the medieval fantasy equivalent of a twenty-car pile-up.

Even Darakin had to eventually step aside and just let nature take its course.

As the riders started to pile up, jerking reins to a halt and twisting and turning in the middle, he looked over at me in disgust, and I nodded.

"NOW!" I roared, and the trap was sprung.

Legionnaires rose from behind the trees behind us—the group on the left slightly farther back than the group on the right to cut down on friendly fire incidents—and they opened fire. Hundreds of Magic Missiles streaked out from hidden positions. The raiders, caught completely by surprise, had nowhere to run. Half their force was already down, and the rest found themselves getting taken down by multiple blows each.

One raider, apparently their leader judging by his slightly better armor, managed to rally a small group for a desperate breakout attempt. I waved to the legionnaires to stop, then fired a barrage of five Magic Missiles up and over the group to slam into the farthest-back riders who were just getting turned around.

They fell. The darts slammed down from above into the crown of a head, the side of a neck, and, for the last, directly into an upturned face.

Then I moved to intercept, Darakin a step behind me.

The raider leader saw us coming, and his eyes widened in recognition—not of me, but of the god at my side. "Impossible!" he screamed, his blade wavering.

***"Merely improbable,"*** Darakin corrected, his voice carrying easily across the battlefield. ***"Surrender, and you may yet live to see another dawn."***

For a moment, it seemed the man might actually consider the offer. Then his face twisted with rage and desperation. "Never! *Charge!*"

His men hesitated, clearly more sensible than their leader.

He turned, snarling at them, "Attack, you cowards!"

It was the last order he ever gave. Darakin's blade swept out in a perfect arc, as he launched himself forward.

The movement was so fast I could barely track the motion. The raider's head tumbled from his shoulders before his men's horrified eyes.

The god planted his blade in the earth and looked at the remaining raiders. "***Is anyone else feeling particularly heroic today?***" he hopefully asked into the sudden silence.

# CHAPTER THIRTY-SIX

“Honestly, I expected better.” I sighed ten minutes later as we wandered back into the center of the small encampment. “I mean, I'm sorry for wasting your time, Lord Darakin. If I'd realized they were this pathetic, I would have never called.”

I shook my head, looking back at the seven survivors who were currently caught between whimpering and begging, and in the case of one idiot, actually trying to pretend it was all a mistake and he was part of the caravan really.

*"Alas, not your fault, though perhaps an invitation to a real battle was a little much to hope for,"* Darakin replied wistfully. *"Long ages it has been since I marched the fields of war, in truth."*

“I bet.” I sighed. “There are those days when you just really want to let off a little steam, kick someone who deserves their teeth in, and then, it's like this. A damn disappointment.”

*"Indeed."* He sighed, before smiling. *"But, this was ever simply a diversion and a happy chance. The real event is yet to be. I have no doubt that you shall not disappoint."*

“I damn well hope not. It'd be bloody embarrassing if I did,” I admitted.

*"Quite!"* With that, he waved one hand and the ground started to rumble in the center of the camp. *"I shall prepare a worthy arena!"*

*"Jax, perhaps another time?"* Oracle sent to me, flying over and smiling at us both.

I shook my head. *"As much as the timing ain't good and we've got a lot to do yet today, this is the best chance for me to face Illoth. I need to learn, and Darakin is..."* I just shrugged.

*"He's a god, and it's best not to annoy him,"* Oracle finished. *"I know. It's just that..."*

*"That he's a friggin' god and I'm just me, and I'm probably going to be beaten like a red-headed stepchild publicly?"* I retorted, sending a mental kiss with it to let her know that I wasn't annoyed, and I damn well agreed.

This had seemed like such a good idea a few hours ago.

The ground trembled beneath my feet as Darakin swept his arm in a casual gesture. Soil and stone forced its way up, the tiny stream and pool displaced and sinking into the muck. More and more rock flowed up, called by the literal hands of a god.

The mass of rubble shifted, reshaping itself into a perfect circle maybe thirty meters across. The earth at the edges rose to form low walls, creating a natural arena in the center of the encampment.

“This will suffice,” he announced cheerfully, his voice carrying the weight of mountains. “A proper field for our contest.”

Oracle hovered nearby, her concern pulsing through our bond, even as a hint of pride glimmered as well. After all, I was *her* man. A man who was picking fights with the gods.

"My prince, shall I have the legionnaires keep everyone back?" Daralen approached, with a wary eye on Darakin.

"Please." I nodded. "And make sure the caravans get water and rest, any injuries are taken care of, and we'll, uh, move out as soon as we're done here, I guess." I tried to be both cheerful and upbeat, but fuck me, I had the feeling I was about to get my arse kicked and that it would be embarrassingly one-sided.

"As you command." She hesitated, then ducked her head and muttered, "Good luck."

The God of Battle stood across from me, his massive frame silhouetted against the afternoon sun. He shook himself; the armor he'd worn during our skirmish with the raiders shimmered and vanished, leaving him in only simple trousers and a sleeveless tunic that displayed arms corded with muscle.

I stripped down as well, removing my armor piece by piece and handing it to a pair of nervous legionnaires who carried it away like holy relics.

I snorted to myself at that, as well as the way that Aellin and a small cadre of the legion's armor-mad nutters were already disregarding the fact I was about to get my teeth smashed in by a god…and were instead excitedly discussing repairs and work they could do on my armor while they had it.

I rolled my shoulders, feeling more vulnerable than I expected without the familiar weight of armor. But my naginata felt lighter in my hands, almost eager for what was to come.

"Are you certain about this, my prince?" Daralen asked quietly, standing at my side as I stretched, ostensibly offering me a waterskin as an excuse to interrupt as another legionnaire did the same for Darakin. "He is a god, after all."

"No," I admitted, rotating my neck until it cracked. "But certain or not, I'm doing it."

The God of Battle, who was fucking grinning his head off, couldn't wait to get started, and had waved the water off.

Worse still was that I realized that I was grinning right back at him. What the hell was wrong with my goddamn life, never mind my mind!

The legionnaires had formed a ring around the arena, keeping the rest of our people at a respectful distance, but still being able to see. I could see the mix of awe and concern on their faces, probably because their idiot of a prince was about to take on a literal god in combat for shits and giggles.

Oracle hovered near the edge, her worry still pulsing through our bond even as she tried to mask it with confident smiles.

Sehran stood next to her. The look on her face said it was fifty-fifty whether she was jealous and wanted to join in, or was considering distracting Darakin with something. Oracle saw my look, sensed what I was thinking and stepped in close, speaking to Sehran in a low voice.

It wasn't until I stepped into the ring that it occurred to me that Oracle might have misunderstood and decided Sehran helping me cheat was a great idea.

I mean, she wouldn't do that, right?

Darakin twirled his swordstaff in lazy circles. The weapon seemed to flow like water in his hands. The blade caught the sunlight, scattering refracted patterns across the packed earth and stone.

*"The rules are simple,"* he called out, his voice carrying effortlessly to every ear. *"We fight until one yields or can no longer continue. I have constrained my divine power to match your somewhat mortal frame, Prince Jax, but not my skill."* His smile was predatory. *"That would defeat the purpose of our sparring, after all."*

"Understood," I replied, taking a final deep breath. "I'm ready when you are."

*"Oh, I've been ready for centuries."* He laughed, the sound joyous as he grinned at me. *"I remember sparring with Amon. I remember the joy of battle in those days, and I have sorely missed it! Come, show me what the heir to the empire can do!"*

I strode to the center of the arena, naginata held comfortably at my side. Darakin met me there, grinning like a lunatic. Up close, I could see the countless tiny scars that marked his skin—a roadmap of battles won and lost across millennia.

*"Begin when you're ready."* His voice dropped to a conversational tone. *"Do not hold back. I will know if you do, and Lagoush watches, ready should you need healing."*

I nodded, then exploded into motion.

The naginata whipped up in a sweeping arc aimed at his midsection, a testing blow to gauge his reactions. He barely seemed to move; his swordstaff simply shifted into the perfect position to deflect my strike with insulting ease. The clang of metal reverberated through the arena.

*"Predictable,"* he commented, not bothering to counter. *"Again."*

Gritting my teeth, I launched into a series of rapid strikes. The naginata blurred as I worked through combinations I'd drilled countless times. Each was met with the same casual defense: Darakin's weapon always exactly where it needed to be…no more, no less.

*"Better,"* he allowed. *"But still reading from a book everyone knows."*

He suddenly stepped forward, his swordstaff moving in a pattern so fast I barely tracked it. I backpedaled, desperately parrying, the impacts jarring up my arms. His final strike slipped past my guard and stopped a hairsbreadth from my throat.

*"Dead,"* he announced cheerfully, withdrawing. *"Let's try that again."*

I reset my stance, frustration building. This time, I waited, looking for an opening. He raised an eyebrow, then attacked—the exact same pattern as before. I recognized it now, meeting each strike with more confidence, though still driven back by the sheer force behind them.

*"Better,"* he said when his blade again stopped at my throat. *"One more time."*

To my surprise, he launched into the identical sequence a third time. This time, I was ready—my defensive movements more economical, my footwork more precise. When his final thrust came, I managed to deflect it and counter with a strike of my own that he barely had to move to avoid.

*"There,"* he said with approval. *"Now you begin to learn."*

I didn't waste my breath answering, instead pressing forward with my own attack. I flowed from high to low strikes, trying to find a weakness in his defense. There were none. Every movement I made seemed anticipated before I'd even thought of it.

*"You fight like you're drowning,"* Darakin observed, casually blocking a flurry of attacks. *"All fury and desperation. There's power there, but no patience."*

"Hard to be patient when you're getting your ass kicked," I grunted, narrowly avoiding a counter that would have taken my head off if he hadn't pulled it.

A rumble of laughter answered me. *"Fair point. But patience is what separates warriors from brawlers."*

He stepped back, twirling his weapon in that hypnotic pattern again. *"Observe."*

His next attack was measured, deliberate—almost slow compared to his earlier movements. I blocked it easily, wondering whether this was some kind of trick. His second strike came from the opposite direction, equally measured. Then a third from yet another angle.

*"Feel the rhythm,"* he instructed. *"Battle is a dance, not a tavern brawl."*

I shook my head, then caught the next blow, deflecting to the side and punching forward with the metal-clad base, aiming for his right ankle.

He stepped over the blow, barely seeming to notice, and instead shoved the haft of his swordstaff against my own and sent me staggering off-balance.

I swore, catching myself, then noticed he stood in the same place, calmly waiting for me. As I stepped up, he started again, the same blows over and over.

With each impact, I grunted and swore internally. He was a fucking god. He'd limited his body to the same as mine in sheer stats, much as the gods would ensure that Illoth did when I faced her. But the difference between what could be done with skill and careful thought, and the way that I'd ended up making my "build" through the realities of life?

That was huge.

Instead, as I batted the blows aside, barely deflecting them, I remembered something. The trick that Tommy and I had learned. The fighting trick that West had beaten into us both and that Flux and then Restun had reiterated. That almost-meditation-but-not of the neutral.

It made little sense to anyone who hadn't managed it, and I'd personally found it first referenced in an old book I'd loved, *The Dragon Reborn*. I couldn't remember what they'd called it in the series, but it was essentially pouring everything, all the distractions, all the fear, all the thoughts and all the ego, what I'd heard described by West once as the id.

All of *that*, all that made you, *you*—you poured into a mental flame until nothing remained.

What was left over, in that calm, brittle silence, was instinct, and when there was nothing that was getting in the way, all your training, all your natural abilities, could come out.

Something clicked in my mind, and I found myself anticipating his fourth strike before it came. Our weapons met with a satisfying clang, and I caught a flicker of approval in his eyes.

*"Better! More!"* he barked.

I mimicked his pattern, attacking from the same three angles he had demonstrated. On the third strike, he deliberately left an opening, allowing my blade to stop an inch from his shoulder.

*"Good."* He nodded. *"But remember—"*

Before I could register what was happening, his free hand had seized my wrist, yanking me forward as his weapon swept my legs from under me. I crashed to the ground, breath exploding from my lungs.

*"A pattern recognized is a weakness exploited."*

I rolled to my feet, dust coating my sweat-slicked skin. "Got it. No patterns."

*"Wrong,"* he corrected, resuming his stance. *"Master patterns, then break them. Surprise comes from established expectation."*

We circled each other, the intensity building. I was beginning to understand his approach—teaching through combat rather than instruction. Every exchange contained a lesson, if I was sharp enough to grasp it, though I damn well knew that should I fuck up, should I do something as disrespectful—like not put in the very best effort that I could?

He'd seriously hurt me.

I also knew what he was doing was warming me up and getting ready for the fight. This was the spar, not the battle.

For the next several minutes, we fought constantly: no break, no quarter, and no conversation. I could tell he was still holding back, but less obviously now. Each time I adapted to his style, he would shift, presenting new challenges. It was like fighting a living combat manual.

*"Your weapon,"* he said, finally allowing me a brief pause as we reset, *"is an extension of yourself, not a tool you wield."*

"Poetic," I wheezed, trying to catch my breath. "But what does that actually mean?"

His response was another attack, this time targeting my grip, forcing me to adjust my hand position repeatedly. When I finally lost my grip on the naginata, sending it skittering across the dirt, understanding dawned.

*"It means,"* he lowered his weapon as I retrieved mine, *"that separation should be impossible. The naginata moves as your limb moves, without thought or hesitation."*

I nodded, adjusting my grip. "Show me."

What followed was the most intense ten minutes of training I'd ever experienced. Darakin demonstrated subtle adjustments to my stance, grip, and movement—not with words, but through combat. Each time I made a mistake, his blade would find the weakness created. Each time I corrected, he would acknowledge with increased intensity.

The spectators had fallen completely silent, watching the display with rapt attention. Even Oracle's concern had given way to fascination through our bond.

*"Enough. The warm-up is done,"* Darakin suddenly declared. *"Now we fight in truth."*

He didn't wait for my response, launching into an attack so swift and complex I relied purely on instinct to defend. My naginata became a blur as I parried, dodged, and countered, driven back step by step across the arena.

A strike slipped through, opening a shallow cut across my ribs. I hissed in pain but kept moving, pivoting to avoid his follow-up. I could hear murmurs of concern from the watching legionnaires, but forced myself to focus solely on the god before me.

*"First blood to me,"* Darakin acknowledged. *"But you learn fast, prince, and I am not disappointed…yet."*

I feinted high, then dropped into a sweeping attack at his legs. He jumped, as I'd expected, and I used the momentum to spin, bringing the butt end of my naginata around toward his temple. He blocked it with his forearm, but I saw the flicker of surprise in his eyes.

*"Better."* He grinned. *"Much better."*

We fell into a rhythm then, a deadly dance of thrust and parry. I was now fighting purely on instinct; my conscious mind slid aside, put into neutral and just…idling, observing. I noticed patterns in his movements—subtle tells that preceded certain attacks. When I successfully countered based on these observations, his smile widened.

*"Yes,"* he encouraged. *"Read the body, not the blade. Ever three steps ahead!"*

I was rapidly tiring, my limbs growing heavier with each exchange. Sweat poured down my face, stinging my eyes. Darakin, meanwhile, looked like he could continue for days without breaking stride.

In a desperate attempt to create space, I triggered Mana Overdrive, channeling energy into my limbs. The sudden burst of speed caught him by surprise, allowing me to land a solid strike across his shoulder—not deep, but definite contact.

*"Second blood to you,"* he acknowledged, genuine pleasure in his voice. *"Well struck."*

Rather than back off, I pressed the advantage, hammering at his defenses with everything I had left. For a brief, glorious moment, I drove the God of Battle backward, his expression shifting from surprise to fierce joy.

Then reality reasserted itself. He adjusted to my enhanced speed, turning my own momentum against me. A lightning-fast sequence of strikes ended with my naginata flying from my grasp and his blade at my throat.

*"Yield,"* he commanded.

I stood there, chest heaving and blood trickling down my side, completely disarmed. Every muscle screamed in protest. I could feel the eyes of the legion upon me, waiting to see what their prince would do.

"Fuck that," I gasped, knocking his blade aside with my forearm and throwing a wild punch at his face.

He caught my fist easily, but laughed—a booming sound of pure delight. *"Excellent! The battle doesn't end when you're disarmed!"*

What followed was barely a fight—more a lesson in humility. Darakin effortlessly countered every desperate attack I launched, tossing me around the arena like a child's toy. I landed a single lucky strike to his jaw that probably hurt my hand more than his face, before finding myself flat on my back, pinned with his knee on my chest and his blade once again at my throat.

*"Now,"* he said, eyes gleaming with battle-lust, *"do you yield?"*

I lay there, utterly spent; every fiber of my being screamed in exhaustion and pain. But I met his gaze steadily, panting for air, sweat and blood seeping into my eyes and blinding me.

"Not…while I…breathe," I managed.

For a long moment, he studied me, his expression unreadable. Then, to my surprise, he withdrew his blade and extended a hand.

*"Then let us call it a draw,"* he announced, loud enough for all to hear. *"For a warrior who refuses to yield has never truly lost."*

A stunned silence fell over the arena, followed by a hesitant cheer that quickly grew into a roar of approval. I took his offered hand, allowing him to haul me to my feet. My legs nearly buckled, but I forced myself to stand straight, facing the God of Battle as an equal, at least in spirit if not skill.

*"You fought well,"* Darakin said quietly for me alone, clasping my shoulder. *"Better than I expected, in truth. There is much for you to learn still, but the foundation is stronger than I had hoped."*

"Thanks," I wheezed, trying not to collapse. "I think."

He smiled, a surprisingly gentle expression on his battle-scarred face. *"Remember what you learned today. Illoth will not be as forgiving as I, nor as straightforward. She fights with tricks and deception, not blade and courage."*

"Any specific tips?" I winced as I probed the cut on my ribs.

*"Fight in an open space,"* he advised. *"Deny her shadows to hide in. And never, ever let her retreat to gather her strength. Once committed, you must pursue until the end."*

I nodded, committing his words to memory.

Oracle flew to my side, concern and pride warring in her expression. "My Lord Darakin, Prince Jax, may I heal you both?"

Although I nodded, noting the formality and the wide smile on her face, Darakin smiled and shook his head that there was no need, blurring slightly and standing healed and relaxed again.

"Fuck me, I need to learn that trick." I grinned weakly.

Darakin turned to address the gathered crowd. *"You have witnessed true combat today!"* he proclaimed. *"Your prince stands tall and true still, yet he fought to a standstill, because of his heart, not his head, nor his skill. Remember this when you face lesser foes!"*

The legionnaires roared their approval, weapons raised in salute. Even the freed slaves joined in, caught up in the moment.

The God of Battle turned back to me. *"I must return. We cannot walk the land in physical form for long without breaking the terms of the truce,"* he said. *"But know this, Prince Jax—you have earned my respect this day. Few mortals can make that claim."*

"Will I see you again?" I asked.

His smile was enigmatic. *"Of course. After all, who else will push you so? Tomorrow night, when you make your camp, reach out to me, and we shall fight again. Each night shall we face each other until the battle is won and Illoth lies dead at your feet."* He clasped my arm in a warrior's grip. *"Until then, fight well. Fight smart. And above all—"*

"Fight to win," I finished.

*"Precisely."* With a final nod, his form began to shimmer, divine energy swirling around him. *"Oh, and Jax?"* he added in a quieter voice, one that I suspected was just for the two of us.

"Yes?"

*"Next time, try not to leave your right side so exposed. It's a habit that will get you killed."*

With that parting shot and a booming laugh, the God of Battle vanished, leaving only scorched earth where he had stood.

I swayed on my feet, exhaustion finally catching up to me. "Well," I said to Oracle as she steadied me. "That went better than expected."

"You're bleeding from at least six different places," she pointed out. "Still."

"Exactly." I grinned at her, fighting to keep my legs straight and not pitch onto the ground in exhaustion. "I expected at least twelve."

That earned me a much put-upon sigh, and then I was being escorted from the ring to the side of a nearby parked wagon, and wonder of wonders, a fucking drink.

Zyenna and Marteen, Othair, Toren, Annabeth, Aellin, Daralen and Sehran were waiting for me, as was a damn seat. I collapsed into it gratefully.

"You were magnificent!" Marteen said quickly, the first to speak up, and I snorted.

"I got my ass kicked," I corrected. "Damn, even Restun's training sessions were less painful than that!"

"I would disagree," Daralen said. "Jax, you fought Darakin, the literal God of Battle, and yes, he could have dispatched you. Yes, there were times when he allowed an opportunity to pass, many of them."

"Wow, thanks for the pep talk," I muttered.

"Jax, he is a god." She went on flatly. "A literal god, and specifically the God of Battle—the one god above all others who you should wish to never, ever face in single combat. You held your own against him. How many mortals can say that they have fought a god? You have faced two!"

"Four," Oracle corrected absently, examining me and using our Complex Healing weave to work through my body.

"What?" Daralen frowned.

"He's fought four of them. Jenae, Tamat, Nimon, and now Darakin," she replied. "Dammit, Jax, you've strained every muscle in your body, and not just slightly. No wonder you're so tired!"

"You fought the goddesses Jenae and Tamat?" Zyenna asked with an edge of brittle calm in her voice.

"Yeah, we had an argument—me and Jenae, I mean," I admitted, before rubbing at my face and wiping sweat from my brow. "I wasn't very respectful and she lost her temper. That one's on me."

"And Tamat?" Daralen asked carefully.

"Oh, yeah, bit of the same there except that one was squarely her fault…" I muttered.

Oracle smacked me across the back of the head.

"What?" I asked, confused, then remembered the fiction that we'd sort of been playing along with since then, and I sighed. "Though I was a bit rude to her too," I allowed.

"You fought them like that?" she asked in a low voice.

"Oh no." Oracle shook her head.

"That's a relief…"

"It was a lot bloodier when he chased Tamat down. But we're not going to talk about that as they've agreed to be friends and allies now."

"I've promised her Illoth's avatar's head," I reminded them all wanly.

"Why?" Marteen asked, eyes wide.

"She's going to make a goblet out of it. I've got one made from Nimon's avatar's skull." I shrugged. "Then we're gonna get pissed."

"You're going to get drunk with the Goddess of Assassins, while drinking from the skulls of your enemies?" Zyenna chortled.

"Even the demon realm is going to choke on that," Sehran said proudly. "Oh, and Jax? If you ever want to sell that goblet? I think there's a few demon kings who would pay pretty much any price."

"I bet. No, though." I smiled. "I'm going to have a full set, one for each god I kill. And then, when the Pantheon of the Flame come to visit for holy days or whatever, I'm going to have special goblets ready for each of them."

"I think some might not want to use such things," Zyenna said slowly.

"You'd be surprised." I snorted. "You should have heard the way they talked when I threw Nimon's altar out of the window."

Thunder rolled at that and the sky darkened suddenly, making me glance up and growl, before waving an upraised finger in the general direction of the clouds.

"You got nothing better to do than listen in on private conversations?" I called upward. "Shows what a shitty god you are. Even the turd spider's busy!"

"Jax…" Oracle sighed. "Half your body is torn and beaten from your training session with Darakin—please don't start a fight with the God of Death…again."

I grinned at her, as the thunder rolled again, then faded. The sun filtered through again.

"Okay, I think given your present condition, and that you're planning to train again each evening between here and Sonra, perhaps we could sort the caravan out, and you could get some rest while we travel?" Daralen suggested.

I nodded gratefully as she went on.

"Okay, as before, Toren leads the caravan itself, and is responsible for the wagons, the beasts, and the wagon drivers. Horace is a waggoneer and guard, but has travelled these parts before, so I suggest you work with him," Daralen said, and Toren nodded, opening his mouth and gesturing to Annabeth.

"Yes, I know you want to include Annabeth in things." Daralen sighed before gesturing to him to explain to me.

"Annabeth is the daughter of the former caravan master, Jared," he said. "I wasn't sure if you knew, but it was his wish that she learn the life of a caravan master, and that she be ready one day to take his place. I'd like to honor that wish."

"Go on." I sighed. "And yeah, I've heard."

"What I'd like to do is take her as my assistant, and Zyenna's. She'll spend all day with one of us, then the other, and she'll learn to run the caravan. Then, when all of this is over, perhaps a small number of the caravans could be returned to her as part of the payment you promised?" he suggested nervously.

I stared at him flatly.

"You said that we'd all be paid a fair fee for the goods and caravans you were taking, that's all," he said, clearly uncomfortable.

"Yeah, I did," I agreed. "Considering that I captured them all, that 'fair fee' may not be what you're thinking, but all right. Train her, see if she can do the job, and we'll talk about the future when we're ready, and yeah, it was never my intention to pauper you all, but right now I genuinely don't know what I can give you, that's all."

"Thank you," Annabeth whispered, her face pale as both she and Toren saw that this really wasn't the time to have brought this up. But judging from the look on Daralen's face, there was a reason.

"Zyenna will continue to run the 'people' side of the caravan and the merchants, with Othair and the aid of her son Marteen, as well as making sure of supplies and so on." Daralen went on, "With myself taking over the command of the legionnaires overall, and our new recruits."

"Do we have many?" I asked.

"Many…?" she prompted.

"Legionnaires and new recruits."

"Two hundred and one legionnaires, though we are short on equipment for them, and some two hundred and seventy recruits. I'd recommend, as we briefly discussed before, we simply fold the various classes of fighters into the legion as aspirants, and we train them as such.

"That way, we—and they—fit into the command structure; we gain a disciplined force, and we have experience at training the next generation. The other alternative is that we maintain our forces as two separate groups, 'legion' and essentially 'not-legion'…along with all the issues that would cause," she finished, looking to me in question.

"Do it," I agreed. "Back on Dravith, we have a similar structure. The cities have the guard, and there's the armies, but they are all under the banner of the legion and they all do legion-style training. It tends to shut the idiots up a lot when they annoy someone and get sent to legion advanced training for the day." I smiled fondly at the thought of the state of some of the trainees as they fell and wept while Restun screamed blue murder.

"Excellent." Daralen smiled at me. "I wasn't sure if you'd see the advantage straightaway, hence wanting to discuss it now."

"Before I got any rest, you mean?" I snorted.

"Essentially." She smiled.

"Fucking knew you were a primus," I grumbled. "All right, anything else you need?"

"No. We'll be making camp in two hours, as I believe we'd do better to move away from both the main watering hole for the area and the location of so much spilled blood. I suggest you rest for the next two hours, travel in the wagon, and then when we set up for tonight, you permit one of the legion to bring you your meals, then rest again."

"I should…" I started and she spoke over me, even as Oracle reached out and squeezed my hand to shut me up.

"My prince, you've shown the legion and the caravan that you care, and that you're one of them when it comes to shouldering the same burdens. However, now is the time to be a leader, not a guard. Please understand that you have already won the hearts of these people with your actions.

"Now, if you are to truly fight and train with a god each night at camp, before you face one in a fight to the death? Please, rest, recover, and prepare," she said.

I paused, hearing what she was saying. Then I deliberately pushed down my working-class background, the way that I was raised, and that I should be out there suffering the run with the others. That no man was better than his fellows and that I'd be embarrassed to act like a noble shitstick and hide in my wagon while the others did all the work.

Instead, I accepted that actually, training and meditation, alchemy and rest were the order of the day for the next few days, because when we reached Sonra?

The shit was going to hit the fan.

# **CHAPTER THIRTY-SEVEN**

The wagon rocked gently beneath me as I stretched out on the bed in my shorts a little while later. It was almost absurdly luxurious compared to what I was used to, with silk cushions and ornate wooden panels carved with scenes of pastoral life that seemed mockingly peaceful, considering it'd belonged to a slaver before me and he'd probably both raided dozens of farms and stolen the paintings.

The irony wasn't lost on me—resting my battered body in comfort purchased through others' suffering.

"You look like shit," Sehran observed helpfully from where she perched near the window.

"Thanks for that insight." I groaned; every muscle screamed in remembered protest as I shifted position. "Really needed to hear it."

Oracle spoke up as she moved around the wagon's interior. "She's not wrong," she said, more gently. "Darakin didn't hold back much."

"That *was* him holding back." I winced. "Fuck me, I'd hate to see him going all out."

"No, you wouldn't," Oracle said seriously. "Because you'd be dead before you realized what happened."

I couldn't argue with that. The God of Battle had systematically taken me apart, exposing weaknesses I didn't even know I had. And we were scheduled to do it all again tomorrow night. The thought alone made muscles I didn't know I had twinge in terror.

"Rest," Oracle insisted, sensing my thoughts. "Daralen has everything under control. The caravan is moving, and we'll make camp in another hour or so."

"I will." I sighed. "Why the hell do I still feel like crap, though?" I grumbled half to myself, only to have Oracle respond.

"Jax, do you remember when we started using the Genetic Drift Examination and our other spells to try to 'fix' you?"

I nodded, putting my hands behind my head and watching her as she moved to sit by my side on the large bed.

"We did that because no matter the being, there are a huge number of variants that you encounter." She slipped into lecture mode unconsciously. "Your literal 'ideal' condition is changed by poor or good foods, access to the vitamin…things you told me about…the air around you when you grew and now as you age. The quality of the mana that you use, and how frequently you damage your mana channels, the exercise you take, sun and starlight damage…a billion possible combinations." She trailed off. "All of them, though, are holding you back, even only slightly.

"What I think you did during the fight with Darakin is that you channeled your mana into your body at a subconscious level, repairing and improving yourself to keep up with him. Think of the way that Amon had done the same thing in the past, adjusting your body and breaking it, then healing it a quarter of a second later, over and over again. He could jump, using your muscles, and land a thousand meters away without effort. Your muscles and tendons, your bones and yes, blood vessels and more, aren't capable of taking that kind of pressure and force. They broke, snapped, and failed—and yet he instantly repaired the damage.

"I think you were doing the same thing during the fight, though unintentionally, and it wasn't until you used your Mana Overdrive that I realized it."

"Why?" I asked.

"Because you were constantly draining your mana," she said. "When you triggered Mana Overdrive, I realized it because I thought you'd already been using it. When I saw that you hadn't? That's when I knew."

"Then why do I feel like crap, if that's the case?" I asked. "Surely I should feel great?"

"Two reasons," she said softly, taking my hand in hers. "First, as much as I know you're wonderful and incredible, you're not perfect. There's a lot of changes that are happening all at once and your body needs both the chance to adjust and fix itself, and it needs to accept the changes, as everything is slightly off."

"It feels like I'm wearing a skin suit that's slightly out of fit," I muttered. "Like it's too big in places and too small in others."

"Exactly." She smiled.

"Okay, if that's one reason, what's the other?"

"The other is that the gods started this change in you after you damaged yourself with summoning so much mana through your imperial ability, and when they healed you after Nimon had hit you with that lightning."

"I remember that," I said. "Fuck, I remember the days after that. It felt like I had ground glass in my joints."

And I did. I'd been in pain with every movement, though it'd healed as the hours passed, getting a little easier each time, and since then...

If I thought about it, I realized that I'd been a little bit...more, since then. Faster, stronger...all of it. I'd picked up from hints and the way that the gods had danced around my questions in the past that they really shouldn't have done what they did, but that they could, partially because Nimon had broken the rules as well.

Now, as I thought about it, I was fairly sure that I *hadn't* been channeling into myself, and... I looked at Oracle, and I saw the look in her eyes.

Yup.

She knew it, and I knew it.

It hadn't been me. I'd not been doing it at all, as far as I knew, consciously or unconsciously. I knew she hadn't been either, and that left only one other who it could have been.

Darakin.

He'd been "fixing" me, getting me ready for the fight, because as I'd had pointed out previously, the genetic ideal and what I was currently were pretty far apart.

And whatever avatar Illoth created? She wasn't going to create a fucking flawed body, I had to bet.

"Guess I'd better just relax and sleep it off then," I said slowly, getting a smile from Oracle when she saw that I wasn't going to say it out loud and possibly ruin the game.

Instead, I nodded, then settled back, relaxing and forcing myself to just chill. Oracle started to work on my body, and not in the way that I liked.

Sehran started to sing, and instead of the usual lust-filled override that her singing fueled, a warmth suffused me, a general feeling of contentment and relaxation. Finally, I surrendered to the exhaustion that pulled at me like quicksand. Sleep claimed me almost immediately, dragging me down into safe, warm darkness.

When I awoke again later, the wagon had stopped moving. Flickering firelight filtered through the small windows, painting the interior in warm hues. My body still ached, but the edge had been taken off. Oracle's healing, combined with a few hours of actual sleep, had done wonders.

"Welcome back to the land of the living," Sehran said, sprawled across a chair she'd somehow procured. "Hungry?"

My stomach answered with an embarrassingly loud growl. "Starving," I admitted. "How long was I out?"

"About three hours," Oracle replied, moving up to sit beside the bed. "We've made good time. Camp is set and everyone's settling into their meals."

A knock at the door interrupted us. At Oracle's word, it swung open to reveal Daralen, her armor dusty from the day's travel but her posture impeccable as always and a solid smile on her face.

"Jax." She greeted me with a crisp salute. "I trust you rested well?"

"As well as can be expected after being used as a god's training dummy," I replied, forcing myself into a sitting position. "Anything you need to report?"

Oracle placed a tray of food beside me, and I smiled my thanks, realizing that it was this that had woken me, the smell of food, before glancing over it. It was simple fare, but it smelled amazing. I tore into a chunk of bread while Daralen spoke.

"The caravan moves at good speed. No sign of pursuit or trouble since the raiders. We've assigned patrols in rotating shifts, with our most experienced scouts ranging ahead." She gestured vaguely eastward. "We should reach Sonra on time in the next day or two if we maintain this pace."

I nodded, swallowing. "Right on time. Any casualties from the day?"

"None. Though on a side note, the prisoners we took from the raiders have been put to work under guard—simple labor, nothing they can sabotage. Several have already requested to take the oath."

"Seriously?" I paused mid-bite. "After we slaughtered their friends? Fuck, I'd forgotten about them."

Daralen's lips twitched in what might have been amusement. "They seem to have reconsidered their career choices after witnessing you and Lord Darakin in action."

"Smart of them." Sehran snorted.

"Not sure what we want to do about that," I admitted. "I had planned on killing them all…"

"But now that the fight has passed, it becomes a case of there were no witnesses to them committing crimes beyond threats, and they claim to have been forced into their situation. I suggest ten years hard labor as legion aspirants, and then we look at their service and make a decision from there."

I gestured to the food. "Sounds good," I agreed. "Except the leader…"

"Ah, yes. My apologies, sir. He attempted to escape during your fight, and came down with a nasty case of 'dead.' I should have said."

"Nah, it wasn't important." I shrugged. "Fair enough. If they're low level and there's no evidence beyond that, I suppose we can't kill them all, as much as I'd like to. Will you join us?"

Daralen shook her head. "Thank you, but I'll eat with the legionnaires later. There are some matters of training I wish to discuss with them." She hesitated. "Aellin and his team still have your armor. They're quite excited about the opportunity to work on it, but are you okay with…"

"I bet they are," I muttered, remembering the gleam in their eyes. "Yeah, that's fine, but tell them not to fuck with it too much. I'm going to need it soon."

"I'll convey your orders," she replied with a faint smile. "Will you need anything else tonight?"

I shook my head. "Just peace and quiet. Tomorrow, I need to work on some alchemy. Can you ask Zyenna to see me in the morning?"

Daralen nodded, saluted again, and withdrew, closing the door behind her.

I turned my attention fully to the food, suddenly aware of the hollowness in my stomach. Oracle settled beside me while Sehran prowled around the wagon's interior, examining the previous owner's possessions with undisguised curiosity.

"This is good," I said between mouthfuls. "Who's cooking?"

"Some of the freed slaves," Oracle replied. "Zyenna and Toren organized them into work groups. It's impressive how quickly they're adapting."

"People are resilient." I thought of my own journey from Earth to prince of an empire. "Give them half a chance and they'll surprise you."

The rest of the evening passed in quiet conversation. Oracle and Sehran filled me in on the details of camp life—who was emerging as leaders among the freed slaves, which of the legionnaires were adjusting well to their new abilities and spells, the ongoing repairs to wagons and equipment, and that the idiot mage was at his carving and enchanting again.

We'd lost a perfectly good wagon wheel to an explosion when he'd tried to make it stronger, despite being told not to, so tomorrow he got to run alongside Daralen as "an opportunity to learn."

I listened, occasionally asking questions, but mostly just grateful for the normalcy of it all.

As night fell, I found myself drifting off again, my body demanding more rest to recover from the day's exertions. The last thing I remembered was Oracle's gentle touch on my forehead and Sehran's quiet singing starting up again from the corner of the wagon.

Morning arrived with another knock at the door. This time it was Zyenna, looking tired but composed, with Othair behind her.

"Jax." She greeted me with a straight back and a firm smile. "Primus Daralen said you wished to see me?"

I nodded, noting that Daralen got the formal naming while I didn't and snorting in amusement as I gestured for them both to enter. "Morning, you two. Okay, I need ingredients for alchemy. Herbs, minerals, whatever we have. Knowing you, you'll have a list of it all already. Am I wrong?"

She looked thoughtful. "We have some trade goods that might serve, but they're expensive. I was planning on using them to help our infiltration in the markets of Sonra."

"Those will help," I acknowledged, "but I need fresh components too. Can you organize a foraging party? People who know the local plants?"

"Of course." She nodded briskly. "Several of our freed people were farmers before their capture, and I believe from conversation with the primus that the legion often supplemented their income by collecting and selling herbs. I'll have a team ready to start scouting within the hour."

"Perfect. Have them report what they find to me directly. I'll be working here while we travel." I gestured around the wagon. "No point wasting time."

"Anything else?" she asked, and I shook my head. "Excellent. Then perhaps tonight we can have a discussion on the various trade goods we've collected?"

I hesitated, then growled to myself. "Of course. Sounds good." I forced a smile.

"No it doesn't." She snorted. "Listen, boy, if you want me to deal with it all, I can, but you should at least have a rough idea of what we have to trade, because Sonra's riders are going to want to know. If all you do is declare you're here to free all the slaves and fight a goddess in the middle of their camp? They're going to ban you outright."

"Dammit," I snarled.

"Tonight, I'll give you a brief breakdown of the trade goods we have, their relative values and why. Then you can hand it over to me and at least you'll know enough to follow along and make decisions."

"You know I don't care," I said softly. "The trade goods—there's going to be either a fight, in which case we claim everything we can, or we try to take Sonra over and make them part of the empire, in which case it's all ours."

"Trade's the lifeblood of the cities and the continent, boy. If your people can't trade, they'll be left starving or making everything they need by hand every time. You want them to be happy and live good lives? This is how you do it…not to mention taxes. You'll be able to tax us all to your heart's content."

"If you don't mind an opinion?" Othair interjected diffidently.

I glared at him, making it clear that I was tired and I damn well did… Then I waved him to continue.

"Yeah, right." I sighed. "I'll listen."

"An understanding of the caravan now may save hundreds of lives later," he said softly.

"Fine," I growled after a few seconds, exasperated and knowing that he and Zyenna were damn well right, which made it even worse.

"That's all I ask." She nodded, then headed to the door. She spoke over her shoulder as if the thought had just occurred to her. "You know, you could appoint a minister for trade for the empire. I'm probably too old, I know, but I'm sure Marteen…"

"We have one," I said firmly. "Two, actually—a master of coin and a master of taxation, or at least how to avoid it." Then I grinned. "I can't wait for you to meet Hannibal and Hanau, though feel free to suggest an additional member to them."

"Hmph." She grunted, then stomped out, annoyed that she'd been beaten to it.

After she left, I set about transforming the wagon's main space into a makeshift alchemy lab. Oracle helped, as did Sehran, vanishing to other wagons and returning with a collection of tables, chairs, and basic equipment where needed. By the time the caravan began to move again, I had a workspace that, although crude, would serve my purposes. And it had at least a fifty-fifty chance of not collapsing on me while I was boiling highly dangerous compounds. It was a win, really, as my life went.

That was when I unpacked the alchemy kit. It'd travelled with me for a hell of a lot of miles now, and as I'd travelled, I'd looted replacement parts. But mainly, it was the same kit that I'd looted from the drow ages ago, with a few minor changes when I'd broke a bit or found a new alembic or crucible I liked.

I still had an aim of getting my grubby little paws on a really good set, something that was enhanced and had more bells and whistles. But honestly, for the time I actually got to myself to "play" with it, I'd probably end up passing it off to others who could dedicate real time to it anyway.

The day passed in focused concentration. The wagon's gentle rocking and the shouts and sounds of the people outside became background noise as I settled into the work. Time blurred as I experimented with some ingredients that I'd never seen before.

Most weren't that different: a slightly broader leaf on this plant, a weaker effect—or a stronger—than I was used to from this root or that. But Zyenna hadn't wasted any time in getting me a supply chain going.

Apparently, alchemists weren't as rare on this continent as they were back on Dravith, but equally there were more healers as well, which was great…and more bandits, dickheads, and wars.

That meant that a good alchemist was *always* in demand. And when Zyenna realized that I wasn't fucking around and could actually make real potions? Well, that was a game changer.

Out came the rarer and more costly herbs and ingredients, and boom. The day really turned into a blur.

Partly because in the process of making a new potion, I made a wonderful discovery.

I say wonderful… I had a vague memory of everything being wonderful, and exciting, and oh so sparkly…right up until Oracle hit me with a heal and kept pumping it in, as Sehran, wearing a cloth drenched in water across her face, managed to bottle up the three vials I'd made.

The hallucinogen was a new one for me. I'd done some playing around with drugs over the years—I mean, who hasn't—and as long as the dealers weren't playing silly buggers with the compounds and they paid the fee for protection, Tommy and I had let them work.

That being said, what I'd come up with was a bit of a nightmare, partly because I'd not drank it. I'd not got it on my skin or anything, and neither had I noticed any fumes coming off it.

It'd been completely inert, or so it'd seemed. I'd been planning on letting it cool and then I was going to see whether it'd worked out.

I'd been merrily washing out the various apparatus, noting what a great day it was, how bright the sun had been, and how generally lucky I was to live such a charmed life, when Oracle and Sehran had hit the place like a wrecking ball.

Mind you, when I'd sobered up, come down and the side effects of a horrific headache and insane farts had died away, I'd examined the bottle.

| Mercandor's Delight | | Further Description *Yes*/*No* | |
|---|---|---|---|
| **Details:** | | Mercandor was an alchemist obsessed with making as much coin as physically possible. The secrets of his "Delight" potion were slow to be revealed, but, when a shipping container was dropped at the wrong place and at the wrong time, it was mixed with both nightbloom and arinsinia's bane. The unholy resulting mixture was responsible for the devastation of the city of Narendor. Mercandor was found to have acted irresponsibly and was only saved from the gallows by a personal intervention by Svetu Himself…on behalf of his gnomes, who wanted the recipe. | |
| **Rarity:** | **Magical:** | **Durability:** | **Potency:** |
| Rare | Yes | 100/100 | 7/10 |

I read it over twice, when I'd sobered up and decided that this was going to be a special gift to Giint, should I ever be in a situation where I could hand it over and then get the fuck outta there.

Then I realized that, considering how powerful it was, it was probably not intended to be chugged, and that would be the mad little bastard's first reaction.

I resolved to put a tiny bit in an incense-smelly thing I'd seen in the movies years ago, the kind of thing that priests had choirboys holding for them.

I carefully then didn't think about the other things that priests traditionally had choirboys hold.

Once I'd fully recovered, four more hours passed in another, more productive blur. I managed to make a grand total of three new discoveries in the field of patterns, which cheered me up no end.

### *Congratulations!*

**For staying true to your choices and for walking the Path of the Creationist, you have gained three points of Intelligence!**

*

### *Congratulations, Journeyman!*

**You have taken further steps to a wider understanding of the art of the Alchemist!**

**Where mana is the lifeblood of the realm, perhaps it's time to make that blood a little cleaner and healthier?**

**The Path to Mana Pattern Mastery has continued! 19/100**

*

### *Congratulations, Journeyman!*

**You have taken further steps to a wider understanding of the art of the Alchemist!**

**Once again you find that a cure can be as deadly as a poison, should it be misapplied.**

**The Path to Poison Pattern Mastery has continued! 34/100**

*

### *Congratulations, Journeyman!*

**You have taken further steps to a wider understanding of the art of the Alchemist!**

**Your dedication to your art has taught you that no ingredient is one-sided. Poisons can heal, and healing potions can kill, depending on the circumstances.**

**The Path to Healing Pattern Mastery has continued! 27/100**

That was the way of the day—or it was once I sobered up some more, anyway. The innocuous herb that, when added to anything else, seemed to aerosolize the mix was almost banned outright, due to the damn danger it posed, right up until I realized the potential of it.

Grenades and aftershave.

As a poison grenade, it'd be fucking incredible. And added to a local equivalent of an aftershave? I could make a poison cure that would literally keep me safe no matter what I ate.

I decided that I'd still draw the line at Grizz's chili, though.

I ground herbs, mixed tinctures, and systematically worked through combinations. It was tedious, repetitive work, but necessary. If I was going to face Illoth, I needed every advantage I could create, and even if it was just another single point of damage I could do, it was worth it.

"You're making more poisons?" Sehran asked from where she lounged nearby, watching with idle curiosity.

She'd sat in the window frame again, a neat trick in itself considering how small it was. But she'd bent herself into the narrow gap, and was relaxing, watching as the miles rolled by under the wheels, a gentle breeze entering the wagon…

And being totally lost in the overwhelming stink of alchemy.

"Among other things," I replied, carefully measuring out a pale powder. "I've made forty healing potions, sixty-four mana, sixteen regular poisons, just in case, and then those three bottles of Delight; a special treat that's guaranteed to get even Giint off his tits. Then I thought, fuck it. I've got a load of antidotes and general cleansing potions, so I thought I might as well. Spiders use venom. Seems only fair to return the favor."

Oracle stepped up beside me, examining my work. "These won't affect her divine essence," she cautioned.

"No," I agreed. "But they might slow her avatar down. Every little bit helps. And besides…I think the bitch deserves it."

The foraging party returned mid-afternoon, bringing even more sacks of herbs and roots. Some I recognized from our travels across Dravith; others were new to me. I spent the rest of the day categorizing them, testing properties, and adding them to my growing collection of preparations.

It wasn't groundbreaking work, but I could feel my skill increasing with each successful mixture. By the time we stopped to make camp, I had a dozen small vials ready—poisons, healing draughts, and a particularly nasty concoction that should burn like hell if it got in someone's eyes. Or multiple eyes, in Illoth's case.

Finally, I used the last and most evil of everything I had, and I made up what turned out to be a totally new potion, netting me an extra point of Intelligence, and best of all, the opportunity to name it.

### *Congratulations!*

**For staying true to your choices and for walking the Path of the Creationist, you have gained three points of Intelligence!**

| Payback's a Bitch | Further Description *Yes*/*No* |
| --- | --- |
| **Details:** | The potion of Payback's a Bitch is unique, created by a budding alchemist on the path of creationism. It has four effects. First, the victim is struck with a sense of extreme confidence. Second, they develop a slight, though increasing sense of inertia. Third, their health begins to drop at a rate of five points per second for fifty-four seconds, and then finally, what may be the most memorable for any of its victims, activates.<br>The fourth stage—projectile vomiting—is unfortunately not limited to a single orifice, and is judged likely to prove to be decisive in any battle, as well as terminally traumatizing. |

| **Rarity:** | **Magical:** | **Durability:** | **Potency:** |
| --- | --- | --- | --- |

| Legendary | Yes | 100/100 | 8/10 |
| --- | --- | --- | --- |

I'd wanted to name it Illoth's Surprise, but as Oracle pointed out, if she was listening and saw that, then she might prepare for that surprise, and I'd end up dying in a most unpleasant way.

As the sun set, I packed away my supplies and prepared mentally for what was coming next. My muscles had mostly recovered from yesterday's beating, but I knew they were about to get a fresh set of injuries.

Daralen was waiting outside when I emerged from the wagon. "He's already here." She simply nodded toward the edge of camp.

I followed her gaze and saw him—Darakin, God of Battle, standing on a small rise overlooking the caravan. This time, he'd manifested in slightly different armor, ancient plates of a style I didn't recognize. As if sensing my attention, he turned, smiled widely, and raised a hand in greeting.

"Fuck me," I muttered. "Round two."

"You don't have to do this," Oracle said quietly at my side.

"Yes, I do." I rolled my shoulders, feeling the muscles protest. "Illoth won't give me a rest day."

The training session that followed was, if anything, more brutal than the first. Darakin seemed determined to push me beyond my previous limits, attacking with combinations that left me constantly off-balance. Each time I adapted to a technique, he would shift to something new, forcing me to learn on the fly.

*"Your footwork is improving,"* he commented during a brief pause, circling me like a predator. *"But you telegraph your strikes with your eyes."*

I nodded, gasping for breath. "How do I stop that?"

*"Practice,"* he replied, then attacked again before I could respond.

By the time we finished, I was bleeding from a dozen small cuts and my right shoulder felt like it might be dislocated. But I'd lasted longer this time, even managing to score a hit on the god's thigh that had earned an approving nod.

*"You learn quickly,"* he acknowledged as we concluded. *"Tomorrow will be our final session before you face Illoth. Rest now. Meditate on what you've learned."*

I staggered back to our wagon. The cheers of the crowd—who apparently loved the "cabaret" I was providing—rang out, and I waved them off with an exhausted hand, before collapsing into a seat.

Oracle was ready and waiting, having said that she wanted to wait until I wasn't going to try anything stupid like walking when she started healing.

After the worst of my obvious injuries were addressed, I sat cross-legged outside the wagon, focusing on my breathing as I settled into meditation.

The camp moved around me—quiet conversations, the clatter of cooking, the soft grumbling, farting, and chewing of various animals and legionnaires—and I let it all fade into background noise as I centered myself.

Oracle drew from my manapool, using it to summon a dozen healing fountains, and to work on fixing me up.

The hours passed, and I worked on my meditation as well, forming my boxes and sliding them into place, my discovery in meditation helping immensely with the jump in my mana, and then adjusting, holding them in place for great stretches of time. Oracle worked on me, inch by inch—and not in the right way—until finally, we both gave up and went to bed.

Tonight was, by unspoken agreement, a night that Sehran was anywhere else but in our wagon. Frankly, as much as she was a tease and a pain in the ass with such things, I was happier with her elsewhere and it being just Oracle and me.

The sex was kind, slow and tender, and by the time we fell asleep, my mind was clearer than it had been in days.

We knew that tomorrow night I'd need to rest as much as possible, and so sex was off the table. Tonight, we'd planned to break the walls if we could, but instead ended up being gentler than I could ever remember.

The next day followed a similar pattern. I rose early, worked on alchemy through the morning hours, and found myself making actual progress. One mixture in particular—a sticky, caustic substance that combined several of the local herbs with minerals from our trade goods—showed promise as both a weapon and a trap. I created several pots of it, carefully sealing them for later use.

It wasn't anything new or revolutionary. Instead, it was essentially a form of pitch, incredibly sticky and flammable, and best of all? When it burned, it got *hot*.

Not "hot"—fucking *hot*, hot enough that water wouldn't put it out. We ended up having to cover it in dirt and stamp it into the ground until the flames suffocated.

I'd basically come up with a local variant on Greek fire, and I smiled as I considered the uses I could make of it when I faced Illoth.

Sure, I was aware that there were probably going to be rules about weapons and so on, but if she got to use fangs and venom—she was a spider queen, so there was no fucking way she wasn't going to have venom, after all—then I wanted something to even the odds.

By afternoon, I'd created a small arsenal of preparations. Nothing that would win a fight against a goddess on its own, but together, they might give me the edge I needed.

As evening approached, I prepared for my final training session with Darakin. This time, I didn't dread it as much. My body had adapted somewhat to the punishment, and my mind was sharper, more focused on the lessons rather than the pain.

The God of Battle waited in the same spot as before, though this time he wore simple practice garments rather than armor. *"No weapons tonight,"* he announced as I approached. *"Hand to hand only."*

I nodded, setting aside my naginata. I liked the idea of the change; this'd be interesting.

What followed was less a beating and more a masterclass in close combat. Darakin moved with impossible grace, demonstrating holds, strikes, and counters that I struggled to follow, let alone duplicate. But slowly, painfully, I began to adapt, my body learning what my mind could barely comprehend.

*"Don't think,"* he advised, after throwing me to the ground for what felt like the hundredth time. *"Feel the movement before it happens."*

I managed it—oh, maybe ten times over the oh, *three fucking hours* of training he put me through, but it was worth it.

By the time we finished, I was drenched in sweat but oddly exhilarated. I'd managed to land several solid strikes and even executed a throw that had caught the god by surprise.

*"You're ready,"* Darakin said finally, helping me to my feet. *"Not to win easily, but to have a chance. And sometimes, that is all a warrior can ask for."*

He placed a hand on my shoulder, and a surge of warm energy flowed through me. *"My blessing upon you, Prince Jax. Face Illoth with courage and cunning. Remember what I have taught you—read the body, not the blade. Strike when least expected. And never, ever yield while breath remains in your body."*

With that, he stepped back, his form already beginning to shimmer with divine energy. *"Until we meet again, warrior."*

"Thank you," I managed, clasping my fist to my chest and sinking to one knee in salute. "For everything."

His smile was the last thing I saw before he vanished, leaving me alone in the sparring ring, surrounded by hundreds who stood silent under the stars.

Oracle flew to me then, still staring at the empty space where a god had stood. "Come on, my love," she said gently. "You need rest. Tomorrow, we reach Sonra."

I nodded, following her back to the wagon, where a hot meal and clean bandages waited. As I ate, I found my mind already turning to the coming confrontation. Illoth would be waiting. The drow Goddess of Spiderkin, weaver of webs and darkness. I would need everything Darakin had taught me and more. And honestly, as much as I'd not admit it to anyone, I was a little scared.

She was a fucking *goddess*, after all. Facing Nimon? That'd not been planned. That'd been an opportunity born of rage and sheer fucking aggression. He'd made a hell of a mistake, and I'd exploited it.

He'd also been unprepared, as was I.

This time around? We were both as prepared as we could be, and yet, in my case? That didn't really feel like much.

That night, despite my aching body, despite my worries and the fact that I might have less than twenty-four hours left to live, I slept deeply and without dreams.

Dawn broke clear and bright, the sky an iron grey that threw rain like it had decided vertical rivers were the way forward for the continent. The caravan moved with practiced efficiency now: wagons formed up, scouts ranged ahead, legionnaires maintained protective positions around our people. And as for me?

I spent the morning reviewing my alchemical preparations, ensuring each was properly labeled and secured. My weapons had been cleaned and sharpened, my armor returned by Aellin's team looking better than it had in weeks.

"They fixed some of the damaged plates," Daralen explained as I examined it. "Said they couldn't resist the opportunity to work on 'historical pieces.'"

"Historical?" I snorted. "Fuck's sake, it's…" Then I sighed and nodded. "Yeah, all right, it's seven hundred years old. I'll take that one."

She just smiled, then left me to dress.

I'd put everything away. I'd taken some time to speak to Sehran, not really willing to accept why I was doing it, just that there was the need. I'd thanked her for her service, and I'd made her promise that no matter what happened today, she'd get Oracle out, and that she'd get her and our unborn child back to Dravith and safety.

I didn't doubt she'd do it, especially when I made a little deal with her that if she had to go back through the demon realm—which I'd not realized was an option for her—then she could use my skull goblet as payment to one of the kings of hell.

She'd promised me that if it came to it, that kind of an artifact in the hands of a demon king would be worth them forming portals and storming through to protect anyone I wanted.

It was shitty. It was, because both Sehran and I both knew that if she had to do that, she'd not be permitted back to this realm herself. She'd be kept there, in hell, watching through the dimensions and wishing for her lost love. But to save my unborn child, she agreed.

She swore, and I held her, thanking her, then offering her a little of my blood as an additional thank-you.

Oracle and I spent some time together, saying little…just, well, being close.

We talked of names, of places and plans; we talked about making the tower into a center of learning and a home for people. We talked about the empire.

We talked about my hopes, and we agreed that as much as I'd named Augustus my heir, we both, and he, knew that he'd be a caretaker.

The first chance he got, he'd bend the knee to our child. I had no doubt that of all the people in the world, he'd be the least likely to end up as the classic evil vizier.

Weirdly, and for a change for me, the leadership cadre of the group were mounted now. It wasn't a big thing, not really. It hadn't been a case of us not having the horses to ride until now, but it'd been more down to training.

If I ran alongside the wagons with the people and the legionnaires, it was both an extra bit of training, and an opportunity for me to show that we were all in it together.

In some ways, that attitude had been worn down since the start of the trek—the luxurious wagon, for example—but in other areas, I'd been happier the way it was.

Riding a horse was guaranteed to fuckin' cripple me at this rate. And as much as I was a fairly good rider—I'd had training back in the baron's lands, after all, and there it'd been a chance to get out and away from the majority of the dicks who lived there—I just wasn't comfortable.

That date with the ex just kept reminding me of bruised balls.

As Othair had pointed out, though, Sonra's outriders would be expecting us to be mounted, and although a great many of the slaves didn't even have shoes beyond the homemade grass ones, we couldn't afford to stand out any more.

How we presented ourselves would be how they reported us, and if it was as paupers, that wouldn't start things off well at all.

As such, the entire leadership cadre, and as many others as could be, were mounted. We didn't have enough for everyone, not even for half, but it made a hell of a difference. And it was only possible because so many mounts had been captured from those idiot raiders.

As the sun climbed toward its zenith, a smudge appeared on the horizon, gradually resolving into the sprawling tent city of Sonra. From a distance, it looked almost beautiful—colorful canopies catching the sunlight, banners fluttering in the breeze. Only as we drew closer did the reality become apparent: Hundreds of caravans encircled it, and tens of thousands of animals. The path we'd trotted along all day had been deep with shit. And as far as we could see, literally flowing back toward the horizon here, as flat as this stretch of land was, was devastation.

Practically every blade of grass, every plant, and every bush had been eaten. There were low stone walls that we passed that marked what had once been a farmstead, and the long rows in the earth showed that it wasn't something in the deep past. This had been a working farm a week or less ago. But now?

It was like a plague of locusts had descended, and a manure truck had dumped its load across every square inch to just complete the effect.

The very air had a haze to it. And breathing it in? You could practically chew the fucker.

The last detail that stood out, and horrifically so, were the flies.

There were clouds of them that rose with each footfall. My people walked with hands that covered their mouths to stop them breathing them in. I just knew that the healing done tonight, even if everything went perfectly, was going to be insane.

"Lovely place," Sehran commented dryly as we gathered at the head of the caravan.

"It's a hellhole," Oracle whispered. "I don't know how it started but it's horrible."

"And just to make it better, it's a nest of slavers and worse," I added, my eyes scanning the approaches. "Then, as the cherry on the top, somewhere in there, Illoth waits."

Daralen joined us, her expression grim. "We've been spotted. Riders approaching from the east."

I looked where she pointed and nodded, seeing that not only were there a good dozen riders already on an intercept course from at least four different groups, but two larger groups of riders were headed toward us as well.

"The little ones will be looking to see what we've got to trade," Zyenna guessed, waving some of the flies aside. "Probably hoping to get a deal done for anything, or anyone valuable before the others can get close enough to make counteroffers."

"And the others?" I asked.

"The outriders of Sonra." She grimaced. "They're supposedly honest, but if you upset them, we're not getting into the city without fighting for every inch."

"I'll be diplomatic," I assured her, then frowned at the looks I got from everyone. "I will!"

"Perhaps instead I could start the conversation?" Zyenna suggested carefully.

"Oh yes please," Oracle said quickly. "All in favor of Zyenna's diplomacy rather than Jax's, please raise your hand!"

Everyone's hands went up. Hell, even Horace put his hand up.

Sehran damn well put *both* hands up.

"I hate you all," I muttered, as I tried to ignore the smiles.

# CHAPTER THIRTY-EIGHT

The riders from Sonra approached our caravan in a staggered formation. Their horses moved with precision that made it clear they'd spent a lifetime in the saddle. The main group—twelve riders in total—wore matching leather armor detailed with intricate patterns in blue and gold thread. Their mounts were equally impressive, gleaming coats and braided manes that suggested these weren't just transportation but status symbols.

"Riders of Sonra," Daralen murmured beside me. "The blue and gold mark them as the Suntari clan."

"The warriors?" I looked over at Othair, who nodded. "Just what we need."

"Ah, perhaps I wasn't clear before, my lord. The Suntari clan provide *all* of Sonra's warriors. Perhaps 'clan' is less accurate, and 'class' might be easier to understand?" he said quickly. "As in, they are the warrior class of Sonra, rather than a specific paladin or other class."

I grunted, then forced a smile, seeing that the damn place just got more complicated by the day.

As the riders drew closer, I could clearly see their faces—weathered skin, sharp eyes, and a bland expression that said 'I've seen it all, and you rank just below a pimple on my horse's arse, in terms of how much I want to see you.' Their leader, a broad-shouldered woman with a damn impressive scar that ran from her left temple to jaw, raised her hand to halt her group about twenty paces from us.

"That's close enough," she called, her voice carrying easily across the distance as she came to a halt and slipped a hand into a pocket. "State your business in the lands of Sonra."

I opened my mouth to respond, but Zyenna stepped forward before I could speak. We'd agreed on this approach, but it still galled me to keep quiet.

"Well met, riders of Sonra," Zyenna replied, her voice taking on the practiced cadence of a seasoned merchant. "I am Zyenna, master of this caravan. We bring goods from the southern kingdoms and the eastern settlements to trade."

The scarred woman's eyes narrowed as she scanned our group, gaze lingering on the legionnaires in their distinctive armor, then on me. "A trading caravan with legion escort? Unusual."

"These are dangerous times," Zyenna replied smoothly. "The Legion Primus Daralen and I agreed that combining our forces would benefit us both on the journey. They seek supplies, while we sought protection."

The riders exchanged glances that made it clear they weren't buying the story. The leader's lips curled into a thin smile that held no warmth.

"Legion," she acknowledged with a nod toward Daralen. "You know and accept the rules of Sonra?"

Daralen saluted, fist to chest. "We do, Guardian. The peace of the camp is sacred. No violence within the rings. No interference with the slave trade beyond the second ring. And all disputes to be settled by Sonra's law."

"Good. See that your people remember them." The guardian's gaze swept over our caravan again, lingering on the freed slaves who were trying—and mostly failing—to look like typical caravan workers. "Your…merchant friends should know them as well."

"Of course." Zyenna nodded, trying to get the conversation back on track. "We're simply here to trade, nothing more."

The guardian's expression hardened at the attempt. "In my experience, caravans that arrive with legionnaires are rarely 'simply here to trade.' Instead, be it intentional or not, they tend to cause uproar and deaths, in the very best of times. And this…" She spat on the ground. "Is not the best of times. I'll ask once more. Name your true purpose."

Zyenna hesitated just long enough to be noticeable. "As I said—"

"Enough." The guardian cut her off, pulling her hand out of a pocket and holding up a small stone that glowed with a bright-red light. "The leaders of Sonra value truth above all else. Lie again, and you will be designated as raiders, permanently banned from Sonra and treated as enemies. Is that what you wish?"

There was a long silence as we all looked at one another.

*"Don't do it,"* Oracle sent me.

I couldn't help but smile, despite everything. I'd been about to shoot an identify spell off aimed at the rock, and she, as always, knew it before I did.

"Perhaps you'd like to take a minute and reconsider your story?" she asked coldly, looking from one of the group to the next.

The air between us crackled with tension. Zyenna's shoulders tensed, and I decided that the whole diplomacy and subtle entrance to the camp was always a vain hope, considering that they fuckin' knew we were coming. That meant it was time to end this charade. I stepped forward, inclining my head in greeting and pulling my helmet off so that the rider could see me eye-to-eye.

"I think we're done with the pretense." I moved my horse forward to stand beside Zyenna. Every rider's hand immediately moved to a weapon, and I raised my palms to show I meant no threat. "I am Jax, Prince of the Empire and Lord of Dravith. I've come to speak with the leaders of Sonra on matters that concern us both."

The lead rider's expression didn't change, but her posture did, straightening slightly as she glanced from the stone to me and back again. The red light had shifted and now glowed a steady blue instead as she studied me more carefully. "The empire fell long ago."

"And now it rises again," I replied.

The way that she looked from the stone in her hand—still glowing a steady blue at my words—and then back to me didn't go unnoticed.

A ripple of murmurs ran through the riders. A rider stationed behind the leader barked something I missed, and the group returned to silence.

"And what matter could be so urgent that a claimed heir to the imperial throne travels to Sonra with legion escort?"

"That's between me and your clan leaders," I replied, meeting her gaze steadily. "If they want you to know, they'll tell you."

Her eyes narrowed. "You think we grant audiences with the clan leaders to those who appear unannounced? Many wait years for an audience with them."

"And we both know I'm not 'many.'" I shrugged, calmly projecting a confidence I didn't entirely feel. "The clan leaders will want to hear what I have to say. Trust me on that."

The stone pulsed blue again.

She hesitated, before swearing under her breath, then raised her voice and spoke over her shoulder to one of her riders. "Keth, return to the inner ring. Inform the council that a man claiming to be a prince of the old empire requests an audience. Describe him, mention the legion presence, and that the truth-stone verifies. Then await their instructions. Inform them that until permission is granted, I have declared an exclusion around them, and none may enter."

The rider nodded, wheeled his horse around, and galloped toward the distant city.

"You will abide here," she informed us. "Set up a provisional camp if you wish, but come no closer until we receive word. You may communicate with none beyond the members of your caravan, and none may leave."

"And how long will that take?" Daralen asked.

"As long as it takes," the guardian replied unconcernedly. "The council meets at their own pace. In the meantime…" She gestured to the remaining riders, who spread out to form a loose perimeter around our caravan. Each of them attached a bright-red pennon to the end of the long spears they carried and fixed their lance, butt first, into a holder on their saddle.

We all looked at the snapping and popping pennon, and I guessed that was the local equivalent of police tape, or flashing lights.

*"We're being watched by others as well,"* Oracle said through the bond. *"I feel the touch of magic. Be careful what you say."*

*"Moreso than that fuckin' shiny rock?"* I asked, and I felt the eyerolling.

"Was this necessary?" Zyenna asked under her breath. "We could have maintained the merchant story, entered the city normally, and then sought out the leaders."

"They already knew you were lying, and I doubt we'd have seen the leaders this side of Christmas." I shook my head. "Better to lay our cards on the table. Besides, this way, we enter with our purpose known, not as infiltrators."

"If they let us enter at all. And what is this Christmas?"

I shrugged. "They will, and forget about it—sorry, holiday from back home, that's all." I waved her off when she tried to ask again, then turned as Horace moved up to stand off to one side, clearly waiting for permission to approach.

I waved him in, and he hurried to my side, speaking in a low voice as he clearly tried to keep it private.

"Lord, uh, we might be here for a while. I've heard of them making caravans they don't know wait for days to prove a point with them. Iffin you don't mind, might be time to start feeding the people and seeing to wounds, cleaning away infections an' so on?"

"Are there many?" Oracle moved in closer.

"Beggin your pardon fer interruptin', but there will be. Marchin' over all this"—he gestured out to the mass of shit as far as the eye could see—"even with good shoes, it's not right. And the infections spread, without…"

I nodded as Oracle patted me on the shoulder, kissed my cheek and then started off. Zyenna grumbled as she watched Othair, the former butler and chamberlain, go with her.

I had to smile. Zyenna was determined to be there whenever the people were getting healing and fed. She was good at her job of looking after them, but damn. If she thought I couldn't see her plan where she got people to associate things like that with her, she was badly mistaken.

Back home, with the way that advertising worked, not to mention all that management bullshit head fuckery, she'd be a world-class leader.

Here, with no such concepts trained? She was clearly a natural.

With nothing else to do but wait, we set about establishing a temporary camp. The sun beat down mercilessly, turning the already foul-smelling landscape into a seething pit of animal shit, dust, and flies, with literal maggots crawling across the meadow muffins that lay everywhere. Even breathing through my mouth didn't help—I could taste the stench in the back of my throat.

I felt the Scour taking hold again and again, as Oracle cast it, then sighed, feeling the little suggestion from her.

"I'm going to work on something," I said disgustedly, thinking about how shit like this would be banned under the Geneva Convention back home, and moved over to sit on the top of one of the wagons.

The riders ignored me, sitting atop their own mounts, clearly assessing and examining everything. Four of their number set off, riding down the wagons, two to a side, apparently counting heads or something.

I sat back, thinking on the problem, and for the first time in ages, sat down to start constructing a new spell.

As I normally did this either with Oracle's help, or on the fly, ramming pieces together and just fucking hoping I wasn't killed in the backlash, to actually do it carefully was rare. So I decided to figure through exactly what I wanted the spell to do first.

Kill off the maggots and flies was a firm part, I decided, followed by scouring away anything that shouldn't be there. That led to a thought about what should be there, and how to pick what was right and what wasn't, and I eventually decided to pass that to Oracle.

Maybe we could figure out an organic identifier between us.

Our camp had barely begun setting up when the first merchant approached. He came from one of the outermost rings of wagons surrounding Sonra, riding a rather pathetic-looking mule and wearing the kind of exaggerated smile that immediately announced his intentions.

"Welcome, welcome, esteemed travelers!" he called out, raising his hands in greeting. "I couldn't help but notice your fine caravan! Perhaps I might interest you in some advance trades before you enter the city proper? I assure you, my prices are most reasonable!"

One of the Sonra guardians intercepted him before he could make it any farther, speaking in a low voice that nevertheless carried to where I stood. "This caravan is under exclusion and awaiting council judgment, Merdon. Approach again before permission is granted, and you'll lose your trading rights for a week."

The merchant's face fell comically. "But surely…"

"Two weeks," the guardian snapped. Her hand moved to the hilt of her sword.

The merchant retreated hastily, though not before shooting a speculative glance our way that promised he wasn't giving up so easily.

"Persistent bastards," Daralen commented, watching him go.

"That's putting it mildly," I replied, having spotted at least three more figures approaching from different directions, all with that same predatory merchant gleam in their eyes. "This is going to be a long wait."

And it was. Over the next two hours, at least fifteen different merchants attempted to make contact with our caravan. Each was intercepted by the guardians, though with increasingly severe warnings after a second rider came out to the escort and passed along quiet instructions before riding off again. It became something of a spectator sport for us, taking bets on how quickly each new entrepreneur would be sent packing.

The last attempt came from a well-dressed woman with six guards in matching livery. Her approach was more direct—she simply rode straight up to the nearest guardian and began what appeared to be a heated negotiation, gesturing repeatedly toward our wagons, while trying to offer something she was hiding in her hand to the guard.

"That one's determined," Sehran observed from beside me, making me look up from the thousand-mile stare I'd been treating a section of the wagon to, while I thought about mana costs for the frostfire circle.

"She's also about to get her ass handed to her," I grunted, seeing just how pissed the rider was and the way that she gestured meaningfully to the red pennon.

Sure enough, the guardian's posture grew increasingly rigid as the merchant ignored the unsubtle hints until, with a final sharp gesture, she proclaimed loudly enough for the entire area to hear: "By authority of the Suntari, you are formally warned, Merchant Kela. One more attempt to circumvent the council's will, and you will be permanently expelled from Sonra. Is that understood?"

The merchant blanched, all pretense of confidence evaporating. She backed her horse away, bowing repeatedly, before turning and galloping back toward the city as if demons were on her heels.

"That was satisfying." I grinned.

"It's also significant," Othair pointed out from nearby. "Forgive me, my prince, but a formal warning carries incredible weight here. Whatever this council is considering about us, it's important enough that they're enforcing this strict isolation."

"Or they're just following protocol for potential threats," Daralen countered.

"No, I've never heard of them enforcing this way. Usually, they allow merchants to come and do deals, on the grounds that if they don't trust someone to get closer to Sonra, then they'll at least let the merchants trade with them before they're sent away. This is new to me," Othair admitted.

"Either way," I said, "I think we've made an impression."

Even as huge as the sky was here on the high plains, the sun was dipping toward the horizon when the messenger finally returned. He conferred briefly with the lead guardian, who nodded several times before approaching our camp; the messenger stayed back, watching.

"Prince Jax," she called. "The council has rendered its decision."

I stepped forward, trying not to look too eager. "And?"

"You and your caravan are granted permission to enter Sonra and establish camp in the third ring." Her expression remained neutral. "You've been allocated the northeastern sector three, adjacent to the great herds, and you will be guided to your place."

A murmur ran through the few of our people who had been here before, and even I could tell this wasn't a standard assignment by the way she said it.

"The northeastern sector?" Othair repeated, eyebrows raised. "That's—"

"A position of great honor," the guardian finished for him. "It is considered blessed by the passage of the herds. The council obviously finds your arrival…noteworthy."

I nodded, keeping my expression carefully controlled. "Please convey our thanks to the council."

She inclined her head slightly, then leaned forward in her saddle. "You should know that the northeastern sector is currently occupied by the Falcrest trading company. They will need to be relocated to accommodate your arrival."

"Is that a problem?" I asked, though I could already guess the answer.

A thin smile crossed her face. "For them? Certainly. They've been established in that location for over a week. Moving their entire operation will require significant effort and cause considerable…displeasure."

"And for us?"

"That depends on how much you enjoy having enemies, Prince Jax. Falcrest is not without influence in Sonra."

I shrugged. "One more enemy won't make much difference at this point."

She looked me over for a few seconds, then shrugged as well. "Perhaps not, should recent notifications prove accurate. In any case, we will escort you to your designated area. The Falcrest trading company has already been informed they must relocate by nightfall."

"That's not much time," Daralen observed.

"No," the guardian agreed. "It isn't." She didn't sound particularly concerned about it.

I watched her and the others, having caught the jab about notifications, and yet…she didn't seem particularly upset or troubled by it either.

We quickly broke camp, reforming our caravan for the final approach to Sonra. As we drew closer, the true scale of the tent city became apparent. From a distance, it had appeared as pretty much a solid wall of caravans. Up close, it was a sprawling metropolis of canvas and wood, concentric rings spreading outward from a central hub like ripples in a pond, and weirdest of all, distinct roads that were full of people.

It became clear why they were there in seconds, as people hurried here and there as fast as they could: every other scrap of land was taken up by wagons, beasts, and tents. Ahead, over the heads of the stream of people rushing about, we could see the herds.

The outer ring—which we were entering—wasn't a clean circle but a chaotic sprawl of wagons, makeshift stalls, and hastily erected tents. People of all descriptions moved through the narrow pathways between encampments—trading, arguing, or simply going about their business. The air was thick with the smells of cooking food, unwashed bodies, and animal dung, a grim mixture that made my eyes water.

"Charming place," I muttered to Oracle as we rode side by side, having been discussing the new spell over and over as we went, with her offering advice and showing me details I'd missed.

"It's…vibrant," she replied diplomatically.

"That's one word for it." I snorted. "So's 'shithole.'"

Our escorts led us through the maze of temporary structures, past clusters of traders who stopped to stare openly at our passing as we rumbled along narrow, specially cleared roads that the wagons barely fit through. Word of our arrival had clearly spread; people pointed and whispered, some even following at a distance.

"We're causing quite a stir," Sehran pointed out, leaning in to speak privately.

"Good," I replied. "Makes it harder for Illoth to move against us quietly."

The northeastern sector three eventually came into view. It was a large area of relatively flat ground where about a dozen substantial tents and wagons were currently being dismantled in obvious haste. Men and women scurried about, carrying goods, collapsing structures, and loading wagons while shouting instructions and curses in equal measure.

At the center of this chaos stood a red-faced man in expensive clothing, gesticulating wildly as he berated a pair of Sonra guardians. Even from a distance, his fury was palpable.

"That would be Merchant-Prince Falcrest," our escort noted dryly. "He appears to be displeased with the council's decision."

"I gathered that," I replied, watching as the man's face grew progressively redder. "He looks like he's about to have a heart attack."

"We can only hope," she murmured, then added more formally, "This is where you'll establish your camp. The area extends from that marker stone"—she pointed to a high flag painted with blue symbols—"to the edge of the herd pasture. Do not attempt to move the marker. You're permitted to trade freely within the third ring, but remember the rules. Violence will not be tolerated."

"What about self-defense?" Sehran asked.

The guardian's expression hardened. "If attacked, you may defend yourselves with minimal force until guardians arrive. Anything more will be considered a violation of the peace."

"And if the guardians don't arrive?" I asked.

She fixed me with a cold stare. "They always arrive, Prince Jax. Remember that."

With those parting words, she rejoined her companions, and they rode off toward the center of the camp, leaving us to face the still-raging merchant-prince and his partially dismantled operation.

"This should be fun," I muttered.

Merchant-Prince Falcrest spotted us almost immediately. His tirade cut off mid-sentence as he turned to glare in our direction. He was a portly man with an elaborately waxed mustache and the kind of skin that you got with too much rich food and wine. His fine clothes—silks and brocades that would have looked at home in any royal court—were rumpled and stained. Overall, he looked—well, it was a fifty-fifty proposition whether he was going to get his wagons moved, or whether his heart would give out first.

"YOU!" he bellowed, storming toward us with surprising speed for a man of his bulk. "You're the so-called 'prince' who's stealing my land!"

I dismounted slowly, deliberately taking my time as he fumed. "I'm not stealing anything. The council made its decision."

"After you filled their heads with lies and bribes, no doubt!" He stopped a few paces away, chest heaving. "Do you have any idea who I am? What connections I have?"

"Falcrest," I replied calmly. "And no, I don't particularly care about your connections."

His face purpled alarmingly. "I have exclusive contracts with half the nobility of the Western Reaches! I supply the Kredar family themselves! One word from me, and not a single city will trade with you!"

I stepped closer, my patience already wearing thin. "Let me make something clear, merchant. I didn't ask for your spot. I didn't bribe anyone. I simply stated who I was and requested an audience. The council made their choice. Take it up with them if you have a problem."

"Oh, I will," he snarled. "But know this—you've made an enemy today. By sundown tomorrow, every merchant in Sonra will know to avoid your caravan like the plague." He jabbed a finger toward my chest. "You'll be begging me for—"

Daralen was there even before I could move. She caught his wrist before his finger could make contact, applying just enough pressure to make him wince as she glared at him, and he stared at her in confusion and horror.

"Word of advice," I said quietly. "Don't threaten people you know nothing about. And definitely don't point at them. Some might take it as an insult."

Fear flickered in his eyes for the first time. His gaze darted to the legionnaires who had moved subtly into position around us. Daralen released his wrist and stepped back.

"The...the peace of Sonra..." he started, rubbing his wrist.

"Was nearly broken by you," I pointed out. "Self-defense on our part. And let me make this clear—that was minimal self-defense. Want to see what happens when you try touching me again?"

There was a long moment of silence, broken only when I snorted in disgust.

"I didn't think so. You have until nightfall to clear out," I reminded him. "Get your shit and move, because my mages are going to start burning this land clear. If you're in it when they start? That'd be a shame."

For a moment, I thought he might continue the confrontation, but self-preservation won out. He backed away, straightening his expensive jacket with trembling hands.

"This isn't over," he promised, before turning to bark orders at his workers, deliberately ignoring us.

"Well, that went well," Oracle commented dryly, as she moved to stand beside me.

"Could've gone worse." I shrugged. "He's still breathing."

"Barely. I thought he might burst a blood vessel."

Daralen turned to me. "I don't like this. Being placed here, forcing out established merchants—it feels like we're being set up."

"For what?" I asked.

"Conflict. Resentment. Maybe just to see how we'll handle it." She scanned our surroundings, ever the tactician. "If I wanted to test a potential threat without direct confrontation, this is exactly what I'd do."

I considered her words. "You think the council is testing us?"

"Possibly, or someone involved with the council is," she replied. "Either way, we need to be careful."

I nodded, watching as Falcrest's people continued their frantic packing. "Let's get our people settled, but maintain a full watch rotation. I don't trust our new neighbors not to try something petty."

"And the council?" Oracle asked.

"We wait," I decided. "If they wanted to meet immediately, they would have said so. Let's see what game they're playing first. Let's face it—tomorrow, at some point, I'm going to face Illoth. If they leave us alone until after that?" I shrugged.

"There will be many who wish for that," Othair suggested carefully. "Should you lose, then they will be free to dismiss the caravan, claim it or make offers for purchase, depending on the outcome of the fight."

"Yeah." I smiled. "And when I bitch-slap her into the next time zone, the council's gonna regret that, I think. Plus, think how many stupid little schemes they're putting in place now will dry up instantly when that happens."

"I suspect that's a position that is currently being discussed in the council ad-nauseum." Othair smiled. "Wondering if you should win—forgive me, but there is always doubt, my prince, or there would be no need to fight—but should you win, they will regret their silence most harshly."

"They'll send a representative to us tonight at least," Zyenna said flatly. "If they don't, then they're useless as merchants."

"Why do you say that?" I asked.

"You aim to reduce your risk as a merchant and gain the best possible outcome. If you were a nobody who had somehow arranged this fight, then they would stay clear, or make a point of providing a sacrificial area for you to wait in and ridicule you.

"As it is, and considering even if they choose to view the notifications of the fight that you already won with the Dark God as somehow faked or suspicious, they will be split between believing that you have somehow managed to manipulate the notifications through unknown magic, or that you stand a genuine chance of winning. Should you lose, you can be disposed of. Should you win? You are a Godslayer twice over.

"There'll be those who want you as far from here as possible to reduce any possible backlash from your fight, and still others who wish to turn the situation to their advantage. Ignoring you until the fight is won serves them well if you lose. But should you win? At best, that is seen as disrespectful, and a being that fights and kills the gods isn't someone you want to offend.

"I expect they'll send someone who makes a token gesture of welcome and then they'll offer a formal meeting for tomorrow, at a time they'll keep moving until after your fight. Agree to nothing, and let me speak with them. Stay out of sight as much as possible, and I'll see what I can do." She was practically salivating at the idea, and I couldn't help but smile.

"You go for it," I agreed. "Oracle and I are going to go work on our magic in our wagon. Let me know when there's a clear section and we'll see about making sure it's properly dealt with."

She nodded quickly and Oracle, Sehran, and I returned to our wagon. Sehran flew up onto the roof and stood there, watching the crowds. The legion formed a ring of steel around us. And as for Oracle and me? Well, we hid.

I could claim a lot of things—excuses, reasons…bullshit, mainly—but there was a massive part of fucking hiding from the stench that was involved.

Considering how foul it was, we didn't even try to fool around. Instead, we sat, Oracle in my arms, my back braced against the wall and legs stretched out across the bed.

If anyone was to look in, we'd have looked weird as hell, considering Oracle had a hand pressed to my forehead, her fingers half melted into my brain, and the two of us lay there with our eyes closed, barely breathing.

That was what we looked like from the outside, anyway. From the inside? We were working at a speed that was insane. We examined magic theories, dredged the depths of the esoteric knowledge that Amon had gifted us, and slowly, inch by painful inch, we constructed a new spell.

We didn't get to name it, meaning that it'd been created in the past, but fuck it, the spell that we were left with was still cool as fuck.

***Congratulations!***

**You have discovered a new spell: Environmental Cleanse!**

> **Environmental Cleanse:**
> A rarely used spell, the Environmental Cleanse is capable of being locked onto a moving target to slowly improve the area around it. Primarily used to cleanse an area of hazardous alchemical side effects and poisonous remains, Environmental Cleanse leaves behind freshly turned earth, infused with a beneficial mineral enhancement.
>
> **Cost:** 5 mana per second of spell duration. The radius of the spell can be adjusted depending on the range desired.

Now at first glance, sure, that's not a bad spell, but not a great one. Dig a little deeper? Our Complex Healing spell cost a hundred mana per minute active. This? Three hundred!

Three times what was required to regrow limbs and heal stab wounds was needed to clean the damn ground and make the air less shitty around us. But the reason?

Oh yeah, that was a good one.

First of all, the spell could be locked onto someone or something. You don't fancy moving it constantly? No worries—lock it onto someone else and have them march up and down.

Poisons? Acid spills? Great big piles of honking shit? Not a problem. It created a five meter radius out from the designated point in a dome, and it literally burned the fuck outta the ground and air.

I mean it—it created a swirling vortex of flames around the designated point. But inside?

Clean fresh air, no stress, and you could see through it, no worries.

That was great and all, but the best bit? When we hurried outside a good hour and a half later and got started, selecting a cleared section of ground that just so happened to have a fuckload of literal crap left steaming on it…well.

The spell flowed out, surrounding me in a swirling flame-filled dome, one that set the merchant dickhead's horses and people panicking. I calmly walked along, Oracle on the outside, guiding me, and behind? As the leading edge seared and burned the shit, it also broke it down; then a second layer rolled the earth, a third compacted it, and a fourth smoothed. So by the time my feet crossed it, there was a clear, clean stretch of dry, slightly steaming earth.

Behind me, as the earth started to be exposed with my walk, the caravans moved in, setting up and laying out with literal military precision, thanks to the legionnaires.

Daralen had taken one look at the faces that surrounded us and had ordered a full field fortification erected.

We had ditches going, earthworks, and best of all, a fuckload of very grim-looking, fully armed legionnaires who glared at anyone and everyone nearby.

I started to feel right at home.

As the sun vanished beneath the horizon, our caravan took shape in the cleared space. Tents rose, cooking fires were lit, and our people began the process of making this small patch of the massive tent city our own. Throughout it all, I could feel eyes on us—not just from Falcrest's bitter glances, but from countless hidden watchers among the surrounding encampments.

Somewhere in this vast, chaotic sea of beings and creatures, Illoth waited. I could almost feel her presence, a cold whisper at the edge of my awareness. She knew I was here, just as I knew she was watching. Our confrontation was inevitable now, drawing closer with each passing hour.

I'd said I'd call to her, that we'd face each other at some point tomorrow, but somehow, I doubted it'd be that straightforward.

I stood at the edge of our camp, gazing toward the inner rings of Sonra, where the true power of the city was wielded. The great herds moved: some laid to rest already, others up and moving…braying, lowing, and damn well farting constantly. They made the area between the second and third rings look like something from the documentaries on Africa.

Tens of thousands of animals following ancient migration patterns had shaped this group. Hell, they probably shaped a lot of the civilization that I was going to be dealing with now that the empire had fallen. Their rhythmic movement was almost hypnotic in the fading light.

They *had* to be semi-tamed, I told myself. They were guided by the drovers and they stayed where they were, after all. On Earth, you try setting up a massive tent city around a migration route and you were asking for a lot of broken-limbed animals and a fuckload of dead people and stampeded tents. But here? It all seemed in harmony.

The literal sea of bodies between the second and third rings moved continuously, both grazing and shifting, rutting and fighting. And that meant that when there were so many, it looked, well, like a sea.

"Beautiful, aren't they?" a voice asked from behind me.

I turned to find a slight figure a few paces away—a young woman with dark hair and eyes that seemed too old for her face. She wore simple clothes, unmarked by any clan insignia, but carried herself with quiet confidence. And it was telling that the legion, although they'd apparently let her through, were watching her like a fuckin' hawk.

"They are," I agreed cautiously. "You're not with Falcrest's people."

She smiled slightly. "No, I'm not. My name is Ren. I serve the Matriarch Ilena Vhyrakai directly."

My interest sharpened immediately. "The leader of one of the three great clans."

"The same." She studied me openly. "You've caused quite a stir, Prince Jax. It's not often someone claims imperial lineage these days, especially not with legion backing. And even rarer that a stone verifies their claim."

"I'm not claiming anything," I replied. "I am what I am."

"And what exactly is that?" she asked, her tone genuinely curious rather than challenging.

I considered my answer carefully. "Someone trying to restore what was lost."

"A noble goal," she acknowledged. "Also, an impossible one, many would think."

"What they think is up to them."

She laughed softly. "Diplomatic. That's unexpected, given the stories already circulating about you."

"What stories?" I asked, though I could guess.

"That you decimated a raider band with the help of a god. That you travel with a legion sworn to the old oaths. That you seek to challenge powers beyond mortal understanding." Her eyes glinted in the fading light. "Exciting tales, whether true or not."

I said nothing, letting her study me.

Finally, she nodded, as if confirming something to herself.

"The matriarch extends an invitation," she said. "A private audience, tomorrow at midday, in the Sariska'ah-Moru. You may bring two companions, no more."

"Just the matriarch?" I asked. "What about the other clan leaders?"

Ren's expression revealed nothing. "The invitation is from Matriarch Vhyrakai alone. Whether you choose to accept it is, of course, your decision."

I nodded slowly. "Tell the matriarch I'm honored by her invitation and will attend, and provided I'm not busy, I'll be there."

"Busy?" she said carefully, as if not sure how the word tasted. "An invitation from the matriarch is not usually something put aside easily."

"I'll be there, unless Illoth arrives first." I smiled. "If I'm still fighting her, as soon as I've cut her head off, I'll be there."

"Very good." She paused, clearly assessing me before going on. "Many here have seen the notification of a confrontation between you and one of the divine."

She said it very fuckin' carefully, and I nodded to her to continue.

"That you have chosen to have it here has earned you both much anger and much interest. May I ask why?"

"Honestly, I was coming this way anyway, and I don't know much of the continent. I knew of Sonra, and I figured better that we have the fight near here so I wouldn't have to travel. From my side, I agreed to summon her for the fight, so if you have somewhere you'd like us to face each other, maybe now's the time to suggest it."

"I shall inform my mistress," she said slowly, clearly thinking it over. "However, I should inform you, not all are against this event, should it prove as the notification suggests."

"Oh?"

"If you lose, there will be much interest in the event, and the legend of Sonra shall grow."

"And when I win?"

"The detail about the followers of that divine being excluded from the territory is of particular interest," she admitted.

I nodded, getting what she was saying. The drow. Dickbags that they were, nobody wanted them nearby, and considering they were masters of illusion spells, that just added to the issue.

She bowed slightly, clearly watching me. "A guide will come for you when it's time." She turned to leave, then paused. "One more thing, Prince Jax."

"Yes?"

"Whatever you seek in Sonra, be that a fight with a goddess or a deal to be made, proceed with caution. The balance here is…delicate. More so than you might realize." With that cryptic warning, she slipped away into the gathering darkness, leaving me with more questions than answers.

Oracle stepped up beside me moments later. "Who was that?"

"An emissary from one of the clan leaders," I replied, putting my arm around her shoulders. "We have an invitation for tomorrow."

"Just one clan? Not the council?"

"Just one," I confirmed. "Interesting, isn't it?"

"Very," she agreed. "Looks like Zyenna's right then—they're playing it safe."

I nodded, watching the spot where Ren had disappeared. "Either way, things are moving now, so I guess we're on the final countdown."

"Is that good or bad?"

"Well, it was a great tune by a band called Europe." I grinned. "Beyond that? Who knows."

As night fell completely, Falcrest's last wagons finally pulled away, and the merchant-prince shot us a final venomous glare as he left. Our camp was fully established now, a small island of order in the chaotic sea of Sonra's outer ring. Legionnaires stood watch at regular intervals around our perimeter, both as guards and as a clear statement of who we were and what fucking with us would mean.

# CHAPTER THIRTY-NINE

The summons, when it came, was completely unsubtle, despite the bitch herself, and I couldn't help but grin as I blinked awake, seeing the notification that hung before my eyes.

*Let all be aware!*

**Illoth, Great Queen of Spiderkin, Mistress of the Drow and Lady of the Night, has come for the soul of the apostate Jax.**

**Jax Amon, disowned former son of the House of Sanguis, who falsely names himself "Godslayer," must now show himself within two hours at the heart of the Temple of the Nether.**

**Any attempt to flee the Great One's justice shall be met with the full force of her retribution, and as others have granted the whelp succor, so too shall they be judged!**

**Look upon the forces arrayed against you, citizens of Sonra, and choose your side wisely.**

**Fall to your knees, proclaim the Great Lady of the Night your mistress, and swear an oath of eternal servitude, or be food for her brood, even as Jax the Pretender shall forever become a nest for her young.**

**A fragment of the divine shall be claimed by the winner of the fight, as well as dominion over the local area—100 square miles—and all that dwell within those bounds.**

**As this is also a time of war in the Imperial Succession, Prince Jax of the Empire's title and position will be deemed secure for this period, and will transfer to his heir, Duke Augustus of Himnel, should he perish.**

**The Imperial claim shall be judged continuous, unless his successor declares his claim null and void.**

**When the Goddess Illoth wins, then she shall claim a fragment of divinity and the life of Jax of Dravith.**

**Should the pretender Prince Jax of Dravith win, then he lays claim to one tenth of her power, condensed into a fragment of her divinity, and, as per the previous challenge, claims the Continent and strips his opponent of any access.**

**HOWEVER: The continent of Carrmor is currently classed as contested, and not currently under his direct control. As such, each territory that is claimed by the Imperial Throne and Prince Jax shall be cleansed of Illoth's hand only once it declares for him. Should Prince Jax succeed in claiming all the continent, then she—and by right of connection, any others who bear her mark—shall also be removed.**

***The Imperial Succession continues!***

*

***Beware!***

**You have reached a new low.**

**You are now declared a BLOOD ENEMY of Illoth, Spider Queen of the Pantheon of the Dark.**

**Beware the fangs in the night!**

I read them both over, then grinned. I climbed to my feet and stretched, even as Oracle, sitting on the edge of the bed, looking fantastic in the tiny outfit she wore, swore.

She'd refused to strip down for bed, pointing out that she'd damn well never get any rest and neither would I if she was naked.

I had to admit that was right.

So was the minor fact that Illoth would no doubt have timed it so that I was just getting to the point of no return when she'd issue the challenge.

Had she done that, I was likely to go after her naked and in an absolute rage, and that wasn't going to end well for anyone, as I still had recurring nightmares about the danger of going to the toilet in Australia and getting my dick bitten off.

Instead, I kissed Oracle, cutting off her rant about "sneaky spider bitches" and then started to dress. I'd barely got my underwear on, when there came a knock at the door.

"What?" Oracle snapped. "We're busy!"

"Not in the right way!" called back Sehran cheerfully. "I've got a bunch of legionnaires out here, a *lot* of citizens, and there's a load of runners heading this way through the herds. Oh, and a lot of disturbances outside the camp!"

"Fly up and check the outside, and send Daralen in. I've got pants on." I snorted.

"Pity!" Sehran called, leaning in the door and winking at me, before moving back to let Daralen in. She launched herself upward with a powerful beat of her wings.

"My prince," Daralen said formally, bowing her head. "Your legion stands ready. May we assist?"

I looked at her, seeing the way that she stared meaningfully at my armor. I remembered the fight in the arena, where Augustus and the others of the legion who were there at the time had insisted on helping me to wear my legion armor for the first time.

I nodded, and she and Aellin stepped in with three other armorers, firmly closing the door in the face of Zyenna, who'd started to climb the short steps as well.

They didn't say anything, which was a little different. Last time, Augustus and the others had been constantly cracking jokes, but I got it. For the Legion of Dravith and considering where I was, there wasn't a huge risk to me then.

I was fighting in the arena as a distraction to let my forces get ready and so that Mal, the crazy bastard, could both make a fortune on gambling and set up the greatest heist in the history of heists.

Here?

I was about to march to fight a goddess, one-on-one, with only my life and the fate of the tens of thousands around me in the balance.

No real risk then.

The pair were formal as hell, barely responding to my attempted jokes, and clearly uncomfortable as they helped me to lock my armor into place. Of course, it was when Daralen was on her knees in front of me when Sehran landed again, pulling the door open and marching in, then shutting Zyenna and the other lookie-loos out.

I heard muffled swearing from the other side of the door as she started to speak.

"Jax, seriously, we don't have time for that, and I've lost track of how many times I've offered to give Oracle a night off. Seriously, you're going to make a girl feel unattractive." She shook her head, clearly joking, despite the glare and growl from Daralen.

"Behave." I snorted. "Okay, what did you see?"

"We're surrounded," Sehran said. "It's not a few scouts or an advance party. The entirety of Sonra is encircled. It's an army, and the creatures out there..."

"How bad?" I asked, my hands never pausing as I continued to dress.

"Spiders," she said. "More than I could count. From tiny ones that carpet the ground like a living black blanket to monstrosities bigger than houses. Think of the battle for Narkolt Keep, but a hundred times worse. Driders, drow raiders, all of them just...waiting. I don't know where they came from, and even my eyes can only see so far, but..."

"She's brought an army," Daralen concluded, her hand reflexively checking the hilt of one of my swords as she slid it into place over my shoulder.

"Not just an army," Sehran corrected. "An extinction event. If you fall, Jax, they'll sweep through this camp like a scythe through wheat. No one will survive, not unless they worship her."

"That'll be the plan," I growled. "It's to make sure they can get you." I turned to Oracle, and she snorted.

"Jax, I can fly, and I have Sehran. I'll be fine, but these people? I won't abandon them."

"No," I agreed flatly. "But if I fall, nothing you do is going to stop a wave of drow, not when that spider bitch herself will be running amok as well. I should have thought about the consequences. Shit, I'm sorry."

A heavy silence fell over the wagon. I finished settling my sabatons, then rolled my shoulders to settle the under armor again properly. The damn stuff rode up like nobody's business until it had the weight of the armor attached.

"Daralen, alert the legion. Full battle readiness, but no visible panic. We don't want to start the party early. Have the legion prepare. If I fall today, you need to be ready to get as many people as possible out of here."

She nodded and moved to carry out my orders.

Oracle moved closer, her expression troubled. "Jax, I don't like this. It feels like a trap."

"Of course it's a trap," I agreed, checking the edge of a dagger before sliding it into its sheath. "But it's a trap I'm walking into with my eyes open. We always knew she'd do something. The only thing we could do as we couldn't prepare for everything was to train, to be ready, and to set up that shield, so that's what we did."

That was something that I'd been damn thankful for when Toren had brought it to me. The shield that the slavers had in place over their original camp was a nasty thing, powerful, but it drained mana at a hell of a rate, and it'd been designed to be run attached to a mana collector. In this case, the mana collector had been missing or sold, and instead a group of slaves had been chained to it, drained continuously until they passed out and more were attached in their place.

We'd not done that. Obviously.

What we had done, though, was ask for volunteers. We'd pointed out that doing this was essentially power-leveling your manapool. Both Intelligence and Wisdom were essentially getting the same kind of a workout as if people were at the gym, going full bore.

The deal we'd offered was that after the fight with Illoth, when it was all calmed down, those with the greatest manapools would be trained with a spell or two to help to protect the camp. As we'd been travelling, Oracle had made good on that promise, sitting in the wagons as I ran; she rode hour after hour, day after day, teaching those we could.

It meant that right now, we had roughly a hundred of the thousand plus citizens who could cast Magic Missile, and twenty more who could cast Complex Healing.

I'd have preferred the way we'd done it in Dravith, where we gave everyone Complex Healing, Magic Missile, and Explosive Compression, but we had neither the time nor the mana, and so we'd done our best.

Instead, we'd done that, and we'd given fifty of the legion all three spells now, and the rest were slated to get it as soon as possible.

As it was, if we came under attack again, there were going to be a *lot* of very surprised enemies when a thousand or so Magic Missiles were launched in a single barrage.

Outside, I could hear the darkened camp coming back to life, the usual middle of the night sounds replaced with a current of fear and confusion. Word was spreading, and with it, panic.

I stood in the middle of the small group as each piece of my armor was attached almost ceremonially, gleaming under a fresh coat of oil. The red and black of the Praetorian Guard, the ancient protectors of the emperor himself, was burnished to a deep luster that caught the firelight.

Aellin personally supervised the whole process, fussing over each buckle and strap. The other armorers moved around me in a choreographed dance, lifting greaves, vambraces, and pauldrons in sequence.

As the final pieces were secured and the armorers left, Othair entered, his expression tight with concern, and I could hear Zyenna outside arguing with someone.

"Several of the clan representatives are gathering outside," he reported. "They demand entry to speak with you before you proceed to the inner ring."

"Let them wait," Daralen cut in. "The prince prepares for battle."

"If we alienate them now, they may decide to sacrifice us all to save themselves," Othair cautioned.

I considered this as Aellin tightened the last strap on my gauntlet. "How much time until I need to be at the Temple of the Nether?"

"About an hour and a half," Oracle admitted. "I don't know how far it is from here, though."

"Then I'll speak with them if they get their arses in fast, I guess." I snorted, feeling almost cheerful as I realized that once again, I wasn't scared anymore. "How many are there?"

"Eleven representatives, and one council member," Othair said as calmly as he could.

"Bring them in—but only those from the ruling clans. I don't have the time to waste arguing with an entire council."

Othair nodded and hurried out.

I flexed my hands in the gauntlets, feeling the familiar weight of the armor settle around me. It was old, as the armorers kept saying, but damn it felt right.

"How do I look?" I asked Oracle, half-joking.

Her expression softened. "Like a warrior-prince of legend. Like someone who's going to tear off the head of a spider goddess and bury her remains in a latrine."

"That's the plan," I replied, bending to kiss her, the touch of her lips like cool silk against mine.

The door opened again, and four figures entered—representatives I guessed from the major clans of Sonra. Their rich clothing marked them as high-ranking members of their respective houses. Their expressions ranged from barely concealed panic to cold calculation.

"Prince Jax," the eldest began, a grey-haired woman whose bearing suggested decades of political shitstorms. "You have brought catastrophe to our doorstep."

"I didn't start the fight with Illoth," I replied calmly, checking my dagger as I slid it into place on my right ankle. "She's been hunting me for months."

"Yet you chose to come to Sonra," another cut in, a rotund man with elaborate facial tattoos. "Knowing she pursued you."

"I came to rescue my legionnaires and look for information," I countered. "The challenge could have happened anywhere. At least here, the conflict can hopefully be contained within your Temple of the Nether, whatever that is."

The representatives exchanged glances at this.

The youngest among them, a sharp-featured man barely in his thirties, leaned forward. "That doesn't make this better—it makes it worse! Since the time of the cataclysm, the inner ring has been sacred. No outsider has been permitted within its bounds, not in the hundreds of years since the establishment of Sonra. Yet now, because of your quarrel with a goddess, we are expected to allow you—a stranger— into our most hallowed ground?"

"Did you see me picking the place of the fight?" I asked him bluntly. "Did I even fucking know what it was called? No, I was asked to meet a representative of yours tomorrow at a location I can't even pronounce, so fuck you, and fuck Illoth, and feel free to go and complain to her directly."

"But, but..." he spat, clearly trying to find an excuse to blame me for the fight to come.

Worst of all, although he might not know it, he damn well had cause, because it was me who had picked the location as Sonra when I'd been running my mouth.

I didn't know anywhere else, and I knew that I had to be here roughly around this time, so I'd gone for it. And right now, with the lives of tens of thousands in the balance, it was looking pretty fucking stupid of me.

"Would you prefer I fight her in the open?" I asked. "With how many thousands of your people and the herds caught in the fight?"

"We would prefer you had never come at all," the fourth representative, a stern-faced woman with some kind of ritual scarring across her cheeks, said bluntly. "But it is too late for that. The question now is what happens after, assuming you survive—which most doubt."

I met her gaze steadily. "If I win, I've already sworn to protect those who stand with me. The empire rises again, and Sonra could be an ally rather than another conquest."

"And if you lose?" the elder woman asked.

"Then pray that my legion can evacuate as many as possible before Illoth's forces descend," I answered honestly. "Because make no mistake—she intends to slaughter everyone here, regardless of who they are or what agreements you might try to make with her."

The representatives fell silent, weighing my words. Finally, the elder woman nodded.

"You will have passage to the inner ring," she declared. "The Temple of the Nether will be prepared for the contest. But know this, Prince Jax—the clans of Sonra do not forget, for good or ill. How this day ends will determine our relationship with your empire for generations to come."

"Well, let's face it, either I die here and so do you all when Illoth murders everyone like the cheatin' bitch she is, or I win the fight, in which case I'm a Godslayer twice over, one of the most powerful beings on the continent and in the middle of your holiest place.

"Add in that the only place that anyone's going to be safe from the drow and all her other scumbag followers is in *my* territory, because Sint, that fuckin' legend, managed to get her to agree that any territory that swears to me, she and all of her kind are banished from? Well, I think you've got some serious thinking to do, haven't you?

"On one side, you've got me and the legion—who, I know, you treat differently because of some dark secret in your past. And on the other you have Illoth, the queen of the murdering scumbag whisky-dicked drow. You get to pick a side here, and the wrong one means you're all dead, so yeah, feel free to have a good long think about your position."

"You threaten us?" the youngest spat.

"Are you fucking stupid?" I glanced at him, then turned to face him fully, standing tall in my armor, my naginata in hand, every inch the warrior/would-be-emperor and towering over him. "No, pal, I'm not threatening you. But I'll make this clear—I'm not threatening you...*yet*. In the empire, slavery is illegal. You know this, I know this, and while you all pay lip service to the notion, you do fuck all about the slaves who are bought and sold around you.

"You have to know the legion were constrained by oaths that forced them to act against their will and all good sense. No single legionnaire would attack a camp if they had the choice, and yet you know they did it in the past, forced by those self-same oaths to try to rescue the slaves you turned a blind eye to.

"No. I'm not threatening you. Not now. I'm making you a fucking *promise*, my son. In three hours, I'm going to have Illoth's head mounted on a fucking pike, and then I'm going to free every slave I can.

"I'm not going to send my legion out, though I could. I'm not going to physically march out and chop each and every slaving scumbag into kibble. Oh no. Because as the fuckin' formally acknowledged Scion of the Empire, as the PRINCE, I have access to imperial abilities. So, take this as a friendly warning. If you've got a *single* slave inside Sonra, one single person, they will be freed, no matter where you hide them.

"If you've been faking it all this time, then the bill is gonna come due." I looked around, then nodded at the silence, the fear, and the anger that radiated off these people.

"If you're truly against the slavers, as you claim? Then get ready, because when I do this, those slavers are going to find they're surrounded by freed slaves, each and every one. Every control device, every fucking leash and chain is going to destroyed. And those who clutch to them? They'll meet the same fate. So, now's your chance, and it's your last one.

"Either you're with me, and you'll swear allegiance to my throne and my empire at the end of this fight, and you'll all be protected when I claim this territory, or you won't, and Illoth will fucking kill any of you she can.

"When I'm finished, I'll rule here, and that's either going to be atop a pile of corpses of the motherfucking drow, and with whoever of your people survive what comes as the lowest of my citizens, or it'll be with your masters as my valued allies. Pick one, and don't waste my time."

"How *dare* you…" He snarled, stepping forward, only to stop as the swords of three legionnaires rested against his throat. "The peace of the camp…" he started hoarsely.

"Was already fucked in the arse by Illoth surrounding us with a fucking army, now wasn't it? Don't forget, boy, this isn't you I'm making the offer to, is it? It's your masters."

"Saru, apologize," the older woman who'd spoken first growled, before looking at me. "You are correct. But be aware, 'Prince,' we shall pass your comments to those we serve, and they shall make the decisions that serve Sonra best, not simply those that you demand. Many have attempted to wrest control of Sonra since the beginning. Their bones litter the plains."

"Well, considering I've got a goblet at home made out of the skull of the avatar of the God of Death, feel free to try me." I smiled. "Listen, was this the way I'd planned on this conversation going? No. I wanted to come to you and be nice, make friends and hopefully convince your people that joining the empire again was for the best. Illoth screwed that up for all of us, so now we get to make the best of it we can. As such, I suggest you all get a move on, because whatever happens, tonight's going to be memorable. Either a goddess dies, or the prince of the empire does."

They departed with the same offended stiffness with which they'd arrived, but noticeably a lot of grumbling and arguing now as well, leaving us to complete the final preparations. Sehran vanished and returned again a few minutes later, her wings folded tight against her back as she passed the narrow doorway.

"The legion is ready," she reported. "Though some of the caravan merchants are already trying to flee, and they're having issues with their oaths. The Sonra guards are marching around, ordering people to prepare to fight as well, but insisting that anyone who leaves their camp will be killed."

"The only choice to make in the circumstances." Daralen nodded. "A mass exodus now would cause chaos, and the enemy encircles us—where do they expect to go?"

I checked my weapons one final time. My naginata, cleaned by Aellin's team, gleamed as I checked the edge, smiling to myself. I pulled a potion out and liberally doused it with the liquid, before grinning to myself even wider as by some magic of the weapon, it soaked it in, and left a marker on the weapon in my mind, telling me that it had five uses of the poison.

God, I loved magic.

Various daggers were attached across my armor, a mace on the left hip, and my swords over my shoulders, before finally my other vials of poison, the naphtha, some mana potions, and healing potions were checked and confirmed in my bag of holding.

I was as ready as I was ever going to be.

I took a deep breath, centering myself, then said the words that I knew would ring in the minds of all those who heard it as possibly the last words of the prince of the empire. "Welp, let's not keep the spider bitch waiting."

We stepped out of the wagon to find the camp transformed. The legion had formed up in ceremonial order, creating a path from our position to the main thoroughfare that led toward the inner rings. Legionnaires stood at attention, weapons at the ready, their faces grim with determination.

Twenty-five stood on either side, clearly intending to march with me. The rest were spread out around the camp, clear in their armor or where it was missing, in their bearing.

Beyond them, the people of the caravan and curious onlookers from nearby encampments had gathered, forming a tense crowd that whispered and pointed as I appeared. Word had quickly spread, and I could see the mixture of fear, awe, and hope in their expressions.

Daralen stepped forward, saluting formally. "The honor guard is prepared, my prince. Fifty of my finest legionnaires will accompany you into history."

I nodded. That was going to make it a fuck-ton easier to get through the crowds, at least. "Thank you, Primus. Legion! Let's move out," I called, and got a clash of steel against steel as the legionnaires crashed their fists to their chests in salute.

We set off to the center of Sonra, our small party flanked by legionnaires in full battle mode, glaring around, ready to fight anyone and anything, and led by Ren, who I'd met a few hours ago.

She'd said nothing, simply slipped out of the crowd and took up a position in the lead, and I'd nodded to the others to follow her when Daralen looked to me in question.

The crowd parted before us, some bowing their heads in respect or fear. Others glared at me with naked hostility, spitting on the ground or hurling abuse as we passed.

I felt the stiffening of the legionnaires each time that happened, but it was the fifth time, when one of them finally realized that the oaths being removed meant something important and decided to cut off the rising aggression before it got any higher.

One of the crowd stepped in the way and sneered, trying to show off to others that he wasn't scared of us, and presumably believing that thanks to the stupid fuckin' oaths that had constrained them, the legion would have to walk around him.

I glanced at him as his friends picked him back up and stared wide-eyed at us as we marched past, then shrugged. A good healer could probably regrow those teeth for him, but whether he could afford one was another matter.

The effect it had on the crowd was clear, though, and rather than standing almost hard against the legionnaires as they passed, they suddenly decided to back the fuck up.

That wasn't to say that it was all doom and gloom, though. Several groups that we passed cheered and waved, and one, a group I mentally marked up as someone to have a chat with later, should I survive, all fell to one knee as we marched past, proclaiming me as their prince and calling out the oath of imperial citizenship.

I felt the twitch as Oracle hesitated, looking to me, and nodded slightly even as I reached into my pouch, pulling a mana potion free and chugging it. She spun the spell out, infusing their words and linking them to me.

I didn't have the time to stop, not even for the few minutes it'd take to formally accept their oaths and give my own in return, but Oracle activated it. And now, as I felt the burgeoning awareness of them growing, then settling back in my mind, I knew I'd be able to find them again and I'd damn well thank them for their trust when I did.

Zyenna fell into step beside me, her face set in determined lines, her son farther back in the small group who accompanied me. "The merchants are split," she reported quietly. "Half believe you've led us all to slaughter; the others think you might actually win."

"And what do you think?" I asked.

She smiled thinly. "I think I've backed the winning horse, Prince Jax. Don't make me regret it."

Othair walked on my other side, periodically murmuring information about the sections we passed through, having been led sideways along the path rather than straight across the fields for some reason by our guide. "This section of the ring ahead is primarily controlled by the merchant guilds," he whispered quickly.

"This is limited to the highest outsiders and only those with long years of trust and relationships already. You'll note that there's been no sign of anyone who could be even slightly connected to slavery for the last hundred meters. They're kept well outside these areas.

"We're about to cross the herds. That's a symbolic demarcation between the outside and Sonra proper. Then, beyond that, and you can see it by the twisting in the air, is the barrier to the inner ring. Few have seen what lies within, and none, to my knowledge, who weren't born of Sonra."

I nodded that I understood, and I did. What was clearly visible rising in the distance from the middle of Sonra wasn't just a symbolic line or a collection of fluttering pennants like in the rest of the camp.

Instead, there was a clear twisting of the air, and a blurring effect. Looking up at the few clouds that scudded past, I noted their telltale shifting as they were drawn to the left and right, marking that whatever caused the barrier around the inner and second ring extended high enough that it either cast the illusion of touching the sky, or it damn well did.

Personally, it seemed wasteful, and I felt Oracle's agreement. Using enough mana to cast a spell that high continually seemed bloody stupid, in fact, but it was what it was. And it certainly made sure that nobody was just going to use a scrying spell or have a flier pass overhead and report on the secrets.

Either way, the spinning air that formed the barrier meant that nothing beyond could be seen through the vortex of cloud that seemed to touch the ground and reach for the heavens at the same time.

I sent a quick 'land when you need to' message to Sehran as she flew overhead. Having her up there keeping watch was great, but as packed as the passage here was, I was willing to bet she couldn't see much. And when it came to passing through that? Better she was by my side and walking than being thrown arse over tit.

Oracle remained close to my side. The bond between us bubbled with tension, concern, and love. I could feel her anxiety through it as well, stifled as best she could, but also her unwavering support as she tried to keep upbeat and cheerful despite everything.

The herds were just weird to cross, I had to admit. Although it only took a few minutes, the stench, I was afraid, might be with me forever.

I was a city boy back home, or town at least, having grown up in an area that held a million or so people, but well spread out. Since coming to the UnderVerse, I'd spent a lot of time in the wilderness or in cities. But the one place I'd never thought to spend any time was in the middle of a herd of highly flatulent, overfed cattle, strangely enough.

What I found as we started to cross what I mentally named as meadow muffin central, was that to make *this* much mess, with only a few thousand cattle currently in sight, they had to be feeding them something deliberately.

I mean, there was just no way that anything could survive here. The air smelled like it was ninety percent methane, and something that I'd noticed and dismissed before suddenly made a lot more sense.

There were very few open flames anywhere.

Okay, fair enough, it's a tent city—I get flames and canvas walls aren't simpatico at the best of times, but now? I was seriously thinking that they should ban any naked flames to prevent an explosion.

I'd seen movies where they blew up enemy ammo dumps and the resultant mess was what I'd started to expect would be left here if someone lit a cigarette.

That's how bad it was.

By the time I stepped out of the herds section, I noticed two things.

First, a low-level spell that was set into the ground. Stepping on it as the guide directed us, I felt a sucking sensation, and despite my immediate hope, it was centered on my feet.

More accurately, my sabatons, as every trace of the filthy mess was ripped free and compressed.

"Nice," I muttered; the guide glanced over, then inclined her head in acknowledgment. "Do you burn it?"

"We do," she admitted, apparently surprised that I'd noticed. "It produces a useful and convenient fuel for many things."

The second thing? There were a hell of a lot of people that clearly knew we were coming, and not all of them were happy.

As we approached the boundary of the second ring, a new and far more formal delegation of Sonra officials met us. They wore the colors of all three major clans, suggesting this was an official escort rather than representatives of any single faction.

"Prince Jax," their leader greeted me with a formal bow. "We will guide you to the Temple of the Nether."

Our procession continued, now led by Sonra officials, and I noted the way that where most of the people in the crowd we passed now looked on curiously, there was a lot less of the naked hostility that had marked the outer ring.

The second ring was markedly different from the outer areas in terms of setup as well. A lot of the tents we passed looked less like they were special things designed to get attention and show off. Instead, they showed both a better quality of build, and a hell of a lot less ostentation and ornaments.

Similarly, the people here were a mixture of better and more professionally dressed and well...*families*. Their expressions were more guarded as they watched our passage, but again, more curious and hopeful on average than the rest.

The closer we got to the inner ring, though, the more that changed.

Families looked to be grouped together, with everything from storage areas and butchery platforms, to cooking and cleaning, and production centers built around mobile forges came and went, each with specific areas that were very clearly delineated.

As we approached the final section before the inner ring, the shift came about again. More and more of the people were better dressed and glowering at us.

"The wealthy don't appreciate having their comfort disturbed," Othair observed quietly.

"They should try being in the outer ring and surrounded by an army of spiders," I muttered back.

We had covered perhaps three-quarters of the distance to the inner ring when I felt Oracle tense beside me. I tore my gaze from the towering wall of clouds that streamed past forming that barrier as Tamat sent a warning that I shared with Oracle and Sehran through our bond as I got it.

***"Movement in the shadows. To your left and right."***

I gave no outward sign that I'd received her message, but I triggered Hyper Cognition, scanning the crowded walkway for threats. Hundreds of damn hard fights had taught me to trust in Oracle beyond anyone else as she started to cast a spell, even as Sehran swooped in closer. I quickly passed the word to Daralen, torn between decisive action and maintaining calm, unsure whether this was an attack or…

The attack came with devastating precision. Two dozen shadows detached from a nearby pavilion, moving with inhuman speed. I caught a glimpse of pasty white skin and silvery hair, and grinned. Drow assassins, their weapons gleaming with what I instantly recognized as poison.

# CHAPTER FORTY

"Ambush!" I roared, leveling my naginata in a single fluid motion and lunging forward.

The legionnaires had seen them as well, and they reacted instantly, twisting to form a solid wall as shields locked together. The assassins weren't just focused on me as they had in the past, though, and that was the first mistake we all made.

Arrows were launched in fast bursts. The powerful bows that the drow were famed for took Sehran out of the sky even as she cried a warning, and more hammered in on us.

The local guides and officials were caught between the drow and the legion, and half of them died before they even knew what was happening.

More died as the spiders burst free, scuttling forward in a wave from freshly opened boxes and containers.

"Oracle, circle!" I barked. "Legion, form a wall!"

The arrows slammed into shields and worse, past them. The legion shields were strong, a tall tower design that were vaguely reminiscent of the Roman design, though a hundred times more advanced.

The problem was that they were designed to be carried and used, and nobody in their right mind carried a shield that was taller than them. It'd be like carrying a door.

As such, when the legion turned to present their shields, they had two options. They could slam the base into the ground and lock the edges together to form a wall, as they did in the turtle formation, where the second row would rest their shields on the top, angled backward and forming an almost solid wall that the legionnaires could see and stab out of, but that stopped the vast majority of anything coming in.

Or, they held their shields up, then they ducked down behind and would set themselves, usually forming into small groups and working together to keep as much of the team covered as possible.

Both strategies had massive benefits, and they both had drawbacks.

The biggest one, as I found out there, was that the order to form a wall was the one that resulted in the shield hitting the ground. The legionnaires hunched down, half squatting behind their shields, waiting for the next order and ready to fight…and unlike my usual companions, not everyone who stood with me in the center were battle-hardened veterans.

Zyenna twisted around, trying to see what was going on, even as I roughly grabbed Othair, shoving him to the ground. She was just outside of my reach, and with my Hyper Cognition activated, time seemed almost to slow as the arrows screamed inward.

She spun and grabbed her son Marteen, shoving him back and down out of the line of fire with a strength that surprised us all.

I knew what was coming, and I saw in a brief, shared glance that she did too.

The first to hit her was in the left shoulder. It staggered her back, and I snarled, pushing myself forward harder, triggering Mana Overdrive and again reaching out, determined to also get her down, before the second and third arrows hit.

The shoulder wound, even poisoned as the sickly green gleam on them showed they were, could have been healed.

Probably.

The hit to her chest? Possible, though unlikely. But the arrow that took her in the eye, snapping her head back and sending her to the ground finally was a step beyond anything I could heal, though. And I already knew, as she collapsed like a puppet with its strings cut, that she was gone.

That was when the first explosion hit. A dart of black light punched into a legion shield, before it exploded. The legionnaire crashed back, blood spraying and his shield reduced to flinders.

The legionnaires on either side were thrown as well, and through that gap they came.

Sehran was down somewhere out of sight, but I felt the pain of the poison rippling through her. I snarled in fury, caught for a split second between one of my closest friends falling, out of sight already, and the people around me I *could* save.

Oracle was fine; hell, I'd seen in the seconds as I barked the order to Daralen that she'd taken my orders to protect Oracle above any other to heart. She and three of the closest legionnaires had spun and backed up around Oracle, their shields presented outward, the legionnaires' bodies hiding my love from any harm.

I picked four mages out in the crowd; others nearby stared in horror as those they'd believed friends and family were exposed as their worst enemies. I started to cast, my voice rising and falling, fingers shifting around the haft of my weapon as I gestured, calling and forming my mana.

That was when Oracle shouted something aloud, and yanked her hands out and down, making a gesture like slamming something down into the ground. A circle rippled out that shone with power.

Hundreds of spiders had been racing forward, headed for us, and in an instant, they were incinerated as the Circle of Frostfire flared to life.

The drow screeched and twisted. Those inside the ring frantically tried to avoid the semi-sentient flames, even as more legionnaires were sent flying as a second and third black bolt crashed inward.

At the same time, I noted two of the nearby legionnaires—and I guessed others I couldn't see—were grabbing and throwing free the innocent locals who were still inside the circle as well.

I gritted my teeth, realizing that for them, not sworn to me, the circle was a death trap. I was damn thankful that they saw that, and reacted accordingly. Even though they were fast, some still paid the price.

Screams rose, and at least one of those who was hurled free landed too close to the spiders, being attacked by them instead.

"Legion, split!" Daralen roared. "First file, protect the imperial family! Kill those mages! Second file, advance and melee!"

The "file" side of the command was new to me, but the legionnaires were used to it; it evidently meaning something like "squad" as the remains of the fifty who had surrounded me as an honor guard split.

The ring around us fell back, tightening. I finished my spell, and five Magic Missiles flared to life in my left hand, then streaked out. The first mage I'd identified sneered as the missiles impacted a half second apart.

His shield turned black, hiding him from me for a second. Then, as it cleared, the second burst; my dual cast that I'd launched straight up streaked around and slammed down.

His shield popped. The final missile made it through to slam into the side of his head, tearing an ear free and sending him to the ground, roaring in pain.

Then, as he lost control of his own spell, the backlash sent him to his back, quivering and howling.

I wasn't the only one, though. Although I was a lot faster than the majority, the legion around me all had that spell now. The firelight around us was banished in a bright golden flare as dozens more roared free from the first file, impacting the running drow and the mages at the back, taking down their support and returning fire on the archers who had expected to do more damage before they retreated.

They weren't only at risk from the legion, though. Even as the second file sprinted forward to get to grips with the incoming melee fighters, the citizens and clansmen of Sonra made their fucking rage known.

The drow were faster and stronger than most—I'd found the first time I'd faced one that they'd almost been the death of me, their agility proving a nightmare—but they vanished under piles of stabbing, kicking people before they could do more than scream.

I twisted, already summoning my third set of missiles when I heard screams as people started to run in fear to my left and behind us, turning to face whatever new enemy it was… I grinned evilly.

A drow was grabbed by a clawed hand and yanked inward, screaming as a boiling cloud of darkness, claws, wings, and glowing eyes shrieked in fury.

I checked my party sense, double-checking, then nodded, leaving Sehran to work out a little rage on the pissant drow, seeing exactly what she'd meant when she'd said that she'd evolved, thanks to feeding on the SporeMother awhile back, and the effect that'd had on her usual form.

I'd not been able to see her clearly, not through the smoke and shadow of whatever she was doing. But I damn well knew it was her, and I recognized the SporeMother's signature darkness at work.

Whatever her evolution was, she'd been terrified that Jian would turn away from her when she'd shown him it. But he'd instead accepted it as only a man who was in love with a succubus and a wisp with two bodies could.

Like a fucking boss.

I turned back to the fight, seeing that the melee was tight and fast, and clearly able to go either way.

Daralen barked out more orders, directing the first file.

Oracle slammed out a circle again as the first failed, and the remaining spiders that had held back or that had survived through the first circle failing now ignited.

Another black bolt of power screamed in, this time hitting the legionnaires around Oracle, and sending two staggering.

Aellin rose from the ground, his helm missing and blood streaming from a cut across his forehead. He threw himself into the gap a half second before another bolt impacted. He was sent back into the others, and I heard Oracle cry out, staggering and being shoved backward by the bulk of her protectors.

I saw the mage, and launched my missiles in response. The fucker sprinted sideways through a gap between tents, left hand slashing at a woman with long blonde hair who was snarling and swinging for him with a dagger.

Others launched behind me, streaking across and popping his shield even as mine served to make it solid.

The drow took three direct hits, screaming, before his opponent drove her dagger into his eye and spat in his face, shoving him backward.

I saw her speed as she snatched the drow's sword from his loosening grip, and I turned back, searching for another target.

Others' missiles had cut more of the drow melee fighters down, and I twisted to check on Oracle, wanting to get into the fight myself, beyond magic, and knowing, damn well knowing, that the entire point of this was to make me do that.

This let Illoth circumvent the rules by taking me down before the fight even began.

That was when Aellin, standing nearby, took a throwing knife to the eye. The blade sank up to the hilt and killed him instantly.

The street erupted again into chaos as others from camps farther back and that had blatantly been hidden in the herd raced inward in a second wave.

Civilians screamed and fled as the legionnaires formed a defensive perimeter around me at a shouted order, falling back and reforming as a hail of blades, arrows, and spells were launched again, this time from farther out.

Oracle dropped to the ground, kneeling to present a smaller target and sent to me as the legionnaires around her formed up again, *"I'm shielding and refreshing the circle. I'm fine. GO!"*

That was enough for me. I knew they wanted me in the fight—I knew it. But I also knew that if I stayed where I was, I was adding fuck all that the legion weren't already bringing to the fight.

Additional bursts of missiles lifted and streaked through the night. I darted forward, joining the line as Oracle ordered Daralen to do the same. She looked at me for my orders, and I nodded once. Oracle had her shield, and this was clearly getting worse before it was going to get better.

The first wave of clansmen who had counterattacked the drow in their midst were almost all dead now. The second wave of drow came in behind them, taking them down as fighting spread out through the camp.

Daralen fought like a woman possessed, her sword a blur of motion that claimed two assassins in rapid succession, even as she barked orders.

I ducked under a poisoned blade, coming up inside the guard of a female drow whose speed nearly matched my own. My armored gauntlet crashed into her face, shattering delicate features, but she barely seemed to notice, her knives seeking any gap in my armor.

Oracle's warning saved me as another assassin materialized, somehow already behind me. I spun, the naginata's reach keeping him at bay, but more were coming— at least a dozen now. Their coordinated attacks pushed us back against a cluster of merchant stalls, even as semi-sentient flames leapt and danced, burning the limp-dicked bastards from their stealth.

"Protect them!" Daralen roared, blood streaming from a cut on her forehead, her helm somehow missing. "For the empire!"

The drow merely laughed, their movements becoming ever more fluid and deadly. Three more legionnaires fell; their armor provided little protection as fresh weapons appeared, ones that glowed like nineties' club rave lights and somehow pierced the strongest defenses.

I was fighting four assassins simultaneously when the air around us changed. A pressure descended, like the moment before a lightning strike, and the very ground beneath our feet trembled.

A voice like thunder rolled across the battlefield: *"ENOUGH!"*

The desperate fight broke as a new figure entered the fray, slamming into the ground like a meteor from the heavens. Every eye turned toward the source of that commanding voice. Straightening from the impact was a figure that radiated power—tall, broad-shouldered, clad in armor that seemed to drink in the light around it—and I grinned evilly as I recognized him.

Darakin, God of Battle, had taken physical form.

The drow assassins hissed in recognition and fear, backing away instinctively.

Darakin strode forward, each step leaving smoldering footprints in the earth. *"Illoth!"* he bellowed, his voice carrying across Sonra and beyond. *"You cowardly wretch! Is this how the queen of spiders conducts herself? Sending assassins to murder her challenger before battle is joined? Where is your honor, Weaver of Webs?"*

The air shimmered, and a disembodied voice responded, dripping with malice: *"Honor? What use has a goddess for the concept? The weak hide behind honor; the strong do what they want!"*

Darakin's laughter was like the clash of armies. *"Spoken like a true coward. If you fear to face him in honest combat, simply yield your claim and slink back from your betters!"*

A hiss of rage was the only response, but I could feel the malevolent presence retreating from the immediate vicinity. The remaining assassins seemed to waver, unsure without their goddess's direct guidance.

Darakin didn't hesitate. His sword—a massive blade that hadn't been there a moment before—swept through three assassins in a single motion. Their bodies crumbled to ash on contact. The rest scattered, melting into shadows and fleeing.

*"Prince Jax,"* Darakin greeted me, still clearly furious. *"It seems your opponent lacks the courage for honest battle."*

"I'm not surprised," I replied, checking my armor for damage. "She's a fucking coward."

*"Indeed."* The god's gaze swept over our small force, lingering on the bodies of the fallen. *"Your companions fought well."*

I looked to where Zyenna lay, her remaining eye now vacant, and Aellin beside her. Anger burned through me anew. "They deserved better than treachery."

*"Yes,"* Darakin agreed solemnly. *"Which is why I shall accompany you to the Temple of the Nether. If Illoth wishes to face you, she will do so under the observance of the Pantheon."*

As if summoned by his words, more divine presences manifested around us. Sint, God of Light, appeared in a blaze of radiance that forced many to shield their eyes.

His form was less overtly threatening than Darakin's, but no less imposing—a figure of perfect proportion, clad in armor that seemed crafted from solidified sunlight.

*"The Spider Queen has broken faith,"* Sint declared, his voice full of anger and disgust. *"Illoth, you were always a coward, but to do this before a true challenge? Pitiful!"*

Beside him, moving like a shadow between shadows, came another figure—feminine, lithe, with eyes that seemed to absorb rather than reflect light. Tamat, Goddess of Assassins, acknowledged me with the barest inclination of her head before melting into the crowd, her presence felt rather than seen as she began to hunt any remaining drow.

*"I shall clear a path, and for each drow I find, I shall take a bounty in blood. Walk without fear, Prince,"* Tamat hissed.

I bit back on the comment I wanted to make, which was that I wasn't fucking scared and she could have pulled her finger out of her arse sooner and dozens of people wouldn't be dead…but I didn't.

Darakin nodded to his divine siblings, then turned back to me. *"Shall we proceed, Prince Jax? Your opponent awaits, and we have established that neither patience nor honor are among her virtues."*

I forced myself to nod and thank the gods, before I turned to my fallen companions.

*"Jax, I am sorry, we were distracted elsewhere, clearly intentionally, but now, you have little time before the time for your meeting has passed. Illoth will no doubt attempt to wriggle out of it, and you know not the cost to my brethren to march beside you. Please, trust that your fallen will be taken care of, and hurry."*

It was Jenae, and through the contact, I sensed that she was both injured and frantically trying to hide it. She and the others were fighting, even now, and despite that, they'd sent the two strongest of their warriors and the literal Goddess of Assassins to clear my path.

I locked eyes with Oracle, knowing she was all right, but tired and currently full of her species' equivalent of adrenaline. We both felt the fury, rage, and despair that Sehran was battling, even as she forced down her changes, hiding from sight in a damaged tent.

I forced down my anger, and turned to Othair. "Ask the survivors to help. Take our people back to our camp, as quickly as you can, and send word. I need everyone to pray to Lagoush. Every single point of mana they can spare, they need to send to her using the relics Sehran brought. Spread the word and do this *now*."

He saw the look in my eyes and nodded quickly. "I will, my prince. Good luck, and I have faith!" he swore, before twisting to face the others and the slowly recovering clansmen on all sides, raising his voice as he called for aid.

"Daralen, send back the legion with our dead," I ordered. "I'm sorry that they won't be with us, but I want our dead to be honored, and the gods themselves are escorting us. I want you with me, and pick another four, but that's it." I opened my mouth to say more, then shook my head. "I'm sorry for your losses. They were brave and true, and they will be goddamn remembered."

She nodded, her eyes hard. She started to bark orders even as I pulled Oracle to me, holding her a brief second, before we had to move.

I spoke to Marteen. "Marteen, I'm sorry for your loss," I said. "Your mother was a good woman and hard as nails. Go with her."

"No," he whispered, standing from her corpse slowly. "She wanted us to be with you, and I will be."

"I'll take her back," one of the legionnaires assured him, resting a hand on his shoulder.

The young merchant nodded his thanks, before squaring his shoulders and turning to me.

We resumed our march toward the inner ring, now with divine escorts that transformed our procession from impressive to utterly fuckin' awe-inspiring.

The people of Sonra kept falling to their knees as we passed. Some wept; others offered hurried prayers to gods they had thought distant and gone.

The boundary to the inner ring loomed before us. The shimmering wall of air that distorted everything beyond it constantly shifted and moved like a living curtain.

I could see why almost no one had ever seen what lay beyond; even standing directly before it, the barrier hid everything, and in a solid ring around it were warriors, most with beasts that snarled and bared fangs.

Some were cats, though big as fuck. Others looked to be something like horses with claws and fangs—varm, I guessed—though, by far, the majority were some kind of hounds.

Huge fucking hounds that topped out at my shoulder and glared at me like I was a snack.

They took one look at the gods, though, and cowered.

Our Sonra guides hesitated at the threshold, clearly torn between their duty to escort us and their lifelong prohibition against entering the sacred space.

"We…ask that your companions step aside, Prince Jax." Their leader winced, knowing that it wasn't going to fly, even as he said it. "No one from outside the trueborn families may enter the inner ring, by ancient law."

Darakin stepped forward. His presence caused the barrier to ripple like water disturbed by a stone. *"The laws of gods supersede the laws of men,"* he stated simply. *"All who choose to accompany the prince may pass."*

There was a brief pause. And even as pissed as I was right now, I had to admit the fucker had balls, trying to stare down Darakin. But he dropped to his knees after a bare hesitation and nodded soberly.

The barrier parted before him like a curtain drawn aside at Sint's gesture, revealing what lay beyond. I stepped through after Darakin. Oracle, Sehran—who appeared so suddenly bounding out of the gathered staring crowd that she nearly got her head lopped off by Darakin in the process—Daralen, and the remaining members of our party—four surviving legionnaires, Marteen, and Toren—followed close behind.

The inner ring of Sonra defied all expectations. Where I had anticipated more tents, perhaps larger and more elaborate than those in the outer rings, instead stood dozens of huge caravans, each that looked to be ancient beyond belief, though fixed on a regular basis.

As we passed between two of them, I saw the faces of what had to be hundreds of beings, and most of them weren't human. Hell, elves, dwarves, and humans were pretty much everywhere in the realm now, with the various furry races sprinkled about as well, and occasionally Minotaurs, naga, and more.

In here, though, most were races that I barely recognized. I saw dozens of gnomes. I saw stooped blue men and women who looked to barely have the strength to breathe unaided. I saw massive creatures that looked like they were the original grove guardians.

And by original, I damn well meant it. Almost everyone I could see looked to be so old, they were on their last legs. And speaking of legs?

Centaurs. There were a handful of them standing with arms folded flat across their chests, glaring at me and avoiding the gaze of the gods in equal measure.

There were a fuckload of different species, but by far the biggest number were the fucking goblins and orcs.

For every other representative of a species that I picked out, there were three of the goblins and at least two of the orcs, and although the others were mainly old, these were of all ages.

"It's a fucking ark," I whispered, seeing them all. "You're all hiding in here, because…"

*"Because out there, the nobles and more would kill them on sight."*

Jenae's voice was low, pitched for only our group, but Sint and Darakin simply strode forward, making us hurry to keep up as the people moved aside.

In the middle of the ring was a perfect circle of ancient pillars, each taller than three men. Within this circle, the earth was covered in grass of impossible vibrancy, untouched by the herds that surrounded Sonra, and I somehow knew that this place moved *with* the herds.

This place… I drew in a breath, tasting it, feeling it, and knowing that even breathing this in was making me just a tiny bit healthier.

"Ashante," I whispered, recognizing the feeling and seeing not only that the pillar nearest to me had a symbol that looked sort of like hers on it, but that so did the others.

As we passed the nearest, I saw a thousand, thousand variations on her symbol and that of the other gods had been carved into them, each trying to reach the old gods, and holding faith when they failed to elicit a response.

The faces I passed stared at the gods in equal parts hope, desperate joy, and dismay. That they'd devoted centuries to trying to reach them and they'd failed, and this idiot who brought war to them had succeeded had to be fuckin' galling.

Then, at the center, stood the Temple of the Nether.

It wasn't a hall in any conventional sense. Rather, it was a structure of gleaming metal and crystal, octagonal in shape, that seemed to hover slightly above the ground. Its walls were etched with runes that pulsed with inner light, and at each of its eight corners rose a slender spire that crackled with contained energy.

"An imperial artifact," Oracle breathed beside me. "I don't know what it is, but I recognize it."

*"It is an Elsecaller,"* Sint declared, his radiance dimming slightly to avoid overwhelming us all. *"The last remaining one, and it links the realm beyond with this one. Once, there were dozens scattered across the realms, allowing the Emperor's chosen to enter and speak with those of other realms in a neutral territory as well as to bring life and healing to barren places."*

*"Be wary,"* Darakin added firmly. *"This one leads to a pocket beyond the veil. Those who you have lost may appear to you. They may call, but remember who you are and who they are. Remember the love that you bear them and ask yourself if one of them would truly ask of you as some will. The offers made are yours to judge, but beware those who lie and hide.*

*"It has been long centuries since this one has been activated, and Illoth knows well the temptations that will be placed before you, as well as the distractions. It will be as a beacon for the lonely dead, and they will come to it. Do. Not. Listen."*

I paused, then nodded, guessing that it'd make a lot more sense when I stepped through.

The leaders of Sonra stood before the entrance to the Elsecaller, three figures of striking appearance. The woman could only be Matriarch Ilena Vhyrakai, her silver-streaked hair bound in elaborate braids, her bearing regal despite her age. Beside her stood twin men, clearly the brothers Daven and Malik Kreonar, their matching faces distinguished only by the patterns of ritual scarring they bore. The third, a warrior in armor that bore signs of frequent use rather than ceremonial wear, I guessed would be Lord Commander Reth Suntari.

I also noted that unlike the tales that I had heard outside, there were four others with them, making it clear that they didn't rule alone. The other four, though, were non-human—two goblins, an orc, and a centaur—and I guessed that they hid here too.

They all bowed deeply as our procession approached, though I noted they directed their respect more toward the gods than to me. Though, if I were honest? I kinda couldn't blame them for that.

"The hall is prepared," Matriarch Vhyrakai announced, her voice surprisingly strong for her frail appearance. "The Goddess Illoth awaits within."

*"Good,"* Darakin replied. *"This ends today, one way or another."*

I turned to my companions. "Oracle, Sehran, stay with Daralen and the others. If this goes badly—"

"It won't," Oracle interrupted, as she reached out to grip my armored hand. "But we'll be ready regardless."

I nodded, then faced the entrance to the Elsecaller. Its door stood open, revealing only darkness beyond. I damn well knew that wasn't the way it usually was, considering the way the locals were shooting concerned glances at it.

Sint placed a hand on my shoulder, his touch warm even through my armor. *"Remember all that you are, Jax. You are more than you need to be to win this fight. Had I not believed this, then we would have steered you aside. We trust in you. I trust in you, my ally, and my friend. Stand tall, hold to who you are, and why you fight, and you shall prevail."*

"Thank you," I whispered, before drawing in a deep breath. "Not allowed to come inside, I guess?" I nodded toward the doors, and he shook his head, even as Darakin spoke up.

*"Unfortunately not, Jax—only you, your weapons, and your own abilities are permitted within. You may use potions, should you have the chance, but no external magic, and both sides are limited to the same number of attribute points in their form.*

*"Lastly, you may choose to hide the fight, should you desire it,"* Darakin said loudly.

"And if I don't?" I asked.

*"Then I would share it. I will use my power to show it to all those who surround us. And though it shall cost me greatly, I ask only that, in return, when you can you spar with me again, on occasion."* The façade of formality slipped then, an almost boyish grin on his face that was quickly smothered.

"I understand," I confirmed, stifling my own grin. "I would be honored to spar with you again, Lord Darakin, regardless, but please, do share the fight."

He nodded, and as he did, I realized the other side of what he was offering. By sharing the fight in real time, however he did it around Sonra, it meant that if Oracle and Sehran had to run? They weren't delayed, and they'd instantly know to do so.

That was a relief, although the fact that I couldn't use my spells was a ballache.

Then I cursed inwardly. I also might be blocked from Mana Overdrive, I realized. That was borderline intrinsic to me, and borderline a spell. Fuck it, I'd find out in a few minutes one way or the other, I guessed.

As if reading my thoughts, Darakin leaned closer. *"Your body is your greatest weapon now,"* he murmured. *"Until you learn all that you are, use that which you have. The spider relies on size and venom, but her first weapon will always be trickery. Remember that as you face her in the Desert of the Soul, and bring her down to your level."*

I checked my naginata one final time, ensuring the blade gleamed with the poison I'd applied—a little insurance policy that technically didn't violate the rules as I didn't know them until now and nobody said anything about it.

Then, with a final nod to my companions, a quick kiss to Oracle and a hug for Sehran—who looked a bit haggard but more or less back to normal—I stepped into the darkness of the Elsecaller.

# <u>CHAPTER FORTY-ONE — THE FINAL CHAPTER</u>

The interior of the Temple of the Nether, the Elsecaller as they'd called it, was bigger than it looked from outside—*much* bigger.

The central chamber was a perfect circle perhaps a hundred meters across, its ceiling a mosaic of glass that showed shifting clouds of red and grey, black thunderheads and the occasional movement of something massive that roamed beyond.

The floor was polished stone inlaid with metal and manastone that formed intricate patterns that occasionally pulsed with inner light.

Eight archways led from the chamber, each identical and equidistant from its neighbors. From these openings flowed constant figures—wraiths long dead, and most reduced to bare shadows, where here and there others glowed with strength and vitality in comparison.

The strength they held, though… I knew it. I *felt* it. Amon had warned me of these bitches. Fuckin' *liches*.

I'd faced a few, and here, even here in a tiny pocket of the great beyond, they stank the place out.

I saw them gesturing; I heard their voices, calling, as they tried to get me to come to them, to come within reach. There was a line, I noticed, one that ran around the room about three-quarters of the way from the center to the outside. Although they pressed up against the line, they sure as shit didn't try to put a toe over it.

I heard voices that called my name, that begged me to go to them, hints of loved ones' voices…the gruffness of Cam's voice, the timbre of Stephanos. I started to look; I couldn't help it.

As soon as I did, though? A dozen others called out the same. Suddenly I couldn't tell which direction the voice had come from, but in an instant, it became clear.

Cam wasn't here, neither was Stephanos. No, they were mimicking him, and it was just like the spider bitch to make sure that they could. I had no doubt that neither of my friends would be here, in truth, ready and waiting by an amazin' coincidence, just in case I popped in for a chat.

Oh no, they were fucking at rest. And these? These were imposters trying to get my attention while she attacked.

I turned and glared at the center of the room, finally allowing myself to see her for what she was, and where.

She was magnificent and terrifying in equal measure. Her upper body was recognizably feminine, though scaled to enormous proportions—perhaps three times the height of a human woman. Midnight-black skin contrasted with hair like spun silver that writhed with a life of its own. Her face was hauntingly beautiful in its alien perfection, with features that seemed carved from obsidian and eyes—eight of them, arranged in a perfect arc across her forehead—that burned with violent crimson light.

Below the waist, her form transformed into that of a monstrous spider. Eight legs, each thicker than my torso and tipped with chitinous spikes, supported a bulbous abdomen marked with intricate patterns in venomous green and red. As I watched, the patterns shifted and changed, forming runes that made my eyes water when I tried to focus on them.

All told, she stood nearly twenty feet tall, towering over me like a living monument to the power gap between mortal and divine.

*"So,"* her voice rasped, somehow both seductive and repulsive, *"the pretender arrives at last."*

I stepped fully into the chamber; the door sealed behind me with a sound like a tomb closing. We were alone now, god and mortal, in a space between the realm of the living and that of the dead.

"Oh, don't you worry, pet. No pretending required," I snapped. "I'm exactly what I claim to be—the prince who's about to add another divine kill to his record, that of Lolly, the goddamn turd spider!"

Illoth's forced laughter was like broken glass scraping across stone. *"Brave words from such a small creature. Lord Nimon was distracted and enraged, betrayed by those he once trusted and busy on the greater planes that your kind cannot even imagine. I am here in truth, and I am neither."*

"And yet you sent assassins," I pointed out sarcastically, shaking my head, beginning to circle her, keeping my naginata low and ready. "Because trying fucking everything to avoid the fight just screams about how eager you are, doesn't it!"

Her multiple eyes narrowed. *"You are marked as my enemy, little one. That my chosen should decide to strike at you, here, when they can finally be sure you won't flee? Had they not, I would have punished them."*

"Yeah, because we all know you're afraid," I taunted, watching for any reaction that might telegraph her first move. "Lolly the Turd Spider, fucking shaking in her nest."

I'd expected rage. What I got was worse—calculation. One of her front legs tapped thoughtfully against the stone floor, the impact sending small vibrations through the chamber.

*"I will enjoy watching my children hatch from your corpse,"* she said conversationally. *"Perhaps I'll keep your Oracle alive long enough to witness it. The spawn always feed more eagerly when their incubator still lives. And then? Then I shall permit my new brood to gestate in her. They shall feed on your bastard offspring, and prevent the twisted monstrosity ever being born!"*

Now it was my turn to feel rage, but I choked it down. That's what she wanted—blind anger, impulsive action. I forced myself to maintain the same measured pace, studying her form for weaknesses.

"You know, you fucking talk too much," I said finally. "Are we going to fight, or are you hoping I fall asleep and you can creep off and hide? Come on, Lolly. Let's get this over with. I've got fuckin' important shit to do today!"

Her attack came with blinding speed. One moment, she glared down at me. The next, she lunged forward, two massive forelegs stabbing down toward me like spears.

I dove sideways, feeling the air move as they missed me by inches and cracked the stone floor where I'd been standing.

I hit the deck, rolled, and then dove again before rolling to my feet, naginata already sweeping upward in a counterstrike that caught one leg as she withdrew it.

The blade bit into the chitinous armor, drawing a line of ichor that steamed where it hit the air, but the wound was superficial at best.

Not a problem, though, because I'd hit her, and she knew it.

"First blood!" I called to her in a mocking tone, suddenly seeing what I'd missed when I'd been distracted by her huge size.

As before, both sides were limited to the same number of points. The gods obviously weren't going to grant me a billion points to take me up to godhood or whatever, so that meant that she was restricted to the same as me.

Normally, that'd have been a problem. It sure as shit was in the fight with Nimon and here, it wasn't good. But what *was* good?

Although she'd obviously used the same trick, creating an avatar with no need for mental stats or Charisma, Perception, and so on—instead putting all her points into Agility, Constitution, Dexterity, Endurance, and Strength—she'd fucked up.

Her avatar was huge, sure, but that meant that to make it as strong as it'd have to be, as powerful as she'd want it to be, it was slower than Nimon had been. She'd not learned a fucking thing from that fight!

Illoth hissed, more in annoyance than pain, and pivoted with impossible grace for something her size. Three legs lashed out in sequence, forcing me to retreat in a series of desperate dodges. Each impact with the floor sent shock waves that threatened to unbalance me.

*"You are quick, little fleshling,"* she acknowledged, her voice unchanged despite the exertion. *"But speed alone will not save you."*

As if to prove her point, she suddenly reared up, raising her front half toward the ceiling.

For a split second, I thought she was exposing a vulnerability—then I saw the glands beneath her abdomen pulsing. I threw myself behind one of the room's many pillars just as a spray of webbing shot forth, hardening instantly where it struck the stone.

*"Hide all you wish,"* she called, moving again with that unnerving quickness. *"This chamber is my domain now. I can sense every vibration, every breath."*

I didn't doubt it. I needed to change tactics—fighting defensively would only prolong the inevitable, because as big as she was, I was betting a single hit from her was going to do a lot of damage. Darakin had been right; I needed to bring her down to my level.

I darted from behind the pillar, feinting toward her left side before cutting sharply right as she responded. The naginata's reach let me score another hit, this one deeper, slicing through the joint of one rear leg. Illoth screeched, the sound reverberating painfully in the enclosed space.

"Second blood to me," I called out, pressing the advantage with another strike that she barely deflected.

*"A flea may draw blood,"* she snarled. *"It remains a flea."*

Her counterattack drove me back, running across the chamber; her chitinous legs crashed down as I dodged left and right, swinging my blade warningly. She was fast, though, and it was only as I reached the outer ring, that I realized I'd been deliberately driven back.

She reared up and sprayed a web out, forcing me to dive aside and roll. I screamed in agony as something suddenly touched me. My health, stamina, and mana all flickered and dropped by at least ten percent.

I ran, ignoring the mocking laughter of Illoth as I looked over my shoulder, seeing a specter shuddering in delight, even as it was mobbed by others of its kind.

Looking back, I barely ducked another sweeping leg in time, leaving a long slash and a shallow wound in it as I sprinted toward the nearest wall, while dumping my naginata into my bag.

My abilities, my training, and all that I'd learned—not to mention the damn upgrades in terms of stats and the touch of the gods—helped every inch of the way as I jumped, catching a decorative protrusion and hauling myself upward. Illoth launched a stream of webbing that missed me by inches as I climbed higher.

*"Running already?"* she taunted. *"I expected more from the so-called Godslayer."*

I didn't waste breath responding. Each handhold required total concentration, and Illoth wasn't making it easy. Webs struck the wall around me, some close enough that strands caught on my armor, pulling at me like sticky ropes as I desperately dodged and climbed.

Finally, I reached the ledge I'd been aiming for—a wide band of metal that encircled the chamber about thirty feet up. From here, I had a perfect view of Illoth below, and more importantly, I had a gamble to make.

Either this was going to work or it wasn't, but I'd been fast as hell climbing, and the reason for that?

*My Soaring Majesty still worked.*

She realized my plan too late. I launched myself from the ledge even as I yanked my naginata free and dove directly toward Illoth's upper body.

Her eyes widened in surprise as I descended, naginata extended before me like a lance. She raised her arms to defend herself, scuttling back almost contemptuously, then hissed. I adjusted my path; momentum and gravity were on my side and I shifted in the air. The blade sank deep into her shoulder, black ichor spraying as I wrenched it sideways on impact.

I swung around, boots crashing into her stomach. I yanked hard, bracing myself and feeding mana into the weapon, making it flare with fire as again, I bent the rules, not broke them.

I wasn't casting a spell, nor using an outside focus: I was internalizing my mana, feeding it through me, from one hand to the other. The only difference was that I happened to be holding a naginata between those hands.

Illoth's scream was deafening at such close range. One of her hands caught me, fingers crushing around my torso with enough force to make my armor groan in protest. She hurled me across the chamber, and only a desperate midair twist saved me from a spine-shattering impact with the wall. I still hit hard enough to drive the air from my lungs, sliding to the floor in a clatter of armor.

*"Clever,"* she acknowledged, ichor flowing freely from the wound in her shoulder. *"But futile. Hiding that you can fly gained you a hit, but you are small, and I?"*

She smiled widely, fangs on display.

*"I am the queen of spiders!"*

I dragged myself to my feet, ribs screaming in protest. I gathered my mana up and pushed it into myself, feeding it into my bones, into my blood and flesh.

My naginata lay halfway across the chamber, where it had fallen from my grasp. Illoth scuttled across to position herself between me and the weapon, her smile revealing rows of needle-like teeth.

*"Injure me, cut me, break the skin of this form—it matters not! I have a thousand of them, ten thousand! You think the driders are a natural evolution? I created them! All of them! I can slip in and out of them whenever I wish. And you?"* She advanced slowly. *"You are nothing before a goddess."*

I lifted my helmet partially and spat blood onto the stone floor. "I've heard that before. Right before I gutted Nimon."

*"Nimon was a fool,"* she sneered. *"I am patient. Methodical. You will not find me so easily provoked."*

I started to laugh as the chamber suddenly shook. The red and black clouds beyond the glass dimmed, and she looked up, blanching.

"Looks like your boss didn't like that, Lolly." After another spat of blood on the floor, I tugged the helmet back down as I straightened up.

I was already feeling the relief of my bones settling and binding together, even as I reached down and tugged a bottle free of my belt, then poured it over first one, then the other of my gauntlets.

Then she paused, her multiple eyes narrowing as they fixed on the liquid. *"What is that you carry, mortal? That little vial…it reeks of magic."*

"Just a little something I brewed up. Want a taste?"

Her laughter was dismissive. *"Your petty poisons cannot harm me."*

"Maybe not," I agreed, stoppering what was left in the vial smoothly. "But there's only one way to find out."

I hurled the vial with all my remaining strength. Illoth's hand lashed out, smashing it aside with contemptuous ease.

*"Is this truly the best that…"*

The glass shattered instantly. To be fair, not many bottles would have stood up to a full-on slap like that from a goddess, so it was hardly surprising, and it splashed across her body.

Sod's Law, I'd been hoping to get her face or the wound on her shoulder, and it got neither. But I also remembered that I'd already stabbed the bitch repeatedly with my naginata coated in it, and I grinned inside my helm.

"Oh no, I'm so ashamed of my throw," I said loudly, not even bothering to hide my sarcasm.

The potion—my special brew 'Payback's a Bitch'—wasn't just a poison. It was a complex alchemical nightmare specifically designed to attack flesh, and its first effect was probably the most dangerous.

It generated a massive amount of confidence in its victim, making it harder for them to tell that something was wrong, and I was really hoping that was still the case right now.

The second effect was a growing level of inertia. Admittedly, I wasn't seeing that right now, but the third was a fast-dropping level of health. In her case, she was unlikely to really care about that, and eight legs kinda countered inertia a lot.

No, it was the fourth effect that I was really hoping for. But for now, and just in case she'd not got enough in her yet—she was a goddess in a mortal avatar's body, after all—it was time to play my trump card.

I sprinted forward, diving into a roll that made it look like I was heading for my naginata. She screeched in triumph, crashing down, clearly thinking to crush me…but I'd pushed hard with both my Soaring Majesty and my Mana Overdrive at once.

The result was that I burst out from under her on the far side in a blur, planted my feet, and flipped, twisting my body and rocketing at the back of her head.

She spun, lifting and trying to get her legs under her again, wobbling slightly as she did, and managed to get only halfway around, before I crashed into her.

Her back was larger than my body, but she was also a spider queen drider thingy.

That meant that when I braced myself and grabbed hold of a projecting section of her spine, she felt it.

She also hissed in both fear and outrage, because she'd just found out the downside of mortal avatars.

Bodies matter.

She twisted, trying to reach me, and found that with her hips fused into what would have been the head of a giant spider, she couldn't turn very far.

She also couldn't reach me, so I started to pound my fists into her. The sound of cracking chitin, and then breaking bones rung out.

She shrieked and squirmed, legs scuttling as she twisted in circles aimlessly at first, just focused on me. Then she screamed and ran at the nearest line, and the hungry wraiths that hovered beyond.

I jumped clear, landing and rolling as she spun, clearly crowing that she'd managed to get me off her back. Then she screeched again as first one, then two more wraiths managed to claw at her, touching divine flesh and bursting with power and life.

She lurched forward, collapsing into the 'safe zone' again and shaking her head, stunned. The wraiths beyond exploded into motion, savaging each other and feeding, the reality of these foul spirits clear for all to see.

I wasn't standing still, though. I was already on the move, blurring across the short distance and skidding with a sound of metal on stone. I braced, sticking my foot under my naginata and flipping it up into the air, and then sprinted back at her.

She was pushing back up, shaking her head and clearly dazed as I arrived, hacking left and right. My naginata was powered with a surge of mana and it flared to life, imbued with fire.

The crack of chitin was almost drowned out by her scream. Her front left leg collapsed, the damage and her weight on it making it crack, pitching her forward.

I spun to my left, hacking into her right foreleg and grinning to myself as the hungry blade sank deep. I felt it, as the hot ichor washed over the blade. I twisted, dragging it upward, instead of out, making her howl again in pain; then I rammed it deep into her side. I channeled fire again, harder, and I saw the glow that shone through her skin.

"Feel it, bitch!" I roared as the blade sank deep, and I viciously twisted it a final time before wrenching it free.

Illoth partially collapsed, her legs buckling. She caught herself with her remaining good legs, her arms wrapped around the wounds in her side and shoulder, still towering over me but now listing heavily.

*"You…dare…"* she gasped, green foam bubbling from between her lips. *"I am eternal… I am divine…"*

"You're bleeding out is what you are," I corrected, circling to her wounded side. "Divine ichor makes a hell of a mess, doesn't it?"

She darted forward, snarling, and an arm swept toward me. I dodged, but not quite fast enough: her fingers caught my left pauldron, tearing it clean off along with a chunk of my under armor. The pain was immediate and intense, but I forced myself to ignore it.

*"I'll devour your soul,"* she promised, her voice weakening. *"I'll trap your consciousness in eternal torment."*

"Heard that one before too," I replied, looking for my next opening. "You evil types really need some new material."

Another sweeping attack forced me back, but her movements were growing sluggish, and I couldn't help but grin. The potion was doing its work, and my strikes had hit vital areas. Black ichor pooled beneath her, spreading across the stone floor in a widening circle.

She was a divine being, sure, and her avatar was just that—a vessel for her consciousness. But as she suddenly paused, looking down at her stomach in confusion, I really started to grin.

"You know, Lolly, the thing is, your flesh? It's not that strong. It just isn't. Nimon—now, that was a fucking beast. *He* was good at it, really went for gold. But since then? Fuck, I didn't even have to dig deep for this one."

That was kinda bullshit, I had to admit, even if only to myself. It was a hard fight, but the level I'd been expecting? Nope.

That was when it hit me.

I had a fragment of divinity, and although it enabled me to capture and hold another with a divine fragment close enough to force the fight, I'd been thinking that was it.

That was all it did.

I reached out and in, feeling for it, and found it exactly where I expected it.

The divine shard was a fragment of death's energy, the energy of all the dead, everywhere.

Nimon was the master of the dead; he fed on their power, and I had literally ten percent of what he had.

Now, ten percent against ninety? Game over. In a one-on-one fight where he could use his abilities and powers properly, I'd never stand a chance.

Here, though, in the fucking crossover point between the lands of the living and the dead, I was surrounded by more death than I'd ever known. The patch of land outside of Himnel that I'd bonded the fragment in, was like me standing in the middle of the Sahara and looking for water in comparison.

It was like searching a politician's soul for honesty and integrity, there was so little.

Here? I reached out, and I pulled, *hard.*

The energy that Illoth had lost to the wraiths was even now being spread far and wide, as hundreds of the evil dead fought for scraps.

Instead of allowing that, as I unknowingly had, I simply hooked my fingers and *pulled.*

*"No…"* She hissed, mingled fear and disbelief clear as I drank it down. Hundreds of wraiths wailed as they collapsed, fading from even this pathetic faded existence.

The others fled; every wraith in the room fled in abject terror.

"Oh yeah." I grinned at her, then slid my naginata into my bag, and started forward.

She'd unconsciously dropped her hands, cradling her belly as some really nasty gurgling sounds started to get louder.

"It wasn't just a poison, Lolly," I told her calmly. "You remember when I told you that I'd make sure they remembered you? That the legion and all the empire would call you Lolly the Turd Spider from now on?"

She groaned, then retched—or tried to.

Her body was a divine avatar, after all; it wasn't like she'd spent the night at an all-you-could-eat kebab van. No, there was nothing in there to come up, but fuck me that didn't stop her body from trying.

Cloned as it was from the "lesser" driders, it came with everything that was needed for life, including, but not limited to, *a digestive tract.*

I stood there for long minutes, watching her, making sure that the others could see it, that everyone from the drow to the goblins to my people and the gods, the humans and even her own driders, could see her losing control and trying the fastest diet in the world.

Then I stepped in and grabbed one of her limbs as it shook.

I reached down inside myself, triggering Mana Overdrive, infusing myself with everything that it gave me and more, and I fed the power I'd ripped from her into it as well.

My armor suddenly struggled to hold me, but that was fine. I only needed it for a few seconds.

I yanked sideways. The sound of her chitin cracking rang out in the new silence of the Temple of the Nether, the realm beyond life that Darakin had called the Desert of the Soul, and she screamed.

The effect was ruined slightly when, halfway through it, she choked, her body trying to vomit, and I braced a foot against her stomach as she fell, crashing to the ground.

"Almost over…don't worry, Lolly," I said cheerfully. "I think your people are starting to get the picture now, or at least I hope so. Because after this? I'm coming for them."

*"You think this ends with the death of this form?"* she rasped, green foam flecking her lips. *"My children will hunt you…they will…"*

"Your children are next on my list," I promised, batting aside another weakening swing. "After I make a fuckin' goblet from your skull and toast the true gods!"

*"You…you…cannot…"*

"Clearly, I fuckin' *can!*"

I flipped her limb around, the pointed tip of one chitinous leg pointed right at her heart, and then grabbed her arm as she tried to hit me, gripping it tight and showing that I could, that she couldn't pull free. Before? She could have…if we were to start the fight over, she could have. But now, poisoned, with a third of her very life force ripped free and then fed into me, and more besides, with her blood loss and her stupidity in spreading her points out to make a creature as big as she was fast as well?

It was almost laughable.

I rammed the point home, then pressed harder. The hope and misplaced confidence faded from her eyes, even as the tip of her leg erupted from the far side of her chest. The wound grew wider and wider as I pushed it all the way through.

Her eyes—all eight of them—found mine, disbelief warring with hatred in their crimson depths.

"Game over, spider bitch." I reached down to my hip and the dagger I had sheathed there. "Say hello to your boss for me, and remind him, I'm fucking comin' for him."

# <u>EPILOGUE</u>

When I stepped out of the Elsecaller, it was to the light of the slowly rising sun.

The gods were gone—not far, I knew that. The fragment of divinity that I'd taken from Illoth was nestled inside me, not yet bound, but waiting, ready, and a part of me so long as I lived. Through it, I felt…more.

I felt the strands that bound my people, that linked them to me, me to them, and all of us to the gods.

Illoth might have styled herself the "spider queen," but I knew better now, having seen fragments of her past. I absorbed it—hints, flashes of inspiration that I damn well knew would take time to make sense and work through—but what was important was clear.

I had a second fragment of divinity. The gods had been distracted by some trick, some attack on their side, and they'd survived. They felt stronger; their connection to the world sure as shit was. But the Pantheon of the Dark?

Belief was a massive thing to the gods. They drew their power from it, from the mana that all those who believed in them unconsciously offered up.

They needed that. They were both powerful creatures in their own right, and they were the living embodiments of their image, their element or…

It slipped away. I could feel it, some greater truth that I was inching closer to getting, to understanding, but again, it was gone.

It didn't matter. Today was a day that was going to be full, regardless. I had people—*friends*—to mourn, I had citizens and land to claim, and fuck me sideways if I wasn't going to damn well get a bath at some point.

No, the important point in the belief structure side of things, I knew, was that the gods had made sure that these people, and at least the army of drow and driders that surrounded Sonra, had seen Illoth, the spider goddess, get taken apart and slaughtered.

I stepped out into the real world in time to see a last fading image, and it was of me, wiping her guts off my boot, on her side.

That was probably why, when I looked around, seeing the hundreds of people close by, and the tens of thousands of people in the distance, the spinning vortex of the inner circle dispelled, I wasn't entirely surprised at the call that rang out.

*"Hail Prince Jax!"* It rose from the throats of thousands. *"All hail, Prince of the Empire!"*

## **THE END OF BOOK EIGHT OF THE UNDERVERSE**

Jez Cajiao

# <u>THANKS!</u>

Hey everyone! Well, I'm sorry for the delay with getting book 8 out to you all, I know it's been a while, so I hope it was good for you too—cue smoking cigarette image while catching our breath in bed—but I have new of more.
Oh yes I do!
So, at the time of writing this, book 9, The Tower of Gaij is in edits, and I'm writing book 10 currently, so to make up for the big delay I'm working my butt off to get more of the story sorted out as well.
You know what I really need though, and what would help a huge amount? If you could leave a review, a rating, or even share the book on social media—with the kind of sick twisted people you know would love it, obviously—because the faster we spread the bad word, the better!
(Also Amazon's algorithms decide if they should hide or promote a book depending on how many people have rated and reviewed it, so there is that!)
Seriously though, I just hope you enjoyed the story, and hopefully I'll see you at LitRPG Con in Denver around July or DragonCon in Atlanta around September again.
Hope to grab a beer with you there, and as always, thank you so much for your support.
It matters more than you know.

-Jez
02/06/2025

# **<u>PATREON</u>**

Hi everyone! Okay, when this launches in June all of my Patreon supporters will have already read it, and some will have already finished book 9, and will be on the next book I've been working on as well, which is UnderVerse 10!

The highest tiers also have access to a secret project, and will be busily reading literally as I finish the chapters. So, if you want to read them perhaps 4-6 months ahead of release? Come join us on the dark side!

HOWEVER: I do want to point out one thing everyone, the app stores on apple and android platforms have enforced that a 30% mandatory percentage goes to them for any purchasing done through the **app**. So the app store Patreon subscription has increased by that amount automatically, PLEASE sign up through the website instead, it's still Patreon's website, and the increase doesn't apply there.

There's several of those wonderful supporters out there that I have to thank personally as well; ASeaInStorm, Mischa, Niall, Kevin, Lex, and Steve thank you all!

TO REPLACE WITH CURRENT MEMBERS

# **<u>https://www.patreon.com/Jezcajiao</u>**

# <u>UNDERVERSE 9: TOWER OF GAIJ</u>

By Jez Cajiao

***Jax never goes down without a fight. But in the aftermath of his latest battle, it's not just his secrets hanging in the balance.***

With the winds dispelled and secrets exposed, Jax has to convince those that survive that the best chance at safety is with the Empire. The best way to prove it? Eliminate the deadliest threats hunting them all.

Jax, Oracle, and Sehran have survived the scorching desert and conquered the untamed wilds. Now they face their most treacherous challenge yet: unraveling the dark truth behind the succubai within the Tower of Gaij.

This fortress of secrets stands besieged on all sides, its inhabitants have no reason to trust outsiders, especially when the old nobility have already staked their claim and tried to take control.

In a tower ruled by demons of debauchery, where pleasure and pain are currency and betrayal lurks behind every smile, it's time for Jax to navigate a labyrinth of backstabbing, bullets, and brutality.

***When everyone wants what you're after, the only way out is through a trail of bodies.***

*Note: This is a Dark Fantasy Epic LitRPG. Expect graphic violence, strong language, and morally complex themes. Reader discretion is advised.*

**<u>*Preorder on Amazon*</u>**

# A FOREST OF VANITY AND VALOUR

By Adam Beswick


**An aggressive debt collector banished from the kingdom. Now his life depends on his ability to help the less fortunate...**

Vireo Reinhold relishes collecting his monarch's proper dues. Working hard to prolong and fund the king's never-ending war, the self-centered official revels in the perks of luxury that come with his unorthodox role. But his world upends when he unearths an ancient spellbook that promises to unlock a shadowy, forgotten magic.

Embroiled in a secret affair with a fellow noble's wife, Vireo is mortified when he's forced to commit an unthinkable act. Driven into exile, no longer able to coerce the vulnerable, and with the powerful tome in his enemy's hands, the fallen agent's only shot at survival hangs on his skills at saving others.

Can Vireo redeem himself as the people's champion before they all fall to a sinister fate?

*A Forest of Vanity and Valour* is the dark first book in the Tales of Levanthria fantasy-retelling series. If you like fast-paced action, evil-to-good transformations, and classic stories with a twist, then you'll love A.P Beswick's ominous tale.

Buy Now!

Jez Cajiao

# BATTLEFORGED: FIRST CLEAR: A LITRPG APOCALYPSE ADVENTURE - BOOK 4

By MH Johnson

How to negotiate in the post-apocalypse:
**1. Always try make a strong first impression.** *— And few things say strength like an army of undead revenants EAGER to begin slaughtering at your command!*
**2. Be clear and concise when making your diplomatic offers. Let everyone know all the wonderful benefits they'll enjoy by doing things your way!** *— If they play their cards right, they might even get to keep their heads!*
**3. Speak softly, and carry a BIG CANNON!** *— Because the best negotiations are when your competitors are looking down the barrel of your gun!*
**4.** *If all else fails, you can always pull out your **DINOSAUR COLLECTION** to impress all your new friends!*
Eric has a little problem.
Someone he cares about has been kidnapped by sadistic goblins working with corrupt bureaucrats who are eager to make him pay for interfering with their plans of military conquest and economic dominion.
Good thing Eric has a BIG ARMY!
An army that's absolutely PERFECT for crushing ANNOYING little problems that threaten any girl silly enough to fall for a guy like him.
Sadly, his mother has made it clear that negotiation is the best path forward when dealing with corrupt administrators. Especially when SMART negotiations just might give his sister the breathing room she needs to fortify her own growing kingdom.
Eric is forced to agree. If nothing else, this is a great opportunity for him to level-up his Negotiation skills. And he can think of no better negotiating tactic than **GROWING HIS UNDEAD LEGION TO MASSIVE PROPORTIONS!**
Preferably by including everyone's childhood favorite: **DINOSAURS!** - *Lots and lots of hungry dinosaurs!*
*Eager for a fast-paced adventure with a survivor determined to get the best of everyone trying to kill him? Then read on!*
Order Here

# FACEBOOK AND SOCIAL MEDIA

If you want to reach out, chat or shoot the shit, you can always find me on either my author page here:

**www.facebook.com/JezCajiaoAuthor**

## *OR*

We've recently set up a new Facebook group to spread the word about cool LitRPG books. It's dedicated to two very simple rules;

1: Let's spread the word about new and old brilliant LitRPG books.

2: Don't be a Dick!

They sound like really simple rules, but you'd be amazed…

Come join us!

**https://www.facebook.com/groups/LITRPGLegion**

I'm also on Discord here: **https://discord.gg/u5JYHscCEH**

Or I'm reaching out on other forms of social media atm, I'm just spread a little thin that's all!

You're most likely to find me on Discord, but please, don't be offended when I don't approve friend requests on my personal Facebook pages. I did originally, and several people abused that, sending messages to my family and being generally unpleasant, hence, the author page:

**www.facebook.com/JezCajiaoAuthor**

I hope you understand.

Jez Cajiao

# **<u>LEGION</u>**

Okay everybody, if you've not yet seen or heard! My wife Chrissy, and our friend Geneva and I have launched the Legion Publishers!
We're taking on new authors, as well as experienced ones, focusing primarily on the LitRPG side of things, but we're open to anything really, with one very clear rule that guides our company:

***Don't be a dick.***

That's it. Our contracts aren't hidden behind layers of legalese, you can find them here:

**<u>https://www.legionpublishers.com/legioncontract</u>**

If you want to reach out and ask any questions, get an idea of the support we offer, and possibly become part of the family? We'd love to hear from you, just tap the link and fill in the form:

**<u>https://www.legionpublishers.com/contact-and-submissions</u>**

Hope you're having a good one!

-Jez, Chrissy and Geneva


If you want to read any of our amazing authors work then go get them!


<u>Theft of Decks</u> By Lars Machmuller **<u>Buy on Amazon</u>**
<u>Quest Academy</u> By Brian J. Nordon **<u>Buy on Amazon</u>**
<u>Wandering Warrior</u> By Michael Head **<u>Buy on Amazon</u>**
<u>Knights of Eternity</u> By Rachel Ní Chuirc **<u>Buy on Amazon</u>**
<u>Scarlet Citadel</u> By Jack Fields **<u>Buy on Amazon</u>**
<u>Welcome to the Dark Ages</u> by Malory <u>Buy on Amazon</u>

# <u>LITRPG!</u>

To learn more about LitRPG, talk to other authors including myself, and to just have an awesome time, please join the LitRPG Group

**<u>www.facebook.com/groups/LitRPGGroup</u>**

# <u>FACEBOOK</u>

There's also a few really active Facebook groups I'd recommend you join, as you'll get to hear about great new books, new releases and interact with all your (new) favorite authors! (I may also be there, skulking at the back and enjoying the memes…)

**<u>https://www.facebook.com/groups/LitRPGlegion/</u>**

**<u>https://www.facebook.com/groups/GamelitSociety</u>**

**<u>https://www.facebook.com/groups/LitRPG.books</u>**

**<u>https://www.facebook.com/groups/LitRPGforum/</u>**

www.ingramcontent.com/pod-product-compliance
Lightning Source LLC
Chambersburg PA
CBHW071424190726
48292CB00001B/97